Praise for Adam Levin's

MOUNT CHICAGO

"A bravura dramatization of grief and the paradoxes of storytelling. . . . Incandescent passages of philosophical inquiry, arresting insight, pathos, and hilarity." —*Booklist*

"*Mount Chicago* is a bawdy, mournful, deeply funny, metafictionally ingenious, psychotic, ridiculous, and majestic shaggy dog joy. When Levin leads the way, every rabbit hole is a glory hole for the mind, and a secret tunnel to provisional bliss and permanent wisdom. Also recommended for parrot lovers." —Sam Lipsyte, author of *The Ask*

"The author achieves a sustained, operatic balance of comedy, grief and despair. . . . A genuinely breathtaking achievement [that] brought tears to my eyes." —*The New York Times*

"*Mount Chicago* is a riveting story of municipal and personal apocalypse: a searing exploration of bad breakups, behaviorism and analysis, chocoholism and depression, neurotic pets, twisted liaisons, the art of writing, loss and true love, pop culture, and marriage. Comparisons may be made to Roth, Pynchon, and DeLillo, but Adam Levin's work is inimitable, ineluctable, and unique." —Rebecca Curtis, author of *Twenty Grand*

"I come away from Adam Levin's books with a greater appreciation for literature, the infinite power of storytelling. Yes: he is Chicago's best novelist. With *Mount Chicago*, however, Levin has entered a higher realm. This book contains the tingling mystery of genius. I put it down and saw the world differently for three days. I was lighter on my feet, funnier, filled with love. This book will change you for the better. We will read Adam Levin for centuries. We will always start with *Mount Chicago*." —Gabriel Bump, author of *Everywhere You Don't Belong*

"Follow Adam Levin into a hole in Chicago, ignore the signs that either he's crazy or you are, and you'll emerge somewhere gloriously strange and brilliantly funny. Like the lunatic, the genius, the acidhead, and the mystic, Levin pursues the grooves of his brain to their remotest reaches, where they begin to form a map of the world."

—Adam Ehrlich Sachs, author of *The Organs of Sense*

"With *Mount Chicago*, Adam Levin has gifted us that rarest of modern joys, the genuinely raucous literary object. What starts as tragedy opens into a catalog of human comedy that is brilliant, furious, and thrilling. Speaking plainly, it's the funniest American novel in years, and I swallowed it more or less whole."

—Kyle Beachy, author of *The Most Fun Thing*

"Flaubert's parrot, Loulou, has found a true literary heir in Gogol, the parrot at the emotional heart of Adam Levin's brilliant, funny, emotionally complex examination of what happens to us when we suddenly realize life is upheaval and no one is safe."

—Jill Ciment, author of *The Body in Question*

"[*Mount Chicago*] blends philosophical speculation with literary fillip to thrilling effect. . . . It's a refreshingly different take on metafiction that considers the relationship between humor and existential despair, amongst other philosophical issues."   —*The Quietus*

"*Mount Chicago* captures an important element of the city that rarely has been shown in fiction. And when it comes to taking a big swing on the absurdities of our modern life, no one does it better than Adam Levin."   —*Chicago Review of Books*

Adam Levin

MOUNT CHICAGO

Adam Levin is the author of *Bubblegum*, *The Instructions*, and *Hot Pink*. His writing has appeared in numerous publications, including *The New Yorker*, *McSweeney's*, and *Playboy*. He has been a New York Public Library Young Lions Fiction Award winner, a recipient of a National Endowment for the Arts Literature Fellowship, and a National Jewish Book Award finalist. He lives in Chicago.

MOUNT CHICAGO

MOUNT CHICAGO

A Novel

Adam Levin

ANCHOR BOOKS
A Division of Penguin Random House LLC
New York

FIRST ANCHOR BOOKS EDITION 2023

Copyright © 2022 by Adam Levin

All rights reserved. Published in the United States by Anchor Books,
a division of Penguin Random House LLC, New York, and distributed in
Canada by Penguin Random House Canada Limited, Toronto. Originally
published in hardcover in the United States by Doubleday, a division of
Penguin Random House LLC, New York, in 2022.

Anchor Books and colophon are registered trademarks of
Penguin Random House LLC.

Page 577 constitutes an extension of this copyright page.

The Library of Congress has cataloged the Doubleday edition as follows:
Names: Levin, Adam, author.
Title: Mount Chicago : a novel / Adam Levin.
Description: First edition. | New York : Doubleday, 2022.
Identifiers: LCCN 2022019201 (print) | LCCN 2022019202 (ebook)
Subjects: LCGFT: Novels.
Classification: LCC PS3612.E92365 M68 2022 (print) | LCC PS3612.E92365
(ebook) | DDC 813/.6—dc23/eng/20220425.
LC record available at https://lccn.loc.gov/2022019201
LC ebook record available at https://lccn.loc.gov/2022019202

Anchor Books Trade Paperback ISBN: 978-0-593-46672-8
eBook ISBN: 978-0-385-54825-0

Book design by Michael Collica

anchorbooks.com

Printed in the United States of America
10 9 8 7 6 5 4 3 2 1

for Camille

In order to grasp what was taking place within me
at that moment, let us imagine that we each have an
inner self ~~of which the visible us is the sheath, and
that this self, brilliant as light, is also as delicate as a
shadow.~~

—Balzac

And then the storm of shit begins.

—Bolaño

Je chiais la nuit,
Je chiais le jour,
Je chiais partout,
Je chiais toujours!

—*Man Bites Dog*

MOUNT CHICAGO

Carrying Pictures of
Chairman Mao

None of this happened. None of it will. The events I'll describe, most of which will be set in the early twenty-twenties, will all be described in the late twenty-teens. The characters who those events will affect do not exist outside these pages, not even those characters who'll strongly resemble certain people I know, and not even in those cases where the characters resembling people I know will have the same names as the people they'll resemble. It'll all be made up. I'm making it up.

No one I've been close with has ever died. I've met a couple Schutzes, but never an Apter. Not a single Gladman. I have never had more than $106,019.00. I have usually had less than $4,000.00. Today—February 2, 2018—I have a little less than $30,000. The seventeenth of November, 2021, will not fall on a Sunday, but a Wednesday. The Rainbo Club doesn't serve Corona. Quentin Tarantino's *Inglourious Basterds* wasn't released till 2009. The Grant Park Lollapalooza Festival never takes place before the end of July. I have never had tenure or nieces or nephews. I've known comedic actors, but none of them were stand-ups. My dealings with mayors have not been extensive.

Once, at a Chicago Public Library ceremony honoring the author Don DeLillo, my wife shook the four-and-two-thirds-fingered hand of Mayor Rahm Emanuel, who, later that evening, in his speech to those gathered, twice pronounced *DeLillo* like this:
    Duh-lee-lee-yo.

—

Two decades–plus prior, when I was fourteen years old, summer-jobbing downtown at my father's insurance firm, I spotted the city's second Mayor Richard Daley, i.e. Richard *M.*, a quarter block away. I was out on my lunch break. He was walking up Wacker with a couple other men, and he appeared so very squat and red-faced that I, who had started eating acid earlier that year, thought that maybe I was finally having a flashback, and so I approached him to get a closer look. I got closer than I'd meant to.

I wasn't, it turned out, having a flashback.

I've never had a flashback. I no longer think that flashbacks are real. The only people who ever report having flashbacks are people who have had bad trips on acid.

Bad trips are panic attacks one has while on acid. If someone is on acid the first time they suffer a panic attack, they don't think, "I am having a panic attack," but rather, "I am having a bad trip." And then, the next time they suffer a panic attack, they think, "This is kind of like that bad trip I had. I am having a flashback," and that's what they tell people about their panic attack: "I had a flashback."

And people believe them. And the ones who like acid but who haven't ever had a bad trip on acid imagine that a flashback will not feel like a panic attack, but like whatever being high on acid had felt like to them—like some kind of fun. So they imagine a flashback must be some kind of fun. But they never have flashbacks. There's no such thing.

I have had bad trips, which is to say that I have had panic attacks while high on acid. But I didn't have my first panic attack while *not* high on acid until I was nearly thirty years old, by which point I'd long since quit taking acid, and had long since worked (and, not so long after that, quit working) as a psychotherapist.

As a psychotherapist, I worked with a number of clients with anxiety disorders, which is to say a number of clients who suffered frequently from panic attacks, so when I had my first one while not high on acid, I wasn't confused: I knew it was just a panic attack. It wasn't pleasant, but it wasn't as terrible as having a bad trip. Not remotely.

Bad trips are worse than anything. Mine were, at least. Unrelenting fear and pain. A sense of being on the verge of inflicting permanent damage on yourself. A sense that if you aren't vigilant enough, you might—to pick just a couple examples—you might accidentally choke on your tongue, or swallow your lips or portions of your cheeks before having even realized you'd chewed them off.

I had all my bad trips at the age of seventeen. Three out of three trips in a row were bad. I'd taken acid some eighty-ninety times before that. I'd thought the world of acid, had faith in acid. I believed that taking it was central to who I was, and I suspected I was God. Not metaphorically.

I suspected that I had made the universe, filled it up with things and beings, and that I, wanting to experience my creations *as* one of my creations, had inflicted amnesia on myself, then birthed myself as the human being Adam Levin, and that when all was said and done, my amnesia would lift, and I would know what the experience of the universe I'd created was like for those who weren't God, i.e. for those who I'd created. That seemed to me like something that God would really want.

When I was not high on acid, I didn't *feel* like an amnesiac God, but often I would think as though I were—I'd been doing so since the age of four or five. Why? I'm unable to say why exactly, though I think I remember the moment it started.

My mom and I were watching *Sesame Street*. Or *The Electric Company.* I don't recall which, but we were on our couch, watching one of those shows (or maybe it was *The Great Space Coaster*), and one of the puppets on the show kept saying, "I think therefore I am." Repeating the phrase, over and over, changing the intonations and stresses. "I think therefore I *am. I think* therefore I am. I think *therefore* I am? *I* think therefore *I* am." Etc. It went on for a minute, maybe two.

Confused, I asked my mom to explain what the puppet was saying.

"It's saying," she said, "that because it knows it thinks, it knows it's real."

"It's a puppet, though," I said. "It doesn't think."

"But we're supposed to forget it's a puppet while we're watching the show. We're supposed to pretend that the puppet can think, and that since it knows it thinks, it knows it's real."

"That's true?" I said.

"Well, not for the puppet, unless we pretend. But what the puppet's saying is true for people. They know that they think, so they know that they're real."

"I know I'm real because I know I think?"

"Yes."

"How do I know I think?" I said.

"Because you can hear yourself think," she said.

"That's it?" I said. "That's the only way?"

"Why are you making that face?" she said.

"What about you?"

"What about me?"

"How do I know that *you* think?" I said. "I can't hear you think."

"I'm telling you I do."

"But I can't hear you doing it."

"You can hear me talk," she said. "What I'm saying is the sound of what I'm thinking."

"How do I know that?"

"Because I'm telling you."

"That doesn't mean . . . That doesn't make sense."

"Calm down," she said.

"I can hear the puppet talk."

"Calm down," she said.

"I can hear the puppet talk and the puppet isn't thinking!"

"I'm not a puppet, Adam. I'm real."

"I can't hear you think!"

"Baby, come on, calm down," she said, and hugged me close. I don't know what happened next. I assume I calmed down, but I don't remember. I asked my mother recently if she remembered, and she said she didn't. She didn't remember the conversation at all. She suspected, she said, I'd made the whole thing up.

"Why would I make that up?" I asked.

"No idea," she said. "I've never understood why you make things up. You *or* your sisters."

But that incident with the puppet reciting the cogito—right then is when it started, I think. The suspicion that I was an amnesiac God. Perhaps it was easier to harbor that suspicion than it was to contend with the possibility that the world was merely a dream I was having.

—

When I was high on acid, I not only suspected I was an amnesiac God, but I *felt* like an amnesiac God. I sensed connections between things and beings that I believed I couldn't have sensed if I weren't God, and I was happy to sense these connections and to think of myself as God. I believed the connections were *real*, were *true*. I was a serious boy, a boy who wanted as much truth and reality to be revealed to him (or by him) as possible, so I took the stuff whenever I could. It was the central occupation of my high school years, and I thought ill of people who'd had bad trips. I thought they were weak, and maybe even ugly, deep down in their souls (I believed in the soul). Which is why, after my first bad trip on acid, which lasted something like forty hours—far and away the worst forty hours of my life—I took acid twice more. One time a week later, the other time a month or so after that. I wanted to prove to myself that I wasn't weak or ugly deep down, that that first bad trip—and, later, the second one—had been anomalous, and that the source of the badness could be discovered and thereby repaired by taking more acid.

I failed.

I've since become pretty sure that the bad trips' badness had everything to do with my digestive system, which by then I'd all but ruined with hundreds of food-free breakfasts starring coffee and cigarettes, followed by hundreds of midmorning, evening, and late-night snacks of Rolaids and Tums. These intestinal abuses had begun to add up, and the thought that had announced the onset of all three bad trips was: "My guts are breaking down."

I didn't accept that at the time, however—the ruined digestive system hypothesis. I remembered the pain that triggered me to think "My guts are breaking down" as clear as I remembered the thought itself, but I insisted on believing that the pain and the thought were outcomes of the badness of the trip, not its causes.

In case this hasn't come across already: I was very much a mind-over-matter kind of fool, a question-beggar, a chicken-or-the-egger. If someone accused me of putting the cart before the horse (many did; most often when I'd bring up the whole amnesiac God thing), I would deny the accusation by way of pointing out that a horse-pulled cart, if its driver so wished, could be deployed in the transportation of horses. As in: maybe other horses, bound for the glue factory, were *riding* in the cart behind the driver, lying on their sides, perhaps, half-dead. Or maybe the horses who were pulling the cart were all very sick, and were, themselves, to be turned into glue: maybe there were six of them pulling that cart, a cart that one healthy horse could have pulled, and the driver was planning to spend the cash the factory would pay him for these half-dozen horses to buy a new healthy one to pull him and his cart back home to the farm.

Were these irrelevant points to make in response to the initial accusation? Pretty much. Sure. Yes, of course. That is: unless they were full of so much brilliant insight and irony and paradox as to render the accusation itself irrelevant, which, by the time I finished making the "points," they would have seemed to me to be. Furthermore, they would, in most cases, have seemed that way to my accuser as well, for he would not have likely heard me going off about my probable amnesiac Godhood to begin with—much less would he have bothered to attempt to argue about it—unless he'd been as high on acid as I.

Were I, at this writing, in a less self-sympathizing mood, I would delete the preceding couple of paragraphs, and just say I was an idiot. A solipsistic, juvenile idiot. But I wasn't an idiot. Or I wasn't *just* an idiot. I was at least, I would say, an *interesting* idiot. The premises I worked from were often false, my reasoning nearly as often unsound, and yet my dedication to both was uncommonly rigorous. I was, as I said, a serious boy.

A *committed* boy.

I was hard on myself. For six months or so after the third bad trip, things were . . . tricky. I believed myself to be a coward, and that was, I thought, the only consistent thing to believe, and, as such, the only courageous thing to believe. The only belief that could demonstrate to me the courage of my convictions was to believe myself a weakling with an ugly soul who was too afraid to face the truth, i.e. too afraid to keep taking acid.

And I *was* afraid. Afraid enough to quit taking acid. I haven't taken it since then. I wouldn't take it again for ten thousand dollars (twenty thousand maybe, fifty thousand for sure—I'm running out of money— but that's neither here nor there, unless you're offering, whoever you are).

I still think I'm a coward at times, but for reasons having nothing to do with drugs, which I still enjoy with some regularity—mostly alcohol, occasionally benzos, less frequently opioids, opiates, and MDMA. I think I'm a coward when I catch myself allowing that there might be some good, intelligent people—people as good and intelligent as any I care for—who have read my fiction without having loved it. When I catch myself thinking, "Good taste varies."

We all know it doesn't. Deep down, we know. We of good taste.

Perhaps I've gotten off track. What I was aiming to get at it is that the first time I encountered a mayor, it was the second Mayor Daley, on Wacker Drive, and because he appeared to be as squat and red-faced as an agitated piglet in an old cartoon, and because I was just fourteen years old and newly fanatical for LSD, I was hoping first and foremost that his exaggeratedly Daley-ish appearance signaled the onset of an acid flashback, and, curious as I was to explore the possibility that the mayor was somehow *triggering* the ostensible flashback—what did I know about the workings of flashbacks?—I moved closer to him.

Closer than I'd meant to.

And just as I had come to realize that despite the mayor's color and dimensions, everything else appeared normal as ever—which meant I wasn't, alas, having a flashback—the mayor addressed me.

"Hi there," said the mayor.

"Mayor Daley?" I said.

"No kidding, huh?" he said. The men with him laughed. "What's your name?" said the mayor.

"Adam Levin."

"Oh yeah?" said the mayor. "I *know* some Levins. Lots of Levins. We got a couple-three over there in just the Education Department alone. One says it like *leaven,* though. The New York way, you know? Like the—the process behind that Passover crackerbread . . . *Holly?* . . . *Menorah?* Help me out, Adam."

"Matzah?"

"Matzah! Right. But so you're not *his* kid, 'cause you say it the Chicago way. You related to any of my other guys in Education, though?"

"I don't think so," I said.

"Well, they do a good job. All the Levins, no matter how they say it. Maybe you probably know that firsthand. What school you at?"

"I live in the suburbs."

"All right," he said. "So what suburbs you live in?"

"Highland Park," I said.

"That's a very nice suburb. Very nice place. I got a lot of friends with homes in Highland Park."

I said, "I like Chicago better."

"'Cause you got good taste," he said. "Greatest city on Earth. Now, tell me something else before I get going, though. What exactly is going on with that haircut there?"

"Going on with it?" I said.

"It's funky," he said.

"Funky?" I said.

"We better get to lunch," said one of the men.

"You're right. He's right. We're running late, Adam. We got this lunch. But just so you know, I wasn't saying anything, or insinue-ing either. About your haircut. I just think it's funky, and you don't seem druggish or in other ways scummy. Your shirt's got buttons and it's tucked in your slacks. Your shoes could be my shoes. You look like you're at work. That's interesting to me. I find it interesting. I find it surprising. I have to get going now. Thanks for saying hi. Keep up the good work."

That's as close as I've ever come to a mayor. It was a foot or so closer than I would come to Rahm Emanuel in 2012, when my wife shook his hand in advance of his having twice said *Duh-lee-lee-yo* before an audience of five hundred people, including Don DeLillo.

While Mayor Daley and I had spoken on the sidewalk, my father and his partner in the life insurance firm were doing business in their offices in the 150 North Wacker Building, twenty-seven floors above us. My father's partner's name was Donald Dann. Dann's brother's son had been married to then divorced from a woman named Laurie Dann, who, three or four years earlier, had entered a suburban grade school and shot some children, broken into a nearby house, shot a person who lived there, and then shot herself.

I'm told that I was, during my infancy, at a company barbecue that she had attended.

And that's as close as I, now forty-one years old, have ever come to a tragedy that made the nightly news. But I *have* published books and taught creative writing. I *do* hold a master's in clinical social work. My wife *is* Parisian. We *do* go to France every year around Christmas. Dozens of blister packs of benzodiazepenes *are* stacked neatly in a drawer in my office. I *am* incapable, by all indications, of learning French, or, for that matter, any other second language. The Quaker parrot I live with *is* named Gogol. Gogol *does* seem to care for one of my sisters almost as much as he cares for me.

And, of course—need it even be said?—I *am* a Jew.

My first novel, *The Instructions,* is about a ten-year-old Jew who might be the messiah. He leads what is either a violent uprising or terrorist attack or both a violent uprising and terrorist attack depending on the point of view you take. Toward the end of that book, Lake Michigan parts for him, right down the middle.

Among the protagonists of the stories in my story collection, *Hot Pink,* there's a young gay man whose father invents a doll that vomits, a wheelchair-bound lesbian fifteen-year-old attending the University of Chicago, an octogenarian who insists on discussing analingus with a group of other octogenarians, and a guy in finance who poisons his dog and worships a crack in the wall behind his bed that perennially oozes an opaque gel.

People ask me whether my work is autobiographical.

When people ask me whether my work is autobiographical, I know they're not asking me whether I am or ever have been a lesbian, an eighty-some-year-old man, a ten-year-old messiah-terrorist, or a person with a bedroom wall that oozes gel.

Sometimes they're asking me where I get my "ideas." The true answer to this version of the question is dull and narratively malnourished: I don't have "ideas," but rather a desire to undermine ideas. "Ideas" get in the way of art. I am anti-idea. Maybe that's an idea. Sure. Okay.

Usually, though, those who ask me whether my work is autobiographical aren't asking about where I get my "ideas." Usually, they're asking me from where I derive the authority to write about the characters and contexts about whom and which I write. In so doing, they're asserting—or at the least suggesting—that a fiction writer can be granted authority (or that a fiction writer *must* be granted authority) over the subject matter with which his work contends by something or someone other than the work itself. They're asking for credentials. They're seeking bona fides. Attestations to *lived experience.*

I'm not interested in that stuff. I don't find it interesting.

It's not that I don't think the life I've lived has informed the ways I think about my characters and the stories I tell about them—how couldn't it have?—but rather that I think the ways in which my life has informed the ways I think about my characters and the stories I tell about them are neither mappable nor worth a reader's consideration. If they were, I'd have included descriptions of the mappable parts of my life in the works of fiction themselves. Like I'm doing right now.

I write down lies that are, hopefully, pleasing to read, lies that are meant to seem—to *feel*—to those who read them, truer and realer than facts even as I admit the lies are lies by calling them *fiction.* I've been writing down lies since I was five years old, and I've been doing it for three to nine hours a day every day since I was seventeen years old. Every day for a quarter century or so. When I'm not writing down lies, I'm often reading lies that are meant to feel truer and realer than facts even as those lies' authors admit they are lies, and when the authors succeed—when their lies feel truer and realer than facts—I am thrilled.

That I want the lies I write down to feel truer and realer than facts even as I admit they are lies via calling them *fiction* is, I believe, the only biographical information about me that a reader of my fiction should need to possess to be thrilled by my fiction. Am I saying I believe that by virtue of my having called this book that you are reading *fiction,* I've delivered all the autobiographical information you should need to possess to be thrilled by this book? Yes, I am.

And so why include this introduction, then?

Because, first of all, I lack the courage of my convictions. It's true. I'm a coward, reader. I question the goodness of my taste. I think that's important for you to know.

I think that it's important for you to know that I fear the lies this novel comprises would thrill you less if I weren't to include this introduction. Perhaps that's obvious enough already, given that I've included it. Then again, seeing as how readers have asked me whether my previous work was autobiographical despite my *not* having included autobiographical information in that work, perhaps it can't be made obvious *enough.*

—

Also, I'm a nihilist. A misanthrope, too—though I guess that probably goes without saying. To be the first is to be the second. Being the second, you might as well be the first.

To be either, let alone both, is generally considered juvenile, solipsistic, idiotic. I know. And I know that to *say* that you are either, let alone both, regardless of whether your claim is true, probably *is* juvenile.

I feel equally compelled, embarrassed to admit, and embarrassed to feel compelled to admit to being a nihilist and a misanthrope. I do.

Nonetheless: a nihilist and a misanthrope, I. I think life is meaningless and people are terrible. I suspect you do, too. And I suspect you are, too. I don't mean that in a bad way. At least, I'm trying not to. I'm trying to agree with you. And my reasons, I assert—the reasons for my nihilism and misanthropy—are just as good as Gladman's. Apter Schutz's are, as well. I trust yours are, too. Our reasons aren't, however, nearly as compelling or thrilling as Gladman's. Mine aren't, at least.

So I'm making Gladman up instead of writing an essay or a memoir. And I'm making Apter up because Gladman needs a foil—all of us do; all readers and writers, non- and fictional alike. And because a foil must be more than just a foil to feel, to a reader, realer than a fact, Apter will have to be more than just a foil. And I'm writing this essayesque, memoirish intro to this novel that I'm about to start writing about Gladman not only because I question the goodness of my taste, but because life is meaningless, and you are a person, people are terrible, and I believe you agree. Don't you agree? I think you must agree. I'm not just talking to myself here, am I? I mean, aren't people terrible, reader? Except for those who you love, I mean? Except for those who *I* love, I mean?

WRONG BODY

Somewhere out there or in there was a bit involving a duck and pants. The bit, once he grasped it, Gladman strongly suspected, was the bit with which he would close his next show.

He was sitting at his desk, trying to grasp it—he'd been trying every day for almost a week, been trying for nearly four hours that morning—when a physical unpleasantness announced itself to him.

This unpleasantness, unspeakable but ultimately harmless, was more an aggravation or discomfort than a pain. A *flare-up*, he would've probably had to call it were he somehow compelled to refer to it directly.

While it didn't demand he seek medical attention, he knew from experience that stress could make it worse.

He figured he'd better stay home that afternoon.

He found his wife in their bedroom, dressing. She asked him what he thought of the shirt she was wearing. He told her he liked it, that he liked all her shirts. Then he said he was sorry to have to cancel last minute, sorry in fact to have to cancel at all, but that he couldn't make the brunch/Art Institute excursion they'd been planning with his parents and sisters for weeks. He was feeling unwell.

"Unwell how?"

"*Mauvais corps,*" he told her, lying.

Gladman was desperately in love with his wife, to whom he'd been married for almost nine years. His wife was Parisian, but he didn't speak French. He'd tried to learn French, but just couldn't do it, the French wouldn't stick, and that seemed to him to mean that something was wrong with him, and sometimes he feared that his wife thought the same, that she thought he was unintelligent or lazy or that he didn't love her or love her enough, so he'd use the French words he did know when possible, especially when he was disappointing her, hoping that would show her he was trying his best.

Mauvais corps, literally *wrong body,* was the phrase the French used to describe the weak and achy feeling that often preceded a cold or the flu. Gladman and his wife used it that way also, but often they used it to mean, "I'm depressed," which for Gladman always meant, "I'm depressed for no reason, and I'd rather not discuss it; I'd rather we behave as though I have *mauvais corps* in the original sense."

For Daphne, however, the *I'm depressed* sense of *mauvais corps* meant that only some of the time. The rest of the time it meant, "I'm depressed and I'd like very much to talk to you about it, but I don't want to burden you by saying so outright, so please take some initiative and push me to expand."

Gladman had wanted that morning's *mauvais corps* to come across to his wife in the original, French sense. Yet because his *mauvais corps* was a lie in any sense, and because he wasn't very talented at lying in person to those who knew him, he thought it wiser, when his wife then misinterpreted his lie, to act as though she hadn't misinterpreted anything.

"You're depressed?" his wife said, misinterpreting his lie.

He said, "I'd rather not discuss it."

"You don't look depressed," she said.

"You think I'm making it up?"

"All I meant was that your face looks alive. Fully animated. Undepressed Gladmanface. No one will know you're depressed unless you tell them. No one will try to talk to you about it. We'll have a nice meal, we'll see some Giacomettis, we'll see some Dubuffets, we'll be back here by five, six at the latest, and we'll order a pizza and watch Larry David."

"That last part sounds good," Gladman said. "If we could skip to the last part . . . But we can't. And it's not about having to explain myself, really. It's the volume, you know? They get so loud. I don't have the energy. I can't match my dad's . . . spirit. I can't raise my voice."

"Do you want me," she said, "to put your cock in my mouth?"

"I *want* you to, sure, but I doubt it'll help," he said. "Probably I'll still have to stay at home. Then you'll feel betrayed and hate me a little."

"I don't think I'll hate you."

"A little," he said. "It's happened before."

"Maybe," she said. "But only a little. You don't want to try?"

"Yes, I want to try," he said. "Of course I want to try."

The head was transporting. His unspeakable flare-up seemed at first to diminish, and shortly thereafter to completely disappear. His wife left to brush her teeth when it was over, and Gladman lay on the bed for a minute, a couple of minutes, pain-free, grinning, and—what was this? *Hungry.* Hungry for potatoes and bacon and syrup, hungry for an omelet, ready to *brunch.* Looking forward not only to eating some brunch, but also to the having eaten of some brunch. To fighting off the drowsy after-brunch bloat via striding with his family through his favorite museum on this gray and chilly November Sunday. To the warm, balanced lighting there, the thick, scentless air, and especially the noise. That cottony noise of humans in motion trying not to make noise. He loved that noise. The thousands of shoe soles padding on the hardwood, occasionally squeaking. The thousands of pantlegs rubbing each other, some of them swooshing. The in- and advertent cracking of knee joints. The murmured comments, the half-swallowed laughter, the sibilant whispers of nervous parents sharply admonishing handsy toddlers. All of it aggregating, averaging out, then fizzing through the ear canals, into the brain, relaxing the nerves, aiding digestion.

Did he really *love* all that enumerated noise, though? Was thick air—was any air—ever truly *scentless*? Perhaps the endorphins released by his jizzing had made the coming outing seem overly rosy. He paused to consider the possibility, but owing, perhaps, to those same endorphins, dismissed it just as quickly, fell back into reverie.

They'd walk around and look at art till they were hungry again, or able to imagine being hungry again, and then Gladman, hand in hand with his wife, who had never—he'd learned this just a few days earlier—she had never once, not in *thirty-four years* of living on Earth—she had never once drank a chocolate milkshake, or, for that matter, any kind of milkshake—she hadn't ever tasted one, not even a *sip* of one—Gladman, hand in hand with his wife, would tell his family it was time to call it a day, and his father would offer to drive them back home, and Gladman would tell him the bus was right there, and his father would insist, and they'd be driven home, and that would be that, and that would be great.

But that wouldn't be that! Gladman decided, smiling on the bed. That *would* be great, yet that wouldn't be *that*—what would be would be *better*. Better than great. They wouldn't go home. Yes, they'd be driven home and, yes, they'd go inside the building *as if* going home, but they wouldn't go upstairs. Once they'd entered the entrance hall, he'd grab his wife's sleeve and tell her to wait, and, as soon as his father's car had pulled away, he would open the door and they'd go back outside, and they'd get in their own car, and take a short drive. They'd drive to the Humboldt Park milkshake spot he'd recently read about, and buy a couple milkshakes.

There'd be brunch, then art, and then there'd be milkshakes, and, after that, pizza and Larry David episodes, or maybe a Chaplin film, or something sci-fi. Whatever Daphne preferred. They had all the channels. They had all the digital on-demand services.

He rose onto his elbows and shouted for his wife, shouted out to tell her the blowjob had worked, that he'd be able to make the excursion after all, and that he had, furthermore, a nice post-excursion surprise in store for her.

"Daphne!" he shouted. "Hey, Daphne!" he shouted. But even before the second *Daphne* was out, the physical unpleasantness had flared back up.

He lay back down.

Sounds of spitting and rinsing, of the tap shutting off. Daphne returned.

"You called out to me?" she said.

"I just wanted to let you know how much I love you."

"And?"

"I can't shake it."

"Good," she said. "I can't either." She pinched his big toe and wiggled it around.

"You . . . what? Oh. That too," he said. "But I meant the *mauvais corps.*"

"Oh," she said.

"As soon as I feel better, though, I've got a nice surprise for you."

"Cool," she said.

"You hate me a little."

"Yes, a little," she said. "It'll pass soon, I think."

"I'll call them," he said, "and say we aren't feeling well."

"*We?*" she said.

"Well, I wouldn't expect you to go without me. Unless—do you want to?"

"I have to," she said. "I already spoke with your sister on the phone—right before you came in. She called to tell us they were stuck in some traffic. I expressed enthusiasm. We joked about how much bacon we would eat."

"I see."

"I think it's probably better not to call them. When they get here, I'll tell them you woke up feeling not great, but were excited to go, and then you started feeling worse, and still wanted to go, so you took some cold meds, but now you're too zonked to get out of bed."

"Maybe tell them you need to stick around to nurse me?"

"No," Daphne said. "That's going too far. They wouldn't believe it."

"How come?"

"I couldn't sell it."

"Why couldn't you sell it?"

"Because it isn't right."

"How is it any less right than the rest?"

"They're your family, Gladman. I'm your wife."

Though Gladman didn't see how that answered his question, he could tell by her tone that if he pressed for greater clarity, she'd get more upset.

"Okay," he said. "*Pommettes?*" he said.

She pursed her lips and exhaled audibly, but leaned a little closer and allowed him to kiss her over and over along both cheekbones.

Once Daphne had left, Gladman took to the internet in order to seek advice on his unspeakable but ultimately harmless condition. The advice hadn't changed since the last time he'd checked, six or seven months earlier. You either went to the doctor to make sure that your problem wasn't worse than it seemed, or took stress-reducing measures and got more sleep.

The three most popular stress-reducing measures were: daily low-impact exercise and stretching; cutting out or cutting down on caffeine, nicotine, and alcohol intake; and, lastly, consumption of benzodiazepines such as Xanax and Valium, which, although controversial (a certain humbug minority claimed that such drugs, however temporarily relief-providing, delayed recovery, and even, in some cases, worsened the condition), was Gladman's favorite measure, the one he'd most hoped to find was still recommended in the forums he visited.

His smaller desk drawer contained stacks of French Xanax. Some nearly two hundred fifteen-count blister packs of .25-milligram ovoid tablets. About half of them were past their use-by dates, but benzodiazepines never turned poisonous. The worst time could do was steal some of their potency, which itself was unlikely if you kept them out of sunlight.

Gladman nonetheless popped the pair of tablets he would swallow from the youngest of his blister packs, one of the dozen that he'd gotten in Paris the previous Christmas.

He washed the pills down with some milk in the kitchen, then returned to the office, printed out the notes that he'd written that morning, brought the notes to the bed, and fell asleep reading them.

Shortly thereafter, he dreamt he'd grasped the bit about the duck and the pants, and awoke to write it down, but by the time he'd found a pen in his night table's drawer, the bit had mostly faded.

It had had to do with anger. That much he remembered. Anger was key. Anger was the engine that powered the bit. Anger on the part of the duck, regarding pants.

But not *just* anger. It was something more complex. Something to do with the expression of anger. How the duck expressed anger or . . . didn't?

Didn't.

Didn't, but wanted to. Or didn't want to, but should have. One or the other.

The duck should have been angry and wasn't angry about something having to do with pants, or the duck was entitled to show that it was angry about something having to do with pants and was in fact angry but wouldn't show it. Both, perhaps, somehow.

But what it was about pants that had made the duck angry or should have made it angry, Gladman couldn't remember at all. Was it trying to buy pants? If so, from whom? Maybe it was trying to have pants tailored? Maybe the tailor or the seller of the pants refused to treat the duck with the kind of respect that customers deserved?

Or maybe the duck was itself a seller or tailor of pants but customers refused to take the duck seriously because it wasn't a man but a duck? or because it wasn't a raven, but a duck? or wasn't a chicken? because ravens, or chickens, in the world of the bit, were the ones who normally sold or tailored pants?

Were the customers ravens, or chickens, themselves? Perhaps there were a number of animal species of customer, none of whom were willing to take the duck seriously in whatever capacity it wished to be taken seriously, and these customers revealed their contempt for the duck via haggling cynically over the money the duck said they owed it for the sale of the pants or the tailoring of the pants, many of them adding insult to injury with microaggressive puns about bills, the kinds of bills you pay vs. the kinds that ducks all had on their faces? And maybe the duck was a mild-mannered duck, and contempt rolled off its back like water. It was used to being treated with contempt by its customers, but what it couldn't stand—what made the duck angry—was hearing those same stale puns about bills, day in, day out, over and over, and seeing how the customers' eyes lit up when they made their puns, how they seemed to think their puns about bills were inspired, inspired and original. And what made the duck even angrier than that was the knowledge that if it chose to display its anger to its customers by winging their necks or biting their bodies, or even if it just failed to politely laugh at their worn-out fucking puns about bills—even then, they'd believe they'd ruffled its feathers, and their satisfaction would drive the duck—

No. No no. Forget it. That wasn't the bit he'd been dreaming about. It was lost for good.

Gladman fell back asleep.

When next he came awake, it was dark outside, his empty stomach was rumbling, and his life had become a meaningless tragedy.

A little more than an hour earlier, at exactly 4:09 p.m., the Earth had opened up under downtown Chicago. The eighty-three-story Aon Center was laid low and folded and southwardly dragged across Millennium Park, which, rapidly sinking, sucked in at the edges, pulling the Art Institute into itself. As the taller building impaled the shorter, Prudential Plaza collapsed and slid south. Then the Crain Communications Building split and toppled, and the Symphony Center caved and toppled, and all the structures on the four-block stretch of Michigan Avenue between the Crain and the Symphony Center, all of them leaning and trembling or buckling, fell eastward at once as if shoved from behind, and a chain of increasingly destructive explosions down in the continually deepening crater blew apart and set fire to and melted and boiled much of the steel and brick and concrete and all of the people and wildlife and plant life from Jackson to Lake between Columbus and Wabash, and Gladman's wife and Gladman's parents and Gladman's sisters and Gladman's nieces and Gladman's nephew were, every last one of them, lost to Gladman forever.

But Gladman didn't yet know what had happened downtown. What he knew was he was hungry, a little bit high, and free of any unspeakable physical unpleasantness. What Gladman felt compelled to consider first and foremost was whether the pizza he would order momentarily should be all pepperoni or half-pepperoni/half-ricotta–black olive.

Daphne preferred ricotta–black olive to pepperoni, but only if the pizza was extra well-done, since otherwise the slices, overburdened and soggy, fell apart when you lifted them.

And it was easy enough to order extra well-done. The dispatcher would adopt a put-upon tone, but he'd get the word to the ovenman anyway. The trouble was that extra well-doneness always caused some charring of the pepperoni discs. The charring didn't quite *ruin* the pizza for Gladman, though it always did disappoint him a little. It probably disappointed him just as much as a slice of pepperoni's not being a slice of ricotta–black olive disappointed Daphne.

So one of them would have to be disappointed, and he had to choose who. That was Gladman's dilemma. And since neither of them deserved to be disappointed, the question at the heart of Gladman's dilemma was: Who was entitled to enjoy their pizza more that evening, Gladman or his wife? Gladman knew the answer instantly. The answer was: his wife. Of that he was certain.

Being Gladman, however, he resented certainty, even his own. Especially his own. Except in art. In art he liked certainty. Demanded certainty. Great art, Gladman thought, was always certain of something. In fact, that was the point of it: to be great while being certain, which for people was impossible.

I can't say if I agree with some or all or none of that. It sounds a bit canned. It also sounds a bit quoted, perhaps a bit *mis*quoted. Like something I might have heard or misheard at a lecture from a certain professor I studied with in grad school, who, like Gladman, was feeling expansive, though, unlike Gladman, wasn't high on Xanax. The professor I'm thinking of didn't use drugs.

But Gladman, in any case, spent a couple minutes attempting to convince himself that Daphne was no more entitled to enjoy their pizza than he. To his credit, he failed. He would order, he decided, a large half-pepperoni/half-ricotta–black olive, extra well-done. When he lifted his phone, though, and his phone lit up, he couldn't see the lock-screen photo of his parrot.

Gladman's parrot's name was Gogol.

His name had been Gogol since 2007, for all fourteen years that Gladman had owned him minus ninety minutes at the very beginning. For an hour after Gladman had first bought Gogol, Gogol's name had been Monkey.

Then he'd called his mom to say he'd gotten a pet, a baby Quaker parrot, and she'd asked what he'd named it, and he'd told her, "Monkey."

His mother's response had been, "Don't be an asshole," which Gladman took to mean, "Monkey is an undignified name for a bird."

His mother had a Chihuahua whose name was Chi-Chi. Before that she'd had a frost point Siamese cat whose name had been Frosty. Before that, there'd been Pom-Pom, a yappy Pomeranian. She hadn't suggested that Gladman was an asshole since the 1990s, since Gladman was fifteen or sixteen years old, so he immediately took what she'd said to heart, unnamed his parrot Monkey, and, half an hour later, renamed it after the author of "The Overcoat," his favorite short story.

Some people thought this was embarrassingly pretentious of Gladman. It seemed to those people that Gladman had chosen to name his parrot after a nineteenth-century Russian author in order to appear more cultured than he was, and that he'd thereby demonstrated, inadvertently, how cultured he wasn't. Gladman understood that. He might have thought the same of someone else, had they named their parrot, or any other pet, after Nikolai Gogol, or any other author. But the reasons he had for naming his parrot after Nikolai Gogol had nothing to do with how he wished to be perceived. Rather, he imagined—correctly, it turned out—that Gogol would be an easy name for a parrot to pronounce, and he hoped that his parrot would behave like the work of Nikolai Gogol: he hoped his parrot would be funny and tender and spirited and weird and no more antisemitic than its milieu.

If Gladman's having named his parrot Gogol was embarrassing, it wasn't because it inadvertently revealed that Gladman was pretentious, but rather because it failed to conceal his ever-increasingly frequent tendency to sentimentally anthropomorphize animals.

All of which, for a while, had confused his wife. Daphne hadn't understood why someone who behaved as gooily loving toward his pet as Gladman would have named that pet Gogol, a word that in French was short for *Mongolien,* which in English meant *Mongoloid,* and thus led her to translate Gogol as *retard.*

The same image of Gogol waving hi from a perch had been the lockscreen photo on every smartphone that Gladman had owned. He'd bought his first smartphone in 2010. In the decade since, he'd owned a total of five. The only other time that the photo had been completely obscured by notifications was in 2011, when Gladman had won a national prize for his second novel. After the ceremonial dinner at which the prize had been announced and awarded, he had eleven vigorous vertical swipes' worth of congratulatory text and voicemail notifications from people who had read on the internet about his having won.

The power of the association was . . . powerful. Gladman, in his bed, looking at his phone, forgot about pizza. His tranquilized heart had begun to flutter. Perhaps he had won something. But what could he have won? It had to be something huge, he thought, swiping vertically. So many of the phone numbers from which the texts and voicemails had been sent were +33'd. Daphne's family, every member it looked like, both their French publishers, many of their friends . . .

What prize or grant or fellowship announcement made while he'd been napping could have reached so many on a Sunday afternoon—a Sunday night in Paris—and been so big a deal as to inspire so many attempts at contact in so short a time?

He hadn't applied for anything since a couple-three years after having published that prizewinning novel. He hadn't published anything since he'd published that novel. He'd gotten tenure and quit writing fiction in favor of performing. So the prize or grant or fellowship he'd just ostensibly won would have to be the kind one didn't apply for, and those kinds were awarded not for *a* work, but for the work of a career. Obviously (was it really so obvious? yes—yes it was), he hadn't won the Nobel Prize. But the $625k MacArthur Foundation Genius Grant? That seemed within reach, and he'd heard rumors of his nomination in previous years.

The MacArthur Grants were always announced in October. What was the date today? He tried to remember. Couldn't remember. He was higher than he'd thought! He adjusted his gaze by micrometers. "11/17/21," read his lock screen, just above the northernmost notification. And so that meant: no. The MacArthurs had already been announced weeks ago. Who had won? He couldn't remember.

But so what about a $125k Lannan Foundation Grant? Could that be it? He hadn't a clue as to when those were announced. They weren't very publicized. Plus, wouldn't he have heard from the foundation before the announcement? Well, maybe not. A few years earlier, the list of MacArthur Grant recipients had leaked a few weeks prior to the scheduled announcement. Maybe the names of this year's Lannan Foundation Grant recipients had leaked. Maybe the foundation itself had leaked the names in advance of having contacted the recipients precisely in order to drum up the high level of national publicity that the leaking of the names of MacArthur Grant recipients had drummed up when—

A call was coming in. Daphne's mother.

"Hello?" said Gladman.

"*Baruch Ha-Shem!*" said Daphne's mother.

Baruch Ha-Shem is something observant Jewish people often say to express relief or joy. It translates from Hebrew as "Blessed God." Nonobservant Jews like Gladman say it, too, to express the same feelings as observant Jews who say it. Not always, but usually, the nonobservant Jews who say *Baruch Ha-Shem* hope to produce a light comedic effect, saying it at times when observant Jews would find the invocation of God to be inappropriate, or even offensive.

Daphne's mother was neither an observant nor a nonobservant Jew, nor was she Muslim, but she, in common with many citizens of France, often said *Inshallah* to express the hope that something she just mentioned would come to pass. *Inshallah* translates from Arabic as "If God wills it."

The non-Muslim French who say *Inshallah* tend, when they say it, to be seeking a light comedic effect that is similar to, if not identical to, that which so many nonobservant Jews seek when they say *Baruch Ha-Shem*.

"The pizza should be here any minute, *Inshallah*."

"*Baruch Ha-Shem*, the pizza has arrived!"

That sort of thing.

It had happened that the first time Gladman heard Daphne's mother say *Inshallah*, which was the first time he'd heard any non-Muslim say *Inshallah*, was also the first time Daphne's mother heard Gladman say *Baruch Ha-Shem*, which was the first time she'd heard anyone at all say *Baruch Ha-Shem*. This was just before the holidays, in 2014 or maybe 2015, six or seven years before the Earth had opened up under downtown Chicago and killed their favorite woman.

"My pharmacist was out of brand-name Xanax," Daphne's mother had said to Daphne, "and so I bought Gladman generic alprazolam for Christmas this year."

And Daphne had said, "I'm sure it works just as well. He won't be disappointed."

And her mother had said, "*Inshallah, inshallah.*"

They'd been speaking in French, and all Gladman had picked up were his name, and *Inshallah*. He asked them what they'd said.

Daphne's mother told him.

"More drugs for Christmas!" he'd said, and hugged her. "*Baruch Ha-Shem!* Jeanne, you're the best."

"What is it, *Baruch Ha-Shem*?" she'd said.

Gladman told her what it meant, how he and other Jews used it, and she liked it, so she'd started using it herself.

"*Baruch Ha-Shem* backatcha!" said Gladman to Daphne's mother, over the telephone, on November 17, 2021. He was certain now that he'd won something major. "All is well in Paris?" he said.

"Now it is, yes. Very much yes. We've been so frightened. Daphne has not been answering her phone, and we feared the worst. She is with you, yes? May I speak to her, Gladman?"

"The worst?" said Gladman.

Politics and the Chicagoan Language

No one from the mayor's office ever said *sinkhole*, except for one gal, just once, over internet: "Our thoughts and prayers are with the families and loved ones of the victims of the sinkhole."

By the end of the workday, that gal had been shitcanned.

The mayor'd liked the gal, too. Liked the gal a lot. The gal didn't get it, though. The problem with *sinkhole*. Or acted like she didn't. One or the other. Same difference in the end. She either really didn't get it—in which case: incompetent—or played dumb when he explained to her—in which case: fuck you because at least have the dignity.

Sinkholes were for Florida. They made you think of swamps and they made you think of armpits. Swampy armpits. Meth, opossums, thrush, and swamp-ass. People in mourning did not need that. People trying to sympathize with people in mourning did not need that. Not in the least did the City of Chicago need that at all. And thereby and therefore: gal, shitcanned.

You know how many hands he could count the regrets on?

He could count the regrets on exactly no hands.

For a week or so, they said *the seismic event*. Which was sufficiently solemn and science-y sounding, sure, except then it began to seem too . . . *earthquakian* for the mayor. Maybe only to him. Hard to know for certain. Epistemical roadblocks and so forth. But who hears *seismic* and doesn't think *earthquake*?

The way the mayor saw it was that the way that people saw it was where once there was an earthquake, there will probably again be a whole nother earthquake, and probably sooner rather than later. People were negative. People needed hope. The city needed to heal, and then it needed to grow, always needed to grow. And it *hadn't* been an earthquake. Basically, what it had been was a sinkhole. So inaccuracy, too.

Then top it all off with by the end of that week *the seismic event* was already getting shortened to just *the event*. For a little while, the mayor thought: Good. The mayor thought: You drop the *seismic,* you eventually lose the earthquakian overtones.

But that was pie-in-the-sky on the part of the mayor. That was a pipe dream the mayor was having. That thinking was wishful.

It was wishful thinking.

No one forgot what *event* was short for. They heard *event* with their ears, but in their brains they were adding the *seismic* in front of it. And a *seismic* unsaid, was, in a way, more affecting than a *seismic* unsilent.

Like the one-drop in all your best reggae music. A beat is missing—the drummer leaves it out—so you supply it yourself, inside your brain. And that beat that wasn't there was made there-er than there. You danced to that beat that wasn't there. Unless for some reason you didn't like reggae—probably not you were racist, probably more like you were too shy to really let go enough to feel the primalistical islander rhythm, or too embarrassed to express the kind of feeling that rhythm made you feel—and refused to dance at all.

Reggae always made the mayor want to dance. The mayor's wife, too. She had a beautiful dance she would do to some reggae.

Or another way to say it, he explained for those staffers who seemed like maybe they didn't dance to reggae, was that *event* sounded a step or three too deliberately removed. Sounded like they were trying to hide something. Like generals saying *collateral damage* for *civilian casualties* for *civilian deaths* for *women and children blown to pieces by mistargeted missiles* for *women and children blown to pieces by properly targeted missiles.*

You say *civilian deaths,* or even *civilian casualties,* maybe you're a sensitive general who's trying to protect citizens from having to vividly picture women and children bleeding, in pieces. But you say *collateral damage,* not only do you cause the citizens you're talking to to think extra long about what you mean by *collateral damage,* which gets them to picture dead innocents more vividly and horribly than if you'd just said *civilian deaths* or *civilian casualties,* but you sound like a general trying to cover something up, to cover even his own ass maybe. Is the point.

"And we got nothing to cover up for, here," the mayor, at the meeting he'd called for the purpose of discussing the terminology, continued to explain for the benefit of staffers who might not love one-drop the way he loved one-drop or might have gotten lost while he explained about the generals. "We got nothing to cover up, because this tragedy was not our fault. Not by a long shot. And as much as citizens like to feel that their cities are being managed by government, that is also exactly just how much if not even more than how much they *dis*like to feel that they, themselves, are being managed by government. They hate it, understand? It insults their intelligence. I know this because I am first and foremost a citizen, and when someone tries to manage me, there stands my intelligence beside me, red-faced and clenching its fists and insulted, looking to me to set things right. And how do we set an insult right? By talking things through? By trying to change the insult's mind? No and no. There's no talking to insults. It's what makes them insulting. By vengeance is how we try to set insults right. And if we are civilized and not violent animals that means going to the voting booth with vengeance in our hearts and acting in accordians with the vengeance in our hearts by voting against whoever insulted us. So you understand the problem with *event*?"

Silence.

"My question," said the mayor, "was not what some call a rhetorical question. I am wanting you to answer it to demonstrate you get what my problem is with *event*."

"It's not the right euphemism," the staffer who'd been hired to replace the gal who'd said *sinkhole* said. "It works against itself. Undermines its speaker." His name was Apter Schutz.

"Undermines, exactly," the mayor said. "Works against, too. And times a million. *Event* is like a euphemism for *seismic event,* and *seismic event* is like a euphemism for *seismic catastrophe* and that one there is its very own self a euphemism for *violent earthquakian act of God,* which all of us here in this room know means *widest and deepest sinkhole maybe ever and for sure in Chicago in recorded history which killed many thousands of unsuspecting innocents in just a couple minutes.* Which is not acceptable. It is bad karate and I do not accept it. So . . ."

"So don't say *event*," Apter Schutz offered. "Or *seismic event.*"

"You guys are the best," the mayor said. "That's why you get to work here, for the City of Chicago, in the office of the holder of its highest public office. Now keep your thinking caps on, and let's order some pizza and figure out the right name for this miserable fucking disaster we have suffered and are suffering and will continue to suffer together as a team."

The last fire at the site of the terrestrial anomaly burned itself out on December 21. By then, Apter Schutz was the mayor's main guy. Not only had he been the one to come up with a catchy yet solemn and science-y name for the disaster that was both non-Floridian (high number of syllables) and anti-earthquakian at its very core (*anomaly*, which, arrived from the Greek or the Latin, meant: never happened before, and wouldn't happen again), he was a total Jew. And that sounded maybe antisemitic if you said it, the mayor knew, and the mayor wasn't that, so he didn't say it, but he wasn't ashamed that it was what he thought. He thought, in fact, that continuing to think it made him something like brave. Brave *because* of how so many people these days, if they heard him saying it, would say that he was antisemitic. So it demonstrated courage. Courage of convictions. It was a silent expression of his ability and willingness to possess the courage of his own convictions, his thinking that Apter was a total Jew even though some would call it antisemitic.

Moreover, though: affection. *Total Jew* was an expression of affection. He thought "total Jew" with affection in his heart. In thinking "total Jew," he was giving a compliment, however silently, and when he looked at Apter and thought "total Jew," he did so with a smile on his face, a certain kind of a warm and friendly but also a knowing and murderous smile, which he'd only recently learned how to smile by observing guess who. That's right. Apter Schutz.

You had to squint both eyes the same amount at the start, but then one of them—the one on the side that you were leaning toward, which was the same side the person you were smiling at was standing on—you *un*squinted it right in the middle of the smile, hiked its corresponding eyebrow and lip corner, too. The effect was: We both know I could have you killed, but since we both know I'll never have you killed, isn't the reminder I could have you killed very flattering for both of us? Like: Aren't we very cute together, heterosexually?

The mayor's wife had noted the new way he smiled, and she herself had said, "It's kind of like Apter. Very Jew-like, but in a good way. Not like you're trying to seem like a Jew." She wasn't being sarcastic, either: she wasn't saying he *was* trying to seem like a Jew, or implying that he wished that he was truly a Jew, or more like a Jew. Why would the mayor ever want to be a Jew? The mayor was the mayor. The last mayor'd been a Jew, and the people'd mostly hated him.

No, the mayor did not wish he was a Jew, though maybe, if he couldn't have been exactly him, if he couldn't have been the mayor who he was already, he might have been someone who wished he were a Jew.

These were, after all, the inventors of the gray area, the Jews. Or if not the inventors, then the ones who named it. Or if not the ones who named it, the ones who named it most often, who described it the best. What area couldn't a Jew turn gray? What gray area of any prominence hadn't the Jews been *the first* to turn gray? They crucified Jesus, which, historically speaking, was probably the shittiest thing anyone ever did to anyone else ever, but, same time, and speaking just as historically, if Jesus hadn't died on the cross, there wouldn't be any Christians, just a bunch of Greek or Roman pedophiles everywhere. Maybe Arabian ones, too, because could there be any Muslims without there first being Christians spreading the idea of just one God? A lot of people didn't think so, the mayor had heard, and the mayor was among them. So any time you said, "The Jews murdered Jesus," you might as well have said, "The Jews started Christianity," which might as well mean, "The Jews started Islam." And three ways vice versa. All those statements, as far as the mayor was concerned, were equally true. That was gray as it got.

And what it was with the Jews was the Jews were raised knowing this right from the beginning. "We're Christ-killers, which would normally mean we were the shittiest people, but since our Christ-killing has ended up leading to the salvation of so many hundreds of millions of souls, not to mention preventing countless little Greco-Roman boys from getting sexually violated in baths and saunas, how shitty can a people like us really be? Not so fucken shitty, after all, looks like." And if that's where you're starting from, a young Jewish schoolkid, having to contend with the all-time grayest of the grayest areas, you're just a lot more likely than the average jagoff—than even, really, the above-average jagoff—to end up becoming a genius at articulating all the right words together. Which were the most important things to be able to articulate. Especially of lately.

These days, more than ever before, people needed to believe you were oppressed before they were willing to give you more power than whatever power you already had, even if you deserved that extra power anyway, and so anyone with any political sense knew how to play oppressed while standing on a throat. Only a Jew, though, could pull off playing oppressed while standing on a throat and at the same time pointing his finger at a guy who's standing on another throat—or even the same throat—and calling that other guy an oppressor. And it was only a very rare few of them like Apter who could (or so the mayor imagined) do all of the above while the throat that he was standing on was *yours*.

Complete and total Jew. Complete and total compliment.

Another mayor's lesser Jew would have thought of Christmas on December 21. Another mayor's lesser Jew would even have probably thought of all the Jews in the media who'd think about Christmas. But would that other mayor's lesser Jew have thought as instantly as Apter had about the other media Jews who'd think about Christmas? The mayor didn't think so.

On December 21, when CFD Chief O'Leary called the mayor from the site of the terrestrial anomaly to pronunciate the last of the fires extinguished, the very first thing that Apter Schutz said into the speakerphone's mike was, "Keep the hoses going, and send no one home."

O'Leary said, "Now why would I do that, and who the fuck is speaking?"

And Apter leaned toward the mayor, across the mayor's desk, and smiled the smile the mayor had learned from him, but this time added a nod to it that said, "Trust your Jew. Back your Jew up."

Which the mayor did.

"That," the mayor said to O'Leary, "was young Apter Schutz who was talking there, Ryan, and he's absolutely right. Keep those hoses hosing till further instructed, and keep your heroes in place, looking busy. I'll explain it all later."

O'Leary said, "We already turned those hoses off."

"That's okay," Apter said. "Just turn them back on."

"That's *okay* with you, huh?"

"More importantly, Ryan, it's okay with *me*," the mayor said. "I see no reason to shitcan your ass for turning off the hoses before you should have. People make mistakes, right?"

He ended the call.

"So?" he said to Apter.

"Helicopters," Apter said. "Weather and traffic. If we're waiting till the twenty-fourth to announce, we don't want anyone *before* the twenty-fourth to know that the last of the fires is out. That would blow the Christmas miracle."

"Miracle?"

"Not miracle, you're right. That's too much. But *blessing*," Apter said. "The Christmas blessing."

"Right," the mayor said. "The Christmas blessing. That's better." He was only just getting it. He hadn't had the chance to think of it yet, of waiting till the twenty-fourth to announce. He would have thought of it, eventually, probably inside the next couple minutes—he wasn't an idiot, just wasn't a Jew—but he loved that Apter'd figured he'd already thought of it. Sign of a truly fantastic mayor–staffer working relationship with strong overtones of mentorship.

"The citizens of Chicago need and deserve a nice sign from above," the mayor told Apter in order to aid in the corroboration of Apter's assumptions in regard to the Jewish speed the mayor possessed when it came to the calculation of truly next-level political decision-making there. "Some helicopter-riding media turd blows the blessing aspect of our goodly fortune by breaking the news of the extinguishment early? That would cause the warm cockles of my heart to colden. Not to mention some runnier media turd than that who maybe has it in for me could hold on to captured images he's taken of the hoses not hosing till *after* I make the announcement on the twenty-fourth? And then he makes it look like I held out word of the extinguishment on purpose to manage perceptions? citizen perceptions? which varietal of management I very publicly, as you well know, am completely against?"

"Bingo," said Apter.

"It's a privilege," said the mayor, "to have you on the same page as me, Apter." Then they did the smile at each other for a while, and started working on his statement.

No one could talk to the people like the mayor. When people tried to talk like how the mayor talked to the people, it sounded like they were making fun of the mayor. Sometimes they were, the mayor knew. That was part of being mayor, or any public person, and the mayor was okay with that, he had a good sense of humor about it, just so long as while whoever it was who was making fun of the way the mayor talked to the people wasn't also making fun of the people at the very same time. Or making fun of the way the legendary mayors of Chicago throughout the whole history of the last century-plus of legendary mayors of Chicago spoke to the people, which is how the mayor spoke to the people.

For that he would not tolerate.

Apter Schutz understood and recognized all of the above, the mayor greatly appreciated. They'd worked on a couple-three statements together, and Apter hadn't ever once even tried to write down a whole sentence for the mayor to say because that was not how the mayor worked effectively, and Apter knew that, intuitively, from studying how the mayor'd worked on statements with other staffers.

How the mayor worked effectively was by knowing the bullet points, plus maybe a couple or three-four buzzwords, and then just going out there for the people and winging it. With feeling.

And so it was, with then as with always, how they effectively worked on the Christmas Blessing Statement.

He delivered the statement at 1 p.m. on December 24, 2021, in Daley Plaza, between the big Picasso and the beautiful Christmas tree that, for the first time since the year 2015, had not been lit in Millennium Park.

"Ladies and gentlemen and gender-nonconforming members of the press, thank you all for coming. I bear welcome news," the mayor stated to the gathered and aforementioned.

"This morning, the heroic men and women and gender-nonconforming members of our Chicago Fire Department extinguished the last of the fires at the site of the terrestrial anomaly. For nearly six weeks now, they have labored tirelessly in our service. They have spent long hours in gas masks and helmets and hazmat suits, peopling hoses and ropes and ladders and pulleys, peopling forklifts and shovels and humble crowbars, jerry-rigging structures of bent steel and broken concrete to get better angles of approach into perilous zones of unknown menace, sweating outside in the freezing cold, disposing of and/or destroying toxinating material before it could make its way into our lungs, into our water. Creating perimeters. Securing those perimeters and keeping them secure. These men and women have, in summation, contained and fended off many kinds of present dangers to themselves and prevented even more kinds of other *potential* dangers from arising *to* ourselves. They have kept all of us safe.

"Tonight, they will get to go home to their families—most of them will. And tomorrow, many of those who are going home tonight will get to sleep in late, late as they want, many for the first time in a while, I'd think. And that's the least they deserve."

Applause.

"Now I would be remiss in pretending that I'm not aware of the timing of this last of the extinguishments, especially what with our beautiful three-story Douglas fir so tenderly strung with its multicolored lights in the plaza right next to me here, so I will not be remiss. I will not pretend.

"I will not pretend that when I learned the last of the fires was extinguished this morning, I didn't think, 'Christmas blessing.' I *did*. I thought, 'Christmas blessing. A reward for hard work. At last, at last. We keep on doing things right,' I thought, 'and maybe things will continue down this path of taking more turns for the better.'

"And I tell you true, the very moment I thought that thought, I realized that even here, even now, even in the wake of our tragedy, there was much to be grateful for. There *is* much to be grateful for. Much. There are blessings to count.

"First and foremost of all: the timing of the anomaly. The whole Novembery Sundayness of it. Had it been less rainy or cold on 11/17, statistics show—and I had my guys look this up, believe you me— attendance at the Art Institute (and this goes more than double, a *lot* more than double for visitations to Millennium Park) would have been higher, a *whole lot* higher, and we could have lost as many as twice as many people as we lost. And had our tragedy occurred just two days earlier, or one day later, so many professional people who work in offices would have been at work in their professional offices, and we could have lost as many as *ten* times as many of the people that were lost. That is first and foremost. That is something to be grateful for, to count as a blessing: all those lives that were saved by the anomaly's timing.

"And then there is of course what was *not* destroyed. What was spared. How is it, until this morning, I wondered this morning, that it had escaped my appreciation that, for example, damage to our El was so minimal? The answer is: it escaped my appreciation because it is hard to count blessings when you're counting victims. Blessings are wonderful, victims are tragic, and in the midst of the tragic, the area beyond the mental line of awareness across which a blessing must cross before it can be wondered at with enough sufficiency to be recognized as a blessing—a line that we call, in my family, *the wonderline*—is very blurry. But, as of this morning, that area has started to clear up a little. The fog, or even the smoke, so to speak, has started to lift. The news of the final extinguishment has shall we say *dissipated* the fog or smoke that was covering the area beyond my wonderline, and now I can all the better see some of the blessings that have gotten across it, such as, like I was saying, the minimal damage to the El.

"We have had to reconstruct struts and reinforce pylons on portions of the Red Line between Lake and Jackson, and it was costly, but we made that happen, and we made that happen in a very timely fashion. That work was finished nearly three weeks ago. And the truth is that the Red Line is up and running and better—and *safer*—than ever, now. And what about the Blue Line?

"Untouched by the anomaly.

"The Pink Line?

"*Also* untouched by the anomaly.

"The Green, the Orange, the Purple, the Yellow: each line as equally untouched as the Blue and the Pink.

"By the anomaly.

"And how about our beloved, much praised, and often popularly sung-about Lake Shore Drive? the world-class waterfront highway of every Chicagoan's fondness and pride, the damage to which, like the damage to all of the aforementioned lines of the El with the exception of the Red, was *nil*?

"How about *that*?

"These are only some of the blessings I counted this morning, and they are an even smaller fraction of all the blessings that I plan to count, and that I plan to share my counting of with you as we stand together in these coming weeks and months overcoming this sad chapter with our can-do, big-shouldered attitudes as the poet would have had it had he been alive to witness the ways we have come together to overcome the aforementioned sad chapter and the ways we will continue to come together to overcome that chapter. *This* chapter.

"If I can leave you with one thought to think about this holiday season, then the thought I would hope to leave you with is this: Chicago isn't going anywhere. We are, every one of us, all-star NFL linesmen in our souls, and yes it is true that I wish, like I'm sure all of you wish, that there had never been any chapter that required our talent for the overcoming of it to be demonstrated, but we have demonstrated that talent, in spades, we have put our big shoulders to the task of tackling this chapter that needs to be tackled, we *have* tackled it in fact, and we will keep on demonstrating even more of our talent in even further spades, we will keep on tackling it till the game is over or it can't get up, whichever comes first, and if you want to know why, I will tell you why, even though I think you already know why: because this is Chicago and we are Chicagoans, and that's what we do here. Everything we can. That is what we do. And I count that as perhaps the greatest blessing of all. You really cross my wonderline, Chicago. Merry Christmas, and a very Happy Chanukah."

Statement made, Christmas Eve officially about to arrive, the people of Chicago assuredly comforted and maybe even hopefully uplifted somewhat, the mayor called Apter Schutz into his office and poured them each a twenty-one-year-old Scotch, and they sat there, on opposite sides of his desk, inwardly warming, mostly quiet, sharing their smile together at each other.

Some months later, looking back and reflecting, it would seem to the mayor like they'd shared that smile all the way through the rest of the winter and first part of spring. Like, if someone ever made the mayor's biopic and paid him to consult on it, that's the image he'd suggest that the filmmaker use to mark the passage of time. Apter and the mayor sharing the smile while the strip of snow on the window ledge behind the desk started glowing, at first just a little, like the sun was coming out from behind some clouds and lighting it up, except then the strip would get brighter and brighter, brighter than the wintertime sun could ever make it, and artful white light would spread across the screen till that's all you could see.

When the next scene started, they'd still be sitting there, sharing the smile, but wearing different clothes, and the mayor'd have a beard, and the strip of snow wouldn't be there anymore because of how, in the biopic, it was supposed to be spring now, spring of 2022, which, historically speaking, might seem a little false to certain viewers because the spring of '22 in Chicago would have been rough, a spring during which the snowfall in Chicago would have actually been heavier than that of the preceding winter. But the mayor would figure that wouldn't be a problem. The mayor would figure that if someone cried foul about how the snow strip should still be on the ledge, or how the snow strip on the ledge should even maybe be a couple inches taller than before the transition with the artful light, he'd just gently remind them that biopics were forms of art, which meant that those who made or consulted on biopics were supposed to be granted artistic licenses, which worked in basically the same exact way as poetic licenses worked for poets, giving them a pass on always being literal because sometimes being literal prevented you from being liter*ary*. Ironic? *Certainly.* It was maybe ironic. Who could argue with that?

ANIMAL PSYCHOLOGY

Every year since they'd met, Gladman and Daphne had spent the winter holidays in Paris. Depending on Gladman's teaching schedule, they'd visit for either four or five weeks.

While they were away, Gladman's younger sister, Kayla, would stay at their condo and take care of Gogol.

It was nice for everyone. The condo was relatively recently rehabbed, modernly applianced, spacious, and clean. The places where Kayla had lived as an adult were rarely more than two of those things, never in a neighborhood as lively as Gladman's, and often inhabited by at least one roommate who annoyed or depressed or annoyed and depressed her.

More importantly, Gogol was nuts for Kayla. Just days after Gladman had first brought him home, Kayla'd broken up with her live-in girl-friend and had spent the better part of the next couple months crashing on Gladman's living room couch. Her continual presence encouraged the parrot, who was still a fledgling and was thus still learning who belonged to his flock, to form a substantial bond with Kayla, a bond that was second only in power to that which he had formed with her brother.

If granted access to two or more almonds, sometimes Gogol would pick up one almond and hold it with his beak, then pick up a second almond with a foot and drop the second almond into Gladman's cupped hand. That was something that Gogol had never done with Kayla, but in everything else, he'd treat her same as he would treat Gladman. He'd climb onto her shoulder to preen her kinky hair or whisper in her ear, he'd lie on his back in her palm and sleep, and he'd learn to whistle bits of songs she'd teach him: the opening measures of the *Andy Griffith* theme song, the opening measures of the *Superman* theme song, nearly half of "The Imperial March."

Four winter breaks prior to the anomaly, though, Gladman's mother was turning seventy, and Gladman's father, to celebrate her birthday, brought her and Gladman's sisters and Gladman's sister Naomi's children to Paris. They were there for two weeks.

During that time, a former student of Gladman's stayed at the condo and took care of Gogol. This student, Ann, had been one of Gladman's favorites: a talented writer, a gentle human being, and the first woman unrelated to Gladman who Daphne had meaningfully befriended in America. She'd been over for dinner any number of times, and Gogol had screamed far less often in her presence than he had in the presence of any other guest except for Kayla. During some of Ann's visits, he'd even left his cage—the cage was kept open whenever Gladman was at home and awake—and repeatedly greeted her by raising a foot and saying, "Hi!" and saying, "Hello!" whereas usually, when guests who weren't Kayla came over, he would pose with defensively out-puffed feathers on the perch inside the cage that was farthest from the door.

By the time Gladman's family arrived in Paris, he and Daphne had been there for nearly three weeks. Kayla, who'd stayed at the condo during those weeks, reported that Gogol had been in fine form when she'd left. He'd learned a new measure of "The Imperial March" and the opening notes of Guns N' Roses' "Patience"—she played them videos she'd made on her phone—and although he'd screamed for five or ten minutes when Ann showed up for the changing of the guard, he soon calmed down, came out of the cage, and whistled a little *Superman* for her.

After buying Gogol, Gladman had spent a couple months reading up on parrots. All the sources agreed that Quakers were especially resilient. *Hardy* was the word that kept coming up. One of the more informative (however clumsily overwritten) books he'd consulted was *Every Parrot Owner's Guide to His or Her Parrot,* and its entry on Quakers contained the following sentence: "In the mind of the Quaker parrot, the only nest-building parrot species on Earth, one readily finds a psychological analog to its hardy physicality."

In part, no doubt, because he so enjoyed words like *hardy*—words it seemed he'd known forever, yet had somehow never spoken aloud—the thought of Gogol's being hardy operated almost magically on Gladman. In the first few months during which he owned Gogol, he was overly concerned about the bird's health. Gogol might, for example, scream nonstop for an hour at a time, remove food from the bowl and drop it on the floor, or chew at his claws in a way that seemed excessive, and Gladman, fearing such behaviors signaled illness, would begin to feel anxious, but before his anxiety could reach too high a pitch, he would remind himself that Quaker parrots were *hardy,* and the thought would provide him a measure of steadiness. It would steady him enough that he'd remember the vet—he'd remember he could always call up the vet. And he would. Once every nine or ten days or so probably. More often than not, the vet would tell Gladman over the phone that whatever behavior had alarmed him was normal, that Quaker parrots were very *hardy.* And those times when he did bring Gogol in for an exam, she'd always conclude that everything was fine, that, even for a Quaker, Gogol seemed particularly *hardy.*

Gladman would believe her and, soon enough, he became less nervous. His calls to the vet became less frequent, *infrequent* even. He'd learned to take Gogol's hardiness for granted, so much so that he didn't text Ann to see how Gogol was doing till three or four days after his family had arrived in Paris, and he did that much only because Daphne had told him that it wouldn't be polite if he didn't check in.

Ann had replied that all was well, that Gogol was "awesome," in response to which Gladman sent her the "hardy physicality" quote from *Every Parrot Owner's Guide.* He thought that Ann would find the quote funny.

"LOL!!!" she texted back. "And amen."

But when they got back from Paris, Ann was waiting for them just past the threshold, wringing her hands. "Before you see him," she said, "I want you to know that he's getting better, he's visibly healing, and the vet said he'll almost definitely be completely fine in a few more weeks, a couple months at most. The treatment is working. It looks a lot more severe than it is."

Gladman pushed past her, went to the cage.

"I would have called," Ann continued. "I was *going to call,* but the vet said there was nothing more you could really do if you were here, so don't ruin your vacation, and I . . . now I'm not sure I should have taken her advice. Gladman? It's okay. He'll be okay. Are you okay?"

He was not so okay. It *did* look severe. Worse than severe. From crop to cloaca, Gogol's front was entirely exposed. Entirely skin. Bare of feathers. Pink and bumpy. Bumpy and glossy. Glossy pink and bumpy skin that could have passed for that of thawing, raw poultry.

A few pinfeather tips Ann took pains to point out—these were the evidence the treatment was working—were beginning to poke through a few of the bumps, like blackheads on acne. The bumps themselves, of which there were hundreds, were, Ann explained, all active follicles. Active was good.

"Active is *good*," she said. "Active is *great*. The damage isn't permanent. Most of those bumps weren't there even yesterday."

Gogol hadn't vocalized, let alone moved, since they'd entered the condo. Hadn't even turned his head to look at Gladman. Just stood there on his sleeping perch, alarmingly postured, leaning radically forward, neck maximally stretched, beak agape, tongue slightly raised, staring down into the floor of his cage.

"Step him up," Daphne offered.

Gladman tried to. He formed his right hand as if for a karate chop, set the hand before Gogol, and said, "Step up."

The parrot kept still. It was as though he'd been hypnotized. No, not that. More like loaded on antipsychotics. He had the fixed gaze of certain very sick patients who Gladman, in his clinical social worker days, had faced in group therapy. Except, no, come to think: it wasn't like that either. Not exactly. The gaze wasn't empty. Gogol wasn't spaced out. His pupils were pinned, and his breathing was rapid, and—was that his pulse Gladman saw? Was that throbbing in Gogol's bare neck his racing pulse? Why should someone be able to see Gogol's *pulse*?

The bird wasn't high or in some kind of trance. He was frozen in panic.

Gladman, removing his hand from the cage, started to wobble. Daphne and Ann took hold of his shoulders, eased him off his feet, sat him on the floor. Daphne brought him some water, then brought him some whiskey. Then she poured two more whiskeys for Ann and herself, and they all drank their whiskeys, sitting on the floor, looking up through the bars at poor, petrified Gogol clinging to his perch while Ann explained what had happened at length.

On the second evening she'd stayed at the condo, she'd noticed some feathers at the bottom of the cage, but she'd assumed it was normal, figured Gogol was molting. It wasn't until two mornings later that she noticed a patch of fluffy white down on the bend of his keel bone, which had formerly been covered in vaned, gray feathers. A dime-size patch on a dollar-wide body.

She called up the vet, spoke with the receptionist. Dr. Bleet couldn't see the bird till ten the next morning. Should she call the emergency clinic? she asked. The receptionist told her that it sounded like Gogol *might* be plucking, but he might only be having "a rough time molting," which could lead some birds to "preen a little too zealously," and plucking wouldn't be an emergency, anyway, not unless there was also bleeding.

There wasn't any bleeding.

Ann made the appointment.

Over the next few hours, she observed what she hoped was only "zealous preening," but soon came to see could not have been merely that. Gogol was ripping healthy feathers from his chest, often two at a time, chewing on them some, then casting them aside, pulling more feathers. Ann assumed he was upset and tried to calm him down, to comfort him some, but he wouldn't let her near him. He'd scream when she approached, back into the farthest corner of the cage, and bite her, *hard,* if she tried to reach in to offer an almond or rub him on the head.

Briefly—for an hour or so—she'd attempted to distract him by clapping, shouting, dropping books on the hardwood. The parrot would startle, would freeze for a moment, but once the moment passed he'd pluck even more frantically.

She consulted the internet. The forums on plucking, of which there were scores, advised he be given organic, plant-based matter to chew at and tear. Popsicle sticks and boxes of Kleenex. Chopsticks, paper towels, and twine. Ann offered them up, but Gogol only backed away from them. Their presence in the cage seemed to make him afraid, and he plucked at himself with greater frequency and violence. By sundown, his chest was bare of vaned feathers, and patches of skin were beginning to show amidst the fluffy white down that remained.

She ate dinner early and covered the cage and shut off the lights. She spent the rest of the evening as quietly as she could, the idea being to get the bird to sleep until the appointment. This, it turned out, didn't work either. In the morning, nearly all the down on his chest was gone, and what little was left he plucked in the car on the way to the vet's.

In the waiting room, he started on one of his legs. Dr. Bleet, once they got into her office, watched him go at the leg for a couple of minutes, asked a few questions, and quickly deduced from the answers Ann gave that he was, in all likelihood, anxious and depressed over Gladman's absence. Bleet remembered Gogol from previous visits, she said. She remembered how bonded he and Gladman had been—remembered watching Gogol stand on Gladman's shoulder, allopreening his beard— and had even expressed concern to Gladman that they might have bonded more deeply than was optimal, that Gogol might believe that Gladman was his mate.

Bleet said parrots often plucked in response to trauma, to emotional as well as to physical trauma, and that emotional trauma could be inflicted on a parrot by a change in its environment as seemingly minor as, for example, a rearrangement of its perches or toys. She knew one parrot that had started to pluck when its owner hung an abstract pen-and-ink drawing on a formerly undecorated wall near its cage. The owner took the drawing down, and the parrot stopped plucking.

The vet told Ann that she would run some blood tests just to be safe—the blood tests, Ann told Daphne and Gladman, had all come back negative—but she was all but certain that Gladman's absence had traumatized Gogol, was *traumatizing* Gogol. "Poor little guy," Dr. Bleet had said to Ann. "Probably thinks he's been abandoned by his number-one favorite person for good!"

Bleet explained to Ann that once Gladman returned, the trauma should lift, but that unless some decisive early action were taken, the plucking behavior might unfortunately continue. Despite how painful the plucking looked, and even despite how painful it probably was, it comforted Gogol. That's why he kept doing it. The pain of it was preferable to whatever he felt while he *wasn't* plucking, which was again (in all likelihood) depression and anxiety over Gladman's absence. In other words, pluck-ing was a coping mechanism. To some degree—a significant degree—plucking *worked* for Gogol, it allowed him some relief or distraction, but he was only just beginning to learn that now. He was only just learning how effective it was. The trouble was that the behavior could generalize; that it would become the bird's go-to coping mechanism for stress, any and all stress, major and minor. The wailing of a car alarm. The smell of cooking meat. A dinner guest with a threatening haircut. An unfamiliar drawing on the wall.

So the trouble they were facing was not so much the damage Gogol had already done himself—if they could get him to stop, he'd recover soon enough, regrow his feathers—but the damage he could eventually do. If plucking *did* become the way he dealt with stress, then once he ran out of feathers he was able to reach, he would pluck at his skin, destroy his follicles, and cause himself to bleed, which was a triple threat for par-rots. Not only did they need their feathers for the healthy regulation of their body temperature, and not only could their open wounds become infected, but they had trouble clotting. They could bleed to death slowly from a cut that on a human would have healed in a day or two.

Bleet removed the parrot gently from his carrier and set him atop a perch on the desk. He stiffened defensively, but, after a moment, started going at his leg again. She cupped her gloved hand over Gogol's head, holding his beak shut and shielding his eyes, then misted him twice—once from below, and once from above, both times at a distance of roughly six inches—with a patented solution trade-named DON'T!, which contained aloe vera and balsam of Peru.

When the vet removed her hand from his head, Gogol went at his leg again, but then stopped before he'd even pulled a single feather, and began, instead, to chew at each of his claws, one after the other.

He was trying, said the vet, to scrape the bitter taste of the DON'T! from his mouth.

Which wasn't possible.

In fact, it probably made the taste worse, for the DON'T! had coated the claws themselves. After a minute, Gogol left the claws alone. He stood on the perch in just the same way that he was currently stand-ing in his cage in Gladman's kitchen—leaning radically forward, neck maximally stretched—and stared at the floor, rapidly breathing, beak agape, tongue slightly raised.

The vet took some blood and put him back inside his carrier, on the perch of which he immediately adopted the same disturbing pose. The vet said this was good. Gogol, she said, was beginning to learn that trying to pluck his feathers would fill his mouth with a bitter taste, a punishing taste. She said the reason he was standing the way he was standing was that he'd already—instantly—learned to associate the aloe-vera smell of the DON'T! with the taste, and was positioning his nares as far away from his DON'T!-coated parts as he possibly could.

She handed Ann a sealed bottle of DON'T! to pay for out front and told her to spray him twice a day—the first time an hour after uncovering his cage in the morning, the second time an hour prior to covering it at night—until his feathers all returned. If, after that, he ever started plucking again, he should, she instructed, be reminder-misted for a day or two.

"It seems terrible, I know," the vet told Ann. "But short of some seriously expensive behavioral therapy, which isn't all too friendly-looking in itself, DON'T! is, as it were, the best solution we have right now."

"'As it were'?" Ann said.

"Well, DON'T! is a solution in the chemical sense as well as in the sense of—"

"Oh, got it," Ann said.

"It's too soon for levity, I guess," said the vet. "I know it's hard to see him standing like that, but I'm afraid you're going to have to get used to it. He'll do so for a while after each time you mist him. Maybe twenty-thirty minutes. Maybe even more than that. One cockatoo I work with used to stand that way for hours after having been DON'T!ed."

DON'T!ed.

Gladman believed in the lame "as it were" bit, but he suspected the vet hadn't really said *DON'T!ed,* suspected that Ann had made that up herself. It was just the kind of word that anyone close to him—especially any onetime star creative writing student whose work had been subjected to his heavy-handed line edits—would know he'd get a big kick out of hearing.

But perhaps he was being a little too skeptical. He was, it seemed, more than a little bit drunk. He hadn't slept one wink on the plane, and the glass of whiskey that Daphne'd poured him, which was now almost empty, had been nearly a triple.

Plus, what did it matter? He *did* get a kick out of hearing *DON'T!ed*. A small thrill in imagining the way he'd spell it. To suggest Ann had fibbed about *DON'T!ed*'s provenance would be to look a gift horse right in the mouth. So instead, Gladman asked her, "How long has it been since you DON'T!ed him last?"

"I DON'T!ed him just before you got here," she said. "He'll be fine, Gladman. Really. The vet was *certain*."

The vet was proven right. In part. Gladman DON'T!ed Gogol as Bleet had prescribed, and by the end of that winter all the feathers on the parrot's chest had grown back.

But he *had* started plucking a couple times since.

The first time, Gladman and Daphne were away in New York City, attending a wedding. Kayla caught the flu the night before their departure and couldn't leave her bed, so Ann had to stay with him.

The second time, they'd gone to a funeral in Florida—Gladman's grandpa's—which Kayla, of course, had to go to as well. Ann had moved to L.A. by then, and they'd had to board Gogol at Dr. Bleet's office.

Both these times, when they came back home, white patches of down showed on Gogol's chest, and Gladman had had to reminder-mist him twice a day for nearly a week before he'd entirely quit trying to pluck. The second time, the circumference of the patch was significantly larger than it had been the first time, which meant Gogol hadn't learned any long-term lessons from the DON'T!ing, which in turn meant, according to Bleet, that he almost certainly never would.

In other words: he could be made to stop plucking via being DON'T!ed, but he couldn't be prevented from starting up again the next time he experienced the trauma of Gladman's absence.

And in yet other words: if Gogol were never to see Gladman again, he'd either slowly and painfully pluck himself to death, or have to suffer the terror of being DON'T!ed twice a day for the rest of his life.

And that was why Gladman, since 11/17, despite possessing the means and desire to kill himself painlessly, had continually decided not to do so. That was the one and only reason.

A Young Jewish Schoolkid

Back in eighth grade, in 2008, Apter Schutz decided to run for student vice president of North Side Secular Jewish Day School. Until the very moment that he made this decision, late the night before the nomination forms were due, a run for vice president had never crossed his mind.

Earlier that night, he'd jerked off to the memory of rubbing Sylvie Klein's bare vagina at the movies six Saturdays prior—*Inglourious Basterds,* second matinee showing—and, after he spent himself, he lay in bed wondering, not for the first time, if maybe he had made a big mistake with Sylvie Klein. If instead of parting ways with her outside her front door, he should have gone into her house and fucked her, which is what she'd proposed.

It wasn't like he hadn't wanted to fuck her. Apter loved to fuck, didn't get to as often as he would have preferred, and he'd definitely been very into Sylvie. In addition to being a phenomenal kisser and possessing a vagina the rubbing of which had just kept him rock-hard through four separate comes over almost three hours, she was doubtless the funniest person he knew.

However: a virgin.

Sylvie'd been a virgin, and her parents had been home, and even if Mr. and Mrs. Klein would have been too involved in their weekend backyard gardening activities to notice whether Apter, as Sylvie had put it, "[were] inside their house, let alone their daughter," it had happened to be Apter's grandmother's birthday, her *sixty-fifth* birthday, in celebration of which there would be a fancy dinner downtown at the Gage at

7 p.m., so there would not have been time to do the thing right. They would have had only twenty minutes or so, maybe half an hour if he got himself a cab, which not only meant they'd have needed to rush through the fucking proper, but that he wouldn't be able to stick around and hold her for more than a couple of minutes after finishing, which could have left her feeling lonesome, and bad about herself, and you only got one first time and so forth.

And, sure, when Apter had explained all that, Sylvie'd insisted she didn't mind the rush, that she wouldn't feel lonely or bad about herself, but Apter hadn't believed she could know. How could she have known? She'd never been laid. So he'd stood his ground. He'd told her they should meet up again soon, as soon as possible, sometime when they'd have at least a couple of hours, *tomorrow* if she wanted, then he'd kissed her goodbye, and said that he'd call.

"You're a jerk," she'd said, and punched him in the arm.

He'd thought she was kidding.

He'd thought she was *flirting*.

The punch left a bruise.

He called the next morning, but she didn't pick up. He texted her, too, the day after that. Texted four times in twice as many hours.

Hi pretty sylvie klein!	1:11 p.m.
How's your day, sylvie klein?	3:00 p.m.
i sense a disturbance in the force, sylvie klein	9:07 p.m.
star wars? dorky. you make me act dorky.	9:07 p.m.

No response.

The following day was the first of the school year, a Tuesday, and she passed him in the halls without even nodding. Wednesday: same. Thursday: same. Friday? On Friday, Apter blocked her path, and she *rolled her eyes* when he said hello.

"Did I do something wrong the other day?" he asked.

"Don't talk to me," she said. "Don't ever bring that up again either."

He didn't understand.

—

When Adi, his sister, made her weekly call home from Harvard that Sunday, Apter, seeking insight, told her all that had happened.

"Come on, man," said Adi. "What's the big mystery? *Hell hath no fury.*"

"That's real?" Apter said. "I thought it was just like a condescending thing that sexist guys say. Plus I didn't *scorn* her."

"It's both," Adi said. "And yes, you did scorn her. You humiliated her."

"My ass!" Apter said.

"She wanted to sleep with you. Wanted you to be her first. And she told you that, Apter, and what was your response? 'I can't be late to dinner on *Bubbie*'s special day.'"

"That's not—"

"'I just can't miss the appetizers, Sylvie. *Bubbie* really likes to see that I eat. Maybe some other time.'"

"I was trying to be sweet."

"I believe you. I do. You've always been a nice boy. But if I were her, I'd probably hate you, too. No offense. Boys your age are dumb. Boys my age, also. Especially nice ones."

"You think she *hates* me?" Apter said.

Adi just loudly exhaled through her nose.

Then the following Monday, there was Sylvie in the lunchroom, grinning while massaging Mikey "Basketball Schwartzy" Schwartz's trapezii.

That had been a month earlier, more than a month, and still they were together, Sylvie and Schwartzy, for sure they were fucking, and Sylvie had yet to do anything other than flare her nostrils and hide her violet eyes whenever Apter appeared within twenty-five feet of her. Apter'd been thinking that he'd mostly gotten over her—in the interim he had fucked Jenny Shell and 69'd (twice) with Bathsheba Kwon-Levy—but, lying there in bed, now, stuck by his drying load to the top sheet, he couldn't soften down while thinking of Sylvie, and he found he didn't want to stop thinking of Sylvie.

So maybe he loved her. This might have been love.

What could he do? Something had to be done. Perhaps he had to apologize to her. Perhaps his sister'd been right. About *hell hath no fury*. Maybe he'd scorned her. Probably, even. He could see that now. Well, actually, no. He couldn't *quite* see it. But he couldn't come up with a better explanation.

He typed and deleted texts for two hours. Texts of apology. Hard to compose. Impossible maybe. How do you apologize for unintentionally humiliating someone? You acknowledge, without decoration, that you did so, and you sound conceited, like, "I guess I just didn't know my own strength." You say, "I didn't mean to, I meant something else, I was trying to be nice, there was a misunderstanding," and that makes the other person sound oversensitive at best, at worst like a moron. And then even if you somehow balance it out and come across humble and regretful and so forth, you're still bringing up something they'd rather not think about. You're still making them remember their humiliation. Rubbing it in. Plus maybe they're almost over it, too. Maybe they've told themselves that no one else noticed their humiliation, and that there's no humiliation if there aren't any witnesses. Which is true. Kind of. *Could be* true. Except here you are saying, "I noticed. I remember. I am your witness." Doesn't that kind of *re*humiliate them?

Impossible, then. Not maybe. For sure. It was impossible for Apter to apologize to Sylvie for unintentionally humiliating her. He didn't know how to. He couldn't imagine how anyone would.

But still. Something had to be done. He couldn't do nothing. He couldn't just wait. It was definitely love. You don't spend two hours sweating an apology if it isn't really love.

So what about a joke then? Apter wondered. A joke out of nowhere. A text from the void containing a joke. Get her to laugh. Sylvie liked laughing. More than the next girl. *Valued* laughing. A joke that made her laugh would make her see he understood her. Or understood her sense of humor. Understood her taste. Which was all the same thing, right? Maybe. It might have been. It might have been, and maybe . . .

A couple days prior, Apter, taking a break from homework, had been clicking around on a white power message board—this was just something that he did sometimes—when he landed on a clip of a stand-up comedian he'd never heard of.

Guy was middle-aged—thirties, maybe forties—but he costumed himself like an elder Jewish snowbird. A sort of Hebrew Magoo on some Florida pool deck. White comb-over wig with crusty melanomas peppering the otherwise shiny pink dome. Large-lensed, heavy-framed, gray-tinted eyeglasses. Orthopedic sandals with Velcro closures. High, beige dress socks bunching at the ankles. Darker-beige Bermudas elastically waistbanded well above the waist. Tucked yet ballooning linen button-down T, inside the much-too-open collar of which appeared to be (and was) a graying merkin taped to his breastbone. Braided gold Star of David the breadth of a Snapple cap and studded with a diamond, depending from a ropy golden chain around his neck, nesting in—or maybe more like nesting *on*—the merkin.

The costume wasn't convincing—was, it seemed to Apter, meant to read "bad disguise." And the guy did this *voice* that matched the disguise. Performed his whole act in it. This constipated *Yiddishe* grandpa voice. Gravelly and skeptical. Arbitrarily vexed. *Tenemental.* Declaratives uptalked as often as not. Middle-syllable *r*'s hard to come by. Terminal *r*'s impossible to come by. *Just last Satuhday, I went to a wedding, and I saw this young fiddla playing such Klezma as you neveh eveh heard in yeh life befaw(?).*

This comedian was Gladman, but the clip was from one of his earlier performances, so according to the summary under the clip, his name was Bernie Pollaco, for that had been Gladman's stage name back then.

Not coincidentally, Bernie Pollaco was also the name of the protagonist in Gladman's short, unpublished novel, *Play Your Straightman.*

A former U.S. infantry soldier who was present at the liberation of Dachau, the Pollaco of *Straightman,* on returning from the war, had a brief, though highly influential career as a stand-up comedian that concluded with an equally influential series of onstage meltdowns. The novel is set some fifty years after the end of that career, on the dementia ward of a nursing home for the extremely wealthy, where Pollaco, a resident, claims that he is "faking the dementia" in order to have everyday access to people who, despite having heard his very limited set of exclusively *number-themed* jokes many dozens of times, aren't able to remember the punchlines, and therefore continue to find him hilarious.

Interspersed between sections of the novel proper (i.e. the story of present-action Pollaco in the nursing home dementia ward), appear fictionalized quotes from well-known Jewish-American comedians and authors, including Lenny Bruce, Andy Kaufman, and Philip Roth. These quotes, which make up a sizable portion of the text, serve to describe

Pollaco's outsize impact on comedy and Jewish-American identity, as well as to debate the very nature of his act and the meaning of his meltdowns.

All the writers and comedians agree that his material was terrible. All of them agree that it was the voice in which he delivered that material—the same overblown *Yiddishe* grandpa voice in which he narrates *Straightman*—that made him so hilarious (and, to many Jews of the time, so controversial). But what the comedians and writers differ on is manifold: the degree to which Pollaco understood the voice-material dynamic; whether his voice was "authentic" or a put on; whether his late-career onstage meltdowns were "authentic" or put-ons; whether his experiences during World War II should inform the way his act was interpreted; how his (mis)understanding of the dynamic and/or the (in)authenticity of his voice and/or the (in)authenticity of his meltdowns and/or his presence at the liberation of Dachau did or didn't determine whether he was antisemitic or philosemitic or neither or both; when, in short, one was laughing *at* Pollaco vs. when one was laughing *with* him . . .

But I won't continue attempting to summarize, for no summary could do that novel any justice.

Suffice it to say that Solomon Gladman's *Play Your Straightman* was a work of perfect genius; the only work of perfect genius that Gladman had written, though Gladman didn't know that. That is: he knew it was genius but he sensed it was flawed. He couldn't quite put his finger on the flaws—how could he? they didn't exist—and so he couldn't repair the flaws. But he was determined not to publish the novel until he discovered flaws and repaired them: until he'd rendered his (already perfect) work of genius perfect.

By 2008, it had been seven years since Gladman had finished the (unbeknownst-to-him) perfect draft of *Straightman,* and he had, in the interim, published two books: a novel, and then a collection of stories. The novel was a flawed work of genius, the collection a perfect work of mere greatness.

After finishing the novel, he'd gone back to *Straightman* for nearly six months, failed to perfect it to his satisfaction, then worked on the collection. After finishing the collection, he'd spent another six months attempting to perfect *Straightman* to his satisfaction, and failed again, which, this time, drove him half-mad with frustration. Something was missing, and he didn't know what. He needed new eyes, a new angle of approach. A theretofore unGladmanlike approach. And what would that be? Well, he'd never been a "write what you know" kind of writer, had in fact held that commandment in contempt ever since he'd first heard it. Also: research. He hated when novelists talked about research, hated novels that felt all . . . *researched*. The most unGladmanlike approach he could take, then, would be to do some research toward the cause of knowing something that had to do with his novel.

Stand-up? Yes, that was it. Stand-up.

He could try his hand at stand-up. He could try his hand at stand-up *as* his novel's protagonist. He could try his hand at stand-up as Bernie Pollaco. Go out and perform Bernie Pollaco's act.

He could, so he did.

And he came to enjoy it. Although it never solved his original problem—*Straightman* remained unpublished, unsubmitted—performing as a stand-up somehow allowed him to let go of that problem. He put *Straightman* down to write another novel, a nearly great flawed one, which won him his national prize and early tenure, which allowed him, in turn, to quit writing fiction in favor of performing, which he had, decisively, come to prefer a few months earlier, when he'd dropped both the Pollaco name and persona and begun to appear onstage as Solly Gladman.

But that last part wouldn't happen for another few years—Gladman wouldn't publish his prizewinning novel till 2011—and, as far as eighth-grade Apter was concerned on that night in his bedroom back in 2008, the name of the comedian in the video was irrelevant. It would have been irrelevant even if Gladman had performed as Gladman, for Apter hadn't ever heard of Gladman, much less read any fiction by him.

The dimwits who posted on the white power message board didn't know what to make of Pollaco/Gladman, their comments ranging from "lynch this kikefaced SEWER RAT" to "We needa make this paracite famus as poss. Could rallie the cause."

Apter, however, had thought that Pollaco/Gladman was hilarious. What's more, his material was actual jokes, almost joke-book jokes: near-joke-book jokes that were all about *numbers*. The jokes were bad, but on-purpose bad. They were just the kind Sylvie herself liked to tell. Dad jokes, really, like,

> What did 0 say to 8?
> "Nice belt!"

and

> On July 21, AD 1837, Napoleon III sentenced 9 to the guillotine for sheltering a gang of radicals. Three of them!

Apter typed both of these jokes into his phone, but neither of them seemed as funny as he'd remembered, not even as on-purpose-bad dad jokes. Maybe that owed to his knowing them already, but then maybe they just weren't all that funny. It might have only been Pollaco's voice that was funny.

He considered sending Sylvie a link to the video.

But no. Bad idea. There was a reason he hadn't thought of that first. It was . . . it wouldn't show enough effort or something.

Plus a joke from the void—somebody else's joke, no less—might not, on second thought, be the best move here. It could seem blasé. Disrespectful. Could make her even angrier at him. Like, "What makes you think I want to laugh at stuff with you, after what you did to me?"

Shit, she probably wouldn't even read a text that he sent. Just delete it straight out. For all he knew, she'd blocked him.

Apter gave up. Felt sorry for himself. Wistfully, he scrolled through their last exchange of messages, the one they'd had during *Inglourious Basterds*.

About ninety minutes into their embrace, Sylvie'd pulled down her skirt and left the theater without explanation. Apter'd figured at first that she'd gone to take a piss, but after a minute he'd started getting nervous that he might have hurt her, like scratched her vagina accidentally or something—his nails had been trimmed, but he had a couple calluses (ping-pong, pencil) and the rubbing had been going on for a while— and, after five minutes, he got worried she'd ditched him, or was hiding in the bathroom, considering ditching him, and decided he'd better make a cocky-slash-insecure quip about it.

I guess you're sick of kissing me	2:17 PM
Kissing got me thirty.	2:17 PM
Thirty years in the can?	2:18 PM
*ThirSty.	2:18 PM
And: Ha! Not in can. Buying water. Long line.	2:18 PM
I think you didn't like the kissing	2:20 PM
Stop fishing. Watch the movie.	2:20 PM
Don't want to watch the movie	2:20 PM
Already seen it twice	2:20 PM
Describe me as a kisser	2:20 PM
Apter	2:22 PM
Yes?	2:22 PM
*Apter	2:22 PM
Huh?	2:22 PM
ARGH	2:22 PM
*APT. As a kisser, you are apt.	2:22 PM
Puntastic!	2:22 PM
Rimshot!	2:22 PM
For real. It was a good one	2:22 PM

She'd returned a minute later with the bottle of water, given him a sip, and then taken his hand and put it back where it had been and . . .

And now she was fucking fucken *Basketball Schwartzy*? Basketball Schwartzy, the king of spent taglines? The guy who, whenever somebody nearby him ate a donut, would point at the donut, pat himself on the sixpack, and say, in a low voice, "Mmm . . . donuts . . ."? who every time he scored a free throw in Gym would shout, "Say hello to my leetle basketball!"? who, only the week before, during homeroom, had passed Apter a printout that featured an image of a handgun-bearing, tuxedoed Daniel Craig, over which image, in Olde English font, appeared the words "Schwartzy. Basketball Shwartzy." and then asked Apter if he thought it might be "too, like, subtle?" and who, when Apter responded, "Too subtle for what?" had said, "For my campaign flyer-poster things, duh. I should've explained that first, I guess. See, there's another version, too, but I forgot it at home. It uses the same exact picture as this one, but the words at the top of the picture are different. More informational. 'Basketball Schwartzy. Student Vice President Basketball Schwartzy.'"

That's who she was fucking? An aspiring vice president of student fucken government?

Wait.

By the end of third period the following morning, Apter'd acquired the forty signatures he needed and turned the nomination forms in at the office. At lunch, he went online in the library, image-searched stills from *Inglourious Basterds*. He found scores of the maniacally grinning Eli Roth in his role as "The Bear Jew" Donny Donowitz, lethal bludgeoner of Nazi elites, and chose one of Donny holding a ball bat with bone and brain matter stuck to the shaft, bloodstains streaking his sleeveless shirt, fresher blood and matter shining up and down his arms.

Apter copied the image, pasted it into an MS Word doc, centered the cursor on the line above the image, selected *22* from the font-size menu, typed *Schutz for Vice President,* then centered the cursor on the line beneath the image, selected *48* from the font-size menu, and typed out the slogan he'd come up with last night, the inspiration behind his campaign: *Apter than the next guy.*

Printed one hundred.

Stole the roll of tape off the checkout desk.

Ditched sixth period to decorate the halls, affixing his flyer to the immediate left of every last Basketball Schwartzy one he came across.

He handed out the rest by the buses after school.

How far would he have taken this? He hadn't any interest in winning the office. He hadn't any platform. Would he have—as he'd imagined he would the previous night—would he have answered every question he would have been asked at the coming debate by stating his slogan and ceding his time? even if pressed to quit joking around? *Look, I already said what I have to say. I'm Apter than the next guy. That's all there is to it. That's all you gotta know.*—would he have, really?

He never found out.

Sylvie called him up just a little after midnight.

"Sylvie Klein?" he said.

"If you want to know why clothespin peddler Mendy Mandelstam is so up in arms over the mass-market proliferation of two thirds, I'll tell you why he's so up in arms about it, bubbeleh: two thirds is irreducible," she said. "Two thirds gets schmutzy? It starts to smell? You wash two thirds, then throw it in the dryer. Mendy's losing lots of money on the mass-market proliferation of two thirds."

Apter laughed into his pillow. Once he'd gotten his breath back, he said, "I almost sent you a link to that video *yesterday*. I miss you, Sylvie. I miss you so bad."

No response.

"I love you," he said.

No response.

"I mean it. I'm in love with you. I have been for a while, but I only just realized just last night."

Still no response. He looked at the screen. She'd ended the call. When had she ended it? What had she heard? He called her back. She didn't pick up. He snuck out of his house, got on the Red Line, got off the Red Line, walked to her house, stood in the alley next to her house, threw pebbles at her window. She snuck him inside.

At school the next day, he pulled down his posters, withdrew from the election, and, during passing period between fourth and fifth, got shoved into the wall by Basketball Schwartzy.

Apter launched a fist, grazing Schwartzy's outer shoulder, caught a punch in the chest, caught another in the ear, and sat on the floor, leaned back on a locker.

Basketball Schwartzy hoisted his backpack as if he would leave. Instead he loomed. Crying a little.

"How could you?" he said.

"We're not friends," Apter said.

"No shit," said Schwartzy. "But I thought we kinda were."

"That's weird of you," said Apter.

"She told me she loved me."

"That so?" Apter said.

"She *loved* me," Schwartzy said. "Fuck you, 'cause she did."

"Okay," Apter said. "Well, she doesn't anymore."

"And what she also loved she told me was the taste of my cum."

"Yeah yeah," Apter said. "All right. Okay."

"That taste when you kiss her's the taste of my cum. And also of my dick."

"Schwartzy, you're a fucken idiot, you know that? For a second, I almost felt bad for you, but now?"

"Yeah?"

"Now . . ." Apter said, but he didn't get to finish.

Basketball Schwartzy, smiling through tears, clutching his book-jammed backpack's hanging loop, swung the bag mightily into Apter's face, knocking Apter out cold and meanwhile producing, to no one's greater surprise than Schwartzy's, an oozing horror show of blood and torn flesh. Something on the bag's exterior—a rusty strap adjuster? one of the zipper pulls? the house key tied through one of the zipper pulls? the snapped-off edge of the novelty dog tag ("Schwarty, Basketball. Point Guard. Jewish.") chained through one of the other zipper pulls?—*something* on the bag had, at impact, punctured Apter's cheek, gums-deep, then scooped out a ragged furrow on the follow-through.

There were multiple witnesses. A cellphone video. The whole thing was settled in just a few days. Basketball Schwartzy, as the Schutzes' lawyer put it, was a *double scion*. His mother came from old-world tex-tiles money, and his father owned the Midwest's second-largest chain of Audi/Volkswagen/Porsche dealerships. The Schwartzes agreed to pay Apter's medical costs—emergency room, reconstructive surgeries—plus fifty thousand dollars for his trouble and pain.

Schwartzy was expelled from North Side Jewish Secular. He enrolled at Francis W. Parker, to which the Schwartzes endowed a pair of merit-based fellowships for children of immigrants. A few weeks later, on the advice of his therapist, he wrote Apter a three-page letter of apology that—both in spite and because of how it closed with the sentence "I hope the next time I run into you, I'll be able to say, 'Let's hug it out, bitch,' and we'll get it hugged out."—seemed weirdly sincere.

They neither heard from nor saw one another again till winter break of their senior year of college at a Nobunny show at the Empty Bottle, where they stood side by side at the end of the bar, waiting to be served. The barmaid asked Apter what he wanted to drink, and Apter, gesturing at Basketball Schwartzy, who he had no idea was Basketball Schwartzy, said, "This guy was first. Go on, man. You're up," and Schwartzy, who had no idea that Apter was Apter, said, "Kindness of strangers! I'll take it! *Thanks*, bro," then ordered a shot of Jaeger and a Pabst, at which point the girl who'd brought Apter to the show appeared from behind him.

This girl was not Sylvie, nor did she really look much like Sylvie, but something about her incited in Schwartzy a nostalgic and full-bodied longing for Sylvie that set off a chain of more complicated feelings that by the end of the show would lead Schwartzy to decide not only to break things off with his fiancée, but to switch his major from Marketing, which he sucked at, to Business, which would require he attend an extra semester of college but which he didn't suck as much at, and just go to work for his dad when he graduated.

"I want you to dance with me, *now*," Apter's girl said, and tugged at his elbow, and goosed him a little, and Apter stepped away from the bar and obliged her.

Following the beating in 2008, Apter missed nearly two months of school. He underwent four surgical procedures. The first, in the emergency room, went badly. His wound became infected, and he had to stay in the hospital a week. Even through the painkillers, his cheek stung and ached, grabbed and pinched, itched and burned, woke him in the night. It hurt like hell, except for those times when the whole left side *went completely numb.*

Unpleasant as *that* was, he knew he'd get through it. He was young and strong and surrounded by doctors. The infection would pass. What really tortured Apter during that week were the terrifying thoughts of what he might look like once all was said and done.

Numerous consultations about the numerous surgeries that he would soon undergo were had with numerous reconstructive surgeons by his hospital bedside. The surgeons' prognoses, though generally optimistic, featured a large enough number of disclaimers concerning complications that might arise due to *the mysteries of nerve damage* and *the mercurial nature of adolescent flesh on the mend,* not to mention *the recovery of proper function in traumatized salivary glands,* to cause Apter full-blown panic attacks. Waking nightmares of permanent deformity. Of a twitchy cheek with puckered, eerily glossy skin: a wet-looking face that jumped around, drooling. Drooling and chapping. Chapping and flaking. In perpetual need of being blotted and wiped. These waking nightmares jacked his pulse to so alarming a degree as to garner him benzo and beta-blocker injections.

And when he wasn't freaking out about how he might look, he was depressed by how badly how he might look freaked him out. Prior to the beating, he'd had no idea how vain he was. How *shallow* he was. And he could, it seemed, berate himself for being vain and shallow all day long—he did berate himself all day long—but that didn't lessen any of his fears. It only made him feel like more of an asshole.

Very much related to all of the above, and, in many ways, even more depressing, was Apter's reluctant realization that, if given the chance to do it all over again, he would *never* have done it all over again.

And that went for well beyond his having egged on Schwartzy.

Though extremely horny and accordingly promiscuous, Apter had always believed in true love. One should, he believed, be willing to suffer a torn-open face—and more, *unto death*—for the sake of true love. Yet during that first stay in the hospital, whenever he'd attempt to comfort himself with the thought of Sylvie Klein—the thought that she was or would be his redemption; that no matter how deformed he ended up, no matter how much fear and pain he was suffering, their being together would make it more than okay, would retroactively justify all of it—he found no solace. Not a drop. He tried and tried to and failed and failed to, and, soon enough, he admitted the truth to himself: if it would've meant an intact face, he'd have gladly never even *met* Sylvie Klein.

And so he had to accept at least one of the following two conclusions:

1) True love wasn't really all that great.
2) He and Sylvie had not found true love.

Conclusion 2 was marginally easier to contend with, but, for that very reason, Apter mistrusted it. At least for a while.

None of which is to say that he wasn't willing to fool around with Sylvie a bunch. Once he was out of the woods, infection-wise, she started visiting. She visited him at home every day that he was home, and twice when he stayed overnight at the hospital for two of his three remaining surgeries.

They couldn't kiss until after the third one, nor could Apter go down on Sylvie—obtruding bandages, fear of bacteria—but she'd suck on his penis while he rubbed her vagina, and sometimes they'd fuck.

Though they weren't very good at that.

Not as good at it, for instance, Apter realized, as he and Jenny Shell or Becky Steiner had been.

Not as good at it, Sylvie Klein realized, as she and Basketball Schwartzy had been.

Sylvie thought they would probably get great at fucking as soon as they were able to kiss again. The same thought occurred to Apter at times, though he found it pretty dubious.

Anyway, they didn't get great at fucking. They got a little better, but it wasn't good enough.

The final Saturday of Apter's convalescence, Sylvie found a second clip of Pollaco on YouTube. It was thirty seconds long. They watched it on her phone, lying next to each other in Apter's bed.

Pollaco told no jokes in this one. Just stood on a tiny, spotlit stage, and, in a mixture of English and pseudo-Yiddish, shouted at the crowd, "You *guhplatzagig* scumbags. You *narshkevival* cunts. You're a bunch of dirty goddamn Jews, the lot of you!" and then, to scattered applause, faked a heart attack.

They replayed the video half a dozen times. They laughed till they coughed. They curled up and kicked and chewed on their knuckles. "Once more," Apter said, getting hold of his breath, but Sylvie didn't comply. Instead she lay back, her head on his shoulder, her laughter subsiding into softening sighs till at last she said, "If you want to know what's really *narshkevival*, Apt, it's this conversation that we keep not having."

Apter waited.

Sylvie went on. "I tried to write you a letter. For days I've been trying. I can't seem to end it."

"How does it start?" he said.

She opened the draft on her phone and showed him.

> Dear Apter,
> I'm sad and confused because we aren't in love, and that doesn't make sense. We did all the right things. We were hot for each other, we had a great time, then you hurt me by accident, then made a grand gesture to get me to forgive you, and the grand gesture worked, and then you got your ass kicked because of how it worked, you got your ass kicked BADLY, and even though you maybe were going to be disfigured, that

didn't scare me off, I kept coming around, I've kept coming around, just to be with you, it's been two months, and we have a good time, a great time sometimes, and we have this great story, and you AREN'T disfigured, but

"Okay," Apter said, returning the phone.

"Okay what?"

"We aren't in love, and that's sad. It sucks. I agree completely. We need to break up. But I don't think we have to have a whole conversation."

"No?"

"What's there to say? I don't have a lot to say. You've been good company. I mean—a lot more than just that. And you never made it feel like you were doing me a favor."

"I wasn't," Sylvie said. "I've had a good time. You're sweet to me, always paying attention, making me laugh."

"We've tried our best," he said.

"We've done all we could," she said.

"And no one's giving you trouble at school, right? Nobody's blaming you for me and Schwartzy, or slut-shaming you or something like that?"

"Only the ones you'd expect," she said.

"Those schmucks don't count."

"No," she said. "They don't."

"And my face," he said, "is pretty much all right, now. It looks all right, doesn't it?"

"It came out great, Apt. You're really very handsome."

"So it's fine," Apter said. "We're gonna be fine."

"So then why are we crying and hugging each other?"

"Don't know," Apter said. Which was true. He didn't.

I don't know either.

"Why do *you* think?" he said.

"Maybe it's *because* we'll be fine?" Sylvie said. "Because us being fine means life is *narshkevival*? I mean, if you and I can't fall in love with each other, then what's the point of anything? How can we hope to ever fall in love with anyone, you know?"

"It does seem impossible," Apter said. "Family and present company excluded, people are *guhplatzagig*."

"A bunch of dirty goddamn Jews," whispered Sylvie.

—

Apter went back to North Side the following Monday, caught up on all his schoolwork before winter break, kept his name on the honor roll, and graduated on time from eighth grade.

None of his waking nightmares had come true. There wasn't any drooling. There wasn't any twitching or too-shiny skin. His reconstructive surgeons had proven themselves, as Apter's *bubbie* had said, "real facial Michelangelos." The scar they left him was thin and straight and long as a kitchen match, running at a gently sloping diagonal beginning at his bite line and ending just below. Soon enough, if he wanted, he could grow a beard to cover it. In the meantime, he looked like he'd been in a duel.

Except for this scar, and a painless, though permanent hitch in his nerves that caused him to squint his left eye when he smiled, Apter fully recovered from his wound.

In fact, he came out even better than new. His smile, which, before, had been a nice enough smile, was now, with the added squint, *magnetic*. Especially when he smiled it while tilting his head just a touch to the left in the viewer's direction.

The mayor of Chicago wouldn't be the first man who'd try to make it his own. Not even the first who worked at City Hall.

THE DOWNSIDES

Gladman had been staying nearer-by for months, passing most waking hours in the living room or kitchen, in sight of the cage, and sometimes even spending the night on the couch. If he left the apartment, he'd return within minutes. If someone came by, he would send them away. Nobody else was around anymore to compete for his attention, let alone his affection. He was making the good, soft sounds more than ever.

But there were of course a couple of downsides, too, to Gogol's post–terrestrial anomaly life.

One downside was the snacks. Not the number of snacks—it wasn't that. He and Gladman snacked together a lot. The variety, though. There was far less variety. A bit of pizza crust here, an almond there, the occasional grape—the classics, basically. Once in a while, there'd be a buttered elbow, true. And buttered elbows were good. Delicious even. But a buttered elbow was no more or less delicious than an oiled spaghetto, and, lately, whenever Gogol ate a buttered elbow, he couldn't shake the sense of its being a kind of dull or deformed or even *failed* oiled spaghetto.

A kind of second-rate oiled spaghetto, in any case.

You clutched it, bit it, turned it, bit it, maybe turned it once more—though probably not; you'd turned it twice already, seen all the best ways it could ever catch light—then polished it off. Light-catching-wise, a buttered elbow may as well have been a popsicle stick. May as well have been a nutritive pellet or a twig. Really.

Not really. Those were overstatements. Sure.

—

But a buttered elbow's limited capacity for reflection was only one aspect of its inferiority to an oiled spaghetto. A minor aspect, too, when compared to the others. To eat an oiled spaghetto was just so much more involved. So much more involving. There wasn't any *challenge* with a buttered elbow. Nothing to master, or pretend to master. A buttered elbow never seemed like it was trying to escape. You couldn't wiggle a buttered elbow into dancing. You couldn't tie a buttered elbow in a knot. Gogol *liked* to eat a buttered elbow, he did—for the flavor, for the texture—but inasmuch as it wasn't an oiled spaghetto, a buttered elbow, lately, made him want to scream.

Sometimes he would.

It hadn't always been that way.

It used to be different. Back when Daphne'd been around. It used to be a buttered elbow could get him to *not* scream. Could get him to stop. Back when Daphne'd been around, he'd been no more likely to receive a buttered elbow than an oiled spaghetto. Or, for that matter, a gratinated gnocco. There'd been all kinds of snacks. There'd been hazelnuts and chunks of apple. Green pepper slivers. A grain of rice stuck to a soft black bean. Very occasionally, a madeleine nearly the size of his breast would be held before his beak so he could bite at the edge, and he'd bite at the edge—sometimes he'd bite twice. A couple of times, the edge had been crisp. Of all the snacks he missed, he missed madeleines the most.

What he didn't really miss were the little corners of hard, sliced cheese that Daphne used to give him. Those were basically, like, antinutritive pellets: near-zero absorption, went right through him, provided less energy than they took for him to process.

Gogol'd only ever eaten those corners of cheese because—well, he didn't like violence. He tried to avoid it. If he hadn't eaten the cheese that Daphne'd proffered, he'd have had to bite her on the hand for getting in his space without a proper offering. Otherwise she could have gotten the wrong idea, i.e. that she could get in his space without a proper offering.

The hierarchy of dominance was steep. Its slope was *slippery*. One day you allow your inferior to enter your space with an insufficient offering, the next day she's trying to enter your space with *no offering at all*—and then you *really* have to bring the violence. Multiple bites. Deep ones. Blood.

So if he hadn't eaten the cheese that Daphne'd offered, he'd have had to get violent, since if he'd declined to eat the cheese *and* declined to get violent—if he'd dropped the cheese, say, or ignored the cheese—she might have started to imagine that she wasn't on the bottom.

Which would have benefited exactly no one, because she'd definitely been on the bottom, Daphne, and right from the start. This was the proof: Gladman'd preened Gogol and Gladman'd preened Daphne, and Daphne'd preened Gladman and *tried* to preen Gogol, but Gogol hadn't ever let Daphne preen him, and Gogol would have never in a million years preened or tried to preen Daphne—Gogol'd only ever preen Gladman.

Well, not *only ever.*

Sometimes Gogol'd also preened Kayla, that's true. Gogol'd preened Kayla and let Kayla preen him. But that had all started years before Daphne'd joined the flock. At that time, Gogol himself had been the bottom. It wasn't all that happy a thing to think about, but that was the truth of it. Or that's how it seemed at least: that on top had been Gladman and Kayla, and Gogol on the bottom.

What was confusing to Gogol was that Gladman and Kayla hadn't preened each other, nor ever tried to, but they'd both preened Gogol, so how had Gogol known that Gogol'd been the bottom? Why hadn't Gogol thought that Gogol'd been the top? Gogol, after all, had received the most preening. That's why that first life wasn't an entirely happy life to think about. Because Gogol'd been dumb. It was shameful, really. Because Gogol'd been the top but he hadn't known it, unless maybe Gogol hadn't been the top because he should have been the top but had been too dumb to know it.

No matter what—whether he'd been happy not being the top while he could have been the top, or he'd been happy not knowing he'd been the top while he actually had been the top—he shouldn't have been happy and yet he'd been happy, and so he'd been stupid, and that was shameful.

Then again, you only live a few times, so why not be happy? Why be hard on yourself? Why be hard on yourself for who you had been in a previous life? Why be hard on yourself for who you had been before you'd understood the laws? Especially when you couldn't—if you were being honest with yourself—you couldn't *really* be sure you understood the laws *now*? Like maybe the laws weren't even really laws? Sometimes Gogol thought they might not be.

Most of the time, Gogol thought he knew the laws, but other times Gogol thought he didn't really know the laws and wouldn't or perhaps *couldn't* know the laws till he was more grown up—till his arms became legs or his wings became arms or he lost the beak or lost the feathers, or maybe not even till *all* of that happened, i.e. maybe not until he'd *finished* growing up—and then sometimes Gogol thought that there weren't any laws to know to begin with. When he thought about his second life, for example—the life during which Kayla'd stopped living with Gogol and Gladman, but Daphne hadn't yet been living with them either—when Gogol thought about his second life, the laws Gogol thought he knew when he thought he knew the laws didn't seem to apply.

When Kayla'd stopped living there, the hierarchy changed, or seemed to change. At first Gogol and Gladman were (or seemed to be) equals— neither one on top, neither one on the bottom: Gogol preened Gladman, and Gladman preened Gogol, and that's all there was to it. But then things got weird.

Weird inasmuch as Gogol started to notice that sometimes he wanted to preen Gladman or be preened by Gladman, and Gladman wouldn't preen him or make himself available for preening. Like, Gogol'd jump off his cage and walk over to Gladman, and Gladman would not preen him or let himself be preened: he'd just put Gogol back on his cage. And sometimes he'd even *lock* Gogol *in* his cage!

But whenever Gladman *went* to Gogol's cage while Gogol was on it, Gogol would preen him or let himself be preened, whichever Gladman signaled Gladman wanted.

And having noticed all of that changed the hierarchy. Or at least it changed Gogol's understanding of the hierarchy. The law was supposed to be that who preened who—and who let himself be preened by who—determined the hierarchy, but now it turned out there was also this whole second matter of *when* you preened and were preened by who. If you wanted to be preened by or to preen another member of the flock with whom you had a long-standing preening relationship but that member of the flock did not always honor your preening desire when you signaled, and you, on the other hand, *did* always honor *his* preening desire when *he* signaled, well, my friend: you were not equals. And if you were not equals, one was higher and the other was lower. If you were not equals and there were only two of you, one of you was on the top and the other on the bottom.

And maybe it would seem obvious to a less intellectual person than Gogol that the one who was on the top was the one who *always* got to get into some preening when he signaled he wanted to get into some preening, but Gogol came to believe it might be more subtle than that. Because there was additionally a matter, it seemed, of how *intensely* you wanted to get into some preening. The more intensely Gogol wanted to get into some preening, the better it felt to get into some preening, and Gogol had to believe it was the same for everyone. And Gogol's desire to get into some preening was always much higher in the wake of Gladman's refusals to get into some preening: whenever Gladman refused to get into some preening with Gogol, Gogol's desire to be preened by Gladman only intensified, and the next time Gladman *did* get into some preening with Gogol, it felt, for Gogol, even better than it usually did. And that feeling seemed pretty unbottomly to Gogol.

And because Gogol never refused Gladman's signals to get into some preening, Gladman's desire to get into some preening wasn't likely ever as intense as Gogol's most intense desire to get into some preening, which probably meant that Gladman never got to enjoy getting into some preening as much as Gogol enjoyed getting into some preening when Gogol got into some preening while most intensely desiring to get into some preening, which intensity of desire Gogol was capable of feeling only when Gladman had previously refused to get into some preening.

So, maybe Gladman was on the top, but, if so, then maybe Gogol preferred it that way. That is: maybe it was less important to Gogol to be on the top than to continue to enjoy getting into some intensely desired preening. Maybe that, in itself, was shameful, but . . .

Whatever, right? YOLAFT. Plus also: beside the point. That point being: Gogol didn't miss the cheese. Gogol'd eaten the cheese because Daphne'd been the bottom. Because she'd been the bottom and he didn't like violence, Gogol'd *eaten* the cheese, but he'd *never* missed it.

—

None of which was to say, however, that Gogol's eating the cheese Daphne'd proffered had been *entirely* compromise and nuisance. After all, whenever Gladman had seen it happen, he'd laughed, which was what you did when a tailfeather shake was called for but you didn't have tailfeathers. And what was more worthy of a tailfeather shake than when the bottom flockmate acted all . . . bottomly? Not much. Maybe nothing at all. So Daphne'd feed Gogol cheese and Gladman would laugh and Gogol'd tailfeather shake, and that was a good thing.

Other hand, though, a lot of things had made Gladman laugh and Gogol tailfeather shake, e.g. Daphne acting all bottomly by bringing Gogol an offering that Gogol *did* want (e.g. an oiled spaghetto), so: no, it wasn't all compromise and nuisance, but he really could have done without all that cheese.

Anyway, among the two downsides to Gogol's post–terrestrial anomaly life, the diminished variety of snacks was the bigger.

The smaller was the laughter. Not the amount of it—Gladman had been laughing as much as he'd ever laughed, maybe even more than he'd ever laughed—but the kind and location.

He had a new kind of laugh that sounded like choking and went on forever, and whenever Gladman would do the new laugh, Gogol'd tailfeather-shake, over and over, but Gladman never saw. Except for one time—the first.

That first time Gladman laughed the new choky-sounding laugh, he was sitting on the couch, and Gogol was standing on his index finger, looking right at him. Gogol'd not only tailfeather-shook a few times, but tried to do the new choky-sounding laugh himself—it seemed, some-how, especially important to master very quickly—and he'd done, he'd thought, a pretty good job: it wasn't *exactly* right, wasn't quite as chesty or something, but it was *almost* the same, it was really very close. Yet Gladman hadn't told him "Good birdie" or given him a snack or an extra-thorough preen or anything like that. He'd just sat there staring at him, continuing to laugh the new laugh for a minute while Gogol continued to attempt to master the laugh, and, very briefly, Gladman laughed the old laugh, but only very briefly, and then he went right back to the new laugh and stood and put Gogol on his cage and went to the office or the bedroom (Gogol couldn't remember which one).

Normally, Gogol would have taken it badly, but he'd noticed that Gladman, while he was laughing, had somehow gotten something in his eyes that his eyes were trying to flush out with water, and that was never a pleasant feeling to have—it stung—so when Gladman set him down on his cage (that is: set him down on his cage instead of being extra-nice, as Gogol would have expected him to be because Gogol'd nearly mastered the new choky laugh), Gogol'd just figured Gladman had needed to go away to concentrate his efforts on clearing his eyes out.

After that first time, Gladman never did the new laugh in the same room as Gogol. Sometimes he'd start to—two or three soft, choky sounds—but before Gogol would even realize that Gladman was doing the new laugh, Gladman would leave the room, or, if they were in a room that wasn't the kitchen, he'd take Gogol to the kitchen and put him on his cage and go to the bedroom or go to the office and close the door.

So that first time had also been the last time he'd ever really seen Gladman laugh the new laugh. But it was far from the last time he'd heard Gladman laugh it. He heard Gladman laugh it kind of a lot.

He would have liked to see Gladman laugh it again.

More than that, he would have liked to see Gladman laugh the old laugh more often than Gladman had been laughing it since Gladman had started laughing the new laugh.

The only time Gladman laughed the old laugh anymore, he seemed to be asleep, or something like asleep.

Time Management

The Xanax and whiskey that Gladman consumed in the months succeeding the terrestrial anomaly did little to mitigate his constant awareness that every last person he'd loved was dead, but when he mixed them in the proper ratio (what *proper* meant varied, was seemingly random, a matter of luck or hydration or stomach content) the intoxicants blurred him out enough to permit him intervals—minutes, even hours, at a time on occasion—during which he could forget how much longer he would likely have to go on.

According to *Every Parrot Owner's Guide . . .* , the average life expectancy of a Quaker in captivity was twenty-three years.

Gogol'd hatched in '07. He was barely fourteen.

The volume of whiskey Gladman drank in a day ranged from zero to eight fluid ounces, and he drank it on an "as needed" basis. The Xanax, however, he swallowed more methodically.

By the middle of February 2022, his intake was up to three milligrams daily. Three milligrams meant twelve quarter-mig tablets, twelve quarter-mig tablets four fifths of a blisterpack.

GLADMAN'S XANAX CONSUMPTION SINCE 11/17/21

Period	Pills/mg Per Day	Pills/mg Per Week	Pills/mg For Period
Weeks 1-2: 11/17/21-11/30/21	3/.75	21/5.25	**42/10.5**
Weeks 3-4: 12/01/21-12/14/21	4/1	28/7	**56/14**
Week 5: 12/15/21-12/21/21	5/1.25	35/8.75	**35/8.75**
Weeks 6-8: 12/22/21-01/11/22	6/1.5	42/10.5	**126/31.5**
Weeks 9-12: 01/12/22-02/08/22	9/2.25	63/15.75	**252/63**
Weeks 13-15: 02/09/22-03/01/22	12/3	84/21	**252/63**

Total Pills/mg Consumed between 11/17/21 and 03/01/22: **763/190.75**
Total blisterpacks consumed between 11/17/21 and 3/01/22: **50.8666667**

The second morning of March, Gladman woke up cramped. Clammy in the bends of the elbows and knees. Sore in the jaw. His sleep the night before had been fitful: he'd been too hot, and then too cold, and his legs had insisted on flexing and twisting. Worse, he'd slept for only nine hours. He had come to count on eleven a night.

And so he decided to up his dosage by 25 percent. Three more pills a day. Instead of six in the morning and six after dinner (*dinner* had come to mean, for Gladman, the only meal he ate each day, usually between 5 and 6 p.m.), he'd take eight in the morning and seven after dinner. He'd take, in total, a blister pack a day. 3.75 milligrams a day.

Was that too much?

Gladman didn't know.

He didn't, in fact, really understand the question. But it seemed a responsible question to ask. Sounded like a question that Daphne would have asked him. A question she'd have hoped he'd consider were she absent.

Which, of course, she was.

Some people were prescribed two milligrams a day. The drug was even available in 2-mig tablets: pills eight times as potent as the ones that Gladman had in his drawer, pills he would not have had to swallow even two of a day to get to where he was trying to go.

If someone told you he ate a dozen eggs a day, you would think he was eating way too many eggs. But if he went on to explain that the eggs came from quails rather than from chickens? You might still think his egg consumption was a *little* excessive, but you wouldn't worry for him. You wouldn't worry a cardiac event was imminent. You'd probably just think he really liked quail eggs, or that he somehow *needed* quail eggs. For the protein, maybe. Perhaps he was just a vegetarian, you'd think. Like Adolf Hitler.

But Hitler had nothing to do with the question.

Though Hitler must have eaten plenty of eggs. Probably a couple a day at least. As for how he'd preferred to have them prepared? Gladman wanted to believe he'd preferred them soft-boiled. That every morning, Hitler took a tiny spoon to the summits of his pair of soft-boiled eggs and tap-tap-tapped, then scooped, ya, scooped, smiling all the way, smacking his lips.

But that was just a lazy cartoon of Hitler.

—

When you allowed yourself the time to really think about Hitler eating his eggs, it seemed more likely he'd prefer them *hard*-boiled. That he'd carry them—two of them—in the front right pocket of his uniform's jacket, and he'd peel and eat them, one after the other, while he walked through a forest.

The first egg, Hitler would eat unseasoned, in two or three bites, whereas the second one he'd take more time to savor. He'd methodically nibble away at its white, till the white was no more, and then, with a shaker that he'd remove from the pocket opposite the pocket he carried his eggs in, he'd distribute pepper evenly across the mushy surface of the blue-gray ball of yolk he'd uncovered. He'd then return the shaker to the designated pocket and bite the ball of yolk in half. Never quite precisely in half—that would have been impossible—but as close to precisely as a human could manage: close enough to allow Hitler to feel comfortable in thinking about the ball of yolk as having been "bitten into hemispheres." That's how Hitler would think of it. "My yolk is in hemispheres."

His first hemisphere of yolk he would chew conventionally, however slowly, but the second one he'd hold behind his pursed lips—flat side teethward—and suck through the spaces between his incisors. The spaces were thin, and this part of his egg-eating practice (his favorite) would thus take some time, a minute or so, and during this time Hitler'd nod to himself, looking up into the sky, really tasting the yolk. Once the gluey streams had ceased to flow through the spaces, he would, with a powerful swirl of his tongue, comprehensively cleanse from his mouth's forward quadrant the sandy residual film of mashed yolk. And that would be that. He would turn back around. Having finished his eggs, Hitler'd turn on his heel, hands clasping one another at the small of his back, and leave the forest, sated, aglow.

Two milligrams a day, though. Some people were prescribed two milligrams a day. Two milligrams a day to contend with anxiety that prevented them from functioning normally. Two milligrams a day, then, to function normally. To go to work at the office, to eat and to sleep, to gaze on a screen beside a spouse on a couch. Two milligrams a day on doctor's orders.

In that light, as well (i.e. as well as in the quails'-versus-chickens'-eggs light), 3.75 milligrams, to Gladman, seemed only a *little* excessive.

Much, perhaps, but not *too much.*

And you couldn't really overdose on Xanax alone. You couldn't, that is, really overdose to death. Well, you *could,* but it was hard. Very hard. That was one of the reasons the drug was so popularly prescribed. There were records of people taking as much as two thousand milligrams— two *grams;* more than five *hundred* times the most Gladman had ever taken in a day; more than ten times the sum of *all* that he'd taken since 11/17—without going into comas or causing any permanent organ damage, much less dying.

On the other hand, if you drank too much on top of even just a few milligrams of Xanax, you had a reasonable shot at killing yourself. Yet that didn't make 3.75 milligrams a day *too much,* either. That would be like saying a pint of beer was too much because you might decide, after drinking a pint of beer, to drive really fast near a nursery school overlooking a mountain cliff. It seemed. To Gladman. Who didn't like driving.

But the one major drawback to Xanax—to all benzodiazepines—that Gladman couldn't deny, which is not to say he was trying to deny anything, was the withdrawal from Xanax. Xanax withdrawal was even harder on the body, and far longer-lasting, than, for example, the much more notorious heroin withdrawal. It was also more likely to kill you.

Alcohol withdrawal was the worst of all withdrawals—was more likely to kill you than Xanax withdrawal—but to experience withdrawal from alcohol, let alone fatal withdrawal from alcohol, required years and years of preceding alcohol dependency, years and years of *heavy abuse.* Xanax withdrawal, on the other hand, could happen after only weeks of dependency, and could be fatal even when the dosages on which one depended were relatively low.

Gladman's mother, who had never once taken drugs for pleasure, had become addicted to Valium—another benzo, one that carried a significantly *lower* risk of addiction than Xanax—after having taken just one milligram a day (half of a 2-mig pill; the lowest-dosage pill that Valium came in; one-quarter the dosage her doctor had prescribed her) for three months following her hysterectomy some thirty years earlier. With the help of her doctors, she'd tried to wean herself off the stuff multiple times—used a razor blade to cut the pills into quarters, sixths, eighths, *twelfths*—but each one of those times, she ended up with insomnia, stomach pains, untenable depression, and she'd never kicked. One mig a day. A dose smaller than that which you'd feed your nervous Schnauzer on the fourth of July.

So in *that* light, Gladman was taking too much Xanax, for he'd been taking it longer than his mother had taken Valium prior to her first attempt to quit; he'd been taking it for about three *and a half* months. He was probably, in other words, addicted to Xanax, physically dependent.

Then again—once again—that wasn't the issue. That had little to do with the question he was trying to answer. It might have, true, had everything to do with the question he was trying to answer if Daphne had been the one to ask the question, but Daphne *hadn't*. Daphne was gone. Daphne was gone, so Gladman wasn't wondering whether taking Xanax every day meant that he was taking too much, nor whether being addicted to Xanax meant that he was taking too much. The question "Was that too much?" had been, he'd come to see, poorly phrased.

A better phrasing of the question would have been: "If Gogol's life span will be the average life span of a captive Quaker, do I have enough Xanax to take 3.75 milligrams a day until Gogol dies?"

or

"Do I have nine years of Xanax?"

And although the question was better phrased that way, it wasn't quite yet properly phrased because Gladman would continue, he imagined, to up his dosage every few weeks, and, furthermore, even if he didn't *ever* up his dosage again—even if he stuck to a blister pack a day—it was obvious that he didn't have nine years of Xanax. He wasn't great at math, and he was even worse when it came to spatial relations, but a blister pack a day for nine years, he knew, would amount to 365 x 9 blister packs, and that was a far greater number of blister packs than his Xanax drawer could hold, and thus a far greater number of blister packs than his Xanax drawer, which was no longer full, contained.

The proper way, then, to phrase the question was: "Do I have enough Xanax to last me till I can get hold of more Xanax?"

That question itself contained subquestions. Two of them:

1) Exactly how many days of Xanax do I have?
2) How long will it take me to get hold of more Xanax?

To answer the first subquestion, he counted his Xanax. One hundred and forty-four full blister packs plus one more that was missing twelve tablets: 2,163 tablets in total: 540.75 milligrams. So his current stocks represented 144.2 days' worth of Xanax if he didn't up his dosage. Fewer days than that if he did. And he probably would. By how much he didn't know—how could he know?—but he felt that it was safe to say his stocks could last him seventy-two days. Seventy-two days was ten weeks and two days.

To answer the second subquestion, he consulted the internet. A search for "Xanax without a prescription" brought up nearly half a million hits, many of which linked to online pharmacies. The delivery times they promised varied. As few as three days from receiving the order to as many as six weeks.

Assuming all proceeded swimmingly, then, Gladman would have more than enough Xanax to last him until he got hold of more Xanax.

But it wasn't ever safe to assume that all would proceed swimmingly, especially when it came to anything involving the mail or internet commerce, let alone both, and it seemed to Gladman that while he probably did have more than enough Xanax to last him until he got hold of more Xanax, he might have only *just* enough Xanax to last him until he got hold of more Xanax.

So Gladman spent most of the afternoon of March 2 filling out forms and placing orders on the first couple dozen pharmacy websites that seemed legit.

By sundown he'd spent just a little bit more than $5,000 for three thousand milligrams. He would have gone on to place further orders—tabs were still open, he had a rhythm going, and the forms were becoming easier to manage, his browser's autofill function more efficient—but Gogol began to jabber and whistle, breaking Gladman's concentration.

He went to the kitchen, fed the parrot a grape, and narrated at him for a couple of minutes.

Apart from "Step up" or "Hello" or "Good birdie" or "Gogol"—to which Gogol would usually respond in kind while either stepping up onto Gladman's hand or waving a leg or tailfeather-shaking—what Gladman said to Gogol was all the same to Gogol as long as it was said to him in comforting tones, so usually he'd speak to him, in comforting tones, about whatever the first thing that came to mind was.

This time it was realism. Being realistic. In comforting tones, Gladman spoke to the parrot about what it would mean, as regarded the Xanax, to be realistic.

Between bites of the grape Gogol held in his foot, he'd peer out from behind it and rapidly nod. To someone who'd never met a Quaker before, the bird might have appeared to be conveying how very reasonable he found all that Gladman was telling him. But the nodding was not an affirmation of anything—at least not anything more complex than the fact that Gogol was alive and functioning normally. Quakers just rapidly nod sometimes.

Other times they shiver, especially the young ones.

Their shivering is more often referred to as quaking. That is why they're called Quaker parrots.

Once Gogol got down to his last nub of grape, Gladman summed up what he'd been trying to say about Xanax and realism:

That he hoped, of course, that he'd receive all the Xanax he'd just ordered from the internet, but that he didn't expect to receive more than half of it. That he imagined that frequently being ripped off was the price of doing this kind of business, and the price was one he could easily afford.

Gogol chomped on grape and nodded.

I'd have nodded, too. I think most people would have.

Over the years, Gladman's father, who had been a general agent for the Centurion Life Insurance Company of America, had purchased multiple life insurance policies on himself, Gladman's mother, Gladman's sisters,

Gladman's nieces and nephew, and Gladman. He'd sold Gladman and Daphne policies on one another, and he'd sold Naomi, who had been divorced for nearly a year prior to the terrestrial anomaly, policies on herself and her children.

Gladman had been listed as the primary beneficiary on several of these policies, and as a secondary or tertiary beneficiary on some others. For those on which he was not listed as a beneficiary, he had been next of kin.

After 11/17, he inherited all the benefits of all the policies that weren't on his life, and he inherited the cash values of all the whole life policies that were. He inherited the savings, the stocks, and the mutual funds that had belonged to his parents and his sisters and his wife, and he inherited his parents' house in Highland Park, his parents' North Side rental properties (one six-unit building, two four-unit buildings), his parents' house in Florida, his parents' time-share on Grand Cayman, his parents' rental properties on Grand Cayman (two luxury units on Seven Mile Beach), and Naomi's house in Evanston. He inherited his mother's collection of jewelry, his mother's car, Kayla's car, and Naomi's jewelry (Naomi's and his father's cars had been parked in the underground Millennium Park garage, and destroyed by the anomaly, for which destruction Gladman received $21k and change from their car insurance companies). He also came to own, free and clear, the condominium in which he lived, for which he'd previously paid a mortgage to his parents, who had lent him the money to buy it for cash, on a short sale, back in 2011.

Carefully aggressive was how Gladman's father's accountant described Gladman's father's way with money to Gladman, to whom that sounded equal parts correct and nonsensical.

In early December 2021, the accountant, who had also been Naomi's accountant, had called Gladman to offer his services to him and to better apprise him of the details of his wealth.

Gladman's father's attorney, who had also been Naomi's attorney, had already called Gladman a few days beforehand to do the same—i.e. offer his services to Gladman and apprise him of the details of his wealth—but Gladman had been "basically unresponsive," the attorney had told the accountant, and had needed, it seemed, to be apprised a second time, as well as, most likely, offered more services.

"Unresponsive like . . . ?"

"Like he said, 'Thank you. Maybe some other time,'" the attorney had told the accountant. "And then he just hung up. I think he might be on drugs."

"I'd be on drugs," had said the accountant. "What a raw deal. What a fucking tragedy. You know, thinking about it just . . . I really miss you. Are you free tonight?"

The attorney and the accountant had met one another through Gladman's father some four decades earlier. The two were secretly homosexual, had fallen secretly and instantly in love, and had, ever since their first meeting, carried on an affair without the knowledge of their wives or children or anyone else save Gladman's father, who could have, it seemed to them, seen through walls if he'd concentrated hard enough. And because Gladman's father hadn't ever looked down on them, even back in the early 1980s when the majority of Americans of his generation most certainly would have, and because he didn't fire either one of them upon figuring out that the two of them were lovers—which, given the capacity for duplicity they'd demonstrated together, and the fact that their jobs entailed the handling of his money, would not have been at all unreasonable—both the attorney and the accountant, ever since they'd begun their affair, had been deeply loyal and grateful to him, had valued him not only as a client, but as a tried-and-true friend. So they earnestly hoped to be of service to his son, who, despite the small waves of controversy surrounding him, and despite the opinions that some of those close to them might have held about his "act" (both the attorney and the accountant were Jewish), had been, they both knew, his father's favorite child. And they agreed it was their duty to protect that son the only way they knew how: by preventing him from making the kinds of rash and stupid financial decisions that so many tended to make while grieving.

The accountant, when he'd called in December 2021, had mentioned Gladman's father's being *carefully aggressive* in the course of attempting to allay the alarm that Gladman had expressed—"That's too much to look after. Too much!" had said Gladman—in the wake of hearing, for the second time (or in the wake, at least, of *being told* for the second time), about all he now owned. The idea the accountant wanted to bring across, the accountant continued, was that Gladman shouldn't feel rushed to do anything with what he'd inherited. The stocks and mutual funds were growing steadily, the homes gaining value, the jewelry gaining value, and the rental properties not only gaining value, but profiting handsomely.

"Handsomely how?"

The accountant explained: the money that the rental properties were earning covered a) the mortgage and tax payments on those rental properties, b) the monthly fees owed to the property management companies in Chicago and Grand Cayman that managed those properties, and c) the mortgage and tax payments on the houses in Highland Park and Florida. Even after paying for all of that, d) five thousand dollars a month was left over, which was more than enough for Gladman to pay the mortgage and taxes on Naomi's house in Evanston, which, again, the accountant reminded him, was gaining value, and so worth holding on to.

"What about the cars?" said Gladman.

"The cars? I don't know," the accountant said. "An old Lexus SUV, and a slightly less old Honda hatchback? Those, if you don't want them, you might as well sell them. Probably you could get twelve, maybe fifteen k."

"Could you do that for me?"

"Do what for you?"

"Sell the cars?"

"I'm an accountant, and I don't really do that. It's not really my specialty. I wouldn't know . . . If you want me to put you in touch with someone who—"

"That's all right. No. I think I'll just keep the cars."

"No harm in keeping them. They'll lose some value over time, but not much more than they have already, unless you drive them a lot, and in that case, well: you're getting some use out of them. We *should* talk about investing some of your cash, though. Much of it, really."

"Why?"

"It's a lot of cash, and it loses value just sitting there."

"The cash does."

"Yes."

"I guess I knew that. But I never understood how cash lost . . ."

"Well, there's inflation for one, and—"

"Got it. No, I got it. I remember now. My dad explained it once. But how much value could it really lose, do you think? I mean, didn't you say I had millions in cash?"

"After the estate taxes, it'll be about 10.5 million. And there's another 1.9 in the market—I think it's best to let that ride, though."

"*The market* includes the real estate or . . ."

"No. The real estate is separate," the accountant said.

"And the real estate is worth . . . some more millions?"

"Correct."

"So how much do you think I need?" said Gladman.

"How much do you *need*? Depends what you want."

"I want to not think about money. I want to not *have to* think about money."

"I understand. For how long, do you imagine, will you want to forgo thinking about money?"

"As long as possible," said Gladman. "Probably forever. Right now for sure. It's so boring to me, you know? It always has been. Not just boring, either—I mean, I'm forty-four years old, and I don't have a credit card. I've never had a credit card. And do you know who did my taxes up until now?"

"Me," said the accountant.

"That was you?"

"Your dad was very well-off, kiddo, but he didn't need more than one accountant."

"So you understand. And thank you, by the way. What I'm trying to say to you is: I'm not doing much here. Nothing special. I'm not doing more here than eating and sleeping, and I have no plans to do anything special, and I have no children, and I don't want any children, so all I really want, if it's possible, is to do whatever needs to be done to make sure I don't have to think about money, whether that's paying bills, paying taxes, collecting dividends or not collecting dividends or paying down loans or paying off loans, or keeping up on insurance payments if I have any of those, or retirement payments, or any other kinds of payments. Anything to do with any of that kind of thing, I would like to be as far away from as possible. Thinking about that stuff, I get . . . violent. I don't know why, but that's what happens. I get some bill? I have to find the checkbook—I can't remember where it is. It's always in the same place, I remember, but I can't remember where that place is. There's just some block. I lose my mind. Start punching walls. You should see me.

You shouldn't. I just—I don't want to get ripped off, but even more than that I don't want to have to think about protecting myself from getting ripped off. I want that taken care of for me. That's all I want. Does that make any sense?"

"I think I understand," said the accountant. "How about this: you get in touch with me if you start to feel like you want to invest your money, and then I'll advise you. Until then, I'll just keep an eye on things for you, and if anything pops up that I feel needs addressing, I'll let you know. Meantime, I'll get you set up with as many autopay options as are available, and when they're not available, I'll make sure to contact you when bills and the like come due, and we'll take it from there."

"You'll contact me by email?" Gladman said.

"*Or* telephone," the accountant said.

"I'd prefer email," Gladman said.

"That's fine," the accountant said. "I love email."

Then Gladman suddenly started to weep. Except for Gogol, the attorney, food-delivery people, liquor-store clerks, and, once, Daphne's mother, the accountant was the first person to whom he'd spoken since the terrestrial anomaly. It was hard. Not the speaking so much as the hearing himself. His voice. He hated it. Why wasn't he screaming? Why wasn't he mute?

"Hey," the accountant said. "Hey there. Hey now."

"I'm sorry," said Gladman, catching his breath, clearing his throat, swallowing and swallowing against a rising nausea. "I didn't mean"—swallow—"didn't mean to offend you. You've been really patient."

"I'm not offended at all," the accountant said. "I understand. You've been through a tragedy. You're *still* going through it. You're grieving. We all are, but especially you. Plus you're new to having such substantial personal wealth—"

"You seem like a very nice person," Gladman said.

"Well . . . thank you," the accountant said. "I hope I am. I'm trying to be. Your father was a friend to me. And your sister Naomi—I adored her. Inasmuch as I can, I want to make sure you're going to be all right. I want to help you out."

"Hold on," Gladman said, and, covering the receiver, rose from the bed to go vomit in the bathroom. On the way there he burped, twice, three times, and the nausea, like magic, completely disappeared, but the vertigo that had accompanied the nausea now became overpowering and he stumbled at the wall, into the wall, then slid down the wall and lay on the floor. It took him some time to find his ear with the phone.

"I think I'm really going to have to get off the phone in a second," said Gladman, "but just to be clear—you're my accountant, now, right?"

"I'd be more than happy to be your accountant."

"You'll just pay yourself the same fees my father was paying you, and take care of all that stuff I just said?"

"Sure," said the accountant. "I mean: pretty much. I'll need to send some papers over in the next few days so you can grant me some limited power of attorney, and you should show those papers to your lawyer, then sign them, and—"

"I don't have a lawyer. I need a lawyer, I guess."

"How about the lawyer your father and your sister used?"

"I don't know him."

"He called you. A few days ago, I think."

"I don't remember. Is he good? Did my father like him?"

"He was your father's lawyer for over forty years."

"Must have liked him. Think he'd be my lawyer?"

"Do I think he'd—"

"Such a stupid fucking question, I know—"

"No, no, no," the accountant said. "I mean, it's not stupid. And, yes, I think he'd be happy to be your lawyer. Do you want his number?"

"His *phone* number?"

"*Or* his email address," the accountant said.

"Yes," Gladman said.

"I'll get it to you, and, you know, I could contact him in the meantime, tell him you'll be writing to him, and kind of, I guess, prep him or what have you, so you don't have to do so much explaining about what you want. Unless that's too forward. I don't want to assume—I mean, it just seems like you're not really enjoying the whole explaining-what-you-want aspect of . . ."

"That would be great," Gladman said. "Thank you. Please do those things."

"I will," said the accountant.

"Mmm," said Gladman. Then he passed out.

—

When he awoke on the couch some three hours later, he didn't remember having crawled to the couch. He didn't remember passing out in the hall or crying on the phone or hiring an accountant or learning that he had become a wealthy man. He had no memory of playing any part in the conversation detailed above. He didn't remember that there'd been a conversation.

Yet, at the same time, he knew that he'd inherited millions of dollars in cash and property; that to manage his wealth he had an accountant who had been both his father's and his sister's accountant; that he liked that accountant. And despite being unable to recall how he'd come to know any of these facts about himself, he didn't question their facthood. They felt like facts. They felt just as factual as, for example, the fact that his date of birth was December 11, 1976. (He didn't remember how he'd learned that, either: surely someone he'd trusted had told him, likely one of his parents, but when? where? what had he imagined it meant when he was told? what had he imagined *to have been born* meant?)

Nor was he troubled by the failure of his memory, for it was easy to explain. It was an outcome of being perpetually loaded on Xanax and whiskey and irresolvable grief. Furthermore it accompanied the state of mind he'd been seeking to produce: the blurry state during which he could forget that he'd likely have to live for another nine years.

Suchly blurred, he could lie there on the couch and just . . . think. Assess and remember and remember some more. Free-associate away with no interference, without hesitation. Without any fear that a fond recollection of something irretrievable might arise too crystal-clearly. Without any worry that such a recollection might cause him to long for the past too painfully.

So that's what he did, lying there, nice and blurry, on the couch, beginning with a thought that went something like this: "I don't know how I know I've inherited millions, but I know I have millions and I trust my accountant, who I don't remember having ever had a conversation with. Does this mean I'm coming out of a blackout?" He'd always been under the impression that blackouts were total, but maybe that was wrong. Maybe some blackouts were only partial. Maybe these were called *brownouts*. *Brownout*, he thought, sounded like *brownstar*. One of the apartments where Kayla had lived had been up the street from Betty's Blue Star Lounge. A terrible place, a 4 a.m. place. "The best place in town," Naomi'd once said, "to have your chocolatini roofied by a pork bellies trader in a fitted Cubs cap lip-syncing Moby." Or maybe she'd said *cinnatini* and *Enigma,* or *raspberry cosmo* and *Fatboy Slim.* When she'd said it, they'd been driving Kayla home from the theater—opening night of one of those shows her commedia troupe would go on to catch hell for, though never quite as much hell as they'd been trying to court. *A Doll's House? The Blacks? A Raisin in the Sun?* He'd loved that troupe, as long as it had lasted. He'd loved them even before they'd started doing commedia, had even helped them find funding for one of their earlier productions. *Helen Keller: The Breakdancing Spectacular.* But the date-rape joke: it wasn't really Naomi's style. She'd always been the stable, social justice–y sibling. Not that she hadn't had a good sense of humor. Had Kayla or Gladman himself made the joke, she'd have probably laughed. You just wouldn't have expected Naomi to make it. You didn't expect her to think those kinds of things. Off-color things. Yet by that same token, it was just her kind of joke. The kind you didn't see coming. Anyway, Kayla, from whom you always did expect a joke, would call the place "Betty's *Brownstar* Lounge," which had never failed to get Gladman guffawing. The first time she'd said it in front of Daphne was just a week or so into Daphne's second visit to Chicago—the visit that had been originally scheduled to last three months, but ended up becoming permanent, becoming a *move* rather than a visit when, ten weeks in, they'd wed at City Hall—and Daphne laughed along with the Gladmans, but it turned out she didn't understand what was funny, and later that night, back at the condo, just the two of them alone, giggling and drunk, she asked Gladman to explain it, and Gladman stumbled to the pantry, found a bar of Ghirardelli, and used it like a crayon. He drew with the chocolate a dense stack of asterisks on the back of a hardcover copy of a novel by a friend of a friend he'd been pressured into blurbing, and above the Vonnegutian asterisk stack, he had written it, the word, in all-caps: *BROWNSTAR.* And Daphne had smiled, proclaimed the Gladmans disgusting, and kissed him on the cheek, and Gladman had blushed, realizing just how very drunk he was, and knowing that, had he been sober, or even slightly less drunk, he would never have drawn an anus for Daphne, much less in chocolate, wouldn't have even said the word *anus,* for he didn't want her (or anyone, really, but especially her) to in any way associate him with the concept of *anus,* didn't want her to think about his even having an anus, for that might lead her to think about the fact that he shat, which could in turn lead to conversations down the line about one or both of them shitting, a topic that had, in the past, some fifteen years earlier with the previous woman he'd been in love with, proven to be off-putting and ultimately, he often thought, ruinous. In any case, things had started to go downhill for them—for Gladman and the previous woman he'd loved—right around the time they'd started getting comfortable discussing shitting. Passion. Mutual physical attraction. Sexual things. All downhill. That might have been only a coincidence, he knew, and his feelings for that woman hadn't remotely been as intense as those which he had developed for Daphne, so even to Gladman it seemed a little square, a little uptight and deco-rous, maybe even a little bit lacking in faith to so vigilantly work to keep the topic of shitting away from his and Daphne's discourse, but better safe than sorry, he'd decided, and after the brownstar-drawing episode, he'd stuck with that policy. Better safe than sorry. Well, except for just once. He'd broken with the policy one more time. Or it might have been more like a thousand more times. Depended on the way you chose to count. But having rented, a year or so into their marriage, the 1992 Belgian mockumentary *Man Bites Dog,* a movie Gladman hadn't ever watched before, they encountered the famous scene in the hospital room in which the very old man who just shat his gown sings his simul-taneously mournful- and prideful-sounding song to the disapproving nurse who's there to change his linens:

> Je chiais la nuit,
> Je chiais le jour,
> Je chiais partout,
> Je chiais toujours!

which translates to:

> I would shit in the night,
> I would shit in the day,
> I would shit everywhere,
> I would always shit!

and Gladman, laughing himself into a coughing fit, repeatedly rewound the scene till he had the lyrics phonetically memorized, and, nearly every day during the year or two that followed, he would, at some point, and often more than one point, sing the song to Daphne till she'd laugh or sing along. But that was it, though, as far as breaking with the policy went. And it wasn't like they'd been Victorians or something. Genitals and fucking, and all the many words there were for genitals and fucking—those came up with regularity (*regularity*, not so incidentally, a word that Gladman never used in front of Daphne) . . . all the words for genitals and fucking and the topics of conversation they engendered came up with regularity, came up whenever even the slightest opportunity to pun arose. That cookie U.S. groceries imported from France? The butter cookie stuck to the square of chocolate embossed with the schoolboy? The Schoolboy Cookie—that's what it was called on the American box. On the French box, it was the Little Schoolboy. *Le Petit Ecolier*. And Gladman's first and only pun in French was *Le Petit Enculé*. The little assfucker. (Anal *sex* as a topic was, strangely or not, entirely permissible.) Just before they'd gotten married, they'd gone to Whole Foods, and just before they'd gone to Whole Foods, Daphne had mentioned she'd been feeling a little bit homesick for Paris, and when they got to the c(ookie)racker aisle, Gladman pointed out the boxes of Little Schoolboy cookies and said, "Would these, do you think, help you feel better? Some *Petits Enculés*?" And the question, in itself, it seemed, had made her feel a little bit better. And some time not very long after that trip to Whole Foods, maybe even the very same evening, they went out to dinner, and, when they got to the restaurant, a neighborhood-famous upscale diner called A Little Bite, Daphne started laughing, and she took out her phone to snap a picture of the sign hanging over the door, and sent the photo to her sister. The word *bite*, in French pronounced *beet*, meant cock. Penis. Dick. Prick. And what got Gladman laughing when Daphne explained this wasn't so much *bite*'s meaning in French, but that she didn't use any of the aforementioned words for male genitalia to explain the meaning. Rather, what she said was "In French, *bite* is *wang*." Beet is wang. "Beet is wang!" he'd all but shouted across Western Av, then kissed her on the cheekbones, on the freckled *pommettes*. And there, on the couch, browned out and blurry, he could feel it on his lips, his once-living wife's face, cool and smooth, could even smell her shampoo, so different in her hair than how it smelled in the bottle, and her palm on his jaw, her fingertips light on the back of his neck . . . But then he just couldn't. Just as quickly he couldn't. Couldn't feel or smell anything no longer there. And he rose from the couch, and poured himself a whiskey and knew he was a millionaire and had an accountant and didn't know how he knew or try to remember or see any need to.

By spring of 2022, the provenance of quite a lot of knowledge he'd acquired since 11/17 was just as lost to Gladman as the December conversation he'd had with the accountant.

He knew, for example, that after the estate taxes had been paid, he'd been worth 16.4 million dollars. That after paying the balances of Daphne's mom's and brother's and one of her sisters' mortgages in Paris (the other sister, who lived in Lyon, refused to accept any money from Gladman), he had been worth 14.8 million dollars. He put, he knew, 1.5 million dollars in a trust for Daphne's niece—the daughter of Daphne's sister in Lyon—and made Daphne's mother the trust's executor. He'd paid off, he knew, Ann's student loan debt—about 100k. And another 100k or so, he knew, had gone to pay the accountant and lawyer fees required to conduct the aforementioned transactions. He knew he'd made decisions to conduct these transactions, and that he'd relayed those decisions via emails and texts with the lawyer and accountant, who had sent him messengers and sometimes mobile notaries bearing documents requiring his signature. He knew, as well, that he'd signed those documents. He didn't, however, remember sending the texts, sending the emails, meeting the notaries or messengers, or writing his signature.

He didn't remember quitting his job at the university. He did, however, know he had quit. And he knew the university had continued to pay him his annual salary of 93k in biweekly installments, and would continue to pay him through fall of 2023, as the school owed him two full-paid yearlong sabbaticals, wanted to continue to list him as a faculty member on the website, and hoped that by the time these "sabbaticals" were over, he'd change his mind and return to his job. Although he assumed that he must have had at least one conversation regarding these matters with someone at the school—the dean of faculty, perhaps, or the chair of the English department—he didn't remember having had any such conversation.

And although he had, by spring of 2022, long since stopped accepting phone calls from anyone whose number he was able to recognize, he still accepted phone calls from numbers that he did *not* recognize, for much of the Xanax he'd ordered online (he remembered doing that) had not yet been delivered—he'd received 1,200 milligrams so far, assumed that he had another 300 coming, and hoped that he had another 1,800 coming—and sometimes the person delivering his pills needed him to sign for receipt of those pills, and sometimes he'd ordered a pizza, too, and he always left instructions in the "Special Instructions" windows on websites to call him on delivery rather than buzz because the sound of his building's front door buzzer caused Gogol to scream his most deafening scream for minutes at a time.

So when an unknown caller rang his phone on April 13, 2022, Gladman thought it might mean more pills, and hoped that it might mean a pizza, though he didn't remember having ordered a pizza. He accepted the call.

"Hello?" he said.

"Mr. Gladman?" said a man.

"Down in a minute," Gladman told the man, and ended the call, and got up from the couch, and fell to the floor—his legs were asleep. Both of his legs. He rubbed them with vigor.

The phone rang again.

"Just putting on my shoes, here," Gladman answered. "Another twenty seconds."

"Mr. Gladman," said the man, "my name is Apter Schutz. I'm with the mayor's office, and I was hoping we could talk about Mount Chicago."

"Mmm," Gladman said, and hung up, and passed out.

A Portrait of the Apter
Schutz as Young Men

1

The first man from City Hall who attempted to make Apter's smile his own was Reginald Glibner. Glibner had been the mayor's right hand since the mayor's election in 2019, and prior to that his campaign manager.

He was the person the mayor had ordered to fire the staffer who'd used the term *sinkhole* on social media.

Early into the evening of November 20, 2021, Glibner and Apter were sitting one stool away from each other at a bar in Ukrainian Village called the Rainbo. Seeing Apter smile when he ordered his whiskey, Glibner wondered who Apter was, and whether he should know him.

"Should I know you?" he said, not meaning to be creepy, nor even clever, but rather having misspoken.

"I don't think so," said Apter.

"I wasn't—" Glibner said, and cleared his throat, blushing. "That came out sounding like I was trying to pick you up."

"You aren't?" Apter said.

"I like 'em a little ruggeder than you, and with much bigger tits. Tits out to here."

"A tit man," said Apter. "I never would've guessed."

"No," said Glibner. "Actually, I'm not. I don't know why I said that. What I meant to say, though, was: *Do* I know you?"

"It's possible," Apter said, "but I doubt it. Usually, having to ask that question means—"

"Right. Sorry. Jesus . . . I'm like the most disingenuous person tonight."

"Cheer up, man. Come on. Really. I'm Apter. I was being a dick. Now I'm buying you a drink. What are you having?"

Glibner said bourbon, Apter asked him what brand, and Glibner, who'd been suffering wild fits of itching lately—they'd come on suddenly, these itching fits; could prevent him from sleeping; had begun, in the last couple weeks or so, to startle him awake in the middle of the night—recalled some advice that the mayor, having noticed Glibner scratching, recently gave him about "the heightened sensitivity of the middle-aged body to various toxins and toxinating substances that used to be tolerable or even, in certain cases, warmly welcomed, such as spray-on antiperspirizing deodorants, inorganical detergents with perfumes in them, suicide chili, suicide wing sauce, or the cheaper alcohols, especially the brown ones, which now, alas, may need to be both entirely and conclusively foregone out of one's diet and habitat owing to what is almost akin to something like allergies or, in any case, allergic-like reactions to the toxinating properties they inflict on one's aforementioned middle-aged body's cellular developments as if out of nowhere," and so, rather than naming a brand of bourbon, told Apter that he'd changed his mind, that actually he'd just have an Absolut and soda with a wedge of lime, and Apter bought him his drink, and they got to talking. They talked for hours.

Apter liked to talk to strangers at bars nearly as much as strangers at bars liked to talk to Apter. He liked to hear about the lives of strangers, especially their jobs, especially lately. He, himself, though only twenty-seven, had already walked away from two successful careers, and was trying to figure out what to do with his time.

Like Gladman and me, he believed that life was meaningless and people were terrible. Unlike Gladman, he didn't feel that life's being meaningless meant that his life was not worth living. Nor did he think that people's terribleness needed to interfere with the pleasure he took in observing and interacting with people. Generally speaking, Apter enjoyed himself.

He liked, in addition to hearing about the lives of strangers he met at bars, to tell those strangers about his own life, which he conceived of as a series of five long anecdotes.

—

The first of these anecdotes concerned the events described in *A Young Jewish Schoolkid,* and needn't be further detailed here.

Except to say a couple of things.

Number one: Apter ended the anecdote on a different note than the one on which I ended *A Young Jewish Schoolkid,* for Apter's anecdote wasn't about how he came out of everything with a supernaturally charismatic smile, but about how he got the scar on his face.

Number two: he spent more time than I have describing the Bernie Pollaco videos. Often he would, in the Pollaco voice, tell as many as half a dozen of the number jokes. On occasion he'd even go so far as to rise from his barstool and impersonate Pollaco faking a heart attack.

2

The second anecdote concerned the only major falling-out he'd had with his parents.

At the start of Apter's junior year of high school, i.e. September 2011, Gladman's second novel made the long list for the national prize that it would go on to win a couple months later. By the time the announcement of that long list was made, someone who called himself Gummo Rickles had been curating an unofficial Bernie Pollaco channel on YouTube for over two years.

Just prior to the announcement, the channel, *Nice Belt,* which had 5,201 subscribers—Apter had been the ninety-seventh—consisted of 126 videos, organized across three playlists:

1. *New Bits!* This playlist featured cellphone videos of performances in which Pollaco made at least one joke that had not previously appeared in any of the other videos on the *Nice Belt* channel. There were twenty-two videos here.

2. *Redundancy Department.* This playlist, consisting of sixty-three videos, featured the earliest-posted cellphone video of every available Pollaco performance that did *not* contain at least one joke which had not appeared in an earlier video on the *Nice Belt* channel.

3. *Department of Redundancy Department.* This playlist featured alternate cellphone videos (forty-one total) of Pollaco performances that had already appeared on one of the aforementioned playlists. If there were, for example, three available cellphone videos of Pollaco's performance at Whackadoo Lounge's Open Mike Night on 10/23/2010, the first one posted would be featured on either *New Bits!* or *Redundancy Department,* depending on whether it contained a previously unrecorded joke or not, and the remaining two would be featured on this playlist, i.e. the *Department of Redundancy Department* playlist.

Gummo Rickles labeled all the videos on the *Nice Belt* channel to indicate their audial and visual properties, as well as the points of view from which they'd been shot. E.g.

PIEHOLE JOHNNY'S OPEN MIC NIGHT, 08/09/2010, UPLOADED 08/11/2010 BY WILLIAMBILLYBILLYBOY, 3RD VERSION POSTED (OF 4)

B+ sonics. Clean. Laughter of videographer or proximal companion drowns out delivery of Dry Cleaner bit from 6:12 to 6:19.

B- visuals. Focused, standard definition, but v. shakey. Also: thumb in upper right corner during opening 87 seconds.

A+ POV. Front table, center stage. Captures more gestures and facial expressions than other three vids of this gig, almost as if Pollaco's performing FOR *Nice Belt* subscribers.

As ever, if you have posted a Pollaco vid that does not appear on *Nice Belt,* that is only because I have not found it yet. Please send me a link, and I will gladly post it, whatever the quality, whatever the performance.

—Gummo Rickles

Apter wondered, at times, if Gummo Rickles was on the autism spectrum. Other times he wondered if Gummo Rickles was Pollaco himself (he wasn't). What else could drive someone to so obsessively and systematically aggregate and label recordings of a comedian who had, in total, just thirteen minutes and forty-one seconds of material?

Then again, Apter was neither on the spectrum, nor, obviously, was he Pollaco, and he'd not only watched every video that Gummo Rickles posted, but as soon as one was made available, he'd download it to his own computer and back it up to an external hard drive just in case *Nice Belt* were ever deleted.

So maybe pot and kettle.

Three days after the national prize long list's announcement, Apter, during a morning free period, went beneath the viaduct across the street from North Side Secular to smoke a cigarette and, hopefully, flirt a little bit with the lovely, emo Fruma Wexler, who played drums and sang for a post-punk band, Evening Redness in the West, had a voice like Ronnie Spector, a Naked Raygun tattoo on her forearm (the pilot from the *Jettison* album cover), and claimed she was only interested in girls, but seemed to touch him—his hands, his chest, his *face*—every time he came within reach.

Fruma wasn't there, though—she was home with a cold. So Apter took out his phone, scrolled through a couple social media feeds, got bored quickly, and checked *Nice Belt,* to which, he discovered, to his great surprise, Gummo Rickles had added a fourth playlist: *Hold Up, Wait a Minute!*

The playlist featured just one video, the first on *Nice Belt* that Gummo Rickles had created himself. The format was split screen, the duration one minute. On the left side appeared a series of fifteen different close-up stills from seven different Pollaco videos. Each still remained on-screen for four seconds. On the right side appeared a series of three professionally photographed portraits of Gladman, and each of these remained on-screen for twenty seconds.

Gummo Rickles's description of the video read:

DO YOU SEE WHAT I SEE?

On the left, of course, is a compilation of stills I've taken from Bernie Pollaco videos that appear on *Nice Belt.*

On the right are photos of a man named Solomon Gladman, the author of three books, and a creative writing teacher at the University of Illinois at Chicago. I am a kind of big reader of literary fiction, and I have heard of this guy before, though I have not read him. His latest novel is longlisted for a pretty major prize that just got announced, and the first photo is from the press release that announced the longlist. The second is from the *New York Times* review of his story collection, which came out two years ago. The third is from the flap of his debut novel, which came out four years ago.

I think Gladman and Pollaco are the same person. If not, they're twins. The resemblance is crazy, unless maybe I am crazy (I'm not!). Does anybody know for sure, though? Have any of you ever talked to Pollaco at any of his gigs? If so, has he ever said anything about being a writer? I'm thinking probably not because someone would have mentioned it by now, but . . . maybe?

If I lived in Chicago, I would hit every amateur night at every comedy club until I solved this mystery, but I live in Los Angeles and I don't have the money or vacation time to fly there. If you have any information about this matter, please let me know. And if you get to see Pollaco perform now or in the future, please ask him if he's Gladman and . . .

Let me know what he says!

In the meantime, I've written Gladman at his university email address, and asked him, myself. Hopefully he's not too busy to respond.

—Gummo Rickles

MAJOR (MAJOR!!!) UPDATE: 9/13/11

Gladman wrote back today! Just twelve hours and forty-one minutes after I sent him my email. And I wrote HIM back, and he responded AGAIN! Three hours and four minutes later! And he's really nice! And he IS Pollaco! And not only that!

Not only is Solomon Gladman, author of three books of fiction and professor of Creative Writing at UIC also the beloved amateur comedian, Bernie Pollaco, but he's another amateur comedian, too: SOLLY Gladman!

Which solves another mystery that some of you subscribers to *Nice Belt* and I have been wondering about for a little while now: "Why does it seem like fewer and fewer videos of Pollaco have been getting posted to YouTube in the last six months or so?" The answer is: Gladman has been in the process of "retiring" the Pollaco character. He is performing just as often as he ever was, but he's been doing so as Solly Gladman most of the time.

If this news makes you sad, I understand: believe me. It made me sad, too.

For about three minutes!

That's how long it took me to find a Solly Gladman video and watch the first two and a half minutes of it.

People, Solly Gladman is great. Maybe even the greatest. By now, I have watched nearly three hours of his performances. He is not always as funny as Pollaco—though sometimes, at least to me, he's even funnier than Pollaco—and he doesn't even seem like he's always TRYING to be funny, but what he is, I am saying it, is: important. (And I'm not saying Pollaco ISN'T important!)

He is doing a new thing. He is doing something that other comedians don't do, and it is something that most comedians can't be expected to do, since they're trying to earn a living as comedians, and Gladman isn't: he is doing whatever he feels like doing whenever he feels like doing it.

Some of his material seems like it's written. He does have a couple openers and closers he uses pretty habitually, and a lot of times he challenges the audience to help him come up with a punchline to "what might, if we get it right, turn out to be the most antisemitic joke of all time, which starts like this: 'You hear about those three Jews that tried to rape the white woman?'" but the rest is just him going off about whatever is on his mind.

Sometimes he talks about his wife. Sometimes he talks about parrots. Sometimes he talks about Jews. BF Skinner.

Drugs. Blowjobs. Duck confit. His favorite parks in the city of Paris. Pizza. Socialism. One of his sets is just him doing impersonations of famous impersonations (Gottfried's Dice Clay, Ferrell's Bush, Little's Carson) and impersonations of impersonations that should but don't exist (Ringo Starr doing Yasser Arafat, Kevin Spacey doing Hitler, Drunken Catherine Zeta-Jones doing Kirk Douglas before and after Kirk Douglas's stroke). Another of his sets, he comes out, and he says, "I am going to prove to you that I am the most improvisational stand-up comedian alive," and then he does! He proves it! How? Simple! His entire ten minutes consists of him mocking and riffing on bits performed by three of the five amateur night comedians who appeared onstage immediately before him.

In other words: unless having no schtick can be considered a schtick, Solly Gladman has no schtick.

Suffice it to say, I am curating a new channel: *Gladman UnSchtuck.* So far, it's got twenty-nine videos covering twenty-four performances. Over three and a half hours of footage featuring two hours and forty-one minutes of non-redundant material. I hope you'll all check it out, subscribe, and spread the word.

—Gummo Rickles

Having read the description, Apter instantly decided to skip the rest of the school day and head back home to watch every video on *Gladman UnSchtuck.* Once he was through, he ate a late lunch of cold schnitzel in the kitchen, ordered all of Gladman's books online, found his university email address on the UIC website, and spent an hour writing him a letter.

Dear Professor Gladman,

Without resorting to superlatives, there is no concise way to tell you how hilarious and brilliant I think you are, and superlatives, as you riffed about just last month at your Julio's

Yokebarn gig, make those who use them sound stupid, which can't help but undermine the credibility of the praise the superlative-user is attempting to convey.

So I will just say this, then: I have been an avid fan of your Bernie Pollaco work for nearly three years. I had never heard of Solly Gladman until this morning, and as soon as I found out he was you, and you were Pollaco, I watched every Solly Gladman video on YouTube. Since doing that, I have ordered all your books. I imagine I'll have read them within the next two weeks.

I have never written fan mail before. I have never understood the purpose of fan mail. I would like to think this isn't just fan mail. I am, in fact, writing with a purpose.

I live in Chicago and I want to see you perform live. Not so I can come up to you and bother you with my fandom. I just want the experience of seeing you live. I wanted that even before I found out who you were. I wanted to see Bernie Pollaco live even though I'd memorized all the jokes, and now I want to see Solly Gladman live even more than I wanted to see Bernie Pollaco live.

As I'm sure you must know, you don't make it easy for anyone to see you live. I cannot say I understand why you make it so hard, but it is your right, and I do not question that. The thing is, though, I am sixteen years old, and I look, at most, seventeen years old. I have had two (expensive!) fake IDs taken from me by doormen at comedy clubs where you've been known to perform in the past, clubs where I have gone in the hope of catching your act on open mic night. Older-looking friends I went with were able to get in, and they told me that you didn't end up performing on either of those nights, so it was either doubly lousy to lose the IDs (you weren't even there!) or half as lousy as it could have been (at least I didn't, on top of losing the IDs, miss you).

(I'm not saying I blame you.)

What I'm getting at, Professor Gladman, is that I know that every once in a while you perform at cafes and all-ages alt-clubs like the Yokebarn, and I would be forever in your debt if you would let me know the next time you were going to perform at one of those venues. I give you my word, I will tell no one else that you told me, if that is your wish.

Thank you for considering this. I won't bother you again. I wish you all the best, and can't wait to read your books.

Sincerely,

Apter Schutz

An automated response arrived ninety seconds later.

Dear You,

If you are a student of mine, this is no longer the address at which to reach me. You should have received an email containing my new address. If you haven't, you can ask anyone else in your workshop for it. And you can ignore the rest of this email, as well.

If you're one of those people who have written to disparage my ethnicity, to shame me for the way my sharing your ethnicity seems to you to disparage that shared ethnicity, to threaten my physical well-being, or to threaten my life, please ignore this autoresponse in favor of going outside and finding someone with whom to have consensual sexual relations, or, if that's too hard for you, which I can see how it might be, then please go outside and eat some pizza or ice cream, unless maybe you're very fat, in which case I'd advise you find and snort or inject some meth—you can smoke it, too, though it's hard on your lungs and I wouldn't suggest that— unless perhaps you're too broke for meth, in which case you can't afford to be online, wasting your life, bothering me, and you should, please, go get yourself a job, you deplorable fucking loser, you. Get that money. I know it's hard, but you can do it. Just like suicide. Don't be afraid.

If you are not a student of mine, but you mean well in writing to me, please forgive this autoresponse. It is, unfortunately, necessary. In the last few days, I have received a lot of email, some of it, like yours, well-meaning, some of it not. I am no longer going to read email sent to this address, and I will no longer respond to email sent to any address of mine unless it is from a friend or a student of mine.

I take my job as a teacher very seriously. I want to do it as well as I can. That requires many hours of work. Writing and performing require even more hours, as do spending time with those I love, going to the movies, reading books for pleasure, traveling, etc. Like everyone else, I am going to die. So I just don't have the time to respond to your emails. I truly wish I did. I hope you understand.

Nearly all of you have asked me when and where I will be performing in the future. I am flattered that you want to know, but I cannot tell you. I can see how that might be aggravating to you, so I'd like to try to explain myself here.

I don't know when or where I will be performing until just hours, sometimes just minutes, before I get onstage. I only perform when I feel like performing. When I get the feeling that I might feel like performing, I go to some venue that I think would give me stage time, and then, if it turns out, once I've arrived, that I do feel like performing, I tell whoever is managing the venue that I would like some stage time, and usually—at least for the last year and a half or so—I'm given that stage time. And then I use it.

Not only don't I know when or where I'll be performing in the future, I don't WANT to know when or where I'll be performing in the future. My plan is to never receive any billing, much less appear on any marquee. I plan never to perform when I don't feel like performing, and never to perform any bit I don't feel like performing. I don't want anybody paying to see me. I don't want to have to think about meeting, surpassing, or disappointing the sorts of expectations that come along with having paid to see a specific performer. I want to do exactly what I want to do, and I want to do it exactly when I want to do it. In other words, I don't want stand-up to be my profession. I *have* a profession. I have two, really. Two really good ones. I'm a teacher and a writer. Those are the right professions for me. I don't need another one. Don't want another one. Don't want to ruin a good thing. When I get onstage, I don't want to work. I want to play around. I want *to play*. I want to play, and I want you to enjoy it. That's all I want from this.

Another, perhaps simpler, way to say all that: I really do hope you'll get to see me live sometime, and I'm certain that if you do get to see me live sometime, my performance, whether or not it's any good that night, will be immeasurably better than it would have been if you knew in advance that you were about to see me live—better than it would have been if *I* knew that you'd known in advance that you were about to see me live. It will be better enough to justify my risking your never getting to see me live, much as I hope you'll get to see me live.

In the meantime, shoot all the videos you want of my performances, post them wherever you feel like posting them, watch them all you want, and please expect nothing further from me.

—Gladman

Apter was, of course, a bit disappointed not to receive a personal response after having spent so much time on his letter, but he didn't blame his disappointment on Gladman. He blamed it on the terribleness of people in general, and, more than that, he was impressed by Gladman's dedication to his art. Above all, he was happy to learn that

Gladman would, by all indications, continue to perform, which meant that Apter would, by all indications, continue to be able to see new Gladman performances online, for free, and maybe one day luck into catching him live.

By fall semester of his senior year of high school, Apter had read all of Gladman's books. He had read the second (by then, national prize-winning) novel once, the first one twice, the story collection once as a whole, and its three best stories four or five times each. He had read every print interview with Gladman that he'd been able to find (there were scores), and he had listened to and watched every audio and video interview with Gladman he'd been able to find (there weren't that many, just a dozen or so).

He'd read many of the contemporary writers whose work Gladman had blurbed, and all the contemporary writers who had blurbed Gladman's work. He had read, in the journal *Cultural Anthropology,* a chapter from Gladman's wife's forthcoming book—a microethnography of the Taylor Street Bocce Courts—and he would have liked to read her earlier books (especially the microethnography of Corsican poker dealers at the ACF gambling club in Paris), but neither of those books had been translated yet.

He possessed two shelves of books by writers who Gladman had praised in interviews: DeLillo, Kafka, Pacheco, Roth, Elkin, Paley, O'Connor, Percival Everett, Saunders, Cervantes, Hannah, Aira, Paul Beatty, Houellebecq, Bordas, Vonnegut, Millhauser, Padgett Powell, Ellison, Ellroy, Castellanos Moya, Bernhard, Bove, Lydia Davis, Nicholson Baker, Helen Dewitt, Christian TeBordo, Adam Novy, André Alexis, Rebecca Curtis, Jeff Parker, Emmanuel Carrere, and, of course, Gogol. He had started to read at least one book by each of these writers and he planned to complete reading at least one book by each of these writers.

He had watched recordings of live performances and films that starred or were written by comedians or comedy writers who Gladman had praised in interviews: the Marx Brothers, Chaplin, Seinfeld, David, Pryor, Iannucci, Gottfried, CK, Cosby, Klein, Allen, Tati, Carlin, Wright, Baron Cohen, Fields, Glazer, Chappelle, Nichols and May, Stiller and Meara, Burr, Foxx (Redd), Gregory, and Silverman (Sarah).

He had more than twenty hours of Pollaco/Gladman videos on his laptop's hard drive.

He had memorized all the Pollaco number jokes, and who-knew-how-many Solly Gladman bits without having meant to—he just watched them that often.

He hadn't yet managed to see Gladman live.

Ever since he'd found out that Pollaco was Gladman, he'd done so much reading of and thinking about fiction, so much viewing of and thinking about comedy, that he thought he might one day become a writer, and while he suspected that only thinking he *might* probably meant that, in the end, he wouldn't, that wasn't the reason he didn't go to UIC to study creative writing with Gladman.

He planned to go to UIC to study with Gladman. He applied and got in. He had, however—mostly to get his parents off his back—also applied to better universities, the sort he'd always been expected to attend—Northwestern, Berkeley, the University of Chicago, Princeton, Cornell—and visited the ones to which he'd been accepted.

Princeton was the only one to reject him.

The University of Chicago didn't have enough girls.

Cornell's girls were fine, but Ithaca was sleepy, too far away from any real city.

His whole visit to Berkeley had been . . . uptight. He kept getting the impression that the students he spoke with wished he would use a softer voice, or curse less frequently, or not gesture so much with his hands when he talked—something like that. No one would tell him what it was about him that put them on edge.

Nothing about Northwestern appeared objectionable. It was ranked Top 20, there were plenty of smart girls there, and the campus was in Evanston, which bordered Chicago, the city he loved. Yet Solomon Gladman didn't teach at Northwestern.

The only school Gladman taught at was UIC. Not a bad university, no, but not a great one either, not like the others. It wasn't even, according to his father, the second best of the Illinois state schools. "And I tell you so *as a graduate* of UIC!" his father shouted across the dinner table, the evening Apter told his parents he would go to UIC.

His mother didn't yell, though he almost wished she would have. Instead she trembled with panic and contempt, seething through her teeth, and there were tears in her eyes, as though the strain of attempting to reason with her son about which college that son should attend were reawakening memories of wartime traumas she'd suffered as a child then suppressed for decades.

How many classes would he even get to take with this Gladman?

Who knew if this Gladman was even that great a teacher?

How often did those who made great art—if this Gladman's work could even be called that; she didn't think it could, nor did his father; she thought Apter'd outgrow it, whatever it was, and so did his father—how often did great artists end up being great people, or even good people, or, for that matter, not *total shitbags*?

Total shitbags was a new one. Not the kind of phrase he knew his mother to deploy. Hearing her use it shocked him a little, even though he knew it was meant to shock him, but he held his ground anyway. He thought his parents were being snobs—UIC was plenty okay. Plus didn't their failure to appreciate Gladman call into question their capacity to predict what would make Apter happy?

For a week, things were cold all through the Schutz house. Cold and acrimonious. Even dinner was cold. Cold-cut sandwiches. Salad with cold cuts. Crackers and tuna. Tuna salad on lettuce. His mom wouldn't cook. Wouldn't, for that matter, ladle or slice.

Then his parents went out on their Sunday date—a matinee and Benihana—and, after that, the energy changed. His father came home from work the next evening bearing a big brown box of Chinese, and they made him an offer. They offered him a bribe. If he were to attend any of the other schools that had accepted him, they told him, they would choose to understand that as a sign of wisdom and maturity, and would allow him full access to the money from the Schwartz settlement a full seven years earlier than they'd initially planned to, i.e. on his eighteenth rather than his twenty-fifth birthday.

That $50k, they let him know, had, in the interim, been shrewdly invested. Had more than doubled.

Apter hadn't known the money would ever be his. He'd assumed they would use it to pay for his college if they hadn't used it already to pay for Secular, or Adi's college. And while the thought of having that kind of money was thrilling to Apter—the places he'd travel between semesters, the apartment he'd rent after sophomore year—it wasn't so much the money itself that swayed him, for he'd always had the sense that, one way or another, he'd always find enough money to get what he wanted. No, what swayed him was the parental desperation the money signified.

As far as Apter could tell, the Schutzes were comfortable, even *well-off*, but not so well-off that $100k+ was a drop in the bucket. Not even close. His mother cooked dinner six nights a week. His father, an accountant, bought all his suits and ties on sale. Both drove older-model Japanese sedans. The summer between her third and fourth years at Harvard, Adi'd had to wait tables at night to pay rent in Queens in order to intern at *Harper's Magazine*. For Apter's bar mitzvah, they'd thrown a Pita Inn–catered lunchtime reception in his father's partner's Skokie backyard for fifty-five guests, forty of them family. Since the start of ninth grade, he hadn't had an allowance. They vacationed once a year. They vacationed in Florida.

So the decision to offer him a $100k+ bribe—*any* monetary bribe, or any bribe at all, really—could not have been one that they came to lightly. That he go to what they thought to be a proper university was just that important to them.

Nor could he say they'd ever steered him wrong. They'd been good parents. Supportive parents. And tolerant, too. He'd had to keep his grades high and show up for dinner Sunday through Thursday, but in exchange they were laissez-faire about girls—about, e.g., girls spending the night—and far from strict when it came to curfew. Until a week earlier, they'd never had a meaningful conflict with him.

Plus even Gladman, he imagined, would think him an asshole to turn down the bribe. And if not, Apter reasoned, then Gladman himself would have been an asshole. And an asshole, Apter wasn't. Nor probably was Gladman.

So he accepted the bribe.

He went to Northwestern.

He hadn't fallen out with his parents once since.

3

Apter's third anecdote concerned his first career.

From the very beginning of his freshman year at Northwestern, 2013–14, social justice had been on certain people's minds. By his sophomore year, it was on most people's minds. Students were awake. Awake and angry. Many'd been awake and angry for a while. It was looking as though same-sex marriage might soon be made legal in all fifty states, and that was good, but too many unarmed people of color were being murdered by police, federal funding for women's healthcare was under threat, every new day brought a new mass shooting, student loan debt was crippling the prospects of middle-class youth, far too large a proportion of money was being earned by far too small a proportion of people, the oceans were eating away at the coasts, and the white nationalist movement was gaining mainstream political momentum.

Apter attended demonstrations, protests, and lectures on campus and throughout the city. Some were more inspiring than others. This depended less on the speaker than the audience. The kinds of people he found himself surrounded by.

He met any number of sharp, energetic, analytical people who seemed to earnestly wish to lessen their suffering and the suffering of others. Who wanted to hear and discuss the best ways to do that, then act. But he encountered plenty of awful people, as well. Overwrought people who seemed to want to suffer, to want to get credit for having suffered, to be *invested* in their suffering, in establishing the inferiority of the suffering of others to their own. And then there were those people who, more often than not, proudly called themselves *allies*, people who claimed to suffer by proxy, to suffer from the shame of living in a world that privileged them and privileged those like them at the cost of others' suffering. These allies seemed to Apter to be less invested in relieving others' suffering than in making other people who called themselves allies feel ashamed of not feeling ashamed enough about living in a world that privileged them.

There were safe-space people and trigger-warning people. There were people who told you their race, ethnicity, nationality, gender, economic status, sexual orientation, pronoun of preference, and (when applicable) medical condition in order to contextualize and/or justify their beliefs, which they referred to as their *truths*. There were people who used phrases like *enthusiastic consent* or *nonconsensual sexual advances* in such a way as to suggest that anyone who had to ask what such phrases meant was likely guilty of sex crimes himself. There were people who claimed that mathematics was *white* and empiricism *a discourse of white supremacy*. And then of course, there were the anti-Zionists (comprised of flagrant anti-Semites, crypto-anti-Semites, and ostensibly unwitting anti-Semites), the vast majority of whom were supporters of the BDS movement, a few of whom were Holocaust deniers, and a downright surprising number of whom—mostly African-American men, though it was certainly inadvisable to voice that observation—believed the *Protocols of the Meetings of the Learned Elders of Zion* to be an authentic record of a meeting held by learned elders of Zion back around the turn of the previous century.

Apter would listen to and, occasionally, provoke these idiots in much the same spirit that, as a boy, he had clicked around and trolled on white power message boards. He didn't fear them—not really—at least not during freshman or sophomore year. He didn't think they would, or could, gain any meaningful traction in America. It was more like he felt embarrassed to discover how often they were on his side when it came to other issues—the issues that occasioned the rallies and marches and talks he attended.

Black lives, Apter thought, did matter. So did gun control matter, and women maintaining their reproductive rights, and healthcare becoming universally accessible, and the country *not* becoming a plutocracy—or at least not becoming *more* of a plutocracy. It all mattered enough to stand side by side with the aforementioned idiots if that's what it took to bring about change. And there probably weren't that many of them, anyway. It probably only seemed like there were. The most-rattlingness of empty cans, etc.

—

Then sophomore year ended. He used some Schwartzy settlement money to tour western Europe for most of the summer, and, when he came home at the end of August, he found a much greater proportion of his fellow Americans to be . . . shitty. A much greater proportion than before he'd left. More of them were shitty to talk to. More of them were shitty to hear. And the shittiness had, itself, gotten shittier. Gotten less tolerant. More intolerable.

That's how it seemed, at least. It might have been him, though. It might have been Apter. Hanging out in Europe might have changed his outlook.

The people he'd befriended over there were far less screechy and sanctimonious than those back home. Especially in Paris, where he'd ended up spending half of the summer. Parisians weren't, he knew, any smarter than Americans. He'd met lots of French idiots, of course he had—most people were idiots—but the idiots in Paris seemed much less intent on expressing their idiotic notions. They were less self-assured of being right. Less likely, overall, when acting like idiots, to incite those around them to act like idiots. The French valued pleasure. They sought pleasure out. They tried to have fun, and they weren't ashamed or embarrassed about that. They'd have rather, it seemed, been laughing than offended. They'd have rather been considered amusing than righteous. They'd rather crack a joke at an idiot's expense than attempt to correct him. *Art de vivre,* or whatever.

Then again, maybe none of that. Maybe Europeans were, on average, as shitty to talk to and hear as Americans, and Apter, through luck, had only just happened to fall in with groups of less shitty ones. Or maybe the groups he'd fallen in with *were* just as shitty, but Apter, foreign, didn't (couldn't) catch what to a native would have indicated their equivalent shittiness.

Then again, again: Occam's razor. The increased American shittiness that Apter perceived upon returning from Europe might have had little or nothing to do with any change in his personal outlook—it might have been real. That is: Americans might have just become shittier. A lot had happened in the previous few months. A lot that, for varying reasons, could very well have emboldened, for better and for worse, Americans across the whole political spectrum. Just weeks before he'd left the U.S., there'd been Freddie Gray's murder and the Baltimore riots, and, while he was away, gay marriage had been legalized, Sandra Bland had died in holding, Caitlyn Jenner had posed on the cover of *Vanity Fair*, a white supremacist in South Carolina had murdered nine African Americans at church, and Independent senator Bernie Sanders had announced he'd be seeking the Democratic Party's nomination for president.

On his way home from Europe, Apter'd stopped in Brooklyn, to stay with his sister for half a week. Adi'd been in high spirits. Two novels she'd pulled from the FSG slush pile had been published over summer to critical acclaim, which had gotten her promoted to associate editor, and her longtime boyfriend, Sidney Baran, a London-born freelance technical illustrator with a part-time teaching position at Pratt, an Olympic bronze in diving, and a well-endowed trust fund, had, as everyone had hoped he would, proposed to her only a few days before.

Although they had always gotten along well—Apter had always looked up to Adi, Adi had always looked out for Apter—they were nearly seven years apart in age, and, before Apter'd gone to visit her in Brooklyn, they'd rarely, if ever, socialized together away from their parents. But by the time he'd boarded his plane to O'Hare, all of that had changed. They'd drunk beer and whiskey, smoked cigarettes and weed, aimlessly roamed from park to bookstore, from pizza to bagel to ice cream spot, conveyed half-abashed Schutz lore to Sidney in tandem, lost track of the hour, and laughed and laughed.

It turned out they were *friends,* the best of friends. What's more, it had occurred to them both—and maybe it was true, maybe it wasn't, it didn't matter—it had occurred to them both that, despite not having previously realized it, they'd *always* been the best of friends.

For the next few weeks, brother and sister, amid the excitement of their new (or just newly acknowledged) best-friendship, communicated frequently. Though Apter was becoming ever more disenchanted with his fellow Americans' narrow-minded behavior, the news out of Brooklyn kept him afloat. Adi's already well-going life seemed only to be getting better by the day, better even by the hour some days.

She had been submitted a thousand-page novel called *Money Changing Hands* that she claimed would become the next *White Noise* or *Blood Meridian,* and she was sure that to edit it would make her career. She'd been sending the manuscript around to her colleagues to build the consensus she knew she'd need to convince her bosses to green-light an offer, and the earliest responses had been uniformly positive. She forwarded all these responses to Apter, who read them with more than a little interest: he found that he cared. He cared about this novel that he'd never read, and was invested in its and Adi's future success almost as if that success would be his own.

And no less involving than her career was her dog. Just a day or two after Apter's visit had ended, Adi and Sidney had fallen in love with and impulsively bought a six-week-old Shiba Inu, Stanz, so named because the tenuous, nearly interrogative-sounding squeak it emitted in advance of barking had, from the very first time they'd heard it, reminded fiancé and fiancée the both of a noise that the actor Jason Alexander, in his role as *Seinfeld*'s George Costanza, habitually made when about to deliver a sideways taunt.

Adi sent videos of Stanz being cuddly. Of Stanz spazzing out. Stanz doing the squeak. Apter watched all the videos all the way through, sometimes twice, often chuckling to himself, and shortly came to feel as though Stanz were partly his, like his nephew or something. Looked forward to meeting him.

Third week of classes, fall 2015, Apter received an email invitation to sign a petition that demanded the firing of a tenured professor of creative writing. As the screen caps included with the invitation showed, the professor had, in a series of posts she'd made to social media over the last couple years, pronounced Ta-Nehisi Coates's latest and much-lauded book to be "unreasoned, swollen and purple"; referred to Cheryl Strayed's hiking memoir as "Self Help trash for crypto-Randians"; called Roxane Gay's collection of essays "self-aggrandizing, borderline-illiterate trash"; and Lena Dunham's whole oeuvre "trash, trash, trash." According to the authors of the petition, these posts served as evidence of the professor's being a "dangerous, oppressive, and violent force on the Northwestern campus who [was] not only causing untold harm to people of color, people with unruly bodies, and women, but destroying the dreams and undermining the achievements and aspirations of countless Northwestern student readers and writers such as the undersigned."

Apter forwarded the email to Adi, thinking she'd find it as hilarious as he did.

The day before, she almost certainly would have, but, this day, she wrote back, "People are terrible. I hate the world so much, little brother." Apter called her up to find out what was wrong.

Two things were wrong.

The first wrong thing was that *Money Changing Hands* had, the day before, been decisively rejected by her new editor-in-chief. He had not read it, and seemed happy to admit that he had not read it, explaining to Adi that he didn't need to read it to reject it, that despite any literary merit it might or might not possess, it was just too long. The sales force, he insisted, would not get behind it; reviewers wouldn't have the patience to contend with it; and according to the coverage Adi'd written of the book, it was neither young adult, nor dystopian, nor written by a person with "an interesting point of view."

Adi protested that, as her coverage explicitly remarked upon, the novel's point of view was beyond interesting, was truly unique, was its greatest asset, and the new editor-in-chief's response was, "The point of view I'm concerned with is, I repeat, the novel*ist's,* not the novel's," which statement Adi asked him to clarify. "The novelist," said the editor, "is a middle-aged cis white man who has published fiction for fifteen years. The world has heard from him before. A number of times. The world has heard from many just like him before many thousands of times. His point of view is therefore not interesting, would not be celebrated, would not, if we published his book in the current climate, lead to our house being celebrated, therefore would not garner any prizes, and so wouldn't have a prayer of earning out."

"The author is gay and Jewish," said Adi, desperate. "The son of Russian immigrants."

"I'm well aware of that," the editor told her. "And, just to be clear, here: I enjoyed his first book, his second as well, and I personally appreciate the ambition he's showing, but the market calls for someone with his background to be humble. The very times we live in call for that. To be ambitious is, I'm sure you won't disagree, the opposite of being humble. We will not make an offer. End of discussion."

And that had been the end of the discussion.

The second wrong thing was that Carter Hath, the executive editor who'd hired Adi—the person at the company who'd lobbied hardest to get her her promotion—Carter Hath had just let Adi know that, after too many recent experiences similar to the one she'd just undergone with the new editor-in-chief, he'd lost all faith in literary publishing, and was leaving FSG to lead the calendar division of a novelty publisher based in St. Louis that would pay him triple his present salary.

"The *calendar* division?" Apter said. "Like wall calendars?"

"I guess calendar sales are way up lately," Adi said. "Last couple years. Not so much wall calendars, really. More pocket and desk calendars—you know, like, the word-a-day kind? Exotic-animal-a-day. Recipe-a-day. It's a nostalgia industry. A new-old way to not look at screens. A tool to *unplug* with. Carter offered to bring me along. The company he'll be working for's expanding. They're in the middle of making some massive push. He says they've got a contract with a printer in Michigan or somewhere who developed some new kind of ultrafast, ultracheap POD machine that can do small-batch print jobs at a fifth the cost that they previously yadda yadda yadda, and, I don't know, 'serve hundreds of unexploited niche markets' or something. I only half paid attention to what he was telling me. The money's pretty great, but no way I'd move to St. Louis, you know? Abandon the dream? I was just so sad to hear he was leaving."

"You're having a real shitty week, huh?" said Apter.

"I'll be fine," Adi said. "There'll be other books, right?"

"Hell yeah," Apter said. "And plus there's Stanz."

"Stanz! What a guy."

"I can hardly wait to meet him."

Later that week, at an informal meeting of Sanders supporters being held in the lobby of Apter's dorm, the topic of fundraising was being discussed. Apter proposed what he thought to be a great idea: a social justice desk calendar. The tearaway kind with a spine of thin glue and a hard plastic bottom. Very old-school. Like the word-a-day kind, except, instead of a word-a-day, it would be an important social-justice-event-a-day. Better yet, two-a-day. A good one and a bad one so as to bring across that while there might be much to celebrate, there was at least as much to mourn, and even more to set right. Like, for instance—Apter tapped at his phone—like for instance, January 15 was not only Martin Luther King Jr.'s birthday, awesome, but it was also the day in 588 BC that Nebuchadnezzar II laid siege to Jerusalem, a siege that lasted over two years.

"What does ancient Jerusalem have to do with social justice?" said Braden Handey, whose proposal to raise funds via selling *Feel the Bern* bumper stickers with letters done in rainbow colors had, moments earlier, been rejected on grounds of 1) co-optation of the LGBTQ rainbow by people (i.e. Braden, Bernie Sanders by proxy) who weren't members of the LGBTQ community, and 2) encouraging the driving of fossil-fueled cars, which activity helped destroy the environment.

"I don't know exactly," Apter said. "I'm not an expert on ancient Jerusalem, but being under siege tends to leave the besieged pretty terrorized. Pretty underserved. Certainly *vulnerable*. And, anyway, it wouldn't have to be the siege of Jerusalem that gets commemorated—that's just the first thing that came up on my phone. I mean, people have always been terrible, right? So I'm sure there are plenty of other instances of social injustice that took place on January 15, and we could use any one of those."

"But putting one on a calendar, same day as King's birthday?" said Braden. "Doesn't that kind of like shit all over the face of MLK and every last thing that MLK ever stood for?"

"Yeah, isn't it like an attempt to completely erase him?" offered Jessic Proveen, editor of the *Daily Northwestern* Opinions section, and coauthor of the petition Apter'd forwarded Adi. Jessic had been the one to initially point out just how violent Braden's bumper sticker idea would be to the body of any self-respecting sexual and gender minority they'd ever known, including themself.

"Kinda like saying . . ." offered Thunderhorse Cohen, whose truth was that—all appearances, birth certificates, and "busted-ass blood tests" aside—she'd been adopted as an infant by her crypto-oligarchic Zionist pig parents from a Cheyenne teen mother they'd met as AmeriCorps workers in southeast Montana. "It's kinda like saying, 'You might think it's really important that MLK was born, but here's something else that was so much more important, and you never even knew, which means you're a fool, so just forget MLK.'"

"No," Apter said, "it isn't like saying that at all, or shitting on anyone, or trying to erase anyone, which, come on—MLK is not *erasable,* let alone by way of a desk calendar that commemorates his birthday. And maybe certain days, like MLK's birthday, if someone really feels strongly about this—maybe certain days could only have one entry on them. But the main thing is that my sister's in publishing, and we were just talking about how, for any number of reasons, there's this whole nostalgic thing happening right now for desk calendars, and there's also this new kind of print-on-demand technology that allows you to print them cheaper than ever. She knows a guy who does that for a living, and I bet he'd help us out. Help us print them for cheap. Then we'd sell them to people—lots of people, probably—for a pretty high markup, and score a bunch of money for the Sanders campaign."

"Sell it to who, though?" Thunderhorse said. "That's what really concerns me. Don't you think there are people who might buy it *because* it seems to be saying stuff like, 'Martin Luther King is not as important as this siege on Zionist-occupied ancient Palestine'?"

"In a word," said Apter, "who gives a fuck who buys it? I mean, if some MLK-hating person bought it, they would be supporting an MLK-loving primary candidate. In fact, it would almost be *better* if MLK-hating people bought it. They'd have less money to donate to Bush or Cruz or Trump or whoever."

"It's bad optics, Apter," Braden said.

"I don't think you understand what that means," said Apter.

"*I* understand what Braden means," said Jessic. "And I agree with what he means. But I sure wish he had said it differently. I mean, that was fucking *violent*, Braden."

"I don't see—" Braden started saying to Jessic.

"Now you're gonna be a fucking wiseass with me?" they said. "You need to check your fucking privilege, man."

"A wiseass?" said Braden. "Jessic, please. I didn't mean to be a wiseass. Please just speak your truth to me, Jessic."

"It's not my job to *educate* you, Braden!" shouted Jessic. "I can't fucking be*lieve* this."

"Don't you pay attention to anything, Braden?" Thunderhorse said. "Jessic was just talking about their unsighted cousin like just twenty minutes ago. I mean, *bad optics*? Shit's ableist as hell."

"Fuck," Braden said. "You're right. You're totally right. I never thought about how ableist of a phrase it was. I'll never use it again. Thank you for educating me about Jessic's truth, Thunderhorse. And also about Jessic's cousin's truth, too. And, Jessic, I'm sorry I didn't let you let me hear your truth when you were first trying to let me hear your truth before, if you even were trying, which I'm not saying you were, and you definitely shouldn't have to feel like I expected you to, or will in the future expect you to, because it is not your job to let me hear it to begin with, or your cousin's job, either. It is my job to learn it, to educate *myself,* and so I'll always be grateful for your effort, if there was any effort, to help me with my job, and, even if there wasn't any effort, I'll always be grateful to even get to *have* the job of learning your truth. And your cousin's truth."

Braden's gratitude for having the job of learning Jessic's truth and Jessic's cousin's truth garnered double-fisted finger-snaps from some of the others in attendance at the meeting, but not from Jessic. In fact, Braden's gratitude for having the job of learning Jessic's truth and Jessic's cousin's truth really triggered Jessic, Jessic explained to the room, because it proved that Braden's job was, for Braden, just a form of *tourism;* it proved that Braden was a *trauma tourist,* which was so problematic that it was dangerously violent.

As they began, in greater depth, to educate those in attendance on the ways in which *trauma tourism* and applause for *trauma tourism* aided in the perpetuation of sighted cis white supremacy and thereby caused violence to Black bodies, biracial bodies, gender-nonconforming bodies, and unsighted bodies, Apter exited the meeting and headed to class.

The class that Apter left the meeting to attend was a 400-level American Studies seminar called 21st-Century U.S. Stand-Up that was taught by Mickey Leary, a prematurely dewlapped assistant professor whose PhD dissertation had been an ethnography of the local alternative comedy scene. Apter'd lacked the prereqs to enroll in the course, but had—by way of a seven-hundred-some-word email conveying both his passion for Gladman's work as well as a sideways, very carefully worded, not-quite-lying-but-nonetheless-dishonest suggestion that he had read the one chapter of Leary's dissertation that Leary had published (in the *Oklahoma State University Journal of Performing and Performance Arts*)—convinced the professor to admit him.

The first week of class, they'd watched Louis CK's most recent special. The second week, it had been Tig Notaro's. In one of the only two interviews in which he had talked about stand-up comedy, Gladman called CK "the best thing going." In that same interview, he'd said that Notaro's much-lauded cancer set had been "sizably influential" on his decision to leave the Pollaco persona behind for "a more autobiographical, or even—*ick*—confessional approach to stand-up. Not to say that the set itself affected me much. But the response to it really opened my eyes to what I might be able to get away with onstage. That is: pretty much whatever I felt like, as long as I was feeling it."

Because both comedians had mattered to Gladman, Apter had already seen hours of their performances, had somewhat complicated thoughts on their work, and so could have said a lot during class discussions. But because about half of the students enrolled were graduate-level (the rest were seniors), he felt intimidated, and mostly just listened.

After the second (the Notaro) class meeting, Leary'd taken him aside, informed him that he hadn't been pulling his weight, and reminded him, gently, that participation in discussion wasn't optional: it was, in fact, worth half the grade. "Lucky for you, though, I'd imagine," Leary'd said, "we'll be watching some Gladman clips next week. I know you have some thoughts on him. I strongly recommend that you share them."

Next week became this week, and Apter thought he was prepared. He'd rewatched some of his favorite clips and gathered his thoughts and even took some notes in preparation to speak about any or all of the following topics:

- Gladman's spontaneous/improvisational approach to performance
- the ways in which the fiction of Solomon Gladman did and didn't correspond with the stand-up of Solly Gladman
- Gladman's refusal to perform at venues that wouldn't let their patrons record his sets
- the comedians who had influenced Gladman
- the comedians who Gladman had lately seemed to have influenced.

And just in case that wasn't enough—who knew how many of the aforementioned topics Leary might exhaust in the mini-lecture he'd give in advance of the discussion?—Apter'd printed out copies of Gladman's three-year-old email autoresponse, which, he imagined, he could pass around to the other students and/or offer to read aloud.

None of Apter's preparation proved useful, however.

By way of introduction to the clips he'd compiled, Leary said, "The comedian whose work we'll be viewing this week is, by far, the least well-known of any who we'll be discussing this semester. According to the survey I had you fill out on the first day of class, not even a third of you have heard of Solly Gladman, and only one of you has seen his comedy. Some of his work has been a bit controversial, and I've spent the last week considering the degree to which I should speak about that prior to showing you these clips.

"On one hand, I want to, as usual, warn you about potential triggers. On the other, those of you unfamiliar with Gladman's work—which is to say: nearly all of you—you have the opportunity here (an uncommonly rare opportunity, I might add) to experience the work of someone who I think is an important comedian without the interference of many, if any, preconceived notions about that work, which I think might greatly benefit the quality of the discussion we'll have after viewing that work.

"So I've decided to split the difference. That is: if any of you are feeling particularly vulnerable to being triggered by *any* kind of subject matter that a man telling jokes on a stage might address, you are, by all means, free to leave class right now without suffering any negative consequences to your grade."

As two of the thirteen members of the seminar gathered their belongings and tiptoed out, Leary continued. "For the rest of you, the one thing I'll add, so as to avoid any unnecessary confusion, is that the first eight minutes of video consist of highlights from three different sets that Solly Gladman did during the first part of his career, which lasted from 2009 to 2011. During that time, he performed in costume, using the stage name Bernie Pollaco. The rest of the clips are from the second—the current, uncostumed, nonpseudonymous—part of his career. That's all."

Then Leary shut the lights and hit play on the projector.

Two minutes into the second Pollaco clip, Jory Gutman-Klamschitz, a first-year performance studies MA who, for reasons that Apter had (more than a couple times) wondered about, seemed to keep his eyes shut whenever he spoke—Jory Gutman-Klamschitz rose from his chair, blocked the screen, clutched his temples between the fingers of one hand, whipped off his glitter-threaded terry-cloth headband with the

other hand, dabbed his neck with the headband as if with a handkerchief, held the headband under his nose, inhaled deeply of the headband, dabbed some more neck, then held the headband forward like a
trophy, wagged it a little, lowered his temple-clutching hand, and, with,
as usual, both eyes closed, said: "Mn-mn. Nuh-uh. Just no. Just. Mn. Just
no. Just. I mean."

Leary, by then, had paused the video, turned on the lights.

"Jory?" he said.

"Just."

"We can give you a minute."

"I don't need a minute," Jory said. "I'm just. I just want to *say*. I'm
pan-Semitic. I'm what a lot of people call a *Jew*, okay? And I have a
grandfather. And my grandfather—*he* is a Jew. He is *definitely* a Jew.
And he might have *cancer*. He might be . . . Oh God. He might be *dying*,
okay? There. I've *said* it. He might be *dying*. He might die any day and
he doesn't even seem to *know* it. He's over seventy years *old* and, any
day now, he might get a checkup and be told he has *cancer*, and it might
be untreatable, and I don't need . . . The *last* thing I need . . . The last
thing I need right now is *this*. This Gladman Pollaco whatever he's called
reminding me that . . . I mean . . ."

"If you'd like to leave, Jory, please don't feel like you have to—" Leary
said.

"Like to?" said Jory. "I *need* to. I need to leave *now*. I need some help.
Will someone just please walk me to the counseling office please? I'm
afraid to be alone, and I need to be counseled, and it's always so busy
there, it's so . . . *busy*. Where's the *funding*? I mean where is my tuition
even *going*, you know? All of our tuitions. Where is it even *going*. Someone in my condition. I cannot *advocate* for myself in my condition. I
need someone to take me there and advocate for me. I need to see a
counselor *right now* and I am asking for someone to volunteer. Will
someone please do what is right here and help me get to the front of
the line at the counseling office? I think my insulin is . . . Does anyone
have any chocolate or pastry? I think I might collapse. I mean . . . Can
you see how I'm *sweating*? Am I as pale as I feel? I think I'm *trembling*.
I need someone to give me something sugary to eat and make sure I'm
not alone and get me to the front of the line *right now*. Please?"

"I'll walk you over there," said Fatima Ahmad, a second-year PhD candidate in communications with an Oxbridge accent who Apter'd fallen half in love with for the first fifteen minutes of the first day of class, then had, just as suddenly, lost all but strictly prurient interest in when, during the ice-breaking exercise following Leary's introductory remarks, she'd revealed, rather smugly—as if she'd believed the revelation would mark her as edgier, or *naughtier,* than others might suspect—that, while her favorite comedians were, "of course," Dane Cook and Ellen DeGeneres, sometimes, when she was "feeling, ehem, *silly,*" she preferred Aziz Ansari.

"Maybe we should take a moment, here," Leary said, once Fatima and Jory had left. "Maybe we should hold off on viewing the video, and process—"

"I cannot say I fully comprehend what Jory Gutman-Klamschitz was on about," said Malik Adams, senior Journalism major, "but this Gladman person and his so-called *comedy act* disturbs me deeply, as well. I do not find it funny at all. Nor do I find it *acceptable.* Neither the so-called comedy itself, nor the cynical exploitative appropriation of Black culture."

"Appropriation?" Apter said.

"This Gladman's whole biddy-biddy-bomming—"

"His what?" Apter said.

"His whole biddy-biddy-bomming, oy-vey, chopped-liver-on-matzah-chomping, so-called comedy routine is nothing but a lot of Zionist cooning. It's a Zionist minstrel show. His schtick's built on the backs of Amos 'n' Andy, Stepin Fetchit, little Buckwheat, Farina and . . . shall I *go on?* Shall I list for you all the many Black comedians who, throughout the history of this nation, have had no other way to express themselves comedically for profit—relatively *meager* profit, I might add—than to perform in Blackface and *virtual* Blackface? How many names will it take to get you to open your eyes to this fact?"

"Slow down there, brother. You're suggesting—"

"You just call me *brother*?" said Malik.

"What?" Apter said. "No. I would never do that. That would be problematic, for me to call another guy *brother.* Microaggressive. I called you *biddy.* I was trying to call you *biddy-biddy-bom,* but, you know, oy vey, all this matzah I'm chomping got caught in my throat, so I had to swallow the second *biddy* and the *bom* the both. My bad."

"Right," Malik said. "So that's how it is."

"I really don't know what you mean," Apter said, "but before you got confusing, I think you were suggesting that African Americans were doing comedy about being African Americans before Jews were doing comedy about being Jews. Do I have that right? Is that what you were suggesting?"

"What I'm *saying*," said Malik, "is this Gladman has appropriated tropes, if not in like 'empirically observable' actuality, then at the very least, in *essence*, from Blackface comedy. He is doing, let's call it, *Jew*face comedy. And that is appropriation. Which is a tool of white supremacy, and is therefore *racist*. Aka a virtual lynching. And that is that. End of discussion."

Three students, by then, were miming finger-snaps, the rest of them nodding in reverent slo-mo.

"So Jewface comedy is racist," Apter said. "A virtual lynching. That is that."

"Condescend to me all you want," Malik said. "Go full Seinfeld. I can take it. I'm strong. I'm used to this kind of violence. You, though, *boychick*—your hands are shaking."

About Apter's hands, Malik was right.

Apter walked out.

What else should he have done? Appealed to the nearest authority for help? Whined for Leary to intervene on his behalf? Apter wasn't a narc, and he could fight his own battles, thank you very much. Anyway, Leary was not the kind of person who even the stooliest, rattiest tattle would ever consider turning to for backup. Throughout the whole exchange, he'd kept his gaze all soft and distant while pursing his lips and caressing his dewlap, unconvincingly attempting (or so it seemed to Apter) to project a kind of scholarly placidity to cover up the panic he obviously felt at the thought of doing his job as a teacher and calling bullshit on the bullshit claims the only Black student in class kept making.

Not to say that Apter, in walking out of the classroom, felt much satisfaction. *Jewface* and *boychick* and *matzah-chomping*—the further away he got from the moment, the more those seemed like they might have been fighting words. Were they? Was there any such context in which they might not have been? Was the context in which Malik used them such a context? What about *full Seinfeld*? Should he have—what— struck Malik? He'd wanted to, sure—Malik, with those words, had left him feeling bullied. But did the feeling mean that he *had* been bullied? Perhaps the bullied feeling owed to Apter's own failure to appreciate the context in which . . . No. Fuck that. He should have struck Malik. He should have. This is how he knew: if Malik had spoken that way to another Jew, Apter would have cheered if that other Jew had struck him.

But had Apter struck Malik, he would have gotten arrested, maybe kicked out of school.

But still, you had to stand up to bullies.

Didn't you have to stand up to bullies?

Why did you have to stand up to bullies?

Standing up to bullies—that wasn't any way to beat them anymore. Maybe it had never been. But then how did you beat them? Apter didn't know. Perhaps you *couldn't* beat them. It seemed like you couldn't.

Except you couldn't join them, either. You wouldn't want to. Unless you were, yourself, a bully, you'd have to become a Braden to join them. Apter was certain he didn't want to be a Braden, and he was nearly as certain he wasn't a bully. *Was* he a bully?

Stupid question. He wasn't a bully. A bully would not have tried to argue with Malik. A bully, rather, would have bitched and moaned about how Malik's anti-Semitism had hurt his feelings. Would have gone on to insinuate, or even claim outright, that to hurt a Jew's feelings was to hurt the Jews. That to hurt a Jew's feelings was *to do violence to Jewish bodies*. What a bully would have done, in sum, was accused Malik of being a bully, which . . .

Whatever.

But if you couldn't beat them, and you couldn't—or wouldn't—join them, what could you do? Wait them out? Try to ignore them? Walk away and laugh at them? Fuck with them sometimes? Exploit them a little?

Yes.

The 2016 Real American Page-a-Day Desk Calendar.

Upon returning to his dorm, Apter made four phone calls.

The first was to Adi, for Carter Hath's number.

The second was to Carter, for the number of his company's printer in Michigan.

The third was to the printer, who quoted printing and shipping costs, then, five minutes after the phone call ended, emailed Apter a link to download some proprietary software with "a number of boilerplate design templates to choose from and modify."

The fourth call was to Sidney. "How much," Apter asked him, "would I have to pay you to draw me a monochrome American flag?"

"Like one of those arm patches tactical soldiers wear on their uniforms?"

"Exactly like that."

"I don't know," Sidney said. "Nothing? Yeah, nothing. I mean, you're gonna be my brother-in-law, right?"

"What if I wanted a hi-def scan of it by tomorrow afternoon?"

"Then you'd have to promise to buy me a pint next time you're twenty-one or older, and in Brooklyn."

"Thank you, Sidney," Apter said.

That evening, he looked through the printer's templates and chose the most basic, which was called BASIC 1.

The bottom fifth of each page of the BASIC 1 calendar showed the day and the date in white type on a black background, whereas the upper four-fifths of each page was blank, unless the day was a holiday, in which case the holiday was named in black letters, like:

INDEPENDENCE DAY
NATIONAL HOLIDAY

MONDAY MONDAY MONDAY MONDAY
JULY 4 JULY 4 JULY 4

Apter spent a couple hours going through the calendar, deciding which holidays to keep, which to remove, and with what, if anything, to replace those he'd removed. He deleted, for example, Holocaust Remembrance Day, and replaced it with Rhode Island Independence Day. Rosh Hashanah became Child Health Day. Kwanzaa became Day After Christmas

Day. The remaining non-Christian religious holidays were all deleted and replaced with nothing. Except for Columbus Day and Thanksgiving, any holiday evoking Native Americans was deleted and replaced with nothing. He left the secular holidays he adjudged "neutral" alone: Mother's Day, Father's Day, Secretary's Day, etc. For Arbor Day, he flipped a coin, landed on tails, deleted Arbor Day, replaced it with nothing.

About whether he should delete *Martin Luther King Jr's Birthday* from the January 15 page of the calendar, there wasn't any question—he should, he did. But he wasn't so certain about the way to handle the holiday that observed King's birthday, which, in 2016, would fall on January 18. He briefly considered replacing it with Robert E. Lee Day, but racism that open wouldn't do the trick. Maybe, he thought, he could *add* Robert E. Lee Day to Martin Luther King Jr. Day, except . . . no, because . . . still. It was still too obvious. Too *macro*aggressive. Would require too little semiotic detective work to be worth anyone's indignant while.

Yet if he deleted Martin Luther King Day and replaced it with nothing, that might look like a mistake, an oversight—might fail to exasperate. The January 18 page needed to be both too subtle and too obvious at once; it needed, in other words, to convey an all-too-obvious *attempt* at subtlety. It needed not to be clever, but rather "clever," and . . .

There it was.

Within a few keystrokes,

MARTIN LUTHER KING JR. DAY
(OBSERVED)
NATIONAL HOLIDAY

MONDAY MONDAY MONDAY MONDAY
JAN 18   JAN 18   JAN 18

became

NATIONAL "HOLIDAY"

MONDAY MONDAY MONDAY MONDAY
JAN 18   JAN 18   JAN 18

The following afternoon, after Sidney sent the scan of the monochrome flag he had drawn, Apter pasted the image into the white space of each page of the calendar.

He then attached the file he'd made, along with Sidney's scan, to an email to the printer. In the email, he requested one hundred calendars (the minimum order) be printed and shipped to his parents' address, and specified the following preferences:

1. that each calendar be mounted on the cheapest black plastic frame available
2. that the cardboard box that would package the calendars be high-gloss white
3. that the title appearing on the cardboard box be arranged in three centered lines of 24-, 36-, and 24-point Times New Roman font as follows:

The 2016

REAL AMERICAN
Page-a-Day Desk Calendar

4. that REAL be blue, AMERICAN red, and the rest of the words of the title black.

The printer called Apter a few minutes later. "When do you want these by?" he asked.

"How soon can you send them?"

"Today's . . . Thursday? We can have them to you as early as Tuesday, but that would cost you an extra, let's see . . . ninety-two cents a unit. Otherwise, it'll be ten business days, so . . ."

"To have them by Tuesday, it's five hundred ninety-two dollars, you're saying?"

"Right."

"That's good," Apter said. "I want that."

"And now, also, are you sure you want the sides and the backs of the boxes to be blank? Like you don't even want to print the price on them anywhere?"

"Oh, yeah," Apter said. "That's a good idea. Yes. Please. Print the price."

"Okay. So what's the price?"

"What do you think?" Apter said. "I mean, what's a good price?"

"That's a complicated question. Not really my area of expertise. On one hand these kinds of calendars tend to retail for anywhere from $13.95 to $27.95, but their cost per unit is usually lower than yours, since we usually print them in much larger batches . . ."

"I think . . . I guess I like $19.95, then," said Apter. "That's like fourteen dollars profit per unit."

"Well. Except then you've got shipping and transaction fees."

"I thought shipping was included in the $5.92 per unit," Apter said.

"Our shipping to *you* is included. If you're gonna sell these online . . . that's what you told me you were doing, right?"

"Right," Apter said.

"Well, then you've gotta pay to ship them to the consumer, okay? And you've gotta pay for the boxes they get shipped *in*. Plus, like I was saying, you gotta pay the credit card companies or PayPal or whoever a transaction fee, which probably comes to seventy-five cents, give or take, so . . . depending on the speed you want to ship them, that's probably another four to seven bucks or so per unit."

"What if I charge separately for shipping and handling, though? I mean, isn't that—"

"It's an option, sure. But I hear people don't like that option so much. They see a price, decide to buy, then they get whammed on the checkout page for shipping and handling that makes the price go up another, what? another third or so in this case? and a lot of them, I think, decide not to buy then . . ."

"Okay, you've convinced me."

"Of what?"

"I'll charge $25.95."

"And you want that on the front of the box? back of the box? side of the box?"

"The side."

"Which one?"

"The right."

"Okay. So let me get your credit card number, and we'll put this in motion. I'll send you a mockup of the box tomorrow morning, and, assuming you're good with it, we'll have your shipment to you by Tuesday."

On Friday, on Wix, Apter, registering as the Real American Calendar Company, paid $120 for therealamerical.com, then "designed" it.

The background was red.

Along the top of the web page, in small black font, was the following message: "We are a small, family-owned, American business. We know our site isn't pretty, but it works. We are working hard to learn the ropes of web design, so please forgive our dust for now, order our beautiful calendar, which we are SO PROUD OF, and God Bless these United States of REAL America!"

In the center of the page was the image of the box the printer had sent, and, beneath the image:

AVAILABLE ONLINE ONLY
ORDER NOW
$25.95.
Shipping and handling included.

Then the PayPal button.

The shipment, as promised, arrived the next Tuesday. Apter stored the cartons in his parents' finished basement, removed a single calendar, and headed back to campus.

On returning to his dorm, he found Jessic Proveen all by themself, lying on the prized common-area recliner. They were scowling up at a paperback edition of Kafka stories they held above their face.

"Hey there, Jessic."

Jessic shut the book, turned its cover toward Apter. "Have you read this asshole?"

"I have," Apter said.

"That story 'A Hunger Artist'?"

"Yeah," Apter said.

"How are they gonna teach us a work of literature, so-called, making fun of anorexia? How is that okay?"

"I know," Apter said. "This whole place is fucked up. And I'm glad I found you 'cause I wanted to tell you: the other day, at the meeting? You were totally right."

Jessic pulled the lever on the side of the recliner, sat up straight. Apter handed them the calendar.

"*Real American*, huh?" they said. "Where'd this come from?"

"Some blue-eyed middle-aged prick by the Davis Street El stop. He was standing behind a table stacked with them."

"A table?"

"You know, like one of those folding tables? Fucking guy. Fundraising. He had one of those Republican elephant pins in his lapel, and all these people were kinda gathered around him, talking Bush versus Cruz on immigration, buying these up. So I stole one."

"That's—"

"Way less than what I *could* have done. I know. I should have disrupted. I should have overturned the table, or at least shouted something, but I was scared to start shit. I was by myself, and there were probably six people gathered around that table, and three of the guys, they were pretty big, and I think they go to school here—one looked familiar, another was wearing a Northwestern cap. There was one point where I really thought I could overturn the table and get away safe—the light was green, I'm pretty fast on my feet—but I worried one of those guys might recognize me, then find me on campus and, you know . . . retaliate."

"There were *students* buying these things, you're saying?"

"You haven't even looked inside yet. Go ahead. It's upsetting, but it's important, I think, to know what we're up against."

Jessic opened the box, started flipping through the calendar.

"A bunch of stars and stripes, huh? Nationalist bozos."

"That's the least of it, Jessic. Check out King's birthday."

Jessic flipped to January 15, clutched their forehead, dropped their jaw. "Nuh-uh," they said. "Nuh. Uh. I mean . . ." They flipped forward three more pages. "You see *this* shit?" they said.

"What shit? No . . . Oh. I didn't even get that far. That's just too . . ."

"'National *quote-unquote* holiday?' No. No way, Apter. This is so . . ."

"Violent," Apter said.

"*Violent*," Jessic said. "They're trying to erase . . ."

"I know. It's hard to even . . . I think we have to do something."

"We need to go back en masse and protest these bastards."

"I wish we could. They're gone, though."

"Gone?" Jessic said.

"Well, I saw them on my way to my parents' place this morning. When I came back: no fascists, no table. But what I was thinking—do you think I could write a piece about this for the *Daily Northwestern*? Like an editorial? I could start out talking about my problematic social justice calendar proposal, and then like segue into how I didn't understand why it bothered everyone, even though I tried to listen, but now—now that I've seen this piece of shit calendar—I've realized, firsthand, how the problematic can and will become violent. Or . . . I don't know. Something like that. Something has to be done. People need, at least, to be warned."

"You're right about that last part. And maybe—yeah, an editorial would work. I'm not sure, though, that . . . I don't think you're the right person to write this editorial . . ."

"I don't have a lot of experience, it's true."

"And you're not really the one being erased. You're not the target of the violence."

"Not to mention all the silencing," Apter said. "You're right."

"Exactly," Jessic said. "The silencing. So for you to write it might be too . . ."

"Too ironic," Apter said.

"Bingo," Jessic said. "We can't participate in that sort of discourse. It only contributes to platforming white ironic modes of thought."

"Those modes of thought exactly," Apter said. "You're just . . . right. It's better for someone like me to step back and, you know, *just listen*."

"I think so, too. I'm glad you agree."

"Well," said Apter, Apterly smiling. "So I'm listening."

"You're . . . ? Oh, you mean . . . well, you know. Yeah," said Jessic. "That's not a bad idea."

Jessic's editorial, "The Everyday Racist Violence of Every Day of the Year," went up at 8:37 a.m., Thursday morning, on the *Daily Northwestern*, alongside a photo of *The 2016 Real American Page-a-Day Desk Calendar*.

For much of the morning, Apter, deploying a variety of usernames, posted links to the editorial on dozens of alt right and white power message boards and websites, with accompanying comments like "And here's the latest dispatch from Multiculti College"; "The great snowflake meltdown's upon us"; "Libtard University doesn't wike ow calendew"; "Now the SJWs are whining that our calendars don't whine enough."

Apter bumped and liked and trolled all his threads and posts and comments. He asked the communities if anyone among them had any idea how to purchase the calendars, replied to himself by linking to the RealAmeriCal website, called himself (i.e. his fake-usernamed self) names for not just googling "2016 Real American Page-a-Day Desk Calendar," made fun of how cheap the RealAmeriCal website looked, scolded himself for ragging on the website, trolled himself for scolding, trolled himself for trolling.

By 11 a.m., authentic user activity had outpaced his own in most of the venues. Some users claimed to have already owned the calendars, some that they'd just gone online to order them.

One of those in the former category—on the website 14wordwarrior .com—said the calendar he'd received was just the right size to fit inside his son's Christmas stocking. Apter liked that. Took it and ran with it. Started posting variations on the following back-and-forth all over the place:

> **JonnyWhite51:** This calendar seems like a perfect stocking stuffer.
> **DarthFucker:** Isn't it a little early in the year to be thinking about Christmas, Grandpa?

DarthFucker: And their website looks like a subhuman built it in 1997 too.

JonnyWhite51: Christmas is the best! I try to think about it as much as possible.

Super88: JonnyWhite51, I'm with you on Christmas. DarthFucker you're a cuck. RealAmeriCal is a small family business. No slick Jew media conglomerate to design their website. These calendars are probably selling like crazy by now, and how many are there? How many could there be? They're probably selling out as we speak.

DarthFucker: Super88: RealAmeriCal's highest-paid shill.

JonnyWhite51: Depends Undergarments' most wettest Grandpa.

JonnyWhite51: DarthFucker, I am no one's Grandpa yet, though I might be your father. I thought I shot off in your mom's ass—I know that's how we started—but I was definitely drunk, so maybe I'm confused.

DarthFucker: [GIF of naked, masturbating man in plastic Darth Vader mask ejaculating fulsomely all over lens of camera]

JonnyWhite51: Super88, you make a great point. We should all be promoting this company for free! I hope they do sell out cuz they deserve to.

By 12 p.m., Apter *had* sold out. He called the printer to order five hundred more calendars. The printer reminded him that an order of one thousand would get him a 10 percent discount per unit. Apter, watching the orders come in on his screen, told the printer he'd think about it and call him back. While he'd been on the phone, there'd been fourteen more orders.

By 1 p.m., he had 783 orders, some for multiple calendars, and they kept coming in, didn't seem to be slowing down. He called the printer back, ordered three thousand calendars, and the printer reminded him that an order of five thousand calendars would get him an additional 5 percent off per unit.

"Fuck it," Apter said. "Five thousand then."

"You want me to charge it to the same card?"

"I do, but hey, listen, something just occurred to me—this is confidential, right?"

"What's confidential?"

"Like if someone calls you up, asking questions about the calendar, you wouldn't—"

"I am an ethical businessman," the printer said. "I will keep all your information private unless otherwise instructed by you."

"Including my name."

"Including your name."

Jessic, in the meantime, had been receiving death threats by email, scores of death threats. They'd screen-capped and tweeted them as they came in, every one, and their followers went from 678 to over 16,000 before they'd had lunch.

By 2 p.m., "The Everyday Racist Violence . . ." had been picked up by *HuffPo*.

By 3 p.m., a listicle titled "The Top Eleven Most Heroic Student (T)He(y)roes of Social Justice Today . . ." went up on *BuzzFeed*, and every (t)he(y)ro on the list was Jessic Proveen. Each item featured a photo of Jessic that they'd posted on Instagram, a link to "The Everyday Racist Violence . . . ," and a bit of biographical information derived from their archived editorials and tweets, e.g. "Hates Themself for Loving Kanye, Loves Themself for Loving Chance" and "Doesn't Even DO Ice Cream" and "Wants you to LISTEN."

Peak interest in Jessic was marked by the listicle, which according to the counter, had 1,500,000+ shares. Still, it seemed to take a couple of days for online media outlets to realize the furor was subsiding. More specifically, it took till late on Sunday afternoon, when news had spread of Martin Shkreli's having jacked up the cost of the toxoplasmosis pharmaceutical Diapram by over 5,500 percent, at which point Shkreli became the focus of most of the woke internet's impassioned energy. Shkreli was just more compelling as a villain than ever could be Jessic as a (t)he(y)ro, more compelling as a villain than ever could be a calendar.

But during those couple days, they gave interviews by FaceTime, telephone, text, and email (about thirty in total) to any and all of the obvious online outlets, gave an interview on NPR's *Weekend Edition*, received a nod from Amy Schumer in her SNL monologue, and acquired a literary agent who would, two weeks later, sell a book of their personal essays on race and gender, titled *Always Educating: A Personal Theirstory,* to Harper Perennial for ninety thousand dollars.

The media were interested briefly in Apter, as well, though they never got his name.

Numerous reporters and web editors sent emails to the contact address on the RealAmeriCal website, seeking comments from and interviews with "the proprietor." Apter, rather than responding to these emails directly, added a note to the web page, under the PayPal button:

> We truly appreciate the interests certain of the better media organizations such as Fox News and Breitbart have shown in our calendar. But we are a small family business made up of humble God-fearing folks who value our American right to privacy and we have lately been receiving enough rude and crude harassments that we are afraid of what granting interviews and giving comments on even the good articles might lead to in terms of personal exposure and so in terms of our pursuits of happinesses and also our safeties. And so we will not.

By the end of that first weekend, Apter had sold over four thousand Real American Calendars. This was already far too many calendars for him to ship and handle on time without help, the orders weren't slowing down, and Christmas was still more than three months away.

He called the printer, offered to pay him an extra twenty-five cents per unit, plus the cost of shipping and handling to ship the calendars directly to Apter's customers.

"Fifty cents per," the printer said.

"No way," Apter said. "You've got infrastructure or whatever. The most you'll need to do is hire a part-time minimum-wager or two—if even that—to label and package."

"I do have infrastructure, but—"

"This is a good deal I'm offering you. The cost of sending the calendars to me is built into the unit cost, right?" Apter said. "And you will no longer be sending the calendars to me, but I'm gonna pay the same for each unit as I've *been* paying you, *plus* shipping and handling to the customer, *plus* a quarter per unit. Tell me that isn't more than fair."

The printer agreed it was fair.

In 2015, Apter sold 27,905 *2016 Real American Page-a-Day Calendars,* profiting a little over $375,000. He donated all that remained after taxes to the Bernie Sanders campaign and pro-Bernie super PACs.

In February 2016, he sent the first round of monthly emails offering previous calendar-buyers a three-dollar discount on 2017 calendar preorders, which he list-priced at $26.95.

Mid-March of 2016, it came clear to Apter that the Make America Great Again campaign would secure for Donald Trump the Republican nomination for president, and when Apter sent his April email to previous calendar-buyers, he offered not only a discount (one dollar, now) on *2017 Real American Page-a-Day Calendar* preorders, but a second calendar for full-priced preorder.

This second calendar was identical to the first, except that, on the box, it said *Great* instead of *Real.* I.e. it was *The 2017 Great American Page-a-Day Calendar,* and it listed for $27.95.

By the end of June 2016, Apter had preorders for 1,300 2017 *Real*s and 4,900 2017 *Great*s, all but the very latest profits from which he'd donated to pro-Bernie super PACs in $10k chunks.

In July 2016, Bernie Sanders conceded the Democratic nomination for president to Hillary Clinton.

Apter did not like Hillary Clinton, nor the idea of a President Hillary Clinton.

Even if he had liked Hillary Clinton, he did not think it was any more a good idea for the wife of a former president to be elected president in 2016 than it had been for the son of a former president to be elected president in 2000 or 2004.

Hillary Clinton, Apter believed, would be a better president than would Donald Trump, but she would, nonetheless, be a terrible president, and while he knew that he would, in the end, vote for Clinton, he wished he didn't have to, and he certainly didn't want to give her his money. Besides, she wouldn't need it to beat Trump, anyway. She would be elected president, no matter what.

Everyone Apter knew agreed.

September 9, 2016, Hillary Clinton called Trump supporters "a basket of deplorables," causing a stir.

September 10, she walked her statement back a little.

September 11, Jessic Proveen, just days before the much-anticipated publication of their *Always Educating: A Personal Theirstory,* published an editorial in *The Guardian* titled "Wake Up, People! Trump Supporters *Are* Deplorable."

The editorial was shared 4.5 million+ times.

Jessic spent, once again, a few days in the spotlight, preselling books to the sympathetic while drawing the ire of the online nationalist/white power communities, which had, over the course of the previous couple months, grown by orders of magnitude.

There were plenty of alt right message-board OG's who remembered Jessic and the *Real American Calendar* dustup. They were happy to remind the ones who didn't remember, and, in the course of the reminding, the newbies got informed, as did members of the more traditional conservative communities, all of which informing served to drive unprecedentedly high volumes of traffic to realamerical.com, the mysterious proprietor of which, it was soon widely rumored, anonymously donated all the profits from the sales of his calendars to the Donald J. Trump presidential campaign.

By January 1, 2017, Apter had sold 28,569 2017 *Real American Page-a-Day Calendars* and 69,801 2017 *Great American Page-a-Day Calendars*.

His 2016 profits had topped $1,350,000.

He was twenty-one years old.

4

Apter's fourth anecdote concerned the dawning of his second and third careers.

On January 5, 2017, he pretended to drunk-text Sylvie Klein, who, by the looks of her Instagram, had been home from Stanford—where she'd gone to study math—since mid-December.

They hadn't fucked since the final quarter of high school: a disappointing encounter born of nostalgia, or, perhaps, of the anticipation of the nostalgia they expected to be overcome by after graduation. In either case, the sex was only marginally better than it had been in junior high, and left them both feeling awkward in one another's company till the winter break of their freshman year of college, by which point they were able to laugh it all off.

But then, the previous summer, i.e. the summer before their senior year of college, Sylvie'd stopped in Chicago for a couple of days on her way back to school from a Birthright trip, and she had drunk-texted Apter. Despite Sylvie's having sent the text ("You awake?") after midnight, Apter hadn't imagined—given what he'd thought they'd both learned the last time—he hadn't imagined she'd been looking for sex. He'd just figured that the weeks she'd spent in the Holy Land had monkeyed with her clock: jet lag, insomnia. He invited her over to the Lincoln Square apartment into which he'd moved only a couple weeks before, made himself a coffee, cleared the boxes from his couch, set a laptop atop them, and cued up Season 3—Sylvie's favorite—of *Curb Your Enthusiasm*.

When her Uber arrived just twenty minutes later, she'd looked better than ever. *Extremely* kissable. But kissing, in that context, would have probably led to fucking, and thereby awkwardness, not to mention that she was, Apter'd realized soon enough, pretty drunk indeed.

He showed her to the couch.

She said, "What the hell is this? I didn't come here to watch bald Jews on a computer."

"We don't have to," Apter said. "I mean—why don't I get you some water, and then you tell me about Israel?"

"You're saying you want to hear about my Birthright trip? No one wants to hear about anyone's Birthright trip."

But then she went on to talk about her Birthright trip, which was boring for both of them. So instead they started arguing about the Palestinians, which argument ended with Sylvie shaking her head and saying, "You can't know unless you've been there. You don't know how it is."

Apter showed her to his bed, placed a glass of water on top of a book box he'd arranged like a nightstand, then returned to the couch and fell asleep watching *Curb*. When he woke the next morning, she was no longer there.

"You alive?" he texted.

An hour later, she texted back: "Enough."

Pretty sure she meant "Alive enough" rather than something more like "I've had enough of you," he responded to her text with a smiley emoji.

Nothing came back. They'd had no contact since. He'd called a couple times but hung up on her voicemail.

And then, nearly four months later, and all at once, on January 5, 2017, 2:19 a.m., eight hours or so after having finished filing for taxes, an hour or so after having said good night to his date to the Nobunny show at the Empty Bottle, at which, unknowingly, he'd run into Basketball Schwartzy, Apter realized he needed to talk to Sylvie Klein. Or wanted to. Wanted to badly enough to seem to need to. He was a millionaire, now—barely, but still—and though he'd known he was a millionaire since a couple or three weeks prior to Christmas, dealing with his tax return had shored up the fact of it, and, for the first time in a while, the meaninglessness of life was . . .

He wasn't comfortable with it. It depressed him a little.

And, except on the whole Palestinian issue, Sylvie was the only person he personally knew whose sense of humor had always been reliable. Apter needed, he believed, to tell her he was rich, that he'd gotten rich off the terribleness of people. Apart from his immediate family and, now, the U.S. Treasury and the State of Illinois Department of Revenue, no one else but the printer knew he was rich, much less how he'd gotten so, and he needed Sylvie to tell him it was great that he was rich, or at least that it was fine, and then make him laugh. He was sure she could do that. Wasn't sure, however, that she would.

Hence: the "drunk" text, the double-false pretensions. She needed an opportunity to reject him.

U in Chi, Sylvie Klein? I want talk.	2:19 a.m.
You want talk. After 2 AM.	2:27 a.m.
Come over. Hang out.	2:27 a.m.
That's a sailed ship, motek.	2:38 a.m.
Be my friend again.	2:39 a.m.
Come over here. I miss you.	2:40 a.m.
Come over here and TAK to me.	2:43 a.m.
I'm free tomorrow to talk over coffee.	2:47 a.m.
Tomorrow sucks.	2:48 a.m.
Another day then. I'm home till Sunday.	2:49 a.m.
I'm not BUSY tomorrow.	2:49 a.m.
Just tomorrow's far.	2:49 a.m.
Tonight is here!	2:49 a.m.
I'm going to sleep, now.	2:50 a.m.
Tomorrow where when then?	2:50 a.m.
I got a car now so wherever.	2:50 a.m.
Pick me up at my parents at 1.	2:52 a.m.
12 instead and brnch?	2:52 a.m.
Ok. Goodnight.	2:52 a.m.

First thing after Sylvie got in the car, Apter apologized to her for the texts.

"I've missed you since last time—I've missed talking to you—and I guess I got that confused with the other kind of missing you, which . . . I'm sorry. I was pretty drunk, and I can see, now, how it was smart of you not to come over, even if it hurt me a little."

"You don't have to be sorry," Sylvie said. "I've missed you, too, and it's—I know how it goes. It's the same for me sometimes. Obviously. 'So you paint it green,' right?"

" 'So you nail it to the *vall*,' " he said, and squeezed Sylvie's hand.

With that, they were settled. Old friends, Apt and Syl.

—

The lines they quoted came from a bit that Gladman used to open with, back in the anti-joke/shaggy-dog-story period that had immediately followed his abandonment of the Bernie Pollaco stage persona:

Moishe and Saul, two senior citizens with strong Yiddish accents, are sitting on a park bench.

Says Moishe to Saul: Hey Saul! I just remembered a joke!

Says Saul to Moishe: So tell me this joke already!

Moishe: So I vill! Here goes: Vat's green, hangs on the vall, and vistles?

Saul: I don't know. Vat is it? Tell me vat it is vat's green and hangs on the vall and vistles, Moishe.

Moishe: A herring!

Saul: A herring? But I don't . . . A herring isn't green.

Moishe: Ach! So you paint it green.

Saul: Okay. Yes. Sure. You paint the herring green. But still. A herring—it doesn't hang on a vall.

Moishe: So you nail it to the vall!

Saul: I see. Okay. And yet. I still don't understand. I don't see the humor. I don't get the joke. A herring painted green and nailed to the vall—this herring, Moishe, doesn't vistle. No herring vistles.

Moishe: And so it doesn't vistle!

Apter started the car. Started *Anecdote 3*. Didn't finish telling it till they were halfway into their omelets at Nookies.

Sylvie pushed her plate toward the middle of the table, fixed Apter with a stare. "Ethereum," she said.

"I don't know what you just said."

"It's a cryptocurrency. Like Bitcoin. You've heard of Bitcoin, right?"

"Heard of it, yes. I don't get how it works, but—"

"You don't have to get how it works," Sylvie said. "You just have to get it. You have to listen to your friend Sylvie who's endlessly better at math than you. Ethereum's like Bitcoin, but it's even further away from peak value than Bitcoin is. It's hovering around ten, and you need to buy some, Apter. You need to buy a lot of it."

"You're giving me investment advice?"

"I'm giving you *excellent* investment advice. Congratulations on your net worth, too. I should have said that first. You pulled some nutsy stuff off—it's hard to believe. I mean I wouldn't have guessed that a hundred thousand people in the entire country owned *any* kind of page-a-day desk calendar, let alone . . . What you just told me doesn't really seem real to me yet, I'm saying, and my reaction to it is, I can tell by the way you're looking at me, disappointing to you. Once it starts seeming real, I'm sure I'll have a better thing to say about you being a millionaire. For now, though, as long as it *doesn't* seem real to me, it's like there's a window here, an opportunity for me to be very unclouded, very cold and rational. I'm thinking I should, for your benefit—for my vicarious benefit, as your friend, as someone who wants the world for you—I'm thinking I should take advantage of this window. Use the cold rationality. So congratulations, I say, but now buy Ethereum. Buy Ethereum ASAP."

"I guess . . ."

"Don't blow this off. You know how many grads at Stanford—just in my department—are rich off Bitcoin?"

"Tell me."

"Well, I don't know how many, actually. But I've had three TAs this year who are all rich off Bitcoin. And how exactly rich varies. Not as rich as you, yet, I don't think—they'd have probably stopped TA-ing if they were, right?—but they're richer every day, and they'll catch up to you and more. It's near eight hundred a coin right now, Bitcoin, and the growth has been aggressive, but steady—the bubble hasn't even really started to inflate."

"I don't—"

"Ethereum, though, is right around ten bucks. I think it's gonna stay there a little while, but when the bubble comes—and it will . . . Put it like this: my parents, last week, for my twenty-first birthday—"

"Ah, fuck! Happy birthday, Syl. I didn't even—"

"No, no. Who cares. I don't care. Listen. My parents, for my twenty-first birthday, they gave me the money I'd gotten for my bat mitzvah. Not the bonds, but the cash. About five k, right? I bought this beautiful Ace and Jig top you see me wearing today, then spent all the rest on Ethereum. Four hundred and seventy-nine Ethereum."

"Well . . ."

"Still the wrong attitude, pal. This is no time to hesitate. And this cold, rational window of mine isn't, I don't think, gonna close till you close it. Tell me you'll buy a lot of Ethereum, Apter, and then I think it'll close. I'll become very happy and emotionally receptive and all, and we'll talk about why the long face as much as you want."

"I'll buy a lot of Ethereum," he said.

"At least fifty k of Ethereum," said Sylvie.

"Fifty k!"

"That's less than five percent of what you've got."

"That's a brand-new Porsche."

"First of all, no, it's not a brand-new Porsche. Or maybe it's a low-end Porsche before sales tax, but . . . since when do you want a brand-new Porsche? Or any kind of Porsche? I mean, if you're suddenly this Porsche guy, why'd you take me to Nookies in a used VW? You're a millionaire, Apter. You've got fifty k to play with. More than fifty k to play with. Put it into Ethereum ASAP."

"Fine."

"Fine?"

"Yes. Fifty k."

"And you won't sell it off till I tell you, all right?"

"Fine."

"And you don't act like my making you richer is a favor you're doing me."

"I missed you, Sylvie."

"Me too, Apt," she said, and kicked him under the table. "And you're good, you're all good. This weirdness you have about the money? It's understandable, of course, it's all new, but also, let me tell you, the long face—it's not the right response. It's kinda silly, to be honest. You think anyone, rich or poor, deserves what they have?"

"Right. No. I don't," Apter said. "I never have. But then . . . Trump."

"Trump what?"

"Trump won," Apter said.

"Because you got rich? Because of your calendar? *That's* why Trump won?"

"Well, he didn't lose because of it."

"You took money off a bunch of assholes who would have otherwise given it to Trump."

"Maybe. Probably in a lot of cases. But in other cases, maybe the calendar encouraged them to give *more* to Trump. Ignited their passions for—"

"Their passions! Come on, dude. Listen. I love you. You're someone I love who loves me back. Even if you *had* done something wrong, I'd probably be happy that you'd gotten rich, that's true—and, by the way, I can feel the window closing, the happiness coming on, we have to go get day-drunk, I'm thinking, very day-drunk—and I know that you knowing I love you compromises your opinion of my judgment here, but I'm telling you honestly, you did nothing wrong. If you were anyone else, I'd say the same. If you want to feel bad about something to do with the election, feel bad that you launched that moron Jessic Proveen's career. Even that, though—whatever. I mean, they might have helped fire up Trump's base a little, sure, but their role was wide open. Begging to be filled. Like, if it hadn't been Northwestern's most devotedly on-brand theirstorian who'd seized the day, it would have been Princeton's, or Yale's, or, I don't know, maybe even Oberlin's, right?"

"Well, but except my calendar's what set off—"

"If it hadn't been your calendar, it would have been a coffee mug. Or some problematic grilling apron. Some problematic GIF. The moment was *ripe*. The context demanded that something, that *anything*—Do you see what I'm getting at here?"

"I think so," Apter said.

"What am I getting at?"

"That I—"

"Ethereum," said Sylvie, "is what I'm getting at."

"Ethereum," said Apter.

"Ethereum," said Sylvie. "Now take me somewhere to *drink*, my newly wealthy friend. Take me somewhere way too expensive. Somewhere special. Somewhere preposterous. Treat me like your most favorite birthday girl."

They searched on their phones for a place that fit the bill. That early in the day, their options were limited, but four of six spots at the Logan Square microbar MumbletyPeg—the second-most expensive establishment they found—were, with a deposit of $60 per spot per hour, available from 2 to 6 p.m.

Apter reserved two spots for three hours.

On the way to the bar, while stopped for a red at Damen and Fullerton, Apter turned to Sylvie to say something funny, he didn't know what, and before he could think of it, they'd started to kiss. They kissed till the light changed, then acted, for a bit, like the kiss hadn't happened. Sylvie said she loved the song playing on the radio, Apter abidingly raised the volume, and neither said another word till they were out of the car.

"Shit, the window," Sylvie said, having just shut the door.

Thinking she'd meant the figurative window of cold rationality she'd spoken of at Nookies, Apter said, "It opened again?"

"Again?" Sylvie said.

Then Apter understood. He got back in the car and raised the half-closed window.

"Apter and Sylvie?" the barman said, as Apter and Sylvie entered MumbletyPeg. The barman was a towering, silver-haired man who wore steel-rimmed, tinily oval-lensed glasses that made you want to refer to them as *spectacles,* a philtrum-bare mustache you would likely spell *moustache* and perhaps pronounce *MOO-stosh,* a sharkskin suit-vest, and garters on his sleeves, yet he didn't, somehow, appear to be in costume. Whatever his look was, he really pulled it off. In part, Apter thought, because he seemed ageless. He could have been thirty and prematurely gray, could have been fifty and youthfully complected.

"We've been kissing," Apter told him.

Sylvie punched him in the shoulder.

"It was great," Apter said. "We have a great time kissing, Sylvie and I. We always have. But for reasons I won't get into with you, the kiss has confused us."

"It sounds like you kids need a drink," said the barman.

The bar was shaped like the barman's mustache, turned upside down, and with the philtrum filled in; like half of a hexagon; somewhat like this:

$$\backslash\_\_/$$

There were two stools per side.

On the side I've represented with the left-leaning slash, two Brazilian women spoke Portuguese, softly.

Sylvie led Apter to the side I've represented with the right-leaning slash, chose the stool on that side that was farther from the underscore, and Apter, of course, sat down right beside her.

The barman brought them cocktails, a different one for each of them. Apter's cocktail, ruby red and stirred, came with a long spike of ice in a Collins glass. Sylvie's, shaken, in a double old-fashioned glass, was butterscotch-colored and highly opaque with a razor-thin layer of bright-white foam atop which something black had been drizzled.

"No menu?" Apter said.

"Way it works here," said the barman, "is I pick your first drink. You don't love the drink I picked you, you don't pay for that drink, and I give you the menu. You do love the drink, you pay for the drink and I give you the menu, or maybe you decide to skip the menu and I bring you the next drink I think that you'll love. Up to you entirely."

"I like that system," Sylvie said. "How do you determine what drinks you think we'll love?"

"I've got a talent," said the barman.

"A talent," Apter said.

"That sounds pretty douchey, I know, but it's the truth. I've got a rare talent, and I don't believe it's mystical or anything like that, but I couldn't explain how it worked if I wanted to. I get a glance at a person, I can tell what they'll love. To drink, I mean. That's all there is to it. I know of seven others like me in the world. Maybe eight. Depends on how you count."

"How do you count?"

"Well, there's a gent in London, a dame in Vegas, a gent in Vegas, a gent in Recife, a dame in Abu Dhabi, and then there's a couple of gents in Tokyo—those are all for sure. They glance, then mix. That's seven. But then also there's this other gent in Tokyo—a possible eighth—and what he does is, he doesn't make your drink till you've answered three questions, and I don't know how I feel about that. I don't know if that's the same talent as mine and the other seven's. So I don't know if he counts."

"Three questions?"

"Three," the barman said. "First question is, he asks you what color his eyes are. Second question is, he asks you what color *your* eyes are. Before the third question, he has you turn in the direction of his window. Now, his establishment isn't quite as large as mine, he only has five stools where I have six, but the place is laid out near exactly like this one. Square room, bar along one wall, entrance through the opposite wall, door to the lav on the wall opposite the fourth wall, which is the only wall that has a window—the fourth wall, I mean. Just like in here. And just like in here, sturdy handmade wooden shelves stocked tight with bottles cover every available inch of wall, floor to ceiling, and just like in here, the window's covered too, with shelving, and that shelving is backless, just like in here, and different kinds of light from outside the building pass through the bottles in front of the window—light from the sun, or, at night, from a streetlamp, or traffic. So the gent in Tokyo, after you name for him the color of his eyes, and after you name for him the color of your eyes, he has you turn to face in the direction of the window, so you're looking at that shelving in front of the window, and he asks you to tell him what color the light is."

"And once you've answered the questions," Apter asked, "he's able to figure out the best drink to serve you?"

"Exactly," said the barman.

"So I think that, you know—if you want my opinion . . ." said Sylvie.

"Please," said the barman.

"I think he counts. That is, I think you should count him. I think I'd say that he's got the same talent as you and the other seven you mentioned."

"Same here," Apter said.

"Go on," said the barman to Sylvie.

"Well, this eighth guy," she said, "he figures out the best drink to serve by acquiring some information that, to me at least, seems just as arbitrary as whatever information I'm imagining you must use to figure out the same thing, okay? You glance at a patron, you know what drink that patron will love. *He* hears a patron name some colors, and he knows what drink the patron will love."

"Could be you're right. If that's how it really is. Only, what if he's hypnotizing you?" said the barman.

"Hypnotizing you?" Apter said.

"Hypnotizing you into loving whatever he serves you."

"With the questions, you mean?"

"Yeah, what if he's asking the questions to hypnotize you into loving whatever it is that he serves you?"

"Is that what he's doing?" Sylvie said.

"Who can know?" said the barman. "I'd heard of the gent from the dame in Abu Dhabi, and I went to his establishment to check it out. I answered his questions, and he mixed me a drink, and the drink was just right. Just like it should be. It was just what I wanted, and I hadn't known I'd wanted it until I was drinking it. By the time the first sip was at the back of my tongue, I didn't care anymore if I'd been hypnotized or not. I didn't bother to consider it. *Forgot* to consider it. I loved that drink. It didn't matter why."

Here, Apter and Sylvie, who'd been certain the barman had been pulling their chains, both became, suddenly, a lot less certain, and they found they were happy to be less certain, and they smiled broadly at each other and the barman.

The barman smiled back, mostly at the gent, not wanting to appear too flirtatious toward the dame, who he found more attractive than any other dame he'd laid eyes on in ages, and to whom he'd been considering slipping his number at the first opportunity until this very moment when he realized he was trying—only semi-voluntarily—to mirror the squint of the gent's left eye, and figured (correctly) that he (Floyd the barman) was not in possession of the dame's romantic interest, not *that* afternoon, and that even if he were in possession of her interest, and even if that interest could lead somewhere nice, he would not have wanted to play any part in the heartache he imagined the gent would suffer should ever such interest come to light. "Second thought," he said, "those two are on the house, you love 'em or not. I'll grab you some glasses of water, now. Enjoy."

Of course, Apter didn't know the barman's thoughts, and so whenever he conveyed his fourth anecdote to someone, it contained very little of the information I've chosen to include in the paragraph above.

Apter and Sylvie did love their drinks, and took sips from one another's and enjoyed these sips thoroughly, and Apter admitted that although Sylvie's drink was no doubt the second-greatest drink he'd ever tasted, the drink the barman had chosen to serve him was patently superior, and Sylvie said she felt the same way about her own drink as Apter had said he felt about his, and they talked about the flavors they tasted in the drinks, and the flavors they named were not often the same, and when they'd finished naming flavors, they studied their eyes and the pale and shifting candy-colored light that came through the bottles in front of the window, and they named the colors of their eyes and the light, and they joked about whether they'd undergone hypnosis, and whether it mattered, and after they'd finished their first round of drinks, they asked the barman to bring them a second according to his lights, and while the barman was mixing their second round of drinks, they talked about the kissing they'd done in the car, agreed it was better not to kiss anymore, but that, because they were celebrating, it was fine that they'd kissed, even better than fine, it was something they were certain they'd remember fondly, and then there was a gap in the conversation, a minute or so during which nothing was said, during which they were trying to determine—or, at least, during which Apter was trying to determine—whether their having just agreed that they would fondly remember the kiss in the car possessed so melancholic a flavor because the kiss would be their last or because they both knew that the kiss would not be their last even though the kiss *should* be their last; that despite their better judgment, they would go somewhere to fuck after leaving the bar, and the fucking would be as disappointing as ever, and both of them knew it would be disappointing, which would mean they'd been lying to each other and themselves by agreeing they'd fondly remember the kiss, pointlessly and wishfully thinking aloud, trying to believe that the kiss in the car would prove to be their last and unable to believe it, failing to convince themselves they'd be fine.

The barman set two shots on the bar. Apter's shot was milky. Sylvie's was colorless. The barman said the shots would "condition [their] palates" for the second round of cocktails, and they shot their shots, and he brought them their cocktails, and after they'd cheers'd and traded sips and agreed that this round was even better than the first, Sylvie told Apter to unlock his phone and hand it over, it was time to buy Ethereum, and Apter, after having done as instructed, watched the barman mix drinks for the Brazilians, and was satisfied to see that the drinks were different than any of those that he and Sylvie had been served.

It was right around then that Apter entered what he would afterward come to think of as a *fog;* what Gladman—had Apter described it to him—would have probably thought of as a *brownout.*

The next morning, on waking, he came out of the fog. He was lying in his bed, in the dark, on his back, between Sylvie (fully clothed) and an empty box of pizza. He was a little bit dry in the throat. Slow to blink. He couldn't recall any of the cocktails he and Sylvie had drunk past the second round. He remembered, however, having spent $600, and that the cost of each cocktail had been $40, and he was certain he wouldn't have tipped the barman more than 50 percent, which meant they'd had no fewer than twelve cocktails between them—the first two having been on the house—and he may have tipped as little as 25 percent, which meant they'd had no more than fourteen cocktails between them. So six or seven cocktails apiece. Plus how many palate-conditioning shots? Where was the headache? Where was the nausea? How was he able to perform arithmetic? Could the barman's mixological talents have possibly been of so high a caliber that you could drink yourself amnesiac on what he served you without suffering for it at all the next day? It seemed the answer to that question was: yes.

To the bathroom he went, and took a long piss, did some cursory ablutions. When he returned to the bedroom, he was surprised the alarm clock read 4:37. He unpocketed his phone, confirmed the clock was right, and saw he had an unread text from the printer in Michigan. The text had arrived at 6:40 p.m., and read, "FYI. Seeing lawyer first thing tomorrow morning."

Lawyer?

He sat on the bed, scrolled up to the top of the exchange with the printer.

	Buy me out. Make an offer.	3:47 p.m.
525k		4:01 p.m.
	I wasn't clear. Make your BEST offer. Website, title, email list, everything. I made 1.35m last year.	4:03 p.m.
525k CASH. The bad guy won. Backlash coming. You will never make that much dough again.		4:05 p.m.
	Okay, forget it.	4:05 p.m.
600k. That's my best offer.		4:13 p.m.
	600k cash, but you handle ALL the lawyer stuff. You send me papers, I sign, you pay me, you pay both our lawyers.	4:17 p.m.
We're on.		4:19 p.m.

Though he didn't remember having made the decision to sell RealAmeriCal, nor the amount he'd hoped the printer would offer, he sort of remembered wondering whether he should sell RealAmeriCal, and wasn't troubled to learn that he'd sold it for $600k. In fact, he felt good. He felt *really* good. Loosened up. Unencumbered. Like a thousand knuckles cracking.

He closed his messages, and saw that he had a new app on his home screen. Its icon was a dollar bill–colored boar with bloodstained tusks and a piggybank-signifying slot along its spine. The app was called WalletSafe. It was—he half remembered, and half deduced—the means by which he could access his Ethereums (or were you supposed to say *Etherea*?).

Sylvie had installed it while the barman (Apter vaguely recalled having thought)—she'd installed it while the barman, likely feeling sorry for Apter, whose gorgeous date was playing with phones instead of flirting over their $40 cocktails—while the barman, having come over to Apter, in order, it seemed, to keep Apter company—while the barman and Apter had small-talked their way toward someplace interesting . . . till they'd gotten to the barman's telling of a fun and rather compelling story about why he'd named his bar MumbletyPeg despite having never played mumblety-peg (which was some kind of game involving a knife) nor having ever seen anyone else play mumblety-peg . . . Sylvie had installed, on Apter's phone, while the barman told the story, the WalletSafe app, and made Apter the owner of roughly $50k of Ethereums (or *Etherea*).

But the point of the barman's story—i.e. the true, and presumably fascinating provenance of MumbletyPeg's name—was lost to the fog, as was any memory of the instructions Sylvie may or may not have given Apter about how to use WalletSafe.

He tried, there in bed, lying on his side now, to open the app.

It asked for a password.

He tried his usual password—*Pollaco#8*—but it wasn't any good.

He tried *MumbletyPeg* and *mumbletypeg*.

Those didn't work either.

"What—" Sylvie whispered, then sighed, cleared her throat, and started over: "What are you doing?"

"Trying to remember my WalletSafe password."

"*AMSSA2019*. All caps. Don't sell yet, though, Apt—you said you wouldn't."

"I'm not," Apter said. "I just want to see." He typed in the password. The app asked for his thumb. He thumbed the home button. The screen read:

WalletSafe

BALANCE

cryptocurrency

5,150.00	ETH
0.00	BTC
0.00	DASH

fiat currency

0.00	USD
0.00	EUR
0.00	GBP

EXCHANGE STATS TRANSACT

"This doesn't tell me much," he said. "What does it tell me? I have fifty-one hundred fifty Ethereums? Is it *Etherea* when it's plural? What is it worth? What do I do with it?"

"When it's plural it's . . . who cares? Just call it Ethereum. You've got fifty-one hundred fifty, yes. Purchased at $9.71 a coin. I'll explain how all of it works again later, cold storage and Coinbase and anything else you might have forgotten. After coffee, though, all right?"

"I'll make coffee in a minute. Two questions first. I'm having trouble remembering—"

"We did," Sylvie said. "We did have sex, but then we put all our clothes back on to eat pizza."

"Good one, Sylvie Klein. Question one, though: my car."

"Still parked on Milwaukee. We Ubered back."

"Okay. Good. *AMSSA2019*."

"What about it?"

"How does it sound familiar, but I don't know what it means?"

"Really?" Sylvie said. "Look, I'll meet you in the kitchen."

Over coffee in the kitchen, Sylvie explained that *AM* was the acronym for master's degrees granted by the University of Chicago, and that *SSA* was the acronym for the University of Chicago's School of Social Service Administration, the school to which Apter had decided to go in order to get his AM in social work, which he would receive—assuming he got the application out before the end of next week, then enrolled in SSA in the fall of 2017—in the spring of 2019.

AMSSA2019.

"I was *drunk,* huh?"

"By the end," said Sylvie, "you were drunker than I've ever seen you before, but when you said you'd become a social worker, that was actually pretty early on. I was sure you meant it."

"Why would I want to be a social worker? Where did I even get that idea?"

"I think Floyd convinced you."

"Who the fuck is Floyd?"

"The barman," Sylvie said.

"The barman convinced me to become a social worker."

"Well, a psychotherapist. You guys were having some conversation about how he became a barman. I didn't pay much attention to that part—I was busy getting you set up with your Ethereum—but the impression I had was that his path to owning MumbletyPeg was winding, and by the time I really tuned back in, you were telling him about Gladman, how Gladman's path to comedy had been winding, how he'd been a writer before he'd been a comedian, and that before he'd gotten published, he'd been a psychotherapist, and then Floyd told you that he thought *you* would make a good therapist.

"He said that there was something about you that 'made a fellow want to spill his guts right out.' Said he hadn't told a story as long as the one he'd just told you since he'd divorced his wife, and that he hardly ever even talked to a patron of MumbletyPeg about anything other than *amari* or whatever. Said something about that violating the ethics of microbar proprietorship, which, I think he misspoke, maybe meant the *aesthetics* of microbar proprietorship—I don't know. Anyway, it was a little pretentious the way he phrased it, and he was probably exaggerating a little, too, because that story he told us about the six or seven other bartenders—you remember that, right?"

"Colors," Apter said. "Hypnosis."

"Well, that seemed pretty well rehearsed to me, that story. I can't imagine he hasn't told it a hundred times by now. But still he seemed to really mean what he said about you. That he thought you should be a therapist, and I agreed with what he said. I thought it was insightful. People always seem to be confessing stuff to you, don't they? You're always getting chatted up, and you always seem interested. Therapist made sense."

"And so . . . what?" Apter said. "I just agreed with you and Floyd and decided to become a social worker, just like that?"

"It didn't happen *quite* that fast. First, I went to the bathroom, and while I was in there, I guess another couple came into the bar, and Floyd had to work, so you got on your phone, looked up Gladman on Wikipedia, and saw that *he'd* gone to SSA—that he'd been a social worker. Then you went to the SSA site and found out that a master's in Social Work was terminal, and it only took two years to get one, and maybe right around then you started texting with your printer. Trying to sell him your company. I don't know. I didn't know what you were doing at the time. But then we drank some more, and I was starting to feel pretty drunk, and I remember I tried showing you how to work WalletSafe, but before I'd even really gotten started, you got a text, said you couldn't believe how much you'd just been able to sell your company for, and you demanded that before I showed you anything, I had to reset your password to *AMSSA2019* because you were retiring from the alt right calendar-making business, and you would go to SSA to become a social worker."

"Okay . . ."

"That's what I said. 'Okay, Apter. Sure.' But you insisted you meant it, that the decision had been made, that it wasn't just the alcohol. Your face was like . . . glowing. And you gave a little speech about how you were a nihilist and a misanthrope except when it came to individuals, but you were also rich."

"A misanthrope except when it came to individuals? Is that even . . ."

"I don't know, Apt. You said a lot of stuff. And you know, I wasn't exactly sober myself. The gist of it, from what I understood, was that you didn't like groups of people, and that even though human suffering was as meaningless as anything else, you didn't like human suffering, but you did like listening to people tell you stories, and you would never have to work to earn money again, so you might as well get yourself, as quickly as possible, into a position where you could help decrease the suffering of individuals by listening to them tell you stories, even though it wouldn't be all that remunerative. Financially."

"I guess that makes some sense," Apter said.

But Apter wasn't being entirely honest. For all the reasons Sylvie said he'd given, and more, becoming a psychotherapist made *perfect* sense to him. He wanted to enjoy what he did with his life, wanted to be good at what he did with his life, and—if such a thing were possible—he wanted to be good *for* doing what he did with his life. From that moment forward, he had no doubt he'd get his AM at SSA and practice psychotherapy.

He didn't want to, however, admit that to Sylvie. He didn't like the idea that Floyd the barman, or any barman—or maybe even anyone else at all—should have been able to see what he should do with his life (what he *would* do with his life) before he'd been able to see it on his own. It embarrassed him a little.

On top of that, he'd been, for the past few minutes, coming to see how backwardly he'd assessed his physical state: he hadn't been hungover, no, but that was only because he'd woken up half-drunk. The coffee he'd swallowed was doing violence to his guts, and he was rapidly getting sweaty and vertiginous. He had to cut the conversation short.

"Sylvie," he said, as he rose from his chair, "you're my favorite person, and you should please make yourself as at home here as possible, but right now I have to go be alone with my bathroom," and he staggered down the hall to be alone with his bathroom.

A couple hours later, Sylvie cleaned him up, tucked him in, and caught the train home.

A couple days later, Apter drove her to O'Hare and, after he'd set her bag on the curb, they hugged goodbye, long and unawkwardly.

A couple weeks later, having signed all the papers, RealAmeriCal was no longer his, and then a couple months later, over Spring Break, he visited his sister and Sidney in Brooklyn.

He sensed, immediately, that something was off, wrong, going unsaid. The newlyweds laughed along with his jokes, but didn't crack more than a few of their own. And they cooed and awwed when Stanz behaved adorably, but the sounds seemed perfunctory, almost strained. Their energy was low.

At first, Apter thought it might have had to do with kids. With the having of kids, or the not-having of kids. He knew they both wanted kids, yet they didn't have a kid, and Adi wasn't pregnant. Maybe there'd been problems? Maybe she'd miscarried? Maybe one of them was having cold feet about kids?

Soon enough, however, it occurred to him that it probably wasn't kids, or anything like kids—that wouldn't make sense. He talked to Adi on the phone at least twice a week, and they talked about things like that, like kids. She'd have said if it were kids, or anything like kids. And what was preventing him from asking?

Sidney? His presence?

After breakfast on the second day of his visit, Apter and Adi took Stanz for a walk, and Apter said, "So what the fuck? Why the long face?"

Turned out Adi, the morning before Apter'd arrived in Brooklyn, had lost another hard fight for a novel she loved, *An Oral History of Man,* and, during the editorial meeting at which she'd gotten the news, she blew her top, railed and ranted, impugned her boss's judgment too directly, in front of far too many subordinates (one would have been too many; four had been present), and was now expecting to be fired next month, when she came up for her semiannual review.

"I haven't seen you blow your top since you were sixteen years old," Apter said. "That time some boy called and you were in the bathroom, and I told him you were in the bathroom, then forgot to ask his name when I took the message."

"Jason Kaufman," Adi said, laughing, giving Apter a shove. "I *think* that's who it was. I never found out. But yeah. I've got a cool temper. I like my cool temper. That's why I didn't want to mention the meeting. I'm pretty embarrassed."

"But so what did it look like? This blowing of your top?"

"I just said I was *embarrassed.*"

"Still, though. You should tell me. Your embarrassment is definitely worth the satisfaction of my curiosity."

"Well, I don't think it *looked* like much, really. It was mostly just me calling my boss, in so many words, an unimaginative coward, then railing on about *Money Changing Hands.* Did you read it yet, by the way?"

"I haven't. But I bought it."

"Well, everyone *bought* it," Adi said, and, just then, as if the universe itself wanted to corroborate his sister's overstatement, they passed not one, but two guys—a couple? had to be—who were sitting side by side on a bus stop bench, reading *Money Changing Hands*. And yet it wasn't that surprising. That is: these weren't the first people Apter'd seen out in public with the tome. An independent press in San Francisco had published the book in early February, and, in the weeks since, Apter'd witnessed its being read on trains, in coffee shops, even once in a bar. It had made the cover of the *New York Times Book Review*. Was on display in most bookstore windows.

"You think anyone'll buy this new novel you love—the one that dick just rejected?" he said.

"I hope so," said Adi. "It needs to be published."

"You ever think about starting a press?"

"Who doesn't?"

"Do you want to?"

"Who doesn't?"

"What would you call it?"

"I don't know, Apter."

"I bet you do," Apter said.

"Fine. You're right. Antic."

"Antic Press."

"Antic *Books*."

"That's better," Apter said. "How much would it cost to start Antic Books?"

"A lot. To do it right, at least."

"How much is a lot?"

"I don't *know*, Apter."

"I'll give you half a million dollars to start Antic Books."

"Half a million dollars, huh?"

"That's not enough?"

"I'm sure it's more than enough. Don't be crazy, though."

"I'm not being crazy. Plus I never got you a wedding gift."

"You gave us fifty grand."

"I gave Sidney fifty grand. I owed him fifty grand. At least fifty grand. Sometimes I think I shorted him. That flag was on everything. Every last page of every last calendar. If you want to start a press, I want to give you half a million, and full control."

"This doesn't seem real."

"I know," Apter said. "But that's only because it's great and it's smart. The world's terrible and stupid and we've gotten too used to it. I'm twenty-one, Adi. A twenty-one-year-old millionaire. You're my only sister and my closest friend and one day we'll die and you want to start a press. Not only do I think you'd start a great press, but I like the idea of helping you start one. If I don't help you, I'll regret it. I know that for sure. And I know you'd do the same for me if our etcetera and so on."

"Publishing's risky. We could lose a lot of money. We could lose all the money."

"Don't make me say that cliché thing about risk and reward. Anyway, I've got enough money. Start a press with half a mil of it. Make a huge splash and pay yourself well. Have Sidney do the covers. Publish only great things. I'll own a third and won't interfere. If there's profit, pay me back. If there isn't, no worries. At least I'll have helped to publish great things."

"I don't know, Apter. It sounds really wonderful . . ."

"*I* know," Apter said. "And it's as wonderful as it sounds. The one thing is, though, I'd really prefer you to start immediately. Like Monday, I'm saying. I don't really understand it, but Dad and I were talking just the other day, and he told me that it would be better, taxwise, if I had a business up and running before the end of this quarter."

This last part was a lie. Apter hadn't had any such discussion with their father.

"When's that?" Adi said. "The end of the quarter?"

"I can't remember—it's soon, though," said Apter. "It's any day now. It would be very helpful to me if you didn't hesitate."

A year or so later, on January 27, 2018, on Sylvie's advice, Apter sold his 5,150 Ethereum, originally purchased at \$9.71/coin, for \$1,103/coin, i.e. at a profit of 11,259 percent.

He might have, had he held out one more day, earned as much as \$800k more. He might have, had he sold a couple weeks earlier, earned as much as \$1.9 million more, but he didn't hold any of that against Sylvie Klein. She sold her Ethereum at the same time as he had—took a slightly worse "hit" than he had, percentage-wise (she'd bought \$4,700 of Ethereum at \$9.81/coin, sold it all for \$528k)—and in just a little bit over a year had turned \$50,006.50 of Apter's money into \$5,680,450.00.

Had he earned the extra $1.9 million, or even just the extra $800k, he'd have probably followed through on the plan that he'd hatched a few weeks earlier (the day the value of Ethereum first exceeded $1,000/coin): to buy Sylvie a Porsche 911 Carrera Coupe, stick a check for $500k in the glovebox, and have the car shipped to her in Palo Alto. But because his having not earned the extra $1.9 million coincided with Sylvie's not having earned what would have been an extra $200k or so, he skipped the I-bought-you-a-Porsche-as-a-kind-of-joke joke, and wired her $700k instead.

The following September, the same week Antic Books shipped its first title—*An Oral History of Man,* hardcover print run of thirteen thousand—Apter started his second year at the University of Chicago School of Social Service Administration.

5

The fifth and, by far, the longest of the anecdotes, wasn't one that Apter'd told often. In fact, prior to encountering itchy Reggie Glibner from the office of the mayor that night at the Rainbo, he'd told Anecdote 5 only five times ever: once to Adi, once to Sylvie, once to his parents, once to an ex who'd called him for comfort sex he didn't want to have with her, and once to a stranger at the Gold Star Tavern whose name Apter wasn't able to remember, so drunk had he become in the course of telling her the earlier anecdotes.

One reason he hadn't often told the fifth anecdote was that he didn't believe it could be of much interest to anyone with whom he wasn't very close—let alone to a stranger—unless such a person were to hear the other four anecdotes first, and, even though Apter, when he told those anecdotes, wouldn't convey more than a fraction of the information contained in my descriptions of them, their telling tended to leave him fatigued, tired of his voice, tired of himself: too tired to go on.

Another reason he didn't tell the fifth anecdote often was that he felt it was missing something. He wasn't sure what. Perhaps, he thought, the ending wasn't really the ending. That is: perhaps he was still in the middle of living out the ending, or, for that matter, living out the middle.

Then again, maybe he *had* lived out the ending, but lacked the perspective needed to tell it well.

Or perhaps the whole anecdote was lacking in perspective. Whereas the Apters of Anecdotes 1–4 appeared to Apter to be Apters other than the Apter who was telling them, the Apter of Anecdote 5 did not. The Apter of Anecdote 5 appeared to Apter to be the same Apter as the Apter telling it, and, as someone must have—or should have—once aphorized,

> You may know the true story of who you once were, but you can't know that of who you've become.

Although, on second thought, he may have had the ostensible aphorism backward. Its inversion, after all, rang just as true.

> You may know the true story of who you've become, but you can't know that of who you once were.

The fifth anecdote, in any case, wasn't much of an anecdote. It contained some engrossing-enough fragments, sure—I wouldn't bother telling you about it if it didn't—but the fragments were scattered. Apter told them out of sequence: jumped forward, tracked back, inserted lengthy asides—his intent in doing so often unclear.

And no two fragments possessed quite the same tone, plus, telling to telling, each itself varied tonally. A fragment that had seemed a lament in one telling sounded more like an affirmation in the next. A fragment that, in winter, had arced toward a cry of anguished frustration, had, in spring—despite containing the same information—arced toward a cry of joyous relief, and then, in summer, didn't arc in the slightest, but aridly meandered toward something like a punchline.

The form of the fragments varied broadly as well. Here was some action, there a meditation. Here was some gossip, there a semi-academic refutation of dominant philosophies of human psychology. Nor was there much correspondence at all between the causal relevance of what was being described and the number of words being used to describe it. A major decision Apter had reached—one with real-world, life-impacting consequences for him—could be arrived at with little or even no elaboration—could be arrived at *in the white-space,* made *off-screen*—and then immediately followed by, say, an intricate description of a public fountain.

Really, it was more like a novel than an anecdote. One of those novels that might just as easily be a work of genius as a work of madness as a wholly pretentious piece of garbage. Campy or kitschy. Dadaist or doo-doo-ish. Gogolian or *gogol.*

Suffice it to say that the people who had heard Anecdote 5 were, all of them, *engaged* with it while Apter told it, but once he'd finished telling it, none of them seemed to know what to do with it. None of them seemed to know how to react. Should they laugh? Commiserate? Deploy cheerful clichés? What did Apter want from them? What was his point? Did he have a point? If he'd had a point, had they missed the point? Perhaps he'd failed to make his point?

When he'd finished telling Anecdote 5 to his parents, they said they loved him and fed him some soup.

When he'd told it to Adi, she'd sent him two hits of molly in the mail, along with a box of manuscripts recently submitted to Antic.

Sylvie, after hearing it, took him to Honolulu for a week, where they ate Adi's molly on the beach and got sunburned.

The ex who'd called for comfort sex he didn't want to have with her told him that she thought she had a better understanding, now, of why their relationship had fallen apart, and thanked him for the closure.

The woman at the Goldstar blew him in the men's room and, for reasons he couldn't for the life of him remember—reasons he suspected he'd rather not remember—slipped him twenty bucks before she got in her cab.

Glibner misquoted Hunter S. Thompson and, as I'm sure you must have guessed by now, offered Apter a job at the mayor's office.

Whatever response he may or may not have sought those few times he'd told it, Anecdote 5 concerned Apter's career as a clinical social worker.

During their first year at SSA, students were enrolled in three classes per quarter and worked in the field fifteen hours a week.

One's first-year field placement was determined by the school. Apter had been assigned to the Partial Hospitalization Program at St. Anatole Hospital, across from Douglas Park. There he did casework and led open group therapy with clients who suffered from chronic mental illness (e.g. schizophrenia, schizoaffective disorder, bipolar disorder). All the clients were unemployed, highly medicated, and highly impoverished. A few lived with family, but the vast majority lived in one of two nearby, state-run psychiatric nursing homes.

It was a depressing gig. Apter wasn't bad at leading group therapy—he got the reticent talking, the talkative listening—but it felt nearly useless. The purpose of the partial hospitalization program—the *mission*—was twofold: a) to prevent at-risk clients from requiring inpatient care, and b) to ease the transition of those clients who'd just been released from inpatient care back into a not-so-heavily/noninstitutionalized existence (i.e. to keep them from returning to inpatient care).

In other words, his job was less about helping people improve the quality of their lives than helping them reduce the cost of their lives to others: their families, the hospital, the nursing home, the state. Less about relieving suffering than helping those who suffered to tolerate their suffering.

Which was, he supposed, better than nothing, but.

On top of all that, he didn't hear many stories—didn't feel he really got to know his clients. Perhaps a couple of them "possessed insight," but, if so, they weren't able to express that insight. Nearly all of them were mis- or overmedicated, about a third of them were developmentally disabled, more than half were addicted to alcohol and/or street drugs, and the few who fell into none of those categories were, nonetheless, all too aware of how helpless they were, how helpless anyone at the PHP was to help them.

And there wasn't any helping them. Not meaningfully. Not unless better medications were developed, or social welfare budgets got raised by orders of magnitude.

Many of the clients professed Catholicism, and, hard as that was for Apter to relate to, harder yet was trying to understand what prevented the rest of them from killing themselves.

By the end of the school year, two of them had.

His PHP colleagues wept about that—both times, they wept.

Apter . . . didn't.

Which wasn't to say he didn't hate that the suffering of two of his clients had been so terrible as to drive them to suicide, but rather that, given how terrible their suffering had been, suicide seemed like a reasonable solution. The tragedy was the suffering, the suicide the end of it. The tragedy the cause, not the effect.

Or maybe the effect was also a tragedy, but certainly not one as great as the cause.

And it took him some effort to understand how his colleagues could become so very upset by the effect when, previously, while the cause did its causing, they'd been able to maintain their emotional balance.

Did their tears come from feelings of personal loss? Apter doubted it. In the couple of months between the two suicides, another client had suffered a grand mal seizure in her nursing home's stairwell and died of the injuries (broken neck, internal bleeding) arising from the fall. This was a middle-aged woman who'd been receiving treatment at the PHP for at least as long as either of the suicides; who was no less knowable or *likable* than either of the suicides; whose death was certainly no less sudden than theirs. None of his colleagues shed tears when *she'd* died.

Was it a religious thing, then? Did they cry at the damnation of the suicides' immortal souls?

That seemed unlikely. Only two of his colleagues were Catholic, one of those lapsed, and the other two were Jews, neither of them practicing.

Probably, thought Apter, their tears were in response to feelings of failure. From feeling they'd failed to save the suicides from suicide.

And there wouldn't, Apter thought, be anything wrong with that. Especially not if they knew that that was why they were crying. Yet they didn't seem to know it or even suspect it—at least, they didn't say it—and when Apter, in a group supervisory session held in the wake of the second suicide, was confronted by his colleagues for his "apparent failure to process his feelings about Shanda's suicide," and he, in response, frankly (but gently!) expressed his thoughts on causes, effects, and relative tragedy, he was accused of lacking empathy.

"For who?" he asked.

"For *Shanda*," he was told.

"But I empathized entirely. I really did," he said. "I empathized, above all, with her desire to kill herself. Her life was pain with occasional breaks she was expected to understand as pleasure. If I'd had her life, I'd have done the same thing. I believe I'd have done it much earlier, actually."

All around the supervisory circle, this remark was met with widened eyes, flaring nostrils, slo-mo side-to-side shakings of the head: total contempt.

And why? Why contempt?

Because, Apter thought, *you're* the ones with whom I'm failing to empathize; you think I have contempt for *you*.

And the truth of it was, he . . . did.

He might not have before the supervisory meeting—he didn't think that he had—but now? Yes. For sure. Contempt. Who were they to judge him?

"Maybe this kind of work . . ." the PHP manager stammered just a few hours later, during their one-on-one supervision session.

" 'This kind of work . . .' what?" Apter said.

"That's not what I meant. Not 'this kind of work,' but 'this kind of *client.*' It's . . . You've shown a lot of talent for leading Group, and your casework is conscientious—you've done a lot of good here, advocated well for those clients in your care, they're in better shape for having gotten to work with you—but maybe working in this context, with this population . . . I'm thinking maybe it isn't for you."

Luckily it was already mid-May. Apter's placement was scheduled to end three weeks later.

During a student's second year at SSA, while enrolled in two or three classes per quarter, he worked twenty-five hours a week in the field at the placement of his choice. Apter chose the Jewish Family Services Center in West Rogers Park, on Chicago's North Side. He did therapy there with individuals, couples, and families, some of them Jewish, many of them not, most of them poor or on the margins, few of them afflicted with chronic mental illness.

He was far better suited to the Center than he had been to the PHP. His clients at the Center had it hard for one reason or another, but even in those cases where they appeared nearly hopeless, they were never wholly hopeless—they were, after all, coming to therapy of their own volition, even paying for it (sliding scale). They frustrated Apter sometimes, sure, but he was, for the most part, optimistic. He believed he could help, and, as far as he could tell, he'd been having some success.

Once every week or two, for forty-five minutes, he would meet with each of his clients in his office, listen to their stories, and aid them in acquiring and wording new insights into the sources of their joy and their suffering. And the depressed ones appeared to become less depressed. The anxious ones appeared to become less anxious.

A self-harming teenage alcoholic who'd been raped by an acquaintance a couple years earlier wept and hugged her father and stopped ditching school, stopped using her flesh to extinguish cigarettes, started attending weekly AA meetings.

An elderly woman, the loneliest person Apter'd ever met—widowed and childless, an only child of two only children—reached out to another elderly woman, a woman to whom she hadn't spoken since college—found her on Facebook, sent her a message—and they'd embarked on a romance.

A married couple from Tehran who hadn't fucked in years—hadn't fucked once since they'd emigrated—fucked.

None of which was to say that working at the Center was always, or even usually, *rosy*. One of Apter's clients, Herbie Cohen, age forty-nine, had late-stage, early-onset Parkinson's and major depression. He wasn't a likable person, Herbie. He was bitter and, worse than that, he was boring. The most boring person Apter'd ever been unable to walk away from. When he wasn't complaining about his pain and the difficulties arising from his pain—complaining in the voice of a man thirty or even forty years older than him, complaining with only the barest hint of animation above the mouth (the occasional longblink, welling eyes, rolling tears, hiccupy sniffles—even the way he *cried* was boring; appeared to be more an autonomic response to dust or strong headwinds than to over- or even just whelming emotion)—Herbie was droning on about . . . what?

Apter honestly couldn't say, so occupied was he with fighting off the urge to fall asleep. Fighting off that urge via fantasies of tearing into the man, of shouting at him, "Snap the fuck out of it! This is why no one likes you! This is why you're depressed! You just drone on through your whiney fucking adenoids, inflicting your suffering on anyone in earshot. Read the room, Herbie, you miserable fuck! You flat motherfucker! You dull, frozen-faced, mouse of a man!" Etc.

Twice in twelve sessions, he'd lost the fight. That is: he'd fallen asleep. Once for maybe ten or fifteen seconds—he wasn't sure exactly. And once for eight minutes, which he knew because, upon waking up, he saw that the session had run five minutes over, and he remembered having checked the clock as he was fading; remembered having realized, with a measure of relief, that there'd been only three more minutes to go.

Neither of those times had Herbie seemed to notice that Apter had slept. Which made Apter even angrier at him, and, because of that, angrier at himself as well—his anger was a failure. His client was suffering. He was angry at Herbie for, it seemed, suffering. And this suffering: it wasn't just—nor even mostly—from the crippling depression or dislikability. The Parkinson's, which surely contributed to Herbie's depression (which depression, of course, was itself both a cause and an effect of his being unlikable)—the Parkinson's was its own separate nightmare.

Herbie kept taking spills. Without any warning, the disease would wrest away all control of his muscles, and he'd drop where he'd stood, unable to shift his balance to guide the fall, unable to raise his arms to break it. He came in with new cuts and bruises each week.

To be Herbie was much harder than it was to be *around* Herbie. Apter knew this. He *knew* it. He just never seemed to know it when he *was* around Herbie.

At their thirteenth session, Apter fell asleep again. He wasn't sure for how long. When he woke, though, Herbie, in an uncharacteristically soft voice, almost a whisper, said, "Are you feeling all right? Are you under the weather?"

"Oh," Apter said. "No. Or rather: yes. I'm fine. Just . . ."

"Are you sure?" Herbie said. "You can tell me, you know, if you're not feeling well. We can call it a day. I won't buck at that. It's important a person gets the sleep he needs. Especially if he's under the weather."

"Do you *want* to call it a day, Herbie?"

"Not particularly, no. But if you have a cold or something—I mean I know it's hard enough to listen to me when you're feeling healthy . . ."

Apter waited, not correcting him.

"Those other times you fell asleep," Herbie went on, "I wasn't worried about you. I figured it was just me being a snooze. But something seems different with you this time. I don't know. You look a little pale or something. Under it."

"I'm fine, Herbie," Apter said. "Thank you for asking, though."

"You're welcome," Herbie said.

Apter waited.

"I don't know why I said, 'You're welcome,' like that," Herbie said. "It's kind of an awkward thing to say. An awkward *usage*. I could have said, 'Sure,' or, 'Of course,' and that would have been normal. I don't know. Maybe I'm not in such good shape myself today. Maybe things are getting worse for me. What's new, though, right? I guess they're always getting worse for me. For everyone probably. Definitely for me. It's pretty much all downhill for me. Always has been. Right from the start, downhill," Herbie said. Then went on.

That evening, driving home from the Center, Apter surprised himself with a sneeze-cough. A bright yellow glob splat upon his steering wheel, and all at once his eyes felt swollen, his head was throbbing, he was sweating all over.

He had to stay in bed for the next three days. Chicken broth and orange juice. Lots of TV. A well-meaning but rather *strenuous* blowjob from his girlfriend, Lindsay Biss—the pharmacist who, some sixteen months later, would call him up for comfort sex he didn't want to have with her, only to become the fifth person ever to hear this fifth anecdote.

Had he been feeling at all romantic or charitable at any point during those days spent in bed, he might have entertained the proposition that Herbie was more *tuned in* to people than he—Apter—had previously believed: that Herbie, in spite or because of his suffering, possessed some kind of fine-tuned antenna that could sense approaching pain or illness in others before even the others themselves could sense it. But Apter hadn't been feeling romantic or charitable. If anything, he found himself *blaming* Herbie for the cold. Not for giving him the cold—not exactly that—but for *weakening* him; for making him more available to the cold; for turning him, somehow, into a victim.

Which didn't make a lot of sense, but that wasn't the point. Or was exactly the point.

Herbie missed the next session, not to Apter's displeasure. Apter called him at the end of the day. Herbie apologized for not having called, himself. Explained to Apter that, the previous Sunday, while brushing his teeth, he'd fallen, chin-first, on the lip of the sink, knocked himself out, come to minutes later with a shattered hip, screaming. He'd left his phone in the bedroom ("Fucking moron I am," he said) and had to shout for an hour before a neighbor finally heard him and called 911.

Herbie had to spend two weeks in the hospital. His insurance was good, provided him with a room to himself, and the hospital wasn't too far from the Center. They did their next session there.

Apter was Herbie's first and only visitor. Herbie said so right at the start of the session. He seemed angry about it. Bitter. Which was good, Apter thought. Or probably good. Either way, it was different. Different from boring. Herbie talked about his family. Bitterly. Apter hadn't known Herbie'd even had a family. Crazy an assumption as it might now seem—as incompetent an assumption as it was for him to make—Apter'd just assumed Herbie'd always been a recluse.

But it turned out: not always. He'd been, in his own words, "an absentee father" and "a real cold fish of a husband—a world-class prick." He hadn't spoken to his ex in a decade. All three of his sons lived out of state: one wouldn't take his calls, another would on occasion but had nothing kind to say, and Herbie didn't even have the third one's number. Herbie's younger brothers—there were two—"feared and hated" him. As children, they hadn't ever been close, and since Herbie's early thirties, they'd been wholly estranged. "What it is is I fucked them real good out of an inheritance from our mother. And I didn't need it, either. Not even a little. I made a pretty penny on my own in those days. I had my own accounting firm. Fifteen employees. But I'm garbage," he'd said. "I'm a real piece of garbage. I saw an opportunity to fuck my brothers out of what was rightly theirs, and I took it. That's why no one visits. That's what I get."

"And your father?" Apter said. "Is he still alive?"

"Far as I know. And *fuck*. Him. I mean, *I* stopped speaking to *that* piece of garbage when I was twelve years old, remember? I was the one who chased him off."

"I didn't know that."

"I never told you about that?"

"No."

"You sure?"

Apter wasn't sure. He might have slept through the story, or just failed to pay attention, but he said, "I'd remember."

"I guess you probably would. It's a pretty good story. It's my one good moment I've always been proud of."

"I'd like to hear about that."

"Well, okay, yeah, so I . . . I poisoned him."

"Poisoned him."

"I know. Poisoned my father. Sounds psycho, I know. And I'm not.

I'm garbage, but I'm not some crazy person, I don't think. And I'm not that kind of vindictive kind of person, either, who poisons his father, but I was that day, you know? That day I was. I was really sick of him. I'd had enough. The way he talked to us. He didn't like us. He didn't want to be there, always made it known. He was a brutal fuck. Never hit us—nothing like that—but he said some awful things I'd rather not repeat. Main thing is, though, he didn't want to be there and he always said so, at any opportunity, and he made our mom cry, and me and my brothers, and one day—not the only time, mind you, but for some reason . . . I don't know . . .

"One day, it's a Saturday morning, and he says his brutal shit to us and she locks herself in the bedroom and just stays there, stays there all day, and then it's like five o'clock and she's still in there, so I have to make dinner. And I hate making dinner. Seeing the food before it's ready to be served—puts me off for some reason. I don't know why. Don't care. I hated it back then, I have ever since. But the point is our neighbor had a dog that shit in our yard, okay? And I got some on a stick, just a little bit, and I wiped it on the inside of his sandwich that I made—my father's sandwich. This is brisket left over from the night before. I wiped shit on his brisket and fed it to him, and, a little while later, while he was puking it up in the bathroom, I told him what I did, and he didn't believe me, so I went and got the stick, and I showed him the stick, brought it to the bathroom and held it out, right under his nose, while he was shitting his guts out there on the toilet and puking in the tub, and he slapped it away, then tried, get this—he took a swipe at me. From that position. On the toilet. And he missed, you know? Of course he missed. He's shitting, puking, pants around his ankles, sitting. He's gonna hit me? How's he gonna hit me? He missed and I laughed in his wretched fucking face. He was *weak,* and I told him that. He was a *weak* person and I was not weak. I wasn't small either, I was a *big boy,* an *early bloomer,* almost as big as him by then, and he—he *spit* on me, spiteful cocksucker—spit his vomity spit right on me. Tried to get my face, but, you know, it was all shirt. Shirt's all he got. Still. Poisoned or no, your own father spits on you? Doesn't matter where it lands. That's it. That's that. One line gets crossed, they're all getting crossed. And that's what happened. I gave him a shove, knocked him right off the pot, and he puked a little more, and shit on himself, his dick and his balls, I remember—all shrunken up tiny. And maybe, in this moment, you think to yourself, 'What have

I done?' In one of these art-house movies, you know? About fathers and sons. This would be some kind of moment where I'd think to myself, 'What have I done? I'm an animal. I've turned us into animals.' Not an art-house movie, though, this. No. I felt pretty good. I felt pretty strong. And what I did was, *I* spit on *him*. Not on his shirt. Right in the middle of his forehead. And then I told him I would kill him if he didn't pack it up. I told him I would kill him if he didn't pack his shit and hit the fucken road, and he believed me, Apter, because I hated him and he knew it was hate, and how big a hate it was, because he hated me back in just the same way. We hated each other and he'd have killed me if he thought he could get away with it, I knew that, and he thought I'd kill him even if I didn't think I'd get away with it because he thought I must be nuts—poisoning him, spitting on his forehead. I don't, by the way, think that's so—I don't think I was nuts, and I don't think he was right. I think that, to kill him, I'd have had to know I'd get away with it, but I'm saying what he thought. What I think he thought. And I told him pack his shit and get the fuck out, and then I left the house, myself, left my mother and my brothers in the house—I wish I would have taken them with, but I just thought . . . I don't know what I thought. I left the house on my own, though. I walked for a while, couple hours maybe, I don't know, and I remember I went, when I got back to the neighborhood, I went to the donut place and got a donut, and the place was almost closed, and the girl behind the counter gave me not one, but *two* extra donuts for free. Nothing too fancy. Just glazeds, you know? But this was a kindness I've always remembered, I don't know exactly why. They weren't the best donuts, these donuts, but they were donuts, and . . . I don't know. Anyway, I ate the donuts, went back home, and by then he was gone. Never saw him again. He never came around or called. What a piece of work. What a piece of garbage. I look pretty *good* next to that hunk of junk. Still, I wish I would've taken them to the donut place with me. At least my brothers. They were pretty scared when I left. I mean—of course they were. I knew they'd be fine, though, and I guess I just thought: they need to toughen up. For that I have remorse. I even wrote a poem about it once in college, in a poetry class. How there were three brothers, three donuts, but one of the brothers ate all the donuts. The teacher said it was resonant. *Resonant.* I wish I would have brought my brothers with me when I left, but the rest, like I said: my proudest moment."

—

Apter wasn't sure how much he believed of Herbie's story, but the thought that he'd been lied to didn't bother him much. He certainly preferred a lively lie to a droney complaint. Nonetheless, he figured he should probably bring it up with Herbie—his sense that Herbie had been less than honest. They should probably, he thought, *explore* it together. But that never happened.

After Herbie was released from the hospital, he was—not unreasonably— too afraid to stand up without another person present, let alone to leave his house, so Apter went to him. And they had a really nice moment together. Herbie, sprawled across his living room sofa, had begun the session with his usual mind-numbing droning, but before a quarter of an hour had elapsed, he'd started crying, and this crying was different than the previous crying, wasn't so much sniffley as *chokey,* and, soon, it rendered him completely speechless. Speechless for a minute, then for more than a minute, up until Apter, on a chair beside the couch, found himself scootching forward a little and taking one of Herbie's shoulders in hand, which seemed to calm Herbie down a little, to slow his breathing, after which Apter removed the hand.

Herbie wiped at his eyes with the backs of his Parkinsonianly tremorous wrists, swallowed some phlegm, and said, "So this commercial. That's what I was thinking about, in case you want to know. There was this commercial, back in the 1980s, for this little pendant you'd wear around your neck if you were old. I can't remember what it's called. Do you know what I'm talking about? Probably it wasn't around anymore by the time you were born—internet and everything—but maybe you know the pendant I mean?" Apter didn't know. "Well, so, in case something immobilized you, like put you in danger at home," Herbie said, "while you were all alone—say you start having a heart attack or feeling faint or whatever—you press the button on this pendant and it activates an alert to emergency services so they can send you an ambulance or cop or whatever. There's even these speakers in your house, these like two-way speakers, and you can yell what the problem you're suffering from—Life Call! That's what the thing was called. *Life Call.* That ring any bells for you?" Apter said it didn't. "Well, it's a very funny commercial, this commercial for Life Call," Herbie said. "People laughed at it a lot. Made lots of jokes about it. This old lady in a robe—*Mrs. Fletcher.* She falls down in the bathroom in this commercial. You don't see her fall. She's already fallen, this old lady, and her name's Mrs. Fletcher, which is roughly, I'd say, the most goyische name that a person can have. Like, even my mother, her name was Krischa, like *Christina*, you know, because she lived in Poland when she was a little schoolgirl and they wanted to hide that she was Jewish as best as they could, which—good luck with *her* nose, which is to say, *this* nose, mine, not that it didn't look good on her, it did, she was a very pretty woman, my mother—but that's what they named her. Krischa. Polish for Christina. Not an uncommon practice is my point. Lots of Jewish girls of that era had that name in Poland. Meaning even *Christina*, okay, even *Christina*, I'm saying is less goyische than *Mrs. Fletcher*, I contend. But Mrs. Fletcher, though, this Mrs. Fletcher she's got this crazy, like, over-the-top, super-whiny Brooklyn-Jewy accent, and, like I was saying, she's on the floor in her bathroom in the commercial, and, after she presses the button on the Life Call pendant, she yells out, okay? And what she yells is: 'Haalp! Eye've fawlen . . . and I can't get ahp!' So that's mostly what everyone made fun of about the commercial. Me included. And a lot. Everywhere you went. I mean, there were T-shirts of this lady. Jokes about her on Carson. On *SNL*. So anyway, that's what I was thinking about. The commercial. I guess because since, now, you know, obviously, I *am* this lady. Basically. I'm basically Mrs. Fletcher. Not as old, no, but that's what happened to me, right? I became Mrs. Fletcher. I've become Mrs. Fletcher. And it's horrible, Apter. It's shit. Total shit. This is the worst I've ever felt, and I've felt pretty fucking bad before. As I'm, uh, sure you've gathered from our conversations together. Pretty fucking bad I have felt, and this is the worst. It's just horrible, or as Mrs. Fletcher'd say, you know, 'It's jast *harrible*,' right? But still. To picture her there on that floor, shouting . . . That's what made me laugh so hard just now."

Just now? Wait. *Just now* . . . when?

"You seem confused," Herbie said. "You got a dazed kind of look there. You have no idea what I'm talking about, do you? You think I'm exaggerating. Making it up. Go ahead and see for yourself. Go on." Herbie extended a trembling finger toward the coffee table, on which Apter's phone lay, keeping the time.

And even though the therapeutic value of doing so may have been dubious, Apter unlocked the phone and pulled the commercial up, and he and Herbie watched it several times, roaring with laughter, choking on it.

Mrs. Fletcher wasn't the only funny part. There was also a man who clutched his chest and shouted, "I'm having . . . *chest* pains!" That was almost as good. But what really got Apter and Herbie snorting—though not until the third or fourth viewing did either of them fully appreciate it in all its subtlety—was the spokeswoman. An old lady in a rocking chair, wearing a Life Call pendant of her own. Just before the part with the chest pains guy, she holds the pendant forward for the viewer, and says, joyfully—almost rapturously, really; in a voice not unlike that of Glinda the Good Witch from *The Wizard of Oz*—"Just press this button and speak into the air!"

"The air!" said Herbie, upon the sixth viewing. "The air, my friend! Mumble to your collar if that's your thing, but if you want us to save you, make sure there's *air* between your face and that collar."

"You can whisper . . ." said Apter in a kind of hybrid Herbie/Pollaco voice (he'd lost track of himself, laughing so hard), ". . . you can whisper right into your very own armpit, and just as long as this whispering happens in a breathable environment, salvation will be yours."

"Goddamnit," Herbie said, "whatever else you do, guy, when you press that button and say what you gotta, make sure, for Christ's sake, you don't say it in a vacuum."

The following week, Herbie wouldn't let him in. Or rather, Herbie's home health aide, Rhonda, wouldn't. "He doesn't want to see you, Mr. Schutz," she said.

"Is he unwell?"

"Very," Rhonda said, with a chuckle. "No worse, though, than last week. *Hip*'s healing nicely. But he says he's done with therapy. He says it a lot. Been reminding me not to let you in for days."

"Why?"

"Well, he's dying, Mr. Schutz."

"That's what *he* says, or . . . ?"

"Not in so many words, no. What *he* says is he doesn't have no more time to waste. But he knows he's dying, and that's what he means."

Apter called Herbie twice to no avail. Twice in two weeks. Left a voice-mail the first time.

He could've done more.

He could've tried harder to get Herbie back in therapy. Could've stopped by again or written a letter. Instead—and with, admittedly, a far greater sense of relief than regret—he gave up. Filled Herbie's slot with a client from the waiting list.

This was early in March 2019. Right before the start of Apter's last quarter at SSA. Despite his failure with Herbie—if that's even what it was—he still felt good about the work he was doing at the Center. Felt he was effective. Felt he was helping. And judging by the noises his supervisor made, they would offer him a job there after graduation. He imagined he'd accept.

But when that last quarter started, Apter, owing to scheduling difficulties, had to enroll in Introduction to Behaviorism, a class in which he, like pretty much all the other students at SSA who'd ever seen or read *A Clockwork Orange,* had very little interest.

It was either Introduction to Behaviorism or Advanced Statistical Methods.

Previously, he'd taken classes in the theory and practice of the other three therapeutic paradigms taught at SSA: Family Systems, Cognitive Behavioral, and Psychodynamic.

Psychodynamic theory had its roots in psychoanalytic theory, which posited that every individual was influenced by an unconscious mind that possessed its own will—a mind that, in essence, possessed its own mind—and was, to one degree or another, able to enact that will: a will that was often in conflict with the will of the individual to whom the unconscious mind belonged. It was basically a little man who lived in your head, this unconscious mind: a little man who, himself, had little men in his head, all of whom constantly fought with one another, causing you to feel and think and act, and none of whom had ever been detected, much less measured, by any existing scientific instrument.

Cognitive Behavioral theory treated tendentious hypotheses proposed by cognitive scientists of the previous century as though the hypotheses were inviolable laws, then repackaged them as bootstrapping wisdom-bytes intended to appeal to and "empower" the tech-enthralled layman who liked to imagine his mind was a computer.

Family Systems theory was a homey hodgepodge of both the afore-mentioned needlessly intermingled at random with misappropriated—even abused—terminology from the Systems Theory lexicon: *family system,* for instance, meant the same thing as *family*—it just took longer to say—and *entropic* meant *bad, negentropic* meant *good.*

In sum, the Psychodynamic paradigm was religious, the Cognitive Behavioral paradigm pseudoscientific, and the Family Systems paradigm, when it wasn't pseudo-intellectual, was anti-intellectual. Though Apter wasn't a proponent of any of these paradigms, that didn't concern him. Each one, despite its incapacity to convincingly account for this or that aspect of human psychology, provided him a different lens through which to view his clients and their troubles, as well as a different set of techniques with which to alleviate his clients' suffering—a different set of techniques with which to help his clients heal—so he took from each what he found to be valuable, discarded the rest, and, by the time his final quarter at Chicago rolled around, he had *a well-stocked toolbox* from which to draw.

Had you asked him about it, Apter would have called his approach to therapy *eclectic.* He'd have told you that he didn't understand why therapy worked when it worked, that he didn't believe that anyone truly understood why it worked, but that, when it did work—and it *often* worked, in his experience—he understood *how* it had worked, i.e. *what* he had done or said to help the clients he'd helped to heal heal. He'd have also told you that the more experience he acquired as a therapist, the better he'd gotten at being a therapist. Were you Lindsay Biss in bed beside him, or squeezing his hand in your lap at the bar, he might even have admitted to having occasional daydreams about eventually developing new insights into why his eclectic therapeutic practice was practicable: new insights that, once properly developed and synthesized, would amount to a comprehensive philosophy of human psychology: a comprehensive philosophy of human psychology about which he'd write a book—maybe more than one book—and thereby leave his mark upon the world. That would really be something, he thought. Something good. That would make for a good kind of life. Even, perhaps, a meaningful life.

But then, final quarter, there arose, as mentioned earlier, some scheduling problems, and he enrolled in Introduction to Behaviorism.

After taking attendance on the first day of class, the winningly portly professor, Nathan Booth, filled his capacious cheeks with air, widened his already wide-eyed eyes, then loudly, though gradually, deflated his face, and told Jennifer Ferris—all-star protégée of SSA's Family Systems guru, Sally Ruffles, PhD—that she wasn't on his roster.

Booth apologetically explained that this sort of thing seemed to happen to him all the time, and that, normally, he'd just proceed to teach the class, but that only just yesterday the dean had called a faculty meeting to discuss class rosters as they related to liability insurance: apparently, if a student who wasn't supposed to be in a classroom—i.e. a student who wasn't on the class roster—were to suffer any kind of injury while they were in that classroom, the school's liability insurance wouldn't cover it. And Booth said he suspected that this could not be true. He said that the dean, brilliant as she most certainly was, must have misread some clause in the insurance policy, but the dean was the dean, and the dean was the boss, and so, in short, he was hoping that someone would please volunteer to go down to the office and get him an updated roster: one he was all but certain Jennifer Ferris's name would appear on.

He promised not to start teaching until the volunteer was back, mumbled something borderline incoherent about using the next few minutes to better set up the PowerPoint presentation that would accompany his lecture, then passed out the syllabus, which itself contained a rather glaring error: a five-line string of letters, numbers, and special characters that one couldn't help but wonder how Booth could have missed. Unless maybe he hadn't, Apter thought. Missed it, that is. Maybe, Apter thought, Booth had noticed the error only after he'd already printed all the syllabi, had determined that it didn't interfere with the information the syllabi contained (which it didn't; the string of characters was down in the footer, out of the way), and had thought it better not to waste a bunch of paper reprinting, even if the error would make him appear a little sloppy.

As one would expect, it was Jennifer Ferris, herself, who volunteered to go to the office for the updated roster.

Once Jennifer had closed the door behind her, Booth addressed the class again.

"I've engaged in a bit of deception here," he said. "Jennifer Ferris is, in fact, on my roster. Also, my PowerPoint presentation is entirely set up—and it's *great,* you're gonna love it.

"But many of you are hostile to Behaviorism. Most people are. And that's okay—for the time being, it's okay. We'll talk about that hostility a little later. For now, though, I want to ask that you allow me to provide you a demonstration of operant conditioning's efficacy. In order to do that, I'll need to count on your not blowing my little deception. I'll need you, when Jennifer returns, not to mention anything I've just said or will have said before she returns. Can I count on you? I promise no one will be harmed in any way."

The class assented, a little bit excited, a little creeped out.

"Great," Booth said. "So how many of you have spent time with Jennifer, in class or out?"

Five or six students raised their hands, Apter among them.

"Have you ever seen her do this?" asked Booth, and, as if to halt a sneeze, or signify *mustache,* he pressed to his philtrum the middle knuckle of his right hand's straightened index finger.

None of them had ever seen Jennifer do that.

"Anything like that?"

No. No one had seen Jennifer do anything like that.

"Good," Booth said. "So this is what's going to happen. By the time we take our mid-period break, Jennifer Ferris will be giving herself a fingerstache with the index finger of—do you care which hand? Do you have a preference?"

Silence.

"I'm asking," Booth said.

"The left," Apter said.

"The left, then," said Booth. "Jennifer will, before the break, be wearing a left-handed fingerstache. She will do that because I, while I deliver my opening lecture, will condition her to do that. After the break I'll explain how I did it—how I shaped that behavior. You should feel free to watch me as closely as you like, but please don't, you know, *stare* at Jennifer. Staring probably wouldn't change the outcome, but it could make the whole thing weirder for her than it needs to be."

Within seventy minutes of her return to the classroom—with a few minutes yet to go before the break—Jennifer Ferris wore a left-handed fingerstache.

Apter, as asked, hadn't stared at her—he'd only thrown quick glances—but he'd kept a pretty close eye on Booth, who frequently smiled in Jennifer's direction, and he concluded the entire thing was a ruse, concluded that Jennifer was Booth's confederate. Concluded that Booth had chosen her to be his confederate because she, known protégée of Family Systems guru Sally Ruffles, would seem to the others the least likely member of the class to play the part of a Behaviorist's confederate. Classic snake-oil salesmanship, thought Apter.

What was in it for Jennifer, though? he wondered. Surely Booth wasn't paying her . . .

And all at once, it came clear, or seemed to come clear: Booth had no idea she was a protégée of Sally Ruffles, and when he'd asked her to help him, she'd agreed so that she could undermine him. Yes. That was it. That *had* to be it because: look at her performance. Her performance was garbage. Fidgety and nervous. She was all too aware of being observed. She was unconvincing. So unconvincing that it must have been deliberate. She looked to be on the verge of laughing half the time.

Booth's lecture, on the other hand, was compelling, almost overwhelmingly so. He began by describing some studies. Three of them.

The first study compared the efficacy of variously educated therapists. According to this study, therapists with any kind of graduate degree that led to the professional practice of one-on-one psychotherapy (i.e. PsyDs, PhDs, master's degrees in counseling, master's degrees in social work) were, on average, over the course of six months of once-a-week talk-therapy sessions, equally effective in treating clients who'd been diagnosed with depression and/or anxiety. Therapists whose highest degree was a bachelor's (any social science or humanities bachelor's) were, on average, over the course of six months of once-a-week talk-therapy sessions, 85 percent as effective as the aforementioned in treating clients who'd been diagnosed with depression and/or anxiety. And therapists without any postsecondary education—i.e. therapists who'd gotten no further in their education than graduating high school—were, on average, over the course of six months of once-a-week talk-therapy sessions, 80 percent as effective as the first group (i.e. those with graduate degrees) in treating clients diagnosed with depression and/or anxiety.

"In other words," Booth said, "four out of every five clients whose depression or anxiety is treatable over the course of six months by someone with a professional degree in psychotherapy are just as treatable over the course of six months by someone with a twelfth-grade education.

"In yet other words: you're busting your humps at SSA in order to become, on average, roughly twenty-five percent more effective as clinicians than you would have been the day you graduated high school. But don't get me wrong. I'm not saying that what you've been learning isn't worthwhile. Your undergraduate education and your training here at SSA will, on average, allow you to help twenty percent more people than you would have been able to help had you never had either. That's quite a lot of people. And each person is his own universe. Etcetera.

"Still. We can't ignore the fact that treatment administered by someone without any training is pretty effective. Nor can we ignore that, when we talk about treatment that's administered by someone without any training, we're pretty much obliged to put *treatment* in air quotes, or, better yet, to be more precise and just call it *conversation*.

"*Talking*.

"Two people sitting in a room together, talking.

"And so one question that arises is: How is it that two people, sitting in a room together, talking, alleviates suffering? How is it that, by way of talking with someone, an anxious person's anxiety can be alleviated? How is it that, by way of talking with someone, a depressed person's depression can be alleviated? How does that happen? What do you think?"

"Through empathy," someone offered. "Through the feeling of empathy on the part of the listener, and that empathy's conveyance to the speaker."

"Okay," Booth said. "Can we define that? *Empathy?*"

"An understanding of another person's feelings," one student said. "A *sharing* of another person's feelings," another student said. "Well, kinda both of those things," a third student said. "Both of those things at once. An understanding *and* a sharing. A sharing of the understanding."

"All right," Booth said. "Okay. All right. And how is the *understanding* and/or *sharing* of another's feelings *conveyed*?"

"Through words. Rephrasing." "Through mirroring facial expressions and posture." "Through timely eye contact." "Tone of voice." "All of those things in varying amounts."

"What words?" Booth said. "Rephrase how? Which tone of voice? What exactly is timely—or, for that matter, *un*timely—eye contact?"

"It depends on the feeling." "Depends on the person." "Depends on the relationship between the two people." "Their relative levels of intelligence." "Their affection for each other." "Their rapport." "Their cultural backgrounds."

Booth stood quietly for nearly a minute, waiting for more, twice flashing what seemed to Apter a rather *private*-seeming smile at Jennifer Ferris.

"There are no simple answers," someone finally offered. "Helping isn't really a science—it's an art," offered somebody else. "Well, it's both," said the student who'd said empathy was both an understanding and a sharing of feelings. "It's not just an art," that student elaborated, "and it's not just a science. It's an art *and* a science. There are different techniques. It's hard to sum them up—that's true. We see your point. There are different techniques, and that's where the science is, in figuring out how and when it's best to apply which one. But *all* of them involve conveying empathy. And that's where the art is. That's . . ."

"All right," Booth said. "All right. Okay. So what I'm hearing, here, is that we don't possess a clear, consensus definition of empathy. Nor are we clear on how empathy, however we might choose to define it, gets conveyed from one person to another."

"Well, but another way it's like art," said the *both* guy, "is you know it when you see it."

"Sure," Booth said. "You know it when you see it. Like art. I like that. Okay. Like art. Or, for that matter, like pornography. But let's table this part of the conversation for now because, here's the thing, and, I'll admit, it's a little cheap of me, rhetorically, not to have brought this up earlier—tricky, even. Of me. I did a tricky thing. I left out an important aspect of the study. An important finding. With all my handsome, fast-talking charm, I was able to get you to forget about the control group in the study we're looking at. Perhaps I led you to believe that the group who received therapy from those without postsecondary education was the control group. You're not a bunch of laboratory scientists, you're young social workers, idealistic and trusting, just looking to help, and here I am, your teacher, ostensibly trying to help you become better at helping by telling you about a study, and you saw no reason to suspect me of engaging in rhetorical stunts to bash home what I imagine will seem, to some of you, a cruel, and perhaps, objectionable point. I took advantage of your wide-eyed, do-gooding innocence. That was shady of me. I apologize for that.

"But what I'm trying to say is that the part I left out is that the control group in this study was a group that received *no* treatment for six months. And it turned out that receiving *no* treatment—that is to say: just sitting in a room, alone, for fifty minutes a week for six months—was shown by the study to be seventy-seven percent as effective in treating anxiety and depression as was receiving therapy from those with graduate degrees.

"Now what do we do with that?" Booth asked the class. "What does that tell us?"

Another long silence. Not, perhaps, as long as the first, but definitely more hostile. Sneers. Twisted lips. Heavy nasal exhalations.

"Time heals all wounds?" Apter offered, skeptical.

"Okay. Sort of. Maybe. Kinda? Let's say time heals *many* of the *most common* psychic wounds, *much* of the time," Booth said. "Or, more precisely: in about seventy-seven percent of all cases, six months spent without any intervention is as effective in treating depression and anxiety as six months spent in once-a-week therapy with a trained professional."

"But the other twenty-three . . ." Apter said.

"They are very important, each person a universe unto and so on and so forth," said Booth, "and we'll get to them in a moment. For now, though, the point I'd like to make is this: in at least seventy-seven percent of all cases, if you can't help your client get better in fewer than six months, you've wasted their time and, if they're paying for treatment, you've wasted their money.

"Now, I want you to think about the implications—"

"Well, except what about relapse?" Apter said.

"Hey, all right then," Booth said, clapping his hands together, once. "Someone here is on the ball. That is such the right question to ask," Booth said.

"That is such the right question to ask," Booth said, "that if I were a member of this class and didn't know any better, I'd think that you and I were confederates, that we'd gotten together in some dimly lit, smoke-filled backroom or something and worked out a little call-and-response routine. You've really teed it up for me. Thank you. I mean it.

"So. What. About. *Relapse?* How much more frequently do previously abolished symptoms of our most widespread mental illnesses recur in those who've undergone no therapy than they recur in those who've undergone therapy with a professional? We've got a second study here that examines that very question. The answer, which, judging by the, uh, *vibe,* pervading the room, you're not gonna like—the answer is: *less* frequently. At least over the course of five years.

"And now some of you look a little confused. I'll say what I just said a second time in different words: according to this very large, extremely reliable study, relapse occurs less frequently over the course of the five years following six months of *no* treatment than it does over the course of the five years following six months of treatment by a professional."

"You're saying therapy does more harm than good?" Apter said.

"No," Booth said. "No. If I believed that, I wouldn't be a therapist, let alone a teacher of therapists. First, there's still that other twenty-three percent for whom therapy's more effective than no therapy, and, second, I've once again left out some important information. Have a guess at what that information is?"

"The various kinds of therapy," Apter said.

"Jesus Christ," Booth said. "You want to teach this class? *Yes.* We've so far been looking at studies that examine the efficacy of psychotherapy only according to the varying levels of education of the practitioners. When we subdivide by *approach*—when we get into practitioner methodology, as this *third* study does—this third study, which analyzes the data from the first two studies—the numbers become more complex. They start to tell a different tale."

"According to this third study," Booth continued, "relapse is fifty percent *less* frequent in those who undergo Behavioral therapy than it is in those who undergo no therapy, it is thirty percent less frequent in those who undergo Behavioral therapy than in those who undergo psychodynamic therapy, and it is sixty percent less frequent in those who undergo Behavioral therapy than in those who undergo *Cognitive* Behavioral therapy.

"Can anyone deduce what this third study's findings indicate about the first two studies' . . . *flaws?* And yes, I do realize that most of you are taking this class because it was the only one that fit your schedule that *wasn't* Advanced Stats—that's okay. Let's speak like laypeople."

"The third study suggests," Apter said, "that the first two studies' numbers are skewed by the preponderance of Cognitive Behavioral therapists. You're saying that, among those in the therapy group, far more of them underwent Cognitive Behavioral therapy than Psychodynamic or Behavioral therapy. All three therapies were lumped together for the studies, but they shouldn't have been."

"Should shouldn't, shmould shmouldn't, but yes, pretty much," Booth said. "Yes! And what that adds up to is this: CBT, currently our country's—or at least our country's insurance companies'—most favored form of treatment for our country's most commonly diagnosed mental illnesses is, arguably, as Mr. Schutz put it earlier, doing more harm than good.

"Psychodynamic therapy, on the other hand, would seem to do no harm, and, perhaps even to provide a small, which is not to say a *negligible*, advantage to those diagnosed with our country's most common mental illnesses.

"As for Behavioral therapy, currently the least frequently practiced of the three approaches, it—how should I put this?" Booth said, looking at Jennifer Ferris for just a moment long enough to cue the rest of the class to look at Jennifer Ferris, who was wearing a left-handed fingerstache. "It just . . ."

"It works a lot better," Apter said.

"This guy," said Booth. "What a teacher's pet. Let's take us a smoke break. Back in fifteen. Jennifer—can I talk to you a minute?"

After the break, Jennifer was gone, as were eight of the other students, each opting to enroll in Advanced Stats after all.

Booth seemed unfazed, cheerful even. "Let's get in closer," he said to the seven who'd returned to the classroom.

As they all began to rearrange the tables, Booth's leather briefcase came into view. It was open on the chair beside the one that Booth himself had formerly occupied, and Apter couldn't help but see inside it.

Apter couldn't help but see that inside it was a hardcover copy of *Damage, The End,* Solomon Gladman's debut novel.

"All right," Booth said, sitting back down. "Now I'll teach you how I did my divisive little parlor trick."

—

It was simple, really. Which was not to say *easy*. But it was almost too simple to believe. What Booth had done to get Jennifer Ferris to perform the left-handed fingerstaching behavior was pay to her what he referred to, at first, as "benevolent attention, in timely increments."

"*Pay benevolent attention*, though," he said, "is a lot of syllables, especially considering that half those syllables are uttered in the service of the adjective, another three-eighths in the service of the noun, and the thing to focus on here is the verb. *Pay*. So let's ditch it—*pay benevolent attention*—let's ditch the whole phrase and replace it with *smile. Smile's* not entirely accurate either, but maybe it's close enough: it's certainly fewer syllables, and it's certainly a verb, so the focus is right, plus I did do a lot of smiling at Jennifer, a lot of smiling with the mouth, the eyes, sometimes both. Then again, *smiling* only describes some of what I did with my face to get her to perform the left-handed fingerstaching behavior. Sometimes I just looked at her in a *curious* or *fascinated* way. Sometimes I looked at her in a way that communicated to her that her high level of engagement with the lecture I was giving—*her* high level of engagement *in particular*—was of special importance to me . . . Enough about this. Let's settle this. Let's say I showed her *goodface*. Better yet, let's say I *goodfaced* at her. Yes.

"I kept a close eye on Jennifer while I was giving my lecture, and, to get Jennifer to perform the left-handed fingerstaching behavior, I goodfaced at her whenever she came closer to doing so.

"Initially, she was sitting with both her feet on the floor, her left hand in her lap. With her right hand, she was writing in a notebook. The first couple minutes of the lecture, I would goodface at her whenever I saw the left side of her body move in any way.

"Soon enough, the left side of her body began to move more dramatically, and at a higher frequency. Her left leg, for example, would cross her lap, uncross her lap, recross her lap. As you know, the target behavior—the fingerstaching—didn't involve her left leg at all, so I lowered both the frequency and the intensity with which I goodfaced at her until her left hand began to move, until it came into view: until her left elbow was resting on the table.

"At that point, I goodfaced at her for a longer period of time than I previously had—maybe half a second or so, I don't know, but for longer than I'd goodfaced at her in a number of minutes.

"Next thing was to get her to bring that left hand to her face. So I goodfaced at her whenever her left hand got nearer to her face . . .

"Now, I could blow-by-blow this for you all the way to the end, but I think—I hope—you get the idea. As Jennifer, in increments, came closer to performing the target behavior—the fingerstaching behavior—I positively reinforced that behavior by goodfacing at her. When, at last, she performed the fingerstaching behavior, I goodfaced even more intensely than I previously had, and, for about five-six minutes, I did so at a frequency that was, relative to my previous goodfacing frequency, higher. By then, I had another five-six minutes to go before the break, and I wanted Jennifer to continue to perform the fingerstaching behavior up until the break, but I didn't want her to get creeped out, you know? By all my goodfacing? I didn't want to make her feel uncomfortable. So I tapered off. I kept the intensity high, but I lowered the frequency. As you saw, it all worked out. When it came time to take our break, she was still wearing that left-handed fingerstache.

"So now you know *how* I did my parlor trick. Why did it work, though?

"Well, my goodfacing was what we call the positive reinforcer: the consequence that Jennifer sought to engender. *Sought* in scare quotes. She *sought* that consequence—sought my goodfacing—because in this context, the context of a classroom, the professor possesses the most power, and we humans seek power, we seek to be in the good graces of the powerful—seeking power is a social, if not a biological imperative, a *reflex* even (and we can argue about the degree to which it's useful to distinguish the social from the biological later on this quarter, as well as the degree to which it's useful to distinguish a reflex from any other kind of behavior)—and my goodfacing signaled to Jennifer that she was in my good graces, that she was thereby acquiring, or approaching the acquisition of some power.

"Of course, she wasn't entirely aware of what she was doing with her body—with her arm or wrist or fingers. From where she was sitting, it just seemed like I really enjoyed how attentive she was being. It seemed to her as though her being attentive to me—her keeping her eyes on me, and thereby signaling attentiveness—was what was causing me to goodface at her. And so she kept her eyes on me.

"You see, Jennifer believed she was shaping *my* behavior. And she was. Of course she was. As I've already described, the frequency and intensity of my goodfacing were controlled by *her* behavior, by what *she* was doing with *her* body. So she was, in fact, shaping my behavior. We were shaping *one another's* behavior. She just didn't quite apprehend *how* she was doing it, whereas I did.

"During the break, I told Jennifer about the deception with the roster, then explained to her what I just explained to you regarding the finger-staching, and she decided this class wasn't for her. Which I understand.

"She felt manipulated. She *had been* manipulated. And no one likes to feel like they're being manipulated. No one likes to feel as though their behavior is under the control of anything other than themselves, let alone under the control of another person.

"And although I do, as I said, understand that—and I imagine you all understand it, too—I can't say that I believe it's justified. It hasn't seemed justified to me in years—not since before I began to study Behaviorism, which can't help but cause anyone who studies it to face the fact that, whether we're aware of it or not, we are all shaping one another's behavior all the time—we couldn't stop if we tried—and so we are all shaped by one another's behavior all the time.

"And I mean *all* the time. Even when we're alone.

"Even when we are not among others, the historical shaping of our behavior by others shapes our behavior.

"And it isn't just others who shape it, either. It's everything in our immediate contexts, and every context in which we have ever been.

"Others are only a *part* of our contexts.

"Our behavior is governed by our contexts: our immediate context and our historical contexts. (That's historical with a lower-case *h*, by the way: our *historical contexts* are the immediate contexts in which we have historically been.)

"Furthermore, if we agree to include, under the rubric of *context*, our genetic predispositions and basic biological imperatives—to consume nutrients, to sleep, to breathe air, to remain hydrated, and, yes, to be social—then it can safely be said that we are governed *exclusively* by our contexts.

"That is Behaviorism. We are as we do, and everything we do is shaped by context, and everything we do shapes our context.

"We are as we do.

"Are we ever more than that? Are we ever more than *as we do*? Well . . . I like to think so. In fact, every last person I know—Behaviorist or otherwise—every last person I know likes to think so. We all have a sense of our own interiority, and except, perhaps, for certain very little children and very troubled adults, we all have a sense that others possess an interiority not much different, at base, from our own. We all have a sense that this interiority is the place from which our *will* emanates. We all have the sense that our will comes from within us, and that, at least to some degree, we do what we do in accordance with our will. That seems meaningful, doesn't it? That we all have that sense? That even those of us, like me, who, *on paper,* believe free will is an illusion, possess *the sense* that we have free will? It seems *deeply* meaningful. More than that, it seems unshakable, *undispossessible,* this sense of having a free will, this sense that we do what we do because we choose to do it.

"Even if we posit (not unreasonably!) that thinking is itself a behavior—even if we posit that *being conscious* is but a bodily function, like breathing, or growing hair or growing fingernails—we can't shake *the sense* that it's something more, something *better*. We can't shake the sense that being conscious enables free will. We can't shake the sense that we freely choose. We can't any more easily shake the sense that we freely choose than we could shake the sense that we need to breathe.

"Have any of you ever held your breath until you passed out?"

No one raised a hand.

"Well, I used to do that. I would hold my breath until I passed out. I don't know why. I don't remember. I don't recall the reasons I told myself I had for holding my breath until I passed out. Did I resent the sense that I needed to breathe? that I *needed* to *anything*? Maybe. That's a nice little story. A punk rock story. Makes me sound kind of cool. That part of the story isn't important, though. It has nothing to do with the point I'm trying to make. What's important is that, for a couple of months when I was six years old, I would hold my breath until I passed out, and, every single time, after I'd passed out, I came to gasping. Gasping for breath I indubitably *needed*. And what I'm saying is that the sense that we possess free will—the sense that our interiority, rather than our context, controls our behavior—is like *that,* I think. We can try to ignore it, we can argue it away, perhaps even *convincingly* deny its existence for a moment or two, but it always comes back—it's part of being a person.

"As is possessing the sense—no less shakable; at least not so long as we stand on this planet—that Earth is flat.

"But all of that to say that Behaviorism does *not* deny the existence of interiority. What Behaviorism denies is that interiority can be examined empirically. It denies the possibility of a *science* of interiority. Behaviorism leaves interiority alone. It concerns itself with the interaction between observable behavior and context. Maybe write that down, if you haven't already.

"Now let's pause for a moment to take a good look at Michael Bonaventure here."

Michael Bonaventure, seated to the professor's right, shrugged a couple times under everyone's gaze. The shrug caused a few of the students to laugh, partly because Michael, despite his somewhat prematurely gray hair (he was thirty-four) possessed the benevolently smirking mien of a beloved grade-school cutup, but also because, owing to the way that Michael was sitting—his back flat against that of the chair, both hands on his waist such that each of his arms was bent to form a triangle with his torso—the shrugging itself looked funny, almost like he was trying to flap his wing stumps or something.

"All right, so now," Booth said, "I want you all to take a look at the first page of your syllabus—at the bottom of that page where those lines of what look to be random printer-error noise are. They're no error, those lines. I hid a message in there. I want you to write down every fourth character, unless that character is a caret. If it's a caret, that's a space."

The text to which Booth referred looked like this:

```
J7!SK7CT6!FUHBXD+RWE/?MNBBBTQ@
A^88=SNNNEX)(AIF4T8&#EUU9D:"8^YH%T874OXC2
^*Y&M=QPYKKB^9$ARDV5IBBBGE3#H71HTFFF:~']^.
<9E55TRKN6EP0!C&&NTBV%^%%%PTS+OUVHSWER
TP44U945RB$4E11=,#%*^WMDHRXPA666N678D6HUS
$$$^POLOPILNKIN^0(*WR2DA2C3IPOOSB1YT&(9.
```

—

The message it hid was:

STUDENT SEATED TO MY RIGHT: ERECT POSTURE,
HANDS ON WAIST

"In case it doesn't go without saying, I got Michael Bonaventure here to sit in that silly-looking way—no offense, Michael—I got him to sit in that silly-looking way, with erect posture and both his hands on his waist—not at all a very common position to sit in—via the same good-facing means I got Jennifer Ferris to left-handed fingerstache.

"I did so," Booth said, "while telling you all, Michael included, about the ways in which one does such things—about the ways in which I'd just done such a thing with Jennifer Ferris—and the reasons why one is able to do such things. I did so not because I love parlor tricks—although I do love me some parlor tricks—but in the hopes that those of you who may have persisted in thinking Jennifer Ferris was a confederate of mine—if there were any of you who so persisted—I did so in the hopes that you would become convinced that she wasn't. A confederate. One confederate would be one thing, right? But two? I don't know. Seems unlikely to me, given that I'm *not* a magician, but a professor, and you are not my *audience,* but my class of clinical social work students. That is: given certain salient aspects of our immediate context.

"If you *are* someone who persists in believing I've been dishonest about these two instances of behavioral shaping, however, I urge you to drop the class. There's no time for more tricks. If, however, you believe I've been honest, but are worried that our class is going to be *about* parlor-tricking clients into fingerstaching themselves and/or grasping their waists, please don't drop the class: there's no need to worry about that. I performed those parlor tricks only to demonstrate to you the all-encompassing power of context over behavior.

"I'm here to help you help your clients more effectively. I'm here to help you help them to not be depressed, to not be anxious, to be rid of phobias.

"As I've said a couple of times already: we are as we do. Which also means: we are not as we don't. Thus, those who are depressed are, simply, those who engage in depressive behavior. Those who are not depressed are, no less simply, those who do not engage in depressive behavior. Those who are anxious are those who engage in anxious behavior. Those who are not anxious do not engage in anxious behavior. And those who are phobic are those who engage in phobic behavior. And those who are not phobic are, of course, those who do not engage in phobic behavior.

"So what I'm going to teach you this quarter is how to properly operationalize those behaviors in your clients—those depressive and anxious and phobic behaviors—and I'm going to teach you how to extinguish those behaviors in your clients, after which your clients will no longer be depressed or anxious or phobic.

"And that's all for today. Readings for next week are listed on the syllabus."

Apter downed a small coffee in the cafeteria, then went to Booth's office in the SSA basement and rapped on the doorframe. The professor, at his desk, before an open laptop, said, "Apter Schutz," and, with a both-handed, spread-fingered *ta-da!* kind of gesture, urged Apter to sit in the facing chair. "Apter Schutz," he said again, once Apter'd settled in. "What'll it be then? Encourage or discourage?"

"Excuse me?" Apter said.

"You're my last remaining second-year. You're in your last quarter. What you learned in class today *spoke* to you, yet your approach to the practice of therapy is what the kids these days like to call *eclectic.* Did you come here in the hope that I'd encourage you to do the hard thing, unlearn the false premises, walk the straight and narrow path of capital-S Science, and become a Behaviorist practitioner? Or did you come here hoping that, by the time you left here, you'd be convinced it was too late to change your eclectic ways, despite having just realized, once and for all, that those eclectic ways were intellectually, scientifically, and probably even *ethically* bankrupt?"

"How do you know my approach is eclectic?" said Apter.

"Deduction," Booth said. He turned his laptop around on the blotter. On the screen was the section of Apter's transcript that listed all the classes he'd taken.

"You were looking me up."

"I was curious. And your transcript, frankly, has made me even *more* curious, since I figured you for a Cognitive Behavioral guy. Historically, the very few second-years who I've, uh, *converted*—they were disgruntled CBTs. I mean, I've shaken up a couple-three disgruntled Family Systems devotees, true, yet never have I closed one, and the Psychodynamic second-years always drop by the end of class one. But the eclectics? Not *once* has an eclectic stuck around past the break."

"Why is that, you think?"

"There's no way to answer that question without sounding like I'm insulting you sideways, and that's the last thing I want to do here, Mr. Schutz."

"I'm pretty thick-skinned."

"Well, in that case . . ." said Booth. "In that case, I'll just say that there's a *reason* that none of those studies we looked at in class today concerned themselves with measuring the efficacy of the *eclectic* approach to therapy."

"Which is?"

"Because it's not an approach to therapy. It's an approach to entry-level management consultancy, so-called *life coaching*, or, I don't know—maybe if you're possessed of a certain type of gleamy-eyed magnetism—cult leadership."

"I see."

"So if you're planning to be a therapist, I wholeheartedly encourage your interest in Behaviorism. You ask the right questions. I suspect you've got the stuff. That's the short of it."

"Well, I'm flattered," Apter said.

"You should be," Booth said. "Or maybe it's more polite to say, 'I'm flattered *you're* flattered.'"

"I didn't really come here to talk about Behaviorism or therapy, though," Apter said. "I mean, I'm gonna go home, look more closely at the studies you showed us, and see if I can poke any holes in them, figure things out for myself, you know?"

"Good. In fact: great. That's a better answer to my original question than I'd have ever dared imagine. And let me welcome you, in advance, into the fold, for you will poke not a single, solitary hole. Those studies are solid. So what *did* you want to talk about?"

"This might sound silly," Apter said, "but I saw *Damage, The End* in your briefcase, and, I guess, well, a professor of social work reading a book by Gladman is, to me . . . I don't know what it is to me. But I really love that book."

"Be still my beating heart! He's a Gladman fan to boot."

"You know he went here, right?"

"I was one of his teachers."

"How is that possible? You're not . . . old enough."

"Aha, but I am. One great advantage to being, ehem, *plus-size*, you see, is the wrinkles don't show. Not for the most part. I *was* especially young back then, though: I was one of those early bloomers, started Yale at fifteen and so forth, and they hired me while I was still ABD."

"*Fifteen?*"

"Indeed. Don't be too impressed, though. If that kind of thing meant as much as people imagine, I wouldn't feel the need to mention it, right? And mention it, as you've just witnessed, I *have*. Anyway, Sol was in the very first class that I taught here was my point."

"*Sol*—wow. For some reason, I wouldn't think he'd go by Sol."

"He didn't really. Pretty sure I was the only one who called him Sol around here. See, he was young, too. Like you. Maybe a *little* older. Everyone else seemed to call him Gladman. Even the woman he was dating. I think he told me his family called him Solly. But he felt like his youth undermined his authority—in session, I mean. Which, you know, I very much related to, and, at one point—must have been during his second-year placement, though maybe his first—who can remember?— but his supervisor told him that she was going to assign him at least one older or middle-aged married couple before the placement was over, and that made him *especially* nervous about appearing too young, and he came to office hours to talk to me about it. I remember I suggested he try to grow a mustache. That's what I'd done, and it had seemed to help me. Whether it actually masked my youth, or just made it seem to me that it had—it helped. But it didn't work for Sol. It didn't have the chance to work. The whiskers itched him too much or something, and he shaved it off before he ever sat down with the couple. Short of it is, I suggested he go by a different name when he was working—to kind of remake himself a little, think of himself a little differently. Solomon was too . . . Solomon-y, I guess. So he settled on Sol, and I thought I'd try to help him get used to it, so after that, that's what I called him."

"Was he a good clinician?"

"I couldn't say for sure. I never supervised him. He showed me some of his process notes for class assignments, and I was impressed, I remember that. And he was a very warm guy, and, obviously, a great thinker, too, an *organized* thinker, at least when he wanted to be . . . So I imagine he had a talent for therapy. But, you know, as a writer—as a writer, he was stunning. I actually looked forward to reading his papers, which isn't usually the most exciting part of this job. But I'd always save Sol's papers for last. They were *funny*. And his fiction—obviously that was . . . he asked to show it to me at one point, and of course I said yes. A couple of the stories that he let me read later ended up in the collection—have you read the collection?"

"More than once."

"Well, a couple of those. 'Atticus' and an early version of 'Melancholy Sally Drops.' I really love those stories. I wrote him a recommendation letter for the MFA programs he applied to at the end of his time here. A glowing one. I was proud of that letter. I kept a copy. You know, a lot of times when a student ends up deciding against becoming a therapist, which happens a *lot*—the burnout rate is high in social work, even for students—a lot of times you feel like you somehow failed as a teacher, but with Sol, it wasn't like that at all. It would have been a shame, a *terrible* shame, if he'd become a clinician instead of continuing to write. I think that when he started here, he thought he'd be able to do both, excel at both, but by the time he finished, I think he considered it impossible."

"Are you—if you don't mind me asking—are you still in touch with him?"

"I don't mind at all. But alas: no. We used to email occasionally. Once maybe every couple of years or so. It's been a while, now, though. I attended a reading he did for the story collection, and we spent a few minutes catching up afterward, but we didn't seem to have a lot to talk about, really. I think I was somewhat starstruck by him, which was strange for both of us, made us awkward whereas once we'd been chummy—maybe not quite *chummy*, but *easy* in each other's company, you know? It was a little bit sad for me, really, that evening. Then, some years later, when I found out that he was doing comedy, I emailed him, and the address was dead, the email bounced back, so I tried his university address, and received some kind of form letter in response."

"The same thing happened to me when I emailed him," Apter said. "Sucked."

"Don't get me wrong. I didn't hold it against him," Booth said. "I knew he'd been catching a lot of hell. Undergoing a lot of harassment. A few of the admin students here, at one point, were concerned—or at least *claimed* they were concerned (these were some serious busybodies)— that Sol's having gone here might reflect badly on them, or the school— something—and they scrubbed mention of SSA from his Wikipedia page, even went to the dean to tell her they'd done so, hoping for kudos, I guess."

"Whoa."

"Whoa is right. And woe was I. The dean, too. We've had a few pretty terrible years in this country. A few pretty, uh, *stupid* years. Anyway, the dean, to her credit, went on the page and put SSA back in. So . . ."

"So at least there's that."

"Exactly," Booth said.

Apter, straining for something to say, and sensing he'd bummed his professor out a little—he'd certainly bummed himself out a little—and not wanting to leave on a bummer note, removed from his bag a copy of Antic Books' latest offering: a short novel, *The Comer,* by a debut author named Arden Crepe. "Here, take this," he said, and handed Booth the book. "That's hot off the press. I think you might love it. I know I've been loving it."

"You don't seem to have finished it," Booth said, thumbing the bookmark.

"I haven't yet, but I'm far enough along that a *lot* would have to suddenly go wrong to disenchant me."

"Well, I'd love to read it, man, but you should finish it first."

"Oh! I see what you mean. It's okay—I have a box of them at home. My sister's a publisher. It's one of hers. I'm *supposed* to give it away."

"You're sure?"

"Hundred percent."

"Then . . . thank you, Apter. This is really kind of you. I'll read it as soon as I finish this reread of *Damage,* let you know what I think."

That evening, Apter had, as he'd said he would, looked more closely at the studies Booth had discussed in his lecture.

After failing to poke holes in the studies' methodologies, he tried to find some way to interpret the results differently than Booth had: a way that might allow him to maintain a clear conscience about continuing to practice his eclectic approach to therapy. Failing to come up with such an interpretation, he read other comparative studies, a couple of which looked at Family Systems practitioners in addition to practitioners of the other three paradigms, all of which corroborated the findings of the studies that Booth had discussed, and none of which could he puncture or reinterpret.

There were no two ways about it: the Behaviorist approach was demonstrably more reliable and efficient than any other, *especially* in treating anxiety, depression, and phobia. Not only was relapse far less frequent in those who'd been successfully treated with Behavioral therapy, but, whereas other therapies could—and often did—last for years, a Behavioral therapist was frequently able to help his clients overcome their anxiety or depression within just ten to twelve hour-long weekly sessions, and their phobias in even fewer than that.

If the approaches from which he'd been eclectically drawing weren't, themselves, as effective as Behaviorist approaches, how could the amalgamation of that which he'd drawn from them possibly be any better? Well, perhaps it *could,* Apter supposed. It was *possible* the sum was greater than its parts—possible that a number of suboptimal techniques, if he meshed them together right, could sort of holistically *jell* or whatever—but it didn't seem likely.

By the time he fell asleep that night, it seemed to Apter that the only ethical argument in favor of his continuing to practice his eclectic approach was that he hadn't yet been trained in the Behaviorist approach.

Booth emailed Apter the following Sunday in praise of *The Comer.* He compared Arden Crepe's style to Don DeLillo's and Helen Dewitt's, her sense of humor to that of Paul Beatty and Stanley Elkin, the startling yet satisfying ending of the novel to a number of early George Saunders stories. He asked if Apter'd ever read "The Hat Act" by Robert Coover. Apter said he had—it was, in fact, a favorite—and Booth linked him to an essay he'd pseudonymously published in '98 that argued for "The Hat Act" being an exemplary work of Radical Behaviorist literature.

The essay was really . . . *good.* Not just convincing, but a pleasure to read.

Had Apter just found the mentor he hadn't known he'd sought? It seemed he'd just found the mentor he hadn't known he'd sought.

At office hours a couple days later, Booth gave to Apter a gift-wrapped copy of Skinner's *Science and Human Behavior.* Then they went to grab a drink at Jimmy's Woodlawn Tap. Before the third round, Booth offered him a longish list of supplemental readings. Apter accepted, thanked him, and, from that point onward, they talked about the readings over coffee or drinks at least once a week.

—

Three Mondays prior to the end of the quarter, Booth texted to say he wouldn't be able to get to the coffee shop at which he and Apter had planned to meet, but that if Apter could make it to the Chicago Behavior Modification Institute—the clinic at which Booth worked—they could talk there instead.

When Apter arrived, Booth introduced him to the Institute's founder, Arnold Lung.

Lung was a longtime practitioner of Operant Analytic Psychotherapy, the talk-centered Behavioral approach to treatment that Booth most favored: one that Lung himself had helped develop some twenty years earlier (his treatment manual, coauthored with two of the other five supervising psychologists at the Institute, had been on the reading list Booth had given Apter). After nine minutes of conversation—at least two of which were spent engaged in what Apter felt to be somewhat *strained* small talk—Lung offered Apter a six-month internship that would begin that summer.

Though maybe *offered* wasn't quite the right verb.

"You're one of us," Lung said, "and you need to come work here. You'll receive the education and training you're looking for."

"I'm really flattered you think so," Apter said. "Your *Manual of OAP* blew my mind. I'd struggled a lot with some of the Skinner that Nathan had me read—mainly *Verbal Behavior*—and *Manual* not only made sense of it for me, but really convinced me to embrace it."

"Well, *I'm* flattered, Apter. Thank you. OAP, for the most part, is our focus here. It's the approach you'd be trained in, the approach you'd practice with the clients you're assigned, but, no less importantly than that, you'd help us develop and refine it further. OAP has evolved some since the manual was published, will continue to evolve, and, from what Nathan tells me, and from what I see before me, you're someone who can help us speed that evolution."

What exactly did Lung see before him? Whatever it was, Apter wanted to see it for himself. He didn't think it would be very cool to ask the question, though. Thought it might lower Lung's estimation of him. Plus he felt a little unmanned and embarrassed—disproportionately so, he'd later reflect—for having pronounced *OAP* as *Oh Ay Pee* all this time, whereas Lung, the first and final authority on all and anything OAP, spoke it like *hope* without the *h*.

"This is all kind of overwhelming," Apter said. "Can I have a little time to think about your offer?"

"A little time? Sure thing," Lung said. "And just so you know: if you accept the offer, you'll be the first social worker who'll ever have held this internship. More than fifty psych ABDs applied this year, and I've whittled the list down to four finalists, flew each of them in for interviews last week—flew them in from Yale, Oxford, Stanford, and Cornell. I told them I'd make a decision by the end of *today,* and I intend to. In other words," Lung said, grinning a little, "you can take all the time you need to think about the offer, just as long as you give me an answer before you leave the building."

"I *am* a sucker for the soft sell," said Apter.

"Am I getting this wrong," Lung asked Booth, "or did your student just sarcastically balk at my offer?"

"I don't think he so much sarcastically balked as archly parried," Booth said to Lung.

"*Parried,* you say," Lung said to Booth.

"I think he thinks he should take a few beats to consider the offer, or to appear to be considering the offer."

"How many beats does he want?" Lung said.

"Hard to tell, really, but I'm thinking you should probably make some more sounds."

"More sounds," Lung said, and turned again to Apter. "Okay. So here goes: This isn't usually how we do it. And I *could* give you till the end of the week to decide. I *will* if you tell me that's what you need, but I'd be shocked if you don't know what your answer is already, I'd give ten-to-one odds your answer's yes, a-hundred-to-one that, whatever your answer is, it will not change by the end of the week, and a-thousand-to-one that you will eventually regret it if you don't accept, plus I really would like to get back to the other candidates before the day's out. Having to deliver bad news to earnest young people—I hate that hanging over my head. It's a price I'm willing to pay if need be, but like Bartleby said. Plus *you,* I'd imagine, would prefer to celebrate joining us sooner rather than later—and who wouldn't, life being short as it is? In sum: if you were to accept right now, we'd both come out ahead, and, down the line, we'd like each other better for it, we two decisive men. Now," Lung said, again turning to Booth, "I can make some more sounds if you think he needs me to, but . . ."

"Those were some pretty good sounds, boss," said Booth. "Look at that face. He's about to accept."

Booth wasn't wrong.

They all shook each other's hands, then details were sorted—dates, times, and pay—and they shook each other's hands again.

Walking Apter out to his car, Booth asked him, "So where you gonna take that lovely friend of yours to celebrate?"

Was it indicative of anything that Apter, before he was able to make sense of the question, briefly struggled to recall having introduced Sylvie Klein to Booth? that it took him, in other words, a fraction of a second to understand that the "lovely friend" to whom Booth referred was not Sylvie Klein, but Lindsay Biss, who Booth had briefly met through the window of her car, a few evenings before, when she'd come to pick Apter up from Jimmy's? or that, in the wake of that fraction of a second, some change in Apter's face or pace or posture caused Booth to say, "Shit, I didn't mean to be nosy. I just thought . . . ?"

On later reflection: yes. Indicative.

At the time, however, Apter didn't sweat it.

"Oh no, man. No. Not nosy at all," he said to Booth. "I just hadn't thought about it. This all happened so fast, I'm still convincing myself it's real."

"It'll feel more real after you celebrate. Like all the best things. Go somewhere special."

"I should," Apter said. "You're right. I will."

Somewhere special. It didn't take him long to figure out where. Before even pulling out of the Institute parking lot, he'd booked a pair of stools at MumbletyPeg.

He hadn't been back since his original visit, and he thought it would be perfect to celebrate the internship in the place where he'd decided to become a therapist. He might even, he thought, convey to Floyd the barman the portions of Anecdote 4 in which he'd played a role. "Craziest of all," Apter imagined he might close his imagined monologue by saying, "is that I didn't—and still don't—actually remember your suggesting that I become a therapist. So, as surprised as you probably are to learn, today, that, three years ago, you said something in passing that determined the trajectory of some random patron's life, I—that random patron, himself—was, three years ago, at least as surprised to learn the same thing. Here's to you, Floyd!"

MumbletyPeg, in those intervening years, had become world-famous, and the prices had, accordingly, risen: to reserve two stools for as many hours (he would've booked a third hour, maybe even a fourth, but only two were available), Apter'd had to drop $400.

This was actually a good thing, though.

He and Lindsay's two-year anniversary (the anniversary marking their original hookup; they'd been exclusive for more like a year and a half) had come and gone a month or so earlier without enough fanfare, according to Lindsay, who might have had a point.

For their first anniversary, Apter'd given her a puppy, a black Labrador Retriever, then taken her out to dinner at Schwa. For their second, however, although they'd eaten at Alinea, he'd only bought her a year of twice-weekly private yoga instruction from a person named Ditmar. Private yoga with Ditmar was, to be sure, something Lindsay had wanted since well before Apter had even met her, and was not, by any means, inexpensive—it had cost around eight times as much as the dog—but it wasn't exactly romantic. To make matters worse, his presentation of the gift had been ill-conceived. Between their courses of yam steam and ribeye pebbles, he passed Lindsay Ditmar's service contract—which was twelve pages long—in an eight-by-ten manila.

As she weighed it in her hand, thoughts played across her face, a little stagily perhaps. Apter knew not which thoughts, but they appeared to be good ones.

Then she freed the contract from the envelope, started looking it over, nodding to herself.

"The short of it," Apter said, "is that I got you the platinum deal, which means you're entitled to unlimited reschedulings for up to twelve hours before any session. It also entitles you to unlimited drop-ins on any of Ditmar's regular classes at the studio, and a biweekly—What's up?"

Though she'd continued to nod, the nodding had slowed, and her face had become . . . her face was crumpling. It was pinched and crumply.

"Lindsay?"

"Frankly, I'm a little disappointed here," she said.

"*Frankly?*" Apter said—he was a little bit drunk.

"This is less than what I hoped for."

"Less?" Apter said. "It's like multiple Bertrams." Bertram was her Lab's name. "Eight of them," he said. "Almost nine, in fact. Nine Bertrams, you're saying, is less than—"

"You dick," she said. "I'm not talking about the price. Who cares about the price? You're rich as God. We've been together two years . . . but it's like we . . . I thought this was . . . I don't know," she said. "I guess I thought this was a lease."

"A lease? Well, I mean, it's kind of a—"

"A lease on an apartment, Apter. Not a yogi."

"No," he said. "I know. I knew what you meant. I'm an idiot. I see that. Two-year anniversary, oversized envelope, certain hinty remarks you've made in the last few months . . . I'm a total fucking moron. We should talk about this, shouldn't we? About getting a place?"

"We definitely should *not*," she said. "Now's not the time. I'm annoyed with you, and you're feeling guilty."

"But that's exactly why—"

"In fact," she said, "we're never going to talk about this. I love you very much, but something's awfully wrong here. You either lack the emotional IQ I used to think you had in spades, or you've gotten less sweet on me or—"

"Maybe you've gotten less sweet on me."

"Yeah. Maybe," she said. "I don't think so, but sure: I guess anything's possible. *Something* is off, though. We aren't properly arcing as a couple. Our narrative is flattening. Our story's feeling stale. We are missing the benchmarks. We just missed a major one."

Missed relationship benchmarks (major and—so, presumably—minor the both). Emotional IQ. Flattening narrative. Improper arcing. Apter found these concepts wanting. Found himself struggling not to quibble aloud with them. Suppressing his desire to ask Lindsay to clarify them: to challenge her, in so many words, to functionally operationalize her terminology.

He showed her his listening face and, soon enough, started listening again.

". . . [Y]ou the benefit of the doubt," she was saying. "I'm going to assume that I was wrong about you way back at the beginning. I'm going to assume we're still sweet on each other and the something that's off, here, the something that's getting in the way of our happiness together is your low emotional IQ and my failure to recognize it till now, and I'm going to try to do what those couples therapy manuals of yours all seem to suggest: I'm going to explain where I stand in as *concrete* a manner as I can manage. So here it is:

"Soon—I don't know exactly when—soon we're going to decide whether to spend the rest of our lives together. We're not going to have some big conversation about it. It's nothing worth really discussing, in the end. We either want it or we don't. I know where I stand, and you *must* by now know where I stand, but I don't know where *you* stand, and I'm not sure you know that either. You have to figure it out. So, as I said, *soon*—and I can't say when because I do not know, and even if I did know . . . but *soon,* Apter, *soon,* you're going to have to make a decision, and if you make the decision I hope you'll make, you are going to have to—and in no small part owing, by the way, to this totally fucking tone-deaf envelope I'm holding, and this completely unfortunate monologue I'm giving *because* I'm holding it, this stupid fucking envelope—you're going to have to demonstrate to me that that decision is *yours. Your choice.* A choice you would have made regardless of whether or not you were about to lose me. You're going to have to go big. You're going to have to go big or go home. I have a great career, Apter. I have a great family, I have great friends, I am in great health, and you, till recently, have been nothing short of great for me, but the thing about that is: I don't need a *great* partner, Apter. I need *the best* partner."

Were this scene, Apter'd thought, to be described in a Solly Gladman routine, whatever he next said to Lindsay Biss would almost certainly feature a sideways comment/joke about the impact of certain Trumpian rhetorical devices on romantic discourse in the year 2019.

And he disliked himself a lot for even having had this thought. And he felt a little guilty—not a lot, but a little—for noticing how sexy Lindsay Biss was, all flooded with emotion.

What he said to her was this: "I think what's been happening is, you know, this whole paradigm shift I've been experiencing, as a therapist, is . . . Well, that doesn't matter, actually. You don't need to hear reasons. That's the point. Basically, all I want to ask is that you give me just a little more time—I'll be finished with school in a couple of months, and my head will clear up, I'm sure that it will—and I will sweep you just *way the hell* off your feet. All right? It'll be something. I promise. It'll be . . . huge."

Because Apter was, as had said Lindsay, *rich as God,* a semi-spontaneous evening at MumbletyPeg, despite the price of drinking there, didn't really qualify as *huge,* but it was, after all, still pretty fucking nice there, MumbletyPeg, and, considering the timing—Apter still had a few weeks of school to go, and Lindsay, given what he'd told her on their second anniversary, would not be expecting any hugeness whatsoever this soon—MumbletyPeg was just the right kind of place in which to gesture at hugeness. Just the right kind of place in which to hand her another eight-by-ten manila, one fat with printouts of desirable luxury apartment listings the real estate broker with whom he'd lately been covertly consulting had been forwarding to him for the last couple weeks.

Floyd, it turned out, wasn't tending bar that night. He was out of the country. His first vacation in nearly five years, according to the bar-maid. A first-class, seven-day-and-night stay at a chateau in Cognac paid for by the Louis Vuitton Moët Hennessy Conglomerate: a gift made to him in gratitude, the barmaid reported, for his having granted them permission to post his recipes (along with his byline) for the Triple-Oh-Seven and the Mad Billy Wallace (MumbletyPeg's spin on the Vodka Martini and the Rob Roy, respectively) on their Belvedere and Ardbeg websites.

The bit of disappointment that Apter initially felt at Floyd's absence was, however, soon washed away by the pleasure he derived in witness-ing Lindsay go instantly misty after taking a swallow of the punch the barmaid had recommended the both of them start with. It was opaque, this punch, but crisp of mouthfeel, and somehow golden when seen through the walls of the squat glass mug in which it was served, yet emerald green when seen from overhead.

"I've never had anything like this," Lindsay said. "I'm so glad we're here, Apt."

He squeezed her pretty knee, then gave a blow-by-blow account of his visit to the Institute, and, after having ordered a second round, asked her, "Are you free on Saturday?"

"I've got Ditmar at noon."

"Well, I'm glad I bought you that platinum plan, 'cause you need to cancel. We've got an appointment at ten a.m."

"An appointment?" Lindsay said.

"We've got a lot to look at. Could take all day."

He handed her the envelope. She extracted its contents, shuffled through the pages.

"You *dick*," she said. "I love you so much."

"Are you swept off your feet?"

"Well, I'm sitting," she said, "but . . . Good enough, right?"

On the first of June, Apter and Lindsay moved into a three-bed/two-bath Logan Square rehab, blocks from the California Blue Line station. Three weeks later, the internship started.

Apter spent all of Monday and Tuesday watching live video feeds of Booth's and Lung's sessions, and taking notes. He spent Wednesday morning discussing the notes he'd taken with Booth, Wednesday afternoon doing the same with Lung. On Thursday, they drove him up to Manny's for lunch, where, over brisket sandwiches and thick potato pancakes, they told him they'd determined that, progress-wise, he was eleven full workdays ahead of schedule; that he'd demonstrated to them that he understood how to administer Operant Analytic Psychotherapy as well as anyone who'd never practiced it could, so, unless he objected, he should take a long weekend, and when, on Monday, he came back to the Institute, he'd start seeing clients.

He didn't object.

On Monday, at the Institute, he started seeing clients.

In practice, most non-Behaviorist approaches to therapy—Apter's (former) eclectic approach included—were very similar. You sat across from a suffering client, listened to her stories, and, eventually, helped her interpret, decode, enrich, and reframe various aspects of those stories in such a way as to lead her to suffer less.

Operant Analytic Psychotherapy also saw you seated across from your client, listening, and so didn't, at a glance, *look* much different. However, OAP involved neither as much nor the same kind of listening.

It involved only as much listening as it took to

    a. understand how, precisely, the client's suffering was an outcome of the interaction between her context(s) and her undesirable/undesired responses to specific stimuli within her context(s), and

    b. convey enough "empathy" and elicit enough "trust" to cause her to

        i. accept (non- or explicitly) your more precise description of her suffering and its causes, and

        ii. take the steps you'd recommend toward changing her context(s) and/or her responses to certain stimuli within her context(s).

Perhaps a woman who was abused by her father during her childhood suffers anxiety. She suffers it often, and most intensely, when in the company of her aging parents, around whom she has had a number of panic attacks.

As a non-Behaviorist practitioner of therapy, you might seek to relieve her suffering (i.e. prevent future panic attacks, decrease her general anxiety about the possibility of suffering panic attacks) by helping her turn her tale of abuse into a tale of overcoming that abuse via guiding her toward insights into how the abuse has affected her worldview and/or her interpersonal relationships and/or her work and/or her physical health.

To an OAP practitioner, however, the abuse is mostly beside the point. To describe the original cause of the woman's suffering by saying, "She was abused as a child"—although that description might be accurate—would not, from the OAP point of view, be any more or less *useful* to the cause of preventing or relieving the woman's suffering than to describe it as "she was born to an abusive father" or, for that matter, as "she was born."

A more useful thing to do would be to describe the suffering itself. To say, for example, "Sometimes she has panic attacks. Sometimes she fears she will suffer a panic attack."

More useful than that: "In certain situations, her heart races, her breath becomes short, she begins to feel dizzy, and she believes that she will die at any moment. In other situations, she fears that she will suffer the aforementioned symptoms."

More useful yet would be to describe not only the suffering, but the contexts in which it tends to arise most acutely, e.g. "When she visits her parents, she tends to experience [the aforementioned symptoms], and in the days and hours preceding visits to her parents, she tends to experience fear of experiencing the aforementioned symptoms."

And most useful of all: "When she visits her parents, and her father raises his voice, she tends to experience [the aforementioned symptoms], and in the days and hours preceding visits to her parents, she fears that, when she visits, her father will raise his voice, and that, when this happens, it will cause her to experience the aforementioned symptoms."

Once the client and the therapist have settled on this more precise description of her suffering and the contexts in which it occurs, the therapist will have conveyed enough empathy/elicited enough trust to proceed in instructing her on how to change her behavior. He might, depending on the variables, tell her to do any, or some combination of any, of the following: see her parents or her father more frequently or less frequently or in a different location or at a different time of day or time of the year than she usually sees him or them; cancel visits she has planned to make to her parents; drop in on her parents, unannounced; perform anxiety-defying acts of dominance over her father or parents before her father has the chance to raise his voice; tell her father to quiet down when he raises his voice; laugh at her father when he raises his voice; raise her own voice when he raises his voice; rather than fleeing the room as she usually does when (in the wake of her father's having raised his voice) her panic attack symptoms start, stay in the room as long as possible, breathing slowly.

Perhaps another client says that she wants to kill her herself.

The question of *why* she wants to kill herself would, to nearly any non-Behaviorist practitioner, be of much, if not primary, importance. The therapist, in response to such a statement might ask the client, "What makes you want to kill yourself?" Or, he might make an observation such as "You must be feeling very sad today," which would invite the client to expand on what she believes is making her want to kill herself.

A practitioner of OAP, however, would consider why the client wanted to kill herself to be—if not entirely beside the point—of relatively little import. It would be of little import because the client, who could have, presumably, killed herself or attempted to kill herself, had done neither of those things; had, instead of doing either of those things, *talked about* wanting to kill herself.

Because anything one did or said (i.e. all of one's behavior) was, according to Behaviorism, done or said (un- or knowingly) in order to manipulate one's environment and the people within it (i.e. in order to manipulate one's context), any client's suffering could be reduced to a description of a) the failure of the client's manipulations to manipulate the environment and others in ways the client predicted/desired, and/or b) the client's failure *to be* manipulated by the environment and/or others in ways that the client and/or others predicted/desired. That was it. That was everything.

So instead of asking the client who says, "I want to kill myself," why she wants to kill herself, the OAP therapist would ask her: "Why are you *saying* that you want to kill yourself?" or "Why are you telling *me* that you want to kill yourself?" or "What is it that you, by telling me that you want to kill yourself, are attempting to get me to do or say?"

And the conversation would proceed, productively, from there.

In sum, the focus of OAP was not on helping the client delve ever deeper into the stories the client told to others and herself about herself, but on helping the client more effectively manipulate and be manipulated by her contexts in more predictable/desirable ways, which, as far as story-telling went, entailed the client's climbing *out* from the depths of her long-arc narratives, and observing and more precisely describing her more immediate surroundings and surfaces.

One's surroundings and surfaces were rich and formidable, overpowering if left unattended. And those relevant to the OAP therapist were often there right now, up-to-the-minute, examinable in situ, far more readily and reliably examinable than a person's history (problematically self-reported or otherwise), far more available to being precisely and usefully described. There was the volume, for instance, at which the client spoke. There were the faces she made. The movements of her hands. The frequency of eye contact. Her posture. Her fidgets. The frequency at which she interrupted the therapist. The frequency at which she invited her therapist's reactions. The timing of her head nods, her shrugs, her *Oh*s and *Huh*s and *Mmm-hm*s and *Wow!*s. The aggression she conveyed when expressing disagreement. The obsequiousness she conveyed when expressing concurrence. How she responded to your sitting there, silent.

Apter learned, and learned well, how to notice and describe these behaviors. How to notice and describe how and when these behaviors varied depending on context. He learned—and learned well—how to think of himself, and of those around him, as extremely sensitive and complex beings constantly enacting and being subjected to moment-by-moment manipulations both of and by themselves, their environments, and others. He learned to better differentiate form from content; to more granularly observe, describe, and manipulate. To understand speech as *verbal behavior.*

It was really thrilling. At first it was. He was mastering something, becoming more effective at doing good: at relieving suffering. For sixteen weeks, he practiced OAP at the Institute with a couple dozen clients, all of whom had depression and/or anxiety. On average, his clients were finished with treatment within nine forty-five minute sessions. Nine was the Institute average for clients with anxiety, ten the average for clients with both anxiety and depression, and twelve for clients with just depression.

At the fourth of Apter's monthly reviews, Lung and Booth described these numbers to him, and asked what he thought of them.

"I think they're pretty good," he said.

"They're beyond good," Lung said. "The practical part of your training is over."

"It's *been* over," Booth said.

"You know what you're doing. The numbers don't lie."

"Well, it's great to hear that," Apter said. "Really. I'm really glad to hear you guys approve of my work, but—and I don't want to shoot myself in the foot here or anything—but: What about relapse? No one I've worked with has been out of treatment for more than twelve weeks."

"This faithless fellow. This dubious dude," Booth said to Lung.

"He's a rigorous bastard. I'll give him that," Lung said to Booth. And then, to Apter: "Of course there'll be some relapse down the line, but we've watched the videos of your sessions closely. You've been practicing OAP to the goddamn letter. Do you have some creative moves? Sure."

"You definitely have some creative moves," Booth said.

"Eerily *insightful* moves do you have. But all of them OAP moves.

Administered with a kind of muscular fleetness neither of us has seen the likes of, true, but it's OAP for sure. OAP all the way. We will not be erasing any videos of your sessions."

"We will, rather," Booth said, "be using videos of your sessions to train future interns at our humble institute."

"All of that to say," Lung said, "that there isn't any reason at all to believe that the incidence of relapse among your clients should be any higher than the incidence of relapse among the clients of any other OAP practitioner here."

"That ain't, as you know, a high incidence at all, a fact on which, you also surely know, we practitioners of OAP pride ourselves muchly. And there *is*, in fact, very good reason to believe that the incidence of relapse among your clients will be *lower* than the Institute average," said Booth.

"That reason being the very clear and consistent positive correlation between the average number of sessions an OAP practitioner takes to treat his clients and the incidence of relapse among those clients," added Lung.

"The kid's making a face because we talked stats."

"STAT?" said Lung, with a mischievous, Groucho-like roll of the eyes. "No. We haven't talked STAT. We aren't there yet."

"Not STAT, boss. Stats. He struggles with *positive correlation*. You should have just said: the less time a client's treatment takes, the less likely that client is to relapse."

"Yeah. What Nathan said," Lung said to Apter. "And he was right," Lung said. "It doesn't have anything to do with STAT."

"STAT is a totally different subject," Booth said to Apter.

"All right, you goofballs," Apter said. "What is STAT?"

"You know, it's funny you should ask about STAT," Lung said. "We've been wanting to talk to you about STAT. Perhaps you've heard some talk of STAT lately? Around the Institute?"

"I might have heard Dr. Glint mention it once," Apter said.

"You know what it stands for?"

Apter said he didn't.

"Short-Term Authoritarian Therapy."

"Okay," Apter said. "That sounds a little . . ."

"Yes, it does!" Lung said. "We probably need a new name for it. But the acronym—I really like the acronym, so . . . It's neither here nor there. What's both here and there is this: your OAP training's done. We're calling it a success. You're a dynamo of OAP. You're a dynamo already, and your training is over, and you've got more than half a year of internship left. You could continue here as you have, just helping our clients by way of practicing OAP, but we feel that would represent a wasted opportunity. We would rather you help us develop one of the two new groundbreaking treatments we're working on here. One is STAT, which I'm betting you've heard us mention by now. STAT is our baby—mine and Nathan's—we're hoping it's the treatment you pick because, well . . . we like working with you and we think you're particularly suited to it. STAT is in the very early days. We only started thinking about it last year. We only started practicing it a few months back. The elevator pitch is: one-to-two-session treatment for phobia.

"The other treatment, however, is no less potentially groundbreaking than STAT. That other treatment is OAP2. OAP2 is OAP for clients suffering from severe chronic mental illness, the kinds of folks you worked with at the PHP. Now OAP2: that's Glint's baby. Glint's and, also, to some degree, Malm's. They're no less impressed than are we with your videos, and the truth of the matter is that OAP2 is much further along than STAT. They've been at it for longer—three-four years, now—and they've had a lot of success, and some of what they've done is truly, well . . . beautiful, really. One example: a young man with schizophrenia, early thirties, came in here ranting about the ghosts of Martians and clutching his crotch, and, after seven months of five-times-a-week two-hour sessions with Dr. Glint, this man has a job in the copy room of a law firm—first job of his life—and has moved out of a psychiatric nursing home into a halfway house from which he will move into an apartment of his own next month. OAP2 is important—no one else in these United States is trying to help schizophrenics do anything other than quiet down—and you would, we feel, be able to contribute quite a lot to OAP2's development.

"So we're giving you the choice. You can keep on keeping on with OAP and leave it at that. Or you can cut your OAP load by a third or a half and join Nathan and I in developing STAT, or, alternately quit OAP entirely, and work with Glint and Malm to help them move OAP2 forward. And yes, you can think about it as long as you need. Now go ahead and ask us any questions you want, and we'll answer them as honestly as we're able, but, in fairness to you—and to Glint and Malm—I will once again underline my and Nathan's bias here: we really want you to work with us on STAT."

"You said you think I'm particularly suited to it?" Apter said.

"Yes," Lung said.

Apter waited.

Booth cleared his throat. "There's something we've noticed about you, watching your videos, that we haven't quite figured out how to talk about without potentially making you a little uncomfortable."

"Okay . . ."

"Also, since we haven't exactly operationalized it yet, it's gonna sound kind of New Agey."

"You're weirding me out already, man!" Apter said.

"It's basically, well . . . It's your smile," Booth said.

"We don't even know if *smile*'s the right word," Lung said.

"Like all of us," Booth said, "you have a whole repertoire of smiles. The rueful smile, the joyful, the humored, the humoring, etcetera, etcetera. Smiles you might smile to varying effect in any number of different contexts. But the particular smile that we're focused on here—we've been calling it the *i-smile*—this i-smile is a smile you only smile in one very specific context."

"The context," Lung said, "in which you are about to bring more influence to bear than those at whom you are directing the smile would normally grant you."

"It's an *influential* smile," Booth said. "Hence: *i*-smile."

"And ever since we first noticed it, this smile you smile, we started looking at videos of our own sessions a bit differently. Neither of us possesses a smile as influential as your i-smile, and both of us knew that, but perhaps, we thought, we might possess something *like* your i-smile: we thought there might be something we unknowingly do with our faces or our bodies when we are in the midst of raising the stakes with our clients, i.e. when we are in the midst of instructing our clients to change their behaviors."

"And it turns out we were right," Booth said.

"Or, at least," Lung said, "we seem to be right. That is: there does seem to be something we do, physically, both of us, in the aforementioned stakes-raising context."

"I do this," Booth said, and, touching his lower lip with the tips of three fingers, tilted his head a few degrees to the right, dropped the lip-touching hand, and exposed his gritted teeth, all the while making direct, yet friendly, eye contact.

"Well, not quite," Lung said. "Almost. But you didn't really quite nail it there, Nathan."

"I didn't," Booth said, laughing a little. "It's hard to fake. But in the right context, I can do it. I can summon it when the time comes. And it seems to really work."

"Ditto me mine," Lung said to Apter, "but I can't get anywhere close to it outside of session, and the last time I tried to, Nathan laughed at me, which was a little embarrassing, so I won't even attempt it here."

"I don't . . ." Apter said.

"That's okay," Lung said. "We've gotten off track a little. We'll show you the video of you i-smiling later—we put together a little compilation of greatest hits—and we'll show you the videos of our own, what, *i-moves,* too. For now, let's change track. Talk about STAT. STAT is like OAP, but supercompressed. Instead of conveying empathy so as to get the client to entertain and thereafter accept our descriptions of their suffering, which acceptance in turn elicits enough trust in us for them to want to attempt to change their behavior in the ways we advise, we basically skip the whole descriptive part, forget about empathy and trust, convey and exploit our *authority* immediately, first session—kind of overpower the client with it—tell them what they need to do, usually tricking them a little, and they do it, and that's it. No more phobia."

"Tricking them," Apter said.

"Well, yes. And there's some theater to all of it. We'll show you some video. But the point we're really trying to bring across, is that we think your i-smile induces clients to grant you authority more quickly and effectively than our i-moves, and so we think you could be better at STAT than we are—and we are getting pretty good at STAT, I gotta say—and we want to teach it to you. What do you think? You want to see a video?"

"Of course I want to see a video," Apter said.

Lung explained to Apter that the client in the video—like each of the eighty or so STAT clients Lung and Booth had worked with so far—believed himself to be participating in a study. He had responded to an ad that offered short-term Behavioral therapy for phobia in exchange for permission to tape his session, and, prior to the session, he'd filled out a questionnaire that detailed his phobia.

The video was roughly twenty minutes long. Booth was the therapist. The client was an early-middle-aged man. At the start of the video, Booth told the client that he'd reviewed the questionnaire, but wanted to hear the client himself describe what had brought him to the Institute, and the client proceeded to tell his story:

He was born and raised in Chicago, and he worked as a sales manager at a Chevrolet dealership in Beverly. His trouble was that he was Indianaphobic, i.e. he had a crippling fear of entering the state of Indiana. He had no idea why, had never cared to know why. He'd just always been terribly afraid of Indiana. He explained to Booth that this had never gotten in his way before; he'd never wanted to go to Indiana, nor ever had any need to go to Indiana, had no friends or family or even any in-laws in Indiana, and on those few occasions when people had asked him to go with them to Indiana, he'd found it easy enough to avoid doing so without bringing up his Indianaphobia.

However, he'd lately been offered a job in Hammond, Indiana. More than just a job, really. A bright, solid future at Indiana's #1 Chevrolet dealership. A potentially lifelong career. He would, if he accepted the job, not only be the sales manager, with a salary significantly higher than the one he was currently making at the Chevrolet dealership at which he worked in Beverly, but he would own a stake in the Hammond dealership, which would earn him even more than that.

Six or seven months earlier, when the client had originally been offered the job—he'd met the owner of the Hammond dealership at some kind of Chevy-sponsored top-salesmen convention in Florida— the client's wife, to whom he'd mentioned the offer in passing, had not insisted that he accept, for she'd known the client was Indianaphobic, and, according to what the client had told her—he'd fibbed not a little— the income surplus the job would provide would not have been that high.

That should have been the end of it.

But then, just five days earlier (i.e. five days before the STAT session), the owner of the dealership had called him again. The sales manager the owner had hired for the job he'd originally offered the client wasn't working out, and now the dealership, for the first time in fifteen years, was looking like it might be knocked off its perch as Indiana's #1 Chevrolet dealership. So the owner was hoping that a second, better offer, might convince the client to reconsider coming in. This second offer featured a salary 30 percent higher than the original offer (which, itself, had been 50 percent higher than the client's salary at the Beverly dealership) and a 6 percent partnership stake (the original offer had included a 3 percent partnership stake), the same commissions scheme, but a stronger quarterly bonus scheme if the client performed as the owner expected. All in all, the client would, at minimum, end up making roughly 115 percent more per year than he currently did, and so, for the client, it was a no-brainer. I.e. No fucking way. Earning even 215 percent more money per year wouldn't be anywhere near worth suffering the dread with which Indiana filled him.

But he'd made a mistake. The mistake the client made was having taken the call from the owner in his car, on speaker, with his wife beside him. When she heard the numbers, she clutched the client's shoulder, and cast upon him a "scary look."

In short, the client, because of that look, had, rather than refusing the offer outright, told the owner he'd need a little time to consider the offer, the owner told him he could have till the end of the week, the client said that he would actually need two weeks, and the owner (to the client's grave disappointment) didn't tell him to go climb a tree, but rather—and with only a touch of impatience in his voice—told the client that he could have two weeks. The client ended the call after that, and the client's wife told him that if he didn't figure out how to get over his Indianaphobia and take the job—a once-in-a-lifetime opportunity for them to change their lives for the better—she did not see how she could possibly continue to respect him, *especially* because, she realized now, he'd lied to her in the wake of the original offer (had understated the salary, and hadn't even mentioned the partnership): an offer that she would have, had she known what it entailed, urged him to accept.

The next day, at the Beverly dealership, the client told his boss about the offer, and asked him for a raise and a partnership. The best the owner of the Beverly dealership could do was a 2 percent stake and a 10 percent raise. The client told his wife. She said it wasn't good enough, and that she'd seen an ad on the El on her way to work, gave him the address of the Institute website, and so, here he was, a volunteer in this study of short-term phobia treatment.

Booth asked him if he'd made any attempts to enter Indiana.

The client said he had. Three times in the last four days, he'd tried to drive into Indiana, and each time he'd tried, he became overwhelmed by panic, and ended up turning around before he'd gotten there.

"Overwhelmed?" Booth said. "Describe *overwhelmed,*" Booth said.

"Afraid."

"Of what exactly?"

"Indiana."

"What are you afraid will happen in Indiana?"

"I told you. I don't know. If I knew, then maybe . . . I just have no idea, but the closer I get to Indiana," the client said, "the more I sweat, the more my heart races, and I start hyperventilating. I mean, I guess I think I'll die there."

"You think you'll die if you enter Indiana."

"I don't know. I don't know why I would think that, but—"

Here, Booth did the i-move, briefly, and said, "It doesn't matter."

"Oh," the client said.

"Are you thinking about dying in Indiana when you turn the car around or not?"

"No. No, I'm not. I'm thinking that if I don't get off the highway, I'm going to get to the toll plaza, be too afraid of dying in Indiana to enter Indiana, and end up in some humiliating kind of situation, you know? A situation where I'm so afraid to enter Indiana that I refuse to enter Indiana, and I hold up traffic and, I don't know, get carted off to jail, maybe even a jail *in* Indiana, and I guess because there's no way to turn around by that point, and I won't go forward, and I won't—"

"Okay," Booth said. He did the i-move.

"Okay?" the client said.

Booth held the i-move for another beat or two, and then, from a drawer in his desk, produced a sheet of paper and a pen, handed them to the client, and said the following: "Write this down. It's important you do everything exactly as I say. If you do everything I say, you'll get past all this nonsense, I assure you. First thing: when you leave this office, I want you to drive to Indiana. I want you to keep in the rightmost lane. It's going to be terrible, just as it has been. You're going to panic. I don't want you to fight that. I just want you to keep going till you get to the point that you can't stand it anymore. Not the point where you think you might not be able to stand it anymore, but the point at which you absolutely can't. You *must* get to that point before you take the next steps, otherwise none of this is going to work.

"Now, when you get to that point in your panicking where you can't stand it anymore, I want you to pull your car over onto the shoulder of the highway, turn on your flashers, put your car in park, take your keys from the ignition, exit your car through the passenger-side door, and lock it. Then I want you to climb over the concrete barrier and lie down in the ditch just beyond that barrier, and roll back and forth for two minutes, no more no less. When you get back up, you'll no longer be afraid of Indiana, and you'll get in your car, and you'll get back on the highway, and you'll enter the Skyway, and you'll drive into Hammond, and you'll accept the job in person."

Once the client had finished writing down all that Booth had just said, he looked at him, questioningly.

"Yes?" Booth said.

"I don't have a change of clothes with me. If I go there and accept the job in a dirty, rumpled . . ."

"That's an excuse to delay your treatment. You're a salesman. You can come up with an explanation for why your clothes are rumpled and dirty, and, given what you've told me about this offer, the owner sounds downright desperate to hire you—just about *any* explanation will do."

"I see what you mean. It is an excuse."

"Anything else?"

"Well, yeah, and this might sound stupid," said the client, "but how do I lie down when I get in the ditch? On my back or my front?"

"You start by lying down on your side," Booth said. "Then, like I told you, you roll back and forth."

"For two minutes," said the client.

"No more, no less. Set the stopwatch on your phone."

"And is there anything else I should do, or prepare myself for?"

"You should go. You need to go do this right now."

The two shook hands and the screen went blue.

"You're telling me this worked," Apter said. "No more Indianaphobia for this guy."

"We are telling you that," Lung said.

"So it's like a faith-healer thing, then? You get him to believe in your bullshit cure, he rolls around in a ditch, is convinced he's been cured, and he gets up and suddenly he's able to drive to Indiana?"

"No," Booth said. "That's not how it happened. I *did* get him to believe in what you're so hurtfully calling my *bullshit cure,* but he didn't have to roll in no ditch. I'll tell you what he told me in the follow-up interviews. On his way to Indiana, he started to panic, the panic got too intense, he pulled his car over onto the shoulder, got out of the car, and approached the barrier, but before going over it, much less rolling in the ditch, which obviously wasn't something he was looking forward to doing, it occurred to him that maybe he hadn't done as I'd instructed; maybe he hadn't gotten to the point that he couldn't stand his panic anymore, like maybe he could have stood a little more panic, in which case, he knew, as I'd told him, that the cure wouldn't work, which would mean he'd end up rolling around in a filthy ditch for nothing, so he got back in the car and started driving again, waiting for the panic to get worse than it had, which . . ."

"It didn't," Apter said.

"Hell no it didn't. It didn't even get *as bad,* right? It had crested right before he'd gotten out of the car, plus the thought of getting in a ditch is, now that he's been nearer to doing so, more palpable: more palpably distressing in itself. And so now . . ."

"So now his panic is less intense as he's approaching Indiana," Apter said.

"Right. And soon enough, he's passed the last exit before the Skyway, and he's panicking, yeah, and it's horrible, but it's not *the worst:* he can stand it, *needs* to stand it if he wants the cure to work, so he keeps on going, thinking that getting in the ditch at this point can't cure him anyway; the panic needs to get worse first. And he pays his toll and he keeps on going, and now he's in Indiana, and it isn't pleasant—not just because it's Indiana—and he's almost, at this point, looking forward to the panic's getting to the point that he can't stand it because he wants to just cure himself, you know? Now tell us the rest. You know the rest, right?"

"Well so now," Apter said, "he's exposed to Indiana, for longer and longer, and his panic's getting weaker, and he isn't dead, and he isn't humiliated, and, soon enough, Indiana just kinda sucks, and he gets to the dealership, accepts the job, handshakes, hurrahs, gets back in his car, drives toward home, more Indiana, more Indiana, enters Illinois, gets home to his wife, says he isn't sure he's cured, but he's been to Indiana, accepted the job, they're gonna live like kings now, and they celebrate together, and maybe there's sex or special desserts, whatever, and then, on his first day of work in Hammond, and every day after for a couple-three weeks, he hangs a garment bag with a clean set of clothes in his car just in case he, on his way to work, has to roll around in the ditch and cure himself for good, but he never has to roll around in the ditch to cure himself for good because exposure to Indiana, despite all its smelly, ugly Indiananess, cures Indianaphobia on its own."

"Pretty much," Booth said.

"And that's how STAT works," Apter said.

"When it works," Lung said. "Pretty much. But sometimes it doesn't work. Sometimes the client doesn't follow through on the instructions."

"And you think that's because your i-moves aren't as strong as they could be."

"We aren't sure if it's a matter of the strength or weakness of our i-moves themselves, or the timing of them, or both, but yeah. Yes. Also, obviously, there are some clients who might, for one reason or another, be immune to the charms of our i-moves, and there might be some cases in which our exposure strategies are flawed, but—"

"Okay," Apter said. "I'm in."

"He's in," Booth said.

"I told you he'd be in," Lung said.

"I really think you should change the name, though," said Apter. "I think you should call it Short-Term Exposure Therapy. STET."

"It does sound an awful lot like STAT, and we know we like the sound of STAT."

"He might be on to something there," said Lung.

"I think he is, boss."

"STET."

"STET."

"STET it is."

He went home that evening with a copy of the i-smile compilation video. Lindsay was working second shift at the pharmacy, so Apter, after borrowing her vanity mirror from the bathroom and setting it up on the coffee table, watched the video on the living room's big screen.

The video was over an hour long, and each of the thirteen clips it comprised lasted four to six minutes: two or three minutes leading up to the i-smile, another two or three succeeding it.

Per Booth and Lung's advice, Apter's plan here was, 1) to learn to recognize the i-smile, and then 2) to practice deploying it.

In many of the clips, Apter, in addition to the i-smile, smiled another smile—a non-i-smile—that he struggled to differentiate from the i-smile at first. He struggled because both smiles involved an identical flexing and relaxing of the same facial muscles, which is to say that both smiles were, strictly speaking, the same smile, which, conveniently enough for Apter, happened to be the smile that he smiled most often; most, as it were, *naturally;* the same smile he'd been smiling since recovering from his injury at the hands of Mikey "Basketball Schwartzy" Schwartz; the smile that anybody who knew Apter Schutz, including Apter Schutz himself, would instantly recognize as *Apter Schutz's smile.*

The only thing in the clips that seemed, at first, to mark the difference between his non- and his i-smile was the client's response: the client invariably responded to the i-smile by attempting to mimic the i-smile, whereas the client did *not* attempt to mimic the non-i-smile.

So to better, more granularly compare and contrast the non- with the i-smile, he copied the video to his laptop, which he placed on the coffee table next to the mirror, then he replayed the first clip on the TV, paused it at the part in which he smiled the non-i-smile (the smile the client did not attempt to mimic), and on the laptop he replayed the same clip, pausing it at the part in which he smiled the i-smile (the smile the client *did* attempt to mimic). The non-i-smile on the TV, Apter noticed, was smiled directly facing the client; for the i-smile on the laptop, however, Apter's head was turned a little to the right such that he was in roughly four-fifths profile to the client, and the left side of his chin was slightly raised.

This turned out, in the end, to be the only difference between the two smiles. He compared non- with i-smiles in seven more clips, and although the position of his head while he non-i-smiled varied at random, every time he i-smiled the position of his head was the same as it had been during that first clip's i-smile: four-fifths profile, left side of chin raised.

So perhaps it wasn't as useful to think of the smile as an *i-smile* as it was to think of it as an *i-angled* smile.

He practiced for an hour or two, taking photos of himself with his laptop's camera, until at last he'd nailed it. While practicing, he happened to notice something else: all the clients in the compilation were men.

The next day at the Institute, Booth and Lung confirmed Apter's suspicions: neither his i-smile nor their i-moves worked on women. They had no idea why. The good news, however, was that Dr. Mallory Lint's i-move—Lint was another young clinician at the Institute who they'd recruited to the STET team—*did* work on women. Though not on men. Whether this indicated something universal about STET and gender, or was only a coincidence (i.e. so far they'd only studied the i-moves of themselves, Apter, Lint, and Malm; perhaps the effectiveness of another therapist's i-moves would prove gender-neutral) was unclear, and the role that gender played in the treatment was something they planned to eventually look into, but for now—i.e. for as long as they were still refining STET's methods—they weren't going to sweat it. They'd just pair STET practitioners with like-gendered clients.

Over the next three months, Apter saw two or three clients for STET per week. The rest of the time he spent at the Institute was split between seeing OAP clients and spitballing/tape-reviewing with Booth and Lung and Lint. All of them, since having identified and mastered their i-moves, had become all-around more efficient therapists: deploying their i-moves deliberately while practicing OAP cut down the duration of their like-gendered clients' treatments by an average of 1.1 sessions.

Apter'd cut *his* down by an average of 1.7. A STET treatment manual was in the offing, and he would receive a coauthor credit. Lung had taken him aside to let him know the Institute partners had unanimously decided that, after his internship, they'd not only start him at the highest salary they'd ever offered a first-year hire, but would, for the next three years, assuming he remained employed at the Institute, cover what they imagined were his student loan payments, and that if, after those first three years, he stayed on for another three years, they would pay off the remainder.

Apter, of course, didn't have any loans, but Lung seemed so happy to deliver the news, he decided not to tell him just yet.

—

The short of it was that he was barely twenty-five years old, and he had made a positive, lasting contribution to the world. Had *been making* a positive, lasting contribution to the world. He was, demonstrably, good for people—good at helping them, healing them—and he was better at being good for people than many other people who were good for people, and people whose opinion mattered to him recognized this. His parents were proud of him. Adi was proud of him. Sylvie was proud of him. Lung and Booth seemed to think he was Jesus. And all those people were in good health. No one he loved wasn't in good health. He, himself, was in good health.

And on top of all that, he had so much money. The blue-chip stocks and the mutual funds in which he'd invested, on his father's advice, most of his calendar/Ethereum haul were outperforming all expectations. Antic Books was way up in the black. The more time that passed, the richer he became.

Holy fucking shit, though, was he bored.

He was burning out fast. So fast he wasn't sure he hadn't burned out already.

The trouble, as he saw it, was that the better you got at OAP and STET, the less you cared about your clients.

Or maybe it was more like: the better that *Apter* got at OAP and STET, the less he cared about his clients.

Or . . . no. Not quite. That wasn't quite the trouble. That was an understatement of the trouble.

The trouble, if he was going to be honest with himself, was that caring less about his clients was *essential* to his getting better at OAP and STET. The less he thought of them as human beings whose suffering he wanted to relieve, and the more he thought of them as problems to solve, the better he got. At OAP and STET.

They moved around and made sounds, his clients. Each client moved around and made sounds, and some of those movements and sounds were undesirable—to the client, to others, to Apter himself—and some of the movements and sounds were not undesirable on their own but undesirable when made where or when the client tended to make them: that was the problem.

To solve the problem was to get the client to make different move-ments and sounds or to make their movements and sounds in different places or at different times, often all of that.

His clients saw themselves differently, though: they didn't see them-selves as problems needing solving. They saw themselves as stories. Each saw his suffering as part of a larger narrative that *was* him; a larger narrative the importance of which was self-evident to him.

Yet it was not self-evident to Apter anymore, this importance. It wasn't evident at all. That larger narrative: it was just another story: verbal behavior, patterned and predictable. Operatic howling. Intricate meowing. Overwrought birdsong.

The less he cared about his clients, the better he got at OAP and STET. The better he got at OAP and STET, the less pleasure he derived from helping people. The less pleasure he derived from helping people, the less pleasure he derived from living in general. The less pleasure he derived from living in general, the less motivation he had to help people. The less motivation he had to help people, the less inclined he became to pretend he thought their larger narratives were important. The less inclined he became to pretend he thought the larger narratives of others were important, the less capable he became of believing his own larger narrative was important to others, or even to, for that matter, himself.

Take, for instance, Apter's breakup with Lindsay Biss. There were any number of ways to describe it.

One way was to say that she wanted to marry Apter and he did not want to be married to her. That was the way Lindsay Biss would have described it.

Another way to describe it was: Apter was not in love with Lindsay Biss. That was the way Apter's parents would have described it, and the way that Gladman would have, too, had he been familiar with the cir-cumstances. Furthermore, it's the way that I would describe it, if, rather than writing this novel, I were having a conversation over drinks with you, whoever you are, unless, perhaps, you're the SSA teacher on whom I've modeled Nathan Booth, or, for that matter, if you're my wife, the author Camille Bordas, and, in the course of discussing the trouble I've been having with writing this part of the novel, we were to end up going down the by-now-somewhat-familiar third-drink rabbit hole of *the*

Behaviorism conversation, and we had come to the part where I was trying to bring across to you my heartfelt conviction that Behaviorism not
only allows for the possibility of true love and transcendent literature,
but is the only psychological paradigm that does so with its eyes wide
open—the only psychological paradigm that can account for true love
and transcendent literature without robbing either of any power (the
only one that, in accounting for true love and transcendent literature,
paradoxically manages to remystify the both, again and again)—while
at the same time trying not to depress you by insisting too much on our
lack of free will, or bore you with more examples of the ways in which
the very structure of human languages gives rise to, and perpetually
reinforces, free will's illusion—or bore you at all. I wouldn't want to bore
you at all, Camille. Ever. Come to think of it, that goes for all of you,
whoever you are. I'll move on.

Yet another way to describe Apter's breakup with Lindsay Biss was:
even though he knew things could never work out with Sylvie Klein,
Apter still wasn't over Sylvie Klein. And that was the way Adi would
have described it (the way Sylvie would've, too, were she drunk or high
enough when asked to describe it).

The way that Apter described it to others was that Lindsay Biss wasn't
funny enough, and she didn't find Apter funny enough, yet because they
so consistently fucked great ("had great chemistry," was the term he'd
used when conveying Anecdote 5 to his parents), the realization that
they didn't find each other funny enough was confounded by the laughter they so frequently shared both in the anticipation and the wake of
all the coming they were doing together. Until it wasn't. Confounded,
that is. The realization.

None of these descriptions were, strictly speaking, *untrue,* but neither
did they really bring across the actual breakup event.

The way Apter described that to himself was as follows:

Lindsay Biss, ever since they'd moved in together some seven months
earlier, had more and more frequently been making a face that Apter
disliked. When she made this face, Apter would ask her if something
was wrong, then she would tell him that, yes, something was wrong, and
then she would describe what was wrong—usually something domestic,
e.g. the way he hung his towel on the towel rack after he showered, or
the way he scrubbed or failed to scrub a pan, or the length of time he

would leave his clothing in the dryer after it was dry, those kinds of things—and Apter would tell her, in a soft voice, that he would, in the future, right what was wrong by doing things in the manner she'd prefer him to, and Lindsay would cease to make the face. He did not find her preferences to be unreasonable. He did not find the annoyance that her face seemed to express unreasonable, and he readily changed his ways according to her preferences.

But he didn't like the face. He really disliked the face. He really disliked the face and, no less than he disliked the face did he dislike the sound of his own voice when it softened in response to the face—it softened effortlessly in response to the face—and, as Lindsay more and more frequently made the face, Apter, OAP-trained as he was, couldn't help but notice the relationship between the face and his softened voice. He couldn't help but suspect that—just as he, in using the voice, sought for her to cease making the face—she, in making the face, sought (knowingly or un-; he suspected *un*-) to hear his softened voice.

And to see if he was right, he stopped telling her, when she made the face, that he would do what she said she wanted, but he would still respond to the face by using the softened voice. He did this for four days. And it worked. That is: on the seven occasions that she made the face during those four days, he used the softened voice, but didn't use the words that she ostensibly wanted to hear (i.e. words that would indicate that he would, in the future, change his behavior such that the complaint she'd just made would be resolved), and she nonetheless stopped making the face.

Then, for the next three days, he did the inverse. That is: on the ten occasions that she paired the face with a complaint during those three days, he did *not* use the softened voice, but did assure her (in his regular, non-softened voice—which took him, he found, a lot of effort to deploy) that he would change his behavior such that the complaint she'd just made *would* be resolved. Not only did this fail, every single time, to rid her of the face, but it led to quarreling as well as longer-lasting and more frequent use of the face. By midway through the second day, Lindsay had started using the face at times during which she *wasn't* lodging or preparing to lodge a complaint, and, by the evening of the third day of this sad little experiment, she, while wearing the face, said, "I love you," to which Apter responded, "I love you, too," in the non-softened voice, and the face remained.

"Is something wrong?" Lindsay said.

"No, nothing," Apter said in the non-softened voice.

"You can tell me," she said.

He didn't want to, though. He didn't want to explain.

"It's really nothing," he said in the softened voice.

"Okay," she said, "good," and stopped making the face.

After that, he stopped withholding the softened voice—to withhold it was tiring, and nearly as tiresome as was hearing himself use it—and the frequency of the face continued getting higher, until, at last (about nine days after the last time he'd withheld the voice), the face and the voice were in play more often than they weren't. She'd use the face, he'd use the voice, the face would go away, but then the cycle would always begin again, and the length of the intervals between the end and beginning of it continued to dwindle.

And it wasn't that Apter didn't know how to break the cycle. He did. He knew exactly how. All he'd have to do to break the cycle was vigilantly withhold the voice for a while—a couple-three weeks at most, in all likelihood—withhold it until the face-making behavior was extinguished. But first of all, as anyone who's ever taken Intro to Behaviorism could predict, that would—for the first few days of the withholding, at least—cause Lindsay to make the face even *more* frequently than she had been, which was an extremely off-putting prospect to Apter. Secondly, and more to the point: he just didn't want to be around her anymore.

When he pictured Lindsay, now, he couldn't help but picture her making the face. And even when he was near her and she wasn't making the face, all he saw in her face was its potential to become the face, and all he could do to prevent its becoming the face, and all he could do to undo its having already become the face—and he did it, he did; he kept on doing it—was use the voice.

And just before they broke up, they were sitting at the kitchen table, eating dinner, and Lindsay made the face, and said, "Baby, what's wrong?"

And Apter, who didn't soften his voice, said, "We're breaking up. I'm leaving."

And Lindsay, face intact, said, "What the fuck."

And Apter, still withholding the voice, said, "I don't enjoy us. You don't either. It's been a while. There's no good reason to keep on trying."

And Lindsay, through the face, stared at him. She said, "Where is this coming from?"

"Come on," Apter said. "Look at the face you're making, Lindsay. You don't like this any more than I do. Come on."

There was, on the counter, beside the stove, five feet away and at the height of Lindsay's head, a black microwave oven in the glass of which Lindsay briefly checked her reflection. "I don't," she said. "I don't like it. You're right. It's been hard, but that's . . . Are you *serious* right now?" and, down the still-intact face, there crawled a fat tear.

Apter's urge to use the softened voice, here, was hard to snuff out—it hurt his chest, tightened his throat—but snuff it out, he did. "Don't worry about the rent," he said. "I'll pay the landlord for the apartment through the end of the lease. It's yours. This is all going to be relatively easy for us. All the furniture and stuff we bought for the place: just keep it. Bertram, too, of course. I'm gonna pack some clothes and leave tonight, and I'll get my books and the rest of my clothes after I find a new place—probably next week, maybe the week after."

"Just like that," she said. "Just like *that*? What the hell is wrong with you? It's like you've turned into a robot."

"I know," he said. "I'm terrible. Especially to you. I'm not saying I'm not terrible, that I'm not acting terribly, but that's all the more reason . . . Listen, I've tried here. We both have. We tried, we failed, it isn't going to work. Just because there's no nice way to end, doesn't mean there's any good reason to continue."

Lindsay clutched at her temples, her face pinched and wet, and said, "You sound like a fucking *robot,* Apter."

And in the softened voice, he told her, "You make me want to kill myself," then got up and left.

He figured he'd stay at his parents' house, but as he pulled up in front of it, he changed his mind. It wasn't very late—not even eight o'clock—and they'd still be awake, and he didn't want to make the sounds and the movements they'd expect him to make, and he knew that if he didn't make the expected sounds and movements, the larger narrative they imagined to be his own would, to them, become distressing, which would, in turn, cause him distress—he hated bumming them out—and he didn't want to stay at any friend's place either. Not that he had many friends in Chicago. He didn't, it occurred to him—not for the first time, though perhaps more poignantly than at previous times—he didn't really have any friends at all. He had colleagues and family and favorite baristas, favorite barmen and barmaids, acquaintances he'd made at coffee shops and bars—dozens of those—and there were women he'd slept with before he and Lindsay had gotten serious, and a couple-three sometime European pen pals he'd met in Paris the summer preceding his junior year in college, and maybe some of those people were something *like* friends, but, no, probably not: if any of them had been a friend, there wouldn't be any question about it. Adi, of course, was better than a friend, a sort of superfriend, but, being his sister, she didn't really count. And Sylvie? What was she? He called her his friend, but she was something . . . else. He would have, he supposed, considered going to stay with Adi or Sylvie had either one been within practical driving distance, but . . . no, actually, he wouldn't have wanted to stay with them either. He just didn't want to have to talk about himself. So he drove downtown to find a hotel, parked his car beneath Millennium Park, and checked into the first hotel he came across, a boutique establishment called the Loop Central. He was given a room on the seventh floor. East-facing windows. The concierge had said it was her favorite room. Best view in the building. Michigan Avenue, Art Institute Modern Wing, Millennium Park, Aon Center, and, beyond it all, lake all the way to the horizon. He parted the curtains and had a look, paid especial attention to the glowing Crown Fountain, which had always been his favorite part of the park, and which, although it wasn't founting (this being Chicago in the middle of winter), was nonetheless *on*. The pair of five-story-high video towers—each tower rising from either short end of the fountain's shallow, rectangular basin—continued to project, to cycle through its loop, through its series of faces, one thousand in all, one thousand human faces, five stories high, shown one at a time on each of the towers, every single face slowly puckering its lips, as if readying to blow on or spit at the face on the screen across the fountain, which it would have done, were this spring or summer. That is: were this spring or summer, each screen would have periodically gushed a thick stream of water from the hole in its center, a hole the puckering lips of the face the screen projected was perfectly aligned with. And children, were this spring or summer, would have been standing inside the fountain, facing one or the other of the screens, awaiting one or the other of the thick streams of water, trying to anticipate when exactly a stream would gush forth.

Apter'd only ever been young enough to do this, himself, for a couple of summers. Despite being named Millennium Park, the park hadn't opened till 2004, and by 2006, it wasn't, for some reason, cool anymore for him to play in the fountain. Not that other kids his age didn't. Even older kids did. Even high school kids did. And he didn't judge them. In fact, he envied them a little. But he'd determined that it wasn't any longer for him, that to play in the fountain would be a bad look, that he wouldn't be able to attract the kinds of girls who he wanted to attract if he played in the fountain, and whenever he visited the park after that, he would stay near Cloud Gate, a stainless-steel sculpture by Anish Kapoor that was so finely polished and so smoothly curved it appeared to be a daub of liquid mercury: a seventy-foot-long, three-story high, thirty-foot-deep daub of fat liquid mercury shaped like a bean laid hollow side down, its reflective surface funhouse-bending everything surrounding it, clouds and skyline and plaza and avenue, and funhouse bending you below it, if you went below it, which is what you did. It's what everyone did, adult and child and adolescent alike, when they visited Cloud Gate; they went underneath it, stood directly beneath its concavity's apex, looked up into their funhouse-bent reflections, and, more often than not, snapped a photo or two of what they saw there. It was something to do, and it was not, by any means, a bad thing to do. It was, however, Apter thought, while looking down on the park through the hotel-room window, an odd—which is not to say *sad*, not necessarily—an odd thing to do if what you wanted to do was get wet in a fountain, and you were only just steps away from Crown Fountain. He was starting, he found, to feel a little sentimental. Also hungry. The Gage was nearby. Just a two-minute walk up Michigan Avenue. He hadn't been back since the day he'd rubbed Sylvie's bare vagina at the movies.

The Gage was near empty, no wait to be seated. Apter ordered steak frites and a twenty-dollar bourbon and started to read Gladman's story collection. He hadn't read Gladman in longer a time than he hadn't read Gladman since first he'd read Gladman in 2011. He hadn't read Gladman since he'd started at the Institute. Hadn't, for that matter, read any fiction since he'd started at the Institute. He didn't especially want to read fiction now, but the image of himself eating dinner by himself while staring at his phone was not one he liked, that image had come to him before he'd left his room, and it was past 9 p.m. on a Tuesday evening in downtown

Chicago, which, after dark, became the single deadest megacity center in the West, so he knew the people-watching at the Gage would be paltry, and there weren't any bookstores open nearby, the 7-Eleven around the corner didn't (he called) stock any magazines he'd ever want to read, and the collection was packed in his bag's outer pocket.

He hadn't thought to pack the collection. Rather: he hadn't thought to pack it after having broken up with Lindsay Biss. Apter owned three travel bags—a sleepover backpack, a weekending backpack, a full-size suitcase—and, he kept, in each one, a toiletry kit, a spare set of house keys, a phone-charging cord, and a copy of the book.

The only times Apter'd ever suffer insomnia were the first nights he'd spend in unfamiliar beds. He'd fall asleep fine, then startle tensely awake an hour later, disoriented, desperate, and crazed with loneliness, even if someone were in the bed with him, and wouldn't be able to sleep again till morning. For years he hadn't known what to do about this—he'd tried alcohol, television, ice cream, sex, milk, cookies, jumping jacks, sit-ups, reading, showers, masturbation, counting to a thousand, counting back from a thousand, and nearly all combinations of the aforementioned—until one night, at the apartment of an English major in Paris, he spotted Gladman's collection on her shelf.

Reading had, as noted, failed to get him back to sleep in the past, but he'd never tried reading a book he'd known, much less a book he'd known and loved, let alone one he'd known as well and loved as much as any of Gladman's, so, after waking the girl, who rode him till collapse, then gulping down her last jar of *riz au lait,* he tried the collection, and, halfway into the second story, "Melancholy Sally Drops," he felt the hot clench of his muscles easing, and soon thereafter the sting in his eyes was replaced by a heaviness, and he found himself struggling to get to the end, which had, upon numerous previous readings, caused him to cry more often than not. He didn't get there, though. He fell asleep on his side, and woke seven hours later with his thumb between pages 65 and 66 ("Melancholy Sally Drops" was not a short short story).

He bought his own copy the following day, a used British edition at Gibert Jeune, and, three nights later, suffering insomnia in another new bed, he picked up roughly where he'd left off the last time (he went back to the space break on 63) and, in the middle of a paragraph on 77, he reread a sentence four times in a row, then conked out till morning. Of course, there were other books that Apter knew and loved—other books by Gladman that Apter knew and loved—but why press his luck? The collection had worked, so he kept a copy in each of his bags. It never failed him.

At the Gage, he turned, straightaway, to "Melancholy Sally Drops." He thought he'd read the first section while eating his dinner, then head back to his room, but he didn't want to stop. So he ordered dessert, a second bourbon, and then a third bourbon he hardly nipped at. He closed the place in order to finish.

Though it tightened his chest, the ending didn't make him cry this time, but, after all, he was in public.

Why a series of lies about made-up people that the person who was telling it had admitted from the outset to be a series of lies about made-up people should move anyone to (or, in this case, more like *toward*) tears, let alone Apter Schutz, was not, *generally* speaking, a mystery to Apter. There were principles at work. He knew the principles. He'd read all the B. F. Skinner there was, and Skinner had convincingly—conclusively—accounted not only for literature, but for all other forms of human verbal behavior; for all other forms of all human behavior, and animal too. Generally.

But more specifically speaking? That is: why a particular short story, such as, for instance, "Melancholy Sally Drops," should move Apter to/toward tears—that was beyond him. Which was not to say he couldn't, if he wanted to—if he were willing to spend the entire rest of his life doing so—map all the relevant matrices of conditioning and association between Gladman and Gladman's narrator, Gladman's narrator and the titular Sally Drops, the reader (himself) and all the aforementioned, all the aforementioned and the larger context of literature and the larger context of literature with which Apter was personally familiar and the sounds of the American language, etc. . . . Maybe he could.

But, first of all, maybe he couldn't.

Second of all, why should he want to? What good could it accomplish? What joy could it bring him? Map and territory, right? Like, had knowing the molecular structures of cocoa and butter and sugar and the ways in which their electron rings conducted themselves when the three ingredients were added together and stirred and heated—had knowing that stuff ever made chocolate taste any better? Well, in a certain sense: sure. Okay. Yes. It was undeniable that certain chocolatiers, by way of possessing such information, had been made better able to create some better-tasting chocolate. But that certain sense was not the relevant sense. Apter wasn't a chocolatier, nor an aspiring chocolatier—he just really liked chocolate, and didn't hold that against himself, his just-really-liking-chocolate—and his knowing why it was that chocolate was chocolate (he'd read the Wikipedia entry once, back in high school) had not affected his experience of eating chocolate in the least, and, if anything, only made him feel dumb for having spent time reading about chocolate instead of reading about just about anything else, or eating some chocolate.

Third of all, he didn't want to. Or maybe that was implicit in second-of-all.

In either case, *most of all,* whether he should—or, for that matter, could—map all the relevant matrices of conditioning and association in "Melancholy Sally Drops" was entirely beside the point.

The point was three points.

The first of these points was that, in reading "Melancholy Sally Drops" at the Gage, Apter'd spent something like a hundred consecutive minutes thinking about descriptions of a made-up person, i.e. Sally Drops, without once thinking about that made-up person—or the person who had made her up—as a problem.

Now, to say that meant that he, in some way, *loved*—or even *cared about*—Sally Drops would be absurd. To say that meant that he, in some way, loved or cared about Solomon Gladman would also be absurd, though perhaps a bit less so. His feelings for Sally Drops, or for that matter, Solomon Gladman, had, no doubt, far less in common with his feelings for Sylvie or Adi or his parents than his feelings for Sylvie or Adi or his parents had in common with one another.

However.

However, his feelings for Sally Drops and Solomon Gladman had more in common with his feelings for any of the aforementioned than his feelings for any of the aforementioned had in common with his feelings for his clients, or even, by that point, Lindsay Biss.

And none of that seemed to him to be fucked up. It just seemed *to be.* Now, it *sounded* fucked up, sure. That is: it wasn't the kind of thing he'd expect he'd be *liked* for if he said it to someone. But that didn't necessarily make it fucked up.

The second point . . .

To bring across the second point requires that I briefly summarize "Melancholy Sally Drops." Thus:

"Melancholy Sally Drops," which is told in close third person, and from the point of view of the titular Sally Drops, is divided into a number of numbered and titled chapters, beginning with "Chapter 131,074: Dreams About Swimming," and thereby suggesting, perhaps a bit heavy-handedly (Gladman, remember, was young when he wrote it), that Sally Drops has been thinking about her life as a work of literature for quite a while. The story's set in Chicago, during Sally's first week of her first year at the University of Chicago. What happens in the story is that she and another young woman named Giovanna Bruni fall in true love, and, among other things they do together, they smoke incense that they've mistaken for opium, feel just like they imagine smoking opium makes people feel (i.e. they believe themselves to be high on the fake opium), and while feeling this way, they have a long discussion in bed about true love narratives, about how all the successful ones end in the sudden death of one or both of the lovers, and how that sudden death itself enables the lovers' true love for one another to resonate with the reader/viewer of these narratives (as well as with the narratives' surviving lovers in those cases wherein only one of the lovers dies): the sudden death enables the aforementioned resonance via arriving while the lovers are still in their love's first throes, i.e. before the lovers have a chance to question and become disillusioned by their narrative and fuck it all up. Shortly after Sally and Giovanna have the conversation about true love narratives, Sally leaves Giovanna's room, heads back to her dorm, finds herself either flirting with or just talking to another young woman who bums her a cigarette—the first cigarette Sally Drops has ever tried to smoke—and, as she is smoking the cigarette, this other young woman informs her (maybe flirtily) that she (i.e. Sally Drops) is not inhaling, and then shows Sally Drops (again, maybe flirtily) how to inhale, and Sally Drops, perhaps realizing, as the reader has, that her not knowing how to inhale means that she didn't inhale the (fake, to the reader; real to Sally) opium, *drops* to the floor, and seizes, and dies.

So the story kind of folds in on itself, or eats its own tail, and

Apter—here's that second point I mentioned a couple pages back—
Apter, having just read the story so closely and intently, there at the
Gage, found himself thinking about himself in much the way Sally
Drops thinks about herself, which led him to ask himself a really long
question:

Had he truly, as he had begun to suspect, broken up with Lindsay Biss
in so sudden and cold and cruel a manner because his "worldview" had
been scrambled by too much Behaviorism, or had he done so because
he, like every other deluded schmuck on Earth, couldn't help but think
of himself—despite his faith in Behaviorism—as living out a narrative
that—in even greater spite of his faith in Behaviorism—he couldn't help
but believe that (by living) he at least partly authored, and that, within
this narrative (comprised of a series of anecdotes, the fifth of which
he was presently living/authoring), he could not remain (as he wished
to remain) an empathetic/likable protagonist if he stopped working
as a therapist unless his working as a therapist was itself convincingly
ruining his life/protagonism/capacity-to-be-empathized-with, and *his
worldview had been so scrambled by Behaviorism as to render him incapable of being anything other than sudden and cold and cruel to Lindsay
Biss when he broke up with her* fit the bill well and conveniently enough?

And the third point, at last, was that—whatever his reasons, whatever
the stimuli, whatever the operants and reinforcers in play—he no longer
wanted to work as a therapist. Put another way: he wanted to work as
a therapist less than he wanted to feel whatever guilty feelings might or
might not arise from his no longer working as a therapist. Alternately:
he wanted to stop working as a therapist more than he wanted *not* to
feel whatever guilty feelings might or might not arise from his no longer
working as a therapist.

He knew, in other words, what he wanted.

He knew what he wanted, and desire drives narrative.

He knew what he wanted, and desire drives narrative, unless desire
does not drive narrative, in which case what he wanted didn't matter, in which case what he did or didn't do didn't matter and therefore
shouldn't matter to him, so he might as well do whatever he desired, or
might as well do whatever he would do, which was, according to either
formulation, pretty much the same thing, which is to say: it was all that
he ever *could* do anyway.

6

"So you quit?" said Glibner. "Walked away from the Institute just like that?"

"Not *just* like that," said Apter Schutz. "I still had a few OAP clients in the middle of their treatment, and I went in to work with them until we were finished. Hour here, hour there for three-four weeks."

"Your bosses must have been angry."

"Nah," Apter said. "No one wants to work with a burnout. Definitely not in the helping professions. Burnout's depressing. Contagious, too. I think they were probably disappointed, sure, but I wouldn't say *angry*. They published the STET manual, kept me on as coauthor, told me the door was always open if I ever wanted to return, and so on. We email sometimes, Booth and I. Lung once, too."

Here, the music stopped abruptly. "Last call! Last call!" John the barman shouted out to the Rainbo. "Last call, guys," Tim, the other, nearer barman said to Glibner and Apter.

And they ordered a final round. Their fifth.

"What are you doing now?" Glibner said. "*These days,* that is."

"You mean apart from trading anecdotes with strangers at bars?"

"*Trading* them, you say."

"Come on," Apter said. "I may have used a few more words than you tonight, but I will have come away from our conversation knowing all about one Reginald T. Glibner's brief career in constitutional law, the depantsing trauma he suffered on the junior-high school bus back in the eighties, his so-called 'party kisses' and other fumbling attempts at nineties-rave-scene-inspired bisexuality in the wake of a breakup with the mohawked and coat-hanger-branded girl of his dreams who left him for a SHARP who drummed for a pretty good Oi! band, plus the fundamental role he played in settling the most recent Chicago teachers union strike, not to mention the sadness he's been suffering all evening over having to fire a bright young woman with a heart of gold all because she'd tweeted 'sinkhole' in the name of a mayor who fancies himself a high-caliber semiotician."

"Fair enough," Glibner said, giggling. "But, first of all, our mayor: he *is* a high-caliber semiotician. *Highest* caliber. True, he might not know the meaning of the word, but then again he might. Now, if you were to say *semiotician* in front of him, he'd probably accuse you of making the word up—I grant you that. I do, I do. Nonetheless, the people of Chicago, while they rarely have any idea what he's talking about—how could they?—they love to listen to him. He's operating signs in ways the likes of you and I would never even think to imagine one *could* imagine. He's got an instinct."

"An instinct for operating signs," said Apter.

"He is trans-syntactical," Glibner pronounced.

"All right, you toadie. That sounds a touch psychedelic to me, but I'll take your word for it. And what was second-of-all?"

"*Second-of-all?*"

"You started out saying, *first of all*—"

"Oh, *second of all*—right. Yeah. I . . . I forget. But I was really asking you before. What do you do these days? Since you quit being a therapist? How do you make your living?"

In telling Anecdotes 3–5 to Glibner, Apter, though he'd portrayed himself as having come out *ahead* in his financial endeavors, had vastly understated—i.e. by orders of magnitude—how much he'd earned from the calendars, the bitcoin, and the other investments.

"Not much," he replied. "For a living: nothing. I do a lot of reading. And sometimes I'll read submissions for Antic, help Adi make decisions, that kind of thing."

"And you like that."

"I really do," Apter said. "Seems the more I read, the further away I get from all the . . ."

"Yes?" Glibner prodded.

"I guess the more I read—fiction, I'm saying—the more I read fiction, the more able I am, when it comes to people . . . the more able I am to be . . ."

"Empathetic to them?"

"*Empathetic?*" Apter said. "Is that the vibe you get from me? No. Not empathetic. More like entertained. I was trying, for some reason, not to say *entertained*, but that's the right word."

"*Entertained*," Glibner said.

"Like, this whole time we've been talking here at the bar—most of it—I was interested in the stories you were telling me, and the way you were responding to the ones I told you. You were funny. You were *entertaining*, and I didn't—at least not after the first or second drink or so . . . I wasn't trying to *solve* you, you know? I wasn't trying to figure out what aspects of our present context here at the Rainbo moved your hands and your face around without your knowing it. And I wasn't silently rephrasing your anecdotes to myself in terms of contexts and operants and stimulus responses in order to get a sense of what manipulated you and how you manipulated what, or how any of that informed the ways you were attempting to manipulate me and the way I might or might not attempt to manipulate you. I just sat back and enjoyed the show, entertained by our Glibner-Schutz dynamic, in gestalt. I enjoyed the manipulations, yours and mine the both, and, even just a few months ago—before the fiction I'd started reading again had begun kicking in— I wouldn't have likely been able to do that unless maybe you were Sylvie, or my sister. I wouldn't have been able to enjoy a conversation with someone at a bar."

"And here I thought we'd bonded," said Glibner. "Two strangers, talking it up like old pals."

"In a sense," Apter said, "that is what happened. That's how I'd probably describe it if I were in a rush. But really—and I mean no offense by this—if tomorrow night, I ran into you again, and you started to bore me, I'd feel zero obligation to suffer through it. I'd get away from you as quickly as I could, and try to avoid you in the future."

"Well, ditto," Glibner said. "That's a pretty harsh way to phrase it and all—seems you're putting matters in starker terms than necessary—but, yeah, me too. But, I mean, were you not like that before you studied Behaviorism or something?"

"Like what?"

"Like, before you studied Behaviorism, you wouldn't have avoided me if I'd gotten boring?"

"Sure I would have. Of course. That's something I do. I resent people who don't try to entertain their interlocutor, especially when that interlocutor is me. I even resent them when they do try, but fail. I always have. I mean, unless maybe they were a client—that's a different context—or someone I love. All I was saying is that, after I got into Behaviorism, and before I'd spent however many months reading fiction again, I don't think I'd have been able to be entertained by you to begin with. Our 'bond,' however illusory it is or isn't, would never have had a chance to form, much less set."

"You know," Glibner said. "I just remembered *second-of-all*."

"I'm lost."

"Well, as I'm sure you recall, *first-of-all* was: our mayor's a high-caliber semiotician. And *second-of-all*, I'm saying, is: you should come work with me at City Hall. That is: you should come work for the mayor. We have that vacancy."

"I tell you I'm a hair's breadth shy of sociopathy, and you offer me a job in politics?"

"'Politics is the art of controlling your context,'" said Glibner. "Tom Wolfe said that."

"*Environment*," Apter said. "Not *context*. And it was Hunter S. Thompson."

"So I confused my New Journalists a little, so what? Come work with me at City Hall," Glibner said.

"Doing *what*?"

"Advising."

"What does that even mean?" said Apter.

"Giving advice on pertinent matters while vigilantly avoiding any use of the word *sinkhole*."

"Which matters? What kind of advice?"

"We'll find out," Glibner said. "We'll see where you'd fit. It's pretty loosey-goosey over there. What do you say?"

"You're drunk, man," Apter said. "That's what I say. You're mistaking Toms and Thompsons. You're *numb* drunk. Haven't even scratched at yourself for five-ten minutes."

"Shit, you noticed that, huh?" said Glibner, blushing. "The scratching? It's not—in case you're worried—it's not bedbugs or a rash or anything. I just itch a lot. Have been lately. I don't know if it's—I don't know *what* it is. Sorry about that, though."

"Enough of that *sorry* shit," Apter said. "*I* don't care. But, you know, maybe if you're gonna frantically scratch at your legs, it's better you scratch them *not* under the bar, because it looks a little like maybe you're doing something else."

"You thought I was . . ."

"No, man. Not me. Not for a second. You're the opposite of creepy. Just that, a little earlier, from the other side of the bar, there were some glances cast. And maybe Tim the friendly barman had to put a concerned young woman or two at ease."

"You're kidding."

"Totally. Half. Don't sweat it, though. It's funny. And no one's filming anything in here, so . . . What I was saying before—"

"You were about to accept my offer to work at City Hall."

"I was saying you were *drunk*."

"I'm not sober," Glibner said. "That is true. But I've been at this twenty years, often drunkenly, and I know of what I speak. You're a smart guy, Apter. The right kind of smart. I'd have offered you the job when I wasn't so drunk. I wanted to. Swear. The second you told me how you worked those message boards to sell that calendar, I was right on the verge, but then you just kept going."

"Yeah, I don't know," Apter said. "Honestly, it sounds like a boring job. I don't even know if I want a job, really."

"Come. On. You, my dear new acquaintance, are *desperate* for something to do with yourself. Something uncommon. Something impactful. Anyone with eyes in his head can see that. And *boring*? Forgive me, but that's a stupid thing to say. You know who called me today? Perry Farrell."

"The singer for Jane's Addiction?"

"You a fan?"

"Of course."

"Well, if you'd been working at City Hall this afternoon, it might have been you instead of me who spent a couple minutes on the phone, assuring Perry Farrell—nicest guy in the world, by the way—that you'd find some way for him or Lollapalooza to help Chicago get past this dark chapter in which we have found ourselves. But you weren't at City Hall today, so it was me who did that. *Not* boring. And that's the least of it. We're talking about working for the mayor of Chicago—having his ear.

Having influence over the city's chief executive. Having influence right in the middle of a crisis the likes of which he's never faced, the likes of which this city's never faced, *I've* never faced . . . The earth has *literally* opened up underneath us. Thousands have died. We've suffered billions in damages. Scores of billions. *Untold* billions. And they say the fires will burn for weeks. Citizens will leave. Businesses will shutter. We need to rebuild. The people are lost."

Apter theatrically swiveled his stool around, dragged his gaze across the Rainbo. It was the middle of the week, 1:40 a.m., and there was barely any room to stand in there. The louder patrons were laughing, swaying, gesturing broadly. The quiet ones' eyes were all slack and lusty. *Roiling mass* was a term that came to mind. *Charged-up crowd.* All of them looked like they were trying to fuck.

Apter swiveled back to his original position. "To me," he said to Glibner, "the people appear to be enjoying themselves. Maybe even a little bit more than usual."

"Right," said Glibner. "That's just what I mean. How can they be enjoying themselves at a time like this? They're *lost.*"

"I'm enjoying myself," Apter said.

"As am I! *More than usual.* And the mayor, too, though he'd never admit it. We're all of us men of the people, see? That's my point. My point exactly."

"You're kind of a fucked-up guy, huh, Glibner?"

"Look who's and takes one and great minds think and birds of a feather, etcetera etcetera. City Hall's where you belong. I rest my case."

"Hey, Tim," Apter said to the barman. "Is it especially drunk in here tonight, or is that just me?"

"Oh, it's everyone," Tim said. "Last couple nights, it's like the second threepeat. I guess tragedy has a way of, you know, whatever."

"This guy here," Apter said, inclining his head in Glibner's direction, "is the mayor's chief of staff. He's offering me a job at City Hall. You think I should take it?"

"What kind of job?"

"I want him," Glibner said, "to be an advisor to the mayor."

"He'd get to hang out with the mayor, then?" Tim said.

"A lot," Glibner said.

"The mayor of Chicago, you're saying," Tim said.

"The one and only."

"Well, so . . . Does it pay really bad or something?" Tim said.

"Pays fair," Glibner said. "Pays well, even, I'd say."

"Apter!" Tim said. "Why even hesitate? That fucker's hi*lar*ious. Don't you think he's hilarious?"

"I do," Apter said.

FACE PROBLEM

It's isn't you. It's me. Or, it's both of us, I guess—writer-as-reader, vice versa, and so forth. Mostly it's me, though. You aren't just imagining it, nor is it your fault: this novel has begun to get away from us.

I had intended to finish *Mount Chicago* in four months. I've never finished a novel in less than seven years, but this one was going to be different. First of all: shorter. Secondly: shorter. Also thirdly.

And it will be (well, from where you sit, reading this, it already *is*) shorter, significantly shorter—the others are over three hundred thousand words long—but not as much shorter as I wanted when I started. I wanted it to be a lean sixty thousand words. A two-afternoon read. It is, at this writing, eighty-some thousand words, and—what? just halfway finished? One-third finished? I couldn't tell you. It's begun to get away from us.

You didn't know I was planning to write a short novel quickly, of course—I hadn't said so—but I do believe you *felt* it.

And then there's Apter Schutz. Apter Schutz has gotten away from us. When I started this book, he was supposed to be "more than just a foil" for Gladman, true, but to be "more than just a foil" doesn't take much—for example, Lindsay Biss, and even Arnold Lung, about neither of whom you will again hear, are each, by my lights, "more than just a foil"—and yet, in the course of my pursuit of his "more than just a foil"-ness, Apter has become, let's face it (you already have, I've been reluctant to) a central character in the novel, perhaps (this remains to be seen) *the* central character in the novel.

To be clear, I'm not trying to say that I'm not *good* with the novel having gotten away from us. I *am* good with it—I must be, right? I mean, I keep on adding to it, centering Apter. I just feel that I need to acknowledge these things.

I don't want you to think that I'm . . . on a different page than you.

But I *am* on a different page than I was when I started *Mount Chicago.* It's February 2019, now. About a year since I typed the sentence "None of this happened." Which, not incidentally, still holds.

And a lot has happened since I typed that sentence. A lot more than usually happens in a year. To me. For me.

My "less than $30,000" dwindled to less than $2,000, and has since then grown to nearly $15,000.

My second novel, *Bubblegum,* which, over the course of the six months preceding my "None of this happened," had already been rejected by twenty-seven publishers, continued to get rejected—fifteen more times—over the course of the six months *succeeding* my "None of this happened," until at last a handful of publishers—one of which had been one of the original rejectors (funny story, that)—ended up making offers on it. It will be published (by the time you read this, it *will have been* published) in spring 2020.

And just a month or so before *Bubblegum* sold, my wife, Camille, got an excellent job: a tenure-track professorship at a top ten creative writing program.

And so a couple months after the novel sold, we left Chicago. Moved across the country.

I miss Chicago. Pretty terribly sometimes. So far, though, I like where we've landed. I like that one of us has a steady income again. I like Camille's students and the writers she works with. And *Bubblegum,* it seems, will be well published. Just yesterday, my editor sent me a mock-up of the cover. The art's just right. Loud as hell. Pink on pink on pink on pink. I'm told the jacket will be made to *smell* like bubblegum. No kidding. Printers can apparently do this now.

In sum, I was hopeless and embittered when I started *Mount Chicago,* then I got more embittered, but then things worked out some, and now I'm not bitter.

Yet life is still meaningless, people still terrible, and no one who I've been close with has died. So I am, like I said, on a different page than I was when I began, but, if I may—in the dubious metafictionist tradition of self-consciously literalizing and thereby, presumably, demonstrating "ownership" over clichéd metaphors—strain a (my) clichéd metaphor: it's still the same novel.

Still pretty much the same America, too. Donald Trump is still president. The comedian Louis CK is still canceled. Jeff Bezos is still the richest person in the world. We still have the largest economy in the world. Our average life expectancy is still on the decline. People still use (the same) social media platforms. Healthcare is still becoming more expensive. We still have troops in Iraq and Afghanistan. We still average a few mass shootings a week. The frequency of hate crimes is still on the rise. Jews are still considered white by those who hate whites, and still not considered white by those who hate nonwhites. The final season of *Game of Thrones* still hasn't aired (though that'll change soon—in just a few more weeks), the country still holds its collective breath in thrilling anticipation of the multiple, simultaneous orgasms of total narrative satisfaction the season is guaranteed to provide us, and we're all still hoping—well, many of us, at least, are still hoping—that by way of suchly coming together as a nation, we will find ourselves coming together as a nation. *Liberté, égalité,* the Mother of Dragons.

We're on the same page.

However, one thing that may yet be in need of sorting out—depends who you ask, I guess—is the face problem we're having.

Might be having, that is.

According to Camille, who's just finished reading *Mount Chicago* up through "A Portrait of the Apter Shutz as Young Men," the novel has a face problem: a problem to do with who gets the author's face.

In most works of fiction, there's at least one character to whom the reader assigns the author's face. When there's only one, it's usually that work of fiction's protagonist's face—Buddy Glass gets Salinger's face, Jack Gladney gets DeLillo's face, Arturo Belano gets Bolaño's—but not always. In Gogol's "The Overcoat," for example, you don't put Gogol's face on Akaky—you put it on the unnamed guy at the office who, upon witnessing Akaky being teased by coworkers, recognizes Christ in Akaky. In *Blood Meridian,* McCarthy's face is neither on the kid nor Judge Holden, but rather on Glanton.

In some works, multiple characters get the author's face. In *Infinite Jest,* Wallace's face is on the heads of Donald Gately, Michael Pemulis, and Orin Incandenza. In *Geek Love,* Olympia and Arturo and their father all have Katherine Dunn's face. In works by Kafka, you *frequently* picture Kafka's face on a number of characters. The explorer, the prisoner, and the soldier of "In the Penal Colony," for instance, all have Kafka's face, as do the men at the bar on the pier; in fact, the only character in that story whose face *isn't* Kafka's is the officer.

Six or maybe seven months back, I read a draft of a story Camille had written, and, early in our discussion of the story, it came clear that I'd assigned her face to the wrong character. A few days later, I reread the story, found that I enjoyed it even more than I originally had, and was totally mystified in regard to how I could have been so mistaken about which of the characters did and didn't get her face.

Perhaps my mistakes had somehow owed to my being the author's husband, I thought, but perhaps they owed to a more general incapacity of mine to properly assign to fictional characters the faces of their authors in cases where their authors were people I knew. I hoped it was the former, since, given that I know myself better than anyone else, I didn't like what the latter might suggest about my capacity to get my readers to properly assign my face to my own fictional characters.

To get a better handle on the matter, I surveyed a handful of other authors I know. I sent emails to them in which I explained what I've just explained here, and told them which of the characters in their novels I had assigned their faces to, and asked if I was right.

Here's how they responded:

> Christian TeBordo:
> Characters in literature don't have faces. Not mine or yours or anyone else's. That shit is childish.

> Salvador Plascencia:
> Levin, I suspect this is one of these idiosyncratic things of yours that you pretend is universal in the hope that it will

become universal by way of your pretending, like your whole "*Game of Thrones* will unite us" line, but then again maybe it is universal and I am weird for not having ever wondered which of my characters readers put my face on. For whatever it's worth, I don't think I picture any character's face when I read, let alone when I write. I mean, Belano/Bolaño's, sure, because it's unavoidable. And Zuckerman/Roth, too, and then there's all the shitty present-day American autofiction, but . . . I think those are exceptions that prove the rule. So unless I think a lot about the question, I will not be able to give you an honest answer, even then it probably wouldn't be a useful answer—probably it would be overthought—plus I would rather not think a lot about the question. Are you having some kind of breakdown or something? You sell BUB-BLEGUM yet? Want to get on the horn? It's been forever.

Keith Gessen:

Who is this? How did you get this email address? How're things in Chicago? Rosenblum told me you're moving to Florida. Why are you doing that? How's the parrot?

Jeff Parker:

Interesting question. I've got no idea. Maybe it's like Shaq said Pythagoras said: "There is no answer."

How's Gogol?

Jesse Ball:

This is not a thing to speak of.

We just had milkshakes.

I want another and will meet you there.

Catherine Lacey:

Dude.

Anyway, after having read *Mount Chicago* through "A Portrait . . . ," one of the things Camille said was: "I like how Apter and Gladman both get your face in this book. That's new for you. None of your characters ever get your face."

And I said, "But you're wrong. First of all, they don't have the same face. I gave them only *kind of* the same face. Secondly, each of those faces is only *kind of* my face. Thirdly, I *have* given other characters my face. Vincie Portite had my face. Also, in 'Finch,' Cliff had my face. And Ben in 'Jane Tell.'"

And *she* said . . .

Actually, now that I'm reconstructing the conversation, I realize that what she said was that it didn't matter anyway. She said it wasn't important. We did, however, proceed to argue, which must be why I've misremembered the face problem as being something that troubled her.

What we argued about was the face of Vincie Portite, a secondary character in my novel *The Instructions*. Camille insisted I was remembering him wrong, insisted that Vincie Portite had *her* face.

This was a patently absurd claim for her to make, I told her: We hadn't met till the end of 2011; I hadn't ever even *seen* her face till nearly a year after *The Instructions* was published. And she said, "Don't be dense. When I said that Vincie Portite had my face, I meant that Vincie Portite had the reader's face."

She was right about that, actually. Both of us were right.

In sum: I was incorrect to frame *Mount Chicago*'s face problem as a concern of my wife's. It's not. It's a concern of *mine*. The face problem is my problem. It's important to me that a reader senses the distinctions between the face of Apter, the face of Gladman, and my own face. If I could tell you why, I'd be a much better writer than I am. And if I were a better writer than I am, I might have a knack for describing faces, and in that case I would describe the distinctions between the face of Apter, the face of Gladman, and my own face—I'd have done so already. Of course, I am not a better writer than I am, nor do I have much hope of becoming one before I finish *Mount Chicago,* which is why, in order to address my concern and, hopefully, solve *Mount Chicago*'s face problem once and for all, I'm resorting to photos. Two of them.

Both photos are photos of me, but neither really captures what I look like, nor even what I looked like at the time it was snapped.

PHOTO 1, however, is what Gladman looked like at the age of sixteen, whereas PHOTO 2 is *not* what he looked like at the age of thirty-nine.

And PHOTO 2 is what Apter *will* look like at thirty-nine, but PHOTO 1 is *not* what he looked like at the age of sixteen.

PHOTO 1   PHOTO 2

Hopefully we're clear on who's who, now, you and I.

ANOTHER DOWNSIDE

Although Gogol'd eventually grown accustomed—for the most part, at least—to the paucity of quality snacking and laughter, a far more serious downside to life in the wake of the terrestrial anomaly surfaced: he was able to fly.

His wings hadn't gotten clipped since Daphne'd disappeared—since a number of weeks *before* Daphne'd disappeared. His last clipped feathers fell out around Valentine's, and the feathers that had pushed them out of their follicles had finished growing in on St. Patrick's Day weekend. He'd been partially flighted since the end of winter. He'd been fully flighted since the start of spring. He hadn't gotten used to it, wasn't getting used it to it, didn't believe he could ever get used to it.

He really missed being unable to fly.

Which wasn't to say that he missed getting clipped.

No, he didn't miss getting clipped at all.

For nearly a decade preceding the anomaly, Gladman would, every three-four months, hold Gogol overhanded, like a baseball, use his free hand to spread a wing, and Daphne'd work the scissors on the spread wing's flight feathers. Then Gladman would hold him overhanded in the other hand, spread the opposite wing, and Daphne'd work the scissors on *that* wing's flight feathers. The procedure, though painless, was far from pleasant: Gladman clearly hated to engage in it. His touch was all off. His touch was . . . frightened.

—

And it was shitty to see a flockmate frightened.

To see your favorite flockmate frightened was shittier than that.

Even shittier yet was when the shittiness of your favorite flockmate's being frightened shittified something that could have been a joy. *Should* have been a joy.

Like being picked up and held like a baseball.

When Gladman *wasn't* frightened, being picked up and held like a baseball was the most reliably enjoyable of any of the everyday joys in Gogol's life.

There were two ways Gladman might pick Gogol up. The first way was Gladman would hold out his hand—its fingers pressed together with its knuckles facing Gogol—in front of Gogol's chest and say, "Step up," and Gogol would either step up onto the index finger of the hand or, if he was in the mood, he would say, "Step up," back to Gladman, and then they'd repeat "Step up" to each other till Gogol grew tired of saying "Step up" or tired of hearing Gladman say it, at which point he'd step up onto the index finger.

Good stuff. No doubt. It was great stuff, even.

But being picked up by Gladman like a baseball was even better. Even more pleasantly collaborative a process. Gladman would lower his hand over Gogol, thumb on one side, other fingers on the other, his palm covering Gogol's body from the back of the neck to the bottom of the spine, and Gogol'd reach for the thumb with one hand and grab it, then reach for the ring finger with the other hand and grab it, and then Gladman, signaled by Gogol's hand on his ring finger, would lift his whole arm, and Gogol, braced for liftoff, would rise along with it. Pure harmony of action. A process that you'd remind yourself to picture, beat by beat, to calm yourself down if, for some reason—or no reason at all—you felt anxious or afraid.

A process you fell asleep hoping to dream about.

Yet, lovely as was being picked up by Gladman like a baseball, it wasn't even on the same plane of loveliness as being continually *held* by Gladman like a baseball, for such holding made Gogol feel *so* protected—invincible almost. And *welcomed* to that feeling.

And usually Gladman turned over the hand that held Gogol like a baseball and used his free hand to preen Gogol's head or underbeak area. Often he brought Gogol up near his face so Gogol could preen his beard or head hair. Sometimes, while Gladman did those things, he'd walk around the apartment, listening to music or talking on the telephone. And nearly every time Gladman held Gogol like a baseball—and regardless of whatever else they were doing—they'd make a bunch of soft sounds at each other, call-and-response sounds, squeaks and suction and kissing sounds, hissing and gurgling and whispering sounds, or just say, "Gogol" or "Hi" back and forth, over and over. And over and over! Or whistle at each other. That shit was the best.

The absolute best.

But whenever Gladman would pick Gogol up and hold him like a baseball so that he and Daphne could clip Gogol's wings, the feeling was off. The pick-up was out of tune, hesitant, *clumsy*. And the feeling of the holding? Not in itself threatening, but distinctly inhospitable. The holding *wasn't right*. The feeling of Gladman's hand: not right. Gladman's thumb muscle: overly rigid. The heat of Gladman's palm: a humid heat. The ring finger felt like it usually felt, but the pinky beside it seemed tense or something, seemed almost to vibrate, like it wanted to twitch. It all meant: frightened. Meant Gladman was frightened.

And after a few times of Gladman being frightened while he and Daphne clipped Gogol's wings, Gogol started to recognize signs that Gladman was frightened *before* Gladman picked him up to clip his wings. Sometimes *hours* prior to the actual clipping. Gladman's eyes got wider, taller. The eyebrows were higher. There were breathing sounds, too, longer- and deeper-than-usual breathing sounds. And Gladman's mouth would be closed very tightly, the lips pale and thin, and the thin line between the thinned lips too straight. Gogol would notice these signs and be frightened till Gladman himself was no longer frightened.

But *why* was Gladman frightened? That, Gogol didn't know. Not exactly. That is: Gogol knew that Gladman's being frightened had something to do with clipping Gogol's wings—that much was obvious, for Gladman always stopped being frightened as soon as Gogol's second wing had been clipped—but he didn't know *what* that *something* was. What could happen? What was there to fear about clipping Gogol's wings?

—

Gogol wasn't the smartest—he knew that. But he was the second smartest, and he understood the basics. The basics of fear. That there were basically only ever two things to fear: flocklessness and death. So, obviously, if Gladman was frightened by clipping Gogol's wings, then the clipping of Gogol's wings could lead to flocklessness or death.

But *how* could the clipping of Gogol's wings lead to flocklessness or death? It didn't make a lot of sense to Gogol, but Gogol trusted that Gladman understood things that Gogol did not.

Gladman most certainly *was* the smartest.

Also, he was huge. His hand must have weighed as much as five or six Gogols, and probably more like ten or twelve Gogols. Just his hand! And Gladman was the one who found all their food, who carried all their water, who made the light and made the light go away. Always had been. The only one who *really* knew how to preen Gogol. The only one who understood the person Gogol was. What was Gogol without him? What could Gogol do without him? All Gogol would be able to do without Gladman was starve and dry out and be lonely and die.

Why think about that, though? Gogol didn't want to. Sometimes he couldn't help it, though. Sometimes he couldn't help but think about things he didn't want to think about.

Main thing was this: when Gladman was frightened, obviously Gogol should be frightened, too, even if he didn't understand exactly why. If Gladman was frightened that clipping Gogol's wings could lead to flocklessness or death, then clipping Gogol's wings—even though Gogol didn't know why—could definitely lead to flocklessness or death.

And maybe one time, something like that had almost happened. Gogol thought he might remember a time when the clipping of his wings had almost led to flocklessness, which, almost certainly, would have led to death (Gogol's). He couldn't be sure. If it had happened at all, it had happened so long ago it seemed like a dream. A very bad dream. It might have been a dream.

What wasn't a dream, though, was that early in Gogol's second life—the life between the life with Kayla and the life with Daphne—Gladman used to clip Gogol's wings on his own. He'd pick Gogol up like a baseball, then move Gogol's thumb-holding hand next to Gogol's other hand so that both of Gogol's hands were clutching the ring finger, and, somehow, he'd manage to reach out with his thumb and index finger to spread one of Gogol's wings with the same hand he was holding him like a baseball with while using his free hand to work the scissors on the feathers of that wing, and then he'd set the scissors and Gogol down on the table, pick Gogol up like a baseball in the formerly scissors-holding hand, move Gogol's thumb-holding hand to the ring finger, and clip the second wing with the scissors in his formerly Gogol-holding hand.

That Gladman had done this more than a few times, Gogol was certain—he had memories of Gladman-only wing-clippings that were nothing like dreams—but one time (the last time?), at least according to the memory that *was* like a dream, Gogol had done something stupid.

Right in the middle of the first wing's clipping—while holding tight to Gladman's ring finger with his right hand—Gogol had removed his left hand from Gladman's thumb to stretch his arm, and, in doing the stretch, one of his claws reached a little ways into his flight feathers, and it was right when that was happening that Gladman closed the scissors to clip the feathers, which also clipped a lot of the claw. Stupid!

Neither one of them noticed at first, though. Then Gladman set Gogol down on the table so he could pick him up like a baseball with the other hand and clip the other wing, and no sooner had Gogol put pressure on the clipped claw than he had felt a little sting and been startled and found himself jumping—he'd jumped onto Gladman, clung to his shirt—and he saw that he'd left some blood on the table, a few drops of blood, and that a drop of blood had sprayed onto Gladman's glasses, and a drop on Gladman's hand, and a little blood was spreading on Gladman's shirt where Gogol clung to it, and Gladman went from smiling and cooing and scratching Gogol's head to touching the drop of blood on his glasses and looking at his finger and seeing the blood there and seeing the blood on his hand and on the table and his shirt and becoming more frightened than Gogol'd ever seen him, and then . . .

A blank. A big fat blank.

The dream or dreamish memory went blank, and the next thing he remembered (or remembered dreaming), he was in the small cage, on the seat of Gladman's car, the seat next to Gladman's, and the car was moving fast and he was cleaning the claw, licking at the blood, and Gladman was *screaming* at him. Shouting and yelling and screaming and groaning and making even more frightened faces than the frightened faces he'd been making in the kitchen before the blank. And then the car stopped and they were at Dr. Bleet's, and Dr. Bleet helped Gogol clean his claw, and Gladman stopped being frightened and everything was fine.

For a while after that (unless none of that had actually happened, in which case, just *for a while*), Gladman took Gogol to Bleet to get Gogol's wings clipped whenever the time came for Gogol's wings to be clipped.

And near the end of that while came the start of Gogol's third life, of he and Gladman's life with Daphne. And not long after the start of that third life, Daphne and Gladman began clipping Gogol's wings as a team instead of taking Gogol to Dr. Bleet to have them clipped, which Gogol, though he didn't love being in the cage in the car, would have actually preferred because Gladman didn't get frightened when it was Bleet who clipped his wings, but did get frightened—as has been well established—when Team Daphne-Gladman clipped his wings.

So Gogol figured that maybe—assuming the whole episode with the claw was not a dream—maybe the reason that Gladman had screamed and shouted and yelled at Gogol in the car on the way to Dr. Bleet's was that he was so angry at Gogol for sticking his claw in between the feathers or for bleeding or for both, or that he was so frightened by Gogol's having stuck his claw between his feathers or for having bled or for both, or that he was both so angry about and frightened by any or all of the above that he'd been right on the verge of abandoning Gogol forever, which would have meant that both of them would have been flockless.

And so maybe *that*—again: if it hadn't been a dream—was what Gladman was frightened might happen whenever it came time for him to clip Gogol's wings: Gladman might have been frightened that Gogol would stick a claw into his feathers again and get it clipped and bleed again and make Gladman so frightened or angry or so both frightened and angry again that they'd no longer be able to flock together.

—

But that *may have been* a dream, that time with the claw and the blood, and something else entirely—something that Gogol just couldn't imagine—might have been what frightened Gladman about clipping Gogol's wings. Whatever it was, though, it frightened Gladman, so Gogol was sure that getting his wings clipped could somehow lead to flocklessness or death, and so the clipping of his wings always frightened Gogol, and he didn't in the slightest miss getting clipped.

No, he didn't miss getting clipped at all. Getting clipped was a nightmare. A waking nightmare. But *being* clipped?

Being clipped was a whole nother story.

Being clipped was, Gogol'd lately determined, *worth* getting clipped.

Not that being flighted didn't have its perqs. It did. Being flighted had exactly two perqs.
1. When Gladman was too far away to climb or jump or step up onto, Gogol could fly to Gladman and land on Gladman's shoulder.
2. If Gogol was feeling anxious or depressed or lonely or bored, and Gladman was in the apartment but not within sight, Gogol could quickly and effectively search the apartment for Gladman via flight and, once he'd found Gladman, land on Gladman's shoulder.

These perqs, however, were pretty negligible.

If Gladman was in sight, but too far away to climb or jump or step up onto, Gogol—whether he was flighted or not—could say, "Step up" or "Hello" or "Good birdie" or "Gogol" or scream or whistle or make other sounds till Gladman came over. If that failed, he could jump off the cage while screaming and *walk* to Gladman.

And if Gogol was feeling anxious or depressed or lonely or bored, and Gladman was in the apartment but not within sight, Gogol—again, whether flighted or not—could make the louder sounds till Gladman returned to the kitchen or living room, or he could just jump off the cage, screaming, then search, on foot, for Gladman till he found him.

Gladman would, in most cases, meet Gogol halfway, if not more than halfway, when Gogol, screaming, jumped off the cage. Having heard Gogol scream his jumping-off-the-cage scream, Gladman would often get to where Gogol'd crash-landed on the floor before Gogol had even recovered his bearings sufficiently enough to take his first step toward (or in search of) Gladman.

It was quicker, yes, and more direct to fly somewhere than walk somewhere, but flying was tiring. Required more energy than walking did. Simply being *able* to fly required extra energy. Gogol spent near as many calories a day on *maintaining* his flight feathers as he did on flying. While the feathers grew in, he had to keep rearranging them to keep them from chafing and stabbing his back. Plus he wasn't a slob, so once they'd grown in fully, he had to preen them. This wasn't preening you could do without a beak: wasn't any kind of preening that Gladman could help with. Having so many more long feathers to preen—some of the flight feathers were as long as his tailfeathers—and no one to help you . . . It took a lot of effort.

And no, okay? It wasn't catastrophic. Didn't signal the coming of the end of the world.

It wasn't as though he didn't have access to enough to eat to provide him the calories he needed to maintain his wings, but still: the *grind* of it, you know? The goddamned grind.

The extra preening was a grind.

The perqs of being flighted were negligible. Dubious, even.

And then there were the difficulties.

The difficulties of being flighted, and the dangers.

The difficulties, dangers, and, lately, the confusion.

Gogol wasn't made of stone. Yes, of course it was fun for him to fly sometimes. Sometimes, *while flying,* Gogol even thought that being able to fly was the point of being Gogol, that being able to fly was *freedom.* He didn't quite know what he *meant* by all that, but that's what he'd think sometimes while flying: "This is the point, the reason I'm me, this is me free."

Only sometimes, though. And increasingly rarely. The joy of flight was fleeting, the novelty of flying wearing off steadily. And like with any other joy that you notice to be fleeting, the times you didn't feel it weren't only just times you didn't feel it. That is: they weren't only times Gogol didn't feel joy, but times that, because Gogol'd thought he'd feel joy and did not feel that joy, he'd feel worse than when he'd started—worse than when he'd thought he'd feel some joy. Worse, as in: disappointed. And a little bit stupid. A little depressed.

And in any case, with freedom—assuming that's even what being flighted gave him—with freedom, as everyone knows, came responsibility. First and foremost: the responsibility to protect yourself from the dangers of freedom.

Used to be that when something startled Gogol, whether a sudden noise or strange vibration or the sight of a square of paper towel, flapping—the color white, for some reason, struck fear in his heart, as did anything lacking much depth that *moved*, especially if the movements were twisting or fold-y—Gogol'd jump off the cage, flap his wings, screaming, and fall to the floor. He wouldn't think about doing any of those things before he'd done them, but rather just find himself having done them. Then find himself there on the floor, a little disoriented. He'd take a look around to get back his bearings, see that all was well (all was always well), and, if Gladman weren't there to pick him up or step him up, he'd walk back to the cage and climb to the top—no big deal.

Except now that he was flighted, getting startled was a big deal indeed. He'd respond the same way to being startled, but with different results. He'd jump off the cage, screaming, and flap his wings, but instead of falling to the floor, he'd be flying. He'd *find himself* flying. Flying *top speed*. He'd find himself flying *top speed*, and . . . windows.

Gogol wasn't the smartest—Gladman was the smartest—but Gogol *was* the second smartest. He knew what windows were: walls you could see through. And he knew where all the windows in the apartment were, too: same plane as the kitchen wall facing the cage, same plane as the office wall facing Gladman's desk, same plane as the bedroom wall next to Gladman's bed. He knew what they were and he knew where they were, but when he was startled, he didn't remember—he remembered almost nothing. When he was startled and he found himself flying, he wasn't unlikely to find himself flying—again, *top speed*, with *great strength*—right at a window: a see-through wall.

That had happened at least a dozen times. All but two of those times, Gogol'd come to his senses quickly enough to switch direction without getting hurt. One of those times, though, he'd pulled up too late and bent back one of his fingers against the window—that finger'd hurt for days. And the other time was worse. The other time, he'd smashed his *beak* against the glass, and fell to the floor, far too stunned to land on his hands; he landed at an angle on his crop and his breast, nearly breaking his keel bone, which could have killed him. And no, he wasn't being dramatic. He could have *died*.

A keel bone fragment could have snapped off and pierced his heart and killed him.

And if that had happened, then, before it killed him, he would have been in lots of pain, even more pain than the bruise to his keel bone and the swelling of his crop that the beak-first hurtling into the window— which, talk about *pain*—had ended up causing.

First, it would have *hurt,* and then it would have *killed* him.

If he hadn't been lucky.

But he'd been really lucky. He had. He'd gotten lucky. He'd gotten really *lucky.* Lucky a fragment hadn't snapped off his keel bone and entered his heart to hurt and then kill him. And even luckier than that, actually. Luckier inasmuch as Gladman wouldn't have been there with him while he suffered and died. No soft sounds would have been provided to accompany and comfort him as death encroached. No final preening. No one-last-holding. Gladman wouldn't have been there because Gladman had been sleeping. Had slept through Gogol's screaming. Hadn't been awake when Gogol'd smashed into the window and hadn't woken up when Gogol'd smashed into the window. Gladman had been sleeping on the floor in the hallway, and Gladman'd stayed sleeping on the floor in the hallway. He would have woken up to find Gogol *dead,* had Gogol died. And he could have really died. All by himself! Died all by himself without Gladman and in *pain*! Killed himself while by himself without having meant to. Killed himself by accident! No. Not by accident. Not *really* by accident. Not because some fucking squirrel outside the window had jumped onto a branch really loudly and startled him—that would have been *by accident*—but rather because *when* some fucking squirrel outside the window had jumped onto a branch really loudly and startled him, he had had the ability to fly. Because he hadn't been clipped! He could have just died! He could have just died because he hadn't been clipped! Because he was flighted, he could have *just died*!

Not *catastrophic*? How about: *fuck you.*
This was life or death.
Being flighted was dangerous.
Dangerous and difficult.

Also confusing.

Some weeks ago, Gogol'd started feeling confused, and then he'd started feeling more and more confused. Like: he wanted something, but what did he want? He didn't know. He just . . . wanted. Confusing.

At first he thought that maybe it was Gladman he wanted—something from Gladman—and he'd flown to Gladman frequently, more and more frequently, flown to Gladman's shoulder to get whatever it was he might have wanted, but he didn't ever get whatever that was, he got no satisfaction, which only ended up confusing him more. He'd think, "Maybe what I want is Gladman to hold me," and he'd fly to Gladman's shoulder, and Gladman was usually nice about it—he'd usually pick Gogol up like a baseball and preen him or let himself be preened or make some soft sounds—but it wasn't . . . that good. It wasn't as good as it had been before. Not always it wasn't—not usually, even—and Gogol'd started to wonder if maybe those times when it wasn't as good, Gladman was thinking about holding Gogol like a baseball and preening and making soft sounds etc. in a way that was like the way Gogol used to think about eating Daphne's proffered cheese: like, maybe Gladman wasn't all that into it or something. Like maybe Gladman was holding Gogol like a baseball and preening him and so forth only from a sense of obligation and nothing more: to maintain the hierarchy and nothing more: because if he didn't hold Gogol like a baseball and preen him and so forth, he'd have to do violence to Gogol instead, and Gladman didn't like violence.

Gogol didn't know *why* it had become this way. Why Gladman had changed. He wasn't even sure it *had* become this way. Wasn't even sure that it was Gladman who'd changed. It might have all been in his (Gogol's!) head. He felt very *confused*. What was different? What had changed? Daphne was gone, but Daphne'd been the bottom, so Gladman could not have cared any more about Daphne being gone than Gogol did, which, truth be known, Gogol did care a little sometimes—no more madeleines or oiled spaghetti, etc.—but not a whole lot. So it had to be the wings. Their not being clipped. Gogol's being flighted and/or Gogol's flights had to be the reason why Gladman wasn't all that into what Gladman had usually pretty much always been into. But then why didn't he take him to Bleet to get him clipped? Or clip him the old way? It didn't make sense.

Unless there wasn't any *it* to make sense of. That is: maybe Gladman *was* just as into holding and preening and soft sounds etc. as he'd been when Gogol hadn't been flighted, but Gogol's being flighted was somehow making it *seem* to Gogol that Gladman *wasn't* as into all that stuff any longer.

It was really really confusing.

It was really unpleasant.

And that was just at first. After three or four weeks of this particular kind of unpleasant confusion, a new kind of unpleasant confusion had begun to mount.

The new unpleasant confusion was accompanied by new, uncomfortable sensations. Gurglings in the abdominal region. Unexpected expansions followed by contractions. Involuntary shiftings and flexings of muscles that Gogol hadn't previously known that he'd had. The new unpleasant confusion was, it seemed, *caused* by these uncomfortable sensations, but maybe that was backward; the sensations may have been caused by the confusion.

The new unpleasant confusion was this: Gogol wanted to kind of *get under* something. To kind of like get under something and—what?—and sort of wiggle or something. To get under something and wiggle, but what? Get under what? Wiggle how? To what end wiggle?

Used to be that when he was alone, waiting for Gladman to come back from wherever he'd gone so they could get into some preening or snacking or call-and-response, Gogol'd space out on deep thoughts about the hierarchy, or what the Gladman flock had been like before Gladman'd been around, or what Gladman might have been like back when Gladman had still been small and winged and beaked and feathered and had had to walk on his arms like Gogol, or what it might be like if Gogol weren't there, or what it might be like if there'd never been a Daphne or never been a Kayla, or where he had come from, or where Gladman had come from, or how weird it must be to live like a perpetually startled savage like the sparrows and squirrels who lived in the tree outside the window, or whether those sparrows or squirrels thought that he and

Gladman were the savages when they looked into the window at him and Gladman, or what "Hi" really meant, if it was different from "Hello," whatever *that* really meant, or if maybe "Hi" didn't mean anything at all.

He used to love thinking about things like that when alone, but now it all seemed a little oppressive, to think about that stuff, like, "Is this all there is? Is this all there is to think about? All there is to think about thinking?" or "Are the only things worth looking forward to doing dependent on Gladman? Are preening and snacking and call-and-response the only things there are to think about doing, apart from thinking? Did thinking even count as a kind of doing?"

Now, when alone, he'd start to think about all the stuff he used to think about when alone, but get to feeling oppressed, and get bored with all that stuff before it got deep, and the desire to get under something and wiggle would intrude on the thoughts, *overtake* the thoughts, and, along with that inexplicable desire would come—sometimes right before he noticed the desire, sometimes just after he noticed the desire—the gurglings from within, the shiftings and the flexings, and although he was always able to convince himself that all these new and weird discomforts were just a healthy part of the process of his transformation into a man and that, in the end, it would all have been worth it—for soon he'd be big and strong and Gladman-shaped and able to gather and prepare his own sustenance—he'd occasionally fear he'd gotten sick and was dying.

White Part

1

Now obviously the mayor had not spent all of winter '21–'22 plus the first part of spring '22 sitting across his desk from Apter, smiling at and being smiled at by Apter while they drank good Scotch and the mayor grew a beard.

But, explained the mayor to Apter, who sat across the desk from him on April 21, 2022, smiling at and being smiled at by him while drinking good Scotch with him, same as on so many previous fine evenings since Christmas Eve of '21——*but,* explained the mayor, it did, to the mayor, seem that way almost.

That they'd been sitting like that.

Sitting like this.

There was even what you might call *an artistically licensed truth* to how it seemed that way. For example, if someone who wanted to make the mayor's biopic wanted to pay the mayor to consult on that biopic, one of the suggestions the mayor thought he'd make to that someone would be to artfully depict the passage of time between Christmas Eve '21 and mid-April '22, i.e. just last week, by filming the actors who were playing the mayor and Apter sitting across the mayor's desk from each other, smiling at each other and drinking good Scotch.

The mayor'd thought about this more than once. Especially of lately. It was really vivid to him.

In the first part of that artful shot, it would be Christmas Eve '21, the actor playing the mayor would not have a beard, and there would be a few inches of snow on the window ledge behind the mayor's chair. That snow would steadily get brighter and brighter till it got so bright that the whole screen glowed with bright white light, and that glow would stay at its peak of total whiteness for a second or two. After that, the whiteness would start to recede, and the viewer of the movie would see that the actors playing the mayor and Apter were, like before, sitting across the mayor's desk from each other, smiling at each other and drinking good Scotch, but now both of the actors would be wearing different clothes, the actor playing the mayor'd have a beard, that pile of snow on the window would be gone, and what they'd be smiling about would not be the beautiful speech the mayor gave to the people on Christmas Eve, but the vivid dream the mayor'd had about Barack Obama.

Or, then again, maybe not, explained the mayor.

That is: it depended.

Maybe the mayor would not suggest the vivid, artful shot because maybe the mayor would not want to consult on his biopic at all.

If someone offered to pay the mayor to consult on his biopic and the mayor accepted, that would be akimbo to the mayor authorizing the biopic, which could end up being a crappy movie that because it was crappy would make *him* look crappy even though that wouldn't be the point of the movie.

How this realization came about to the mayor was just last night, when the mayor's wife had made him watch that movie *The King's Speech*.

The King's Speech was, to put it plainly, a snore. *The King's Speech* was boring, and because it was boring, it made the king who it was about look boring, not to mention weak and annoying and totally non-kinglike.

At first, the mayor tried to appreciate it anyway. He gave it a chance. Maybe, he thought, the whole point of *The King's Speech* was to look like a boring quote-unquote important movie, but to actually be a comedy about how annoying and boring the king was, which—a movie like that, the mayor thought he could really appreciate.

But it turned out: no. That was not the whole point. Or even part of the whole point.

The point of *The King's Speech* was more it was supposed to make the king look like a hero who inspired his country by bringing the people of his country together at a very troubling time in that country's world history by giving a speech he had to overcome a disability to give. You could tell that was the point by the music got used. Rousing music.

But the mayor wasn't roused. His wife wasn't either.

Hence: *The King's Speech* was crappy. A crappy biopic.

And penultimately this crappiness of *The King's Speech* caused the mayor to reflect on: a) what if a biopic of the mayor was crappy? and b) what were the odds that it would be crappy? Because that would be a problem. Obviously.

While reflecting on this matter, the mayor naturally thought about other biopics. He tried to think of all the biopics he'd ever seen, and he'd seen a *ton*. And how it turned out is that he had a problem with a lot of them.

Almost all of them, actually.

It turned out he had a problem with so many of the biopics that he had seen, you could almost say *he had a problem with biopics,* and you could almost say that the biopics that he didn't have a problem with were the exceptions that proved the rule that he had a problem with biopics.

Not even just almost. You could. Did. He was. Saying it.

Now, the problem with biopics, as the mayor saw it, was really a matter of . . .

Well, to put it simply: the main problem the mayor had with biopics was how crappy they were.

He could count all the good biopics ever made on exactly just the fingers of one of his hands.

Raging Bull (pointer)
Goodfellas (middle)
The Social Network (ring)
The Fighter (pinky)
The Wolf of Wall Street (thumb)*

He used to would have said *Schindler's List* made the grade also, true, but he was caused to think doubtfully about *Schindler's List* by none

---

* The mayor had never seen *I, Tonya* or, believe it or not, *The Irishman*. He would have liked those, too.

other than Chicago's own favorite filmmaking son, the one and only award-winning writer and director of so many of the more important productions in this era in which we have lived and are living, David "Always Be Closing" Mamet.

When the mayor met Mamet, the mayor wasn't the mayor at that time. The mayor, at that time, was the first-term alderman of the 11th Ward, and it was Daley the Son who was the mayor at that time.

Daley'd had the alderman over to his house for a poker night with Mamet and a couple other aldermen.

It was a truly memorious night, that night.

It happened right after the Oscars of the year that *Shakespeare in Love* won a lot of Oscars, and someone—maybe the alderman himself—said *Shakespeare in Love* should not have won Best Picture, that *Saving Private Ryan* should have won Best Picture, and Mamet shocked all the players at the table by saying he hadn't seen *Saving Private Ryan*.

The alderman told Mamet that Mamet had to see it, and Mamet said that Mamet did not have to see it. Mamet said he knew that he didn't have to see it because it was directed by Steven Spielberg and Steven Spielberg was a "pretentious schlockmeister."

Hearing Mamet call Spielberg a pretentious schlockmeister was even more shocking to the alderman—to all the aldermen present, in fact, and to Daley, too—than hearing him say he hadn't seen *Private Ryan*.

And the alderman told Mamet that he had a theory and he felt he was incumbent to say his theory.

This was his theory: it was the old Steven Spielberg who Mamet was thinking of. The *Jaws* and *E.T.* and *Raiders* Steven Spielberg. But the new Steven Spielberg was who made *Private Ryan*: the same new Steven Spielberg who'd made *Schindler's List*.

After the mayor finished saying the theory, Mamet delivered his third and most powerful shock to each and every one of all the players at the table by telling them *Jaws* and *Raiders* were perfectly okay by him, that *E.T.*, though schlock, was made for children, so its schlockiness was, to some degree, forgivable, and definitely harmless, but *Schindler's List* was a whole nother thing. *Schindler's List* was a monument to schlock. *Schindler's List* was a model of schlock.

"The God of all schlock," Mamet called *Schindler's List*.

—

It was, Mamet said, the kind of schlock schlockmeisters had always aspired to jizz down the throats and all over the faces of "the members (as it were)" of the American Academy of Motion Picture Arts and Sciences.

Schindler's List, Mamet said, was so monumentally a monument and model and God of schlock that schlockmeisters—just like they had been doing ever since Best Picture had gone to *Schindler's List*—would be jizzing schlock just like *Schindler's List* down into the throats and forward onto the faces of the members of the American Academy of Motion Picture Arts and Sciences "for decades to come (so to speak)."

Schindler's List, Mamet went on to say, was the kind of schlock that ruined your clothes—wool, cotton, blends, it didn't matter: ruined.

You had to scrub with steel wool and hydrochloric acid to clean the schlock that was *Schindler's List* off your skin.

You had to shave off your beard if you got some on your beard.

Steven Spielberg's *Schindler's List* was, in conclusion, for jagoffs, Mamet told Mayor Daley and the aldermen. It had turned, said Mamet, one of the greatest tragedies in the history of man into a feel-good movie that made you feel good when you watched it because it made you think of yourself as being like Schindler, or at least kind of like Schindler, when what a movie about Schindler that was not for jagoffs would make you feel like was either a Nazi or a Nazi collaborator because, "according to the numbers," that's what you would have been.

Personally, the alderman would not have wanted to see a movie that made him feel like a Nazi or a Nazi collaborator, and he said so to Mamet and everyone else.

And Mamet said that that was the point: no one wanted to see a movie like that, so Spielberg made a different movie. A movie for jagoffs that everyone wanted to see.

And the alderman asked Mamet if Mamet was saying that the alderman was a jagoff, and Mamet said that he'd only just known the alderman two hours so he couldn't say for sure, but if he had to place a bet on it, he'd bet the alderman was probably a jagoff because, first of all, most politicians were jagoffs, which went double for aldermen, and triple in Chicago, and then, second of all, people with bad taste were jagoffs, and anyone who thought *Schindler's List* wasn't for jagoffs clearly had bad taste, plus thirdly it was the alderman's turn to deal and, instead of deal-ing, the alderman was uncontrollably laughing his ass off (completely true) while being called a jagoff by a short, hairy Jewish man he kept losing all his money at cards to, "which indicates complete and total jagoff," said Mamet.

So the alderman, at length, got ahold of himself, wiped his eyes, dealt, then lost the hand in a heads-up with Mamet, who, when he showed his winning cards, said, "Take that, you skinny, uncircumcised, filthy Irish jagoff," and everyone at the table, Daley included, fell apart laughing, laughing like devils, like masters of the universe, like dangerous men in a Martin Scorsese gangster movie.

No one laughed harder than the alderman himself. Being insulted, jok-ily or no, for having Irish heritage was at that point in history *always* a nonadulterant pleasure that swelled one with pridefulness. Plus the alderman had recently put on a few pounds, and he hadn't been sure how well he was carrying it, so being called *skinny*—it made him feel good.

And *Schindler's List* made him feel good, too. Not the way being called skinny made him feel good—that movie was sad! jerked the tears from his eyes—but moralistically, like Mamet had been saying.

Schindler's List made him moralistically feel good back then, as the full-of-promise first-term 11th Ward alderman, and it still today made him moralistically feel good now he was mayor.

Schindler's List made the mayor moralistically feel good and the rea-son was this: he *wasn't* a jagoff.

The mayor, as the saying goes, *knew thyself,* and he would not have been a Nazi or collaborated with Nazis. Not as an alderman, and not as the mayor. That was the hole in David Mamet's argument. Not everybody in the European country *Schindler's List* took place in was a Nazi or a collaborator with Nazis, so not everybody in the audience for *Schindler's List* would have been, either. And the mayor was one of them. Perhaps it sounded like Shintoism to say so, but a lot of Americans were one of them, frankly.

So he could moralistically feel good without moralistically feeling bad about moralistically feeling good. Like a lot of Americans.

Same time, Mamet was also probably correct in a more worldwide sense of being probably correct: most people in most of the world shouldn't feel how the mayor and a lot of Americans felt when they saw *Schindler's List.* They had no right. Numbers were numbers. Numbers couldn't lie.

But it didn't matter, anyway. Even if *Schindler's List* was a sixth uncrappy biopic, it didn't matter. First: it would have only been the sixth best of the six.

Second, and more mainly: there were only five or six. That was the point.

And the real penultimate point about that was this: out of the only five or six uncrappy biopics, three of them were made by Martin Scorsese, two of them were about boxers, and two about guys with unimaginable amounts of money. The mayor was not a boxer, his amount of money was very imaginable, and Scorsese hadn't made a biopic in almost ten years—he seemed to be out of the biopic business entirely.

He seemed to be making a lot of documentaries.

So however uncrappy the mayor's biography was or wasn't—and the mayor felt it was very uncrappy—the chances a biopic about his biography would be uncrappy were not very good, and when he imagined being paid to consult on his biopic, he imagined he would only accept the offer on one condition: that the biopic's filmmaker agreed to also make a documentary about the mayor's biography.

Unless the filmmaker was Martin Scorsese.

Or, if it was one of the other directors of the two or three good non-Scorsese-directed biopics who asked the mayor to consult on the mayor's biopic (these other directors, the mayor felt, were probably one-hit wonders, biopicwise, but: benefit of the doubt), he *might* still accept their offer to consult if it didn't include an accompanying documentary, but only on the one condition that he could record a commentary track that you could listen to while the movie was playing.

See, the way the mayor saw it was he had a theory, and this was the theory: the advantage of a documentary was the same as the *dis*advantage of a biopic, and vice versa. That is: explanations. More specifically: explanations causing thinking.

In a biopic, you did not want explanations causing thinking.

In a documentary, you wanted explanations causing thinking.

If it was a biographical documentary, you wanted the subject of that biographical documentary to give explanations that answered pressing questions no one before had ever dared to ask him, and to describe some important incidents he'd never described before. If you didn't have that, your biographical documentary was garbage.

Unless the subject was dead.

If the subject of your biographical documentary was dead, then you needed never-before-seen archival footage of the subject describing important incidents and giving explanations that answered pressing questions that somebody'd asked him before he died.

Unless the subject died before the age of the abilities of recording sounds and moving pictures. Then, if you didn't want your biographical documentary to be garbage, you had to have a combination of an actor reading letters or speeches the subject wrote in a convincing-sounding voice-over during reenactments, and also some experts and/or members of the subject's family and/or of people who used to be professionally close to the subject describing incidents and giving explanations and historical insights that answered pressing questions.

So since the mayor wasn't dead, he'd obviously be the one to do the explaining in the biographical documentary about himself that accompanied any biopic about him that wasn't made by Scorsese if the biopic's filmmaker wanted him to consult on that biopic.

Unless that biopic was made by David O. Russell, David Fincher, or maybe Steven Spielberg. In that case, he'd do the explaining in the commentary track.

Because you couldn't have explanations in the biopic itself. Not unless you wanted that biopic to be guaranteed crappy.

That was the second part of the thing he'd started getting at before. That was the thing he was *really* getting at.

—

The thing was this: explanations in a biopic made the biopic crappy because a biopic was supposed to make you *feel* things, and explanations made you *think* things, and thinking things got in the way of feeling, which, in a certain way, was either very ironic or the very opposite of very ironic.

A perfect example for illustrating this better might be illustrated by something no less venal as a macaroni and cheese casserole.

Suppose your wife says she's about to feed you the best macaroni and cheese casserole of your life. She explains to you the proportions of cheese to milk to noodles she used when she made the casserole, and the thicknesses of the slices of olives and onions and peppers she sliced, the techniques she brought to bear on the layering into the casserole dish of said ingredients, and the heating and cooling and caramelizing methods she applied to the whole thing. Maybe also the herbs and spices and so forth as well. And she also explains what this macaroni and cheese casserole will be like: tells you the flavors it'll taste like, the scents that it will smell like, and the textures it'll feel like to your teeth and to your tongue, and even to your hand as it forks. She explains all that, then gives you a plate full of this macaroni and cheese casserole.

And then now you're eating it.

And maybe it *is* the best macaroni and cheese casserole of your life. Maybe you've never before eaten a better macaroni and cheese casserole, but you are nonetheless still *thinking,* while you're eating this casserole, about how the textures and scents and flavors match up to her explanation of how she said they'd be. And you're also thinking about other, earlier casseroles. You're comparing this macaroni and cheese casserole to other, earlier macaroni and cheese casseroles because you're trying to figure out if it really *is* the best macaroni and cheese casserole of your life, or if it's just one of the really great ones but that because you're eating it right now, in the moment, it seems like the best. (And, by the way, this is just what is meant by the eternal present in which we are all said to live in lately as being a problem, according to certain modern-day philosophers and other kinds of pundits of thought on internet and elsewhere.)

And you're *contrasting* the casseroles, too. You're not just comparing. You're comparing *and* contrasting the casseroles.

So instead of fully feeling the experience of eating what might be the best macaroni and cheese casserole of your life, you're only partly feeling the experience of eating it because part of you is *thinking* about the casserole as a result of the explanations your wife gave you about that casserole.

And in the part of your biopic that's about this casserole, there'd be a casserole-eating scene with actors where the casserole would look to the audience—and sound to them when chewed—like what might be the best casserole of the life of the actor who is playing you.

That's if Martin Scorsese made it.

Or *maybe* one of the other two—or possibly three—directors who have made uncrappy biopics.

But, in the part of a *documentary* on you that's about this casserole, there might be a reenactment of the eating of the casserole or an iPhone video of the actual casserole (if you recorded that casserole) or a still from that iPhone video (if that video exists), and probably it wouldn't look to the audience like what might be the best casserole of your life or the reenacting actor's life because of the angles and the light and etcetera not being ideal, and so an explanation from you would be required either in voice-over or in an interview segment, and during that voice-over or interview segment, you would not only explain that it might have been the best casserole of your life but explain what made it the possible-best casserole of your life: the textures and flavors and smells and plating of the casserole, and maybe also the thoughts you had while experiencing those sensory experiences with the pleasure nerves inside your face, and the methods you used to compare and contrast the casserole with other casseroles. And the audience wouldn't end up *feeling* like they'd witnessed you eating what might have been the best macaroni and cheese casserole of your life, but they would think a lot about how the experience of eating the casserole was an experience you were *explaining* might have been the best casserole-eating experience of your life, and they'd think about whether you were telling the truth, whether you were able to tell the truth, whether you did a good job with the words you used to tell the truth if in fact you were telling the truth, and whether the casserole you said might have been the best casserole of your life would have maybe-been the best casserole of *their* life if they'd received that casserole from their wife or husband or gender-nonconforming partner, or even from someone they weren't romantically involved with in any way, such as their mother for instance, or a sibling.

And that's fine: in a documentary. From a certain point of view or perspective, such thinking-causing explanations such as those are exactly what a documentary's whole point is, which . . .

Which . . .

"I kinda lost my train of thought," said the mayor to Apter, who was nipping good Scotch through the smile he was smiling across the desk at the mayor on April 21, 2022. "I'm . . . wait. I thought about this a lot last night, after *The King's Speech,* and it made a lot of sense. Trust me. But now I'm . . . *I'm* the casserole, or the biopic's the casserole? I guess that, in a way, we're both . . . No . . . We couldn't *both* be the casserole, unless . . . could we? or . . ."

"I think what you were getting at," Apter said, "is that if Martin Scorsese makes your biopic and wants to pay you to consult on it, you'll advise him to depict the two of us sitting across your desk from one another drinking good Scotch on Christmas Eve. And you'll suggest to Scorsese that, in the middle of that scene, the snow on the ledge outside the window should acquire a rapidly increasing glow that soon fills the whole screen with whiteness. When the whiteness fades, it'll be last week, and you'll have just finished telling me about your Obama dream. We'll still be sitting at your desk, drinking good Scotch, but there won't be any more snow on the ledge, and you will have a beard, all of which will indicate to the audience that months have passed. Furthermore, much of what went on in the months that have passed will have been brought across through implication and feeling—via Martin Scorsese's unparalleled filmmaking genius—and the rest of what went on in those months will be brought across in the post-whitescreen part of the scene in which we'll have just finished having discussed the Obama dream."

"All right," the mayor said. "So far so good."

"Well, so, if, however," Apter went on, "it's someone other than Martin Scorsese who makes your biopic and wants to pay you to consult on it, you'll refuse to do so unless they make an accompanying documentary about you. In that case, you'll advise the director to mark the passage of time between Christmas Eve and the day last week when you told me about the Obama dream in the same way as you'd have advised Martin

Scorsese, but then, in the accompanying documentary, you'll *explain* everything that went on *during* the passage of time marked by the white-screen part of the biopic scene because you won't be able to trust that anyone *except for* Martin Scorsese could ever possibly bring across all that went on during that period as comprehensively as Martin Scorsese could, let alone as elegantly as Martin Scorsese could. In fact, you won't trust that anyone except for Martin Scorsese could bring across *anything* in a biopic as comprehensively and elegantly as Martin Scorsese could, so in the documentary, you'll have a lot to say about any number of the events depicted in—or left out of—the biopic.

"*However,* if the director who makes your biopic and wants you to consult on it is either David O. Russell, David Fincher, or *possibly* Steven Spielberg, you—although you won't demand an accompanying documentary be made—you *will* refuse to consult on the biopic unless whichever one of the two or three of those directors that it is agrees to allow you to record a commentary track. If they *do* agree, you will advise them to mark the passage of time between Christmas Eve and the day you told me about the Obama dream last week in the same way you would have advised Scorsese or anyone else, but while that scene of us in your office is playing, you'll explain, *on the commentary track,* everything that happened during the passage of time the scene marks, same as you would have in the documentary. And you'll probably explain some other things on the commentary track as well, during other scenes that might fail to communicate all that Scorsese would have been able to communicate had he been the filmmaker."

"Right!" said the mayor. "You're a great listener, you know that? I couldn't have said any of that better myself."

"Maybe, maybe not," Apter said, "because something's confusing me. How would you be able to get everything across on a commentary track? The scene that we've been talking about, for example—unless I'm misunderstanding something—it wouldn't last more than a couple minutes."

"You know, I see what you're getting at there. Would I be able to explain all that happened in real life *during* the white part?"

"Yeah," said Apter. "What would you say?"

"That's a great question, Apter. A *great* question. Really insighted. Lemme think a few seconds . . ."

The mayor poured them more Scotch and thought a few seconds.

2

There really was a lot to explain. Which begged the question, first of all, of how to begin. And thereby in turn also begged the question secondly of how to more generally orientate oneself towards one's explanations.

Was Mount Chicago, that is, a case of men making history?

Or was it more a case of history making itself? history, which, verily as she rolled along, subsumated men to their predetermined fates?

Was it, in other words, that the mayor and Apter took a many-pronged approach to Mount Chicago, or that destiny's approach to Mount Chicago was a beast of many prongs?

The only certainty at hand the mayor ever concluded to was there was more than one prong. Five prongs at minimum.

Maybe even six or seven.

Enough prongs, anyway, that to count them might require more fingers than the mayor had on either one of his hands.

Right Hand Pointer

One prong for sure was the Glibner prong. The Glibner prong could probably be considered the first prong. It started, in a way, before Apter was hired. Before the anomaly itself, for that matter. Nine weeks before the anomaly? Ten weeks before? It could have been even eleven or twelve.

Glibner started itching was how it started.

Glibner started itching a *lot*.

Scratching, too, as one does when one itches.

Thought he was having some kind of allergic reaction to environmental toxins or pollutants at first. Something in the air. No emergency, though. Figured that it would pass like the weather. Or with the weather.

And when the season changed and Glibner kept on itching, he figured it was just his skin had gotten sensitive to something that it didn't used to be sensitive to. Because the body was like that.

That's just what it was like.

The mayor knew this through his own lived experience. When he was young, he'd eat pizza or a burger and fries for lunch, then some pizza at dinner if lunch had been a burger, or tacos for dinner if lunch had been pizza and he didn't want a burger.

Also often some dinner fries, too, irregardless.

And if he wanted some ice cream after lunch or dinner, he'd eat some ice cream after lunch or dinner. Only time he wouldn't eat some ice cream if he wanted some ice cream was *while* he was eating his lunch or dinner: then what he'd do is he'd order a milkshake. And when he wanted to drink, he'd drink some Jameson and chase it with Guinness or he'd drink Johnny Red and chase it with Guinness.

These were lifestyle choices that had all made him feel good.

But eventually they didn't.

He hadn't been able to eat or drink like that for years. The body wouldn't stand for it. Indigestion in the guts. Reflux above them. Fatigue in the muscles. A fog upon the very noodle of the skull. That was middle age.

That's what middle age was. Higher sensitivities, lower tolerances. Preventive behaviors. Better practices. More salads and fish. Nicer whiskey. No stout whatsoever. Straighter posture in your desk chair, also. Lifting with your legs, even just your briefcase. Yogurt with your breakfast. Fresh fruit for dessert, and flossing right after if the fresh fruit was berries. About your teeth, you came to see the truth of what you'd always been told and known deep down: you only got one set. You simply had to start being more conscionable.

So for his part, the mayor, when he noticed Glibner scratching, figured: higher sensitivities, lower tolerances. He'd suggested Glibner try a gentler laundry detergent, a bath soap without any added perfumes, non-antiperspirizing underarm deodorant.

Glibner tried it all. Nothing did the trick.

But you could get used to anything if you get enough practice. That was middle age, too. The lesson you learn from it.

To furthen an earlier example, for instance: Used to be the mayor's wife would call the mayor at the office around two or three, ask what sort of non-pizza he wanted for dinner, what kind of un–ice cream he'd like for dessert, and she'd give him choices like salmon or tilapia, grapes or plums, and he'd tell her, "Whatever you feel like, honey," which was the nice way of saying, "It makes no difference, all of it is bland, too soft, and wet." But then one day, completely out of nowhere, he found himself getting hungry for tilapia. Now, maybe it was just he was hungry for the capers in the sauce she sometimes flavored and textured the tilapia with, but that was not the point. He had a preference. That was the point.

He'd *developed* a preference.

She called him at the office and offered salmon or tilapia or a new tuna thing she'd been reading about, and he told her, "Tilapia. Not the kind with coconut sauce, though. The lemon and capers one," and she said she could do that, and, what do you know? Just like that he suddenly found himself a little bit looking forward to dinner.

Man was a highly adaptional creature.

Adaptionality-wise, it didn't even have to be you, either. You could itch and scratch all the time and get used to it, of course, but those around you could also get used to it, too.

Many could, at least.

The middle-aged especially. In middle age you had to learn to tolerate your own lower tolerances, and those lower tolerances of others around you as well, or else . . . what? You'd go bananas.

Glibner itched and scratched all the time and got used to it, accepted it. And the mayor got used to and accepted Glibner's itching and scratching. And probably Glibner's wife got used to and accepted it, too, but only to a certain degree. That is: not completely.

Because then she went bananas.

About two-three weeks after Apter'd been hired, so three-four weeks after the terrestrial anomaly, there came a night that Glibner itched and scratched so much, his wife went bananas and kicked him out of bed, made him sleep on the couch.

In the morning, she got him an appointment with a doctor, and he went to see the doctor, who sent him for tests.

Tests came back, and what they said was: cancer.

Hodgkin's.

Either the lymphoma or the nonlymphoma kind, the mayor couldn't keep the medical nom de guerres straight. Stage 3 though. Not the worst, except also not the best. The prognosis was decent, but: chemo.

Right there was when the Glibner prong, whenever history would come to judge it had exactly began, started doing its main effect.

So first of all, chemo. Chemo and all of its many attentive ravishings. Then secondly: the general dispiritedness and malcontentability that sprouts out from those ravishings and causes one to enter into a revaluation of the values one lives by and practices in the course of one's life and actions.

In the first couple weeks after Glibner's diagnosis, the mayor'd heart-to-hearted with him once on the phone, and once also at a lunch that Glibner hardly touched, and in both conversations there was more than the usual amount of themes on the topic of kids—about loving one's kids, spending time with one's kids, not dying without really knowing one's kids or getting one's kids to really know one thyself—and it sounded like maybe, even if he beat the lymphoma, Glibner would not return to work at City Hall.

And nor was it a topic the mayor felt it was appropriate to press Glibner on, either.

And neither did he feel like he needed to, either.

Gal who'd said *sinkhole* on internet aside, Glibner'd put together a great team at City Hall and, since he'd gone on sick leave, that team had rallied, stepped up, was so far taking good care of business in Glibner's absence. Plus by then he had Apter, who saw all the angles even better than Glibner, saw the angles Jewishly and got out ahead of them, cut them off at the pass if they needed the chop.

Now the pointiest part of the Glibner prong, though, was not Glibner himself, or the cancer he had, but his teenage son, Bobby. But before Bobby's role in Mount Chicago got important enough to be explained at this juncture, the other prongs started doing their thing, and the mayor'd have to explain those first.

Suffice it to say for now that Bobby was above-average big on using social media.

Suffice it also to say for now, more specifically, that when Bobby first met the mayor eight years before—when Bobby was seven years old or something like that—it was at a barbecue over at the Glibners' place, and Bobby requested the mayor's and the mayor's wife's friendship on Facebook *while* they were all shaking hands hello.

And last but not least, let's suffice it to say for now with some little bit of totally affectionate jesting that if Mamet wrote a tagline for Bobby to speak in a monologue in a mostly unfictionalized movie about Bobby Glibner, that tagline for sure would be "Always be posting." (The mayor could not take credit for that joke, though. That joke was his wife's.)

Right Hand Middle Finger

Mid-January, the mayor's office received the report from the team of University of Illinois scientists who'd been studying the crater with sensitive instruments. This report was the second prong. It was mostly good news.

The best of it was: the terrestrial anomaly was a terrestrial anomaly. The details of the math and the physics and the chemistry behind it weren't all that clear to the mayor, but that was all right. He got the main thrust. Basically, a combination of very uncommon geological and lake and weather events combined in an even more very uncommon—like, never-before-seen—way, and there you had it: anomaly.

The mayor's favorite part of the report was the disconsenting opinions that came at the end about the odds.

Opinion 1: Before the terrestrial anomaly happened, the odds that the terrestrial anomaly would happen had been one in ten billion. Now, because of the relaxation of the tectonic powers and the settling down of crust layers that resulted from the terrestrial anomaly, the odds that another terrestrial anomaly would happen in Chicago were one in one hundred trillion.

Opinion 2: Before the terrestrial anomaly happened, the odds that the terrestrial anomaly would happen had been one in two trillion. Now, because of the relaxation of the tectonic powers and the settling down of crust layers that resulted from the terrestrial anomaly, the odds that another terrestrial anomaly would happen in Chicago were one in a trillion trillion.

One in one hundred trillion? One in a *trillion* trillion? Not that the mayor wasn't happy to hear it, but what ever happened to *not in a million years*? That wasn't available? Like, who even had a calculator big enough? The calculator app the mayor had on his phone only went up to the hundred millions.

Unless you turned the phone sideways.

But point is: hilarious.

When the mayor, at the presser the following day, summarized the news about the odds to the people, the way he put it was, "Never again." Nobody bucked.

There was also some neutral news in the report. Facts and diagrams and photos of sonograms:

The crater was 123 acres big, and pretty much rectangular. If you could remove all the junk and detritus from the crater, the lowest part, in the middle of the crater, would be about 250 feet below street level, and the highest parts, which were along the crater's edges (Lake and Jackson between Columbus and Wabash; Columbus and Wabash between Lake and Jackson), would be about 150 feet below street level, though sometimes as much as 180 feet below street level because the sides of the crater, which were basically sheer, sloped a little more in some places than others.

In other words: if you removed all the junk and detritus from the crater and then stood right at the edge of the crater at street level, and you dropped a penny straight down into the crater, that penny would, depending on where exactly along the edge you'd been standing, fall 150 to 180 feet before it landed at the bottom of the crater. But if you *threw* the penny toward the middle of the crater, it would fall even more than 180 feet before it landed at the bottom of the crater since the crater got deeper the farther toward the center it got.

As for that junk and detritus: most of it was able to be broken down and removed using basically normal means of demolition—bulldozers, diggers, a little bit of dynamite.

And if you removed all that junk and detritus, all that would be left in the crater would be what the scientists were calling *the cone.*

The cone started rising out of the ground at the lowest point on the surface of the crater, right at the center, and the center of the cone itself was pretty much right directly under where the Cloud Gate sculpture, aka the Bean, used to be.

The epicenter they called it, which the mayor did not call it because of the powerful earthquakian overtones.

The diameter at the base of the cone was five acres. The height of the cone was just over 230 feet. All the scientists agreed in the report that removing the cone would be virtually impossible. The mayor couldn't believe it at first because: *Impossible?* Who tells the mayor of Chicago *impossible?*

Morning after the report was delivered, he called the lead eggheads into his office to dress them down for saying *impossible,* but, turned out, they did not deserve it. They said that, first of all, the cone started down deeper in the earth than the base of the crater. What their report was calling the cone was really just the top of the cone: the part of the cone that showed above the base of the crater. They referred him to page 117 of the report, which had diagrams the mayor couldn't make heads or tails of.

They explained the diagrams:

The bottom of the cone was even bigger than the part that stuck out from the base of the crater, they explained. The bottom of the cone, in fact, was almost as far down *below* the base of the crater, they said, as the top of the cone was *above* the base of the crater, and the farther down it went, the wider it got, till you got to the bottom.

"So I'm thinking about a Hershey's Kiss," the mayor said to the scientists. "You take a Hershey's Kiss, tear the wrapper from the top, but stop tearing halfway. Now look at what you got: if the Kiss was the cone, the brown part's the part we'd see if the detritus and junk got removed from the crater. Silver part's the part we would *not* see unless we dug into the base of the crater surrounding the cone. Would you say my metaphorical suppository's accurate?"

They would. They did.

And this was how come all the detritus and junk created by the anomaly was all in the crater, well below ground level, instead of there being mountains of it piled up above the ground: because everything within the area of the crater got sucked toward the center and down, down, down, toward and/or into the space that the cone was now taking up—a space that, while the anomaly was happening, was an unimaginably hot and pressurous space.

Where the cone was now, the eggheads said, had been the hottest, most extremely pressurous part of the whole anomaly. They said they'd done some calculations, and that the amount of material that was heated and pressured into forming the cone was as much material as the whole Aon building *plus* the whole Art Institute plus even a little bit more material as well. In fact, they said, from the couple of satellite images they'd studied of the anomaly, they did a kind of digital reconstructing or reverse engineering of the way the structures dropped and dragged toward the epicenter and were pretty sure the cone was largely composed of the Art Institute's modern wing and some 70 percent of the Aon building in addition to cars and sidewalk and street cement, and, yes, people and their dogs and their children and so forth as well, but that was nothing anyone wanted to think about, even if you couldn't really help thinking about it, which you couldn't.

"Now correct me if I am incorrect, or wrong in any way," said the mayor, "but what I hear you saying about this cone is that these pressures and heats that formed it inside the space that it now takes up, the way they worked was like with Superman, when he takes a hunk of coal in his fist and squeezes it into a diamond."

"Pretty much," said one of the eggheads.

"Okay," the mayor said. "Okay. And so why is it black?"

"Why is it *black*?" said the other egghead.

"Report says the surface of the parts of the cone you scientifically examined was black and you thought that the whole surface of the cone was probably black."

"The interior of the cone, as well," said an egghead.

"But a diamond," the mayor said, "is not black. Why isn't it a diamond, the cone, is what I'm getting at."

"Well, to begin with, the molecular structure of diamonds," the one egghead said, "is crystalline, and so not only would a uniform exertion of energies be needed to—"

"Never mind all that," the mayor said. "Forget it. But are there diamonds *inside* that cone?"

"I suppose it isn't *terribly* unlikely that some diamonds might have formed, but . . ."

"And what about the people's diamonds?" said the mayor. "Like the diamond earrings and pendants and engagement rings and so forth that belonged to the Chicagoans that got melted and pressured into the cone—are those diamonds still in there, you think?"

"Surely some of them must be, yes," the second egghead said. "Are you wondering about the feasibility of mining the cone for diamonds, or trying to retrieve the diamond jewelry, or . . . ?"

"Mining?" the mayor said. "No. That was just a passing curiosity. A little weird of one, maybe, I am starting to see by the looks you are giving me, which, I'm not too in love with, the looks, tell the truth. I guess . . . I guess it's probably a lot of diamonds that are in that cone is all I'm saying. I'm just reflecting, with sadness and awe, about all the diamonds, all the people who prized those diamonds, and all of them dead and gone, now, you know? I mean, the Art Institute crowd—these were frequently some of our most upscale citizens."

"Well, good, that's good," the first egghead said.

"It's *good*?" the mayor said. "These were *people*. With *families*."

"No, no. Not the people," said the egghead. "That's tragic—the losses. Incomprehensible. I lost a cousin, who, growing up, was almost like a sister, and . . . I was only trying to say that it was good you weren't thinking about mining the cone because we really don't think it would be worth the labor, Mr. Mayor. As we say in the report, we recommend you just leave the cone be. Fill the crater in around it, build on top of it—doesn't matter. Whatever you fill with, and whatever you might build, the structural integrity of the cone will be greater—the cone will support it. The cone will not bend. It will not shatter. It will not melt. Without a diamond-tipped drill, you couldn't even scratch its surface."

"I'm sorry to hear about your cousin," said the mayor. "There is perhaps nothing in the world that is harder to lose than to lose a loved one is. I am no scientist, but I am certain I would venture that is harder to undergo than even the surface of this very cone you have so thoroughly belabored in study for the good of the city."

"Thank you, Mr. Mayor."

"You're welcome. I mean that. Now, let me ask you guys something," the mayor said. "Do you have a better word than *crater* you can think of? A word that's maybe not so totally . . . moony?"

"I'm not sure what you mean by *moony*, Mr. Mayor."

"Not moony. That's not the word. But like the moon, though, you know? Empty. Rocky."

"Desolate," Apter said.

"*Desolate,* exactly," the mayor said. "Apter here always knows what I mean. Can you guys think of a word that's less desolate than *crater* to call the crater?"

"Dr. Chen has occasionally referred to the crater as the *basin,*" said the egghead who hadn't lost a sisterlike cousin.

To the other one, the mayor said, "Now *that* is good. Are *you* Dr. Chen?"

"I'm Dr. Manganelli," said the one who'd lost the cousin.

"Well, please tell Dr. Chen for me that I think he's really on to something. *Basin* works. I think we can do better, but maybe that is just my naturally optimistical nature shining through. *Basin* is definitely good enough for now. Here's what I want you to do," said the mayor, handing his copy of the report to the egghead who wasn't Manganelli. "Before this report or any summary of your findings gets turned over to the press, I want you to take all the *crater*s out and replace them with *basin*s. The people of Chicago deserve to have less desolate feelings when they think about the anomaly, not more. Don't you agree?"

The eggheads agreed. How could they not? They were funny-looking, yes, their haircuts were not exactly good haircuts, and their manners were maybe a little bit autistical, and their voices were maybe a little bit girly, but these weren't bad guys. These were okay guys. From a certain perspective, the mayor admired them.

<u>Right Hand Ring Finger</u>

By the end of February, most of the companies whose offices had been in the buildings destroyed by the anomaly had either relocated to other offices inside the city, or were in the process of relocating to other offices inside the city.

Some companies had moved to the suburbs, sure, and a few had even shuttered, but, for the most part, those companies were either failing or weak-kneed companies that more than likely would have left the city or shuttered within the next couple years, even if there'd never been an anomaly.

At least that's how the mayor chose to see those companies, and how he chose to not stop the people of Chicago from seeing those companies.

Plus also, too, and more to the point: just like if there hadn't been an anomaly, those evacuating and shuttering companies would be replaced by other, better companies. Chicago was, after all, still the greatest city on Earth, and, what that partly meant was: megacity. And what *that* partly meant was: too big to fail. The economic environment was multiply various and full of opportunity. It was important to remember that.

To never forget it.

One window closes, so you open up a door.

And then you go through that door.

And so forth through other doors, and onward into rooms with bigger, better windows that might or might not close, and then you dealt with those then.

Skyscraper-wise, things were also looking positive.

The owners of the Crain Communications Building, the Aon Center, and Prudential Plaza had all a) been well and properly insured and b) they'd committed—both privately in meetings with the mayor, and publicly through press releases—to rebuilding what was lost. In just a couple-three-five-seven years, the skyline would be returned to its former glory. No weird gaps.

In fact, according to the mayor's taste in skylines, the glory of Chicago's might even end up being *more* glorious of a credit to the city inasmuch as he'd never thought very highly of the Crain Communications Building, which had, okay, back when it was built in 1984, looked pretty sci-fi with its diamondy top and disaligned corner—for better or worse, it had really looked like *the future* at first—but, even before all the downtown traders unpleated their suit pants and unmoussed their mullets and started buying Japanese luxury vehicles (1993? '94?), that building just looked like . . . the eighties. Shallow. Unnatural. Trying too hard. President Reagan's too-dark pompadour. Madonna doing movies. Eddie Murphy singing pop songs. Rambo III and Rocky IV. Tofutti brand dairy-free frozen dessert. Crystal Light, Sizzlean, and Oakley Razor Blades.

All that shitty, embarrassing stuff.

You'd look up at the Crain in 1992, say, and you'd think to yourself: The Berlin Wall is no longer standing, so why am I still dressed like this? Why are all the kids still dressing like *that*? Why did I used to watch *Dallas* and *Falcon Crest*? Why do I still watch *Who's the Boss?* and *Cosby*? Why do I have to keep on pretending that Oliver Stone is good at making movies or that Chevy still makes a good-looking Corvette? Why am I still buttering toast with margarine?

CRAIN COMMUNICATIONS BUILDING

You'd look up at the Crain and get a not-so-fresh feeling.

The skyline would, at minimum, recover.

And as for the six-block stretch of buildings along Michigan Avenue and the west side of Wabash? That six-block stretch that was now only so much rubble in the basin?

Chicago would cross that bridge when it came to it. In fact, Chicago might, when the time came, build an actual bridge you could cross there. That was one option. A bridge over the basin. *The New Michigan Avenue Overpass* they'd probably call it if that's what they did.

Remained to be seen.

How that portion of the basin would be dealt with in the future was a question for the future that would not be decided till more of the future became some of the past: till the skyline was returned to its former glory or an excession of that former glory, or was at least closer to being returned to either one of those states of glory, and better-informed decisions could be made. But it could be prime real estate once again, that six-block stretch. Nothing would necessarily prevent that. Only question was the question of when, which was not a question the mayor sweated or would sweat too soon if ever he would even sweat it at all.

The mayor, in short, did not sweat those lost buildings. Those buildings, in short, were not a prong. Or if those buildings *were* a prong, they got only a toe for representation, and the mayor was not about to start going barefoot.

What the mayor did sweat was no Art Institute. *That* was a prong. *That* got a finger.

Third on the strong hand. Aka ring finger.

The Art Institute of Chicago could not be replaced. It could not be replaced because it was irreplaceable, and it was irreplaceable not just because of the problems they were having with their insurers about the great works of art that should have been kept in off-site storage but were instead for some reason kept in on-site storage and so got destroyed and etc.—problems that were going to take forever to settle in court—but because even if they got all the money they said they were owed by their insurers, they could not stock any rebuilt Art Institute that might get built with priceless and extremely expensive artworks that would even come close to approximately substituting for even one-one-hundredth of the priceless and extremely expensive artworks the anomaly destroyed, such as Picassos.

And such as *American Gothics* and *Nighthawk.*

And that picnic at the park made of dots from *Ferris Bueller's?*

The close-up vagina-celebration paintings of the desert flowers from the old Southwest?

All those beautiful Andrew Warhols?

Dream on.

These were one-of-a-kind works of art, the lot of them. *Irreplaceable.* And they were hardly a fraction of what you could take for an example if you needed examples.

Not to mention all the artistic nonart artifacts they'd had in there, too: the finely crafted bronze weapons and armor from the swords-and-shields era of early mankind, the blankets and towels of the Native Americans, the decoratively emblazoned handmade vases from the samurai period of the Chinese emperors, significant African pots and pans, the necklaces and crowns and dueling pistols of the British noblecy—none of it was left.

There was no replacing the Art Institute of Chicago, and that could cause all kinds of negative domino effects.

Pride in the city—yes, for sure: that could go down.

Educational opportunities and cultural understandings for the students and underprivileged youths of the city? Those would definitely go down.

Classy dates with one's romantic partner that took place between 4 and 7 p.m. on a Thursday and didn't cost anything beyond the train fare as long as both of you could show an official form of ID that said you lived in the City of Chicago? How many options to have such dates were any longer available? One fewer than before is how many any longer—that much was for sure.

And it wasn't just the people of Chicago who lost these works of art, but the people of the entire world, including Indiana and suburban Chicago. People who, with there no longer being an Art Institute, now had one less reason—or thousands less reasons, each lost artwork and artifact potentially a reason—to visit Chicago. One or thousands less reasons to stay in its hotels and eat at its restaurants and get some shopping done at its shops. And that was the pointiest part of this prong. The tourist economy. It would be getting dinged. It had already been dung, but that was not the mayor's fault: no one blamed him. What they'd blame him for was if it stayed that way.

So the mayor had to fix it. But how do you fix it? How do you replace what is irreplaceable? How would failing to replace what was irreplaceable eventually, unfairly, reflect on his legacy? How might it—in the sooner immediacy—affect his chances at reelection in 2023?

These big questions and a couple of other associated big ones had haunted the mayor for nearly a month.

For thirteen straight weeks after 11/17, his approval ratings had climbed and climbed, peaking—at 84 percent!—in the wake of the scientists' report on the basin. In the wake of that wake, though, they'd started to sink.

He had kept his face happy and his attitude positive, even in private, but the more the ratings sank, the more the big questions haunted him, and the more the positivity tired him out. And then, one late afternoon, middle of March, just hours after learning his ratings had sunk to 59 percent—the previous week, they'd been at 66 percent—the big questions were haunting him so goddamn much he couldn't stand to keep them to himself anymore. He suggested Apter pour them a second round of whiskey, and once the kid was up and heading for the liquor cart, he asked a couple of those questions out loud. A couple of the not so self-centered-sounding ones, knowing that Apter would know what he meant.

"How do we replace what is irreplaceable?" he asked the back of Apter. "How can we possibly replace the Art Institute?"

Apter brought the whiskeys back to the desk, saying nothing. They raised and clinked their glasses and sipped.

"So?" the mayor said.

"So what?" Apter said.

"I asked you some questions."

"I thought you were just lamenting," said Apter.

"I was lamenting. I am lamenting. But I was also really asking for your thoughts on these matters."

"On how we replace the irreplaceable?"

"Specifically the Art Institute."

"We don't," Apter said. "We don't replace it. It's irreplaceable."

"Do you got, perhaps, a less obvious answer than that?"

"We don't *try* to replace it. We don't even *pretend* to try to replace it. We do something else. Or pretend to."

"Such as?"

"Turn it into a park?" Apter offered.

"A park."

"People love parkspace."

"Well, that much is true, but . . ."

"No one ever comes out against parkspace," said Apter. "In the entire history of big city politics, no political platform has ever included an anti-parkspace agenda."

"Well, yeah. Might as well be an anti-education agenda."

"An anti-*child* agenda," Apter said.

"A pro-crime agenda."

"A pro-Indiana agenda," said Apter.

"I don't know about *that*," the mayor said, "but okay, I'm listening— hey."

Apter'd taken his phone out.

"I said I was listening," the mayor said.

Apter read his phone. "Nearly thirty million people," he said, "visited Millennium Park last year. The Art Institute had fewer than two million visitors."

"Sure," said the mayor. "But they were the *right* kind of visitors, though—the Art Institute ones."

"The *right kind*?" said Apter, still reading the phone.

"I don't," the mayor said, "mean that racistly. I mean it financially. The Art Institute was upscale. Millennium Park—that was . . . admission was free, you know? People came from out of state to go to Art Institute, then stayed at hotels. People came from the suburbs to go to Art Institute, and then they fine-dined."

"Plenty of wealthy people visited Millennium Park."

"But not enough, I bet. Do we have any numbers on the wealth of the visitors? Does it even matter? It doesn't even matter. I mean, are you trying to make me feel worse? Millennium Park is rubble, too."

"Irreplaceable rubble, though?" Apter said.

"Well . . . maybe not *as* irreplaceable, but still, I'd say yes. Pretty irreplaceable. You had the Franklin Barry bandshell there, you had the Bean, Crown Fountain, the BP bridge. All that stuff was . . . that was beautiful stuff."

"It was," Apter said. "I loved Millennium Park. But Frank Gehry, Anish Kapoor, Jaume Plensa—none of them are dead."

"So what? Who are they?"

"The guys who designed the bandshell, the Bean, the fountain, and the bridge. They're all still alive."

"Sure, okay. I gotta say, though, Apter, I just—I don't get where your head's at today. I ask you how we replace the Art Institute, and you're saying rebuild Millennium Park on top of where the Art Institute was. Doesn't compute for me."

"Look, forget about *on top of*," Apter said. "Or—I don't know. Maybe. But that was just a rough draft idea. I'm saying forget about the Art Institute for now. I'm saying we could rebuild Millennium Park. Or try to at least."

"You know how much that park cost to build? How much it cost back in the good old days when the ground wasn't twenty stories below the ground?"

"Around half a billion dollars," Apter said. "Says right here," he said, pointing at his phone.

"Half a *bil*. Twenty-twenty-five years ago, half a bil," said the mayor. "And you know how *long* it took to build?"

"I know it wasn't ready for the millennium."

"It was *four years late* for the goddamn millennium."

"Four years late for the millennium—you're right," said Apter, thumbing upward on his phone. "But the thing is: Who got it built?"

"You know who built it," the mayor said.

"Everyone does. And who was a stronger mayor than him?"

"His father probably."

"That's debatable," Apter said. "But except for his *father*, what mayor of Chicago was in office even half as long as him?"

"I see your point. The Son was great. So what? I'm not him."

"*That's* my point," Apter said. "You are not Richard M. Daley, who was four years late on Millennium Park, who was more than—Jesus, did you know this?—he was more than *two hundred percent* over budget on the park."

"Yeah, no shit. The Son couldn't do it like he said he could do it. The Son, who did *not*, I might add—and who did *not*, I repeat—have to contend with any natural disaster during his time in office that killed thousands of Chicagoans and buried the Art Institute."

"Exactly."

"I am really not following you at all."

"Even Richard M. Daley, in far better circumstances than yours, couldn't get Millennium Park built on time or on budget. He had two years; it took six years. He had $175 million; it cost $475 million. But then he got it built, and everyone loved it."

"Not everyone did. Not at first. At first—"

"But *at last* they did. That's what matters here. Millennium Park, which was much beloved by the time it was destroyed, is, in memory— like nearly everything else that is gone—even more beloved. What I'm suggesting is that you, Mr. Mayor, will announce your intentions to build Chicago a park—a *memorial* park—that will cost *more* to build and *take longer* to build than Millennium Park. And it will cost more to build than you'll say it'll cost and take longer to build than you'll say it'll take, and everyone will know that, and no one will blink. They will embrace you as a visionary. A man of faith in the power of parkspace, the power of beauty. You will build something beautiful that will—not coincidentally—inspire businesses and real estate developers to stay in the Loop, to make the Loop—to make all of Chicago—an even more desirable place to live and to work than it was *before* the anomaly. And look, maybe you'll even hire the same artists and architects to design the park—they're *still alive*. Either way, this memorial park you build will be *better* than Millennium Park. Might even be *bigger* than Millennium Park. No matter what, it will draw more tourists than Millennium Park, and *everyone will love it*. Everyone'll love *you*. And more pertinently than that: they will love you for *planning* to build it. They will love you *while* you are building it. They will love you *at first* as well as *at last*."

"Memorial park. I don't know. Anyway, we do need to start talking about a memorial, I guess. Something like the water tower—something symbolic. I don't know what that would be, though. Everything's . . ."

"It'll have to be a lot more than the fucking water tower," Apter said. "The anomaly was much worse than the great Chicago fire."

"*Worse!*" the mayor said. "Fire wiped out the whole city."

"It wiped out some buildings," Apter said. "Three hundred–some people died."

"That's not true."

Apter showed him the Wikipedia entry on his phone.

Three hundred–some people.

"That is a great surprise to me," the mayor said. "Am I crazy? How many people lived in Chicago?"

"At the time of the fire? Let's see," Apter said, poking at his phone. "In 1871, Chicago was the fifth-largest city in the nation. Population of about three hundred thousand. And look here: ten years later—1880—it was the fourth-largest city. Population half a million. Ten years after that—not even quite twenty years after the fire—Chicago was more than a million strong, and had become the second-largest city in the United States."

"Now *that* is a story that is full of beautiful hope, the story those numbers tell," the mayor said. "I didn't realize the growth happened so fast. This information could be useful in a speech down the line. I am storing it in my noodle."

"Good," Apter said. "You're right. That's good. But I don't think you've heard me. This park I'm talking about: the *promise* of it will win you the next election. You won't have to deliver on that promise for a *while*. Just make it, repeatedly. And then, once you do deliver on the promise—and you *will* at *some* point deliver on the promise, maybe even after the twenty-twenty-*seven* election; you, who aren't Mayor Daley, will be allowed at least as much time as it took Mayor Daley—it'll seal your legacy."

"You're a little worked up this afternoon, Apter. You forget to eat lunch or something? I think you're maybe drunk."

"Not drunk in the least. I had a burger for lunch, a great big burger with bacon and cheese."

"Ah, to be a young man," said the mayor. "Where'd you eat that burger at?"

"Where'd I eat the burger? I ate it at the Blarington."

"Any good for burgers? They weren't open for burgers in my burger-eating days."

"Excellent burgers."

"Fries?"

"Yeah, fries."

"Hand-cut, I'm betting."

"Hand-cut and crisp. A heavy silver boatful."

"I ever tell you what I used to eat fries with, Apter?"

"Why don't you tell me."

"Mayo," said the mayor.

"Mayo. Okay. That's pretty interesting."

"A lot of people do that sometimes these days, I know. With the garlicky mayo, right? the alley-olé? Didn't used to, though. I was a pioneer of mayo on fries. Used to get made fun of for it."

"And look at you now, kicked back in your chair, feet up on the desk, sipping your whiskey, Chicago's chief executive, the king of all French fries."

"Wiseass."

"A park is a good idea, Mr. Mayor. It's the best idea I've ever put forward here, and time is of the essence. We have everyone's sympathy. You want to move on this fast. Secure private donations. Major donations. Host a charity event, or a benefit concert, and—"

"A *benefit* concert!"

"Why not?" Apter said. "Glibner told me that Perry Farrell, right after the anomaly, called him up champing at the bit to do something for the city, and that's the guy who owns Lollapalooza, so . . ."

"Yeah, I remember Glibner mentioned that. But I don't know about that Farrell. He's maybe, uh . . . He seems a little bit *funky*, you know?

And Lollapalooza—that's complicated, my relationship with Lolla-palooza, if you want to know the truth. Anyway, Farrell's not the only guy you have to deal with when it comes to Lollapalooza."

"So forget Perry Farrell. Forget Lollapalooza. It wouldn't have to be a concert. It could be *any*thing high-profile. What's important is to get the ball rolling. We get a significant donation or two for the park, and then . . . Money follows money, right? But it needs to happen soon. Before California falls into the ocean. Before New Orleans starts drowning again, or Puerto Rico, or who knows where else. This can't wait till summer."

"Okay, so I'll think about it."

"Don't humor me," Apter said, smiling the smile.

"I'm not!" the mayor said, smiling it back.

Though he was.

Mostly.

Right Hand Pointer Again and Also Pinky

On the ride home, the mayor got a call from Glibner, who was in great spirits. Beyond great spirits. Kept breaking out into that crying kind of laughter. That morning, some test results had come back. His treatment's success had exceeded expectations. Far exceeded them. Total remission. He would not be returning to work at City Hall. Next fall, he'd be a visiting associate professor of political science at DePaul University, where his wife taught English. If he liked it, they'd probably hire him permanent. If he didn't, he'd figure out something else to do. In the meantime, he'd just spend time with his family, rent a camper and take them on a couple of road trips, see himself some coastlines. The world was his oyster. That's what all this had taught him. It had always been his oyster, the whole entire world. How had he missed it? Why hadn't he known?

"Good for you, Reggie," the mayor said, and meant it. "I knew you'd pull through."

"World's your oyster, too, you know? No less than mine."

"Yeah, my oyster. Except I want a burger. God*damn*, I want a burger."

"I hope we'll stay in touch."

"Sure, we'll stay in touch," the mayor said, which came out sounding less warm than he'd have hoped. "I mean, what the hell, Reg? Of *course* we'll stay in touch."

"Maybe I'll convince you to come to DePaul, guest-lecture my class," Glibner suggested.

"Name the day," the mayor said. "And thank you for calling. Now go be with your family, godsakes."

When he came into the kitchen, his wife was by the oven, drinking white from a goblet. He touched her near the eyes and kissed her deeply on the mouth, but also really gently.

After he stopped, she said, "That was special."

"Glibner's cancer's totally remissed."

"What good news!" she said. "That's great. I hadn't realized you were all that worried, though."

"I wasn't. Least I didn't think I was. But you: I am so in love with you."

"Well, same here, pally."

"The world is your oyster and it's my oyster, too. We have to remember. We should never forget."

"I like the sound of *that*."

"We will not this evening be supping on fish."

"It's already cooking."

"It's going in the garbage then."

"You're taking me out?"

"Verily shalt I."

"I'll put on some lipstick."

At the Blarington, the mayor overdid it on the mayo. Four little silver cups of it that weren't that little.

His wife didn't make any comments on the mayo. When the waiter replaced the third cup with the fourth, she did give him an almost stern kind of look, but the mayor, winking, footsied her foot, and the look completely melted away.

It was a really pleasant moment, that little exchange there. The kind that you hoped you'd remember while you died, if how you died was in a bed, slowly.

Whole dinner'd been full of moments like that. They'd used their softest voices, touched and held hands underneath the table, discussed vacations future and past. But then, a couple bites into dessert—they were sharing a bowl of mixed berries and cream—bloating overcame the mayor all the sudden, a streak of heartburn flashed in his chest, and the focus it took to keep the pressures inside himself from getting outside himself before he could excuse himself was making his pits drip.

"Be right back," he said to his wife.

Ten minutes later, he returned to the table, and he felt a lot better, but not enough better, which, even if he had, would not have made a difference. The mood had been spoiled. He'd spoiled the mood. No love that night would the mayor be making. His wife was fiddling around with her phone.

"What you got there?" said the mayor when she didn't look up.

"Check your Facebook," she said.

"Maybe you remember perhaps," said the mayor, "how someone—some beautiful lady whose name I do not recall at the moment—told me that a certain game on Facebook with bagels and arithmetic was making me *tense,* and how right then and there I immediately deleted Facebook off my phone. To *aplease* that beautiful lady."

"So come here."

He ass-slid himself around the booth clockwise. His wife set the phone on the table between them. What was he looking at? A stack of comments made mostly of words like *brave* and *strong* and *you're amazing* and *proud of you.*

"And?" the mayor said to his wife.

And she made a kind of show of how many times she had to flick the screen to scroll up to the top. Once she got there, he saw that the comments were comments on a post from Robbie Glibner.

The post said this:

cancer & 8time suicide survivor

The mayor was puzzled. His wife was, too. Because what did that mean, *suicide survivor*? Wasn't that kind of an octomoron?

And a *cancer survivor*: Had Robbie had cancer? It did not seem possible. It did not seem possible for Robbie Glibner, the fifteen-year-old son of a friend of the mayor's, a man who'd been working closely with the mayor for almost seven years, to have had cancer without the mayor or the mayor's wife knowing. And for Robbie to have had cancer that remissed on the same day his father's cancer remissed without the mayor or the mayor's wife knowing seemed even less possible. So obviously—obviously?—Robbie must have meant he was a survivor of *Glibner's* cancer, which, okay, seemed like a bit of a stretch, but whatever. *We're pregnant,* right? Words were rubbery sometimes. Gumlike. Words stretched. Especially for the younger generations, and often without the older generations realizing it.

So *cancer survivor* had maybe gummed up and stretched for the younger generations so that now it meant "a person with a loved one who used to have cancer" in addition to meaning "a person who himself used to have cancer."

And so if that's what *cancer survivor* could mean, then maybe that meant that *suicide survivor* could mean "a person whose loved one committed suicide." That kind of followed, right? That is: it was the same kind of stretching, octomoron or no.

Only but except though what about this: If a loved one of fifteen-year-old Robbie Glibner's had committed suicide, the mayor and his wife, having known the Glibners seven years by then, would probably have heard about that suicide, and if *eight* loved ones of fifteen-year-old Robbie Glibner's had committed suicide, there was just *no way* that the mayor and his wife would not have heard about it, right?

Probably the Guinness Book of World Records would have heard about it.

As the mayor and his wife were talking this through, a new comment on Robbie's post went up. A comment from another high school kid called Mai:

> Robbie, your courage is so admirable. I feel so blessed to have a friend like you. I am not a cancer survivor, but as you know I am a Suicide Survivor (19x), and what you may not know is I am also an Alzheimer's Survivor, so if you need an ear or a shoulder please don't be shy about making use of both of mine (or all four!? ☺) and just DM me. I am here for you. Always. Also, I don't know if it would be your kind of thing, but I have found both the **Supporting Survivors of Suicide group** and the **Teen Suicide Survivors Coping Network** group to be really helpful resources for coping and support, so I will send you an invitation to join them, but no pressure. The Alzheimer's Survivors groups I belong to have

been great for me, too, like really really welcoming, and some of the members have shared valuable skills and advice they learned from Cancer Survivors groups they're also a part of, especially **Own Two Feet Cancer Survivors Network** and **Healing After the Cure**. I can't vouch for those groups, but I can vouch for the wisdom and kindness and generosity and gratitude of the people who share what they've learned from those groups, and if you would like to DM with any of them about the groups or anything else, just let me know, and I will connect you. I'm so proud of you!

Mai's post only confused matters further.

First of all: *Alzheimer's survivor.*

If a *cancer survivor* could be someone with a loved one who used to have cancer, then an *Alzheimer's survivor* could assumably be someone with a loved one who used to have Alzheimer's.

But Alzheimer's was incurable. So then . . . what?

An *Alzheimer's survivor* was someone with a loved one who currently still *had* Alzheimer's? And so when you called yourself an *Alzheimer's survivor,* that would mean something like "Every day I am surviving the continuing survival of my loved one who has Alzheimer's"?

Unless though maybe it meant that the loved one who had Alzheimer's was dead from the Alzheimer's and you had survived the death of that person? *Survived,* then, more like in the way an obituary means when it says, "So-And-So McGee, who, earlier this morning, died of complexities arising from whatever, *is survived by* his wife and three children"?

But if that's how it was, then why bother to specificate Alzheimer's? That is: you should be called a *death survivor.* Which sounded octomoronic, sure, but no more octomoronic than *suicide survivor.*

Except . . .

Except Mai's post had made it clear to the mayor and his wife that they had not grasped the meaning of *suicide survivor.* Because, okay: even if fifteen-year-old Robbie Glibner, who they'd known since he was eight years old, could have somehow survived the suicide of eight loved ones without the mayor or his wife knowing about any of them, there was just no way that his friend Mai, who was not only a very pretty A-student-looking girl with nicely cut hair and clean normal clothes and excellent grammar and nothing even a little bit funky about her on the surface at all that might indicate *fruitcake* (the mayor and his wife had clicked on her face and looked through her profile), but was also someone who went to the same small private high school as Robbie, and, by the looks of the photos on her photos page was real-life actual friends with Robbie . . . Even if the mayor and his wife could believe that Robbie had survived the suicide of eight loved ones, to believe that he would attend a small high school with a girl who'd survived the suicide of *nineteen* loved ones . . . it wasn't believable.

Not even if it wasn't *loved ones* but just mere acquaintances who'd have had to kill themselves to count as suicides survived was it believable.

It was too unbelievable for even a moron to ask another moron to believe and think that that other moron would believe it for even a second, and since they knew Robbie wasn't a moron, and since this Mai looked even less like a moron than Robbie, they did not believe they were being asked to believe any of what they'd briefly thought they'd had to try to believe.

So they stopped trying to believe it, and, on the ride back home, the mayor came up with a new theory.

This was the new theory: to call yourself a suicide survivor didn't require you to have a loved one or acquaintance who committed suicide, but just to know of someone whose suicide personally upset you.

In that sense, even the mayor himself would be a suicide survivor. Because back when the mayor was still the alderman—a couple-three years maybe after he'd played poker with Mamet—Dana Plato, who'd starred in the 1980s family sitcom, *Diff'rent Strokes,* killed herself with pills, and the mayor got really sad about it. Sad not so much because he loved *Diff'rent Strokes*—though he'd liked it fine for a couple seasons, up till cute little Arnold got his puberty jowls—but because he had, ten or so years before that, bought the *Playboy* magazine with the Dana Plato spread in it and had admired it *fondly* any number of times (not to be vulgarine, but the bush on her was just very inviting and beautiful and classy), and when he heard about her suicide, he thought about all those pictures in *Playboy,* how much he'd enjoyed them, how happy they'd made him but how upset he now could not help but think Dana Plato really must have been while posing for those pictures even though she looked so carefree and energetic in those pictures. Tears of a clown, but the opposite of that. Giggles of a torture victim or a slave. Which got him really sad.

The mayor's wife did not support this new theory, though. She said maybe she could see how a high school kid could get so upset about this or that celebrity suicide that they'd call themself a survivor of that suicide, and maybe she could see how a high school kid could then get so upset a second time about a second celebrity suicide that they'd call themself a survivor of *that* suicide, too, which would then make them a *two-time suicide survivor,* but for that to happen six more times? *seventeen* more times? Come on. No way. Mai, like Robbie, was fifteen years old. How many celebrity suicides of the last fifteen years could the mayor and his wife even *name* without first googling?

The mayor saw that maybe his wife had a point, but by the way she'd gotten out of the car before he'd even turned it off and kind of stomped into the kitchen ahead of him and poured herself a wine without offering him any, he could tell that she was a little annoyed with him for talking about Dana Plato's blond bush with admiration and longing—annoyed not because she was uptight or jealous about that kind of thing, he didn't think, but more because of how he'd set the mood for making love, eaten too much mayo to make the love he'd set the mood for, *and then* started talking about the blond bush—and she probably would have shot down any theory he might have come up with right then, even if it had been the exact right theory.

"What about, though . . ." he said, in a cautionating tone. When she finally looked at him to hear the rest of what he'd say, he said, "What I'm thinking is what about if this kind of celebrity suicide survivorship could retroactivize?"

"I have no idea what that means," she said. "What does that mean?"

What it meant was pretty clear, he thought. What if you could be a suicide survivor of any suicide that upset you, even if you weren't aware of that suicide at the time it was committed, or even alive? Like for instance, another suicide that upset the mayor was Marilyn Monroe's. He was only a toddler when Marilyn killed herself, and so he didn't even know that she killed herself till years later, and even then it didn't particularly upset him, not until years and years after that; not till after Princess Diana died, and he, like so many others, really thought about what Elton John was trying to say: how Marilyn, just like Princess Diana, had seemed to live her whole stormy life without even a single solitary person to turn to for an umbrella or shelter of any kind. He had, in fact, gotten *more* upset while thinking about Marilyn's suicide than he'd gotten when he'd thought about Dana Plato's. Still did, for that matter, sometimes, when the song played.

Anyway, if this retroactivizing theory of his was correct, then the mayor would be a *two-time suicide survivor,* at *least* a two-time suicide survivor. And maybe Mai and Robbie and others of the younger generations were just a lot more sensitive about celebrity suicide and/or more knowledgeable about the long history of celebrity suicides because of the internet. If the mayor was right, then a teen going through eight or even nineteen survivals wouldn't seem as unlikely anymore.

But, Marilyn Monroe had, like Dana Plato, also coincidentally posed for *Playboy,* and although the mayor'd never spent much time with the Marilyn nudes—they looked almost fake, like paintings or something, plus were completely and totally non-crotch-revealing—he thought it better not to bring Marilyn Monroe up to his wife, and he let the theory go.

"Actually, never mind," he said.

By then, she was already stroking her tablet. He watched her for a minute. Then another minute. Then he shifted in his chair, shifting pressures inside himself, and was just getting up when she started to talk. "I think," his wife said, "that our difficulties might not be coming from *survivor* but *suicide.* I think it might be that *suicide* is the gummy word."

The mayor was lost, but he said, "Could be," in order to aplease her, and also because, well . . . "Be right back," he said.

He did not so much come *right back,* as eventually come back.

Meantime, a bunch of googling had got done. A lot of clicking on the links to the groups Mai's post said Robbie should join. A lot of Wikipedia and Urban Dictionary. Some hashtag-searching on the Twitter, too.

The mayor's wife shared the findings she'd found with the mayor, and she shared them in a voice that made it seem like she was done being pissed with him about the mayo. He told her that her research seemed to really provoke some further questions, and she told him she was happy to hear him say that because she thought so too. And the mayor was happy that she thought so too, and more than that he was happy she was happy, and they researched together, deeper and deeper—the mayor brought his own tablet down from the bedroom—til those questions got answered, at least for the most part.

What their research turned up: that was the fourth prong.

This was the fourth prong:

Turned out that *suicide* and *survivor* the both were pretty gummy, and together they were even gummier than that.

Suicide survivor did used to mean what the mayor and his wife originally thought: a person who had a loved one who had committed suicide.

Same time, there also used to be a kind of person who called themself a *suicide attempt survivor*. This was just what it sounded like: someone who tried to kill themself but didn't end up killing themself.

And then, more recently, there used to be a kind of person who called themself a *suicidal ideation survivor*. That was also what it sounded like: someone who thought about trying to kill themself but didn't end up killing themself, or trying to.

And then, more recently than that, there was a viral social media post by a celebrity vlogger who had come out as a suicidal ideation survivor a few weeks before posting. This post was about the disrespect that suicidal ideation survivors like herself were being shown in the survivor community, especially by the suicide attempt survivors. What the vlogger said was that the main thing that she hoped her post would bring people's attention to was that the difference between thought and action was really thin sometimes, and this was one of those times. The difference between thinking about trying to kill yourself and actually trying to kill yourself was often, she said, just a matter of circumstance and opportunity, like did you have a rope handy or a gun or pills or a razor while you were ideating suicidally or did you not have such suicide-activating items handy? That was often it: all that made the difference.

And so suicidal ideation survivors basically *were* suicide attempt survivors, the vlogger insisted. A suicidal ideation survivor, the vlogger insisted, was a kind of suicide attempt survivor who was unable to follow through on the attempt not because they wouldn't have attempted suicide if they'd had the opportunity, but because they hadn't had the opportunity.

So suicidal ideation survivors may as well just start calling themselves *suicide attempt survivors,* the vlogger said, and not only *may as well,* but *should,* the vlogger said, because first of all, they deserved the same respect, and secondly, it wasn't their job to educate others in the survivor community or any other community about what it meant to be a suicidal ideation survivor vs. a suicide attempt survivor or vs. really any other kind of survivor for that matter, and if they continued to call themselves *suicidal ideation survivors* then they'd be unjustly pressured to educate more than if they went with just *suicide attempt survivors.*

After this social media post went viral, it looked like that's what happened. *Suicidal ideation survivor* stopped being anything anyone called themself. You just had *suicide survivors* and *suicide attempt survivors.*

But then, next-to-last-most recently, some young Republican type called Jory Gutman-Klamschitz wrote an op-ed for the *Wall Street Journal* about the misuse and abuse of the word *survivor,* and the viralness of this op-ed was still contagious to this very day. Even five months after it first got published, people were socially mediating about it, and the way they mediated was very extreme: you had people calling Gutman-Klamschitz everything from "Adolf Hitler" to "a voice that if they listened to it closely enough might just save his generation from the next Adolf Hitler."

The op-ed, titled "First They Came for Our Survivors," was about how Gutman-Klamschitz's great-uncle's brother-in-law, Nathan, had been a prisoner of the Auschwitz concentration camp along with the rest of his (Nathan's) family, and how all of Nathan's family got murdered at Auschwitz except for Nathan, who lived for two years in the camp before he got freed.

Nathan's family, Gutman-Klamschitz said, were victims of the Holocaust, but Nathan himself was not only a victim: Nathan himself was also a survivor.

But not only that: Nathan himself was *not* a survivor until ten years *after* he was freed from Auschwitz, Gutman-Klamschitz's great-uncle, according to Gutman-Klamschitz, had told Gutman-Klamschitz that Nathan had told him (the great-uncle). From the time the Holocaust started till ten years after Nathan was freed, Nathan was a victim, but ten years after he got freed, he married Gutman-Klamschitz's great-uncle's sister-in-law, which was his way of saying *yes* to life, and *no* to being merely a victim of Nazis: *that* was when he became a survivor.

To be a survivor, Gutman-Klamschitz explained, was a two-step process.

1. There has to be something outside yourself that nearly kills you, but then fails to kill you.

2. After the something that nearly kills you fails to kill you, you have to refuse to let other people define you by how you didn't get killed or how you nearly got killed, and you have to refuse to only be defined by yourself by how you didn't get killed or nearly got killed.

Follow those two steps, Gutman-Klamschitz advised, and then you'd be a survivor. Anyone else who called themself a survivor, Gutman-Klamschitz said, was either a victim of something or not a victim of something, but was, either way—whether a victim or something less than a victim—culturally appropriating 1) Gutman-Klamschitz's great-uncle's brother-in-law Nathan's pain and struggles, 2) the pain and struggles of everyone else who was a survivor of the Holocaust, and 3) the pain and struggles of everyone else who was first a victim and then a survivor of other, non-Holocaust attempts to kill them that were made by something outside themselves.

And then last-most recently and finally, the original *suicide survivor* community—the community that was made up of people who called themselves *suicide survivors* because they'd lost loved ones to suicide—collectionally determined together that they were being targeted by Gutman-Klamschitz's viral op-ed for not having lived lives that featured something outside them trying to kill them, and they were among the most frequently socially mediating announcers of Gutman-Klamschitz's Hitlerness, and they said the word *survivor* needed to be liberated from the Holocaust and all the other stuff that was like the Holocaust because to be a survivor was a lived experience that no one could judge the quality of others' feelings of living through by, and that instead people should learn from each other's lived experiences, which was why, as far as they were concerned, anyone who was in any way *suicide-adjacent* could be correctly called a *suicide survivor* if they felt like one, and, for that matter, anyone who felt like a survivor of anything *was* a survivor of that thing, and could and should learn from each other how to better survive, and also how to better demand acknowledgment and respect for themselves and for what they'd been through from those who were privileged enough to be outside the larger survivor community.

And also, they said, Gutman-Klamschitz should be canceled, and so they were canceling Gutman-Klamschitz. And so Gutman-Klamschitz was canceled, they said.

It was unclear if the cancelation of Gutman-Klamschitz had taken.

The bio line at the bottom of his most recent op-ed for the *Journal*—he'd published three since "First They Came for Our Survivors"—said he had a book coming out in fall.

If you were canceled, didn't that mean you didn't get to have a book?

Or did it just mean people would boycott your book if you had a book?

They tried to figure that out, the mayor and his wife, but then, all at once, they got too tired, and found they didn't actually care about this aspect of their research.

Main thing was: they were satisfied that Robbie Glibner'd be fine. The only reasonable explanation for his calling himself an *8time suicide survivor* was that he'd thought about killing himself eight times, which seemed, when you thought about it, above-average healthy for a fifteen-year-old, considering how many times their younger daughter had threatened to kill herself over this or that bit of nonsense—when she wanted a phone, or a later curfew, or more expensive jeans, that kind of thing—back when she was a tween and a teen. And those were threats, which were more serious than thoughts, right? Threats she never even pretended to deliver on. Plus look at her now: about to finish med school, engaged to a lovely young woman with tasteful tattoos and a thriving yoga gym. Robbie'd be fine.

And yeah, the way that young people whose lives hadn't ever really been threatened were referring to themselves as *survivors* on internet did seem precious and overdramatical, but, the mayor thought, maybe it shouldn't seem that way.

Maybe that was close-minded of him. Twentieth century.

The mayor'd had suicidal ideations himself before. He was under the impression that everyone had them once in a while, and he happened to not want people to know that he'd had them, so he never told people. He just didn't think that was a good look on a future mayor, a current mayor, or anyone's father or husband, suicidal ideations. He thought it seemed kind of pussyish, really. But if he *had* wanted people to know about his suicidal ideations, maybe he'd want those people to call him a suicide survivor. Who could know? Epistemical roadblocks, and etcetera.

And maybe his suicidal ideations weren't as strong as these kids', anyway.

Might even be that the measure of the strength of a person's suicidal ideations was how willing that person was to look like a pussy by admitting to them.

Either way, the gummy stretching of the word *survivor* wasn't anything to get bent out of shape about, not with everything else there was to get bent out of shape about.

His wife had summed it up best that very evening, just a few minutes after they watched that vlogger's viral post. In her hilarious old Jewish lady voice where she kind of half frowned and shrugged and used her hands a lot, the mayor's wife said to him, "So they call themselves survivors? Big whoop. Someone's getting hurt by this? No one's getting hurt by this."

And maybe even, thought the mayor, it didn't not just hurt but *helped*.

If there were all these survivors walking around and eating and sleeping and watching TV and going on internet and having sex and drinking coffee and etcetera, didn't that make it pretty normal, surviving?

Like didn't it make being a survivor less depressing?

And wasn't less depressing survivorship a good cause to support?

What survivor wouldn't rather be a less depressing survivor?

What survivor wouldn't rather be made less depressed by other survivors?

And, for that matter, what nonsurvivor wouldn't rather be made less depressed by survivors?

It was half past one when at last they headed upstairs to bed. That was too late, sure, but it had been more than worth it. While the two of them had sat there at the kitchen table, sipping at beverages, stroking their tablets, and calling each other's attentions to new information when the data they had on their screens was relevant, it had felt not a little like one of those scenes in a legal drama where the good-guy lawyers with tensions between them owing to a rivalry stemming from an earlier misunderstanding about a clerkship back in law school or a romance or a relative they have in common run into each other at the all-night library late in the night where one of them's discovered a legal decision in the dusty lawbooks that might help them win the landmark battle for greater justice that fate has united them to work on together, and the other one is so impressed by the discovery that he gets inspired to rethink a lot of other old legal cases he's always been an expert on but now is able to see in a whole different light, and if only they can convince the court to see those old cases in this same different light, the lawyers might just very well end up winning their landmark battle for justice for reasons that will be explained to the audience in the climaxing court scene at the end of the movie in fifteen-twenty minutes or so.

The mayor felt that, during those hours at the kitchen table, he and his wife had experienced together not just one warm, important-feeling moment, but a whole montage of warm, important-feeling moments—moments of discovery, surprise, appreciation, mutual agreement, chuckles and grins, shared looks of concern, comforting shoulder squeezes, gentle elbow ribbings, and nonsexual but tender hand and knee grabs—that the mayor was *certain* he'd remember while he died, if, when he died, he was lucky enough to die slowly, in a bed.

About that last part, however, the mayor was incorrect. That is: he *would* die slowly in a bed one day—on January 7, 2051—but he would *not*, while dying, remember those hours at the kitchen table, nor any other part of the evening described above, nor, for that matter, any other of the many moments that he had ever imagined he'd remember while he died.

Although he would, by the time he died, have been dying of pneumonia in his bed for days, he would not believe that he had been dying; he would believe that he would overcome the pneumonia, just as he had overcome every other illness he had ever suffered, and he would contend with the pain and discomfort the pneumonia was causing by deploying the same strategy he'd always deployed to contend with the pain and discomfort brought on by illness: he would distract himself from the pain and discomfort by picturing various naked women in part and in whole from various angles at various distances.

Now, somewhere out there or in here is a bit about the mayor dying slowly in his bed and Dana Plato's blond bush in command-+'d close-up. The bit entails, I'm pretty sure, the following signifiers: *rosebud, little boy, socrates, anus, bush.*

If I were Gladman, or even just half as good as Gladman, I'd be able to write the bit, but alas: neither Gladman nor even, I fear, half-Gladman am I, so I won't even try.

I have a better handle on the mayor's wife's death.

Like her husband before her, she'll die slowly in a bed—this'll be on March 1, 2059—but unlike him, she'll have advanced dementia.

Despite the dementia, she'll know that she's about to die, and, in her final moments, she will remember, with striking clarity, a television ad for a patented laser procedure designed to reduce menstrual bleeding.

The ad, which will have originally aired in 2027, features a woman standing in an aboveground swimming pool, holding a toddler-aged, water-winged girl by the underarms, and, to the girl's great delight, repeatedly raising the girl overhead and gently re-dunking her.

Because of the dementia, the mayor's wife will experience a momentary feeling of confusion while remembering the ad.

At first, she will think that she is the woman and that her elder daughter is the toddler.

Then she'll think that she is the woman, and her *younger* daughter is the toddler.

Then suddenly she'll realize the toddler is neither of her daughters, nor is she the woman, but that *she* is the toddler and the woman is her mother.

Unless she was right the first or the second time.

Or the first *and* the second time.

Or the first and the second time and also the third.

And she *was,* she will think.

She *was* right every time, she will think.

And she will not feel confused, and then she'll be dead.

And Robbie Glibner will in fact kill himself. He'll dive off a footbridge and into a deep, snowy gorge and break his neck. This will be on January 6, 2031, in Ithaca, New York, in the middle of his second year as an

MFA creative writing student at Cornell University, just minutes before the sun goes down, about an hour after his return from Chicago, where he'll have gone to spend the holidays with his family.

Why exactly he'll choose to take his own life won't be clear to anyone who knows him, not even him. That is: he will be feeling depressed, but not the most depressed he's ever felt—not by a long shot. In the couple weeks prior, he'll have had a really good time with his family. He'll have had a good time with his old pal Mai, as well. They'll have gone bowling together, slept together twice for old times' sake, and gone out drinking and brunching together with a handful of other mutual friends who'll have been home for the holidays.

The footbridge from which Robbie Glibner will jump is one to which he'll have taken a walk nearly every day since his move to Ithaca, a foot-bridge he'll have visited hundreds of times, and from which he'll have thought about jumping at least as many times, yet as far as Robbie will be able to tell on January 6, 2031, he will not have gone to the footbridge to kill himself.

Standing on the bridge, watching the sun set, it will occur to Robbie Glibner, as it will have occurred to him countless times before, that even though life is meaningful and people are basically good despite their so often seeming terrible, he's in a lot of inexplicable pain, a lot of the same kind of inexplicable pain he has been in ever since right around the start of middle school. And as it will have occurred to him any number of times, so it will occur to him that day on the bridge that the only relief he's ever had from this pain has been incomplete and temporary, and that to keep on hoping that prior to his death he might ever experience a more prolonged or thorough feeling of relief from his pain than he previously has would be foolish.

And just as he will have done any number of times since arriving at Cornell for his MFA in creative writing, he will, on January 6, 2031, consider jumping off the very bridge on which he's standing. What will be different this time is that his neck, owing to all the driving he'll have done to get back to Ithaca in the last couple days, will have been hurting for a number of hours, and the Advil he will have taken upon arriving at his apartment in Ithaca will have, just moments prior to his considering the jump, begun to work its anti-inflammatory magic. By this point, however, Robbie will be too preoccupied with his thoughts about inex-plicable pain and incomplete and fleeting relief from inexplicable pain to remember the entirely explicable soreness in his neck, let alone the Advil he will have swallowed in order to relieve that explicable soreness, and, for the first time, the thought of jumping from the bridge will be accompanied by a feeling of relief mixed with fear, rather than just a feeling of fear.

The last thing he'll think is, "I think I want to do this, it could be my only chance," and then he'll have done it, his sore neck will break, and then he'll be dead.

By the time Reggie Glibner and his wife meet their end in a smashup with a concrete-mixer truck on I-94, on St. Patrick's Day, 2043, they'll have long since forgiven Robbie completely for all the pain his suicide caused them. Completely. Really. They will have. And both of them, having become, in the course of completely forgiving Robbie—toward the singular end, in fact, of completely forgiving Robbie—devout Episcopalians, they will, for all 29 (Reggie) and 105 (Reggie's wife) seconds they remain alive in the wake of their collision with the concrete-mixer truck, vividly imagine embracing Robbie in a silver-white heaven. Whereas Reggie's imagining of the embrace will center on the feeling of holding his son, his wife's will center on the feeling of being held *by* her son. They'll be overcome with joy, and then they will die.

Mai will be "temporarily shattered" when she hears about Robbie Glibner's suicide. She'll wonder if she shouldn't have had sex with him over the holidays, or if she should have had sex with him more, or differently, but then she'll decide such thoughts are self-centered, and she'll be angry at Robbie for making her grieve and angry at herself for being angry at him for making her grieve. Mai will live long enough to meet the first two of her eleven great-grandkids, but lots of people, by the time Mai dies, will be living long enough to meet their great-grandkids, and *how* Mai will die—on July 15, 2106—and what she'll do with her life after Robbie's suicide will be even less remarkable than her response to Robbie's suicide, i.e. it isn't worth remarking on any further.

On the other hand, Basketball Schwartzy will die of a massive stroke in front of his very tall, teenage son while shooting a fadeaway jumper in their driveway on September 9, 2038. The stroke will kill him before he hits the asphalt. That is: he'll expire in midair, there by the grace of his own self-propulsion. He won't be picturing anything at the time. One moment, he'll be seeing the ball on its way to the hoop while thinking in words, and the next he will die.

The last words he'll think will be: *Rock in the hole.*

And the rock will, in fact, go in the hole.

I think that's nice. It's nice that he'll make the shot, I think.

So too, incidentally, will Basketball Schwartzy's son, whenever he'll look back on the death of his father. He will not, however, remember what he shouted as the rock went in the hole, just before he realized his father'd fallen. He won't remember having shouted anything at all.

What he will have shouted, though, was this: "*Nice* one, Dad!"

I think that's nice too.

Right Hand Thumb

Fifth prong was the dream. Not the Obama dream. A different dream, which might not actually have been a dream. The mayor didn't remember having any dreams, but the morning after he ate all that mayo, he woke up so sure about Mount Chicago—what it would mean, how it would work, even what it would look like—that it must have been a dream, right? He must have figured all of it out while he'd slept.

Where what had used to be Millennium Park was, they would build a new park. The Mount Chicago Memorial Park. There'd be some kind of bandshell or other open-air kind of theater to hold some concerts in, and maybe there'd be a fountain, too, and maybe a garden, maybe a reflecting pool, or a bridge or something, and maybe it would expand to where the Art Institute had been or maybe it wouldn't—the details of that stuff could be worked out later—but the main thing there'd be was three main things:

First of all: the cone. They would dig out all the junk and detritus all the way down to the bottom of the basin surrounding the cone, and there it would be, this big black cone coming out of the ground, twenty-three stories high and five acres wide.

Mount Chicago.

Secondly: the walls. Most of the junk and detritus in the basin would be carted away, but some of it would be piled up, especially any objects the anomaly hadn't totally melted and pulverized: anything that was still recognizable as what it had used to be before the anomaly. Such as car bumpers, maybe. Steering wheels, too. Bricks and pipes from this or that building. Elevator buttons. Elevator doors. Cellphones and jewelry, tiles and faucets and hunks of sinks, motorcycle handlebars. Bicycle frames. Who knew what remained intact or semi-intact? They'd only find out once they got to work.

But all the intact and semi-intact things that were found while the detritus and junk was getting carted off would be piled up high to mark the borders of the park, and then towering walls of reinforced concrete with windows in them would be constructed to hold the piles in place and allow the park's visitors to see some of what had been destroyed by the anomaly. That would allow the visitors to not only have some sense of the massive scale of the destruction but also some feelings about the people who were destroyed.

There would be a lot of feelings.

The mayor could picture himself, for example, contemplating the complete and total incineration of a boy from Chicago who he'd never get to meet; a boy whose life he could only now imagine by looking at a half-melted push-scooter wheel wedged into the detritus behind the window glass.

And he could picture himself contemplating the complete and total crushed-into-dustness of a woman from Chicago who he'd never get to meet; a woman whose life he could only now imagine by looking at a flattened-down golden tube of lipstick wedged into the detritus behind the window glass.

He could picture himself getting choked up while contemplating such objects and people.

And while he contemplated the picture of himself contemplating such objects and people, he *got* choked up.

These walls would be very moving. The whole park would.

And finally: the engravings.

The parts of the walls that were not glass would be engraved by expert engravers with the names of all the anomaly's victims and survivors.

"Now I don't want the survivors' names to be organized in alphabetical order," the mayor said, as he finished explaining his whole vision for

Mount Chicago Memorial Park to Apter, which explaining he'd started doing second thing as soon as he got to City Hall. (First thing had been he'd gathered the staff to tell them the good news about Glibner's cancer, let them know they'd be celebrating that good news with some on-the-mayor Giordano's pies at lunch, and to ask a volunteer to find out what toppings and crust styles people were in the mood for, then place the order accordingly.) "I want the victims' names to be organized in alphabetical order, but I want those survivors' names," the mayor continued, "to be organized in what I think is a much more creative way that honors their experiences, and lets the visitor know—"

"Wait," Apter said. "I don't mean to interrupt you—you seem really excited about this whole thing, but you've said *survivors* a couple of times now, and . . ."

"Yeah?" said the mayor. "I think I know what you're getting at, but say it anyway because I have a retort."

"There weren't any survivors of the anomaly," said Apter. "Only victims."

"That's what you think," the mayor said. "And here is my retort: what you need to do is spend some more time on internet, Apter. For a young man your age, you obviously don't do that enough. Way I see it, and internet will back me up on this, we got at least tens of thousands of survivors here in Chicago. Maybe more than a hundred thousand, depending how we decide to count."

"More than a hundred thousand survivors," Apter said.

"The families," said the mayor. "The immediate families of the anomaly's victims. There were twelve thousand victims, give or take, right? Between their husbands, wives, brothers, sisters, mothers, fathers, and also I'd say grandpas, grandmas, and grandkids—that's tens of thousands of survivors you got there for sure, but maybe other loved ones count, too, such as aunts and uncles and cousins, boyfriends and girlfriends and nonromantic friends and business colleagues with special affections for each other—*associates* let's call them."

"Again: I'm not sure it's correct to call any of those people survivors," Apter said.

"They have survived the untimely and traumatic death or deaths of a loved one or loved ones, and so they are survivors. Now, some of them are bigger survivors than others, that much is true, and what I'm trying to get at here is I want that to be recognized in their engravings, okay? By the bigness itself. Of their engravings. And also the number of their engravings," the mayor said. "You look confused, like you need an example. Here is my example: say you've survived the loss of a loved one to the anomaly, and say I have survived the loss of two loved ones to the anomaly: my name on the wall should be engraved twice as big as yours. Another example is say you've survived the loss of a loved one to the anomaly and I have survived the loss of five loved ones to the anomaly: my name on the wall should be engraved *five times* as big as yours. And not only that, okay, because there's more. Because the way the survivors' names will be organized on the walls is this: every survivor's name should be engraved under the name of any victim whose death that survivor survived. So if I lost five loved ones and you lost one loved one, and the loved one you lost was one of the five loved ones I lost, our names would both appear under the name of that loved one, my name five times as big as your name, but my name would also appear—just as big—under the names of my four other lost loved ones. So first thing we need to do is find out a way to find out how many loved ones every survivor in Chicago has lost."

"Only in Chicago?" Apter said.

"As opposed to what?"

"As opposed to, I don't know: Milwaukee? Highland Park? Hong Kong? I mean, a lot of the victims of the anomaly were tourists. A lot of those who weren't tourists must have had loved ones who don't live in Chicago."

"That is not an unfair point, but it's only really one not-unfair point, whereas here are not one but *two* not-unfair points with which I respond to your single one with:

"First point: Do I look like the mayor of Hong Kong?

"Second point: Are we talking here about any of the following: the Mount *Milwaukee* Memorial Park, the Mount *Fuji* Memorial Park, or the Mount *Highland Park* Memorial Park? Or is what we are talking here about the Mount Chicago Memorial Park?

"No, I'm sort of half kidding. Down the line—after we figure out who the Chicago survivors are, and all the math and the ratios of how big all their names should be—maybe there'll still be space on the walls to add more names of survivors from other locales, and we can make a decision about . . . You're looking at me with a lot of skepticality right now, Apter, and it's time for you to stop that because this is our move. It's a park like you suggested just last night, but it's more than a park, it's also a memorial, and it's more than just a memorial park—it's a memorial park that's in a basin that's twenty-some stories deep and it's got a *cone* in the middle of it twenty-some stories high that is made of the very human beings and human possessions and great art that got destroyed by the same event that victimized the very same victims the survivors are surviving the loss of. Who wouldn't want to see that? What tourist wouldn't rather see that than even a world-class art museum, if he had to make a choice. There's art museums everywhere, in every major city, world class–level art museums in plenty of world-class major cities. There is only one world-class major city where there is a cone like the cone that is Mount Chicago, though. That city is Chicago. That city is ours. And they won't just come to the park for the cone and the names on the walls and the contemplations the objects behind the walls' windows will inspire. There'll be space for all kinds of concerts at the park. There will be concession stands. Probably there'll be an area for buskers. Probably, too, some kind of beautiful garden and a playground. And there will be multiple escalators down into this park—escalators that will, I would think, be the longest escalators ever built. *Some* of the longest escalators anyway. Kids will love those escalators. Adults will too. They'll come to the park to look at the cone—to look at *Mount Chicago*—and they'll come to look at the names on the walls, to look at *their* names on the walls and the names of their loved ones, and to contemplate the damaged objects piled up behind the windows, to contemplate the people those objects used to belong to, the buildings and artworks and homes and offices those objects used to be a part of. Yes. They will come to do all of that. But also they'll come to the park to do yoga. They'll come to the park to skateboard and scoot and perhaps rent a Segway. To hear some live music. To take a bunch of selfies. To grab a coffee or a pretzel or whatever. They'll ride those big escalators just to hear their ears pop. They'll come to picnic and hopscotch and have a first kiss. Marriage proposals will happen at this park. Weddings themselves will happen at this park. Our park will be a memorial to the anomaly's victims and survivors, yes. It'll stand as a reminder of the horror of 11/17. But it will also be a celebration, understand? A celebration of survival and surviving and of this great city. Of all that the anomaly did *not* take away from us. Of what remains and what we can grow from it. How we grow with it. Of what Chicago does when you hand it some lemons. Have you ever been to Auschwitz?"

"Auschwitz?" said Apter.

"The concentration camp memorial there in Eastern Europe."

"I went during college."

"Some fucking place, right? I mean, I've never been, but I've seen some documentaries, and . . . even on film . . . some fucking place. Like, those shoes, you know? That room with all the shoes. I couldn't even cry, Apter, seeing those shoes, imagining all the murdered kids who used to wear those shoes. Not just the kids. The adults too. I was what you call *beyond* tears. Thinking about everything those satanic Nazi bastards did to your people and other peoples too. I couldn't even cry. And when I woke up this morning, thinking about Mount Chicago, I was also thinking about Auschwitz, too. I don't know exactly why—might have been this thing I read in the *Journal* a little bit before bed. That's not the point, though. Why. *Why* is not the point.

"Point is I woke up today thinking about Mount Chicago, but also Auschwitz. The shoes, the gas, the ovens, the trains, the fillings in the teeth, the candles made of fat, the pillows made of hair, the lampshades of skin, those so-called studies the one doctor did to all those many twins. All those murdered Jewish and Gypsy and disabled and homosexual and probably also transgender people, and even all those murdered communists too. I was thinking of all of that, thinking about Auschwitz, and what I thought was: every memorial should be so moving. That is the one and only measure of a memorial's success. How moving it is. Auschwitz has got to be the most moving memorial in the world. It has to be, right? And I thought, 'The goal of every memorial should be to be as moving as Auschwitz, but at the same time, that does *not* necessarily mean that the goal of every memorial should be to be as depressing.' So what I want, I'm saying, is I want Mount Chicago to achieve that level of being moving, but also, at the same time, to be less depressing."

"Than Auschwitz," said Apter.

"I want it to be a less depressing Auschwitz."

"A less depressing Auschwitz," said Apter.

"*Our* less depressing Auschwitz," said the mayor.

~~Left Hand Pointer~~

Sixth prong was the Obama dream.

But come to think of it, no. No it wasn't. Not in terms of the biopic's white part, at least.

The mayor's Obama dream was the sixth prong in terms of Mount Chicago, sure, but in terms of the white part there was *no* sixth prong because the dream would get explained *after* the white part.

Only took a single hand to count the prongs, after all.

3

Still, it was a lot to explain.

"You know, I'm thinking you're right, as is per according to your custom of being," the mayor said to Apter on April 21, 2022, after having spent a few seconds thinking about the prongs. "During the white part, which I'm thinking wouldn't be more than twenty-thirty seconds, I would not have time on the commentary track to describe all that happened between Christmas and last week in any kind of way that does the right justice to all that happened during the passing of those months. Commentary track just wouldn't be enough. So I guess that, Scorsese nonwithstanding, no matter who it is wants to do my biopic—like even if it's Fincher or Russell that wants to do it—I guess I'll refuse to consult on it unless they make an accompanying documentary.

"Now, with Scorsese I still wouldn't make demands, but I *would* make sure to specificate my opinion that when the white part of the scene ends and it's spring and I've got my beard, the first thing should happen is not just us sitting there, smiling at each other because of how great my Obama dream was, but actually us sitting there a couple minutes *before* that moment, smiling at each other because I'm *telling* you about my Obama dream, just like how I did last week, when I had it. So we come out of the white part, and there I am, beard and all, no snow on the window ledge and so forth, and I'm telling you about my Obama dream, explaining to you how I interpret the meaning of that dream and so forth. I think that would still be extremely artful. Maybe even more artful than the way I've been imagining. There's no reason the dream and the explanation of the dream can't come after the white part, you know?"

"Sure," Apter said. "Makes sense to me."

The mayor waved his glass a little, wordlessly toasting. "So what else then?" he said. "You get anywhere with Gladman?"

"Not sure. I have to go see him."

"When?"

"Depends what time we finish here."

"*We* like you and me, you mean?"

"Yeah."

"Drink up and get out then," the mayor said.

And Apter did and did.

ENDEAVOR

1

On the day back in March that the mayor first mentioned Mount Chicago, Apter backed out of their after-work whiskey. Said he had a hot date, had to get home and change.

"Well, ooh la la," said the mayor. "Good luck!"

Apter didn't exactly have a date. Innertown Pub, however, had a new barmaid he'd lately been flirting with, her shift began at six, he wanted to get there before the evening crowd, and he wanted to talk to Sylvie Klein before that.

Maybe Adi, too, time permitting.

But he called Sylvie first.

He wasn't seeking her help. He just wanted to recount to her—was dying to recount to her—the conversation he'd had with the mayor that morning.

He imagined he'd do so in just four beats. Imagined he'd deadpan beats 1–3: the design of the park (cone, walls), the mayor's understanding of the word *survivor,* the whole harebrained plan to quantify the losses via relative font size. For the final beat, though, he'd hardly speak. Instead, he would message her the sound file he'd assembled during his lunchbreak: a compilation of highlights he'd snipped from the recording he'd made of the meeting. "Now play that," he'd say.

Then Sylvie'd play the sound file, laugh her ass off, and Apter'd go to the Innertown and flirt.

—

Up until he told her, "Now play that," the call went as planned, but the sound file was bigger than Apter had realized.

"Play . . . ?" said Sylvie.

"I sent you—I'm *sending* you a sound file. It's gonna take another minute to get there, looks like."

"Oh, cool," Sylvie said. "Meantime, the answer's probably yes."

"The answer to what?"

"I mean, once I have the relevant data, I could crunch those font-size numbers in about ten seconds—no doubt about that—and I *think* I know a developer who can hack something together to generate the list of the so-called survivors. That's assuming *you* have a list of the victims' names and addresses. You do, right? City Hall must, at least."

"Well, yeah, we've got a spreadsheet, but—"

"Good."

"But I was only calling to tell you about the conversation, Syl. And to send you this crazy sound file, which—Jesus, my phone's slow. I wasn't calling to ask you for anything."

"You don't need to, *motek*. I'm happy to help you. Even toward inane, unseemly ends such as this one. It's like that Charlie Brown T-shirt I used to wear: *Friendship means never having to ask.*"

"I only vaguely remember that T-shirt, uh, *motek,* but I'm pretty sure that isn't what it said."

"Come to think, it does sound a little rape-y," said Sylvie. "The shirt *was* vintage, seventies I think, but yeah, good grief, you're probably right. Anyway, I'm helping. Shouldn't cost a dime, either. The developer owes me. I got him a job."

"That's—"

"Also he's in love with me."

"Oh?"

"I *think*. Definitely a little."

"A little in love with you."

"No, yeah. We're in love," Sylvie said. "For sure."

"Like you never have to ask?"

"*He* never has to," Sylvie said.

Apter ended the call here, surprising himself, then texted, "sorry. weak sig, low batt. try you ltr/tmrw."

"No worries," Sylvie texted back. "Send that spreadsheet whenever."

At Innertown, Apter realized he'd misunderstood: the barmaid wasn't working. When she'd told him, last night, that she'd be there at six, she'd meant that she would be there drinking.

"There he is," she said when he came through the door. She stood to greet him, kissed him on the cheek. Her hair was down. It smelled like almonds.

Just after they'd ordered their second round, Apter launched into Anecdote 1, and no sooner had he gotten up from his stool to impersonate a Pollaco onstage heart attack than the barmaid interrupted him, said, "Speak of the devil," and showed him his phone, which he'd left atop the bar. The screen was lit. Six messages from Sylvie had all arrived at once.

Message 1: "Less depressing Auschwitz!"

Message 2: "Also, talked to Hersh. Hersh is in."

Message 3: "Hersh is the boy btw. Forgot to tell you his name. You ready for this? Makes our names sound like we're daughters of the Mayflower."

Message 4: "Herschel Bobovnikoff."

Message 5: "Herschel Bobovnikoff."

Message 6: "¡¡¡Herschel Bobovnikoff!!!"

While Apter read the messages, a seventh came through, attached to a sound file.

Message 7: "Hersh just made this."

He begged the barmaid's pardon, and went into the bathroom to listen to the sound file. Herschel Bobovnikoff had modified the one that Apter'd sent Sylvie—had looped and autotuned the mayor's voice, snapped it onto a dance beat, added washy synths and a hard-driving bassline—to produce an ecstatically lovelorn-sounding early-'10s-style banger that, lyrics notwithstanding, Charli XCX or Sky Ferreira might have sung:

INTRO
Have you ever
Have you ever
Have you ever been to Auschwitz?

DROP

I was also thinking about Auschwitz, too.

VERSE (X 2)

Have you ever been to Auschwitz?
The concentration camp memorial
There in Eastern Europe

CHORUS (X 2)

I want it to be
a less depressing Auschwitz!
Our less depressing Auschwitz!
Our less depressing Auschwitz!

VERSE (X 2)

CHORUS (X 2)

DROP

CHORUS (X 4)

OUTRO

When I woke up this morning,
thinking about Mount Chicago,
I was also thinking about Auschwitz, too
I was also thinking about Auschwitz, too

The song was three minutes, twelve seconds long. There in the bathroom, Apter listened to it twice, laughed till he choked. Coughed, spit. Coughed a little more. Wiped his eyes. Got ahold of himself. If Sylvie was in love with this Herschel Bobovnikoff . . . If this Herschel Bobovnikoff was even half as funny as the song would suggest . . . If he was half as kind as he seemed to be funny . . . If he was able to get her to . . . If Apter didn't . . . If you can't beat 'em join 'em.

"Just hurt my throat laughing," Apter texted Sylvie. "Bring Herschel to Chicago soon. Ve vill together drinknikoff."

The barmaid, when Apter returned from the bathroom, was talking to Mikey, the owner of the tattoo shop up the street.

"'No *need*,' the man says," Mikey said to the barmaid, "'I'll eat it *here*.'"

Clutching her chest, the barmaid fell apart laughing.

Apter happened to know what the man to whom Mikey'd referred would eat. "'No need, I'll eat it here'" was the punchline to a joke that, in one of Apter's favorite Solly Gladman performances from 2013, Gladman had claimed to have been Charlie Chaplin's favorite joke of all time.

The barmaid really seemed to love it, too.

"That sucked of me," said Apter to the side of her face once she'd finished laughing. "I was rude. I apologize."

"It's all right," she said. "Really. Do you want to get out of here?"

"I wouldn't mind," Apter said.

"Okay," she said. Then she surprised him. When she got up, she hugged him.

That she hugged him at all at that point surprised him, but more surprising than that was how *warm* the hug was. The hug, Apter thought, while he was still being hugged, was the single warmest hug that he'd ever received. How likely was that? It seemed pretty unlikely. It didn't seem true. Perhaps it wasn't true. Perhaps it was a typically nice, warm hug that, in the wake of hearing Sylvie say she'd fallen in love with a guy, or in the wake of hearing Sylvie say she'd fallen in love with a guy who Apter imagined he'd want to be friends with, or in the wake of hearing Sylvie say she'd fallen in love with a guy who Apter imagined he'd want to be friends with but didn't imagine he'd be able to be friends with—or maybe a guy he imagined he *would* be able to be friends with but wasn't sure what that said about him (Apter), let alone whether he liked what it said . . . perhaps it was a typically nice, warm hug, but when you're waiting to find out whether you're relieved or disappointed about something, or when you're trying to *figure out* whether you're relieved or disappointed and you have the sense, delusional or not, that you can *choose* which to be, the sense that you're *obliged* to choose, maybe any typically nice, warm hug will feel like—and maybe even therefore *be*—the single warmest hug you've ever received.

Whether the superlative applied was academic, however, Apter concluded. The hug was certainly nice and warm, and, for whatever reason, he *preferred* to think it was the single warmest hug that he'd ever received—maybe he even *needed* to think that. Maybe it was helpful.

As suddenly as it had begun, the hug ended, and the barmaid, once again, surprised him: "See you next time, I guess," she said, and sat down.

"Later, brother," Mikey said.

"Oh," Apter said. "So. Yeah," he said, and paid, and left.

It was early yet. He headed toward Damen Avenue, headed toward home. Didn't feel like going home. Felt like taking a walk, but it was too cold to walk. Thought about tacos, but didn't very much want any tacos. Not any tacos in walking distance, anyway. He didn't particularly want a drink, either, but he thought that he might, if he had another drink, develop a large enough desire for tacos to convince himself to hail a ride to get a good taco or even to accept a lesser taco from one of the places he could get to on foot, and anyway there across Damen was the Rainbo, and the promise of warmth in the golden-brown glow that swelled from the doorway as a smoker out front made her way back inside was enough to convince him.

One double Maker's later, he wasn't any less taco-ambivalent. He ordered a Corona, checked the time on his phone—it wasn't even eight—and saw that he'd missed two FaceTime calls from an unknown number. The first had come nineteen minutes before, the second only nine minutes before. He googled the number (213) 586-4887. Los Angeles area code, no other info. As he closed the browser, a third call came in.

He clicked ignore, and in came a text.

(213) 586-4887:	Answer the phone.
Apter:	Who is this?
(213) 586-4887:	Ari
Apter:	?
(213) 586-4887:	What the fuck. Are you Apter or not?
Apter:	Who IS this?
(213) 586-4887:	Jesus check yr email get back to me.

Apter checked his email. From Adi'd come a video of Stanz eating grapes; from Sid, the same video of Stanz eating grapes; from his father, a link to an article about password protection; from Glibner two emails, each headed "Introducing . . ."

The latter one from Glibner bore an attachment, so he opened it first.

Introducing . . .
Reggie Glibner 7:09 PM
to me, Ari, Perry

Apter Schutz: meet Lollapalooza Festival coproducers: Hollywood superagent Ari Emanuel and rock star extraordinaire Perry Farrell.

Ari and Perry: meet Apter Schutz, the bright young comer who's taken over for me at City Hall.

As I've detailed in separate emails I just sent to each of you, this is the last you'll hear from me for a while. You're all gonna get along famously, I'm sure of it.

Attached please find a doc containing contact info for one another.

Best,
Reg

Introducing . . .
Reggie Glibner 7:08 PM
to me

Apter!

Long time. As I bet you've heard, I'm healthy and retired. Everything is beautiful.

Tomorrow morning, I'm out of here. Taking Robbie and the wife to Paris. Why? Because I love Paris, I'm done at City Hall, and I received a SPAM four hours ago that offered a great deal on 10 nights in Paris if we leave tomorrow.

Meantime, the mayor just called to ask me to do one last thing: introduce you to Ari Emanuel and Perry Farrell. I'm sure he'll fill you in with more details, but basically, he wants them to make some kind of high-profile financial gesture to help build the Mount Chicago Memorial Park, which he said you know all about already.

Short of it is: I said yes to the mayor, and I'll put you three in contact by email momentarily.

Some things to bear in mind:

1) Perry Farrell, who, if you somehow don't know, is the lead singer of Jane's Addiction and the founder of Lollapalooza—I can't remember if I told you this—contacted me not even 24 hours after the anomaly. He asked that I inform him of anything he or Lollapalooza could do to help the city, and it wasn't pro forma. He is a great talent, a famously generous person, and also a really easy guy to talk to.

2) Ari Emanuel, as I'm sure you MUST know, is former mayor Rahm Emanuel's younger brother, and a co-owner, along with Perry and Live Nation, of Lollapalooza. He is the biggest talent agent in the world. He is a billionaire, or nearly so, and he is not remotely an easy guy to talk to. He is an IMPOSSIBLE guy for the mayor to talk to. I met him and Perry two summers back, when we negotiated—very protractedly—the latest contract between Lollapalooza and the city. Ari made it clear that he felt the mayor's attempts (mostly successful) to gouge Lollapalooza were motivated by the mayor's desire to punish Rahm Emanuel by proxy for having backed a political opponent of the mayor's in the 2019 Democratic primary. Between you and me, Ari was pretty much right about that. In sum: there is no love lost between our mayor and any Emanuel. You will be given some shit about who you work for. Also, he has a thing about video calls.

3) I really need to be done with politics. At least for a while. Life's too short. Am I saying I'll ignore you if you bother me with any of this Mount Chicago stuff? Maybe. But I am definitely saying that I really hope I won't need to. This is nothing you can't handle, I know Perry's gonna like you, and I tend to think Ari will too. Ari likes poise, and you've got that in spades. Show him.

4) FYI, Below's a copy of the email I'm sending to Ari and Perry, and, no, I'm not sending a copy of THIS email to either of them.

Best of luck!
Reg

Dear Ari and Perry:

I've retired from City Hall—just beat cancer—and am getting on a plane to Paris tomorrow, but the City of Chicago, which all of us love, needs your help, so before I head out, I want to connect you to Apter Schutz, the young man at the mayor's office who's in charge of the Mount Chicago Memorial Park, which will be built, at least in part, on the site of what used to be Millennium Park.

It's a massive project that will cost upward of half a billion dollars, and I know you'll want to help in whatever way you can.

Apter's got the details.

I'll send an email introducing you guys in a second.

I wish you both all the best.

Sincerely,
Reggie Glibner

—

Apter went outside and called the mayor's cell.

"What happened?" said the mayor. "You get stood up?"

"Something like that, but—"

"She doesn't deserve you."

"Thanks, but—"

"I mean it. Other fish. Who does she think she is anyway, the tart?"

"Listen," Apter said. "Ari Emanuel keeps trying to call me. Trying to *FaceTime* me, actually."

"Ah, that's great! Glibner said he'd get on it right away, but—wow. He really meant *right away*. Gotta love that guy. So what did the barking little jagoff have to say?"

"I didn't take the call."

"Interesting move."

"I don't know what it is I'm supposed to be doing."

"Getting us some high-profile money for the park. A pledge. A donation."

"What's high-profile mean in this instance?"

"Eight figures."

"Eight? As in ten million dollars?"

"That would borderline on a provenance I privately refer to as *Insult City*. That would be approximately one not-so-big fraction of recession-era profits for a Lollapalooza. *Mid*–eight figures is what I'm thinking."

"I don't know how to ask someone for mid–eight figures."

"Easiest thing in the world. You say you're raising money to build a park that's gonna cost half a billion, minimum, and you're hoping for *a significant donation to get the ball rolling*. If Glibner did his job right, you don't even have to say that 'cause he already said it. If you want to put a finer point on it, you tell that son of a bitch Emanuel that we came to him *before* any Pritzkers, *before* any Crowns. Before Wrigley. Before Boeing. And etcetera."

"Is it even true? Half a billion?"

"I don't . . . What do you mean?" the mayor said.

"Did you talk to anyone? Designers? Architects?"

"I have talked to no one of the kind. I'm following *your* lead here, Apter. What you advised me yesterday. Iron's still hot, tragedy-wise, so I'm striking before the next major natural disaster captures the hearts and the minds of the moneyed. First we'll get the donations pledged, then we'll sort out the rest of the details later."

"I don't—"

"You *do*. Whatever you were gonna say. You do. You can. You will. Just ABC, right? Always be closing. They're already in. Ari wouldn't call if they weren't in. Definitely he wouldn't call so soon. He knows we know that. He's signaling a willfulness. A desire. Now it's just a matter of *how* in he is, and what he'll want in exchange."

"Like tax breaks for Lollapalooza or something?"

"Nothing like that. No favors get done here. This is charity. Charity creates goodwill. Buys it. Buys general goodwill, and public acknowledgment of charity. Goodwill in the bank to exchange for favors later, and one's name on something. He'll expect goodwill, and demand his name on something in exchange, and that's all there is to it."

"And I'm not supposed to ask for anything specific?"

"All you're supposed to ask for is more. Whatever he says he wants to do for the park, you ask for *more*."

"And what should I accept?"

"*The most.*"

"What can I tell him he can put his name on?"

"Depends on how much the most turns out to be."

"So I need to get back to you with whatever that is. 'The most.'"

"Right."

"And then I'll need to get back to him with your response."

"Exactly—What is that sound keeps dinging?"

It was FaceTime. Ari.

"So my role here," Apter said, "is go-between as much as negotiator."

"Nail on the head."

"And you need a go-between because . . ."

"I hate this guy. Even more than his brother. And it's mutual. I'm not asking him for anything, and he's not giving me—Do you not hear that? That ding? It's a dinging? Like *ding-ding, ding-ding*?"

"He's calling again," Apter said. "Fourth time."

"*Fourth* time! Better take it. You *got* this, boyo. Bye."

"Hey hey hey," said Ari Emanuel. "The boy himself. Adapter Shits!"

"And you must be the ex-mayor's little brother, Arnold. You're *really* suntanned, little Arnold."

"Oh, just stop. I like you already. I mean, what the fuck kind of face is that you're making? You looking for a blowjob? A *job* job? Answer your phone when Deb calls, tough guy. Deb!"

"Who's Deb?" said Apter, but Ari Emanuel, after having shown it to Apter, had already used his middle finger to close the chat.

Apter went back inside and drank his Corona.

Ari's secretary, Deb, called half an hour later, while Apter stood in line at the subpar taco joint.

She told him he'd be flying ORD to LAX the following morning at ten thirty for a four o'clock meeting at Endeavor, Ari's agency, then asked him for his numbers: frequent flyer, birthday, social security.

He went outside to convey the information, and by the time that was through, the line had gotten longer, and he'd seen a young woman having trouble picking up after a pit bull that must have been ill, so he skipped the tacos and headed back home. On his way he called Adi to inquire about *Entourage,* the weekly half-hour dramedy series that had aired on HBO from 2004 to 2011.

Adi'd watched *Entourage* all through high school—she'd had what, if pressed, she would have described as a "reluctant attraction" to the show's chubby stoner character, Turtle, played by the actor Jerry Ferrara—whereas Apter, who'd been in grade school at the time, had been under the impression that the show was "for girls" (an uncommon impression to have, it would seem: any number of television critics had designated *Entourage* "*Sex and the City* for lads and bros"), and whenever Adi had turned it on, he would go to the basement to watch DVDs of *Seinfeld* or *Curb* on the older ("the small") TV set.

Hollywood superagent Ari Gold was a character on *Entourage* whose catchphrase "Let's hug it out, bitch!" had become a meme back when Apter was a boy, but Apter, though he'd heard the phrase hundreds of times in middle school, hadn't learned its origins until junior high, when he saw it deployed by a Nazi called Gonzo on a white power message board Apter liked to troll. Gonzo'd injected a "let's hug it out, bitch" into an argument between two other Nazis, one of whom's response to Gonzo had been, "listen to this obama-sucking nigger quoting yesterday's wisdom of the hollywood superkikes," which was bizarre enough a string of words to read that Apter, having read them, was compelled to google "Let's hug it out, bitch," which brought him to a Wikipedia entry for Ari Gold, which said he was based on real-life Hollywood superagent Ari Emanuel, the younger brother of President Obama's then chief of staff, Rahm Emanuel.

That's why Apter, the night before he was to meet with Ari Emanuel, wanted to hear about *Entourage* from Adi.

"What a bad show," was the first thing Adi said when Apter asked about *Entourage*. Then she talked about the show in depth for a while. For long enough a while and at great enough a depth that it seemed like she'd initially been disingenuous. Like she thought that *Entourage* wasn't just *not* a bad show, but that it was a *good* show, or even a *great* one, and was, for some reason, embarrassed to admit it. She kept saying stuff like, "It's totally stupid, I know—it really is—but I find it kind of entertaining to *think about.*"

The first thing that Adi said she found entertaining to think about was that Hollywood superagent Ari Emanuel—who everyone knew was the inspiration for cartoonishly obnoxious Hollywood superagent Ari Gold, who was portrayed by cartoonishly obnoxious actor Jeremy Piven—had not only been the agent of the creator of *Entourage*, but of virtually everyone who was associated with *Entourage*, including but not limited to:

a) Movie star heartthrob and *Entourage* coproducer Mark Wahlberg, on the early portion of whose Hollywood career the show was loosely based.
b) Adrian Grenier, who plays the movie star heartthrob whose early Hollywood career is loosely based on Mark Wahlberg's.
c) Perry Farrell, who, in his capacity as lead singer of Jane's Addiction, sang "Just Because," the song that accompanies the opening credits on every episode of *Entourage*.
d) Jeremy Piven.

Entourage concerns itself, Adi went on to explain, with the sexual adventures, business decisions, and camaraderie of Vincent (Vinny) Chase, a young movie star heartthrob on the rise, and his . . . entourage.

Two members of this entourage have moved from Queens to Hollywood to live with/off Vincent Chase: 1) the scrappy, go-getting Eric, and 2) the chubby stoner, Turtle.

A third member of the entourage is Johnny Chase (aka Johnny Drama), Vincent's older, far less good-looking brother, who moved from Queens to Hollywood a number of years earlier—at some point in the early 1990s—in order to pursue his own screen-acting career, with which he had some minor success (antepeak-TV television), though that career has been on the decline since long before Vincent's arrival in Hollywood with Eric and Turtle, and, like Eric and Turtle, Johnny has no income of his own and lives with/off Vincent.

The last member of the entourage, Hollywood superagent Ari Gold, has great affection for Vincent, believes Vincent capable of becoming the next Tom Cruise, but doesn't live with/off him, as he has his own family and great personal wealth.

Four other things that Adi said she found entertaining (to think) about *Entourage* included:

1. That Mark Wahlberg occasionally appears on the show, playing himself, and that, whenever he appears, he's always with an entourage.
2. That Johnny Chase, who one presumes to be loosely based on Mark Wahlberg's less good-looking, has-been brother, Donny Wahlberg—a former member of the 1980s multiplatinum-selling boy band New Kids on the Block—is played by Kevin Dillon, the less good-looking, has-been brother of movie star heartthrob Matt Dillon.
3. That Hollywood superagent Ari Gold, despite frequently saying foul, sexual things to and about women, is actually a loyal, loving husband and family man, just as Ari Emanuel is reputed to be, whereas Jeremy Piven—an actor from Evanston who Adi said had propositioned no fewer than half a dozen women she personally knew—has always been known to behave (i.e. in real life) toward women in the way that Ari Gold *purports* to behave.
4. In one of the later seasons, Jamie-Lynn Sigler, the actress who starred as Meadow Soprano on HBO's *The Sopranos*—she, like

so many other guest stars on *Entourage,* plays herself—very winningly, and to everyone's great surprise, starts dating Turtle the chubby stoner, who she explicitly finds far more interesting and attractive than Vincent Chase, and, while in the middle of shooting that season, Sigler started dating (i.e. in real life) Jerry Ferrara, the actor who plays Turtle and, thereafter, the two were briefly engaged.

"And *that,*" Adi said, referring to the information contained in item 4, "is especially entertaining to think about because you can't help but imagine that Jerry Ferrara, without having played Turtle on *Entourage,* would never have had a chance at getting romantically involved with someone like Jamie-Lynn Sigler, especially not back then, when she was at the apex of her stardom. And you start to wonder about things like whether Kevin Dillon, by way of his star turn as has-been Johnny Drama, who he kind of already *was* in real life—whether that star turn caused Kevin Dillon to become *less* like Johnny Drama—that is: less like himself. Or maybe more like himself? I don't know. And did Ari Emanuel become *more* Ari Emanuel–ish as a result of viewing Jeremy Piven's portrayal of Hollywood superagent Ari Gold? Less? And what about Piven? Did playing Ari Gold allow him to be more *Piven-ish,* or more Emanuel-ish or . . . Look, it's a stupid show. Sexist, too. But a stupid, sexist show that dialogues reflexively with reality in a pretty entertaining way, I guess is all I'm saying. I mean, you need a lot of extratextual information about mid-aughts Hollywood celebrities and power brokers to really appreciate that aspect of it, and, even if you have that information, the show still fails to achieve anything Cervantes or, for that matter, Hemingway—or Mailer or Roth—haven't already achieved in spades, but . . . it's TV, not literature, so . . ."

Well before Adi began trailing off—well before she'd begun to talk about Turtle/Ferrara's relationship with Jamie-Lynn Sigler, in fact—Apter had realized that most of the information she was conveying about *Entourage* wouldn't likely have much, if any, bearing on the next day's meeting with Ari Emanuel, but he also realized, while roughly midway between the subpar taco place and home, that he was rapidly starting to feel very drunk—too drunk—and he remembered that he hadn't eaten since lunch, and knew that if he didn't fill his stomach with something hot and simple—i.e. lots of pasta—before he went to bed, the next day's hangover would be unbearable, and it occurred to him, upon arriving home, that if he didn't stay on the phone with Adi, the odds were pretty high that he'd allow himself to go to bed and pass out before he had the chance to start filling his stomach, so he encouraged Adi to continue talking until his pasta had finished boiling, at about which point she started trailing off, and Apter, seeing an opening, said, "That was really helpful. Thank you, Adi."

"I bored you," Adi said. "You're handling me."

"Never," said Apter. "Hey, I almost forgot! Just a second . . ." Apter sent her the sound file he'd sent to Sylvie. "I just sent you this recording I made of me and the mayor. A conversation we had today. Context is, he wants to build a park where Millennium Park used to be. He wants it to memorialize *the survivors* of the anomaly, which . . . I'm too drunk to explain what that means right now, but it'll—the recording: you'll still like the recording."

"Hold on," Adi said. "Is this something you usually do? Record conversations you have with people? Are you recording this?"

"Hell no. That would be creepy. Am I creepy? I just record the mayor."

"Is that a good idea?"

"It's not a *bad* idea," Apter said. "It's legal—he's talking to me, Illinois's what's called a one-party-consent state—I looked this up—and I'm one party, consenting, plus I'm not a blackmailer or anything. I mean . . . worst that could happen is he somehow finds out, doesn't like it, and fires me, which . . ."

"But—"

"Anyway, he'd probably be *flattered* if he found out."

"But I still don't—why are you doing it?" Adi said.

"That'll become self-evident once you listen to the recording. I mean, the SNL guy—what's his name? I'm too drunk. Doesn't matter. But that guy's impersonation of the mayor? Pales."

"You're weird, little brother."

"Maybe," Apter said. "For sure, though, I'm dizzy. I gotta eat a bunch of pasta right now."

"Don't forget to hydrate. Love you," she said.

He had two large bowls of buttered elbows with parmesan, chased an Alka-Seltzer with three pints of water, fell asleep before ten, thinking,

"*Herschel* . . . or *Bobovnikoff*?" without really knowing what he meant by that question, and woke the next morning feeling mostly okay.

It was good to be young.

Even better than that: to be young and know it, and know it was good.

As had long been Apter's habit on waking, he reached for his phone, opened YouTube, and checked *Gladman Unschtuck*. Suddenly, he felt even better than he already had, for there hadn't been a Gladman performance—at least not one that any of the thirty-six-some-odd-thousand subscribers to the *Gladman Unschtuck* channel had seen, much less recorded—since early November 2021, which had led to all kinds of comment-section rumor and speculation, none of which had been particularly un- or convincing (e.g. "Maybe Gladman's wife had a baby and he's taking a hiatus." "Maybe Gladman's gone back to writing fiction, and just doesn't have time for stand-up right now." "The UIC website says Gladman's on sabbatical. Prolly he's living in Paris with his wife." "Those last few videos, he looks pretty tired, I think. Maybe SICK AND TIRED? Of working for free? Or of working at all? Let's all hope he's just taking a break. If you're reading this, Gladman, we really miss you, man."), and Apter now saw that, just last night, Gummo Rickles had posted a brand new, seven-minute-long video titled "What Happened to Solly Gladman."

He clicked play at once, and, within ten seconds, his excitement transformed into agitation: the video was not of a new performance, but rather just a compilation of every recorded instance of Gladman and Gladman-as-Pollaco saying the words "I don't know."

"Fuck you, Gummo Rickles," Apter said and then started to type, but got autocorrected on *Gummo* three times in a row (*Gummies* then *Gumbo* then *Gumming*) and closed the app, for he suddenly remembered having thought, "*Herschel* . . . or *Bobovnikoff*?" and knew what he'd meant: What would he call him? *That's* what he'd meant.

Herschel: pudgy-little-brother type, open expression; the softhearted neighbor kid you look out for.

Bobovnikoff: the pale genius in the corner, rail-thin and brooding, appeared to be sneering but that was just his face; the other kind of neighbor kid you look out for.

Apter googled around on his phone, found a bunch of photos: not pudgy, not pale.

More like Paul Newman with a dark, patchy beard.

Newman playing Dylan.

Paul Newman starring as "Handsome" Bobby Zimmerman, welter-weight boxing champion of the world.

Hersh then. Just like Sylvie'd said. *Hersh.*

Well, so . . . good for him.

And her.

Good for everyone, probably.

Apter closed his eyes and fell back asleep.

When next he woke, it was 9 a.m., and he panicked about running late for his flight, but in the shower remembered he had millions of dollars—if he missed his flight he could painlessly buy his way onto the next one, or the one after that, and still make the meeting—not to mention that he wouldn't be checking any luggage, plus the business-class ticket Endeavor had bought him would get him through security quicker than usual, and then he was no longer taking a shower, but kissing the barmaid's fragrant neck, and he didn't want to stop, but he needed to piss, was dying to piss, and he woke from his dream, and it was only seven thirty, and he ran to the bathroom and pissed for what seemed like four or five minutes, but was more like a little bit less than two minutes. For the first thirty seconds, it felt like an accomplishment—a victory even—but shortly thereafter came to feel like a chore.

2

After the pilot had authorized the passengers to use their devices, Apter took a few minutes password-protecting the anomaly victims spreadsheet on his laptop, then attached the file to an email to Sylvie:

Sylvie Klein!

On my way to L.A. for one night—long story, tell you next time.

To open this, you'll need to type:

1) the nickname of the guy who broke my face for love, i.e. *nickname lasty,* in AlTeRnAtInG cApS, followed by

2) the four-digit year it happened, followed by

3) Mendy Mandelstam's least favorite fraction (spelled out, no caps, no hyphen), followed by

4) the name of the barman who inspired me to go to school for the profession I no longer practice (AlTeRnAtInG cApS), followed by

5) the three-letter acronym for where I went to grad school (all caps), followed by

6) the number of times we had sex last night (digit).

Thanks again. Talk soon!

Yours,
Apter

He spent the rest of the flight eating bowls of warmed nuts and watching Season 1 of *Entourage,* which wasn't as bad as he'd imagined it would be. It featured lots of gorgeous women who sometimes were topless; large, expensive houses and sleek, foreign sports cars that seemed like they might be nice things to own; parties at which the male:female ratio ranged between 1:2 and 1:3; celebrity cameos; jokes that, despite rarely being very funny, kept the mood consistently light; and story lines the stakes of which felt roughly half as dramatic as scratching the wax off a one-dollar Lotto card. You could fall asleep near the end of episode 2, then wake in the middle of episode 3, or even episode 7, without feeling lost.

Entourage, above all else, was *relaxing.*

The perfect TV show to watch on a plane.

The limousine Deb had sent dropped him off at the Beverly Wilshire. The driver told him he'd already been checked in, handed him a key to room 1001, and promised to return at four fifteen to take him to his four thirty meeting at Endeavor.

It was half past three.

The suite was three rooms, looking out on whatever.

Apter set his bag on one of the couches, washed his face, then had a club sandwich and a coffee downstairs, on the poolside patio. A couple at the table a few feet in front of his spoke to one another with quiet intensity about a child or a dog they would raise—vegetarian or vegan, that was the debate—but Apter tuned out before discovering which (the answer was neither; they were talking about hiring a live-in maid), so distracted was he by the tops of the ears of the man of the couple, which were tucked inside the band of the man's blue ball cap.

Trying to recall having seen that before, failing to recall ever having seen it, thinking it shouldn't seem all that strange, but nonetheless struck by how strange it did seem, Apter determined that, no, he mustn't have seen it before, and he wondered whether tucking your ears in your ball cap might be *an L.A. thing,* wondered why that should cross his mind, let alone seem to be at all likely, for it did seem likely, *didn't* it seem likely?

He thought it seemed likely, and thought himself insightful, but then, just as quickly, he felt a little foolish for going so far, for the self-satisfaction that going so far and thinking himself insightful had provided him, for why would he figure these two for Angelenos? Why would he assume a couple people drinking beers on an L.A. hotel's poolside patio lived in L.A.? Because drinking on a hometown hotel poolside patio seemed to be *an L.A. thing* itself? Sure. Maybe. And what would be wrong with that? Was there anything wrong with that? Why was he trying to find something wrong with it? The patio was *nice*.

Maybe he had something against Los Angeles? But what could he have against Los Angeles? He'd never even been there before today. And he liked it so far. It was seventy degrees out. Hardly any wind. True enough, the club sandwich, even though he ate it quickly, had become a little too wet toward the end, but the coffee—in a good way—smelled like olives.

Getting up to leave the patio, Apter struck the bottom of the table with his knee. The sudden clattering startled the man in the ball cap, whose neck and shoulders flinched in such a way as to pop his left ear free of the band.

The man turned, glared at Apter, and tucked it back in.

The driver was waiting near the door of the lobby.

Apter asked him where his limo was.

"Don't worry," said the driver, "I won't try to talk your ear off or anything. I'll stay a few steps in front of you the whole way there."

Then the driver led Apter to Endeavor on foot. It was two blocks away. A five-minute walk.

Endeavor was sunny and expensive-looking, like Ari Gold's agency on *Entourage*. The office that Apter was brought to by the woman who met him when he stepped off the elevator—the office belonging to Ari Emanuel—was sunnier and more expensive-looking.

"Ari'll be here shortly," said the woman, pointing to a couch that faced a couple chairs.

"Are you Deb?" said Apter, taking a seat.

"I am," she said. "Thank you."

" 'Thank you?' "

"You're welcome," she said. "The WiFi password for guests is Emanuel."

"Stop sexually harassing each other!" Ari shouted from out in the hall. "What we'd like to do for the City of Chicago," he said, now coming through the doorway, "is, as I'm sure you were counting on, hoping for, maybe even begging old man Elohim for if that's your kinda thing—what we'd like to do is host a benefit concert."

He sat on one of the chairs facing Apter, turned to Deb, and said, "Where's my number-one favorite impresario?"

Deb showed Ari her palms and shrugged.

Ari shrugged back, showed Deb a finger, pointed the finger at the doorway and thrusted.

Deb left, giggling.

"Grant Park," he continued. "June 16. Day before the start of Lollapalooza." From a carafe on the coffee table between them, he poured them each a glass of water. "Day Zero," he said. "That's what we'll call it. A bare-bones event by Lolla standards. Gates open at noon, show starts at two. Single stage. Between six and nine bands—headliners, all—and nonmusical acts between each set. Jane's Addiction will play, full original lineup. Kanye West will play the hits. Pixies will play, full original lineup. Smashing Pumpkins will play, full original lineup. Tricky will play with Martina Topley-Bird. That's all locked down. Radiohead is nearly locked down. We're talking to the Fugees about a reunion—long shot. We're talking to Mike D and Adrock about a project they might or might not be willing to admit they've been working on for years with Thom Yorke and DJ Shadow—long shot. We've even got feelers out to Fugazi about a reunion—except who fucking knows with those guys, am I right? Wouldn't count on Fugazi. But the idea is we start promoting as soon as next week, announce Jane's and Pixies and surprise guests, which will instantly ignite rumors about the Pumpkins and Kanye because: 'How couldn't they?' Chicago, etc. General admission: $175. VIP passes: $700. Come-to-the-after-party-because-otherwise-she-might-not-fuck-you passes: $2,300. Come-to-the-after-after-party-slash-silent-auction-of-signed-instruments-played-at-Day-Zero-because-you-flew-in-from-Monaco-or-Riyadh-or-London-or-Abu-Dhabi-and-she'll-always-fuck-you-but-she'll-wish-you-were-your-dad-or-your-better-hung-brother passes: $15,000. Concessions partners TBD, but we're thinking burgers, tacos, ice cream, beer of course, and maybe a gin-and-tonic tent, maybe a donut bar, maybe some kind of top-your-own-houmous gluten-free vegan chia-seed suck'n'fuck food-truck pavilion deal. Like I said, though: concessions TBD. All profits from ticket sales, concessions, and silent auction go to the city. We retain T-shirt and pay-per-view earnings. We name the bandshell and—"

"What bandshell?" said Apter.

"This Chicago Mountain Park isn't gonna have a bandshell?"

"Right. Yes. It is. Go on . . ."

"As I was saying, we name the bandshell, and we name something else—a promenade or a garden or something. Whatever we want. We get first refusal on naming whatever else you decide to offer naming rights to, which, as I understand it, you don't know what that'll be yet. There you have it."

"Okay . . ."

"*Okay?*"

"You have an office I can use? I need to call the mayor."

"No."

"No?"

"No, you don't need to call the fucking mayor."

"I don't have the authority to negotiate terms with you."

"No problem there. This is our first, last, and best offer."

"Okay, well . . ."

"*Well?*"

"That just doesn't make sense," Apter said. "You flew me all the way out here to make your first, last, and best offer? You could've done that by email. Or FaceTime—whatever *that's* all about. What *is* that all about?"

"I had you flown out here *first class*—"

"Business class."

"That's the *best* that was av*ai*lable. I had you flown out here *best* class and put you up in one of the finest suites in one of the finest hotels in our fine, fair city in order to a) see if I wanted to poach you from your fat-ass, dimwit, crypto-anti-Semite boss, knowing that b) even if I decided I didn't want to poach you, you'd tell him how nicely you were treated out here, which would enable him to reflect on how nicely *he* could have been treated, were he not such a—what's the phrase I'm look-ing for? right—were he not such a *fatassed, dimwitted, crypto-antisemitic piece of shit.*"

"Okay."

"Oh. Kay. What."

"Okay, so *no*."

"You're saying *no*."

"For now, at least, I have to. Your first offer isn't good enough for me to say yes to, and since it's also your last and best offer, that means it's a no."

"Bullshit."

"Look, maybe this could change. Maybe, in another few weeks, we'll have talked to, I don't know, the Pritzkers, or the Crowns, or Zell—whoever—and they'll offer a donation that'll really get the ball rolling for the park, and then this whole Day Zero concert—which sounds like a really great concert, by the way—maybe at *that* point, it could work, if it's still on the table, which of course we hope it will be, and if those naming rights you want haven't been claimed by other donors. See, I'm not trying to say that your offer isn't generous. It is. It's even kind of *almost* there. Like, maybe just a couple tiers away from what we need. I mean, it's worth, what? A few million?"

"Try ten or twelve."

"If you say so, I believe it. But what we need is fifty million to start. *Minimum.* We need that so the smaller money that follows will be, well . . . larger than it'll be if the starting money—the, I don't know what you call it, the *leader* money, I guess? Anyway, we need fifty million to start, at minimum, I'm saying, because we want the money that *follows* that leader money, or rather we want the money that follows the money that follows it—the second- or third-tier donations, that is—to be the kind of money *you're* talking about, and the lower we start, the less that follow-money's gonna be. The higher we start, the higher it'll be. Now given the timing of everything, and the fact that we're talking about proceeds not-yet-earned from a concert not-yet-held, maybe if we announced the benefit concert, we could tell the press that it would be 'a donation worth as much as an *estimated* twenty, twenty-five million dollars' since the auction and concession earnings are so opaque and variable, and maybe they'd swallow it, and maybe other potential donors will swallow it, too, but no one's ever gonna believe the concert could possibly bring in *fifty* million—not without the T-shirts and pay-per-view, you know? Grant Park's big, but it's only so big. You can only sell so many tickets."

"Okay," Ari said.

"Okay what?"

"The city can have the T-shirts and pay-per-view."

"Great, then it's probably a go. I'll talk to the mayor."

"Sure," Ari said. "But just keep your phone in your fucking pocket, all right? You can talk to the mayor when you get back home. That really was the last, best offer—that's all we've got. And just so you know, I was gonna give you the T-shirts and pay-per-view anyway. We can't profit off a benefit concert without looking like assholes. Plus I love Chicago. I loved Millennium Park. I *want* the city to have a nice, new park."

"So you held out on me for . . . form's sake?"

"Partly I held out because it was *fun*. Mostly, I wanted to see how you'd handle it. How long it would take you to tell me how bad it would look for us to profit off a benefit concert."

"It occurred to me to mention it," Apter said, "but it didn't seem like the right move."

"It might have been the right move—woulda been quicker for sure—but I like that you took it in a different direction. Showed some style. I'm being very earnest right now, if you haven't noticed."

"Is that what that faraway look means, Ari?"

"It *is* what this faraway look means, Apter. I'm impressed with you and I want you to work for me."

"As a Hollywood agent?"

"As a budding Hollywood superagent."

"Don't agents need connections? I've got no connections."

"They need a lot more than connections. Good ones do. Anyway, you'd be connected to me, see? What do you think *that's* worth?"

"Probably a lot, if I wanted to be a Hollywood agent, but why would I want to be a Hollywood agent?"

"Asks the guy who works for *duh mayor*, for what? Fifty k? Sixty k?"

"The mayor's hilarious."

"*Hilarious*, you say."

"He is. Not always deliberately, not even usually deliberately—but he's almost always hilarious," Apter said. "And I don't think he's really an anti-Semite, by the way. No more so than his general milieu in any case. If he were, though, that might be even more hilarious."

"You're one of these new young Jews who thinks he's *white*, aren't you? You think Jews are just regular old *white* folks, don't you? That, my friend, is what's hilarious."

"You've got me all wrong."

"Yeah? Well . . . good. I'm *glad*. Job's still on the table, after all. Want it?"

"You still haven't told me why I should."

"Apart from the money?"

"I don't care about the money."

"That's stupid. It's a lot of money."

"I'm set for life."

"I didn't peg you for a trust-funder."

"I'm not a trust-funder," Apter said.

"So then . . ."

"So forget it. Pretend I'm a trust-funder. Apart from money, why would anyone want to be a Hollywood agent?"

"No idea."

"Come on. I thought you were being—what's the word you used?—*earnest*? Be earnest. You love your job. It's obvious. It isn't really just the money, is it?"

"It's *mostly* the money. I mean, *I'm* set for life, too—I'm set for a few lives. Still, making lots of money—very exciting to me. To anyone. Everyone. It isn't *only* that, though. You're right. I'm great at this job. In fact, I'm incontestably *the best* at this job. No one'll argue otherwise, not even behind my back. Doing a thing you're good at . . . it's a pleasure. I'm sure you know that. A thing you're great at? That much more of a pleasure. Only follows, right?"

"It does."

"And getting paid for what you're great at—getting paid *greatly* for what you're great at—getting paid *in accordance with* your greatness . . . Unbeatable. Anyway, you would be great as an agent. I'm certain of it. And I'm the world's foremost expert on the matter."

"Thank you," Apter said.

"By which you mean . . ."

"I'll seriously consider coming to work for you."

"I'll take it. And another thing, just in case it isn't obvious—I've been assuming it was, but you didn't ask, so maybe it isn't: All the stuff on *Entourage*? The parties, the lunches, the pretty faces? It's pretty accurate. In quality, if not quite quantity. You meet a lot of stars, a lot of talented people, a lot of powerful people, a lot of *hilarious* people, too, for that matter, and, as you can imagine, it's a lot of fun, which—ho, ho, ho! Speak of the ding-dang goddamn motherfucking devil!"

Apter's gaze followed Ari's to the doorway. The legendary Perry Farrell came through it, looking just like the legendary Perry Farrell, except for the shirt, i.e. that he was wearing one.

Ari said, "Apter, that's Perry Farrell, musical genius and master impresario. Perry, Apter Schutz, who needs a better job."

"Pleasure to meet you, Apter," Perry Farrell said. "I hope you find a better job, and I'm sorry I'm late."

"So lemme guess," said Ari. "Traffic?"

"The freeway," said Perry Farrell, "was jammed."

"So you get off the freeway and you take the tollway, no?"

"Well, I got off the freeway and the tollway was jammed."

"So you get off the tollway, take locals for a while, get back on the freeway."

"But I got off the tollway, took locals to the freeway, and the locals were congested and the freeway, Ari—the freeway: still jammed."

"So you paint it green."

"You do. You paint it green."

Apter slapped both of his knees and howled.

"You *know* that one?" Ari said.

"Those nonmusical acts for Day Zero you mentioned. Who were you thinking of getting?" said Apter.

Perry Farrell had read Gladman's prizewinning novel, but had never heard of Bernie Pollaco or known that Solly Gladman, who he *had* heard of but hadn't ever seen perform, was the same person as Solomon Gladman.

Ari'd read nothing by Solomon Gladman, nor seen any Solly or Pollaco shows, but he knew of all three, although, like Perry, hadn't known they were connected. He said he seemed to remember having first heard of Pollaco a few years back from a cousin, Shmuely, who'd said that Pollaco's act " 'made people hate Jews.' Does that sound right?"

"Assuming your cousin's a particular brand of humorless moron—it sounds completely right," Apter said.

"Shmuely did flunk the second grade," said Ari. " 'Drooly Shmuely had some trouble at schooly.' They used to sing that to him till he cried. We did, I mean. Me and my brothers. Wasn't very nice of us, I guess. He was always trying to *wrestle* me, though. Big fat kid. Anyway, your boy gets onstage and tells 'Paint It Green'? I can't even imagine."

"You're gonna love this," Apter said. Having found the mp4 he'd been seeking, he set his laptop on the table, pressed Play.

THE OVERCOAT.mp4

Before an audience (off-screen) at Julio's Yokebarn, Gladman paces the six-inch-high stage.

GLADMAN

. . . Anyway, I've got nothing new to say tonight, and I've been having one of those days where I'm thinking that maybe I've never had anything new to say on any night, ever. But still I want to be up here, talking to you, you know? I still have this desire, or need, to be up here, talking to you tonight, and so here I am, up here, talking to you tonight, and what I'm thinking is that, maybe, rather than focusing on doing something *new,* I should just try to focus on doing something *good.* Like, if I were a singer—if I were up here tonight because I wanted to connect to you by way of singing rather than by way of talking—what I'd probably want to do for you is covers. I'd sing a bunch of covers. Covers of a couple or three old, reliable classics. That's the kind of thing I want to do for you tonight. Except, how can I do that as a stand-up, right? I mean, maybe I could perform a few minutes of Gottfried or Seinfeld or Louis CK, but that . . . it wouldn't be . . . It wouldn't feel like a cover. It would feel like an impersonation. Your attention would be drawn to how much or little I sounded like those guys instead of the material. And there's nothing inherently wrong with that, per se—there's nothing wrong with impersonations—but that's not in the spirit of what I'm after, here. So what I'm thinking I'll do instead is—and maybe it's a really bad idea—but what I think I'll do—what I think, I should say, I'll *try* to do—is I'll try to tell you a short story. I'll try tonight to tell you the greatest short story of all time—what *I* consider the greatest short story of all time, at least, and what everyone else who's read it, even if they don't agree with me that it's *the* greatest of all time, never hesitates to call *one of* the greatest short stories of all time. "The Overcoat" by Nikolai Gogol. It might be a really bad idea on my part, but that, weirdly or not, makes it all the more appealing to me. You guys know this story? Just out of curiosity, can I get a show of hands for how many of you have read it? "The Overcoat" by Nikolai Gogol? . . . Really . . . Don't be shy. I'm not gonna like call on you or anything . . . Come on . . .

. . . Not *one* of you. *Not one* among the, what? seventy-five of you? eighty of you? Not one among all you members of the reputedly well-educated alt-comedy audience here at the Yokebarn has read Nikolai Gogol's "The Overcoat" is what you're telling me. I refuse to believe it. No, I'm kidding. I know you educated types don't like to read. But know what? As horrible as that is—as horrible as it is, on the like global scale of things, that none of you present and future cultural movers and shakers have read Gogol's "Overcoat"—it's actually a boon for me. Kinda takes the pressure off. As you can probably imagine. Or, if you can't imagine: it kinda takes the pressure off because this story, in addition to being the greatest short story ever written, is about fifty pages long and, even if you *did* tell short stories—that is: even if *telling* short stories was a thing that people did sometimes onstage *or* off—this one probably wouldn't be the one you'd want to start with. It's really . . . layered. So . . . good. Anyway, I think I'll just go ahead and start now.

"The Overcoat" by Nikolai Gogol.

On his way to work, Akaky Akakiyevich, who—

Quick sidebar, actually: in Russian, this name, *Akaky Akakiyevich,* it means something along the lines of like *Doodoo Poopoo,* or more like, I guess, *Doodoo son of Poopoo. Poopoo's son, Doodoo.* That kind of thing. But maybe, uh . . . Yeah. No. There's really too much punning in the story for me to explain every time a pun comes up—I don't even know a lick of Russian, either, I just heard this lecture once about wordplay in Gogol and . . . fuck it. Let's forget about the name. And the wordplay. The wordplay's a layer we can lose here, right? You can *read* the story for that if you want to— and you should. You should read it, and you should want to, but . . . So . . . Okay. Starting over now.

"The Overcoat" by Nikolai Gogol.

On his way to work, a little man who loves shortbread sees a sign in a bakery window. Sign says—and, well . . . actually . . . no.

Scratch the *little*. He's not particularly little, our protagonist. Or well, *maybe* he's little, I can't quite remember if he's little, but saying so feels . . . embellish-y. Irrelevant. It's irrelevant to the story, whether he's little or not, so I'm just . . . Let me . . .

I'm gonna take a deep breath now and start over once more. Last time. I promise. Last time for real. I'm starting to see that these kinds of doubts—when you're telling someone else's short story, there's just no room for these kinds of doubts, much less all these pauses and asides. I'm gonna stop that now.

Gladman quits pacing.

GLADMAN
"The Overcoat" by Nikolai Gogol.

On his way to work, a man who loves shortbread sees a sign in a bakery window: *GREATEST SHORTBREAD IN THE WORLD BAKED HERE.*

Man goes inside the bakery, says to the baker, "Is it true what your sign says? Is it true you bake the greatest shortbread in the world?"

"Indeed, sir, I do," the baker tells the man. "In fact, I have a pan in the kitchen just out of the oven. Would you like a sample?"

"Please, yes!" says the man.

The baker disappears into the kitchen, returns with a

pan full of lozenge-shaped shortbreads. Sets the pan on the counter in front of the man. "What a nice smell," the baker remarks. And it isn't just salesmanship, this remark—he really does like the smell. He's proud of his shortbread.

"A *wonderful* smell," the man agrees.

"Well, go on," says the baker. "Go ahead and try one."

Man chooses a shortbread. Tastes it. Just a nibble at first. His eyes go wide. One of them glistens.

He takes a whole bite, begins to chew. Rests a hand on the crown of his skull, and . . . leaves it there. Takes another bite, chews some more. He's breathing heavy through his nose, now, *loudly,* and *both* his eyes are glistening.

Swallowing, he gasps a little, sucks at his teeth. "*This,*" he says to the baker. "This is the greatest shortbread in the world. You bake the greatest shortbread in all of the world!"

"I'm so glad you appreciate my shortbread," says the baker.

Man asks him, "May I ask you a question?"

"By all means, please do," the baker says.

"Do you think you might be able," says the man, "to bake this shortbread—this might be too much to ask, I know—but do you think you might be able to bake this shortbread into the shape of the fifth letter of the alphabet?"

"E?" says the baker.

"E," says the man. "That's right," he says. "E. I know it might seem peculiar, but a shortbread of that shape—it's something I've dreamt about ever since . . . well, ever since I can remember."

"Then I have some good news for you," the baker tells the man.

"You *do*?" the man says.

"I *can* bake—and will be more than happy to bake—this dream-shortbread of yours into being."

"Please don't toy with my emotions," says the man.

"I would never," says the baker.

"You mean you really aren't pulling my chain?" the man says. "That might hurt my feelings. It could damage me irreparably."

"I don't kid about shortbread, sir," the baker says. "Now,

tell me: What size would you like this dream-shortbread to be?"

The man, almost furtively, points at the pan from which he'd previously plucked his shortbread.

"Ah, yes," the baker says, "of course. These shortbreads here *are* the perfect size."

"No," the man says. "That is: maybe they are the perfect size. I don't know. You are the expert on shortbread—no doubt. But the shortbread *I* dream of is the size of the pan."

"That is quite a large shortbread," the baker says.

"I understand," the man says. "I do. I'm sorry. It's too much to ask. I've asked too much. What I'm asking you to do just can't be done."

"Please!" says the baker. "Of course it can be done. I can and will do it. I was simply remarking on—"

"Oh, good!" the man says. "Oh, glory! Oh, wonder! And money's no object, if that's what you were getting at. I've been saving. Just name your price."

The price wasn't what the baker had been getting at at all when he told the man, "That is quite a large shortbread."—he hadn't been getting at anything, really, just thinking aloud— but much as the baker *likes* the man, the conversation is beginning to feel long and awkward, so rather than correcting the man's misinterpretation, the baker proceeds to name his price.

The man judges it fair—more than fair—and pops the rest of the shortbread he's holding in his mouth, and, sucking at and chewing it, shakes the baker's hand. The baker tells him to come by any time after four to pick up the shortbread. After shaking the baker's hand a second time, the man leaves the bakery. Goes to work.

Now, our man's a good worker, kind of guy who never calls in sick. Kind of guy who, even if he's feeling a little sick himself, will take on a double to cover a shift if a coworker asks—he's the first guy you call when you need your shift covered. The boss *loves* him.

Anyhow, his shift today doesn't end till six, the bakery's

a half hour away from work, and the thought of the dream-shortbread being ready for two and a half *hours* before he gets to it—it just seems wrong. More than wrong, really. It seems disrespectful. It seems . . . what? Almost like a betrayal. Like a betrayal of himself . . . A betrayal of his dreams . . . It's hard to explain, but it tortures him a little.

So, at lunch, he calls up every coworker he knows who's got the day off, but no one's answering their phone. Then he tries again on the first of his afternoon smoke breaks. Gets through to one guy, but the guy's got a doctor's appointment—can't miss it. Gets through to another guy, but the guy pretends the call gets dropped, then declines to pick up when our man calls back.

And the man's thinking: What?! My dream-shortbread's gonna come out of the oven and . . . just sit there? Sit there just waiting for *two and a half hours*?

Unacceptable. He can't accept it.

So hat in hand, the man goes to the boss just before three thirty, says he has to leave. Boss asks him if he isn't feeling well or something. Our man doesn't like to lie. Will lie if he has to, but really doesn't like to. "It's not that," he says.

"What is it, then?" the boss says. "You got some kind of appointment you forgot about or something?"

"Well . . ." the man says. "You know, I'd rather not say."

"Some *pussy*?" says the boss. "You gonna get yourself some pussy? You got a hot date?"

That kind of coarse language makes our man feel embarrassed, and he's a blusher, our man, a blusher-clammer-upper, and all he can do here is blush, speechless, and look at his shoes.

"Listen," his boss says. "Let me tell you something. Hey. I want to tell you: you're our best worker. You're our best worker here, and everyone knows it. Everyone agrees. You're the best we got and I worry about you. How shy you are. I worry you're lonely. A lot of us do. And I, for one, sometimes I worry you're so lonely you're gonna do something terrible. I worry you're so lonely you'll hurt yourself one day. I worry you're so lonely you've already hurt yourself, and that you hurt so bad that you'll kill yourself one day. And then what, huh? You kill yourself, I'm out my best worker. My other workers? They're out their best coworker. I don't want that. No one wants that. We want nothing but the best for you. It's true. For a couple years, a few years back, me and the other guys used to talk about trying to find you some pussy. That is: whatever *pussy* means to you. *Pussy,* for a while—or so some of us considered—might actually, for you, mean more like *rectum.* Which was fine. *Is* fine. Comple*te*ly fine! Whatever *pussy* meant to you, and whatever *pussy* means to you, I don't know why it is we never actually tried to find any for you, but we didn't. Maybe it's because whenever we found some pussy that we believed might have been nice for you, instead of bringing you and that pussy together, what we'd do is we'd try to make that nice pussy our own—keep that nice pussy for ourselves, so to speak. And we've always felt a little bad about that. Well, I shouldn't speak for the others, I guess. But *I* have always felt bad about that, because I care about you, and I really think all you might need is some pussy. Other hand, last time I thought I found some nice pussy for you and kept it to myself, I ended up getting married, and I'm happily married. I can't say I regret not helping you out that one time—ha! But when I had my brief flirtation with religion last year, I prayed to Jesus Christ for him to get you some pussy—again: whatever *pussy* meant for you, I specified that—and I bet I'm not the only one around here who did that while praying. A little bit of nice pussy can really solve a lot of problems. For anyone, I'm saying. A little bit of nice pussy can solve a lot of problems for *anyone,* okay? But especially for you it can solve a lot of problems, I think, because you're so lonely. That is my philosophy. That is all I'm saying. So I'll tell you what: get the fuck outta here. Go get that nice pussy. And if you want to talk about it, or maybe get some advice or something, I'm happy to do that. To listen. To advise. I'm a shoulder, an ear, and an open book. But if you don't want to talk about it—and, judging by the tomato face you've got going, I'm guessing you don't—that's also fine, too. You don't have to say another word to me at all regarding this matter. I won't be hurt. Just please: go forth and sink the pink, my friend. *Or* the stink. Whichever one it is you prefer. Be it pink, or be it stink, find the happiness to which you are entitled, the happiness that you have more than earned. I am rooting for you always. Go. Go on."

And *just like that,* our man's on his way to the bakery.

Thirty minutes later, he's standing at the counter.

"Perfect timing," says the baker.

"It's ready?" says the man.

"Just out of the oven," the baker tells him. "Be right back."

The baker disappears into the kitchen, returns with a pan containing the E-shaped shortbread. Golden-brown. Buttery sheen. Still steaming a little.

"Oh dear," the man says. "Oh no," he says, breaking, with a kind of honking sound, into a sobbing fit.

"Sir?" says the baker.

The man stands there sobbing. A minute goes by. To the baker, this minute feels like an hour.

"Sir?" he says again.

"It's . . ." the man says in a trembling voice. He scrubs at his face with his sleeves for a second. Sniffles. Throat-clears. "I thought you were kind," he says. "I was convinced. I was convinced you were a kind person who understood me, who took me seriously. Who believed in my dream. Who wanted to help me make my dream come true."

"I am, sir," the baker says. "I did. And I do. What seems to be the problem?"

"I want you to know," the man continues, either ignoring or not having heard the baker's question, "I want you to know that this morning, I really came out of my shell. I took a great risk in doing so, and I believed it was worth it. I believed you cared. And now I see I was wrong. As usual. I'm always wrong. You were only pretending. You led me on. Ever since I first came in here this morning, I thought . . . I don't know. I suppose I found hope. I thought things were perhaps about to get better for me. And now I see how delusional that was. Once again, I see. Once again, I see, and yet it feels like *all at once*. It feels all new. All newly terrible. I opened up, yes, and you led me on, only to mock me. I want to know how you could do this to me. I want to *ask* you how you could do this to me. But that question: It isn't the right question at all, is it? The question I should be asking is: How could I have dared to believe you might *not* do this to me? How could I have ever dared to believe you *would* not do this to me? I should be used to this kind of treatment by now. This is what the world has in store for me. Same as what the world has always had in store for me. I cannot understand why I cannot understand. I must be cursed. I must deserve to be cursed. I must have done something terrible to someone at some point, but I can't recall ever having done anything terrible to anyone. I kicked a dog once, but that was by accident. I was just trying to walk to the art museum, and I didn't see it there. Not till I'd kicked it. The sidewalk was crowded. It was, without a doubt, more crowded than I'd ever seen a sidewalk, and more crowded than I've ever seen a sidewalk since. The subway workers union was striking, you see, and the bus drivers union was also striking, as were the unions of railroad workers and teachers, and this was during morning rush hour, so all the adults who couldn't find cabs were on their way to work on foot, and all of the kids, owing to the teachers strike, couldn't go to school and so, like me, they were all on their way to the art museum. I swear I didn't see the dog when I kicked it. I doubt many did. And when I realized what I'd done—when I felt my foot make contact with something and then heard the high and fearful canine yelp—it wasn't till I'd already kicked the dog that I saw the dog. And even then, I only caught but a glance. And I made an apology. I apologized twice. I crouched down, right in the middle of the sidewalk, and apologized to the dog and, still in my crouch, looked up into the face of the owner of the dog, and apologized to him. And he said, I remember, he said, 'No problem, guy. No big deal,' and I suppose I believed him. And I suppose I felt relieved to believe him, and just as I was about to stand up straight again, *I* was accidentally kicked. A passing pedestrian kicked my shoulder, and I toppled. And the passing pedestrian apologized to *me*, but continued passing—I don't think he realized I'd fallen, I don't think he even realized I was me. That is: I don't think that he saw me, but rather only felt the contact between *someone* and his foot, and knew to apologize, and so apologized. And when I tried to get up, I found I couldn't get up, so crowded was the sidewalk with rushing pedestrians who stepped on my ankles, stepped on my thighs, stepped on my head, and my hands, which broke three of my fingers, and at last on my testicles, at which point I determined that I, in order to survive, had to get out of this line of pedestrian traffic as quickly as possible, and so, one-handedly—owing to my broken fingers—I dragged and scraped and clawed my way *across* the sidewalk, perpendicular to foot traffic, till I finally, luckily, found refuge in the doorway to a stationery store, the owner of which took pity on me, which is the last thing I remember before waking up in county hospital. But I suppose *that* might be why I deserve all this terrible shame and humiliation. I suppose that I didn't feel badly enough about having kicked that dog. I suppose that when its owner said, 'No problem, guy. No big deal,' I was all too willing and all too quick to accept that he was right, to accept that the kick *was* no problem and no big deal. I suppose that *that* must be why I deserve such mocking cruelty from you. I failed to give myself a sufficient beating for having kicked that poor little dog that morning, and so have, ever since, been made by the universe to pay for it."

Now the baker, he's pretty confused at this point, but he's not a hard-hearted person—he's been through his share of rough times, himself—and the man's unbridled display of vulnerability, here: it touches him. He's touched. Who wouldn't be at least a little bit touched, right? So he says to the man—who, by this point, is just kind of slumped over on the counter, right next to the register, burying his head in the space between his crossed arms—the baker says to the man, "Sir, I had absolutely no intention of mocking you, much less doing violence to your dream. In fact, all I wanted to do was make your dream come true. I spent much of today looking forward to presenting you the shortbread you ordered and, for the life of me, I don't understand what's wrong with it, but if you could be perhaps just a bit more explicit about that, I will, if it's at all possible, repair the damage I have wrought. Will you tell me what the problem is, sir? Please?"

And the man, even though he suspects the baker's just trying to set him up for further shame and humiliation, also realizes that he has nothing more to lose, and might as well answer the question. So he does. "It's the case," he says.

"The case, sir? What is the case?"

"I know you're still mocking me, but I'm so wrung out here, and I'm sure I deserve it, so I'll just play along. It's an uppercase *e*. You baked the shortbread into an uppercase *e*."

"I thought that's what you'd asked for, sir," the baker says.

"Come on, now," the man says. "An *uppercase e*? What dream could I have had of a shortbread like that? What good could ever come of a shortbread like that? What benefit to *me* could ever I get from a shortbread like that? What good could you have possibly thought I could ever make of a shortbread like that?"

Baker says, "So if I'm understanding you correctly then: you're saying you wanted me to make you a shortbread the size of this pan, baked into the shape of a *lowercase* letter *e*."

"You make it sound like nothing," the man says. "It's the best shortbread in the world. What I wanted was *the best shortbread in the world* to be baked into the shape of a lowercase *e* the size of this pan. That's what I wanted, and it's all I ever wanted."

"Well, I'll tell you something, sir. If you'll allow me the privilege, I will make that shortbread for you. I have a wedding to cater this evening, but I can have the dream-shortbread ready for you as early as six tomorrow morning. Will you let me have another chance?"

"I will," the man says. "Of course I will, because I'm a fool who can't take a lesson no matter how many times he's been taught that lesson. I'll be here at six. But I want you to know:

if you do anything to me tomorrow that's like what you've done to me today, I really do think that'll be the end of me. I just won't be able to go on anymore."

"I'm confident I won't disappoint you," the baker says. "I'll see you in the morning. And if you'll wait just a moment, I'll wrap *this* shortbread up, and send you home with it today, free of charge."

And here the man gives the baker so chilling a look of terror—or is it contempt? is it *hatred*? the baker can't tell—but this look turns the baker's blood so cold that he doesn't press the matter, just lowers his eyes while the man, in silence, and bearing no shortbread, makes his exit.

Following morning, six a.m. sharp, the man, who went to bed the day before while the sun was still out, and then, for nearly twelve hours, slept a deep, however, nightmare-plagued sleep—they were murdering animals, and he was complicit—appears at the counter of the bakery.

"Sir!" says the baker. "Your shortbread just came out of the oven. It's a *good* one, sir. I'll be right back."

The baker disappears into the kitchen, returns with a pan containing the shortbread. Sets it down on the counter in front of the man.

The man's eyes are shut—scrunched to the wrinkling.

"It's okay, sir," the baker says. "I did just as you asked me to. Please don't be afraid."

The man allows one eye to pop open, points it at the shortbread, opens the other eye. He *sees* the shortbread. It's golden brown, has a buttery sheen. It's steaming a little and it's the size of the pan, and it's shaped like a perfect lowercase *e*.

"My God," the man says. "Oh my God," he says. Holds up a finger, covers his mouth, uncovers his mouth, swallows, swallows. "This is everything . . ." he tells the baker. "This is everything I wanted. Everything I've *always* wanted. This is my dream. You've made my dream real, just as you said you would. Everything is different now. Everything is better . . . You have changed the very course of my life. I was going to kill myself as soon as I left here. I was going to jump from the bridge and drown. I really was. No longer! And no longer will I allow myself to be mistreated as I have been mistreated. No longer will I play this role. No longer! I owe you my life. I'm forever in your debt."

"Oh, nonsense," the baker says. "Pure nonsense. You owe me nothing. I won't even charge you for the shortbread, sir. Not a penny. I'm just so relieved and happy to have gotten it right. The pleasure, I mean this: the pleasure's all mine. Your uncommonly powerful appreciation of quality shortbread inspires me. Your satisfaction in this instance buoys me. Thank you for coming in here and giving me another chance. Thank you for reminding me of what I truly care about and stand for."

"Normally . . ." the man says. "That is to say, *previously,* during such an interaction as we are presently having, right about now is when I would have started blushing and clamming up. But I don't want to do that today. I don't want to do that anymore at all. I don't think I will. In fact, I think I *won't.*"

"You certainly aren't blushing, sir," says the baker, which pronouncement instantly—and to both men's pleasantly light entertainment—causes just a touch of heat to climb its way up the man's neck and cheeks. "Now, if you'll pardon me for a moment," says the baker, "I've noticed I'm out of twine up here, so I'll just run down to the storeroom real quick, grab a brand-new spool, and then I'll box up that shortbread for you, nice and tight."

"Oh, there's no need for that," the man says. "I'll eat it here."

So . . . So that was . . . Well, actually that was *not* "The Overcoat" by Nikolai Gogol. Not really, at least. It was, however, Charlie Chaplin's favorite joke of all time. Sort of. According to the internet.

"Hey, man, you know what?" Perry Farrell said. "I loved that. I'm convinced."

3

Ari FaceTimed Apter some three weeks later.

Radiohead was in, he said, and the Thom Yorke/Beasties/Shadow project would premiere three songs near the end of their set.

Fugazi was out.

White Stripes was in.

Fugees said they were in but Ari didn't trust that they wouldn't back out.

Penn and Teller would introduce an illusion before sundown, revisit the illusion between Tricky and Pixies, and grand finale it *during* Jane's Addiction's set.

John Mulaney, Hannibal Buress, and Bill Burr would alternate introducing bands, performing seven to twelve minutes of comedy with each introduction.

A partial guest list for the after-parties would be "leaked" to the press. In addition to all the Day Zero performers, the list would include Beyoncé, Jay-Z, Bill Murray, Oprah Winfrey, Leonardo DiCaprio, Cara Delevingne, and Michael Jordan. Jonny Greenwood would DJ at the first after-party, Chance the Rapper would DJ at the second after-party. Rumors that any and every Chicagoan or former Chicagoan who'd ever been anyone in entertainment would make an appearance were bound to spread and would be encouraged. For the most part, the rumors would be proved true, as would rumors that the Obamas—all four— would make an appearance.

"Amazing," Apter said. "I'm speechless. You really came through."

"I could not," Ari said, "agree more. I *am* amazing. I *did* come through. To put something like this concert together in so little time, much less for *free*? Amazing. Kind of person who can do something like that—kind of person who *does* do something like that—that's the kind of person who you'd think, if he called you up, you'd definitely take the call. Or if, for some reason, you missed the call, and he left you a voicemail, let alone two *separate* voicemails, you'd call him back. I mean:

Am I right or what? Am I right or am I right? Like, who *wouldn't* call a person like that back? Except, of course, for a novelist, I mean. Or a comedian. Or a novelist-comedian who also works as a college professor because being a novelist-comedian doesn't earn him enough on its own to pay rent. A guy like that probably *wouldn't* call back, right? A guy like that would probably have *bigger fish to fry.*"

"You sound hurt."

"Fuck you. I'm texting over his contact info."

"I don't know if I'm—"

"What's not to know, here? What the fuck is not to know? Ever since our little meeting, Perry Farrell's been sending me links to Gladman videos twice a day. *At least* twice a day. Now along with each and every link Perry sends comes a question, *occasionally* implied, but usually explicit: 'Have you gotten hold of Gladman yet?' And I hate to say 'No,' to clients, Apter. Hate it. I *hate* to say 'No' to clients, let alone to partners, but I'm not a liar, so here I am, saying 'No' at least *twice a day* for nearly a month to Perry Farrell, who is not only a client, but *also* a partner. I lay the blame for this on *you.* This problem I'm having is yours to make right. If you don't make it right, I'm your enemy forever. Is that something you want?"

"Ari."

"Enough with that fucking face already. You want to see this guy open Day Zero more than anyone, so *you're* the guy that's gonna make it happen. You're going to do so, first of all, because I'm finished with this part. Not unless I *really* need someone to get an abortion do I ever leave a third voicemail. I can't recall the last time I left a *second* voicemail. In fact, I can't recall the last time I had *Deb* leave a second voicemail *on my behalf.* And you are going to do so, second of all, Apter, because you want to come work with me, even if you don't know it yet—I think you do know it, by the way—and this is just the kind of thing that working with me will entail. Third of all, as we've already established, you don't want me for an enemy. And last of all—last but not least of all—last but not at all fucking least of all at all—"

"That enumerating thing you're doing with your fingers?" Apter said. "The mayor does that, too."

"Last of all, *you motherfucker,* this will be *fun* for you. It would be fun for you if you *weren't* a Gladman fanboy, but, unless you completely misled us at that meeting, you are *the* Gladman fanboy, and you will *love* doing this. So fucking do it, okay?"

"Okay," Apter said.

"Do it *now*," Ari said.

"I will," Apter said. "I want to, actually."

"So fucking do it!" Ari said.

"Hello?" answered Gladman, thirty seconds later.

"Mr. Gladman?" said Apter.

"Down in a minute," it sounded like Gladman said.

"I'm sorry?" Apter said, but he received no response. He looked at the phone. The call had either been dropped, or Gladman had ended it.

Apter redialed.

"Just putting on my shoes, here," Gladman answered. "Another twenty seconds."

"Mr. Gladman," said Apter, "my name is Apter Schutz. I'm with the mayor's office, and I was hoping we could talk about Mount Chicago."

"Mmm," Gladman said.

"Probably I should explain what that is first. Mount Chicago," Apter continued. "Because you can't have heard of it yet, since we haven't announced . . . I'm sorry. I'm a little nervous about calling you like this—really *very* nervous, actually. I'm such a big fan of yours, Mr. Gladman, and it's just, um . . . I . . . Are you still there?"

No response. He looked at the phone. The call had either been dropped, or Gladman had ended it.

Apter redialed. Went to voicemail. Voicemail box full.

Ended the call. Redialed. Went to voicemail. Voicemail box full.

Tried three more times at ten-minute intervals. Same result.

Was about to try again when Ari FaceTimed.

"*Nu?*" Ari said.

Apter told him what had happened.

"'Down in a minute?' he said?" Ari said.

"I *think* that's what he said."

"So maybe he was at home," Ari said.

"Maybe," Apter said.

"So he might still be at home," Ari said.

"I don't know," Apter said. "*If* he was at home. Maybe he was waiting on a ride, or—"

"Or a delivery," Ari said. "Or a hooker."

"He's married," Apter said.

"But you wouldn't object to the assertion that there's at least a point zero zero one percent chance that he's at home right now," Ari said.

"I guess," Apter said.

"So then the reason you seem so frustrated right now must be because I interrupted you in the middle of putting your coat on, right? You were just about to get up from that ugly, red ergonomic chair you sit on all day in your panel-lit, drop-ceilinged, carpet-stained office with the burnt-coffee smell and the greige metal file cabinets—you were just about to get up to put your coat on, and then hail a ride on your ride-hailing app while *on your way* to the elevator, and here I am, *FaceTiming*, slowing you down."

"Something like that," said Apter, closing the chat, getting up from his desk, and reaching for his coat.

Before his finger had come off the buzzer, a screaming came across the sky.

Not three minutes later, Gladman, in cargo shorts, tilting a little, the backs of his Sambas folded under his heels, thumbs poking through tears in the sleeves of his hoodie, the hood of which was gathered in an almost-ball on one side of his neck—Gladman was standing opposite Apter, just a foot or so away, behind the heavy glass door to his apartment building's entrance hall, squinting and shivering.

Apter smiled his smile and said, "I'm Apter Schutz. I tried calling earlier?"

Gladman pointed at his ears and shrugged.

Apter repeated himself, louder.

Gladman shook his head and opened the door.

The volume of the screaming increased by factors.

"I'm Apter!" shouted Apter.

Gladman shrugged again, and waved Apter inside.

Apter followed him deeper into the screaming. Up three flights of stairs. Into his apartment. As they crossed the threshold, the screaming's

volume peaked, and Apter's left eardrum warbled and purred, losing—
permanently, though he didn't know it—a small range of upper-register
sensitivity. Then Gladman stepped rightward, into the kitchen, and, all
at once, the screaming stopped.

"He has to see me," Gladman said, gesturing toward a small green
bird atop a white wire cage beside the cluttered counter. "He hates that
buzzer. He hears it, starts screaming, I go down to answer it, he doesn't
stop screaming until I'm back. That's why I tell you guys 'Call,' not
'Buzz.'"

"He's so *small*," Apter said. "That something so small could make that
kind of racket . . ."

"I know."

"What's his name?"

"Gogol," said Gladman.

"For the writer."

"What else?"

"I guess . . . I don't know. I mean, I think it's also a French slur for
mentally retarded people," Apter said. "But you probably wouldn't have
wanted to name your bird a slur, so."

"Speaks French, reads Russians, delivers medication—job market
must really be *booming* for liberal arts types these days. You an ex-felon
or something? You know you dress pretty nice for a delivery—" said
Gladman, before getting cut off by a coughing fit that he wasn't able
to bring under control til, having sat in a chair at his kitchen table, he
drank half the glass of water Apter brought him. "I think I might have
forgotten how to talk," Gladman said. "That was the most words I've
spoken in a row in a while." He cleared his throat, drank some more
water. "I must have aspirated spit that I should have, uh . . . *swallowed*.
Anyway, thanks for the water. You'll receive a generous tip momentarily."

"I'm not a deliveryman, Mr. Gladman," Apter said.

"Oh? Oh, right, of course. You know, I don't make these appointments. My lawyer, sometimes my accountant—*they* make these appointments, and they *do* let me know, but I'm just . . . My memory lately's
a little, uh . . . I probably shouldn't talk about my mental incapacities
to a notary, huh? *Being of sound mind I hereby* and all that kind of
nonsense—not *nonsense* . . . I'm not trying to demean your profession,
calling it . . . You know what I mean. Anyway, please," Gladman said,
and gestured at a chair.

And Apter sat down at Gladman's kitchen table, across from Gladman, a few feet behind whom Gogol, yogically, stood on one leg atop the door of his cage, stretching his opposite leg and wing.

"Here you are," Apter thought, "in Gladman's apartment, sitting down with Gladman at Gladman's kitchen table." Then: "You are sitting across from Solomon Gladman." Then: "Across this table from you is Solomon Gladman, also known as Solly Gladman, also known as Bernie Pollaco." Then: "Just a table's width away from you is Solomon Gladman, who you've wanted to meet for most of your life." Then: "Right in front of you, here, is someone whose work you've spent hundreds of hours considering, talking about, and enjoying." Then: "Though this is only the first time you've ever been within shouting distance of the person you're looking at, let alone within whispering distance of that person, that person is someone who's affected the shape and texture of your life more than nearly anybody else."

But try as he might, Apter wasn't able to produce within himself the sense of momentousness he believed he should possess. Any sense of momentousness at all, really. Where was the charge? Why'd he feel so dulled, so muted? He'd been more starstruck by Perry Farrell. He'd been more starstruck by *Ari Emanuel*.

The light in the place was not his favorite kind. Maybe that was the trouble: the light. Apart from the lamp that was clamped to Gogol's cage, which was aimed to shine downward into that cage, the only source of light was the ugly Chicago winter-afternoon light glaring in through the windows behind him, blinds-striped: the light of a sun that forced you to squint but refused to warm you. Light that made you sleepy while preventing you from napping. Groggy light.

Headache light.

The kitchen table's finish, in this light, looked sticky. Gladman's scalp, in this light, looked razorburned. Gladman's glasses: smeared with oils. The tumbler from which Gladman was drinking had whitish lip prints all along its rim, and the bubbles in the water inside the tumbler looked less like bubbles than particles, flakes—flakes of dandruff.

Maybe some of them were. Mustache dandruff.

And maybe it wasn't the light, after all. Or maybe it wasn't *just* the light. On closer examination—not such *very* close examination, either—Gladman's personal hygiene didn't look to have been all too recently maintained. Certainly the light wasn't helping any, but Gladman was . . . a mess. Would've looked like a mess in any light. The top of his neck was less shaven than the bottom. No part of his neck was as shaven as his cheeks. No part of his cheeks was as shaven as his chin. And his eyeballs were nearly as red as white, and his wrinkled lips as white as pink, and these lips were parted in such a way as to suggest he was fighting to suppress a sneeze, and his jaw was set in such a way as to suggest he was fighting to suppress a yawn.

He did not look like a man who had ever had a wife, let alone like a man who was currently married. Where *was* his wife? Apter glanced around furtively for signs of Gladman's wife, and found, instead: two leaning stacks of pizza boxes on the fridge; on the chair to his left, a brown paper shopping bag riotously brimming with corked, empty bottles; and, on the windowsill behind him, a desiccated succulent beside a dead spider.

And just like that, Apter understood everything. Occam's razor. Daphne Bourbon was gone. Daphne Bourbon had left. Gladman's wife had left him, and now he was depressed. This accounted not only for his neglected hygiene and bereftness of star power, but also for why he hadn't performed in so long.

Delivers medication.

Major depression. His wife had left him and now he was depressed.

"It's a little messy in here, I know," Gladman said. "Sorry about that. I wasn't expecting, uh, company today. So you got those papers?"

Apter told Gladman he wasn't a notary, and then, in broad strokes, explained the reason for his visit.

"That's a whole lot of crazy stuff you just told me," said Gladman. "Perry Farrell—man. Jane's Addiction. They were one of my favorite bands. Girl I was hung up on all through high school—she loved to make out to that song 'Three Days.' You know that one? 'Three Days'?"

"Great song," Apter said.

"Amen. Anyway, I suppose that's nice and all that Perry Farrell likes my work—really, it's cheering to hear that—and it's been a pleasure to meet you, Apter, but . . . How do I put this . . ."

"Look, I think I understand," Apter said. "I know you've always refused to appear on marquees. I know you never perform unless you feel like it. Ari and Perry know all of that, too, and we all respect it, and no one's asking you to compromise there. We anticipated reluctance from you, and what we're proposing is this: we don't announce you. Not in the press release, not on the website, not on any flyers. Nowhere. A couple of the *musical acts* won't be announced, by the way—there's a whole 'surprise performances by special guests' kind of vein we'll be mining in the promotion. So you'd come to Day Zero, see how you feel, and if you feel like going on, you've got the opening slot. If you don't feel like going on, you don't go on. Smashing Pumpkins, who're gonna be the first band to play—they're one of the surprise special guests, so please don't repeat that—but Smashing Pumpkins, if you don't go on, maybe they'll start early. Or the show'll start late. Not the end of the world. No promises broken. And your set can be however long you want, by the way. It's a festival, you know? We've got hours of wiggle room. Do ten minutes. Do half an hour. Do *two* and a half—whatever you want."

"Two and a half, he says," said Gladman.

"I know *I'd* love that. I mean it. So would Perry Farrell, I'm sure."

"This is all—it's really thoughtful of you," Gladman said. "And I don't want to seem ungrateful but, well, you know . . ."

"I know . . . what?"

"Come on."

"What come on?" Apter said.

"Do I look like a man who wants to get onstage in front of thousands of people and talk a bunch of *narishkeit* to get them to laugh?"

"In fact, maybe you do," Apter might have answered. Or he might have answered, "You look like someone who needs some help," or "You look like someone who needs a friend," or "You look like the loneliest man on earth"—any of those answers would have been honest—but when Gladman, in asking his rhetorical question, spoke the word *narishkeit,* he did so in a kind of understated Bernie Pollaco voice, which may or may not have been deliberate, but in either case snapped Apter awake to the fact that Gladman really *was* Gladman, thereby infused him with the sense of momentousness he'd failed to feel earlier, and rendered him temporarily incapable of speech, so Apter didn't answer anything. Just smiled his smile.

At which point a screaming came across the kitchen. Gogol'd leapt from his cage, flapping his wings. He flew past Gladman's ear, toward Apter's head, pulled up and hovered helicopter-like above the center of the table for three-four seconds, showing Apter his smoothly feathered, countershaded underside, then landed on the table, raised one leg, said, "Hi!" turned around, and Tramp-limped to Gladman, who picked him up like a landline telephone receiver.

"Sorry about that," Gladman told Apter. "You, my friend," he said to Gogol, "are acting like a maniac. Something startle you?"

"That was nuts," Apter said. "I think he said 'Hi' to me."

"He did. He knows a few words. That's one of his favorites. He doesn't usually get so aggressive, though. I need to clip his wings. He's not used to being flighted."

"I've never had that kind of angle on a bird before," said Apter. "It was more, um . . . *elegant* than I would have thought."

"*Elegant?*"

"No package. No junk."

"Oh, right," Gladman said. "They've got a cloaca—see that?" Gladman held Gogol out toward Apter, pushed its tailfeathers toward its backbone, revealing a downy, shadowy, opening—nothing gross, just . . . nothing. A slit. Gladman let the tailfeathers bounce back into place and the cloaca disappeared. Gogol, his eyes fixed on Apter's face, gave no indication of feeling put out by this. "It does everything, that hole," Gladman said. "Shits, drops eggs, or, if it's a male, launches these *jizz packets*."

"Jizz packets."

"Yeah, the sperm is grouped up inside these kind of delicate bubbles, and when the birds fuck—What am I talking about here? You don't need to hear about this."

"Please. I want to."

"Yeah? Okay. Well, when they fuck, basically, the male stands, really kinda precariously, on the back of the female, and she puts her tail up in the air, exposing her cloaca, and then, usually after a lot of struggle for balance, the male, from the side—like to get around her tail—the male lowers his cloaca, and then the two of them rub their cloacas against each other till the male's cloaca tosses its jizz packets. The female's catches them, and some chemical she has in there makes them dissolve."

"The jizz packets."

"Yeah. No. Just the surrounding bubble parts. Not the whole packet. The *bubble parts* dissolve, and that's when things get really interesting, okay? Each packet, turns out, has different kinds of sperm in it. Three different kinds. The first kind of sperm is basically what you think of when you think of sperm—it's just trying to swim to the egg and fertilize it."

"Conventional sperm."

"Totally conventional. But then there's this second kind of like *assassin* kind of sperm that shoots around in search of any other sperm that might be in the female's cloaca from a previous fuck she may have had with a different bird, and if it encounters such sperm, it attacks it with a series of repeated headbutts, trying to slow it down, or, better yet, kill it. That's only *if* it can get to it, though, because, see, then you have this third kind of *thug* sperm, which is the most common kind, and these thug sperm work as bodyguards for the conventional sperm: while a conventional sperm makes its way toward the egg, these thug sperm form a phalanx around it in order to protect it from the assassin sperms' headbutts."

" 'Make love not war,' " Apter said. "To a bird, that's virtually oxymoronic."

"You lost me on that one," Gladman said.

"Well, they wiggle around and rub cloacas, out pops the dick, in shoots the jizz packets, and maybe, if the female's popular with the guys, there's a . . . battle. A war. Of jizz. To make love, for a bird, then, *is* to make war."

"Ah, right," Gladman said with a charitable chuckle. "That's pretty much it. Apart from the dick. There isn't any dick pops out. These are wholly dickless creatures, parrots. Most bird species are. Dickless. Except for ducks. And swans, I think. And maybe ostriches. Ducks for sure, though. Ducks have dicks. Shaped like corkscrews."

"Corkscrew-shaped dicks. How's that work?"

"Beats me," Gladman said. "Sounds pretty uncomfortable. But *most* birds are dickless, though. All parrots: dickless—Hey," he said to Gogol, who'd turned his head to bite at the tip of Gladman's thumb. "Hey. Take it easy. You want the shoulder?" He set the bird on his shoulder. "Mostly, he just wants me to hold him," Gladman told Apter, "but lately he gets a little antsy sometimes. It's the hormones, I think. You let the wings grow in, some switch gets flipped, and they become more aggressive. Anyhow, oof. I better, uh . . ." Gladman's pallor had taken a sudden turn for the wan. Well, for the *wanner*. There was sweat on his forehead. He wiped at the sweat.

"You all right?" Apter said.

"Oh yeah, I'm fine. Just due for a nap, I think," Gladman said, miming a yawn, or maybe actually yawning, which caused Apter and Gogol the both to yawn. "Getting old in here," he said. "Need my naps. But what an unlikely conversation we've had, huh? You tell me Perry Farrell wants me to open a concert for him, and next thing we're talking about ducks and jizz. Thanks for coming by, Apter. It was a pleasure to meet you."

"Oh," said Apter, rapidly deflating. "I—sure. Of course. I'm just . . . I'm gonna leave you my card here, okay? In case you change your mind about the concert, or want to talk or something."

"Talk?"

"I don't know. I was . . . Doesn't matter," Apter said, and as he rose from his chair and set down his card and said, "You paint it green, right?" Gogol, screaming, jumped from Gladman's shoulder, onto the table, as if to fetch the card.

Gladman picked him back up before he got to it.

"What's that you were saying? Ow!" Gladman said. Gogol was biting him. "What's *wrong* with you?" he said to Gogol, and got up and locked the bird in the cage. "What were you saying?" he said to Apter.

"I just said—" Apter said, and Gogol started screaming again, and Gladman shrugged and pointed at his ears. Apter waved himself off, waved at Gladman, and left the apartment.

He called Sylvie Klein on his way to the El.

"I know, I know," she answered, "and I'm sorry. I was just about to call you. It's almost there."

The *it* Sylvie meant was the Tree of Loss: the document that would, once she had all the data she needed, map the anomaly's victims' relevant surviving relatives according to the size of the font in which their names should be engraved on the walls of the park.

Herschel Bobovnikoff hadn't been able to get his part done as quickly as he had originally predicted. The Social Security numbers of many of the victims were taking longer to uncover than he had originally estimated. Without a victim's social, the shady software tools that Hersh had developed couldn't probe or scour or comb or scrape the web to find that victim's survivors, and the even shadier software tools that Hersh was using to infiltrate the databases that might or might not contain those socials could be deployed only intermittently and moderately since too sustained or flagrant an incursion would set off an alert or an alarm and then antiviral protocols would enact themselves or firewalls would erect themselves and the databases would clench up and get blocked and their further hacking would become impossible and maybe traceable which could lead to things on Hersh's end getting ID'd or zapped or . . .

Something like that.

Apter neither fully understood the holdup, nor really cared to even partially understand it. In fact, he cared not at all about the Tree of Loss or the walls of so-called *survivors'* names. From the moment the mayor'd first mentioned the walls, Apter'd thought the idea—however entertainingly so—was patently stupid and vaguely offensive, or, if not quite *offensive*, then in pretty bad taste, and the passage of time had done nothing to change that. Furthermore, the mayor wasn't in any rush. Even if all the funds required to build the park were to be secured that very day and construction on the park were to start tomorrow, it wouldn't be finished, according to the designers and architects the mayor'd been consulting, for at least three years. The excavation of the detritus alone, they'd said, would be, at minimum, a six-month process.

He'd explained all that to Sylvie a few times already, but it didn't seem to lessen any of the self-imposed pressure she felt to get the job done fast, and, by the technical jargon she used to describe the incomprehensible (to Apter) difficulties that Hersh was having getting the socials, Apter was starting to develop the sense that what she really wanted here— even more than she wanted to help him out—was to get him to admire her boyfriend for his coding prowess or mathematical intelligence or disruptive, outside-the-box thinking or . . .

Something like that.

Which Apter did.

To some degree.

He admired Hersh for being able to do incomprehensible (to Apter) stuff with computers—stuff that, according to Sylvie, most other people who did incomprehensible (to Apter) stuff with computers were incapable of doing—but none of it was stuff that Apter found very interesting, or even knew how to find very interesting.

And so he'd ham it up. He'd enthuse. For Sylvie's benefit. He'd been, for three weeks now, hamming it up, uttering *amazing*s and *wow*s and *that's nuts*es at news of any ostensibly impressive hacking development, but—perhaps to her credit—Sylvie didn't buy it. Didn't *seem* to buy it. Or maybe she bought it, but Apter just didn't want to believe she bought it? Like, maybe he didn't want to believe she could be snowed? Or maybe it was more that he didn't want to believe himself capable of snowing her? Was the difference that important? It wasn't important.

What Apter found important here was this: he derived *hardly any satisfaction at all* from Hersh's stumbling. Really only just the smallest amount. And the moment he'd catch himself feeling even a hint of that minuscule nothing of a modicum of satisfaction at Hersh's stumbling, he'd berate himself; he'd shame the satisfaction into nonexistence. For that, he wished Sylvie'd admire *him*. He doubted she was even aware of it, though, the generosity of his intentions in regard to Hersh. She gave no indication of being aware of it, and there wasn't any way he could think of to make her aware of it without undermining his claim to generosity, if not the generosity itself. If you ask that your generosity be acknowledged as generosity, did that not transform it into something—or *reveal* it to be something—other than generosity?

Enough fucking Talmud.

"I mean it this time," Sylvie continued. "We're really close. We're at eighty-three percent. Well, eighty-two-point-seven. Shouldn't be more than another week tops."

"Who cares?" Apter said.

"Well, fuck you, too, Apt."

"No, no," he said. "I didn't mean it that way. I care. I really do. It's just—you're not gonna believe this, I barely believe it—I just left Solomon Gladman's apartment."

"Fuck you."

"You said that already."

"Are you being serious?" she said.

And then he told her all about it.

"Jizz bags," Sylvie said once he'd finished. "Jizz bags and duck cock!"

"Jizz *packets*."

"Jizz *packets*," said Sylvie. "I wish you had a recording—you know what you should've done, by the way, is played him that 'Less Depressing Auschwitz' file. That's right up his alley. He'd have loved that, I bet."

"You're right. I messed up."

"And you really didn't tell him about the comedy class or the calendar or anything? Or that you went to SSA and studied with his teacher?"

"I wish I had," Apter said. "I wish I'd told him all kinds of things, but I was just getting used to being there, you know, and then he really looked sick all of a sudden. One second, we were joking around—"

"One second, *you and Bernie Pollaco were joking around!*"

"I know, right?"

"*In Bernie Pollaco's kitchen.*"

"No, I know. Totally nuts. That's exactly what I mean. I had to get used to it, and then right when I started to, he just got extremely *afflicted*-looking, and, anyway, he was already, I think, making noises like he wanted me to go. So."

"Maybe he'll call."

"I really doubt that—I think I creeped him out. 'In case you want to talk'—I sounded like a fucken . . . I don't know."

"It's *fine*," Sylvie said. "I'm sure he doesn't even remember you said that. Plus the joke about *make love not war*—I bet he thought that was hilarious. I bet he really liked you. Everyone does."

"You're a really nice person, Sylvie," he said.

"Thanks?" she said.

Back at City Hall, he called Ari's cell. One ring, then voicemail. Before the beep had sounded, Ari FaceTimed.

"Yeah," Apter answered.

"Long face," Ari said. "I don't like a long face."

"So maybe quit with the fucking video calls. Gladman said no."

"And why is that?"

"I think he's got depression."

"Of course he's got depression. He's a stand-up comedian."

"I think his wife left him."

"Of *course* his wife left him. He's a *stand-up comedian*."

"He's not exactly a typical stand-up comedian."

"Fair enough," said Ari. "You'll try again tomorrow."

"That I will not. His 'No' was final. I'm not gonna bother him."

"His 'No' was a gambit. There's something he wants. Maybe he can have it. Or her. It's probably a woman. If he's wifeless, then a woman might be just the thing."

"You didn't see him, Ari. He's in pain. He's sick. He isn't *horny*. He has *depression*."

"You keep saying that . . . Did you tell him how to reach you in case he changes his mind?"

"I left him my card."

"Good. I'll tell you what. Don't try again tomorrow."

"I won't."

"Take a few days and think, except listen to me, now. You're making me out in your mind to be a shark, and that's almost fair because I'm kind of a shark, but this isn't a sharky moment for me here. Short of Seinfeld, Gervais, Rock, and Eddie Murphy—*maybe* short of them—I could, in a phone call, get literally any comedian in the world to open Day Zero. I could get Dave Chappelle to open Day Zero. I could get Wanda Sykes to open Day Zero. I could get Amy Schumer, Kevin Hart, Steven Wright, Zach Galifianakis, or fucking *Ellen* or Jim fucking Gaffigan if I wanted for some reason to get fucking Ellen or Jim fucking Gaffigan to open Day Zero. *In a phone call.* If Gladman doesn't open Day Zero, I will, in a phone call, get Larry David to open Day Zero unless Perry decides Sarah Silverman should do it, which he might. In that case, I'll call Sarah Silverman, and she'll open Day Zero. But I want to see Gladman open Day Zero because he's a freak and an outsider, and the thought of giving him a chance to perform in front of an audience hundreds of times bigger than any he's ever performed in front of—it makes me *feel good.* More important to me than that? It makes *Perry Farrell* feel good. That's why Perry *started* Lollapalooza way back in the nineties—to mainstream the *good* stuff that's getting overlooked. I know a lot of performers, Apter. All kinds of performers. Actors, stand-ups, musicians, *illusionists.* They need an audience. They need to perform. That's why they do it. If they don't perform, they become depressed. If they are depressed, performing can help them fight their depression. It doesn't always work, but it *often* works, and it never leaves them in a worse place than where they started. Never. Especially not comedians. Not even when they bomb. *Especially not then.* When they bomb, they get pissed. It's *energizing.* You say his wife left him. You say he's depressed. I believe you. Why shouldn't I? I do. But so fucking what? So you leave him alone? Is that what you do? Is that . . . what? Is that how you *help* him? He needs to perform."

"Maybe," Apter said.

"What the fuck does that mean?"

"What you're saying makes some sense, but you're selling it a little hard," Apter said. "I'll take a few days and consider reaching out to him again."

"Do that. And don't get all resentful about coming around to my way of thinking, here, either. That was not a hard sell. I just got you to where you were already going faster than you would've if I'd kept my mouth shut. *I'm* not the one who left the guy your card."

An email from Ari came within a quarter-hour.

The subject of the email read, "PEP TALK."

The body of the email read, "REMEMBER WHAT YOU'RE WORKING ON AND CHEER THE FUCK UP."

Attached to the email was a PDF:

TENTATIVE LINEUP

Jane's Addiction + Penn & Teller + closing all-performer covers
medley tbd
Bill Burr
Radiohead/Secret Project
Hannibal Buress
Kanye West
John Mulaney
White Stripes
Bill Burr
Pixies
Hannibal Buress/Penn & Teller
Tricky w/Martina Topley-Bird
John Mulaney
(Fugees)
Penn & Teller
Smashing Pumpkins
(Solly Gladman)

At the start of their after-work whiskey conclave, Apter handed a print-out to the mayor. "For your eyes only," he said. "The first press release won't mention half of those acts."

"You know, this is really impressive," said the mayor. "I've heard of *most* of these people. Why do some got parentheses?"

"Those are *maybes*. The Fugees have a habit of planning reunions, then calling them off, and Gladman—I just met with him today, and he turned us down, but Ari thinks he'll change his mind. Wants me to convince him."

"Fugees I definitely heard of. Girl with the funky dreadlocks, right? But Gladman, I don't know . . . I *think* I heard of him. *Solly Gladman . . .*"

"He's a local stand-up," Apter said. "But also he's a novelist. He won a big prize a little while back."

"*Right*. That's it."

"You've read him?"

"No," the mayor said. "Nothing like that. You know Chucky Kleinfeld from the Public Defender's?"

"I've heard his name."

"Chucky and his wife—they *hate* this Gladman. Hate his guts. We were at this fundraising dinner with them a while back—probably a couple months before the anomaly. It was a fundraiser for a . . . it was a Jewish cause of some kind . . . I can't remember what exactly the cause was. No, you know what? It wasn't for a Jewish cause. It was an ACLU dinner. Or maybe an N double-A C—no. I don't know. But there were a lot of Jewish people there, I remember, and Chucky and his wife, they were talking to some of the other Jewish people at our table, and they were talking about Gladman. They saw a video of him, of some performance he did that their kid was watching, and they said it was antisemitic. And one of the other Jewish couples at the table said they thought he was *great*, Gladman, and that they loved his books, and then, I remember, things started getting kinda loud, and this *third* Jewish couple at the table, even though they said they never saw Gladman or even heard of him I don't think—it was kinda hard to follow, but that's the impression I got left with at least—the wife of this third couple said he sounded like an awful human being, the husband dis-agreed that he sounded like an awful human being, and *they* started arguing in the middle of this larger argument, and, by that point, everyone was getting so loud that Jewish couples from tables that were *next* to our table started arguing about Gladman with each other *and* with the Jewish couples at our table. Yeah. A lot of your people really dislike this guy."

"Well, they're people," Apter said.

"What does *that* mean?"

"People are terrible."

"What the hell kinda thing is that to say? People are *not* terrible. Especially not yours. Your people are special."

"That so?"

"*Special,* your people," the mayor said. "And even if they weren't, you shouldn't say that about your own people—that they're terrible. No one should say that about their own people. Anyway, your people, they dislike this guy *on behalf* of being your people. I mean, they dislike him on behalf of their being *Jewish* people. He offends them right in the Jewish parts of themselves, so."

"So . . ."

"So I'm saying: maybe this Gladman shouldn't do Day Zero."

"First of all," Apter said, "he probably won't—"

"No, I know. I got that. But you said you're gonna try to convince him again, and you're very convincing, in case you don't know, so maybe, I'm saying: don't try to convince him. I'd rather we don't cause an alienation of my Jewish constituents."

"Look, Mr. Mayor, some Jewish people don't like Gladman, or don't think he's funny—that's true. But then some do. And most *would,* I'd think, if they got to see him. I happen to think he's one of the all-time greats. My good friend Sylvie—she'd happily agree. And Ari Emanuel's become a big fan. And Perry Farrell loves him. *Loves* him, and *really* wants him to open the show."

"See, I hear you," the mayor said, "and I understand by your face how this might be a sensitive topic for you, but what I hear when I'm hearing you is: you think Gladman's funny. And that has some value to me, Apter. It does. But you're just one Jew. And then your friend Sally? I don't know Sally. So: she thinks he's funny has not a lot of value to me. Ari Emanuel? That has almost negative value to me to hear that he likes this Gladman—he is not the best of your people, which, as you know, that has longly been my view and of late no lessly. And then you got Perry Farrell, and I don't know why you're even slipping him into the mix. Couple times I met him he seemed like a nice, good person to me and all but he's neither here nor there, right? He's Irish."

"He's Jewish."

"Please. His name's Farrell."

"His stage name," Apter said. "He was born Peretz Bernstein."

"All right. And so you're telling me that's a Jewish name, *Peretz*."

"Bernstein, too."

"Learn something new every day," the mayor said. "Nonetheless, I guess what I'm saying still stands: you've named four Jews who like this Gladman, and I only know three of them, and I only like two of them, and judging by that dinner I was at with Chucky Kleinfeld, enough Jewish constituents seem to hate Gladman that it seems like a bad idea, him opening a benefit concert we're throwing."

"*Fuck* Chucky Kleinfeld, Mr. Mayor, okay?"

"Fuck Chucky why?"

"Talk about *names*. He's an adult called *Chucky*. People *call* him that. He *lets* people call him that. Probably encourages it. Probably introduces himself that way. 'Chucky Kleinfeld, pleased to meet you.' Schmuck."

"Glibner did used to call him *Schmucky* Kleinfeld."

"No *way* he's not a schmuck. And just like every other schmuck who's ever lived, he'd rather feel superior than have a laugh, I'd bet."

"I don't ... I was with you on the schmuck part, but now I'm confused."

"I don't know what you mean."

"I mean: What's the difference?" the mayor said.

"The difference between ... ?"

"I don't want to get all *Deep Thoughts with Jim Dandy* on you here, but ... When you laugh at something," the mayor said, "aren't you, or some part of you at least—aren't you saying, 'I feel superior to what I'm laughing at'? or 'I *am* superior to what I'm laughing at'? Isn't that the whole *point* of laughing? Isn't that the one thing laughter *always* means?"

"No," Apter said.

—

When he got back home from work that evening, Apter drank a pint of water at his kitchen table and, for the someteenth time in less than a month, listened to the sound file he'd sent to Sylvie.

> Have you ever been to Auschwitz? The concentration camp memorial there in Eastern Europe. Some fucking place, right? I mean, I've never been, but even on film . . . some fucking place . . . That room with all the shoes . . . Imagining all the murdered kids who used to wear those shoes . . . I was what you call *beyond* tears . . . I couldn't even cry. And when I woke up this morning, thinking about Mount Chicago, I was also thinking about Auschwitz, too . . . Every memorial should be so moving. That is the one and only measure of a memorial's success. How moving it is . . . And I thought, 'The goal of every memorial should be to be as moving as Auschwitz, but at the same time, that does *not* necessarily mean that the goal of every memorial should be to be as depressing.' So what I want, I'm saying, is I want Mount Chicago to achieve that level of being moving, but also, at the same time, to be less depressing . . . I want it to be a less depressing Auschwitz . . . *Our* less depressing Auschwitz.

If he didn't spit-take, he thought, it was only because he had the whole thing memorized, every last syllable and intonation, and could pace his sipping and swallowing accordingly.

Memorized, and yet: still funny. Maybe even funnier than ever.

And maybe Ari was wrong, maybe he wasn't.

That is: maybe pressing Gladman to perform at Day Zero would annoy or offend him, or maybe it would convince him to perform at Day Zero, which in turn might help pull him out of his depression.

But Sylvie—Apter was certain—was right.

That is: Gladman would love to hear the sound file. It wouldn't likely help much, if at all, with his depression, but it shouldn't annoy him, couldn't offend him, would get him to laugh, and *might*—via keeping the lines of communication open—create an opportunity for Apter to convince him to perform at Day Zero, which performing, again, might help pull him out of his depression.

So Apter attached the file to a text: "Apter Schutz here. It was thrilled to meet you, Mr. gladhand, and the last thing I'd ever want to do is bother you, but I regret not having played you this fording. I think it's right up your alcohol, comedywise, and, yes: the voice really is the mayor's of Chicago's."

He corrected the typos, de-autocorrected the mis-autocorrections, deleted the last two words, and pressed send.

UNBECOMING

As Gogol woke the next morning from uneasy dreams, he found himself perched on his usual perch, but something was wrong. Abdominally wrong. Seriously painful. Something really hurt.

He'd had a hard time falling asleep the night before. He'd felt so confused by that man who came over. The man who could do that thing with his face.

That man, when he did that thing with his face: he became the top.

Or so it had seemed.

He'd seemed like the top, and Gogol'd wanted to preen with him, so Gogol'd tried flying over to preen with him.

Before Gogol'd been able to get to the man, though, the man had stopped doing that thing with his face, and Gogol'd stopped wanting to preen with the man, but Gogol'd still wanted to preen with *someone,* and Gladman had picked him up like a baseball and set him on his shoulder and preened with him a little, and that was all fine, but it was only just fine, and Gogol, while perched on Gladman's shoulder, facing the man, tried to get the man to do the thing with his face, but the man didn't seem to see Gogol trying, or, if the man saw, he didn't understand what Gogol was doing, or he might have understood but didn't care what Gogol wanted, or he just didn't *want* to do that thing with his face.

Except then the man was leaving, and right before he left, he started doing that thing with his face again at last, which made it seem like Gogol'd finally gotten through to him, but then, once again, he stopped doing the thing as soon as Gogol tried flying over to preen with him.

It was really confusing.

And why didn't Gladman ever make the face that the man who had made the face had made?

Was it possible he couldn't?

If he could, then he wouldn't.

But if he could, then he should.

He certainly didn't, yet maybe he could, and so maybe he would.

That was Gogol's hope.

Gogol hoped that Gladman could and would make the face, and, once the man who had made the face had left, Gogol tried, for a while, to get Gladman to do so, but, except for one time when Gladman laughed his old laugh for a minute—which, even though it wasn't what Gogol'd been after, was, to be sure, a pleasant surprise—Gladman didn't seem very responsive to Gogol, and then, not long after that, Gladman went to sleep.

Most confusing of all: What happened to the hierarchy?

When the man who could make the face made the face, Gogol'd *instantly* known the man was the top, but the man wasn't even a member of the flock, so how could the man have been the top?

Could the man who could make the face have possibly become a member of the flock without Gogol knowing? Could that man have been a member of the flock *all along* without Gogol having known? Could a member of the flock who Gogol hadn't even known about till now have possibly been the *top* member of the flock all along? And if so—if that man could be the top of the flock, *let alone* if he could have been the top all along—then how was it that when that man *wasn't* making the face he didn't seem like the top anymore?

Since when did some face you could make make you the top?

Since when could your being or not being the top switch back and forth from one moment to the next?

Since forever? Was that possible?

And if any of that *was* possible, what could Gogol really say he knew about his flock?

Very little!

And if Gogol, at this late date, still knew so very little about his flock, how could he even pretend to begin to understand its hierarchy? How could he even be sure it *had* a hierarchy?

Maybe Gogol was crazy. Or stupid. Maybe both. Maybe all his life he'd been crazy and stupid. Maybe he was too crazy or stupid—or too crazy *and* stupid—to know how crazy or stupid (or crazy *and* stupid) he was. It was too confusing. Impossibly confusing. Too impossibly confusing to sort through.

Which had made it really hard for him to fall asleep.

Or so Gogol had thought till he woke the next morning from uneasy dreams and realized something was seriously wrong with him. Something inside him. Inside his abdomen. Pain. There was pain.

Serious pain.

And at last he understood:

What had made it hard for him to fall asleep had not been his confusion. What had made it hard for him to fall asleep had not been his fear of being crazy, stupid, or crazy and stupid. His confusion and his fear had been outcomes, not causes.

Outcomes of dying.

Gogol was dying.

Had been dying.

Gogol woke before sunrise and realized he was *dying.*

Gogol's pains were the pains of Gogol *dying.*

Gogol's fear and confusion the previous night had been the fear and confusion that came before the pain that meant that you were dying.

And he'd known it all along. Hadn't he known it? He'd *almost* known it. He could see that now.

All the weird gurglings.

The expansions and contractions.

The involuntary shiftings.

The flexings inside him of parts he hadn't previously known were inside him.

He'd *almost* known those for what they were: signs of the fatal illness that would kill him.

He'd stopped himself from knowing, though. Stopped himself from fully knowing. Convinced himself the signs of his fatal illness were only the discomforts of becoming a man. Told himself that this uncomfortable part would end soon, that once it was finished, it would all have been worth it: he'd come out the other side of it shaped like Gladman. He'd be big and strong and wingless and capable.

What a miserable trick he had played on himself.

What a terrible joke.

Now he had to face the truth. The truth was this pain.

All those discomforts had, while he'd slept, gathered together to become *this pain*. They had all *united*. Banded together to become this excruciating ball of pain about which he could no longer lie to himself.

He couldn't even scream from this pain—it was wrong.

Seriously wrong.

How could it be? How could he be dying?

He'd thought he'd have at least five or six more lives to live before he'd die; that for at least three or four of those he'd live as a man.

To have to die now—to have to ever die at all—that was horrible enough; but to have to die before becoming a man? To never get to be a man? Not even for a moment?

Was there anything worse than this? He'd rather be crazy. He'd rather be stupid. He'd rather be crazy *and* stupid than dead. He'd rather find out that he'd never been right, had been crazy and stupid his whole entire life, that there'd never been any hierarchy at all, that he should have eaten everything he'd ever been given and should never have bitten anyone who'd approached him and should have preened with everyone who'd wanted to preen.

The only thing he wouldn't rather do than be dead was continue to die. It hurt too much.

Over there on the couch, asleep, was Gladman. Gogol wanted to preen with him one last time, to be picked up and held like a baseball and preened.

If he screamed, he knew, he'd wake Gladman up, and if he kept on screaming once Gladman was up, Gladman would get angry and cover the cage, and if he continued to scream once the cage was covered, Gladman would eventually remove the cover, open the cage, and pick him up and preen with him.

—

But he also knew that he probably wouldn't make it.

He wasn't even sure he could beat back the pain enough to get *one* scream out.

And if he did get that scream out but couldn't scream more, then the last thing that had happened between Gogol and Gladman before Gogol's death would be Gladman getting angry at Gogol for screaming, and that would be terrible.

Ugly and terrible.

Gogol's death would be that much harder on Gladman.

Gogol knew this because Gogol knew that if their positions were switched and Gladman died right after Gogol'd screamed and woke him and made him angry, Gladman's death would be that much harder on Gogol.

And Gogol also knew that if their positions were switched in the other sense of *positions being switched* and Gladman died right after it was Gogol who'd gotten angry at *Gladman*, Gladman's death would be that much harder on Gogol.

As of right now, the last thing that had happened between them was Gladman loudly laughing the old laugh while Gogol tried to get him to make the face that man had made. It wasn't the best last thing that could have happened—it wasn't preening—but it was pretty good, and it was definitely better than Gladman getting angry at Gogol: endlessly better.

And the pain was getting worse, hurt more with each breath, and, all at once, Gogol knew for sure that even if he were able to scream one time, he wouldn't be able to get enough screams out afterward to get through the covering and uncovering of his cage that he would have to get through to get to some preening, and so he decided not to scream.

And he took another breath, and the pain got even worse, and he realized that if he died on his perch, he'd fall dead to the grate at the bottom of the cage and the grate would rattle, which might wake Gladman, and if the rattle woke Gladman, then Gladman would be angry that Gogol had woke him, and the last thing that ever happened between them would be Gladman getting angry at Gogol for waking him by falling dead off his perch and rattling the grate.

—

So Gogol gingerly started climbing down toward the grate, trying to get there before he died, and, as he climbed down, he saw the ugly fabric box in the corner of the cage in a whole new light. He hadn't even thought about the box in months.

This was an ugly fabric box that was open on the side and that Daphne'd put on the floor of the cage a little while after she'd joined the flock. The box was ugly and stupid and it took up space—it was four Gogols wide and three Gogols high—and, up until now, he hadn't understood why Daphne had put it there. He'd thought she'd put it there out of stupidity. He'd thought she'd put it there because she liked to look at it because she didn't even know enough to know it was ugly.

Up until now, he hadn't understood that the ugly fabric box was a box meant for dying in. But now he understood: Daphne had given him a five-sided fabric box to die in. An ugly, five-sided fabric box to die in. It was kind of her, actually. Not kind to Gogol, but kind to Gladman.

The idea of this box was to get inside it right before you died so that when Gladman found you dead, he wouldn't have to touch your body or even really look at you: he'd go to your cage, see your not-standing body there inside the box, know you were dead, reach into the cage, crumple closed the open side of the box in his fist so the box became the shape of a bag, then remove the bag-shaped box with you in it and throw you away—or whatever gets done.

That the box had come from Daphne was something that Gogol didn't really love, but still: he was glad the box was there. He was glad for the chance to make his death that much easier on Gladman than it would have been if there wasn't any box.

Even more gingerly now than before, he made his way over to the opening of the box, and entered the box.

In the box, he started in on the dying proper. The dying proper gave him no peace. The dying proper hurt worst of all.

It hurt to stand up, so he hunkered down, but then it hurt to hunker down, and so he stood up again, but then it hurt to stand up again, and he had to hunker down again.

After nine or ten cycles of this, however, something changed.

Gogol started feeling better.

He started feeling suddenly a whole lot better. The pain in his abdomen, the horrible pain—it became less serious, a *lot* less serious.

And then it became *so* unserious, it was almost like a pleasure.

And then it *was* a pleasure. It was a pleasure on par with *preening*.

No!

It was *better* than that.

It was *better* than preening. It was *so* much better.

Except then it got worse again. Worse than ever.

Except then it improved again. Felt *better* than ever.

He hunkered then stood and then hunkered then stood. The pain moved, became pleasure, then became pain again.

This couldn't be death. It wasn't. It wasn't! Gogol'd been mistaken!

Rather: Gogol'd been correct!

Rather: he'd been *mostly* correct!

First he'd been mostly correct, *and then* he'd been mistaken.

He'd never been dying. He'd been becoming a man.

He was becoming a man.

He was becoming a man, but it was happening differently than he'd always imagined. He'd always imagined that he'd grow new arms first. Well, actually, he'd imagined that he'd lose his wings first, and *then* grow new arms, but he imagined that he'd grow new arms *before* he'd lose his old arms and grow some legs. But that's not how it would go. That's not how it was going.

The first thing he'd do, before losing anything, was grow his legs.

That's what was happening.

That much was obvious.

If what was about to come out of him were arms, they wouldn't come out of where they were coming out from: they'd come out from some place much closer to his wings.

All this time, that flexing of parts inside him he'd never known were inside him before? They *hadn't* been inside him before! They were new! Those parts were his legs! Those uncomfortable gurglings and shiftings were the gurglings and shiftings of *legs* being made. His Gladman-shaped legs! And here they were! About to come out of him!

He hunkered down then stood up and hunkered down then stood up, and . . .

What came out wasn't legs.

What came out—he didn't know what it was. He had no idea what it was at all. The biggest shit of all time? The hardest shit in history? The biggest, hardest, *roundest* shit ever shat?

He had no idea. All he knew was he'd failed. Instead of making the legs he was supposed to make, he'd failed to make any kind of legs at all, and now he was ashamed. And he was still shaped like Gogol.

He'd fucked up, was ashamed, and whatever this was—this shameful product of his miserable fuckup—whatever this was, he had to keep it hidden. He knew that, too.

JEWISH PROBLEM

". . . And when I got a little closer," the mayor said to Apter, "I saw it was *not* Barack Obama standing in front of the wall of survivors, but another handsome African-American man who I'd mistaken for Barack Obama, and I felt, frankly, like maybe I was one of these kinds of racist persons who doesn't know how truly racist of a person he is, you know? One of those guys who thinks all handsome African-American men look the same but doesn't even realize that that's what he thinks, so he's always thinking every handsome African-American man he sees is Barack Obama. You know the kind of accidentally racist guys I mean, right? They don't mean to be racist, but maybe that makes it worse somehow? Or so I've heard it said? I don't know. Either way it isn't good.

"And I felt like such a jagoff, mistaking this handsome African American for Barack Obama. But then, when I got even closer to him than I'd already gotten—I didn't really walk up to him so much as I was suddenly right in front of him, or . . . I don't know. But suddenly, I'm right in front of him and I realize he *is* Barack Obama. It's him! I was right, then wrong, then right again. And I fucking love this guy. My favorite president for sure. And he's smiling. He's smiling at *me*. I mean, we're the only two people in the whole park, so who else could he be smiling at? No one else. Me. What a good feeling.

"And what Barack Obama does at this point in the dream is he puts his hand on my shoulder in this really warm way—I can't even bring across how good it felt, I mean . . . But he puts his hand on my shoulder, okay? The de factor leader of our party. The greatest public speaker of my political lifetime, and probably also of my nonpolitical lifetime, too. A guy who brought just about as much glory to the City of Chicago as a guy can bring without being Jordan or Ditka, or . . . maybe even more glory than those guys, I don't know. High-profile glory.

"But point is, though, Barack Obama puts his warm hand on my shoulder while smiling at me, and then with his other hand, he makes this like broad, sweeping gesture at the wall of survivors that we're standing next to at the Mount Chicago Memorial Park, and it's like he's trying to tell me, 'What a brilliant idea that you had when you came up with this wall of survivors. What an amazing leap of genius your mind had to take to even come up with the conceptual framework of the park at all, but this wall? Nonparallel! And, my God, Mr. Mayor, the execution of your brilliant idea isn't parallel either! It is all so truly marvelous. If I may use your own words to describe to you what this survivor's wall means to me, I would describe it as this: it crosses my wonderline. *You* cross my wonderline. You are a credit to this city. You are a credit to this country. You have entered the Parthenon of leaders, Mr. Mayor.' And etcetera.

"That's what it *seems* like the gesture is saying, that's what it *seems* like maybe Barack Obama is actually about to say out loud to me, but then, Apter, that turns out to not be an accurate prediction of the circumstances maintaining here, 'cause what happens next is when he opens his mouth to speak, he does not even have *the voice* of Barack Obama is first of all. It's one of the spookiest feelings I've ever felt, the feeling I got when I heard the voice that came out of the face of Barack Obama, because that voice was the voice of the old Mayor Daley. Daley *the father*. And what Barack Obama or maybe Mayor Daley disguised as Barack Obama says to me in the voice of Mayor Daley while he's making this broad, sweeping gesture at the wall of survivors with the one Obama hand, and squeezing my shoulder so warmly with the other Obama hand, is not anything like what I thought he was gonna say. What he says is: 'Not nice.'

"Just that. 'Not nice.'

"And I can't talk, okay? I try, but I can't. I can't get my voice to come out of my face, so I can't even ask him what that means, 'Not nice,' but in all his Obama-Daley wisdom, he reads me, reads me loud and clear: he understands that I don't understand what he means, and he wants me to understand, he really, really wants me to understand, and I know this, and he knows that I know this, and what he says to get me to understand is, he says: 'Bad karate. It's bad karate, Mr. Mayor.'

"Says that in the Mayor Daley voice, okay? But I don't understand still. I don't understand. And that's when I realize I need to cough. And I can. I can cough. So I cough.

"I cough and there's sound, and I feel I got my voice back. I found my voice again. And what I say in my voice is: 'What's that you mean, though, by *bad karate*?'

"And he answers me in *Obama's* voice, now. 'The people,' he says. 'It just isn't very nice for the people, Mr. Mayor. It's bad karate. You need to put aside this bad karate you're doing, and you need to make it nice for the people,' and then before I can ask him how to make *what* bad karate nice for *which* people *how*, I realize Barack Obama has such a nice smile that you can't even tell, when he's looking right at you, no farther from you than you are from me, Apter—he's such a handsome guy with such a good smile that you don't even *have a clue* what he's really thinking about you, not even if what he's really thinking about you is that you're a one hundred percent complete and total jagoff. And I realize in that moment that that's what he's really thinking about *me*. He's thinking I'm a complete and total fucking one hundred percent jagoff, and I'm so angry about that, it wakes me up, *sitting*. I sit straight up in bed, and I'm sweating like a pig, and I'm *angry*, I'm angry at Barack Obama for having those negative thoughts about me, but also even angrier at myself for getting angry at him and for making him angry at me to begin with, and, all at once, I understand.

"All at once I understand that the not-nice bad karate he meant was the names."

"On the wall," Apter said.

"The names on the wall *exactly*," said the mayor. "How they're organized. Well, how we're planning to organize them once the park gets built and there *is* a wall. It *is* bad karate. It'll make the people feel bad and think I'm a jagoff. That's what I realize.

"And I'm sitting there in bed, sweating and angry, and I interpret for myself that what I was trying to tell myself in my dream of Barack Obama I just had was that the wall of survivors should be different than how we've been talking about. The wall of survivors should *not*, first of all, have the names of the survivors in different font sizes depending on how many people they lost to the anomaly—that'll only make the people whose names are in smaller font sizes feel bad. It'll make them feel like the City of Chicago is *not nice* and doesn't admire their survivorship as much as it admires the larger-font-size people's survivorship is how they'll feel. And that feeling will keep people apart or pull them apart further than they are already kept and pulled instead of *bringing them together to heal by taking pride.*

"And no lessly second of all, we are *all* survivors, my dream was saying to me. Every Chicagoan. *Every last Chicagoan* who was alive on 11/17 is a survivor of the anomaly. And if I understand certain genetic DNA studies that I've been reading about, then certain genetic scientists of DNA would even argue that this is even true for every last child who wasn't born yet on 11/17 but whose parents were Chicagoans on 11/17—that all of them were survivors of the anomaly, too. They have all suffered loss and trauma, and they have all survived their losses and traumas. *All* of them. All of *us.* We're *all* survivors. Do you see what I'm getting at?"

"Maybe?" Apter said.

"So tell me."

"We won't have any of the survivors' names engraved on the walls."

"*Won't have any names engraved on the*—No. You did not understand my dream at all," the mayor said. "What we'll do is we'll engrave the names of *every* Chicagoan on the wall: every Chicagoan who was alive on 11/17. Maybe also—all depends on if science can make a final decision about the genetics of handing down trauma DNA to offspring before we start the engraving process—maybe also every Chicagoan who has been born *since* 11/17. We'll engrave all their names in the same exact font size. *That* is the healing karate of the park about which my dream aspired to grant me the awareness of."

"That makes a lot of sense," Apter said. "Of course."

"I knew you'd understand," the mayor said. "And I want to tell you another thing: I'm seeing something else differently than I was seeing it yesterday, and I think you'll be happy to hear. Last night, right after you and I had our little *teta-ted,* I didn't like the way we left it. I told my wife all about it over dinner, and she's got a great head on her shoulders, you know? She's the one, truth be known, who originally came up with the concept of having a crossable wonderline, and she made some good points last night that, frankly, I'm surprised you didn't make yourself. Main one being: Gladman's a Jewish problem, and if Perry Farrell's Jewish, it's a one hundred percent bunch of Jews who are putting Day Zero together, and since it would be unpolitic of an Irishman such as myself to interfere on *any* inter-Jewish matter, much so the less would it be politic of an Irishman such as myself to try and solve the Jewish problem of which aforementioned. So I did a whole three-sixty. You have my blessing. Really. You're a fan of this guy, and so I hope you convince him to open the show. I am cheering for you. But maybe just don't announce him till the concert sells out, huh?"

When Apter left the mayor's office that morning, it was barely 8 a.m. in California, and much as he'd have liked to get it out of the way, he decided that he'd better wait a couple hours to call Sylvie Klein: allow her some time to digest her breakfast before letting her know that all the semilegal pro bono work she'd had her boyfriend perform on Apter's behalf had been for nought.

Just a few minutes later, though, Sylvie called him.

"Hey, Syl," he said, "I'm glad you called. Not so much *glad,* actually, but . . . I'm afraid I've got some news that might upset you a little."

"Is it about Daphne Bourbon?" she said.

"It's the survivor wall," Apter said. "The mayor canceled it. I understand if you hate me a little."

"Canceled it."

"Yeah, I guess what happened is he had a dream about Barack Obama in which it came clear to him that there was an even *more* ridiculous way to commemorate 11/17, and . . . I'm really sorry I wasted your time, Syl. Hersh's time, too."

"Look," Sylvie said, "don't worry about that. I mean, I haven't lifted a finger yet, and Hersh—he won't mind."

"No?"

"Maybe a *little.* But a lot of the code he's been writing to get at the socials is portable. He'll be able to use it for other, you know, endeavors . . ."

"Well, I'm relieved to hear that. Most of it, at least."

"Ha! You've got nothing to worry about. Really. Hersh is a gray hat through and through. Soon as I tell him, he'll delete the list you sent, *and* all the data he's gathered."

"Okay," Apter said. "That's good."

"Yeah. Yes. So, uh, Daphne Bourbon . . ."

"I have no news on Daphne Bourbon."

"No, that's the reason *I* called," Sylvie said. "*She* is, I mean. She didn't leave him, Apt. She died. In the anomaly."

"No," Apter said.

"I know. But . . . she did. Her name's right there on the victim list. Page thirty-one."

"I'm an idiot," he said. "I'm . . ."

"No, no," she said.

". . . a total fucking *idiot*."

"Hey, come on. If you're an idiot, then so am I. I didn't think to check the victims list, either. Not till last night. And I never would've if it wasn't for Hersh. I was just starting to tell him what you'd told me about your visit to Gladman's, and when I got to the part about how it seemed to you like Gladman's wife had left him, I said her name, said *Daphne Bourbon,* and he said he remembered it from the top of a sublist he'd recently made of anomaly victims with green cards—a group whose socials are particularly hard to get at, I guess—and even *then* . . . Even after he said he remembered her name from the list, I didn't fully believe it till I checked for myself. It's hard to believe. So."

"That's not . . ." Apter said.

"What's not . . . what?"

"I sent Gladman that 'Less Depressing Auschwitz' sound file."

"Oh," Sylvie said. "Oh no," she said.

"Indeed," said Apter. "That is exactly what I did. Yesterday, after I met Solomon Gladman—who was nice to me, and who seemed really sad, like sad in a *big* way, sad in let's-call-it an *insurmountable* way—what I did, Sylvie, just as soon as I could . . . What I did, just as soon as I could, was I callously evoked a personal tragedy he recently suffered. The personal tragedy that was, no doubt, the source of his insurmountable sadness. I callously evoked that personal tragedy of his while suggesting, by text message, that he laugh about it. I. Am. An idiot."

"Wow . . . yeah . . . well . . . more of an *asshole,* really," Sylvie said.

"Great."

"You're not, of course. Come on. That is: you *are,* but we knew that already. What I meant was: you're not an asshole for sending that sound file—you didn't know about his wife!—but probably Gladman does think you're an asshole. For sending that sound file."

"Thanks."

"Probably thinks you're an idiot *and* an asshole, actually."

"Sylvie," Apter said, getting his breath back, "I know I'm laughing, but I feel really bad about this."

"Don't," she said. "Not yet, at least. We can't even be sure that Gladman's upset. That sound file's *funny*. He might've found it funny, right? He *is* a comedian."

In- or correctly, it had been clear to Apter, when he'd visited Gladman, that to mention Daphne Bourbon, let alone to *inquire* about her, would have been out-of-bounds. Out-of-bounds because Apter had thought that Daphne'd left Gladman and, judging by the suffering state in which Apter'd found him, a state that he couldn't help but imagine *owed* to Daphne's leaving, he had assumed Gladman wouldn't want to talk about that.

Despite the affinity Apter felt for Gladman, the affinities he knew he shared with Gladman, and the affinities he suspected he had *to* Gladman, Apter and Gladman weren't *friends:* unless Gladman were to have brought it up himself, his relationship with his wife—even if it *weren't* the cause of his suffering—would have been none of Apter's business.

And now that Apter knew that Daphne had *died* . . .

Now that he knew that Daphne had died, to mention her without having first received Gladman's consent would be, Apter felt, even further out-of-bounds than it had previously seemed.

Even if he *were* a friend of Gladman's, the amount of pain that doing so would risk inducing was just too high.

Apter may indeed have been an asshole, but he wasn't a sadist.

Nor did he imagine that mentioning Daphne might open a wound that had healed or was healing: Gladman had obviously not gotten over Daphne's death, Apter doubted he was *getting* over Daphne's death, and, were Gladman *never* to get over Daphne's death, Apter wouldn't be all that surprised.

What Apter did imagine, however, was that Gladman had moments, waking moments, in which his suffering relented a little, maybe even disappeared entirely—while, for instance, he was swallowing food, or falling asleep, or staring at his parrot—and the possibility that Apter, if he were to mention Daphne, could ruin or even delay one of those moments for Gladman . . . that possibility struck him as all too real.

To do such a thing would be indefensible.

All of which is to say that Apter couldn't, without mentioning Daphne, find a way to properly apologize to Gladman for having sent the "Less Depressing Auschwitz" sound file, and so he didn't properly apologize to Gladman.

He didn't improperly apologize either.

From April 14, 2022, to April 19, 2022, he wrote two or three letters of apology a day, but he sent not a one.

On April 20, at 10:41 p.m., having just sat down to try to write another letter of apology, he received the following text from Gladman.

> That thing you sent last week—hilarious! Thank you. Why don't you come by my place after work one day soon. Between 6 and 8, say. Open invite, but tomorrow'd be best. We'll have a drink. Talk about this concert more. No promises, but I am reconsidering.

Me Too

1

Although Gogol's Graham&Swords CinchToClean! 18″x18″x24″ Play-top Birdcage did keep the floor surrounding its stand (sold separately) cleaner than many other brands of birdcage would have, the CinchToClean! itself was no cinch to clean. Droppings adhered to its seed-guard skirt and perches and bars as stubbornly as they would have to any other cage's, and the husks and crumbs and down and dropped pellets the CinchToClean! prevented from falling to the floor found their way into the droppings and adhered to the droppings.

Gogol took a shit every fifteen minutes.

Twice a week—on Wednesdays and Sundays—Gladman replaced the liner in the tray beneath the cage's grate, vacuumed the area surrounding the stand, and scrubbed whatever droppings remained on the floor with a fruit-based, pet-safe solvent called PoopAway. A seven-minute process.

No big deal.

But to clean the cage itself—which required partial dis- and subsequent reassembly, removal and subsequent replacement of select toys and perches, a quarter bottle of PoopAway, half a jumbo paper towel roll, and a sponge—took him an hour if he did it bimonthly, as recommended by *Every Parrot Owner's Guide to His or Her Parrot*.

Not that he had to do it bimonthly.

He only *had to* do it triannually.

It wasn't till after four months without a cleaning that the cage became intolerably disgusting.

However, cleaning the cage triannually—which required *total* dis- and subsequent reassembly, removal and subsequent replacement of *all* the toys and perches, a *half* bottle of PoopAway, a *whole* jumbo paper towel roll, *two* sponges, *and* a scrub brush—would take him three hours.

To spend an hour scrubbing crusted droppings—an hour inhaling fine flyaway particles of PoopAway-scented crusted droppings—left Gladman exhausted, sore in the shoulders, and slightly afraid for his pulmonary health.

To spend three hours doing so was *more* than three times as dreadful: it wasn't just the process itself that lasted longer, but the anticipation of engaging in the process. In the week preceding a triannual cleaning, Gladman, as he worked up the energy it would take him to perform said cleaning, was depressed and anxious.

On the other hand, during the anxious and depressing week preceding a triannual cleaning, the sight of the uncleaned-for-four-months cage would disgust him so thoroughly that, once he *did* eventually get it clean, he'd have a palpable sense of satisfaction and relief; a palpable sense of satisfaction and relief that he did *not* have after getting the uncleaned-for-only-*two*-months cage clean.

The first year or so during which Gogol was in Gladman's care, Gladman, still attempting to follow *Every Parrot Owner's Guide . . .* to a T, had cleaned the cage bimonthly. After that year or so, he had come to believe in Gogol's hardiness, thereby lost the motivation to do everything *Every Parrot Owner's Guide . . .* suggested, and, for the next five years, he cleaned the cage triannually.

And then he met Daphne, and Daphne moved in.

After Daphne moved in, Gladman's pre-triannual-cage-cleaning anxiety and depression would cause *her* to suffer. His face would deaden, he'd whine and snap, sigh too loudly, walk with a slump, start petty arguments, and need to be alone—all of which was unacceptable. Childish, stupid, and unacceptable.

The fifth time it happened, he explained the problem.

He hadn't explained the problem before because . . . because he was not an especially good husband.

He could be pretty selfish.

More precisely: he hadn't explained the problem before because he was ashamed that so small a problem—the need to *perform a household chore*—should turn him into such a monstrous pain in the ass.

But the fifth time it happened—the fifth time Daphne was made to suffer Gladman's pre-triannual-cage-cleaning anxiety and depression—he made her cry.

Then he misunderstood how he had made her cry.

Only after *that* did he explain.

It happened like this:

He'd agreed to participate in a couple of panels at the L.A. Times Festival of Books, and, twenty-two hours before he flew to Los Angeles, which was three days into his week of pre-triannual-cage-cleaning anxiety and depression, he checked in for his flight online, only to discover that, despite his being enrolled in the Global Entry Program, and despite having entered his Known Traveler Number when prompted, the ticket he was issued didn't have the TSA PRE symbol on it, which led to his spending half the morning—first over e-chat, then via telephone—bullying various customer service representatives into fixing the ticket, after which, somewhat bolstered by his having wrested pyrrhic victory from the jaws of bureaucracy (the security line he'd just lost two hours of his life to avoid would have taken but a sixth of that time to get through), he went to fix himself a cup of coffee in the kitchen, where the sight of Gogol's disgusting cage instantly plunged him back into his misery, and Daphne, who was making a grocery list at the counter, asked him what he wanted for dinner.

He said he didn't know what he wanted for dinner. It was 10 a.m., so how could he know?

She said she was about to go to the supermarket, and it would be really helpful if he could tell her what he wanted.

He said it didn't matter; he didn't care what they ate for dinner.

She said that wasn't true. He was picky, she said, and unpredictable.

He disagreed with the characterization.

She offered an example in defense of it. The example she offered was: she'd made boeuf Bourguignon the previous Tuesday and Gladman had loved it, had said it was the best boeuf Bourguignon she'd ever made for him (which had been true), but then, when she'd reheated the boeuf Bourguignon the following night (everyone, including Gladman, knew boeuf Bourguignon peaked in quality the day after it was made), he'd said he couldn't eat it. Hence: picky, and unpredictable.

Gladman objected. He told her that, just as he'd explained to her on the night he'd declined the reheated boeuf Bourguignon, he'd had a stomachache from having eaten so much of it the previous night, and to eat it again would have only made his stomachache worse.

And Daphne said that was neither here nor there; she wasn't trying to say that he should have eaten boeuf Bourguignon that second night when he knew that doing so would have hurt his stomach. All she was trying to say was that the recent boeuf Bourguignon episode demonstrated that, when it came to dinner, Gladman was picky and unpredictable, and, since she was, right now, about to go to the supermarket, she wondered if he might perhaps be capable of *predicting* what would be good for him and his stomach, and thereby *pick* what she'd make for dinner, because that was something she obviously hadn't developed the skills to do *for* him.

At this point, Gladman's head was in the fridge. He had opened the fridge to get some half-n-half to add to the espresso he'd just finished pulling, and maybe the blast of cool air on his face brought him back to his senses—or brought him *partly* back to his senses—but whatever the cause, Gladman realized (not for the first time) that, in all his life, there had never been another person—neither his mother, nor his father, nor either of his sisters, let alone any woman with whom he'd been romantically involved . . . there had never been another person who'd treated him as kindly as Daphne. There'd never been another person, Gladman realized, who'd less deserved to suffer the brunt of his—or anyone's, but *especially* his—impatient and miserably bitchmouthed depressive moods than Daphne. Fuck's sake, she was asking him to tell her what *he* wanted for dinner; she wanted to know what he wanted for dinner so that *she* could shop for the ingredients *of whatever that was and cook it for him.*

And rather than deciding to remove his head from the fridge, look

Daphne in the eyes, and apologize to her for having taken her for granted, Gladman thought it would be better to keep his head inside the fridge and make fun of himself in a manner that acknowledged how much of a dick he was being and how much of a saint Daphne was to even put up with him.

This, it should be said, was *not* the wrong impulse for Gladman to have. Daphne pretty much always understood Gladman's attempts to get her to laugh for what they were: expressions of his love for her and his vulnerability *to* her. And she certainly preferred such loving attempts at comedy to direct declarations of all-too-easily-and-Americanly-oft-stated big feelings such as "I love you so much" and "I'm really, really sorry."

No, the trouble did not arise from Gladman's impulse to keep his head in the fridge and make fun of himself in a manner that acknowledged how much of a dick he was being and how much of a saint Daphne was to even put up with him, but rather from Gladman's rapidly ensuing determination that the best way to *execute* this impulse would be to impersonate Tony Soprano, the most famous and lovable sociopathic mafioso to ever habitually mistreat his wife on prime-time TV.

And so that's what Gladman did: a weak impersonation. While his head was in the fridge.

"Stop breaking my fucken balls already, huh?" Gladman said to Daphne.

And Daphne, who started crying instantly, said, "Don't *say* that to me, Gladman. How can you say that to me?"

And Gladman, still searching around in the fridge for half-n-half, couldn't see Daphne's face, and so mistook the gasp and crack he heard in her voice for part of a shockingly well-rendered and *really* darkly comic impersonation of Carmela Soprano—i.e. Tony Soprano's long-suffering wife—that she was performing in the service of riffing with Gladman toward peace and forgiveness and an end to the argument.

And Gladman replied, "You know, you're always breaking my fucken balls over here! Every goddamn motherfucking chance you get! Stop breaking my balls already! Stop!"

And, having found the half-n-half, he slammed shut the fridge, and saw his French wife, who had never seen *The Sopranos,* crumpled on the floor, weeping into her hands.

—

In French, the phrase "You're breaking my balls" is *Tu me casses les couilles.* Not an uncommon phrase at all.

But to a French person who has never seen *The Sopranos,* the phrase does not usually sound, as it does to most Americans who have seen *The Sopranos,* like a colorful and somewhat humorous way to accuse your wife of nagging you; it tends to sound a lot more like a forthright way to accuse somebody (your wife, if she's the one you're speaking to) of figuratively castrating you.

And so *mock*-accusing your French wife, who has never seen *The Sopranos,* of breaking your balls in order to let her know that you realize you've been acting like the kind of dick who'd accuse his well-meaning wife of nagging him is not likely to be interpreted by your French wife in the spirit in which you intended, especially not if she can't see your face because your head's in the fridge. There are just too many competing levels of signification for the (ostensible) humor to break through.

None of which is to say that a French person who's never seen *The Sopranos* would be *incapable* of imagining that a French husband, who's in the midst of having a domestic argument with his French wife, might tell that wife, *Tu me casses les couilles,* in order to produce a self-effacing comedic effect that might preface or even stand in for an apology, but rather that it would be *roughly as difficult* for such a French person to imagine a French husband doing so as it would be for an American person to imagine an American husband, who's in the midst of having a domestic argument with his American wife, telling that wife, "You need to shut your castrating mouth, you ugly fucking cunt" in order to produce a self-effacing comedic effect that might preface or stand in for an apology.

Because he hadn't known that "Stop breaking my balls" could be so harsh a thing to say to one's French wife who hadn't seen *The Sopranos,* and because she didn't realize that he didn't know how harsh a thing it was to have said, and because he hadn't known that she'd never seen *The Sopranos,* and because she hadn't imagined that she might have been expected to have seen *The Sopranos,* it took a while for Gladman to realize what had upset Daphne, and nearly as long for Daphne to realize that Gladman hadn't the faintest idea about what had upset her.

And because he didn't initially imagine—or secondly or thirdly imagine—that his intention behind having repeatedly told Daphne to stop breaking his balls might have been misconstrued by her, Gladman assumed she was crying because he'd been acting like a dick for three whole days without having ever explained why he'd been acting like a dick, and so he finally admitted to the thing he hadn't wanted to admit to: that he was so frail and namby-pamby and lazy and ungrateful a delicate rose of a person that the thought of having to, triannually, spend a few hours cleaning up after an animal he loved caused him to behave, for a week at a time, like someone who'd just been diagnosed with cancer in the midst of being put through an IRS audit in the wake of discovering his business partner had been stealing from him for twenty years, and he hated himself for that, and hated himself even more for the way that he had been treating people the last few days, especially Daphne.

"I know this already," Daphne said, once he'd finished speaking his weak-ass piece. "You don't think I know this? The cage is disgusting, it needs to get clean, and so you become depressed and act like a jerk until you have cleaned it—that's what you do. You do it every time. It is not surprising. It is typical for you. It's who you are. You're a child, Gladman. You're immature. You're a fucking baby. You sweat the small things, and you *only* sweat the small things. This time it's even worse than the others because you have to get on a plane tomorrow, so you are acting like a jerk for that reason, too. You are always a jerk before you have to fly. For two entire days before you fly. And why? Why do you become a jerk before you have to fly? Because, like a reasonably sane person, you worry the plane might crash? No. You don't worry the plane might crash. You are *certain* the plane will *not* crash, in fact. What you worry is the train won't get to the airport in time. That is why you become this jerk. You worry the security line will be long. You worry the weather will delay the flight. *That* is why you become a jerk. Once the plane is in the air, you eat the Biscoffs and pretzels and you giggle at the screen, no longer a jerk. You *enjoy* the turbulence! You are sitting in a chair in the middle of the sky, next to your wife, and the sky wants to slam us flat into the ground, it wants us to explode, and you *prefer* it that way because it's less *boring*. You are more afraid of boredom than death. You are more afraid of pain than death. More afraid of annoyance than death. You are more afraid of *inconvenience* than death. You aren't afraid of death in the least! You don't believe you can die. You think that death—"

"I do believe—"

"You don't! You say you do. You *think* you do. You write books about it to convince yourself you do, but no one you love has ever died and you don't believe death is real for you. Just like a baby. A newborn baby."

"A newborn baby who writes books?" Gladman said.

"You are *such* a fucking idiot, husband. You are *such* a baby! And I almost *like* that. It is *almost* cute. It is *nearly* comforting. I can almost take heart in your stupid delusions when I become afraid—when the plane starts to shake and dip and rock, or I find a new mole that might not be round, or my mother tells me she fell in the shower, or I learn my sister found a lump in her breast—you are so *fearless* when it comes to what a normal person *should* fear that when I am overwhelmed with those fears, your steadiness momentarily makes me less afraid. But only momentarily. And then your steadiness makes it all worse. Your steadiness itself begins to scare me. I remember where it comes from. I remember it's because you know nothing of death, and I imagine a time when you will—because you *will*, Gladman, you *will*—and I can't help but think that you will be destroyed by knowing. That someone you love will die, and it will overwhelm and destroy you because you can't even wait in a fucking line without going crazy. And what scares me even more than any of that is imagining what you'll do if something ever happens to *me*—if I get sick, if *I* get too depressed, if I get . . . *fat*. How *inconvenient* that would be for you, how *boring*, and I can only imagine you getting so overwhelmed by the inconvenience and the boredom—so overwhelmed that you abandon me."

"I would never abandon—"

"I know you think you wouldn't. And usually I don't think you would, either. I am very upset right now and I am overstating matters. Usually I don't think you would abandon me. I love you. I know you love me. I know we're in love. I would never abandon you—"

"I know that," Gladman said.

"And I know you know it, and what I think is, 'If we're as in love as we say we are, as I *believe* we are, it is mutual, and since you know you wouldn't abandon Gladman, it is the same as knowing Gladman would not abandon you.'"

"Good," Gladman said. "That's true. No *ifs* about it. All of that is true."

"But *this*, you fucking asshole? This way you spoke to me before? I'm *breaking your balls*? You say this to *me*? This is a piece-of-shit thing to say to me. You don't say this to me, Gladman. It is . . . It is . . . *c'est quoi le putain de mot?*—abusive. It is abusive to say this to me. You have abused me and disfigured all of these *pretty feelings* we have just been speaking of. It makes me *ashamed* to be in love with you."

"I didn't mean to . . . I think there's been a misunderstanding," he said.

That night, they ordered pizza for dinner and watched the first three episodes of *The Sopranos*.

In the morning, Gladman flew to Los Angeles. On the flight, there was turbulence. He tried to be afraid of it, and, failing that, tried not to enjoy it, but he couldn't help himself—it felt too much like a carnival ride.

His seat, however, seemed especially small, even for economy, and he had to keep getting up to stretch.

This wasn't the airline he usually flew with.

The panels at the festival were fine. The other writers were friendly. Under 75 percent of the questions from the audience were intended to "tempt" one or more of the panelists to read or find an agent for unpublished work.

He sold a bunch of books and got a free coffee mug.

The online check-in for his flight home was breezy, and, for the first time ever, he purchased an upgrade—paid for a premium economy seat. It was only an extra $78.

He was pleasantly surprised to think of it that way—*only* an extra $78. Having money was new. He'd only been tenure track since fall. His salary was triple what he'd made as an adjunct, and he needed to work only half as much.

Only, only, only.

The premium economy seat proved its worth. His thighs didn't cramp. His back didn't ache. Up didn't his unspeakable unpleasantness flare.

He took a cab from the airport. Forty-two dollars and however many cents plus tip. More than twenty times the cost of taking the Blue Line. And traffic was heavy. He arrived home *later* than he would have by train. And he couldn't wear his headphones without feeling rude. And the cabbie kept saying things.

So, on the one hand: a fifty-dollar lesson. On the other: a lesson for only fifty dollars. And *only fifty dollars*. There it was again. What a nice thing it was to think such a phrase.

No, the cost of the cab was not what got Gladman down.

Between reluctant utterances of whichever monosyllabic form of "Amen" the latest half-heard driverly earful seemed to demand, he thought about undressing Daphne in various rooms, thought of her variously naked in various positions on various surfaces, wondered where they'd fuck next, and, just as the cab was exiting the highway, thought of how infrequently they'd fucked on the living room couch, which was a really great couch: leather and firm, yet supple and highly stain-resistant.

They really hadn't fucked enough on that couch. Nor, come to think, had they done enough fucking standing up in the kitchen. They'd been married for over a year by then, they'd lived together for a little more than that, and, as far as Gladman could remember, they'd fucked on the couch only two times, both times right before going to bed, and they'd only ever fucked in the kitchen once, in the very early morning . . .

So these three fucks were actually *double* outliers: nearly all the fucking they did was in the afternoon, hardly *any* of the fucking they did was in the morning, and one in ten fucks—*at most*—was fucked post-sundown. So it was really very counterintuitive, wasn't it? That is: you'd think that a couple who preferred to fuck in the afternoon would find themselves doing a larger-than-average proportion of their fucking outside the bedroom . . .

Unless, perhaps, they were big-time nappers.

But Gladman wasn't much of a napper at all—not without benzos; naps made him crabby—and Daphne *never* napped . . .

They *had* fucked in Gladman's home office a bunch—probably a bit more often than normal, though not much more often than you'd be likely to predict once you considered their not being nappers along with their preference for afternoon fucking—and also they'd fucked in the bathroom some, but they hadn't fucked enough in the office and the bathroom to make up for the fucking they should have done on the couch or standing up in the kitchen; all their would-have-been-in-the-kitchen-or-on-the-couch fucking had been done in the bed. What might explain that? Gladman wondered, as the cab pulled up in front of their building and he looked at the meter and added the tip and swiped his card in the thing on the seat and declined the receipt and thought, cheerfully, "Only fifty dollars."

Why, he wondered as he exited the cab, hadn't they fucked more in the living room or kitchen? They'd never discussed it. Why hadn't they discussed it? It seemed really weird. It's not as though they avoided the topic of fucking, so . . .

Of course!

Of course they'd never discussed it, Gladman thought as he entered the building and checked the mailbox—empty—and started climbing the stairs.

They'd never discussed it because there was nothing to discuss. The answer was simple and obvious: too simple and obvious for Gladman to think about without being pressed; too simple and obvious for Daphne to imagine Gladman wouldn't have realized on his own. Too simple and obvious, in short, for either of them to have ever bothered mentioning.

The answer was: Gogol.

Daphne was shy to fuck in front of Gogol.

Maybe Gladman was shy to fuck in front of him, too.

Either way, that was it. That was the reason. They'd only ever fucked in sight of Gogol's cage when the cage was covered; the couch and the kitchen were in sight of Gogol's cage.

So the first thing he'd do when he came through the door, he thought as he came through the door, was cover the cage. He'd cover the filthy, intolerably disgusting, unhygienic cage that he absolutely had to clean within the next day or so and . . .

Gladman lost . . . the spirit.

I.e. in his pants.

Just like that.

As he turned the corner into the kitchen, and the smell of freshly baked tarte Tatin filled his nose, and Gogol said to him, "Hi! Hello! Gogol! Hi!" he saw the cage was no longer filthy and disgusting—that Daphne had cleaned it; cleaned it spotless and, furthermore, enhanced it; spruced it up with the addition of a little fabric box that sat in one of the corners; a little plush-lined, fabric box with an opening on the side; the kind of soft, private room that certain parrots loved to hide in or hide certain of their toys or sometimes their food in—and although he had to admit to himself that he was relieved the cage was clean, he also felt guilty;

felt guilty *and* relieved; a combination of feelings he'd never before then experienced; a combination of feelings that, frankly, struck him as *goyische*, distinctly *goyische*, yes, and he didn't even know what he *meant* by that, but he sure didn't like it, nor like that he meant it, whatever it meant, it really got him down, and Daphne, who'd been lying on the couch—having fallen asleep, it seemed, watching *The Sopranos* (Season 2 of *The Sopranos*, it looked like—ponytailed Furio was on the screen, a character who hadn't appeared in Season 1)—Daphne sat up, rubbed her bleary eyes, and sneezed three times.

"You cleaned the cage," Gladman said. "And made tarte Tatin. Baby, you're too kind to me."

"No joke," Daphne said, and sneezed a fourth and a fifth time. "I think I got sick from inhaling—I don't want to think about what I might have inhaled."

She was sick for a week.

They didn't fuck on the couch.

They lay on the couch and watched a lot of *Sopranos*.

Overall, it was actually a joyful week. He remembered it fondly, and knew, while in its midst, that he'd remember it fondly.

But that *goyische* feeling, though . . .

The cost of a brand-new Graham&Swords CinchToClean! was $71.

If he ordered the cages five at a time direct from the warehouse, he could get them for $50 apiece.

The cost of never having to clean the cage again, then, was *only* $150 a year.

He bought five cages. They came in flat cartons. He stored them in the storage space down in the basement. Every four months, he brought one of the cartons up from the basement and unpacked it in the kitchen: powder-coated wire walls, playtop, and grate; scratch-resistant plastic base w/ seed-guard skirt; see-through plastic latch-on bowls. He unfolded the walls, hooked on the playtop, snapped on the base, latched the bowls, and slid the grate into its slot in the base. Then he took Gogol away from the old cage, set him inside the small carrier cage, placed the small carrier cage in the office (the sight of his cage being dismantled had upset him in the past, caused him to scream), returned to the kitchen, and, one by one, removed the items from the old cage (the perches, the toys, the fabric box Daphne'd got him), cleaned them off, and arranged them in the new cage the same way they'd been arranged in the old cage. He took the old cage off the stand, popped the new cage onto the stand, threw the old cage away in the larger alley dumpster, threw the carton away in the smaller (purportedly *recycling*) alley dumpster, got Gogol from the office, and set him on the new cage. This took thirty-five minutes, start to finish.

And every twenty months, he bought another five cages.

2

Six days after having met Apter Schutz, Gladman sat at his desk, piercing blister-pack foil with the edge of his thumbnail and apportioning that day's Xanax dosages—fourteen quarter-mig tablets for the morning, another twelve for after dinner—when a reminder to replace the cage made his phone chime.

He slept the reminder, finished freeing the tablets from their blisters, swept the after-dinner dosage pile into a rocks glass he set on the bookshelf, swept what remained into another rocks glass he brought to the kitchen, took half the morning's dosage with a pint of water, decided to take the second half with whiskey, right then received the follow-up reminder from his phone—which was good; he'd already forgotten all about the cage—and had second thoughts regarding the whiskey.

Setting up a new cage, though it wasn't exactly *hard* to do, demanded a measure of focused concentration, for even a relatively small deviation from the old cage's arrangement of perches and toys and fabric box could, Gladman feared, trigger Gogol to scream and/or bite and/or shit in his water bowl.

Gladman swallowed the rest of his morning dosage with another pint of water, got one of the flat-packed cartons from the basement, brought it up to the kitchen, removed its contents, and put the cage together.

Throughout the process, Gogol was exceptionally quiet. Conspicuously calm. He'd normally have perched atop the open door of his cage and mimicked the snapping and latching sounds that accompanied Gladman's assembly of the new cage, perhaps whistled some "Imperial March" or *Andy Griffith,* said "Hello" or "Step up" or "Gogol" repeatedly, preened his feathers, sharpened his claws, paced, danced. Instead, he just waited, *silently observing.*

Doing so not from atop the open door of his cage, but from in front of the bottom of the cage's opening—from atop the edge of its seedguard skirt, down onto which he'd climbed from his favorite perch the moment Gladman had entered the kitchen with the carton.

He stood there, on the edge of the seed-guard skirt, observing Glad-man silently and making this . . . face.

This funny new face he'd been making for the past few days: beak parted just a touch, he'd tilt his head forward and a little bit sideways and *squint* his nearer eye.

It was Columbo-ish, almost, this face Gogol made. It looked as if Gogol, in making the face, sought to mimic Peter Falk's Columbo.

But Gladman hadn't seen *Columbo* in years. He doubted he'd seen it since adopting Gogol—he'd never much liked it—and Gogol never looked at the television anyway.

When Gladman watched a show—even when he did so with Gogol on his shoulder—Gogol watched *Gladman*.

On closer examination, maybe the expression was more Dallas Winston–ish than Columbo-ish, anyway.

That is: more Dallas-Winston-as-played-by-Matt-Dillon-ish, as in:

or maybe

And Gladman *had* watched *The Outsiders* since adopting Gogol.

Although it wouldn't exactly be correct to say that *The Outsiders* was one of his all-time favorite movies, Gladman had, as a boy, watched *The Outsiders* more frequently than he had any other. Back then, he'd very much wanted to *be* Matt Dillon's Dallas Winston.

If you turn to page 243, and look very closely at Photo 1, you might be able to see, in Gladman's sixteen-year-old face, certain traces—certain fading vestiges of "muscle memory"—of his failed, earlier-boyhood struggle to appear Dallas-Winston-ly "troubled" or "agitated" or "ominous" in repose, as in

or maybe

But Gladman's facial muscles had, thankfully, lost that memory decades ago, and, as far as he was able to recall, the only time that he had watched *The Outsiders* since adopting Gogol (after Daphne, having discovered page 243's PHOTO 1 in one of Gladman's old yearbooks had asked Gladman if he'd been as much of a prick teenager as the look on his face in the photo seemed to indicate, and Gladman had admitted that he probably had been a prick, though maybe not *quite* as much of a prick as the photo suggested, for the look on his face in that photo spoke more of his embarrassing earlier-boyhood desire to be Dallas Winston than of anything else, and then Daphne had said, "Who is Dallas Winston?" and Gladman had rented the movie to show her), Gogol hadn't behaved any differently than he normally would have while Gladman faced the television (i.e. Gogol'd faced Gladman).

Anyway, that was years ago that he'd rented *The Outsiders* for Daphne. No way that Gogol, even if he *had* paid attention to the film instead of to Gladman, would have only *now* attempted to mimic the smile of Dillon's Dallas Winston.

Unless maybe he'd watched the movie more recently with Gogol, but forgotten?

Or maybe he hadn't forgotten having *watched* it with Gogol so much as, for example, forgotten having passed out on the couch in front of another movie, after which the algorithm of the service by which he was streaming that other movie had, once that other movie had ended, recommended Gladman watch *The Outsiders* next, and when Gladman—asleep—had neglected to refuse the recommendation, the service had mistaken Gladman's inaction for consent and gone ahead and played *The Outsiders*?

Whatever its origin, it was funny, this face that Gogol kept making. Gladman had no complaints about the face.

After having put the new cage together, it was time to put Gogol in the carrier cage and take him to the office so as to relocate the toys and perches and fabric box without interference.

As he approached the parrot, who still perched atop the seed-guard skirt, making the face, Gladman attempted to mimic the face: tilted his head, squinted an eye.

"Good birdie!" Gogol shouted.

Gladman smiled.

"Good birdie! Good birdie! Good birdie!" Gogol shouted, and he shook his tailfeathers loudly, repeatedly.

Gladman cracked up.

Gogol tailfeather-shook more.

Gladman did the face again.

Gogol *good-birdie!*'d.

Gladman cracked up.

And Gogol shouted and tailfeather-shook more.

The cycle repeated five or six times.

As his laughter abated, it occurred to Gladman that, with the exception of the few minutes a few days earlier during which he had played, replayed—and replayed twice more—the "Less Depressing Auschwitz" sound file, this was the hardest he'd laughed since 11/17.

That sound file had been *something*. It wasn't just a matter of what the mayor had said—though that was no doubt dazzling—but how *earnestly* he'd seemed to say it while at the same time sounding like he was doing an impersonation of himself, which is to say an impersonation of someone who, to begin with, sounded like he was attempting not merely an impersonation of the second Mayor Daley, but an impersonation of the second Mayor Daley impersonating Barack Obama.

Like if Andy Kaufman were to impersonate Jim Carrey impersonating Andy Kaufman singing "Love Me Tender" as Foreign-Man-as-Elvis.

But without intending to.

Plus the Holocaust.

Yet something seemed wrong. Not so much *morally* wrong, no. Nor something wrong with the sound file itself so much as . . .

In thinking about the sound file, Gladman was possessed by a vague sense of having somehow erred. Having made a faux pas.

Something to do with the kid—Apter. Had he thanked the kid? He couldn't remember thanking the kid. For sending the sound file. And he'd liked that kid. He'd liked talking to him, and then, after he'd listened to the sound file, he'd liked him all the more. He *should* have thanked him, couldn't remember thanking him, and had a pretty strong suspicion that he hadn't.

He took his phone from his pocket to check. What he found was that he'd typed, "This is amzing nd hilarious!!! Thanks you!" in response to Apter's text, but had not, apparently, managed to press Send.

And then he remembered.

Remembered he'd *deliberately* failed to press Send.

He remembered that, just before pressing Send, he'd determined that the kid deserved a better response than "This is amzing nd hilarious!!! Thanks you!"

He'd found himself thinking about how much Daphne would have enjoyed the sound file, how hard the sound file would have made her laugh—which was a further credit to the kid's sense of humor, and so a further credit to the kid—and he'd determined that the kid deserved a more heartfelt response.

But what had happened was that, in thinking about how hard Daphne would have laughed, he started to imagine it: Daphne laughing hard.

He'd imagined Daphne laughing hard, and it had just so happened that, in that very moment, the whiskey he'd been drinking while he'd listened to the sound file began to interact with the after-dinner dosage of Xanax he'd taken an hour earlier, which interaction had eased him into that magical, browned-out state of intoxication he perennially sought, a state in which he'd found himself able to recall not just the sound of Daphne's laughter, and not just the way her laughter would contort her face (he'd recalled those things a million times since she'd died), but this gesture that she used to make when she couldn't stop laughing and really wanted to stop: she'd press the lowest knuckle of her hand—which hand? the right or the left? the right, or . . . yes yes yes, the right for sure—she'd press the lowest knuckle of her right hand's thumb against her two front teeth and kind of forcefully pet or maybe more like gently slap and clutch at her right wrist and forearm with her other—her left—hand, as if doing so could massage or cajole the laughter away, and he couldn't believe he'd forgotten about that gesture till then, it was so beautiful to him, and so suddenly vivid that he couldn't have possibly done other than hold on to it, the image of it, of Daphne making it, of Daphne laughing so hard she really wanted to stop—he couldn't just *let it go* in order to type out some text, he had to live in the memory for as long as he was able, and . . .

After that: blur. He'd probably passed out. Maybe just forgot, though. About the text.

Either way, he'd sent no text. And if he'd owed the kid a better one than "This is amzing nd hilarious!!! Thanks you!" six days ago, now he owed him one even better than that.

So he should, he decided, take more than just a few seconds to write it. And not right this minute. Not while distracted. Not right here in the middle of a cage change.

His finger, on its way to the lock button, slipped, and the phone asked him if he'd like to add Apter's number to his contacts.

Sure, he thought, might as well. Clicked Yes.

And his phone asked him if he'd like to use his new contact's profile photo in his contacts app.

Sure, he thought, might as well. Clicked Yes.

And in the little circle that would have otherwise contained the initials *AS*, there appeared a photo of Apter Schutz's face, tilted and smiling, one eye sort of squinting, which.

"You trying to smile like this guy?" Gladman asked in a comforting tone, and raised the phone to show Gogol Apter's photo.

"Hi!" said Gogol, raising and lowering a leg, not looking at the phone.

"It's okay if you were," Gladman said in a comforting tone. "You shouldn't be afraid to tell me the truth. I wouldn't be jealous or anything. In fact, I'd think it was great. I like when you learn new things, you know?"

"Hi?" Gogol said, waving the leg again.

"All right," said Gladman, pocketing the phone. "Good birdie," he said.

"Good birdie!" said Gogol.

"Step up," Gladman said, with the back of his hand set against Gogol's breastbone.

"Gogol," said Gogol.

"Step up," Gladman said.

"Step up," Gogol said.

"Step *up*," Gladman said, nudging Gogol's breastbone with the back of his hand.

Gogol bit him. Hard. Broke skin. Then he pivoted and jumped to the floor of the cage, and did another unprecedented thing: he ducked inside the fabric box.

Gladman went to the sink to scrub the bleeding bite with dish soap.

"That was fucked up," he said in a tone that was not comforting. "You hear me, man? You hear me?"

"Hello!" came Gogol's fabric-box-muffled scream.

"No hello. No. That was shitty of you."

"Gogol," Gogol muttered. "Gogol. Gogol."

Gladman dried his hands, but the bite was still bleeding. It was *right* between the knuckles. He went to the bathroom, tweezed off the torn, white scrap of skin, washed the stinging cut a second time with soap, bandaged the cut, and grabbed a towel from the closet.

The towel was for Gogol. To drape over Gogol in order to diminish the depth his beak would be able to sink into Gladman's flesh when Gladman picked him up to remove him from the cage.

The towel, however, proved unneeded. Gogol, when Gladman returned to the kitchen, was still hiding out inside the fabric box.

The fabric box was attached to the cage by a pair of fabric strings laced through and tied in a butterfly knot around a few of the bars.

Gladman untied the knot and unlaced the strings. He reached into the cage and crumpled the box's open side in his fist. Pulled the box out.

Gogol emitted frantic whistles and kiss sounds.

Gladman took pleasure in these sounds for a moment, but the

moment passed quickly, left him feeling petty, and his anger at Gogol was overcome by pity.

"Frightened animal," he thought.

He took the box to the table, set it down like a lunch bag, then turned it on its side—as it had been in the cage—and when he unclenched his fist to let the opening gape, something other than Gogol came out onto the table.

That is: something other than Gogol *rolled* out onto the table.

No.

Two things.

Two things rolled out onto the table, then Gogol, screaming, bolted out after them, hopped right over them, got between them and the edge of the table, and squatted in front of them, blocking their path, preventing them from rolling off the edge of the table.

He turned toward Gladman with a look in his eyes that was pleading or murderous or maybe both, then nudged the eggs back into the box with his beak.

Or rather: she turned toward Gladman with a look in her eyes that was pleading or murderous or maybe both, then nudged the eggs back into the box with her beak.

Gladman sat on floor and laughed till his head ached.

3

Half an hour later, the old cage had been dumpstered, as had the carton. All the cleaned-off accoutrements—save the fabric box—had been properly arranged and secured in the new cage. The new cage had been affixed to the stand.

Only then did Gladman move the box to the new cage.

Gogol, who had stayed with her eggs—of which, it turned out, there were six in total—emerged while he was tying the strings through the bars. She perched on the door, made the face, said, "Step up."

Gladman stepped her up, brought her with him to the couch, and let her stand on his shoulder while he preened the feathers on her head and neck and read the "Unwanted Eggs" section of the "Eggs and Breeding" chapter in *Every Parrot Owner's Guide to His or Her Parrot*.

According to which:

1) Hormonal changes that gave rise to egg-laying could be triggered by nearly as wide a variety of stimuli as those that gave rise to plucking could.

   Apart from mating with another parrot, the most common of these stimuli were: change in diet, sleep-cycle interference, cage relocation, over- or underexposure to sunlight, introduction of a new animal or person to the home, subtraction of a familiar animal or person from the home, introduction of a new "beloved" toy to the cage, subtraction of an old "beloved" toy from the cage, rubbing or petting or "scritching" of the rump, rubbing or petting or "scritching" of the abdomen, and new free-flightedness.

2) Some parrots who'd laid unfertilized eggs just left them alone. Other parrots who'd laid unfertilized eggs would sit on the eggs. Other parrots yet would neither sit on the eggs nor entirely leave them alone, but aggressively protect the area in which they'd laid them.

—

Gogol, obviously, was the third kind of parrot. Having been through multiple cage changes over the years, she must have—probably from the moment Gladman had brought the new cage's carton into the kitchen—anticipated the removal of the fabric box from the old cage, adjudged the removal dangerous to the eggs, and therefore bit Gladman to prevent the removal.

As for what had stimulated her to lay the eggs to begin with, it could have been any number of the items on the list of most common stimuli. He should probably, he thought, try to figure it out, but it wasn't his main concern right then. What concerned him most was what he should do about the eggs.

According to the subsection, it was best for the hen if you allowed her unfertilized eggs to remain with her for the average period of incubation minus one week, as measured from the day the first egg was laid; by that time she would have realized that her eggs were not developing, would have thereby lost interest in them, and so wouldn't be traumatized by their removal.

The reader was advised to turn to a page at the back of the book to find a table that listed the average incubation periods for various popular parrot breeds.

According to the table, Quakers incubated for four weeks. Okay.

That meant Gladman should remove the eggs three weeks from the day that Gogol'd laid the first one. Fine.

But when had Gogol laid the first one?

Hard to say. Gladman hadn't, until today, looked inside the fabric box for months.

Then again, Gogol's behavior—the bite, the remaining with the eggs while the box was on the table—certainly seemed to indicate that she hadn't lost interest in the eggs.

So it was safe to assume she hadn't laid the first egg *more* than three weeks ago.

Gladman opened the browser on his phone, searched the relevant terms, and found out that:

1) Quakers laid their eggs in clutches that ranged from four to eight.
2) The eggs in a clutch were laid twenty-four hours apart.

—

This meant:

    1) Given the bite and the hiding in the box (i.e. given that Gogol was still protecting the area in which she'd laid her eggs), the earliest that Gogol could have laid her first egg was twenty days ago: March 31.

    2) But the latest that Gogol could have laid her first egg was five days ago: April 14.

So, problem solved: to err on the safe side of not traumatizing Gogol, Gladman should leave the eggs where Gogol'd laid them till twenty-one days from April 14, i.e. May 5.

He set a reminder in his phone, returned Gogol to her cage, drank a big whiskey, and let the rest of April 19 blur away.

The following evening, just before bedtime, he started nodding out on the couch, but then realized he'd forgotten to clean the pan in which he'd sautéed the elbows he'd had for dinner.

So he got up to clean it.

Gogol was perched on the door of the cage. When he passed her, she said, "Hello!" to him and waved, so he decided to give her an elbow from the pan.

As he handed her the elbow, she made the face, and he made the face back, and she said, "Good birdie!" and he remembered he still had to text Apter Schutz.

He opened the messaging app and reread Apter's text. He noted Apter'd sent it on April 13, and noted that today was April 20, and, as he did fuzzy math in his half-asleep head, he looked into the box and counted seven eggs, which meant that Gogol had laid an egg since yesterday, and suddenly he wasn't so tired anymore.

4

The next morning, Gladman anxiously woke an hour earlier than usual, but resisted the urge to down his breakfast dosage of Xanax with whiskey. He had to stay sharp.

Hoped he had to stay sharp.

It wasn't quite clear.

Apter'd responded to his text the night before with one of those upturned-thumb animations—the one where the two thumbs waggled briefly before turning sideways to touch at the tips and bend themselves into a smile shape—which seemed to be saying, "Sure thing, dude!" which could have meant, "I will come by between 6 and 8 p.m. tomorrow, as you've asked," but just as well could have meant, "Probably I won't make it over tomorrow, though I'm glad you invited me, and will come by as soon as I'm able," or even, "Yeah right! I am smiling at the thought of your imagining I'm eager enough for you to open Day Zero that I'll just drop everything to come by your apartment during your most preferred two-hour window."

Afraid of looking repellently needy, Gladman didn't text back for further clarification.

He took a long shower, evened his beard out, trimmed his fingernails, did a little picking up around the apartment: emptied the garbage cans, cleared the living room and kitchen of empty bottles and glasses and takeout containers. Ran the dishwasher. Changed the sheets in his bedroom. Folded some laundry.

Nothing else needed doing. Nothing he had an inclination to do.

It was barely eleven.

He ordered a pizza that he grazed for eight hours while streaming the acclaimed new docudrama series *Canceled: Woody Allen*.

All ten episodes. He couldn't turn away from it.

—

The moral certainty with which the series' writer/director—the mononymic, self-designated *ingénx*, Çlÿphtís—seemed to tell the story was so unabashed that Gladman wondered whether they (i.e. Çlÿphtís), despite what their universally adoring critics made of the show, might be *mocking* the very notion of moral certainty. Or perhaps mocking the show's viewers for being so simple-mindedly binary, or so hungry to relive, or so hungry to witness—or even to *enact*—public lynchings as to be drawn to such a show. As in: maybe this was actually a work of subversive art. A kind of anti–morality play. Maybe it was arch. But coyly so. *Coyly* arch. The screen equivalent of Sid Vicious's "My Way" cover, autotuned.

No.

The screen equivalent of Thomas Bernhard singing along to Sid Vicious's autotuned "My Way" cover on his deathbed.

Or . . . whatever.

Gripping.

Gripping was the word.

The CGI alone was . . .

Well, not *alone*. You couldn't separate the CGI from the performances.

Take Matthew McConaughey. He did *not* look one bit like Woody Allen—not in repose—yet he nonetheless disappeared into the role, for he did *sound* like Woody Allen, had all the Woody Allen gestures down pat, and was able to expose even the most basic Allenly tics (sniffing, throat-clearing, eyeglass-adjusting, hand-wringing, etc.) for the harbingers of sneering, misogynistic, toxically male, pedophilic doom they'd always been. All credit for *that* to McConaughey, *and yet*, it was the DeeperFaker CGI software—a lesser version of which had been most famously deployed in Scorsese's *Irishman*—that aged McConaughey accordingly, cementing the realism such that, in the scenes where he was playing Allen at forty, McConaughey, who'd been fifty-two while the series was shot, looked just as much like the viewer imagined McConaughey at forty playing Allen at forty would have looked as he looked like the viewer imagined McConaughey would look at eighty playing Allen at eighty in those scenes where he was playing Allen at eighty. Stunning.

Hugh Jackman's Frank Sinatra was even better, and Timothée Chalamet's Dylan Farrow better yet.

The real standout, however, was Mia Farrow's Mia Farrow.

—

According to Ronan Farrow's profile of her in *Vanity Fair*, the former movie star herself thought the role, which had launched her surprise late-career comeback, was "very much completely ironic really," since she hadn't ever sought any sort of comeback to begin with. She'd just wanted, she said, to continue to humbly strive to be the most benevolent, useful citizen of the world she could possibly be. However, the producers to whom she had sold the rights to *I Will NOT Be the One Destroyed by This*—the bestselling memoir/"toxic masculinity–survival guide" (coauthored with Rebecca Solnit) on which *Canceled: Woody Allen* was based—had insisted that she accept the role of Mia Farrow, Çlÿphtís had refused to take the project on without her in the role, and she, despite her reservations, realized she wouldn't be able to live with herself if she were to walk away from an opportunity to contribute to so important and edifying a ten-part docudrama series as Netflix's *Canceled: Woody Allen*.

Gladman was reading the profile on his phone when a text came through from Apter Schutz.

"Downstairs," it read.

Gladman texted him the code to unlock the front door.

No sooner had Apter sat down at the table—he was telling some story about the mayor and biopics while Gladman, at the sink, filled the tank of the espresso machine—than Gogol, screaming, jumped from her cage, flew across the kitchen, and landed on his shoulder.

Drop-jawed, Gladman closed the tap.

Gogol walked across Apter's shoulder toward his face, pressed the top of her head to the side of Apter's chin, raked it up and down repeatedly.

"Is he gonna bite me?" Apter said quietly. "I think he wants to bite me."

"That's the last thing she wants."

Gogol stopped with the rubbing, stuck her beak in his beard, started nibbling methodically.

Apter closed an eye—the one nearer the bird—and whispered, "I'm freaking out a little here."

"She's *preening* you, man."

"I'm really not—that beak is really close to my eyes. I'd really rather . . ."

"All right, okay. Here's what I want you to do," Gladman said. "First, put your hand sideways just under her head, like this . . ."

Apter put his hand just under Gogol's head. Gogol continued to preen Apter's beard.

"No, no," Gladman said. "Tuck your thumb in your palm and turn the hand around so the knuckles are facing her . . . Good. Good. Now say, 'Step up.'"

"Step up," Apter said.

Her beak full of beard, Gogol grumbled, "Step up."

"Say it more insistently. Command it," Gladman said.

"Step *up*," Apter said.

Gogol grumbled, "Step up," and, as she did so, took her beak from Apter's beard and stepped onto his hand.

Apter lowered the hand, moved it some inches away from his chest.

Gogol said, "Hi!" and raised a foot.

Apter said, "Hi," back, and this look came over him—this naked, peace-gorged, shock-of-recognition look. Not all there, but not quite blank. Almost religious. Almost sexual.

A look that you hardly ever get to see on the face of a sober, nonfictional adult who isn't enjoying a bout of psychosis.

You do see it a lot, in movies, though, that look. TV commercials, too. Often in close-up. Usually when a troubled and/or troubling character—in most cases either the offspring or parent of the person whose face is overcome by the look—shows a sudden grace, or sudden greatness, or a previously unknown talent for something unexpected and beautiful. Singing. Chess. Soccer. Mathematics.

Or when a father holds his goop-flecked, newborn child the first time.

The shot tends to be accompanied by swelling strings.

Swelling strings or sudden, total silence: the sudden, total subtraction of the soundtrack, which, right up till the look overcame the face, had been fully swollen with swelling strings.

It isn't a marker of quality filmmaking.

—

But Apter wasn't fictional, and Gladman was moved. Gladman understood.

He'd glimpsed that look on himself in a mirror fifteen years ago.

He and the woman who he'd leave for Daphne half a decade later had tried to sneak out of a house party early, and the hostess of the party caught them before they could get to their coats. Begged them to stay. Told them they had to—of all things—*meet her budgie.*

Back then, Gladman cared little for animals.

He thought of them as ill-designed, malevolent clockworks that carried germs and smelled not-good.

But the hostess insisted and the ex said okay.

The hostess brought them into her bedroom, opened the cage that sat atop her dresser, and said, "This is Sheena."

Sheena bore two lavender, lozenge-shaped markings on either side of her orange beak, but—apart from her scaled, Caucasian-colored legs, and her slightly protuberant, Vader-helmet-esque eyes—was otherwise white as a fresh-plucked Kleenex.

She leapt from one perch inside the cage to another, then to the perch affixed to the door, and off that perch she flew up and across to Gladman's shoulder. She approached his head and tilted her own, tilted it *inquisitively,* and Gladman—not a big weeper by any stretch—felt his ducts bulging, and he looked in the mirror that was over the dresser (to look right at the bird strained his writerly neck), and kind of *witnessed* his face, the look upon it, that above-described look; saw himself experiencing something entirely new and intense and *good.* This wild animal, he thought . . . This thing that can fly, he thought . . . It's standing on you, staring at you. No one's coercing it into doing either thing, and that has to mean . . . It *wants* to stand on you. It *wants!* It is able to want, it wants, and what it wants is to more closely see you. While over there in its cage, it found you compelling, knew you weren't a threat, and so it got closer. And maybe you're compelling, and you're surely not a threat, but how can it know that? How can it know you mean it no harm? *Why* should it know that? It weighs what? thirty grams? You weigh sixty-some *kilo*grams. You are over two *thousand* times larger than her. She should fear you, shouldn't she? Yes. She should. She should clock you as dangerous. You'd clock you as dangerous, if you were her. Things like you—you *eat* things like her. That's what you'd think, if you were her. So maybe she's stupid. Either she's stupid, or she knows something you don't know, something you don't even know *how* to know, and so maybe *you're* stupid. Or *have been* stupid. And maybe you'd rather be. Yes. No maybes about it. That's what you'd prefer. You'd prefer to be stupid. To have been stupid. You'd prefer that she know how to know a thing that you don't. How to know things that you don't. You'd prefer that she know—and if she, then who else? what else? everyone? every animal? . . . You'd prefer to believe the world to be even more complicated than you've always believed the world to be. You've always preferred to believe the world to be even more complicated than you've always believed the world to be. And you can. So you will. Now you'll believe it. It's a pleasure to believe it. It's a pleasure to believe she wants to be here.

Sheena lowered her rump and took a shit on his shoulder.

"Oh no!" said the hostess. "I'll clean that. I'm sorry."

"It's okay," Gladman said. "Really. I don't mind."

And he didn't. It was nothing. A fleck on his sweatshirt. A sticky gray pebble. But the hostess had already stepped Sheena up, returned her to the cage.

For the next three months, he made no headway on *Damage, The End,* a book he'd been working on for over six years—a book that was supposed to be his debut novel. Spent nearly all the time he should have been writing watching home videos of parrots online. Just budgies at first, then all kinds of parrots. Parrots talking to people, talking to each other, singing along to popular music, breaking out of their cages, breaking other parrots out of their cages, identifying colors, identifying shapes, solving three-dimensional puzzles, bringing food to dogs and kids, stealing food from kids and rabbits, teaching words and songs to fledglings . . .

To become a novelist, you had to write at least one novel. Maybe you had to publish it, too. For sure you had to write it, though.

And not only wasn't he becoming a novelist, he *was* becoming—he may even have already, he worried, *become*—a loser.

A bird-obsessed loser.

He said so to his sisters one night at the bar.

Naomi said that, yeah, he sounded pretty loserly. He really needed to finish that book.

Kayla mostly agreed, but suggested that he wasn't so much a bird-obsessed loser as he was a bird-*video*-obsessed loser.

Gladman wondered aloud if the distinction was useful.

"If these were videos of some *woman* that you were spending all your writing time watching," Kayla said, "you'd be a loser. A creepy loser, in fact. If, however, you were spending all your writing time *hanging out with* the woman, you wouldn't be a loser. At least not in the best case. In the best case you'd be a man in love. And because the woman would be in love with you, too, she'd understand you needed time and space to write, and she'd let you have that."

"That's true," Naomi said. "Other hand, if you replace *woman* with something else—a video game, say—the distinction's pretty irrelevant. Like, if you were spending all your writing time watching videos of video games being played by other people, you'd be a loser, right? But you'd also be a loser if you spent all your writing time *playing* a video game."

"Good point," said Kayla. "And thereby and thusly doth the question ariseth: Are bird videos more like videos of women or videos of video games?"

"Better yet," Naomi said, "is a bird more like a woman or a video game?"

"I vote *woman*," Kayla said.

"Hear hear," said Naomi. "Certain British people even call women *birds*."

"He needs to get a bird," Kayla said.

"If you get a bird," Naomi told him, "you'll probably stop watching videos of birds. Or at least stop watching *so many* videos of birds."

"But even if that's so," Gladman said, "having the bird won't help me finish my book, will it? It'll just replace the videos. Or mostly replace them. I'll hang out with the bird instead of watching the videos."

"I don't know," Kayla said. "If we're right about a bird being more like a woman, you'll eventually grow tired of hanging out with it. Or of hanging out with it so much."

"Well, that's not . . . That's dark," Gladman said.

"I don't know that it is," Kayla said. "But so what if it is? Long term, it's probably good for your writing, right? That's the concern here. It's probably better for your writing than a woman, in fact. Because a woman:

if you get too tired of hanging out with her, you get rid of her, and then you waste even more of your time looking for another woman till you find one and the cycle . . . recycles. Same goes with playing a video game, actually. But a *parrot*? A parrot you *adopt*? It's like a kid."

"She's right," said Naomi. "You can't get rid of a pet like that, brother. Not unless you're heartless. You're not heartless. Not *that* heartless. It would be like getting rid of a kid. Or a woman you're in love with."

"*Or a woman you're in love with,* exactly," said Kayla. "So once you start getting tired of hanging out with your parrot, you hang out with it *less,* and there's your time to write."

"Because no way do you, after having gotten tired of hanging out with your parrot, decide to get *a second* parrot," said Naomi. "That would be really fucking stupid. And you're not that stupid."

"My apartment's small, though," Gladman said. "It's not like . . . I mean, hanging out with it *less* would have to mean leaving the apartment, which does not lead to writing."

"Less *actively* is what I meant," Kayla clarified.

"More *passively,*" Naomi further clarified. "Like Mom and Chi-Chi. Think about them."

"Exactly," Kayla said. "Mom and the Cheech. She still carries him everywhere, lies about him being a service animal, makes you admire him for a couple seconds every time you see them, buys him *sweaters*— all that bullshit—but she doesn't, like, act as though Chi-Chi is a part of whatever conversation she's having anymore, and she doesn't, I don't *think,* spend much time, when it's just the two of them, talking to Chi-Chi and trying to teach him tricks or whatever . . . she hasn't done any of that stuff in years, I don't think. She just has Chi-Chi near her. They watch TV together on the couch, you know? Hang out together in the kitchen and eat."

"As one eats and watches TV," Naomi said, "not with any video game, nor with *some woman,* but only with a woman one is truly, madly, deeply in love with."

This comment really cracked his sisters up, and the conversation turned to Kayla's last ex-girlfriend, then Naomi's douchey husband, and Gladman tuned out, got lost in his thoughts, for he'd started, for the first time, to consider what it might mean to *passively* hang out with a parrot. How that might look. In his apartment.

He imagined that if he were to adopt a parrot, he would keep its cage across from his desk, and that whenever he desired a hit of whatever it was that looking at parrot videos supplied him with (or more like—he was betting—*almost* supplied him with), he could—instead of opening his browser and getting stuck inside YouTube for hours—lift his head just a few degrees, adjust his gaze, be instantly satisfied by what he saw, then get right back to work.

It seemed worth a try. He had to try something. Had to finish the book. Plus his sisters approved. Their advice was rarely bad. And he *wanted* a parrot. He really did. The whole conversation, he'd been hoping his sisters would convince him to get one.

He spent the next couple weeks making appointments with various avian breeders, going to their homes, interacting with their fledglings. He met Conures and Quakers and Senegals and Lorikeets. Caiques, Pionuses, African mousebirds—even an Aracari toucan. Fifty, maybe sixty birds in all. He adored every one of them, every last one, and the thought of choosing one brought on tension, panic, paralysis. He couldn't do it.

Then he went to a bird show—a monthly gathering of breeders in a grade-school gym, out in Glen Ellyn—and, at one of the smaller booths along the back wall, a pushy breeder set Gogol down atop Gladman's shoulder. Gogol picked up one of Gladman's hoodie's drawstrings, held it in his (her) foot, and preened it, and Gladman felt the look he'd seen on himself in the mirror at the party coming over his face. And when the breeder took Gogol off Gladman's shoulder in order to replace him (her) with a more expensive Pineapple Green–cheeked Conure, Gogol bit the breeder, jumped/flew back onto Gladman's shoulder, picked up the drawstring again, and that was that. *He* didn't have to choose after all.

Nine months later, he sold his first book.

Fifteen years later, Gogol lowered her hi-foot and made the funny face, at which Apter smiled.

"Good birdie!" shouted Gogol.

"Jesus Christ," said Apter, laughing. "I don't even . . . Should I pet him or . . ."

But he wasn't really asking. That is: he was already going for it—going for it incorrectly—and Gogol warning-bit him on the thumb.

"Hey!"

"Oh no," Gladman said.

"It's all right," Apter said. "It didn't really hurt—just startled me. I thought he wanted . . ."

"She does. She likes you. She wouldn't perch on your hand if she didn't. You startled *her*, though. Your approach. She has to see your hand coming from in front and below. She's wired to fear raptors, so if there's movement from above her—or even from the side—she thinks it's a hawk or an owl or whatever. Panics."

"You'd think the response to a hawk would be to fly away or . . ."

"No, I know. You're right. I explained it badly. See, way before your hand gets to her head, she knows it's not a raptor—I mean, we move in slow motion compared to Gogol. She's already realized your hand's not a raptor, so she doesn't fly away, *but* she's been startled nonetheless—got startled *before* your hand got there—startled by *you*, by *your* hand, and she doesn't want you to startle her again, so she bites you. Not because she thinks your hand's a raptor, or even because she wishes you any kind of real harm—she just doesn't want you to approach her the way you approached her anymore."

"Your parrot is shaping my behavior, you're saying," Apter said.

"Always," Gladman said. "I mean—she's not that great at it, but . . . yeah. She's trying. I think all animals must do that, you know? You give them something they want, they give you something you want so you'll keep on giving them what they want. You usually think of it the other way around—that you give them something they want so they'll keep on doing something *you* want, but it cuts both ways, you know? It must."

"Nathan Booth would be thrilled to hear you saying these things."

"The kid reads Booth!"

"I studied with him," Apter said, "at SSA."

"Me too," Gladman said.

"I know," Apter said. "That's why I went there."

Stepping Up

Over the next ninety minutes or so, Apter told Gladman all five of the anecdotes described in the chapters "A Young Jewish Schoolkid" and "A Portrait of the Apter Schutz as Young Men."

For various reasons, and in multiple ways, they came out differently than usual.

In none of his previous tellings of the anecdotes had Apter hesitated to convey his great affection-for-slash-obsession-with Gladman's work, or the degree to which it had shaped the course of his life.

In this telling, however, his interlocutor's being the very source of that work complicated matters.

For Apter to express the true depths of his affection/obsession would have been to risk seeming . . . creepy. Stalker-like.

But given that one of the reasons he was there in Gladman's kitchen (probably the main—and maybe even the only—reason, from Glad-man's point of view, Apter figured) was to encourage Gladman to open Day Zero, too thoroughly understating his affection/obsession would have been to risk making the affection/obsession he did express seem hollow and salesman-like, which could have, in turn, made Apter seem . . . oily. Sleazy.

And to express none of his affection/obsession for/with Gladman's work was not an option: without it, the anecdotes simply wouldn't have cohered.

Besides, Apter *wanted* Gladman to know that his work had been important to him.

Wanted Gladman to know *him.*

That's why he told him the anecdotes to begin with.

Simultaneously, then, he had to, while telling the anecdotes, guard against:

1) appearing sycophantic,
2) appearing falsely flattering/ulteriorly motivated,
3) appearing too concerned with appearing sycophantic or falsely flattering/ulteriorly motivated, and
4) sounding slight or disrespectful in the course of deploying the narrative and rhetorical strategies that ostensibly guarded against items 1, 2, and 3.

He had to do all of that *and* he had to be—and, it should be said, *wanted* to be (just as any conscientious storyteller has to be and wants to be, but especially when the one-person audience for the story he's telling is an all-time master storyteller himself, and even more especially when that all-time master storyteller's storytelling sensibilities are precisely the storytelling sensibilities the conscientious storyteller has spent his entire storytelling life attempting to make his own)—*engaging,* if not downright entertaining.

He really wanted Gladman to like him.

Another complicating factor was Daphne Bourbon.

Gladman still hadn't mentioned Daphne, let alone her death, so Apter had to assume he didn't want to talk about Daphne.

And Apter had to assume that if he was correct—i.e. if Gladman didn't want to talk about Daphne—then Gladman didn't want to think about Daphne either. Or didn't want to think about her there, in Apter's presence.

Whether Gladman may have, in some way, needed to talk about Daphne—whether or not Gladman's talking about Daphne could have been *helpful* to Gladman—was not for Apter to judge. It wasn't for anyone to judge but Gladman, and maybe Gladman's therapist, if Gladman had a therapist, which was none of Apter's business. Apter wasn't that therapist. Apter was a guest.

Moreover, Gladman looked to be in far better shape than he had the week before. His shave was even, his eyes were clear, the apartment was clean-ish, his energy was up. Perhaps he'd begun to climb out from his depression.

So, in order to respect Gladman's senses of self-determination and personal privacy, as well as to stay out of the way of the progress the man appeared to be making with his grief, Apter not only refrained from referring to Daphne Bourbon but did his best to refrain from referring to anything that might evoke Daphne Bourbon or the kinds of feelings he imagined Gladman must have had for her.

In addition, then, to taking the obvious precaution of avoiding all mention of his specific admiration for any of Gladman's many stellar Daphne-focused stand-up bits, Apter repeatedly stifled his oft-felt impulse to praise Sylvie Klein's beauty and intelligence, and, inasmuch as it was possible, generally played down Sylvie's importance to him, the intensity of the feelings he had for her, and the degree to which those feelings determined so much of the behavior described—and so many of the outcomes arrived at—in the anecdotes.

Then, of course, there was Gogol. Gogol as object, subject, and subject matter. Both the rhythm and the shape of Apter's anecdotes were altered by the parrot numerous times.

Within moments of Apter's having told Gladman that he'd attended SSA, Gogol, still perched on Apter's hand, lowered her rump and shit on the floor. It wasn't nearly as disgusting as it was funny, or, for that matter, as it was weirdly *classy.* The seeming ease and unself-consciousness with which the bird adjusted her posture, obeyed nature's call, and returned to first position without missing a beat—without even slightly averting her gaze . . .

She'd shown the poise of a world-renowned diplomat.

Of an allied nation's foremost diplomat swallowing a belch in the middle of a sentence she was speaking at a dinner being hosted at the White House to honor her visit.

Or something like that.

After Gladman had wiped up the dropping with a paper towel and a spritz from a bottle of something called PoopAway, he brought from his office a portable perch—a piece of T-shaped driftwood glued stem-down to a melamine serving tray—and set it atop the table between them. He suggested that Apter bring the hand that Gogol was standing on near and parallel to the perch's crossbar. "Now tell her, 'Step up,'" Gladman said.

Apter did as advised, but Gogol wouldn't climb onto the perch.

He said, "Step up," again, this time with the stress on the *up*, and Gogol muttered, "Step up," but remained on his hand.

"She really doesn't want to let go," Gladman said. "Here's what you do: first, you put your other hand over her like this."

Apter, making sure to initiate the movement from below and in front of the bird, covered Gogol's neck and spine with his hand as shown.

Immediately, Gogol, reaching sideways with her left foot, wrapped her toes around the base of his thumb, then reached in the opposite direction with her right foot and wrapped her toes around his pinky's middle knuckle.

"Now just lift," Gladman said. "You don't have to squeeze or anything, okay? Just lift her up and kind of lower her over the perch. Good. Great. Now start spreading your fingers, so she loses her grip."

As Apter's digits slipped free of Gogol's grasp, she let her feet—first the left, then the right—fall onto the perch, and grabbed hold.

"You're really cooperative," Apter told her.

Gogol mumbled a series of muffled, throaty syllables.

Unlike, say, a dog or a cat or even a toddler probably would have, Gogol seemed to be under the impression that Apter's anecdotes were being told, whether in part or in whole, for her benefit. She didn't just stand there on her driftwood perch and "allow the adults to talk." She kept her eyes on Apter when Apter was speaking, turned to face Gladman when Gladman spoke, made frequent dipping movements of her head and upper body that suggested she was nodding in agreement with what was being said, shook her tailfeathers and sometimes pronounced, "Good birdie!" when either man laughed, occasionally did a kind of whole-body shivering thing—*quaking* was the word for it, according to Gladman, who explained it was a neurological peculiarity of the species—and, during any pause in speech that lasted more than a second or two, emitted more of those aforementioned muffled, throaty syllables, as if she thought it was her turn to speak.

Gogol seemed, in other words, to think of herself as an *active member of the audience.*

This was all very charming, Apter found, and sometimes—and increasingly—distracting.

Increasingly, Apter found himself paying attention to—and, in some sense, *measuring,* and even, to one degree or another, *responding to*—Gogol's reactions to the various sounds of his voice, the movements of his hands, the angle of his head in relation to his shoulders, the quality of his laughter.

That is: increasingly, Apter found himself thinking of Gogol as though she *were* an active member of the audience. As someone he was, in some sense, performing for.

Somewhere in the middle of Anecdote 3, Apter paused to drink the last sip from the glass of whiskey that Gladman had poured him in the middle of Anecdote 2. He'd underestimated how much was left in the glass, the whiskey wrong-piped him, and by the time he'd finished coughing (which Gogol had mimicked, which had made Apter laugh more, and in turn made him cough more), he'd forgotten where he'd left off prior to the sip. "So where was I?" he said and, while trying to remember, he chewed at his lip and absently started cracking his knuckles.

Craning her neck, Gogol opened her beak and showed Apter her tongue. It was bubblegum pink and narrow and smooth—no visible buds or lines—and looked dry. Clean.

"What a creature," said Apter.

"She's a weirdo, all right," Gladman said. "Crack a couple knuckles in earshot, she yawns."

Apter tried to ask, "Why?" but, although he hadn't initially registered Gogol's behavior as a yawn, having heard Gladman say the word *yawn* triggered the yawning reflex, and he yawned, cutting off the "Why?" before he was able to pronounce the vowel.

Apter's yawn caused Gladman to yawn, which in turn caused Gogol to yawn a second time, which set the men off yawning a second time, which set off a third and final round of yawning.

"No idea why she does it," Gladman said at last. "I didn't train her to or anything. My best guess is she's got some kind of TMJ thing in her beak and when she opens it wide like that, the sound she hears is like knuckles cracking and she thinks we're able to hear it, too—thinks she's mimicking us, that is. Impossible to say, though. A riddle wrapped in a mystery inside an enigma, she."

"You keep saying *she*," Apter said. "I've been saying *he*. I thought—"

"So did I," Gladman said. "Funny story, actually."

"I love a funny story."

"Well, thing is," Gladman said, "Quakers, unlike a lot of other species of birds—Mallard ducks for example—Quakers aren't what's called *sexually dimorphic*. Which means you can't tell by looking at them—Quakers, that is—whether they're male or female. There aren't any markers. There's a test you can do, a DNA test I think, but it requires a blood sample, and they don't clot so easily, birds, which maybe makes it a little dangerous, the test. A little traumatic for the bird either way, 'cause the pain from the needle. Plus, the test isn't cheap. It's more expensive than Gogol was. So if you adopt your bird before, say, you've finished—let alone before you've sold—your first novel, and your only income is from adjunct teaching, you might think, 'Fuck it. What's the sex matter anyway?' So you might skip the test. Just assume the sex is the same as the sex of the Russian after whom you named the bird. That's what I did, at least. So for fifteen years, I think Gogol's male. A little brother. But then, the past few days, she laid a clutch of eggs. Yesterday I found those eggs. All along, my little brother was my little sister. Surprising, you know? For me, I mean. Bizarre. Biologically, though, I guess it's not that bizarre. Or surprising. See, I haven't clipped her wings in a very long time. They haven't been grown-in even close to this much since before she reached sexual maturity. These last couple months—it's the first time she's been fully flighted since before I even met, uh . . . Or . . . Well, rather, let's say, since, before you—if I'm doing the math right—since before you ever got the scar on your face. Anyway, it's the first time she's been able to fly while also being able to reproduce, and, if I've understood what I've read correctly, the release of the breeding or mating hormones or whatever they are—the chemicals inside her that trigger egg-laying—get curbed or diminished or . . . I'm obviously not a biologist. What I'm saying is, it isn't all that strange for a virgin, female middle-aged bird that hasn't been fully flighted in years to suddenly start laying eggs once she *does* become fully flighted. Which doesn't, however, mean it's any good. For her. It takes a toll. Wears her out physically. Maybe psychologically, too—I mean, these eggs, obviously, aren't gonna hatch. So I'm thinking that if I clip her wings, she'll probably stop laying. That's what my book on parrots says."

"But you don't want to clip them," Apter said.

"I really *do* want to clip them," Gladman said. "Her being flighted—I like the idea of it. It's a nice idea. If you're capable of flying, having that capacity taken away from you must be—it's a shame . . . But it's dangerous for her. She just isn't very good at flying. She hasn't had much practice. Not in years. And even birds who are good at flying—it isn't safe for them to fly around indoors. They get spooked by something, sail off through the air, mistake a window for a block of sky, and get banged up—maybe break something, maybe their necks. Their bones are hollow, you know? They break really easy. Not clipping her—it's irresponsible of me. I've been a shitty older brother. And now, with the eggs . . . I gotta just do it. I need help, is the thing."

Apter didn't know what *helping* could mean here. He feared, in a vague way, what it might entail. Pain? Blood? Getting bitten again? He had no idea.

But inasmuch as there wasn't anything especially funny or storylike about the "funny story" he'd just been told—by a man who, if nothing else, certainly knew how to tell a funny story—Apter couldn't avoid suspecting that Gladman, in so expansively dumping all those parrot factoids on him, had all along, however clumsily, been working him up sideways into offering his help, and, if such help *wouldn't* entail some measure of unpleasantness or difficulty, why should Gladman have felt he had to work him up to offering it? Why take the long way around the barn? Why *make a case*? Why not just ask? Apter didn't like it.

Still, this wasn't just anyone seeking his help. This was Solomon Gladman seeking his help. And his wife was dead and he wouldn't (couldn't?) say her name. And he seemed kind of anxious. He seemed to have paled a bit.

So Apter said, "Could *I* help you clip her?"

Turned out wing-clipping was neither difficult nor unpleasant. Didn't seem like it needed to be a two-person job, either.

Maybe Gladman just wasn't feeling well or something.

Maybe he'd been anxious about something other than the clipping.

Or maybe—and this was probably the simplest explanation of all—Gladman was a geek, pure and simple. A bird geek. Maybe Apter, because he held Gladman in such high esteem, had been reluctant to imagine—and thereby late to discover—that Gladman was a bird geek, and so had mistaken signs of Gladman's (over-) enthusiasm for symptoms of anxiety. Maybe all that had happened over the preceding few minutes was that Gladman, as would have any geek allowed half a chance to hold forth at length on the subject matter that his geekery encompassed, had seen his opening and suchly held forth.

Anyway, clipping Gogol was easy. Took about three minutes.

Gladman got a pair of scissors from the knife drawer, handed them to Apter, grabbed the parrot off the perch like a baseball with his right hand, removed his thumb from her grip so that both her feet grabbed one finger—"The ring finger," he pointed out to Apter, for no reason Apter was able to discern—and then, with his just-freed thumb held over her back in order to keep her from flying away, he used the fingers of his left hand to spread her left wing. He told Apter to open and arrange the blades of the scissors on either side of the blue feathers ("The blues are the flight feathers," Gladman said) right along the line where they started peeking out from under the green feathers, double-check to make sure that Gogol's feet ("And this is very important.") were still grasping Gladman's ring finger—that her nearer foot was *not* ("I repeat.") reaching into the feathers—and close the blades ("Like you mean it.") decisively.

Which Apter did.

Blue feather tips sailed down onto the floor.

Gogol didn't seem to notice.

Gladman set her down on the perch, picked her back up with his left hand, and he and Apter did the same with her right wing as they'd done with her left.

Same result.

"Last part," said Gladman, "is I drop her on the floor."

"Why?"

"Because that whole thing we just did was painless for her. She might not realize she's unable to fly now. When I drop her, she'll try to fly, and realize she can't—she can't get any lift anymore—and that the best the flapping of her wings can do now is slow the fall. From this height, she can't hurt herself when she lands, but from higher up she could. Hurt herself. So I do this right now, and, later, if she's somewhere high and wants to leave that place, she'll remember she can't fly, and she'll know not to jump. Or at least she'll know not to jump till she's closer to the ground."

"How would she get that high to begin with, though? If she can't fly, I mean."

"She's a phenomenal climber," Gladman said.

He dropped the bird. She let out a scream and flapped her wings, which slowed her fall, but couldn't prevent it.

While Gladman swept up the fallen feather tips, Gogol demonstrated her climbing prowess. Climbed from the floor to Apter's shoe, climbed his shin till she got to his knee, tramp-limped her way along his thigh to his shirtfront, climbed the placket all the way to the collar, and from the collar stepped sideways onto his shoulder.

Although he wasn't as afraid of his face getting bitten as he had been earlier, he was warier of being shat on. "Step up," he told Gogol, and she refused to step up, so he grabbed her like a baseball and set her on the perch.

"You're good at that," said Gladman. He was washing his hands.

"Hell yeah. I'm a pro."

"No, really. You are. I mean, you didn't even have to look at her. Just grabbed. I'm impressed. Thanks for your help with the wings, by the way. You deserve another whiskey. You want another whiskey?"

"Only if you'll join me."

Ignoring the condition Apter'd set forth, or, perhaps, having misunderstood "join me" to mean "join me once again at the table," or maybe not even having heard the condition over the sound of the running water, Gladman, after shutting the tap and drying his hands, got a bottle from the cabinet, sat down at the table, and poured one for Apter. "So you were telling me," he said, "that Bernie lost the primary, and you didn't think Hillary needed your money."

"Right."

"Can I guess what happens next?"

"Sure."

"You became disillusioned with electoral politics and decided the only way to really make a difference in the world was to help individuals one at a time, so you went to SSA to become a therapist."

"Maybe sort of?" Apter said. "Not exactly, though. No."

That the jumping-off point for Apter's telling of the anecdotes had been his having told Gladman that he'd ended up studying with Nathan Booth because Gladman had gone to SSA was yet another major reshaper of the anecdotes.

Having begun so near to the end of his overall story not only required Apter (i.e. in order to keep things interesting) to splice his fifth (i.e. longest) anecdote into a kind of frame narrative to and from which the other anecdotes sprung and backstepped, but rather substantially bent the arcs of both Anecdotes 4 and 5.

More specifically:

Inasmuch as Apter's decision to study at SSA had always played a large part in Anecdote 4's resolution (the rest of that resolution entailing his extremely profitable sale of Ethereum, and founding of Antic Books with his sister), and inasmuch as Apter's decision to quit working as a therapist played an even larger part in Anecdote 5's resolution, the thrills that Apter's previous interlocutors had ostensibly derived from finding out how the previous versions of Anecdotes 4 and 5 would end could not be counted on to materialize here, for Gladman already pretty much knew how the anecdotes ended: he knew from the start that Apter'd gone to SSA, and he knew, by virtue of Apter's being in his kitchen to represent the interests of City Hall and the Endeavor Talent Agency, that Apter was no longer a therapist.

Furthermore—as Apter discovered only in the course of telling this chopped-up, rearranged, frame-story version of it—Anecdote 5 had a different, far more decisive ending than it used to.

Whereas, previously, the end of Anecdote 5 had seen Apter wistfully gazing upon Millennium Park's Crown Fountain through a hotel window, going to the Gage to eat steak frites, reading Gladman's "Melancholy Sally Drops," and somewhat reluctantly deciding to abandon his career as a therapist in favor of (rather, *presumably* in favor of—it was never all that clear in the earlier tellings) contending more directly with the meaninglessness of life while paying less attention to people he did not love, now the anecdote ended with his *most recent telling* of the anecdote.

That is: now Anecdote 5 ended with his having told the previous versions of Anecdotes 1–5 to Reggie Glibner at the Rainbo, back in November, and being hired on the spot to work for the mayor.

Last, and perhaps most dramatically of all (most dramatically for Apter, that is):

Apter realized, just as he came to the end of telling Anecdote 5 to Gladman, that Anecdote 5 was no longer his final anecdote.

Anecdote 6, like the version of Anecdote 5 told to Gladman, ended with its own telling. But Apter hadn't understood, when telling Glibner Anecdote 5—which had, after all, been his final anecdote when he was telling it to Glibner—that doing so would eventually become the end of that anecdote.

Whereas he *did* understand that his sixth anecdote—which i) began when he came to work for the mayor and thereby became the mayor's right hand, and ii) middled when he agreed to help Ari and Perry raise money for Mount Chicago via Day Zero and thereby wound up contacting Gladman—ended right there in Gladman's kitchen (or, rather, was, as he told it, *about to end* right there in Gladman's kitchen), where, in the course of conveying the first five anecdotes to Gladman, he'd concluded (almost passively—it was more like he "realized he had already concluded") that, whether or not Gladman agreed to open Day Zero, the process of trying to get Gladman to do so had so far been so very thrilling for him (he was sitting in his lifelong hero's kitchen, laughing with him, perhaps becoming his friend) that only a fool wouldn't realize how much he would enjoy being a talent agent, and that he *wasn't* a fool, and that therefore he would, after Day Zero, move to Los Angeles and work at Endeavor.

Once Apter'd finished, Gladman said, "I like that," and poured himself, at last, a neat whiskey. "I really like how you ended that," he said. "How you brought it all together. You tell a good story. A good *bunch* of stories. I'm glad you came by. You almost make a guy want to try something new, you know? Seize opportunity. Change his life."

"Sure," Apter said. "That's me all over. Your friendly neighborhood archaic torso of Apollo."

"No, I mean it," Gladman said. "It's hard to say this kind of thing—at least for me—without sounding arch, or like I'm setting up a punchline, I know that, but that's just . . . my voice, I guess. You've really given me a sense of hope here, Apter. Inspired me. Jesus. Even to me, that sounds sappy. Probably it is. Nonetheless: true. *The case*. You're gonna be a great talent agent, man. You already are. You've convinced me, anyway. I'm gonna try to do Day Zero."

"No shit?" Apter said.

"None. Well, actually, ha, kind of a lot of shit. See, to do this, I need your help with Gogol."

"With Gogol."

"Well, I mean, you know I never schedule a performance in advance. I only ever get onstage when I'm in the mood. Sometimes I've got a beginning, sometimes even an ending, but that middle part, the majority of what I do . . . it's all improvised. So I worry that, come Day Zero, I won't feel it. So what I want to do is try a different approach. I want to write my whole act instead of just improvising. I don't think I'll need long. A week, I'm thinking. Maybe two. And if I get anywhere promising, I'll commit to Day Zero. If that would be all right."

"Of course," Apter said.

"Good. So I need total quiet is the thing. If there's any hope of me succeeding, I need to be alone. Just at the start. Because I'm thinking that writing this act—it'll be more like writing fiction than anything else. And I can write fiction when Gogol's around just fine—I mean, it's actually pretty helpful, her being around—but I never got *started* writing fiction while she was around. First book, I hadn't adopted her yet, and after that one, everything else I started—well, everything else that ever got anywhere—I started while I was away from home."

"You want me to come feed Gogol while you go somewhere? I could do that, no problem. Just show me how."

"I don't want to go anywhere. That's the thing. I don't think . . . I don't even know where I'd go. I want to stay here to work on this. So what I was hoping—I was more hoping you could take Gogol to your place."

"Oh."

"I know it's a lot to ask, but, first of all, I'd pay you. *Handsomely*. I came into some money recently."

"I'm not worried about money, Mr. Gladman."

"Second, she really likes you, man. It's wild how much she likes you. I've never seen her so comfortable with anyone as she is with you. She really kinda can't stand most people, and I mean . . . I'm . . ." Gladman had taken his phone from his pocket, started to scroll it. "There it is. Okay. Look. I'm gonna show you something. It's a little bit disturbing, so don't get upset, but I don't know how else . . . So just . . ."

He showed Apter the phone, on the screen of which was this:

"That's not—?" Apter said. His throat had tightened, cracked his voice. He shoved the phone back across the table.

"It's her," Gladman said.

Apter turned to Gogol, healthy on her perch, and she tilted her head and squinted an eye—you'd almost think she was doing his i-smile—and she said, "Good birdie." Didn't scream it. Said it softly, as if to herself. Almost like a question.

"That's something parrots do," said Gladman. "In captivity. When they're anxious, or depressed. It's something they do to themselves. They pluck their own feathers out. And if there's nothing stopping them, then once all the feathers they can reach are all gone, they pluck right at the follicles. The follicles bleed. They can get infected. Sometimes the bird can bleed to death. Not that often, but sometimes. Also, they can destroy the follicles, and then: no more feathers. Ever. If she doesn't see me for a while—not even that long—she gets upset and she does this to herself. Some years back, I went out of town for a month. I paid my favorite student—a sweetheart of a person, biggest animal lover I've ever met—to come here and hang out with Gogol and feed her. That picture—that's from, I don't know, just, like, four or five *days* after I left. The student took her to the vet, got this spray, this medicinal spray, that got her to stop plucking, but it's like a cure-is-worse-than-the-disease kind of thing. Well, not *worse*. But close. Gogol *hates* that spray. You spray her, she just looks like . . . she becomes almost motionless. Stares down at her feet like . . . I don't know, man. Like, well—those clients you mentioned at the PHP. Overmedicated with antipsychotics. *Lost.* It's fucking terrible. Anyway, she didn't like my student the way she likes you. Except for me, there's no one around who she likes the way she likes you. Believe me, if there were, I would ask *them* to take her. I mean, I feel like I kinda know you, like I know you enough to know you're a *mensch,* but I know I don't really know you enough to ask you for a favor like this. It's a lot to ask. And I'm sorry I had you look at that picture. That was really heavy-handed. Manipulative. I shouldn't have done that. But Day Zero—I really want to do it. I haven't wanted to do much—*anything*—in a while, and I really want to do it, and I want to get started as soon as possible, and I know I can't with Gogol here. I'm sorry I showed you the picture. That was just shitty of me. Too much. I guess I wanted to explain, and I didn't want to falsely advertise and . . . I don't know."

"What if you're wrong about how much she likes me?" Apter said. "What if I take her to my place and she starts mutilating herself?"

"First thing you'd do is spray her with this horrible stuff she hates that I'd give you. That'd get her to stop for six or seven hours. It always does. Next thing you'd do is contact me, and I'd get in the car, pick her up, bring her back here, and that'd be that. I don't want her to hurt herself any more than you do. It's the last thing I want."

"You'd come get her."

"Immediately," Gladman said.

"Okay. And what about the screaming? Not that 'I'm flying' screaming—that sucks a little, but whatever. That alarm screaming she did the other day. When I buzzed. I've got neighbors."

"That's the only time she really does that," Gladman said. "When she hears that buzzer. I couldn't promise you she wouldn't get freaked out by something at your place and do that scream. Usually, though, you can just move her cage to a different part of the apartment, and she stops. Buzzer's the only thing that never worked for. But all of that to say that, if that were to happen—that terrible scream—and you couldn't get her to stop, you'd just let me know, and same deal: I'd come by and get her."

Gladman showed him what to feed her, how to spray her with DON'T! if she plucked, and how to cover her cage at night.

A fabric box on the floor of the cage contained the eggs. Gladman twisted the box's open side shut, wound a rubber band around it, and said Apter should open it after getting home, then leave it be.

He took the cage off its stand, set it on the floor, folded the stand, laid the stand atop the cage.

He placed a two-pound bag of pellets and a Ziploc full of almonds in a file box alongside a bottle of DON'T!, a bottle of PoopAway, a tiny jar of styptic powder, and a paperback titled *Every Parrot Owner's Guide to His or Her Parrot* ("in case you're interested").

From the closet in the hallway, he brought out a navy-blue jersey-knit top sheet to use to cover the cage at night ("if you want to"), rolled it up, and jammed it into the file box.

On the fridge was a magnet with Gogol's vet's emergency contact info on it. He took it off the fridge and tossed it into the file box.

He cleaned the droppings from the driftwood perch's melamine tray, set Gogol on his shoulder, jammed the driftwood perch inside the file box, and closed the file box.

He dropped two almonds into the bowl of Gogol's carrier cage, filled its mounted dropper bottle with water, lowered Gogol inside the cage, closed the cage, and hailed a van with an app.

They brought the large cage and the stand and the file box down to Gladman's entrance hall. Then Gladman went up and got the carrier cage with Gogol in it and brought that down and handed it to Apter.

The van arrived. Gladman packed in the large cage, the stand, and the file box.

Apter got in the van with Gogol in the carrier cage in his lap. Gogol grumbled, "Hello," to the driver.

"I'll send you a photo after I get her set up," said Apter to Gladman.

"Apter," Gladman said, "you're my new favorite person. Thank you for doing this. I owe you big."

"You owe me a performance," Apter said.

"You'll have it. Another thing. I meant to say this before: you shouldn't feel shy about sending me forthcoming Antic books. For blurbs, I mean. If you want to, that is. I flipped out for *An Oral History of Man,* and *The Comer,* too. Your sister's got some taste."

"I'll tell Adi. She'll love that."

"Good. Tell her. And remember: anything comes up with Gogol these next few days, I'm available. Just call or text—whatever. I'll make sure my phone's on."

"Go in, now—you're freezing, man," Apter said. The wind had picked up, and Gladman had shivered, pulled his hood on, crumpled into himself.

"Bye, Gogol," said Gladman.

"Step up," Gogol said.

Wounded Birds.MP4

GLADMAN

So I've had this little parrot, Gogol, for going on fifteen years. Well, she's a *medium-size* parrot. According to, you know, parrot scientists.

If you met her, you'd think of her as little, though. Weighs ninety-one grams. That's a king-size Snickers bar. A little bit less. Minus her tail, she's the length of one, too.

Quaker parrot. That's the species. Also called a monk parakeet.

Once, when she was about a year old, I was clipping her wings—clipping the left wing—and, right when I started closing the scissor blades, she reached her foot back without me seeing, and I lopped off most of her smallest toe's claw.

At first I didn't even realize that anything had happened. She might not have either. But then . . . There was all this blood. All these tiny drops of blood had sprayed everywhere.

I didn't faint, I don't think, but it's good I was sitting. My vision tunneled, I remember that for sure. Whole kitchen blackening inward from the corners. And my face felt . . . *loose* or something. Freezing-cold hands. Pounding in the ears.

All that blood.

I thought she'd die.

Not an entirely crazy thought.

Parrots have a really hard time clotting. I guess all birds do. You read any book on how to care for a parrot, once a chapter, sometimes twice, it mentions how inefficiently their blood clots, how great a danger it is for them to bleed, how easy it is for them to bleed to death, even from just a tiny cut. Which makes some sense. The inefficiency, I mean.

These are wild animals.

Breeder I bought Gogol from told me Gogol's mom was born in captivity, like Gogol, but that *her* mom was taken from a nest somewhere down by the University of Chicago.

A lot of Quaker parrots live down there. They build these massive, intricate nests on electrical transformers. Stadium lights at ball fields, too. Any high-up, sturdy thing that gives off heat, they like to build the nests on.

In warmer climates, they build them in treetops.

Wherever they build them, these nests are remarkable. Got dozens of rooms. Sometimes more than a hundred—no kidding. They're like apartment buildings.

Each nuclear family gets an apartment nest. Three rooms. I'm not making this up. There's three rooms per family. There's a room in the back for the parents to fuck in and lay the eggs and feed the hatchlings, a room in the middle where the fledglings and older offspring hang out, and then the front room, which is more, I guess, like a kind of covered porch-slash-outhouse-slash–entry hall. They stand at the opening of that front room, keep an eye out for predators, and shit down onto the ground from there, too.

The nests are all made of sticks. Fallen twigs. Branches the Quakers chew off trees.

I saw a couple wild ones doing that in Spain once. They ripped this sprouting frond off a palm, stripped the leaves, shaped the ends of it, and bent it a little to get it to fit in the part of the nest they meant it for.

They spent like half an hour doing this together. Working on this one frond. I never saw anything like that. You see something like that, and . . . I don't know.

But the nests can get up to two hundred pounds or something, because, like I said, they have dozens of rooms in them. What happens is a couple Quakers pair off to mate, build their three-room apartment nest, and start a family. Then their kids, when they get to be about two years old, three years old, they either bring back a mate to the original nest and attach a new three-room apartment to it, or they go to the mate's original nest and attach a new three-room apartment to *that,* then start their own families. The nests can last decades.

In Chicago, they're considered a nuisance. Fire hazard. Every so often, ComEd clears them out. They're not supposed to kill the parrots when they do that, but it happens, I guess.

There's always some babies in the nest, and, during the removal, they fall or get crushed. Some of the grown ones get crushed, too. And some of the babies are still alive inside the nests when the nests get removed.

The whole flock gets really fucked up, basically, and there are some people—breeders, usually—who take it upon themselves to rescue the orphaned babies and also sometimes the injured adults.

Gogol's mother's mother was one of those—an abandoned baby or an injured adult. I don't know which. Either way: a wild animal.

A wild *prey* animal.

And that's probably why they're so bad at clotting, Quakers. There just aren't a lot of situations in the wild where, if they found themselves bleeding, clotting well would be much of an advantage. If they're bleeding, it's almost always because some predator's already tearing them apart.

So usually, when you buy a parrot, along with the food and the carrier cage, the breeder also sells you some styptic powder. Comes in a screw-top jar, this stuff. You put a little on a wound and it contracts the blood vessels, slows the bleeding. You have to use it sparingly, though, because it's toxic. You have to be really careful with it.

I don't know how long it took me to remember the styptic.

To remember I should use it.

Could've been thirty seconds since I closed the blades. Could've been sixty. Once I've remembered, though, my head stops swimming. I stop feeling faint. The frame rate's dropped, and my panic's begun to work for me a little. I've become the man of action in slo-mo.

Gogol's back on the kitchen table at this point.

Soon as I'd wounded her, I'd set her down, set her on the table, and then, probably because the pain from the injured claw surprised her when she put her weight down onto the foot, she'd jumped at me, onto me, onto my shirt—flapping her wings, spraying the blood around, these tiny drops of blood, spattering it onto my arms, my glasses—but then that must've hurt her, too, the clinging to my shirt, because she jumped back down, and now, like I said, she's standing there on the table in front of me again.

She's standing on the uninjured foot, holding the other one up and kind of forward the way she does when she waves hello, and this fat kind of bubble or, like, helmet of blood is covering over the top of the toe. And it's pulsing. Dripping. Pooling out on the table. And she seems like she's showing it to me, the toe. Like, "Look at this. Look what happened. What do we do now?"

Man of action in slo-mo, I know what to do. I know everything I'll do for the next twenty minutes. The whole order of operations. The blow-by-blow.

I'll get the jar of styptic from under the sink, open the jar, set it down on the table. I'll pick Gogol up, dip the toe in the jar, set her back on the table. Get the carrier cage from the closet, return to the kitchen, set the cage on the table and open it up. Set Gogol on the perch inside the cage, close the cage. Take the cage to the car, belt the cage to the passenger seat, start the car. Pull out of the spot, do a U, proceed west to Ashland Avenue. Take a right onto Ashland, take a left on North Avenue. Call the vet's office once I'm on North, tell them I'm coming, continue on North all the way to the office, double-park in front of the office. Unbelt the cage from the passenger seat, pick up the cage from the passenger seat. Take Gogol inside so the vet can save her life.

It's all laid out.

I start to follow through: I get the jar of styptic from under the sink, pick Gogol up, dip the toe in the jar, set her back on the table, go to the closet for the carrier cage.

All good.

But then, when I return to the kitchen, Gogol's got the toe in her beak. She's biting at the toe.

Gogol is *eating* the toxic blood-slowing powder.

That is: in addition to poisoning herself with the toxic blood-slowing powder, she's preventing the powder from slowing the flow of the blood from her toe.

She has to stop that, so I offer her an almond. Usually this gets her to quit whatever she's doing. She loves to eat an almond. It takes her a minute or two to eat one.

So I offer her an almond, she takes the almond from my hand with her beak—her beak is like half the size of the almond—then tries to take the almond from her beak with the injured foot, but *winces* when the injury touches the almond.

Then she sets the injured foot down, like to try, I guess, to stand on it so she can hold the almond in the uninjured foot. Winces when the injury touches the table. Raises the injured foot again. Drops the almond onto the table.

She's given up on the almond. Can't deal with the almond. To deal with an almond she needs both feet. One to hold it, and the other to stand on.

She's biting the toe again.

Poison.

Blood flow.

I make a big, angry sound. I punch the fridge.

Gogol, startled, stops biting at her toe. Goes on alert. Draws her head feathers in all flat against her skull so her eyes bug out.

Her beak is crusted with blood and styptic. There's hardly any styptic left on her toe.

I pick her up and she bites me. Hard. Puts a hole in the meat of my thumb. She's trying to escape me. Bites me a second time, then a third.

Any thought I may have had of reapplying the styptic— nixed. Even if I could calm her down long enough to dip the toe in the jar, what would be the point? She'd eat it again.

I don't reapply the styptic.

I shut her into the cage, and we go.

It's a fifteen-minute drive. She bleeds the whole time.

I keep looking over, and she's still on one leg. She won't make a sound, in fact hasn't made a sound since I lopped off the claw, is *completely* silent, which is not . . . it isn't usual at all.

And she keeps returning the toe to her beak. I keep on startling her to get her to stop—punching the steering wheel, slapping the seat, yelling loud as I can, "No!" and "Gogol!" and "Stop!" and "Fuck!" and every time I startle her, she leaves the toe alone, flattens the head feathers, bugs out the eyes, but after just a few seconds, the feathers unflatten, and the eyes go back to normal, the toe bubbles over with another dripping helmet of blood, and she's biting it again.

This was the really painful part. This drive, I mean.

I mean, *you* know Gogol doesn't die in the end. You've known that from the start. But me? I really didn't believe that she'd make it. At any moment, I thought, she'd lose too much blood, or the poison she ate would stop her heart, and she'd wobble and sway and fall down dead.

And it wasn't just that I was losing her and knew how bad I'd miss her, this young animal who I'd spent hours every day hanging out with for months, who I'd planned to continue hanging out with for decades.

Wasn't just that it'd be my fault, either—that she'd die because of my carelessness, my momentary inattention.

All of that was there, sure. Of course it was. I was dreading her loss, dreading the guilt and regret I knew I'd feel when she died, but that dread was in the background.

The real terror in the car—the immediate terror, the *special* terror—came from knowing I was making death harder for her.

See, I was certain that Gogol knew she was dying. That that had to be why she'd gotten so quiet. Because she knew. Animals know, right? They know when they're dying, and that's what they do: they go quiet and try to make themselves small. Try not to be noticed. They go off to die alone if they can.

And I wasn't only *not* letting Gogol go off to die alone, I was making her suffer more. Making her painful, protracted, untimely death—already the single worst thing there is—making the worst thing there is even worse. I was *startling* her. Repeatedly startling her. Frightening her, again and again. At, like, ten-second intervals. Five-second intervals.

Me.

I was doing that. One of the only people she loved.

Maybe *the* only person she loved. The only animal.

Or maybe *love* sounds precious. Melodramatic. It could be. Might be. She's a wild animal, raised in captivity—who knows if she can love? Who knows what she understands of our relationship? Who knows what *I* understand of our relationship?

Could be Gogol thinks I'm her father. Or mother. Her sibling or a mate.

Hell, she might even think I'm a bird. She hasn't hung out with birds since she was six weeks old. She might think we're the same.

She might think she's a person.

I retract the word *love.*

Trust, though. . . . Whatever else Gogol thought or felt about me, I was one of the only people she trusted. The one she trusted most. And that's demonstrable. It's got nothing to do with me anthropomorphizing her—or with her maybe *avio-morphizing* me or however you'd say it.

It isn't precious.

Listen: she's a wild animal, a *prey animal,* who lets me hold her even though I could crush every bone in her body by squeezing no harder than I squeeze a mug of coffee in the morning. Lets me hold her in my hand whenever I want even though I have a mouth. Even though I have teeth. She's seen me use them—my hands and my teeth. She's seen me halve fistfuls of uncooked spaghetti. She's seen me chew almonds. Seen me bite into *chicken.*

Love or no love, I'm the person who Gogol trusts the most, and while we're in the car on the way to the vet, and while I believe she's about to die, and while I believe she *knows* she's about to die, the one thing she keeps doing is biting at her wound, and so you have to figure that biting at the wound must grant her some pain relief, provide her some comfort, that she wouldn't keep on biting at the wound if biting at the wound didn't lessen her suffering. Yet I keep on interfering. Inciting panic. Compounding her fear. Rattling her cage. Punching the steering wheel. Making violent noises and horrifying faces with my mouth full of teeth.

Making it so that the last things Gogol will ever experience, on top of all the pain and discomfort of her fatal injury, are fright and confusion, torture and trauma, and, maybe worst of all, a sense of betrayal.

Among the last thoughts she'll ever have will be that she'd been mistaken. Tricked. That all her life she'd been misled. That the being she trusted most in the world turned out to be a total fucking monster.

Or worse than *that,* she won't feel betrayed, won't think I'm a monster; instead she'll die thinking I'm *angry* at her, angry for reasons she doesn't understand—if she understood, she'd stop biting at the claw, right?—she'll die trying to figure out what's made me so angry, this person she trusts more than anyone else.

And she'll fail.

What else could I do, though? I couldn't think of anything else to do. One moment you've got just enough blood in your body to live, next moment you lose a drop and you're done. One moment you've got just enough hope in you to act, the next moment you lose a drop and you're static. Or maybe I've got that reversed, that second part: maybe going static *makes* you lose the hope. Either way, I didn't know what else I could do. I had to keep the crucial last drops in circulation.

So I kept on startling her all the way to the clinic.

Eventually we got there, the vet cleaned her off, applied more styptic, fed her a drug that made her too sleepy to bite at the claw, and the claw stopped bleeding, and Gogol lived.

Claw grew back inside a couple of months.

Gogol seemed to forget the whole episode. Behaved the same as always toward me.

Not really much of a story, I guess. It was good enough for a while, though, I think.

Good enough till it started slowing down.

Love, trust, feelings, and so forth.

It started slowing down, then it ended too abruptly.

Ended how you knew it would from the start.
Everything was fine at last.

Story used to be better, though. I swear.

I mean, it was always the same story, always detailed the same events, and always ended with everything being fine at last, but I used to *tell* it better.

I did.

I'd almost retraumatize myself while describing that miserable ride to the vet's, and people'd notice how upset I got—hear some shift in my voice or see a look that came across my face or whatever—and they'd be moved by that, and feel they'd heard a good story.

Anyway, for twelve-thirteen years, that was the story of the single worst day of my life.

Which: I know. Pretty lucky life, right? You make it to middle age, and the worst day of your life is a day you thought you might have accidentally killed your pet, but then everything turned out fine at last—pet survived, thrived, etcetera—that must be a pretty lucky life.

It was. I was lucky. No denying it. Never tried to deny it. I was glad to be lucky.

That bothers some people.

Has bothered some people.

Some of them—some of the people it bothers, I mean—are less lucky than I was.

But a surprisingly large proportion of those who are bothered by my luck are just as lucky as I was. In some cases more lucky.

These bothered people, I've noticed, are people who think that by listening to a story, they're doing the storyteller a favor, or, you know, granting the storyteller a "privilege."

They don't really like hearing stories, these people.

They like *having heard* stories, some of them, but they don't really like hearing them.

And they're *always* bad at telling stories, themselves.

Which only follows.

How can you be any good at something you don't know how to enjoy?

All my life, I've stayed away from them as best I could, those people. I dislike people who aren't good at telling stories.

You do, too. I'd stake Gogol's life on it. You don't like those people, either. Even if you're one of them.

Not that you'd know you were one of them.

But not even those people who don't like to hear stories like people who aren't good at telling stories, I'm saying. And when I'm feeling all right, that seems like a curious riddle. Worth a think. The rest of the time . . .

Perhaps I'm getting off track.

That's not a rhetorical *perhaps*.

I'm not sure getting off track is possible here.

I mean, you probably know this already, but in case you don't: these are some of the last words I'll ever speak.

I don't trust I can fully get my head around that—the position it puts you in. The position your position puts me in.

Our relative positions.

I can't tell whether the value of what I'm saying here is—or will be—increased or decreased by my suicide.

Like, on one hand, you might think, "This is the suicidal Gladman: he isn't thinking straight."

On the other hand, you might think, "This is the truest Gladman: the Gladman who, knowing he's about to die, has no reason to kid himself, let alone dissemble for an audience."

On yet another hand, there's, "This is the novelist/comedian Gladman who, knowing he's about to kill himself, is herein making a final attempt to manage his—ick—artistic legacy."

—

Could be I'm none of those Gladmans right now.

Or all of them.

Could be that I shouldn't have even mentioned any of them, which could indicate I've become a Gladman who isn't very good at telling stories. So far, there's some pretty solid evidence for that.

Not for me to know, I guess. Hard to know what you're able to know about yourself.

Ever since the anomaly, though, I've thought of myself as having been a number of Gladmans.

Three. That's the number.

Three different Gladmans. Each one of these Gladmans as distinct from the other two Gladmans as he is from just about any other living person: each Gladman distinguished from the other two Gladmans by what he most recently considered the worst day of his life.

And now that I've said so, maybe I've lived, from your point of view, as *two* Gladmans: this Gladman who's talking right now being a Gladman who thinks he's no more similar to the Gladmans he was before the anomaly than he is to just about any other living person, and the earlier Gladman being the Gladman who used to understand himself as a more holistic, continuous Gladman. That wouldn't be unreasonable of you, I guess.

However you might prefer to think of it, though—however you might prefer to think of *me*—the way *I* see it is that, like I said, I've experienced life as *three* distinct Gladmans.

There's the current Gladman—the one speaking to you—the worst day of whose life was 11/17, when his wife, parents, sisters, nieces, and nephew all died at once.

There's the previous Gladman, the worst day of whose life was the day I started out talking about: the day twelve-thirteen years back when he thought he'd accidentally killed his parrot.

And then there's the Gladman prior to the previous Gladman. The original Gladman. Gladman prime. The worst day of *his* life happened about fifteen years before the Gladman who thought he'd killed his parrot thought he'd killed his parrot. I'll describe that in a minute.

First, though, so as not to create any confusion, I want to acknowledge that I'm discounting someone you might think should count as a fourth Gladman. The child me, ages zero to seventeen years and some change.

I don't think about him much, or even want to. He's just not that interesting to me. He doesn't count.

That kid was never called Gladman, anyway. At least not by any non–gym teacher, he wasn't. That kid was just Solly.

He almost might as well have been anyone, Solly.

Any Jew anyway.

Or any random Jewish schoolkid in America between, say, the first Intifada and 9/11.

Or maybe I'm wrong. I mean, I know for sure that *he* wouldn't have liked to be described that way, but . . .

Look, I barely even remember the boy.

I remember the day he stopped being Solly, though. The day he became the original Gladman.

Worst day of the original Gladman's life.

Solly had the house to himself that day. That week.

Solly's parents had gone out of town with his sisters on the annual springtime family trip to wherever his father had a business conference. Phoenix. Orlando. Some place like that.

Even though he hadn't wanted to join them on vacation— even though he'd had to argue hard and loud to convince them not to force him to join them—his parents must have felt bad about going without him: for takeout and gas, they'd left him two hundred dollars.

Twice, probably, what they thought he would need.

Three or even four times what Solly thought he'd need. He didn't like to eat, ate little more than one meal per day, preferred both the most popular stimulants to food, and, in 1994, in Chicago's northern suburbs, you could get a pack of Marlboros for under two dollars, a bottomless coffee for a dollar twenty-five, and a roll of antacids for fifty-nine cents.

LSD cost five bucks a hit. Solly bought a ten-strip to share with his friends. Each tab had the logo for McDonald's printed on it—the golden arches—but instead of being yellow, the arches were brown.

Cinnamon Arches, the dealer, Armen Arakelyan, said it was called. But Armen himself called the acid *Darches* because the color of the arches reminded Armen of the color of diarrhea, and *Darches,* he said, was like a shortened version of *Diarrhea Arches.*

This really cracked Armen up when he explained it.

Not so much Solly.

Which Armen pointed out. Said that Solly didn't seem to think *Darches* was funny.

Armen was Solly's most reliable connection for acid, so Solly said that, no, he *did* think *Darches* was funny. Just not laugh-out-loud funny. He liked the *idea* of it, but maybe the execution wasn't quite . . . Like, for example, wouldn't maybe *Dire Arches* be a funnier thing to call the acid than *Darches* since *Dire Arches* already sounded enough like *diarrhea* that it wouldn't need to be explained to come across?

Armen didn't think so. Whatever *Darches* might lose in subtlety, he said, it made up for in sound. The sound of *Darches* was funnier than the sound of *Dire Arches.* Plus *dire* was already a "real word," and it meant pretty much the opposite of *funny.*

Solly said Armen made a good point—that probably the only reason *Darches* hadn't cracked him up to begin with was that he'd never been a connoisseur of toilet humor. He'd always been more of a dick-joke guy.

Armen pursed his lips sideways and said, "Sound *pers*onal."

—

Pursing your lips sideways and saying, "Sound *pers*onal" was, at that time, supposed to be a mildly hostile but also mildly funny way to close out a topic of conversation. It meant roughly the same thing as *TMI* would come to mean some years later.

Black people who pursed their lips sideways and said, "Sound *pers*onal" did it for one kind of laugh, and non-Black people did it for a different kind of laugh that had its origins in anti-Black sentiment, pro-Black exoticism, an admiration for Black English, or a condescending attitude toward Black English, which all might have been, at base, the same thing, or might not have.

Hard to say in general.

Impossible with Armen.

Armen was a goof.

Maybe also a prick.

Solly didn't really know him. They weren't really friends.

Anyway, when he pursed his lips sideways and said, "Sound *pers*onal" to close out the topic of conversation, Armen may have been implying that preferring dick jokes to toilet humor was a sign of homosexuality, and that homosexuality was distasteful to him.

But considering their socioeconomic background and the music they listened to and the way they cut their hair, Armen was more likely implying that preferring dick jokes to toilet humor was a sign of *closeted* homosexuality, and it was *closeted* homosexuality that was distasteful to him.

Most likely of all, Armen was archly *pretending* to imply that he was the kind of guy who found homosexuality distasteful. The kind of right-wing jock-type guy who did *not* listen to the kind of music Armen and Solly listened to or cut his hair the way Armen and Solly cut theirs, and who Armen had contempt for.

This is just me talking, here, though.

Unpacking the moment.

I mean, Solly didn't think about any of that stuff when Armen pursed his lips sideways and said, "Sound *pers*onal."

When Armen pursed his lips sideways and said, "Sound *pers*onal," Solly changed the subject.

He asked Armen whether the Darches were speedy.

Armen told him he'd heard the Darches were a little bit speedy, but that he couldn't say for sure because he hadn't tried them. For the past couple weeks, he'd been *cleansing,* he said.

Now, Solly *did* think a bit about Armen's use of *cleansing.*

That is: what Armen meant by *cleansing* was more or less clear to Solly, but Solly'd never heard the word used that way before.

The way Solly'd usually heard *cleansing* used was on the heels of *ethnic,* and Solly acknowledged that by making a crack about understanding why Armen wouldn't want to take acid while cleansing: something about how committing genocide was a lot more fun a thing to do when you were sober, and how the last time he'd committed genocide on acid all the screaming had really annoyed him, and *the smells* . . . Jesus.

Which Armen said he didn't think was funny at all. He said it wasn't cool to joke around about genocide. He was, he told Solly, part Native American.

And Solly asked Armen whether Armen was serious.

And Armen said his grandma was half-Pottawatomie, then looked at his pager and said he had to jet.

Solly found the end of this exchange both comical and weirdly enraging enough that he wrote down the reasons in his little steno pad when he went outside to smoke his next cigarette.

I still have the steno, so I'm just gonna read from it.

"One. Anyone telling anyone it isn't 'cool' to joke about anything.

"Two. A non-Jew telling a Jew it isn't 'cool' to joke about genocide.

"Three. An Armenian with a name more Armenian than my name is Jewish acting offended by a genocide crack not because he's Armenian but because he's 'part Native American.'

"Four. A guy who wanted to abbreviate the phrase *Diarrhea Arches* and couldn't even come up with *Dire Arches* believing his opinion on what's funny should matter.

"Five. Still rocking 'Sound *pers*onal' with the lips however many months later.

"Six. 'Cleansing' for 'staying sober' is precious and pretentious and overdramatic. Like 'loving her' for 'fucking her' or 'pastry' for 'cupcake.' No. 'Pastry' for 'donut.' 'Pasta au gratin' for 'macaroni elbows in powdered cheese sauce.' 'Depressed' for 'sad.' 'OCD' for 'uptight.'

"Seven."

The list stops there. The numeral seven, followed by a dot. I can't remember whether that's because Solly had another reason and his friends' arrival interrupted him, or because he failed to realize he didn't have one till after he'd already written down the seven and the dot.

Anyway, not long after Armen left, Solly's friends came over. Jay Yu and Tess Byrne. Jay brought an unlabeled audio cassette he'd found beneath a floormat while cleaning his car. Tess brought a bag of big sourdough pretzels. They decided they'd drop a hit and a half, then see how they felt in an hour or so.

Solly rummaged the drawers in the kitchen for scissors to cut up the ten-strip, Jay went upstairs to get Solly's old box from Solly's sisters' bedroom, and Tess asked Solly to please have some pretzels. When she'd hugged him hello, she said, she'd heard his stomach gurgle, which would ruin her trip if it kept on happening. She'd worry about Solly's guts, she said. How all the cheap antacids he took with all the coffee he drank with all the cigarettes he smoked were breaking his guts down. Not to mention, she said, that before his family had left for Atlanta, she'd promised Solly's mother to keep him from starving.

So while they sat out back around the patio table, waiting for the acid to start kicking in, Solly ate a number of sourdough pretzels.

Jay's cassette turned out to be a mix that Solly had made for him their freshman year of high school. It was mostly Jane's Addiction, Fugazi, and Nirvana—all of Solly's mixes from freshman year were.

A couple weeks earlier, Nirvana's Kurt Cobain had overdosed while the band toured Germany. None of the news reports had been at all clear about whether the overdose had been deliberate, but everyone had a strong opinion on the matter.

Jay was sure the overdose had been accidental. If it had been on purpose, Cobain would've succeeded: he would have been dead. Plus he would have left a note.

Tess thought Jay was talking shit. Maybe Cobain *had* left a note—for his wife or infant daughter or his bandmates—but whoever he'd left it to hadn't told reporters. Anyway, wasn't it also possible that he'd deliberately *failed* to kill himself? That he'd overdosed on purpose, but didn't want to die? That the nonlethal overdose had been a cry for help? How many assholes did they know who'd done that kind of thing? How many assholes had she herself *dated* who'd done that kind of thing?

Solly said he was certain that Cobain's overdose had been an earnest attempt to die. He could tell by Cobain's singing, he said. Not the words he sang, but the sound of his voice, which was the sound of a voice that was being destroyed by the way that it was being used to sing. You could tell that Cobain was in great pain, that he was completely hopeless about the pain, completely unable to imagine that anyone could help him get beyond the pain, and so he wasn't someone who'd cry for help. He was someone who hadn't seen any point in crying for help in a very long time, and who'd looked forward to dying for years and years, and he'd only just found the energy to kill himself. Solly told his friends that he believed they knew it, too, knew it just as well as he did, but that they didn't want to know that they knew it, they didn't want to know because they loved Cobain's voice as much as Solly did, and they didn't want to know that what they loved would have been less lovable or even maybe unlovable if the person it originated from wasn't suffering enormously. They didn't want to know that the voice would be a less stunningly beautiful voice if Cobain didn't suffer enormously, so they lied to themselves, or told themselves stories about what could and couldn't be known in order not to have to feel bad about delighting in an outcome of enormous human suffering.

Tess said that was childish. Overly romantic. She said she thought Solly was unwilling to believe that an artist who moved him might not be heroic. Cobain had a wife and a baby daughter, Tess said. Risking his life to cry for help was cowardly and weak, and Solly didn't want to see that. If Cobain *had* earnestly attempted to kill himself—that wasn't much better. It was maybe even worse. Either way: not one bit heroic. And *surviving* the attempt? Beyond unheroic. Not to mention embarrassing. What an embarrassment. What a fucken clown.

Cobain's embarrassment—anyone's embarrassment at having survived any authentic suicide attempt—was the last thing that Solly wanted to imagine, so he told his friends that Armen called the Cinnamon Arches *Darches,* which was supposed to be short for *Diarrhea Arches.*

And Jay said Armen should have called it *Dire Arches:* that, at least, was *almost* funny.

Tess laughed so enthusiastically at this, you could tell the acid had started kicking in for her, and once she'd gotten ahold of herself, she said that, as long as they were talking about calling things other things than they were called, she wanted to mention that she'd been thinking lately—or had *seemed* to be thinking lately, but either way was definitely thinking "nowly"—that, if it'd be all right with Solly, she'd really like to stop calling him *Solly,* and instead call him *Gladman,* and would he mind if she did that?

Solly told her it seemed maybe a little Coach Ditka–esque, but sure, why not. He wouldn't mind.

Well, that was *great* news, Tess said, that was really great news, and she asked Jay if he would also start calling Solly *Gladman*.

And, by the way that Jay squinted and bit his lower lip, as if he needed to consider all kinds of serious implications before answering Tess's question, it was clear the acid was kicking in for him, too.

At last, he said that he wasn't sure. He asked her *why* she wanted to call Solly *Gladman*.

And Tess said she wanted to apologize to Solly in advance for being offensive, if what she was about to say *was* offensive—she knew she could sometimes be really offensive and she really didn't want to be offensive, she said— but she thought, she said, that *Gladman* was a very nice name because of the almost like sunny kind of *Glad* part, but even more importantly than that, or maybe not more importantly, but equally importantly, *Solly* was a pretty awful name because it sounded like *sollen,* which meant *gloomy* or *depressed,* and she thought that maybe the reason or one of the reasons why Solly was always so gloomy and kind of depressed, no offense, was because of that—because of how everybody was always calling him by a name that sounded like a word for *gloomy and depressed,* and she wanted him to be more glad and sunny because she loved him, and she thought that Jay should want that, too, because Jay loved him, too.

Solly told Tess that that was all really interesting, that it wasn't offensive, and that, like he said before, she should feel free to call him *Gladman* if she wanted, but there wasn't any such word as *sollen*. Not in English, at least. Maybe in German or something. The word she was thinking of, he told her, was *sullen.*

And Jay said he thought Solly was right about *sollen* and *sullen,* but Tess wasn't so sure. She wasn't sure at all. Tess believed *sollen* was definitely a word in English—she was definitely sure she'd heard it before—and *maybe* it didn't mean exactly the same thing as Solly said *sullen* meant, but it was still a pretty gloomy and depressing word.

Also, Tess said, that shouldn't even matter, though. And it didn't. It didn't, Tess said. It didn't matter if *sollen* was a "real word," because both of the words, *sollen* and *sullen,* when she said them out loud or even just in her head, they bummed her out—just a little, not a ton, but a little, no offense, they threw a little shadow—and that was the opposite of what happened when she said *Gladman* out loud or inside her head, and the most important point that she was making, she said, was that Solly would be less gloomy and less often depressed if they called him *Gladman,* and she thought that if he let himself become Gladman like that, it would only make everyone love him even more.

Jay said he was convinced. From now on, he said, he'd call Solly *Gladman.*

Tess's reasons seemed pretty silly to Solly, but he really didn't care at all what they called him, and he started to wonder if that was a mistake. Started wondering if he maybe *should* care what they called him.

It seemed to him like his friends thought he should. Like they thought he would. Like they expected him to care.

If they didn't think he'd care, then why wouldn't they just call him whatever they wanted to call him? Why would they ask his permission to call him something different?

Unless they were making fun of him or something. Were they making fun of him?

No, they were his friends. They wouldn't make fun of him. Well, they would, of course—the three of them were always making fun of each other—but they wouldn't make fun of him maliciously. They wouldn't make fun of him to put him down. They didn't laugh *at* each other, he and his friends. They laughed *with* each other. It's why they were friends. Or maybe not *why,* but it's *how* they were friends. Or how they knew they were friends. Because they made each other laugh.

It's what they *did* as friends. The main thing they did. They laughed with each other, and a lot of the time they laughed with each other *about* each other.

If his friends were making fun of him, he'd know, and he didn't, and so they weren't.

So that had to mean they thought he should care what they called him. Or, at least, that they expected him to care.

And since he trusted his friends, he thought maybe he should. Care. But why? Why should he care? And why weren't they telling him why he should care? If they thought he should care and he clearly didn't care, you'd think they would tell him. Unless it was one of those things you shouldn't say on acid. One of those dark things you didn't say because everyone was high or about to be high, and the intensity of your thoughts when you were high on acid could grow an unpleasant remark into an unpleasant metaphor that could grow into a whole unpleasant theme or like leitmotif or web that connected with and hijacked other metaphors and rotted out their meaning the way a cancer cell becomes a tumor in one organ then metastasizes to other organs till the organs malfunction and eventually fail and your whole body fails and dies and starts to decompose, tumors and all, like that rotting red fox on the floor of the forest in the time-lapse footage the movies like to use to represent the interiority of characters freaking out on psychedelic drugs.

Unless they put you in an oven and turned you to ashes. Then you wouldn't have to rot like the fox on the floor of the forest. You wouldn't have to rot like you'd rot in a mass grave dug from the floor of a forest—

Wait . . .

Was it wouldn't "have to" rot or was it more like wouldn't "get to" rot? Some Jews would say wouldn't "get to" rot. They believed you were supposed to rot in the ground. But those Jews were religious. Solly wasn't religious. To rot, to Solly, wouldn't be a punishment *or* a privilege, so it wasn't wouldn't "have to" rot *or* wouldn't "get to" rot.

All it was was *wouldn't* rot. You *wouldn't* rot if they put you in an oven and turned you to ashes.

An oven?

The trains.

He'd lost his trains of thought. How you rotted or didn't wasn't the point. That wasn't what Solly'd been trying to figure out. What had he been trying to figure out again?

Ovens . . . his name . . . his friends . . . the dark thing— right!

Solly's friends wouldn't want to evoke the dark thing, whatever it was—if there even *was* a dark thing—for the same reason Solly changed the subject to *Darches* when Tess had said Kurt Cobain would be embarrassed about surviving his suicide attempt, and, for that matter, for the same reason Solly wasn't right now describing to Jay and Tess the thought he was having about veal and Cobain and the music of Nirvana: the thought that enjoying the music of Nirvana was like eating veal while the calf it had been cut from was still alive, crouched in its box, watching you slice off pieces of your portion to share with your friends and loved ones.

Which, on second thought, wasn't what enjoying the music of Nirvana was like at all. No suffering calf ever tried to be veal. Cobain sang his songs on purpose. The analogy was stupid. Was Solly stupid?

Were the Cinnamon Arches making him stupid?

Were they making him smart enough to realize he was stupid?

Was the dark thing the Holocaust?

On one hand, the dark thing was obviously the Holocaust.

On the other hand, wasn't failing to see past the obvious a mark of stupidity?

If failing to see past the obvious was a mark of stupidity, then the dark thing probably *wasn't* the Holocaust. That is: assuming Solly, who wasn't seeing past it, was stupid.

But then if Solly wasn't stupid, he might have already been seeing past the obvious, and if, in seeing past the obvious, what he was seeing was the Holocaust, that probably meant the Holocaust *was* the dark thing and that the reason his friends thought he would care if they stopped calling him *Solly* was that they knew he was named after his mother's beloved uncle Sholem, who'd survived the Holocaust. A year or so before Sholem's death, which occurred a few months before Solly was born, Solly's mother recorded a tape of him describing his experiences during the war—first in the Lodz Ghetto, where he lost his two daughters to malnutrition and tuberculosis, then in Auschwitz, where, just hours after his son had died on his feet while pressed between Sholem and the wall in the cattle car, Sholem's wife had been separated from him and taken to the showers—and just a few weeks ago, his mother'd played the tape for Jay and Tess when they came back with Solly from seeing *Schindler's List* at the Deerbrook Mall.

That was probably why Tess wanted to start calling Solly *Gladman*. Because *Solly* made her think of *Sholem*, which is just what the name was intended to do, and since *Sholem* made her think about the Holocaust, *Solly* also made her think about the Holocaust, but she'd feared that if she said so to Solly and Jay the Cinnamon Arches would metastasize it into massive forest-gravesfuls of decomposing foxes, so she made up all that *sollen* nonsense.

Or maybe Tess's angle on *Solly* vs. *Gladman* had nothing to do with the Holocaust at all. Maybe Solly was misinterpreting things. Overanalyzing the misinterpretations. Overdetermining the overanalyses. Seeing connections where there weren't connections. An illusory pattern. No. An *elusive* pattern. No—

An elusive, illusory pattern—written sideways in block letters, and underlined twice—gets a full page in the steno pad here.

Solly must have thought that was some really heavy shit.

Elusive is spelled incorrectly, though, I think. Two *i*'s, two *l*'s.

Ill usive.

It's a word, no doubt. Of course it's a word. But it's redundant with *illusory*. I mean, they're synonyms, *illusive* and *illusory.*

Solly wouldn't have gotten excited about a pair of

synonyms, let alone a pair of synonyms that possessed the same root. Not excited enough to isolate and double-underline the phrase.

If he confused *illusive* for *elusive,* however—that would make more sense. In terms of the isolation and underlining.

So I'm pretty sure that Solly was thinking of *elusive* with an *e.*

Or that Gladman was thinking of it.

That I was. Me.

Because fuck *this* already, right?

I've been planning to do a whole like *artful* return to first person. I thought I'd wait till I got to this specific moment I'll describe in a minute—this specific moment when Tess slaps Solly's hand and shouts, "Gladman!"—and then after I described that, I'd just start telling the story in first person again, using *I* instead of *Solly,* implicitly suggesting that we'd reached the part of the story where Solly's realized that he's dissolved into Gladman. Thing is, though, I'm not sure that Solly *did* realize he'd dissolved into Gladman when Tess slapped his hand and shouted, "Gladman!" or if the realization came later, or even maybe a little bit earlier. And, more than that, this whole talk-about-myself-in-third-person conceit is feeling kinda tired by now. Kinda tiring. Been feeling like that for a while, really.

Like a *tiring, tired conceit,* double-underlined.

Plus I'm starting to think it was unsound from the start. Like I said a while back, the Gladman who Solly became that day is a different Gladman than the Gladman who's telling you about him, not to mention a different Gladman than the Gladman who thought he'd killed Gogol.

Anyway, I must have thought *an elusive, illusory pattern* was some really heavy shit because, on the next page of the steno, I *explored* it further.

On the next page of the steno, written sideways, in block

letters, and this time underlined not twice, but *three* times, is *an elusive*(with the extra *i* and *l*)-slash-*allusive*(with an *a*) *illusory pattern.*

Deep.

An elusive/allusive, illusory pattern.

I guess I should take a second here to explain the significance of the word *pattern,* in case you've never used heavy psychedelics. Because it wasn't just figurative, that word, the way I was using it. I wasn't just referring to some increasingly paranoid *pattern of ideas* that I was *contemplating.* I was referring to a pattern that I was literally *seeing.*

Some people, when they're high on acid, they hallucinate on a really grand scale, like the Doors in Oliver Stone's *The Doors,* or Hunter S. Thompson in Gilliam's *Fear and Loathing.* They have telepathic conversations with their pets, hear houseplants weeping, laugh at jokes the sky's spelling out for them with clouds. Some people see beings who aren't there at all—aliens, ghosts, inner children externalized. They might argue with these beings. Or follow them elsewhere. Try to hug them. Try to disappear them.

But it's pretty uncommon, in general, for people who're tripping to hallucinate to that extent. Much more common is seeing patterns. Everyone I know who's taken hallucinogenic drugs has seen patterns. I'd taken acid about a hundred times, and I *always* saw a pattern. Every time I tripped on anything. Acid, mushrooms, morning glory seeds—whatever. I'd always see a pattern.

Same pattern every time.

Sometimes the pattern's lines were bolder than other times, or its elements were stretched or compressed more broadly or narrowly than at other times, or they'd be oriented differently along their axes, and sometimes the whole thing would crawl left or right, or rock or rotate, but it was always the same pattern. The drug would come on, and, until the trip was over, I'd see this pattern on top of anything I looked at. It was this kind of phosphene-colored, glowing web or like jigsaw puzzle of interlocking gecko or maybe salamander shapes. Sloppier and more organically rounded—*blobbier*—than the figures in the MC Escher work the phrase "interlocking gecko or maybe salamander shapes" probably makes you think of. And these shapes would throb—or breathe—and I could never quite focus on them. If I tried to stare at them directly, they'd lose definition, fade at the center—almost like those floaters you get in your eyes. An *elusive, illusory pattern*, right?

And not being able to focus on the pattern gave anything I thought of a suspicious-seeming edge, this feeling that a secret or secrets were being kept from me, this sense that I was *almost* understanding something true and important that I'd never understood before, but that I hadn't quite gotten there—the secret was being withheld. The pattern, understand, was alluding to this secret. *An elusive/allusive illusory pattern.*

And not only could I never discover what the secret was, but I could never tell who was withholding it. I might think the secret was that my friends and I were dead but didn't know it, or that I was dead and they were alive and they knew it for sure but weren't telling me. Or the reverse: that they were dead and I was alive but they weren't telling me. Or that *I* knew they were dead, or that all of us were dead, but that I shouldn't talk about it to anyone—that it was me who had to keep the secret, at least until I could prove it was true. That kinda thing.

If this sounds unpleasant to you, you're not hearing me. Or I'm failing to express it properly. I took acid *a lot*. With the exception of fucking, taking acid was my favorite thing to do, and I found the pattern beautiful, and I absolutely loved the sense of suspicion and secrecy—of being right up next to truth and understanding, on the verge of uncovering it.

A lot of times, I suspected I was God, or that all of us were God, me and my friends—I mean, I used to believe in

God—and those times were no more or less thrilling than
the times I thought I was probably dead. One time—the
first time, actually—I thought I was a character in either a
slightly fictionalized memoir, or a highly autobiographical
novel. I couldn't decide if the author was me, or one of my
friends, but everything was so stylized and perfect and in
its right place—Tess's laugh, Jay's devil's lock, the freckles
on the shoulders of our other friend Hannah, the touch of
green I found in my eyes in the mirror, Stephen Perkins's
drumming on Jane's Addiction's "Three Days," even the dark-
ness of the sudden realization I had that Kurt Vonnegut and
Perry Farrell, my favorite writer at the time and my favorite
singer, both had mothers who'd killed themselves—it was all
so ordered and full of good sense and free of rough edges,
I just couldn't imagine that we weren't art. Free will, which
I'd believed in at the time, and which I'd continue to believe
in for a couple more years—suddenly, it just seemed really
overrated. And that was great, too.

I've gotten a little ahead of myself, though. I skipped ahead.
I didn't take out the steno till I got to the bathroom. Didn't
misspell *elusive* till I got to the bathroom. Didn't go to the
bathroom till after Tess slapped my hand and shouted,
"Gladman!"

Before any of that happened, I was still sitting there on the
patio with Jay and Tess, thinking about my mother's uncle
Sholem, about the tape my mother had made of Sholem, and
I was picturing, vividly, and *very* involuntarily, many of the
horrors he'd described on that tape—I'm not gonna describe
them here, don't worry—but I couldn't stop thinking about
the Holocaust, couldn't stop picturing it, and the specific
images Sholem's stories evoked started blurring with other
images of the Holocaust, the documentary stuff I'd seen at
school and Hebrew school and in the movies and on TV,
and it was . . . You know, I'd thought I'd burned out the Holocaust receptors years earlier, but now it turned out I hadn't.

I started getting really upset. Upset about the Holocaust, yeah, of course, but also upset at myself for thinking about the Holocaust at all on acid, or *allowing* myself to think about it on acid.

And all of this, you know, it was happening at the speed of . . . thought. The speed of *racing* thought. Racing thought collaging itself. Faster than time-lapsed decomposing fox-speed. And I knew I shouldn't say anything about any of it to my friends, so I stayed quiet about it and just tried to think of something else. Tried to kind of *pivot,* you know?

But everything was connected, webbed up, overlapping and overdetermined, and the furthest I got in my pivot was Armen. Thoughts of Armen. The end of our exchange. When I made that crack about cleansing and acid, and Armen said I shouldn't joke about genocide.

I started thinking that when Armen said it wasn't cool to joke about genocide, maybe I'd actually hurt him. Like, maybe he wasn't just trying to make me feel bad as payback for making *him* feel bad about *Darches* or his stupid and pretentious use of "cleansing" for "staying sober." Maybe when I made my genocide crack, it caused his brain to cough up overly vivid imagery of slaughtered Armenians or Native Americans or even Jews—same kind of imagery my own brain was coughing up, there on the patio.

So I tried to picture what Armen's face looked like when I made the crack about genocide. I wasn't even sure I'd looked at his face when I made the crack, but I thought I might have, and so I tried picturing it to see if I could determine, by the way it looked, or might have looked, whether I'd actually hurt him or not.

And it wasn't really till that point, I don't think, that I began to understand just how fucked up I was. Because I pictured Armen *crying.* Tears, snot, heaving chest—the whole thing. That's what I pictured when I tried to picture his face, and I *knew* he hadn't cried when I made the crack about genocide—I had no doubt that Armen hadn't cried—but I thought maybe I was picturing him crying because "some part of me knew" that I'd hurt him with my genocide crack.

So I started feeling pretty awful about that. Guilty. Ashamed. Insensitive and stupid. All the bad things. Just really awful. And that's when Tess slapped my hand and shouted, "Gladman!" and I opened my eyes, which I hadn't realized were closed.

I asked Tess why she'd slapped me, and I couldn't hear the words I'd spoken, and I thought maybe it was because I was gasping a little—gasping as if I were crying or something, as if all I could push out of my throat was breath—and then I thought maybe I *had been* crying. *Was* crying. I touched my face. My face was *wet*. I was fucken crying!

But also that wasn't why I hadn't heard myself.

The music was blaring. That was why.

Tess turned the music off, and I repeated the question, and was able to hear it.

What they told me was that I'd closed my eyes, which they'd thought was weird, and they'd tried to get me to open my eyes by saying my name—by saying "Gladman" over and over—and when I didn't respond, they'd thought I was just fucking around because I wanted them to call me "Solly." Like I was refusing to acknowledge that I knew I was Gladman, refusing to acknowledge I knew that when they said "Gladman," they were talking to me.

But then I'd started clutching my forehead and crying, and they'd repeated my name again—"Solly," this time—and I kept not responding, and then Tess had noticed that the cherry of my cigarette was down past the filter, and she became afraid I'd burn my fingers, so she shouted, "Gladman!" and slapped it from my hand.

Neither of them could tell me how long this whole part lasted. It couldn't have taken more than a minute or two they said, but it was weird. It was really weird and they were really worried. Was I okay? Why was I crying?

—

And here's when I noticed that my guts were ... squirmy. Squirmy and almost like *burning.*

I needed to take a shit.

Now, this was complicated.

On one hand, it was good news that I needed to take a shit. It was good news because all the awful stuff that had been going through my head—the invasive Holocaust imagery, the guilt about making the genocide joke, the feeling like I'd made Armen cry even though I knew I hadn't made him cry—all that awful stuff was, it seemed, *emanating* from my guts. It was an outcome of the acid-enhanced discomfort of needing to take a shit while not taking a shit. Or, if not quite an *outcome* of the discomfort, the awful stuff was, at least, made *more* awful by the discomfort. Hard to say. But that all the awful stuff was *connected* to the discomfort—that, I was sure of. The way it came on, it had this kind of *throb* to it, and this throb, I noticed, was in time with the burning clench of my squirmy guts. So it was good news that I needed to take a shit because it meant, presumably, that if I took a shit I might feel less awful.

Other hand, I was terrified of others thinking about me taking a shit. Especially my friends, and most especially Tess— who, often as not, I believed I was in love with, and would sometimes fool around with a little—but even my family. Even total strangers.

Here's a statistic for you: of all the thousands of shits I'd taken in the preceding thirteen years, not a single one of them occurred in a public bathroom. I hadn't shit in a public bathroom since the age of *four.*

And since that last public bathroom shit, I'd never once taken a shit at a friend's house, I'd never taken a shit at home while a friend was over, and I'd *certainly* never taken a shit anywhere at all while high on acid.

I so dreaded the possibility that anyone might associate me with the act of shitting that I didn't allow myself to shit if anyone else might know that was what I was doing, and I was sure they'd know that's what I was doing if I were to do it because, judging by how long it took others to take a shit, fifteen-twenty minutes was a really long time, and that's how long it usually took me. Fifteen-twenty. Not infrequently a whole half an hour. I had to read to shit. I had to be reading, or I just . . . couldn't. And I had to be *involved* in what I was reading. Had to forget—had to hide it from my*self*—that I was trying to shit. I took a while to get started, and then, once I'd finished, I'd wipe like a champ, like the son of a lumber magnate, like I *hated* the Amazon. A lot of times, I'd wipe for longer than I'd shat. Always flushed twice. Flushed *at least* twice. I took a really long time.

Thirty years later, I still have this problem. The problem's gotten smaller, less intense, I've gotten past it, partly—I mean, I've lived with other people, I've had to get *somewhat* past it—but I've never fully gotten past it, and I wouldn't start to get even the little bit past it that I *have* gotten past it for a few years after this day I'm describing.

If I didn't know I'd be dead tomorrow anyway, I wouldn't be telling you any of this.

Anyway, I was in a bind. I needed to shit and I was desperate not to shit, and I had this idea that I could kill my need to shit or at least ride it out if I could constipate myself—it's a strategy that had worked for me in the past. So I asked Jay where the bag of pretzels was, and he said it was inside, that he'd taken it inside, and I got up to get it, and they asked me where I was going, my friends, and I told them I was going to get the bag of pretzels, and they told me there weren't any pretzels left in the bag, that we'd finished the pretzels, that I myself had eaten half the bag—which meant something like six pretzels, seven pretzels, these massive, rock-hard Bavarian pretzels—and didn't I remember eating all the pretzels? And I didn't, of course. I didn't remember eating all the pretzels, I remembered eating two or maybe three of the pretzels, but my mouth, I noticed—my lips and my gums—I noticed they were sore, and dry, I tasted copper, tasted some blood I guess, and just as I started to determine that there's no way my friends would *lie* to me about my having eaten a large number of pretzels, or about the pretzel bag now being empty, I *felt* the pretzels. Inside me, I felt them. They—those pretzels—they were what wanted to get out. They'd wanted to get out while I was sitting there, thinking about the Holocaust, and now that I was standing, they were *trying* to get out.

So this is what I do. I tell my friends that I need to be alone, to think, so I'm going inside, and I don't want them to bother me. I need to sort something out, I tell them.

Tess asks me what I need to sort out.

I say I can't talk about it. I don't want to talk about it.

Tess says she doesn't like that, that she really thinks I should tell them because she doesn't think it's a good idea for me to be alone, the acid's really good, it's strong, and even though I'm not crying anymore, I was just crying not even a minute earlier, and so forth.

And Jay says, "I notice you have a pen there, Gladman."

I forgot to mention: all of us thought of ourselves as artists of some kind. Jay drew and painted, Tess sang and played drums, and I wrote, ahem . . . *poetry*. We talked to each other about paintings and music and books pretty often, and we all thought of ourselves as artists, and what's more we all knew we thought of ourselves as artists, but we never *called* ourselves artists or talked to each other about our own work because, I guess, we thought there was something cheesy and un–punk rock about talking about it, something lame or unhumble or something, and so Jay's mentioning that I was holding a pen, which I was, though I hadn't noticed till he'd said—I was holding a pen I must have fished from my pocket, a pen I was rapidly clicking open and closed—Jay's mentioning that was like him saying to Tess, "He wants to be alone to write a poem, leave him be," and so I said, "So what?" as though Jay, in noting that I was holding a pen, had spoken a non sequitur, which confirmed for them both that I was going to write a poem but that I wanted us to pretend that that's not what I was going to do, and Tess backed off, told me that, okay, they'd give me half an hour alone, uninterrupted.

So I go to my bathroom. I go *upstairs* to go to the bathroom in my bedroom and . . . Look, I know that taking a shit isn't—I know it's rude to talk about shitting. Girls don't like it. Shitting's uncool. I know. I do. So I'm gonna try to do this part as quickly as possible. I am. I promise.

On the way to my bathroom, I grab the novel I'm reading from my bedside table, but my need is so emergent that I don't even have to crack the thing open. Soon as I'm seated, I'm just . . . shitting. For a while. And it's heavy. An opera. All sweat and shivers and eyes going cross. Feels like it might never come to an end. Pushing and rocking and straining and humming. I'm moving mountains. It's *Flight of the Valkyries.*
        Then suddenly it isn't.
        Suddenly it's over.
        Well, I think it's over.
        All movement has stopped. In the guts. In the asshole.
        Feels like I'm done.
        And *yet.* It doesn't. That is: I still feel full.
        Full of shit.
        I still feel full of shit, and I know I'm really high, and that's probably all it is. That's probably why I feel full of shit. I know it's probably a kind of tactile hallucination or whatever, and I really want to be done with this part of the day, so what I do is, I make the decision to *convince* myself that I'm done. I adjust my position, look in the bowl. And what I see there, man—what I see is a single turd the size of a . . . gumball.
        Not a jumbo gumball, not even a full-size gumball, but like the kind of gumball that you put a quarter in the machine and you get *five* of them.
        So, okay. So I am, it turns out, still full of shit. In one sense,

that's actually not-bad news: the reason I feel so full of shit is simply because I am. Full of shit. Means I'm not crazy.

But then in another sense, it's pretty alarming. That whole opera, right? It had really felt like moving mountains, and all it was was, I don't know, moving a pebble? Kicking at sand? Shifting some gravel? Mountains hadn't been moved. And don't get me wrong: it's not like I've forgotten how high I am. I mean, I know I'm on acid, I know I'm not exactly an expert on reality, but I have this thought, okay? I have this *thought,* and when I have this thought, it really kinda sets me off into a panic. I didn't write this thought down in the steno, but I remember the thought, word for word. I'll tell you what it was. You ready? This is what it was:

"You can't remember how to shit."

"You can't remember how to shit."

And what does *that* mean, you know? What does that *mean*? I forgot how to shit? That's like forgetting how to walk. It's worse! It's one of the first things you ever knew. It's like the fourth thing you ever figured out. Or maybe the fifth. One of the first ten things, for sure. You figured out how to breathe, you figured out how to cry, you figured out how to suckle, and then, in short order, though I can't for sure say which order exactly, you figured out how to piss, how to burp, how to puke, how to sleep, and how to shit.

Take it easy, Gladman. Take it easy, I think. You remember how to shit. You couldn't possibly have forgotten how to shit. That's an LSD-type thought. Calm down. You remember how to shit. This is how to shit: read your book and forget about shitting. *That's* how you shit.

My book, it's right there on the counter next to the sink, where I'd set it down so I could undo my jeans. This is *Breakfast of Champions* by Kurt Vonnegut—really fun novel. This is my first time reading it, and I open it up to where I left off. Right near the beginning. Just a few pages into the preface. Night before, in bed, I'd finished another book and started

this one, but then I got too sleepy—no fault of Vonnegut's—
so I had to put it down.

Anyway, I open it, and, first of all, what I find myself looking at is an illustration of . . . an asshole. I don't mean a dislik-
able person. I mean an asshole. An anus.

Vonnegut's drawn an anus in the middle of a page in the
preface of his book.

Basically a bunch of x's or, like, a stack of asterisks with a
black dot in the center.

This is, obviously, a pretty unlikely thing to find in a novel.
A funny thing that, normally, I'd have probably laughed at a
lot. I don't, however, laugh a lot at the asshole. Or even a little.
I'm too distracted by that pattern I mentioned before. Those
Day-Glo, interlocking geckos or salamanders or whatever
they are. They're brighter and squirmier and more defined
than I've ever seen them, and the white parts of the page—
the margins, and the spaces between the words and the
paragraphs—they're really throwing the pattern into relief,
especially in the area surrounding the asshole.

And that phrase, "the area surrounding the asshole," it
loops through my head, round and round, passes through
cycles. And it becomes "the hairy area surrounding the
asshole," and then "the hairy, smelly area surrounding the
asshole."

That phrase is one I *would* write down in the steno. It's
part of a setup for a joke. A joke I was convinced I'd just come
up with. A joke I was, at least momentarily, impressed with
myself for having coming up with, there on the toilet, high
on acid, even though it would, on later reflection, reveal itself
to be not so much a joke I'd *come up with* as a modification
on an old joke, a really hypermisogynistic joke Tess had once
told me.

This was the joke, the one I thought I came up with:

What do you call the hairy, smelly area surrounding the
asshole?

The person.

—

More on that in a minute.

Before I wrote the joke down, I tried to read. No easy task. Between the formation of the joke in my head—that cycling around of the setup I mentioned—and the increasingly active and vivid lizard pattern that it seemed to me I might at last get to have a real *direct* look at, I could hardly pay attention. I got only as far as the sentence under the asshole drawing. That sentence is: "I think I am trying to clear my head of all the junk in there—the assholes, the flags, the underpants."

I knew this sentence was somehow true and important, but I couldn't really grasp it. Was Vonnegut speaking *figuratively*? Did he mean "assholes" like the one in the drawing, or did he mean people who were assholes? Both? And what was this about "flags" and "underpants"? What a weird, like, *juxtaposition*.

And then "clear my head of all the junk in there." Sure, it was common enough a phrase and all, but if you thought about it some, the imagery was just . . . If the assholes and the flags and underpants were the junk in his head, they were metaphorical assholes and flags and underpants, or *representations* of assholes and flags and underpants, so how could you *clear* them? . . . was it clear like *clarify*? . . . Language was weird. Weird was language. LSD. Blah blah, meow meow.

I must have read it twenty times, that sentence. Enough times to memorize it, for sure. I must have read it twenty times, and, like I said, I knew it was true and important, but I couldn't grasp its meaning, and the more I tried to grasp it, the more it slipped away.

Plus it certainly wasn't helping me shit. And I felt just *so* completely, desperately full of shit. Shitting needed to happen and reading wasn't working. Wasn't helping me forget that I was trying to shit.

So I set the Vonnegut beside the sink and reached down into my jeans for my pen and my steno. If reading won't work, maybe writing will, I thought.

First thing I see in the steno is that list. The one I read

to you earlier. All the reasons why it was funny and enraging when Armen said it wasn't cool for me to joke about genocide.

And by the time I finish reading that list, a couple things have happened.

Number one: I'm entirely convinced of the position I'd taken when I wrote the list. More convinced, in fact, than I was when I wrote it. I'm overcome with a sense of righteous indignation. Who the fuck does Armen think he is, and so forth. Guy tells me it's uncool to joke about genocide and now I'm supposed to beat myself up? Suffer guilty feelings while high on acid? No.

And from this elevated feeling of righteous indignation, of refusal, of *Fuck you, no!,* I have an insight—an insight that I still hold to be true. Or true *enough,* at least. True in spirit for sure. Only insight I had that whole day that's worth anything.

This was my insight:

Up until the Nazis came along, the twentieth-century Europeans who hated my people imagined us to be, basically, a bunch of orgiastic Rothschilds. They imagined us to be a mighty cabal of terrifying fat cats with excellent teeth who were sitting around in marble-ceilinged offices and leather-lined living rooms with hideous, incomprehensible art on the walls, counting stacks of money from profits turned by usury, and, above all, *laughing.* Laughing at *them.* The people. The volk. Moneylending, war-profiteering drinkers of blood just roaring with laughter. Guffawing and tittering capitalist devils who gathered together in gentile-built architectural structures and nourished ourselves with agricultural products of gentile labor that were brought to our tables by gentile servants, and all of it paid for with gentile money we'd stolen *in passing,* through parasitic practices that required neither muscle nor hustle, just a little special math we could do in our heads even while we sprayed the cum from our mutilated cocks into the fair and sweet-smelling gentile pussies and pink little mouths and suffering brown assholes and sky-colored eyes of their gentile daughters and sisters and wives and *roared with laughter* at all the many humiliations we inflicted on all of the hardworking gentiles everywhere.

That was the image. That was what they thought of when they thought of Jews. We were well-heeled, cigar-puffing deviants in eveningwear who couldn't stop laughing. We couldn't stop laughing and they couldn't laugh with us 'cause they couldn't get our jokes 'cause they couldn't hear our jokes 'cause our jokes were on them and we wouldn't let them near us if they weren't in livery or weren't in line at our shops or our banks or we didn't have our cocks in one of their holes, and we never told our jokes in front of the help and we never told our jokes in front of our customers and we never told our jokes in front of race-traitor whores. We were fucken untouchable. That's what they thought of us.

Then the Nazis made their cartoons and their posters and movies, and the volk were alarmed and disgusted to learn—though, more than that, they were *relieved* to learn—that we were also the other kind of untouchable. There were fat cats *among* us, and these fat cats ran and ruined everything, sure, but most of us weren't fat cats at all: most of us were loyal servants of the fat cats, and we were unhygienic and craven and weak and we lived in the company of plentiful vermin. Lice jumped in our hair, rats were sleeping in our beds, roaches climbing our walls. We *were* vermin. Repulsive and troublesome—dangerous, too—but not so very superior after all. Rather: small and defective. Grubby and feeble and scrabbling and long-faced. Completely unsmiling. Incapable of joy. Incapable of laughter. Ugly and humorless. Rats. Fleas.

They hated us long before the propaganda started. They'd always hated us. Always. They'd thought we had secret math and secret means and secret strengths that made us superior and *filled us with hilarity.* Same reasons that those who hate us hate us now. They'd hated us long before the Third Reich, had wanted to wipe us off the face of the planet long before Adolf Hitler, but it wasn't *until* Adolf Hitler came along that they believed they *could* wipe us off the face of the planet. It wasn't *until* the propaganda really got going that they learned to think of us as humorless vermin. They didn't *try* to wipe us off the face of the planet till they believed they'd be able to pull it off. And once they believed it, well, then, you know—then they *really* tried.

So for a Jew not to laugh at *any*thing that Jew finds funny, for *whatever* reason that Jew finds it funny—that's a victory for National Socialism.

That was the first thing that came of my reading the list I'd written in the steno—that insight born of righteous indignation.

The second thing? Oh *wow* was I shitting!

I was losing weight. I won't get into . . . there was a lot of shit.

There was really a whole lot. So, so much. And all of it had come out so easily. I hadn't strained, I hadn't pushed, I hadn't even *tried*.

So much shit had come out of me so consistently and easily that, soon enough, I had nothing left inside to shit, and yet I continued. I continued to shit. My asshole, I mean. My asshole continued.

I was shitting nothing, but continuing to shit, and I became afraid I'd forgotten how *not* to shit. How *not to be* shitting. Afraid I couldn't remember how to *stop* shitting. Afraid that I'd lost, in other words, control of my *sphincter.* The ability to still my very own sphincter.

What a word that is. How I hated that word.

I needed to get that word out of my head, and even more than that, I thought, I needed to stop shitting.

And deploying some creative LSD-driven logic, I reasoned as follows:

Reading Kurt Vonnegut on acid didn't help you shit, so you thought writing on acid might help you shit, but instead of writing on acid, you ended up reading words you'd already written, which made you shit, so maybe *writing* words on acid will *stop* you from shitting.

So at the bottom of the page, right under the list, I wrote

some words. Wrote my joke about the person. That is: the hairy, smelly area surrounding the asshole.

That filled the page, and yet I remained unstill of sphincter, so I flipped to a new page, to write something else, something more—I didn't know what.

Now this is an unlined steno, okay? And the pattern, man. On that blank, white, unlined page, that pattern really *popped*. Even more than it had in the area surrounding the asshole in the Vonnegut. It was beautiful. It was beautiful and it *meant* something. Was alerting me to something. Some hidden truth. Some next-level type of understanding. I was right on the verge of it. If only I could look at it directly . . . I just had to figure out how to look at it directly, and I'd get there.

But I couldn't. Just couldn't. I tried but I couldn't. I never could. I never did. The more I squinted for focus, the further the pattern fled the focal point. The more I relaxed my eyes, the more centered it got, true—but the more centered it got, the more it squirmed around and blurred.

I brought the steno toward and away from my face, turned it sideways, upside down. No change.

At last I tried out a new thought about the pattern. I thought that maybe the pattern wasn't itself the secret truth. Maybe it wasn't itself the hidden understanding. Maybe that was the part in the middle. The part that I could look at directly and accurately describe. The part that wasn't the pattern itself, but rather the part unobstructed by the pattern. I didn't want to believe that, though. It was fucken boring, man. I wanted to see the pattern so bad. I wanted to be able to accurately describe *the pattern*. That might, I thought, allow me to see it.

So I tried to describe it.

An elusive, illusory pattern, I wrote. Wrote it sideways across the page in block letters, underlined it twice, misspelled *elusive*.

Then I turned to the next page and wrote—sideways again, and in block letters—*An elusive/allusive, illusory pattern*. Misspelled *elusive* a second time. Underlined the whole phrase *three* times because I must have thought . . . Who cares, actually? I'm sick of talking about the pattern. You must be, too.

The next page in the steno features the last sentence I wrote in the bathroom. I know it was the last sentence I wrote in the bathroom because it was the last sentence I'd written down sideways in block letters. On the remaining fifty-however-many pages of the steno—which contain a description of the majority of the events I've been describing to you here, plus a bit more, which I'll get to in a minute—the writing gets normal again.

But this third and final sideways sentence, which I wrote on the toilet while I freaked out on acid, is special to me. It's the first good sentence I ever wrote. About six years later, with only the smallest edit—I replaced the words *my* and *will* with *her* and *would*—it became the first sentence of my first published short story, "Melancholy Sally Drops."

This is the sentence:

"A wish: that my asshole will please stop kissing at the air."

Not bad for a seventeen-year-old, huh?

I like that sentence.

Sooner or later the wish came true. My sphincter relaxed. Or unrelaxed. I don't know which. My asshole was no longer trying to shit, though. That part was over.

Now it was time for the great fiasco.

Time to wipe.

Wiping took even longer than it usually did for me. The toilet paper was whiter than the pages of the steno, and the pattern was . . .

Well, the toilet paper wasn't *just* white, right? It had a pattern of its own—a textural pattern. The manufacturer's imprint. Which gave it little shadows, gradients, depth. Little shadows that interacted and interfered with the pattern my eyes were imposing on its surface in this way that . . .

I don't think I have the energy for the blow-by-blow.

I wiped and checked, as one does. I wiped and checked and wiped and checked and wiped and checked and wiped and checked, and after the obvious part of the cleaning was through—that part itself required two flushes—and I'd gotten to that far more targeted part of the wiping process where the ass is verging on cleanliness but not quite there, the checking became really effortful. I couldn't tell if I was seeing quivering little brown specks of shit on the paper, or little gray dancing shadows or gullies in the imprint, or the flicking tongues or tails or scrabbling finger-toes of elusive, illusory geckos or salamanders or what. I couldn't tell. Couldn't make the distinction.

All I knew was that I had to err on the side of too much wiping. That is: better to waste a bunch of time and toilet paper and water than to have any shit left over in the crack of my ass.

Now, I wasn't horny. Not at all.

For what I trust are pretty obvious reasons, the thought of the body—especially of the mouth, of its wet heat and smells—was, at the moment, extremely disgusting to me, but I *was* seventeen, and that meant I could count on getting horny pretty soon, at any moment, and since Tess, a lot of times, got horny on acid, especially if I put on Jane's Addiction's "Three Days," we'd probably end up making out at some point, and the thought of her smelling or even *thinking* she was smelling even the faintest hint of shit coming off me . . . I mean, that would be bad enough if we *weren't* so high.

So to have a squeaky-clean asshole seemed more important than it ever had before is what I'm trying to say.

I wipe and check and wipe and check and, eventually, my asshole starts itching. Then it starts burning. Then I think I see tiny dots of red on the paper, tiny dots of red blood on the paper, blood from my asshole, and my heart starts to race. *Blood from my asshole.* But then I stare at the dots a little, and they start looking brown, and I feel a little better. They all flux back to red, true enough, but then they flux again back to brown. So it's all in my head. I'm sure. Pretty sure. Some number of wipes earlier, I thought I felt my asshole kind of swelling through the paper—like *falling out of me*—but that was obviously not happening. How could that happen? That was obviously a hallucination. The dots on the paper—they were like that.

They were just more shit.

I don't know how long I actually spent wiping. Or, for that matter, trying to shit, shitting, trying to stop shitting. I have no sense of how many times I had to rise from the toilet and rub my thighs to get the pins and needles out of my legs. No idea how many times I had to flush.

Too many, though. Too many. Too much.

It wasn't till the toilet paper roll was spent that it occurred to me that I could just take a shower.

That it took that long was especially moronic, given that I was *facing* a bathtub.

I flushed one last time, got off the toilet, stepped out of my jeans, pulled my T-shirt and socks off, and stepped into the bathtub.

Then I heard my friends.

Well, not my friends, themselves, but the music my friends were listening to. *Ritual de lo Habitual* by Jane's Addiction.

It was playing downstairs, on the living room stereo, and it struck me that it *had been* for a while.

My wiping had, in part, been soundtracked—distantly and muffled—through the walls and ceilings and floorboards of the house by *Ritual's* first three songs: "Stop," "Ain't No Right," and "No One's Leaving."

Now the song "Obvious" had started. After "Obvious" would come "Been Caught Stealin'" and after "Been Caught Stealin'" would come "Three Days."

The thought of "Three Days" was the thought of Tess's neck, her chest, her shoulders, her hair, her navel, her lips, her tongue—the parts of her body she'd allowed me to handle and get in my mouth.

And *mouths:* suddenly they didn't seem so gross after all. Standing in the tub, they seemed pretty great.

If I could get down there before the song got going, maybe I could give Jay the look—he knew about me and Tess and "Three Days"—and he'd go outside and draw for a while, or watch a movie down in the basement.

How long did I have, then? "Obvious" was medium long— six minutes, maybe—and had already been playing for a minute or two. "Been Caught Stealin'" was under four minutes. So at best I had about eight minutes to get down there, but maybe "Obvious" was further along than I thought, plus my sense of time was pretty warped, and probably it would be better to get down there a little bit *before* "Three Days" started, more *subtle* or something . . .

So I didn't take a shower. I mean, I didn't take a whole shower. I took a half shower.

A lower-half shower.

Dried off, got dressed, arrived in the living room before the last chorus of "Been Caught Stealin'."

Found myself staring into Tess's spread pussy.

Ginger.

A surprise.

I'd never seen a ginger one, and Tess was a blonde.

It wasn't just that, though.

A couple of fingers were rubbing Tess's pussy, a third kind of lazily sliding in and out of it, and these were not Tess's fingers, but Jay's.

Jay had his back to me. His torso was blocking Tess's breasts and her face. He was wearing a T-shirt and one of his socks, and his knees were on the floor, on either side of Tess's forearms—she was raised up onto her elbows a little. While Jay was reaching back to rub and finger her pussy, he was also very slowly fucking her mouth.

How did they even conceive of this position? Had they learned about it somewhere? From a diagram? A photo? Why hadn't I been taught?

As "Three Days" started, Jay turned his head. Probably, I'm guessing, to gaze at Tess's pussy. When he turned, he saw *me* gazing at her pussy, and jumped off her face. And there was Jay's cock. Another surprise. It was Guinness in the can. A beat cop's Maglite.

"Gladman," Tess said. She'd balled herself up to cover her nakedness. "Gladman," she said. "Oh, Gladman, oh no."

Right then's when I started to have a bad trip.

In case you missed it, that was a punchline.

About the bad trip part, it would be impolite to give too many details. Boring. Like a stranger's dream. Nothing really happened. It was all *in my head*. I felt jealous and also ashamed for feeling jealous, and was, in general, confused and afraid. Everything appeared to be oily and sticky and grimy and clenched and just . . . aesthetically hostile.

Like, think seventies American auteur cinema. Its harshest lighting. Its most jarring sound design. Bug-eyed Nurse Ratched's purpling face while McMurphy strangles her in Forman's *Cuckoo's Nest*. Any nighttime surface in *Mean Streets*. Every *Straw Dogs* chunk and spatter. Any conversation in every Cassavetes film. Everything seemed disgusted with itself and was made more disgusting by its own expressed disgust and it was all in my head or coming out of my head.

At one point I tried to watch some TV. Afternoon reruns on channel 32. I thought—swear to God—that *Taxi* was *Cruising*. Once I realized it wasn't, I thought it was *Serpico*.

The interlocking lizards in the meaningless pattern tried to suffocate then sodomize then gorge on each other.

Probably lasted three hours. Forty-five-or-so minutes on top of however long it took Tess, whose dad was a private practice psychiatrist, to find a bottle of my mother's Valium in my parents' bathroom and convince me to swallow some.

I passed out till early the following morning.

When I woke, my friends were gone in more than one sense—we'd still hang out occasionally, until graduation, but it was never the same between us again—and I had a really serious hard-on.

Tess's pussy getting rubbed while her mouth got fucked—it was such a dirty thing to think about that, but I couldn't shake it, so I jerked myself off, and when I came . . .

Well, actually, when I came it was—it was an orgasm, you know? A teenage one. One of the first couple thousand I'd ever had. That part was a pleasure.

But then hardly three minutes later, there was pain. Discomfort. A throb. An ache. A throbbing discomfort. An aching throb. A throbbing ache.

I lay there in bed, hungover on acid, hungover on Valium, sticky with jizz, in pain and discomfort.

I hurt pretty bad.

And I don't mean my *conscience*.

I'm not talking about my *heart*.

I'm talking about my asshole.

I'm talking about piles. Raging hemorrhoids.

The hellish case of raging hemorrhoids I'd inflicted on my asshole with all that pushing and straining and wiping.

Worst day of my life till I thought I killed Gogol.

Then, morning of 11/17, I was sitting at my desk, when those hemorrhoids flared. *Acted up*.

I was supposed to have brunch and then go to the Art Institute with my wife and family—my parents, my sisters, and my sister Naomi's little kids—but the hemorrhoids flared, so I backed out of going.

I stayed home, ate some benzos, took a long nap—a

couple long naps, actually—and by the time I woke up from the second one, they'd died. All of them. All the people I loved. Worst day of my life.

A couple of punchlines just now became available. Too available not to mention. They're not the best punchlines, but given what I'm supposed to be doing here, I feel that duty compels me to mention them.

The first one is this: "Hemorrhoids ruined my life by saving it."

And then the second one isn't for me to deliver. By the time it becomes viable—in just a few hours—I'll be incapable of delivering it, but you know: you can. If you want to, I mean. You can tell people: "Gladman's hemorrhoids killed him by saving his life."

But I don't find either of those punchlines very satisfying. Their irony's shallow. O. Henry–esque. Sitcomly almost.

More than that, though, I guess: I don't think life's a joke. I never have. A lot of times it's very funny, it's chockful of jokes, but that doesn't make it a joke itself. I mean, it's got plenty of music in it, too, plenty of songs, plenty of singing—does that mean it's a musical?

I say no. I do not think that life is a musical.

I think what it is, it's more a shaggy dog story. A bunch of patterns you can almost make out that seem like they're about to come together to reveal each other fully and form a larger pattern giving rise to a kind of totality of meaning, and then they *do* come together, but in doing so—in coming together—they *don't* form a larger pattern, or more fully reveal one another. In fact they further obscure and sometimes even dissolve one another. And maybe they weren't ever there, you think. Maybe those patterns weren't ever there. Maybe you imposed them.

Or maybe the storyteller himself imposed them, but he was fucking with you. Being hostile toward you.

Then again maybe he wasn't being hostile. Maybe you

misheard what you were being told, or the storyteller misunderstood the way you hear things.

Or maybe there was a larger misunderstanding—a larger, mutual misunderstanding. A misunderstanding that began at the beginning. Like maybe the storyteller thought that you wanted to enjoy a story so he told you a story, but what you really wanted was to relearn a lesson or be affirmed by a slogan or inspired by a sermon, so you listened for a lesson or a slogan or a sermon. You wanted something to live by, not something to live *in*. Not something to live *through*. Not something *to work with*.

Perhaps I've gotten off track again, though.

What I was going to say is that, apart from not thinking life is a joke, another problem I have with either of the aforementioned punchlines is that they're too reductive. They aren't *untrue*, but they aren't especially accurate either.

Seems to me that it's no more accurate to say, "Hemorrhoids ruined my life by saving it," than it would be to say, "The timing of the anomaly ruined my life by saving it," or, "My failure to imagine that I might be seeing my wife for the last time I'd ever see her ruined my life by saving it."

Had the anomaly happened on 11/16, I'd have been with all of them.

Had I, on the morning of 11/17, registered the very real, however remote, possibility that I might not get another chance to spend time with my wife if I didn't spend the day with her and my family, I'd have gone with her, or at least insisted that she stay with me.

Woulda coulda shoulda.

I don't feel guilty. I don't blame myself. I'm not saying that. The anomaly was anomalous. I know it's not my fault that everyone I love died. I'm not asking for a hug.

What I'm trying to say is that I think I've got something better to tell you than "Hemorrhoids ruined my life by saving it."

—

Now, what I've got doesn't clarify fuck-all. It doesn't *shear the dog* one bit. It does, however, kinda knot, or braid, or like, dreadlock the fur by way of allowing me some "sense of personal agency." To be sure: it's a false sense, and I know it.

I know my "sense of personal agency" is an illusion because I know that personal agency itself is a fiction, but still I like to pretend.

I like to pretend, when I can, that personal agency is real, and that I have it. I like to have some sense of personal agency because . . . who cares?

Because I'm a person. Leave it at that.

Anyway, I've had hemorrhoids for thirty years. They're hardly ever a problem. Most of the time I'm not *aware* of them. They're just kinda there. They're just another part of me. Like my liver. My spleen. The central knuckle of my left middle toe.

But then sometimes, like on the morning of 11/17, they flare up. It's really predictable, though I never predict it.

One thing that causes them to flare up is stress. Another thing is sitting down for too long. That morning—morning of the anomaly—I'd been stressing out about a closer. How to close a performance. A number of performances, actually. Hypothetical ones.

Most of my career as a performer, I'd just get onstage and let fly whenever I felt like it. I'd get on, let fly, see where it took me, but I always liked to have a closing bit in pocket, just in case I couldn't find another way to land, which would happen sometimes. And I needed a new one—a new closing bit—because I'd been using the previous one for too long. I wasn't feeling it anymore.

And I was, on 11/17, and for a few days before that, too—I was obsessed with this idea that my closing bit should concern itself with a duck and pants. Why? No idea. I had *a feeling*. I felt *inspired*.

Why doesn't matter really.

Point I'm trying to make is I wrote and I wrote, deleted

and deleted, and I kept on thinking I almost had the bit down—it was right there, I thought, I just had to keep going at it. I *believed*. And so I pushed.

Kept thinking I nearly had it, but kept not getting it, and kept on pushing till I'd pushed too hard, till I'd sat too long.

Boom. Flare-up.

And until it came time to prepare for this performance, I never earnestly thought, "Hemorrhoids ruined my life by saving it," but I did, once or twice, think comedy did. "My work." Whatever we want to call it.

The duck and pants bit.

Or my continuing failure to nail the duck and pants bit. Ruined my life by saving it.

My insistence on nailing the duck and pants bit, I thought—once or twice, at one point or another—ruined my life by saving it.

Again: not true, not false. It's not any truer or any more false or even any more accurate than any of the other aforementioned assertions about what ruined my life by saving it, but that "sense of personal agency"—it's there. And it's better. For me. I like it better.

And in, uh, honor of . . . Well . . . Sure . . .

In *honor* of that, I nailed it. The duck and pants bit.

Nailed it for you.

Sorta.

Really, I nailed it for a young man I met the other day.

Guy who asked me to do this performance.

For you.

Whoever you are.

I like this guy a lot. More importantly, Gogol likes him a lot.

And, I mean, that's *saying* something. It's a really big deal. Gogol really doesn't like most people.

Really doesn't like most people.

Like if she goes too long in the company of people she doesn't really like without also being in the company of a person she *does* really like, she gets depressed and harms herself, physically. Mutilates herself. Tears her feathers out. Tears at her skin. And I told you about the clotting.

Has to regularly be near someone she likes, Gogol, and she's only ever liked three people: me, my sister Kayla—who died in the anomaly—and this guy I'm talking about.

She's with him now.

He's gonna keep her.

Keeping her wasn't something he agreed to, but he'll do it anyway, and, because it wasn't something he agreed to, I've taken some measures to make it up to him. This performance being one among them, the measures.

So the world's on its head, everything's changed—I'm doing the bit about the duck and the pants now . . .

The world's on its head, everything's changed, it's a science-fictional postapocalypse. Warfare and famine and deadly pandemics and a meteor carrying radioactive bacteria that entered the food chain and radically mutated any number of animal species it didn't annihilate have reduced the size of the human population to a handful of millions all living within a hundred miles of Irkutsk, and between all the bombs and tsunamis and sinkholes and earthquakes and floods and the meteor's impact, whole chunks of continents have broken away, and the poles have shifted, north's trending southeast, Brazil's become a quartet of islands, the UK crashed into the coast of Miami, New Zealand is gone—it just started to drift, and then it drowned—Tel Aviv has been overrun by polar bears, armies of chimps fight the elephant tribes who've allied with the badgers on the beaches of Berlin, and on sunny afternoons, if she's in a certain mood, the brooding captain of a pod of bipedal dolphins will crawl her way up to the top of the ruins of Euro Disneyland's Sleeping Beauty Castle and, facing the direction that used to be north, she'll observe, through a pair of birding binoculars, the giant winged lobsters messing around in the verdant canopy that lines the coast of what used to be the southern tip of Greenland, and she'll wonder if the food is better over there, and she'll worry that her filthy crustacean counterpart is wondering the same about over *here,* and she'll clutch at the hilt of her sword so hard that her hand will go numb.

And in the City of Chicago there's a long, scummy river branch that stretches all the way from Humboldt Park to the lake, and along its banks on the Humboldt Park end, dozens of families of mallard ducks are being farmed—mostly for their eggs, though some of the fatter ones are taken away to be burned alive in sacrifice in times of bad weather—by a colony of beavers who hold the ducks captive in a dam-like structure covered by backstops salvaged from the chain-link-fence production facility on Pulaski Road that the reigning King of Chicago's grandfather granted the colony dominion over some fifty summers back.

The King of Chicago is an emperor penguin who's able to fly.

Every penguin in Chicago believes the king's a god, that his father was a god, his father's father was a god, his brothers are lesser gods, his sons are all gods to one extent or another, and their sons will be gods to one extent or another.

Like the penguins and the rest of the kingdom's citizens, the beavers believe the king is a god, that the previous kings of Chicago were gods, and they believe that the brothers and the sons of the reigning king who are able to fly are also gods, but unlike the penguins, most of the beavers aren't quite sure about the other brothers and sons of the king—the unflighted princes—though they keep that to themselves, as do all the other citizens who share the beavers' doubts.

On the other hand, we have the ducks. The ducks don't believe there's such a thing as gods. If there were such a thing as gods, why would all those gods be penguins? Why would none of those gods be ducks? Surely at least one god would be a duck, and that god duck would never allow the penguins to bar the ducks from acquiring citizenship, let alone allow the penguins to allow the beavers to cage and steal from and murder the ducks.

The ducks hate the beavers, fear the penguins, and believe in dumb luck. Accident. Chance. That's what they profess.

Still, they like to tell stories that account for their luck—as if it weren't dumb, as if chance weren't random.

They've got hundreds and hundreds of stories like that.

All their stories are about the old days, their ancestors, how they arrived in the Kingdom of Chicago and ended up being caged by the beavers. The stories lack intertextual harmony, they contradict each other at nearly every turn—what caused what effect, who came before whom from where and why—but that doesn't bother any of the ducks. In fact, the ducks prefer it that way. If the stories cohered, what would they have to argue about? What would they have to refine and embellish? If their stories cohered, they'd all become suicidal with boredom. Apart from telling stories and arguing about them, there isn't much else you can do in captivity. Eat and sleep and fuck. That's basically it. And if you eat too much, you get fat, no one fucks you, and soon the beavers take you away and they kill you. If you sleep too much, that also makes you fat, and the beavers take you away and they kill you. And the more you fuck, the more it breaks your heart when the beavers steal your eggs, so you become depressed and you eat and sleep more and it makes you fat and no one fucks you and the beavers take you away and they kill you.

All the stories are about the old days, and one of the stories is about how, in the old days, the ducks had been caged by a different group of beavers in a different scummy branch of the river in a distant land that they'd eventually escaped to the Kingdom of Chicago from, and in that former cage, their ancestors used to sometimes tell stories that weren't about the ducks who came before them, but those who would come after them, and one of the stories their ancestors told was about a special duck with a speech impediment—a stutter or a stammer—who would free them from their cage and lead them out of the distant land, and, according to the story told in the cage in the Kingdom of Chicago, the story that their ancestors used to tell about the special duck came true: the special duck freed them from the distant land's cage and brought them to Chicago.

Nearly all the ducks in the Kingdom of Chicago think the story about the special duck is bullshit.

Some of them think it's *dangerous* bullshit, and they refuse to tell it to any of their ducklings because they don't want their ducklings to develop any hope of escaping the beavers. Too much hope can, they believe, lead to overeating and too much fucking.

Other ducks who think the story about the special duck is bullshit, however, don't think its being bullshit is dangerous at all, and they tell it to their ducklings to give them pride— "Ducks were *free* once," etcetera. The right amount of pride can, these ducks believe, lead to proper eating and the right amount of fucking.

Of course, there are also some ducks—very few of them, really—who don't think the story about the special duck is bullshit, or at least they *suspect* it isn't bullshit, and it fills them with hope and pride the both, and they tell it to their ducklings for *that* reason.

To one such duck is hatched a runt duckling who shivers a lot. It's neurological or something. The duckling, whenever he becomes afraid or angry or frustrated—he just shakes all over. Which is, the duckling's mother thinks, adorable and peculiar, but above all: *special.*

And during the first month or so of this duckling's life, his mother thinks about her own mother a lot, her own mother who'd fattened and been taken away by the beavers last year, and who she—that is, the shivering duckling's mother— misses terribly.

And one thing she thinks about when she thinks about her mother is something her mother had said just days before the beavers took her away: that maybe the story about their ancestors telling the story about the special duck who freed the ducks from the cage in the previous land and led them into the Kingdom of Chicago had been told and retold and refined and embellished and argued about so many times that it had gotten muddled, gotten confused.

For instance, maybe their ancestors *did* tell a story about a special duck who would come along to free the ducks, but the special duck they told the story about had *not* come along to free their ancestors: their ancestors' prophecy hadn't been *about* their ancestors but about the *descendants* of their ancestors: *them:* the ducks in the cage of the beavers in the Kingdom of Chicago.

Perhaps the special duck, the shivering duckling's grandma suggested to his mother before being taken away and murdered by the beavers—perhaps the special duck would come along one day to free her and her daughter and the other ducks in the cage of the beavers in the Kingdom of Chicago.

And if *that* much had gotten muddled and confused, then other parts might have also gotten muddled and confused, the mother of the shivering duckling starts to think, when she thinks about her mother.

For instance: maybe the prophecy wasn't made by ancestors who'd lived in the previous cage, but by ancestors who'd lived in the current cage.

Or maybe there hadn't ever *been* a previous cage. Maybe the ducks had always been caged in *this* cage: the cage of the beavers in the Kingdom of Chicago.

And maybe, just maybe, the part about the speech impediment had also gotten muddled and confused. That is: maybe the special duck who would come along to free them would not have a speech impediment, but something else about it that made it different from the other ducks in the cage of the beavers in the Kingdom of Chicago.

Like perhaps he wouldn't stutter or stammer but *shiver.*

For a month or so after the shivering duckling's hatch, his mother entertains thoughts like these, especially once the sun has gone down and she's finished telling her ducklings their bedtime stories.

And then, out of nowhere, something unprecedented happens. Two things, really.

Two unprecedented things.

The first unprecedented thing is: a tornado.

One night, a tornado rips through Humboldt Park. The tornado itself doesn't harm any ducks. It doesn't pass directly over the dam-like structure in which they're caged, and the backstop covering the dam-like structure protects them from the worst of the flying detritus.

However, seven beaver kits are killed in a trice, and one of them is Robbie, the eldest son of the beaver chancellor, Sweet Beav the Fantastic.

The following morning, at Robbie's burial, the beaver chancellor, who has already announced to the other beavers that he no longer feels very sweet or fantastic and would, from now on, like them to call him Wrecked Beav the Humbled— the beaver chancellor tells the other beavers that he and they have angered the weather and need to appease it with better sacrifices.

"And what is a better sacrifice?" Wrecked Beav the Humbled asks the other beavers, rhetorically. "Have we not always sacrificed the most fattened ducks?" They *have,* Wrecked Beav the Humbled assures them. They *have* always sacrificed the most fattened ducks. Therefore there exists only one possible way to interpret the meaning of the tragedy the weather has inflicted upon them:

The weather no longer wants fattened ducks.

What the weather wants now is unfattened ducks.

Unfattened duck*lings.*

Seven of them.

The beavers are so relieved to hear that Wrecked Beav the Humbled, despite the loss of Robbie, is still capable of understanding the weather, that they chant his new name. "Wrecked Beav the Humbled! Wrecked Beav the Humbled!"

They chant it seven times.

And Wrecked Beav the Humbled is so moved by their chanting, and so clever a beaver, that when he realizes the number of times they've chanted his name is *exactly equal* to the number of beaver kits killed by the weather, which is of course also *exactly equal* to the number of unfattened ducklings he just told the beavers that the beavers must sacrifice to appease the weather, he understands that the equivalency itself means something, as well, something more than what he's already interpreted, something more than *seven,* and, all at once, it comes to him.

"Seven ducklings *times* seven!" he says. "Seven ducklings for seven days!"

"Seven times seven!" the beavers chant. "Seven times seven! Seven times seven!"

The beavers chant, "Seven times seven!" seven times, then race each other to the dam-like structure to clear the detritus off the backstop and gather the day's seven ducklings for sacrifice.

And that's the other unprecedented thing that happens a month or so after the hatch of the shivering duckling: the beavers start killing ducklings.

One of the first seven ducklings the beavers kill is the shivering duckling's least favorite brother, Todd.

Todd was the first and the biggest of the clutch to hatch. He resented the shivering duckling for being their mother's favorite, and, when their mother wasn't looking, Todd would step on the shivering duckling's foot or clap his bill around the shivering duckling's neck, and sometimes he'd even, with the flap of a wing, knock a bit of food from the shivering duckling's bill and snatch it up from the ground or the water where it fell, or, even worse, *not* snatch it up, but let the food drown if it fell in the water or shit right on it if it fell on the ground—like, he didn't even pretend he wanted the food for himself: he just didn't want the shivering duckling to have it. Todd was a dick.

Still, when the beavers took Todd away to kill him, the shivering duckling was really sad. Also afraid. Todd tried to fight back with all his might—made sounds with his voice that sounded, to the shivering duckling, very dangerous, and even bill-clapped one of the beavers on its tail—but Todd's fighting proved useless. Didn't slow the beavers down one bit. In fact, the beavers laughed while they took Todd away. And if brave Todd wasn't any match for the beavers, the shivering duckling wouldn't stand a chance when they came for him, none of his brothers would, let alone his sister, and the shivering duckling knew it and he shivered.

His mother was even sadder and more afraid than he was. Seeing Todd taken away like that broke something in her. She spent the rest of the day swimming furious circles around the dam-like structure and making incomprehensible sounds that were kind of like softer, completely unfearsome versions of the sounds that Todd had made while he'd tried to fight the beavers, and she'd paused in her circling only twice before sundown, both times near the duck that the shivering duckling and his brothers and sisters had all agreed was probably their father, and when she paused she made sounds that were *just* like the ones that Todd had made while fighting the beavers.

The first time she paused, the probably-father duck was eating a pile of food he'd gathered, and he lowered his eyes and ate it more rapidly.

The second time, which came a few hours later, the probably-father duck was also eating a pile of food he'd gathered, and he ate it more rapidly, but didn't lower his eyes, and the shivering duckling's mother, still making the fearsome beaver-fighting-Todd sounds, kicked some of the food pile into the water, and the probably-father duck clapped his bill around her neck and dunked her head into the water and held it there till the duck who the shivering duckling and his brothers and sisters all agreed was probably their uncle clapped his bill around the probably-father's neck, and the probably-father, releasing their mother's neck, then made a quick and very fearsome beaver-fighting-Todd sound himself, and the shivering duckling's mother turned and swam away to circle the dam-like structure as before.

But it isn't till some hours after sundown that the shivering duckling realizes just how broken his mother has become.

It isn't till some hours after sundown that the beavers stop singing, and the firepits the beavers burned the seven sacrificial ducklings in have finally gone out, and all the ducks in the dam-like structure, their eyes and throats still stinging from the smoke, have fallen asleep—it isn't till then that the shivering duckling's mother wakes him with a nudge and tells him to follow her to the opposite corner of the dam-like structure, where she shows him a hole in the backstop.

Three diamonds of the chain-link have been punched out by a branch or a log the tornado had flung the night before.

The hole is *just* big enough for the shivering duckling to fit through, and his mother tells him that she loves him, that he's special, that he might even be the special duck from the story she tells him at bedtime sometimes, and that he has to get out. He has to, *right then,* she says, climb on her back and go up through the hole and swim as far away as he can from the murderous beavers and the dam-like structure.

The shivering duckling doesn't like this at all. Shivers harder than he's ever shivered before.

He hasn't even learned how to fly yet, he says.

And his mother says that upsets her as well, but that he knows how to swim and he knows how to hide and he knows how to feed himself: those are the most important things to know, and knowing those things should be enough for now.

He says he doesn't want to go, though. He'll be all alone.

She tells him that alone is the only way to go. She wishes she could send his sister and his brothers with him, but they're just too big: he's the only one who can fit through the hole.

But he hasn't even gotten to say goodbye to them, he says.

His mother tells him that she'll say goodbye to them for him.

But that isn't the point! That isn't the point he's making at all, he says. He doesn't want to be apart from his sister and his brothers to begin with, and most of all he doesn't want to be apart from her.

And his mother says that she doesn't want to be apart from him either, and she's sure it's the same for his brothers and his sister, but that any of them could be taken away at any moment by the beavers, then killed, just like Todd, there's no order anymore, nothing they can do to predict or affect their fate, it's no longer just a matter of not getting fat, and so when they'll have to part isn't up to them anyway. It may never have been up to them, but now for sure it *really* isn't. Except for tonight. Tonight they have a choice. Tonight they can choose to part *tonight*. But not after tonight. In the morning, she says, the beavers will find the hole in the backstop, and they'll fix the hole or replace the backstop, and the shivering duck will never have another chance to escape, and if he doesn't escape, he'll never be able to come back to free them, and all of them will die in the cage or the sacrifice pits of the beavers in the Kingdom of Chicago.

"Stop shivering now," she tells him, "and climb on my back, and I'll raise you up, and you'll go through the hole."

He's never been told to stop shivering before, and he tries to stop shivering, but can't stop shivering, being told to stop shivering only makes him shiver more, and his mother claps her beak around his neck, *hard,* and a sound comes out of him that's like a higher-pitched version of the beaver-fighting sound that Todd made that morning, and that sound, at least to the shivering duckling, sounds even more fearsome than Todd's had sounded, and it fortifies him some, and he stops his shivering.

"I love you," his mother says. "Any waterfowl with a heart and two eyes would love you," she says. "Find a new mommy, then grow big and strong and come back and save us."

And he climbs on her back, and she raises him up, and he pushes through the hole and runs along the backstop and jumps in the river and swims away.

He's halfway to the lake when the sun comes up and he spots a bevy of beautiful swans on a tiny island directly ahead of him. He approaches the island, shaking and shivering, and tells them that he thinks they're all very beautiful, the most beautiful birds he's ever seen, and that his mommy has told him to find a new mommy and grow big and strong, so he's looking for a mommy and he wonders if maybe one of them would like to be his new mommy till he grows big and strong.

Most of the swans seem to find this hilarious, and they call him mean names. They say he's the ugliest duckling they've ever laid eyes on, and they tell him that his mommy, who's a *whore*, they say—he doesn't know what that means, but can tell it's unkind—they say that the shivering duckling's whore-mommy hates him because he was born even more retarded than the usual duck, which is why he shivers and shakes like that, like a fucking *retard*, whatever that means. And they say he's *a poultry*, whatever that means. And they say he's *a chattel*, whatever *that* means.

One swan, though, doesn't seem to find him hilarious at all. She steps out in front of the rest of the bevy, and asks the shivering duckling if he would like *her* to be his new mommy, and the shivering duckling says that he would really like that so much, and he steps up onto the tiny island, and, before he understands what's happening to him, the new-mommy swan has clamped her bill hard around one of his wings, the beaver-fighting sound is coming out of his throat, and he's no longer standing on the edge of the island. He's no longer standing on anything at all.

The new-mommy swan has whipped him up into the air in the direction of the nearer bank of the river, and he thinks she's trying to teach him how to fly, and he even thinks he might be learning to fly—he's flapping his wings, and he certainly feels *different* than he ever has before—but he isn't lifting up any higher in the air, in fact he's dropping fast, and he falls on his side, onto the nearer bank of the river, falls right onto the extended wing the tricky swan had just clamped in her bill, and the wing makes a bunch of snapping noises because the wing has just broken.

The wing hurts so much it's like there's more of the pain than there is of the wing.

It's like there's more of the pain than there is of *him*.

It's less like it's *the pain of the shivering duckling* and more like he's *the shivering duckling of the pain,* and the swans are laughing even louder than before and they're shouting incomprehensible insults like "That duckling really granted his king a privilege!" and "What a privilege that duckling has granted his king!" and "Have you ever before seen another creature with so much natural privilege-granting talent?" and the shivering duckling is sure that he'll die.

He doesn't want to die in sight of the swans, so he drags his body closer to the water and hides in the nearest high clump of cattails, and he shuts his eyes and he shivers and shakes while they laugh at him or laugh at his pain or laugh about their incomprehensible insults till one of them shouts out, "Gods in the distance!" and the laughter and insults are instantly replaced by the thumps and crumples and air-tearing roar of the entire bevy taking flight at once.

The King of Chicago enjoys harassing swans, though he doesn't seem to think of it that way. He seems to think of his harassment of the swans as a favor to the swans, or an honor that he's bestowing on them.

The harassment always takes the same form:

Whenever the king comes across some swans, he invites them to fly around in circles with him—to, as he puts it, "grant their king the privilege of taking to the higher air with them"—and, because he's a god, they have no other choice but to accept the invitation.

And like his flighted brothers and like his flighted sons and like his flighted father who reigned before him, the king's flying is ugly—wobbly, spastic, endlessly flapping—and, once they've all gotten up into the sky with him, the swans have to fly even klutzier than he does to make him look good or, rather, to make him feel as though he looks good.

Despite how loudly his retinue down on the ground may applaud—and they always applaud pretty goddamn loudly—no one looks good, and everyone knows it except for the king, and no one else knows it better than the swans.

It's a terrible humiliation for the swans, who pride themselves on their grace above all—even above the beauty of their plumage—so they do their best to avoid it when they can.

The king is not, however, among the waddle of penguins the swans on the tiny island just fled. Had they stuck around, they would not have been humiliated. They would have, in fact, enjoyed themselves.

They would've been given a bunch of free food.

Heading up the swan-scaring waddle of penguins parading up the bank is the king's only daughter, Princess Guin, who likes to stroll in the morning with her friends and give buckets of food away to subjects she encounters.

Her guards push the buckets on a four-wheeled cart.

It's a lot of buckets.

Guin tries to be generous.

The shivering duckling doesn't know about any of this.

All he knows about penguins is what his mother taught him: that the penguins rule Chicago but that doesn't make them gods, whatever that means, because there's no such thing as gods, whatever *that* means.

And all he knows about what just happened is that some very mean swans called him very mean names and then a swan he'd hoped would want to be his new mommy didn't want to be his mommy but wanted instead to be the meanest swan of all so she picked him up and threw him and the other swans laughed and said a bunch of weird stuff and left him to die, and now his wing is broken and he's so afraid and sad and in pain and also *really* angry that he doubts he'll be able to ever stop shivering.

The shivering duckling is shivering so hard, the burst part of the flowering top of the bulrush he's leaning on the stalk of shakes off some of its fuzziest pollen, which expands into a glistening, donut-shaped cloud.

The glistening draws Princess Guin's attention and, waddle in tow, she goes to the cloud to get a closer look, finds the shivering duckling with its broken wing, and her heart balloons. He's the most adorable thing she's ever seen. Is he not the most adorable thing they've ever seen? she asks the waddle. He's so adorable, they can't even speak, just aww and coo.

And the shivering duckling aims his wet eyes at the face of the princess and tries to say, "Mommy?" but bulrush pollen has caught in his throat, and it scrapes like sand, and the scraping of it chokes him, forcing him to cough, and between the coughing and all the shivering, "Mommy?" comes out sounding like, "Mo?—Mo? . . . Mo?—Mo?"

And Princess Guin says, "I think he's telling us his name is Momo! Aw, Momo, dear Momo. Sweet little Momo. You *must* stop coughing. Drink a little water. Wash your little throat out."

So the shivering duckling drinks a little water, washes his throat out, relieving the scrape, and he asks the princess if she'll be his new mommy till he grows big and strong, or until he dies, or at least till his wing heals, and she's so overwhelmed by how adorable his shivering little voice is, she feels an urge to stomp him dead.

Being the princess, that's just what she does.

Not really. I'm kidding. That's too fucked up. Who would ever . . . That's not what's written down here.

Guin does not stomp the shivering duckling dead.

She tells him she'd love to be his new mommy for as long as he'll let her, and she lifts him up from out of the bulrushes, rubs her soft forehead along the edge of his bill, and carries him all the way home to the palace, feeding him bits of food along the way.

When they get to the palace, she goes to her father, the King of Chicago, says, "His name's Momo," which the shivering duckling doesn't bother to protest—he doesn't have a name, always wanted a name, always thought it wasn't fair that only Todd got a name—and the king asserts that Momo the shivering duckling is just way too adorable, blesses the adoption, then calls the best of the palace doctors to the court.

The doctors feed the shivering duckling a potato-based paste that's laced with opium, and once it's kicked in, they set his broken wing and bind it to splints.

Over the next few months, Momo the shivering duckling grows up. Becomes a shivering youth, then a shivering adult. He doesn't learn to fly—although you'd never be able to tell by looking, the nerves in the wing he broke sustained lasting damage—but soon he gets his shivering under control.

He's rarely afraid of anything anymore.

Hardly ever sad, either.

He barely remembers his life in the dam-like structure. His mother and siblings, after coming to seem to him less like birds he'd formerly known and more like characters from half-remembered dreams, came to seem less like characters from half-remembered dreams and more like half-remembered characters from stories that somebody else had told him, and now they seem less like half-remembered characters from stories somebody else had told him and more like facts from a history lesson to which he didn't pay enough attention.

It's pretty much only when he becomes very angry that he really starts to shake anymore, and he doesn't become very angry very often. Doesn't find much reason to.

All the penguins treat him like royalty. They call him a god. They really love him. He's no longer *adorable*, like he was as a shivering duckling, but he's strikingly *beautiful*—the way his emerald crown feathers catch the sunlight, the way his blue and mostly hidden secondary feathers appear to almost like *wink* at you or something when he stretches his wings, not to mention how he glides along the surface of waters without any sign of effort: with his head held high and his feet beneath him so that, even when he's going fast as he's able, you can't detect paddling. Beautiful. Appealing.

So appealing and beautiful do the penguins find Momo that some begin to whisper about it being maybe other than right to allow the beavers to farm his brethren.

Over a period of months, the whispers get louder, become more like murmurs, and the princess, who from the very moment she adopted Momo understood somewhere deep in her heart that it was wrong to allow the farming of his brethren but felt she was too inexperienced and female to broach the matter with her father, the king, hears the murmurs and is bolstered by them.

She goes to her father and tells him of the murmurs, and tells him she thinks that perhaps he should consider getting out ahead of them before they get louder. "Before they graduate from murmurs to rumbles to full-scale loose talk," she says to the king.

Loose talk doesn't frighten the king, let alone do rumbles, nothing frightens the king, but he does love Momo, and, more than that, he loves the princess, and he's moved by the way she feels, he tells her.

If he were to know for certain that the brethren of his adopted grandson were anything like his adopted grandson, the king says, then he would, by royal decree, free them all and make them citizens of the Kingdom of Chicago, but he doesn't know that for certain, does he? And neither does the princess.

The only duck who any penguin really knows, he says, is Momo, who has, after all, been raised and civilized in the palace, and the fact that Momo was able to escape from the beavers whereas no other duck has ever escaped from the beavers would seem to indicate that Momo is special, and, given that the beavers, who no one denies are savage imbeciles, have been able to subjugate Momo's brethren since before the founding of the Kingdom of Chicago—since before the gods learned to fly, in fact—it might just be that Momo's brethren are the same lesser creatures the penguins have always suspected them to be: even more savage and imbecilic creatures than are, for example, those imbecilic savage beavers who farm them.

Wisdom, says the king, dictates the following: that before freeing Momo's brethren from the beavers, a delegation of penguins should visit and observe them in the dam-like structure in order to determine their level—if any—of imbecilic savagery, that he himself should lead such a delegation, and that the princess and Momo will, he hopes, agree to join him.

When she hears this, the princess becomes so happy she does a kind of semivoluntary foxtrot.

The delegation heads out the next morning. Thirty-some delegates plus another twenty-some guards and servants. It's only a ninety-minute journey by foot, but they stop to enjoy a picnic brunch in the marshy crotch between the river's main bank and the bank of the branch that leads to the beavers, and just as their brunching gets under way, the king spots a roving swan in the water, and commands the swan to trumpet for his bevy.

When the bevy arrives, the king asks them for the privilege of taking to the air with them, they tell him they'd be honored, and they fly around in circles for a while.

Momo doesn't know why—he can't remember—but something about the swans makes him angry, and he shivers at the sight of them, shivers even harder at the sound of the joyful laughter they're faking.

The penguins notice. Whisper about it. Didn't Momo

outgrow that shivering thing? They haven't seen him do it in a really long time. How long? Months at least. Maybe a year. Two years, even? It seems a lot different than the way they remember it. They remember it being adorable, endearing. Isn't that right? Isn't that how it was? Yet now it looks . . . Well, it's really a little off-putting, isn't it? Not adorable at all. It looks like something is wrong with Momo. Like Momo has a disease or something. It looks like weakness. It looks . . . not regal in the least. Much less godly.

Momo hears a few of these whispers, which anger him a lot, causing him to shake more. What should he do? Should he pretend he doesn't hear, or should he try to defend himself? How can he defend himself? Each penguin outweighs him by orders of magnitude. Where is his mother? Why isn't she defending him? He doesn't want to ask her to—he'd look even weaker if he asked her to defend him—but he shouldn't have to ask. She should know to defend him. Like, doesn't she hear what they're whispering about him?

In fact, she doesn't.

Princess Guin doesn't hear the whispers.

She's seen her father fly circles with swans before, seen it dozens of times, and it always takes forever and makes her feel embarrassed, so she's slipped away with her favorite guard to a patch of tall grass some twenty meters distant, where she lies with her head between the guard's happy feet and teaches him the art of cloacalingus, which she learned by observing an orgy of bats at the Navy Pier ruins the week before, while out on a charitable food-distribution walk. The sight of those bats repelled her at first but, being someone who strives to keep an open mind, she watched till she overcame the repulsion, till it turned to something else, something like an obsession.

She's thought about the bats nonstop for days now, and, lying in the grass with the guard, she's glad she did.

Those bats, turns out, were *on* to something.

The princess and the guard sneak back to the waddle just as it's finished packing up to leave. She sees Momo shivering. She asks him what's wrong. He lowers his eyes, says he doesn't want to say.

She presses a bit, but that only makes him shake more, and so she backs off, gives him space, allows him to walk a few feet in front of her, puts all her motherly intuition to the task of trying to imagine what's troubling him.

Perhaps he's afraid of what the freedom of the ducks will mean for him? she wonders. Afraid of how the coming liberation of the ducks might affect the specialness of the special place that he holds in the hearts of the penguins of the Kingdom of Chicago? Perhaps he fears that when they see the ducks in the dam-like structure, the penguins will come to think less of him? That they'll make him feel ashamed of who he is?

But that wouldn't make sense. Why would he only become upset about that now? Why wouldn't he have said something yesterday? or, for that matter, *ever before*? Had Momo voiced such concerns, she'd never have brought the topic of duck liberation before the king. Had he voiced such concerns, she would have, without a moment's hesitation, done everything she could to *quell* the spread of the duck-lib murmurs.

And Momo had to know that, didn't he? Yes. Of course. Of course he knew. Must have. So if he had those concerns, he'd surely have voiced them. So that couldn't be it. That couldn't be what troubled him. Where does she even come up with this shit?

Interesting question, she thinks. Good question.

Perhaps, she thinks, these concerns are her own. Are they? Couldn't be. If the concerns were *hers,* she'd never have suggested duck-lib to her father. Also, she wouldn't have hidden them from herself, the concerns. That wouldn't make sense. No one really did that. No one really hid their own concerns from themselves. Why would someone do that? *How* could someone do that, even if they wanted to? That had never made sense to her.

Plus even if it would have made sense to hide her own concerns from herself and she knew how to do so, why would she *stop* hiding them? let alone *now*? No. These weren't her concerns. They simply weren't. She hadn't any such concerns.

But maybe Momo, for some reason—owing to something she'd inadvertently said or done before she'd snuck away with the guard—maybe Momo is concerned she has such concerns? Or that she has concerns that are something *like* those concerns?

Maybe, she thinks.

Perhaps.

May*be*.

But, try though she does, she can't for the life of her remember having said or done anything that might have led him to think that she had such concerns, or *any* concerns, and as the delegation comes in sight of the beaver settlement, and she sees that Momo's shivering still hasn't subsided, she's stricken with panic. She panics at the thought that she's failing him somehow, failing to understand him somehow, that she's wounding him without realizing it, that a breach is forming—has formed—between them and that if she doesn't close it before they meet his brethren in their cage, it will never close, the wound will never heal, and they'll never be the same again.

And she picks him up gently, and looks him in the eyes, and says, in the softest, most tender voice she can muster, that she wants him to know that he can talk to her about anything, no matter how upsetting or strange or embarrassing he thinks it might be. He's her son and she loves him, she's loved him from the very moment they met, and it's because of her love for him—it's because of *him*—that this delegation has embarked on this historical journey, which, if all goes well, will result in great changes to the very texture of life in the Kingdom of Chicago. If all goes well, she says, Momo's brethren will all become citizens. The ducks will be free, just like him, but they'll *never ever* move him out of position, much less will any of them ever stand in for him—he's one of a kind. No one in the world could ever replace him. He'll always be the first free duck in the Kingdom of Chicago, he'll always be the first *anything* in her heart.

Still shivering, Momo averts his gaze.

"Say something," Guin says.

"Put me down," he says.

She puts him down.

"I've done as you've asked," she says. "Tell me what you're thinking, now. Please, Momo. Tell me."

"Your beak smells weird," he says. "It smells really bad. 'What the hell has she been eating?' That's what I'm thinking."

No, no, no. Again. That's not . . . Bad joke. That's not what's written down here.

That's not what happens.

What happens is the princess sets Momo on the ground as he's asked, and he shuffles off ahead of her. "Just leave me alone," he tells her, over his shoulder.

And for the first time ever, she really . . . dislikes him. Even kind of—for just a flash—she even kinda hates him a little.

First time that's ever happened.

She looks down at Momo as he walks in front of her, and it's as if she's seeing through a new set of eyes. Or an ancient set of eyes. A different set, anyway. A set not her own. And what she sees is how small he is. How low to the ground. How unsure of stride. How entirely non-tuxedoed of plumage. "Pitiful," she thinks. "Underbird. Weak. Wretched, shaking, suffering, animal. Someone," she thinks, "should stomp him out of his shivering misery."

But only for a flash does Guin think those thoughts. See through those eyes. Only for a flash.

In the wake of the flash, she just feels really guilty. Ashamed of herself. He's her son, after all.

The delegation arrives at the dam-like structure, and right about then's when things start to get dark.

Some beavers have just pulled a fattened duck up from under the backstop. Two of them hold her, a third binds her legs. Some other beavers a little farther away are getting a sacrificial firepit going.

When the beavers in the first group see the King of Chicago before them, they freeze.

The king tells one of them to untie the duck and bring her over. He tells another one to go get the chancellor.

By this point, Momo and Guin have both stepped to the front of the delegation to stand on either side of the king.

It occurs to Guin that the duck the king has ordered untied might turn out to be Momo's first mother.

It occurs to her that whether the duck the king has ordered untied turns out to be Momo's first mother or not, there's a distinct possibility that Momo's first mother will be among the ducks in the dam-like structure.

And it occurs to her that the reason why Momo's been shivering might be that it's occurred to Momo that Guin would be thinking just the kind of thoughts that she finds herself beginning to think.

Namely: What if Momo loves his first mother more than me? What if I'm jealous? Will I be able to hide it? Will I be able to prevent myself from stomping her dead? Is that even what I'd do? *Would* I stomp her dead? It *is* the first response that comes to mind, but that doesn't mean . . . But how can I know? I do know I'll be jealous if he loves her more than me. I will: I'll be terribly jealous. *I'm* Momo's mother. I'm the one who raised him and made him a god. It's possible that I *will* stomp his first mother dead if he loves her more than me. So if that *is* what Momo, who knows me very well—if that's what he's afraid of, then, well: he's right to be. Oh, let's hope it doesn't come to that! Let's hope he doesn't love his first mother more. Let's hope he hardly loves her at all. Better yet, let's hope she's already dead. I can't believe I didn't, till now, consider any of the awful potential outcomes of this visit. What a miserable failure of imagination! My head's been in the clouds. Rather, it should have been. Where it's been in's the cloacas. I'm a terrible mother. I thought I was good, but it turns out I'm terrible.

Having untied the duck, the beavers come forward, set her down before the king. He asks her name.

She tells the king she doesn't have a name.

"In that, and perhaps even more," says the king, "we two are alike."

Meantime, the beaver chancellor—Comeback Beav the Once Destroyed, he calls himself now—the chancellor of the beavers appears before the king, bowing and scraping. "What an honor to be so unexpectedly paid a visit by—" he says, before the king cuts him off.

"What were you doing to this duck?" the king demands.

While the beaver chancellor explains at length about the weather undergod the beavers sacrifice ducks to appease, the duck the king's saved stretches a leg out and shakes all her feathers, drawing Momo's attention, and Momo takes his first good look at her.

It's the first real look he's had at another duck since his unremembered ducklinghood, and, soon enough, he's overcome with a kind of . . . calm.

No.

Not a calm.

The opposite actually.

The total opposite.

It only seems like a calm for a moment because he's stopped shivering, he's completely stopped shivering, all at once he's stopped shivering, but it's not a calm at all, what's overcome him. What it is is an excitement, a *powerful* excitement. Something is shifting, shifted—something inside him. Something inside him has shifted.

And now the something is . . . outside him.

And it's pink as a tongue and corkscrew-shaped.

Weird. Very weird.

Not that he isn't glad it's there—he is. He *is* glad it's there, whatever it is, but he also has the sense that he should do something with it, or *to* it, yet he doesn't know what.

"Please pardon me for asking," the she-duck whispers, "but did my eyes betray me, or were you shivering just now?"

"I was," Momo whispers. "Then I took a good look at you, and something shifted."

"I can *see* that," the she-duck whispers. "Shifted! That's so adorable. You're so adorable. I'm so happy you're here."

"You are? You're happy?"

"Of course I'm happy. The special duck took a look at me and . . . *shifted.*"

"The special duck?"

"That's what she called you—your sister. She'd talk about you all the time when we were ducklings. Said you'd return to the structure to free us. Others didn't believe her. My parents, for example. But I did. I believed her. And now: here you are."

"I have a sister?" Momo whispers. "I always wished I had a sister."

"Well, no, she's not . . . I mean, your sister—she's . . ."

"What?"

"She's gone. They took her away."

"Away?"

"Last month, they—oh, you're shivering again."

It's true. Momo's shivering. He's shivering a lot, and whatever it was that had gotten outside him has gone back inside and he's very confused.

"I don't understand what's happening to me," he whispers. "And I'm very confused about what you just said. Where did they take my sister away to?"

"No, that's not what . . . That's just how we say it. *Take you away.* When they take you away, it means they . . . Well, it means they kill you."

"What are you telling me? You're telling me I had a sister and then they . . . they *killed my sister*?"

"They did."

"Why would they do that?"

"That's what they do."

"But why, though?"

"The weather."

"That makes no sense."

"No, it doesn't."

"I don't . . . I can't believe I had a sister and they killed her."

"It's hard. I know. It can be really hard."

"What was she like? Can you tell me about her? Did you know her well?"

"She was my closest friend. I'll tell you everything I can. Not here, though, okay? Not right now. Let's fly around when you're finished freeing us, and we'll find some privacy, you know? We'll talk."

"I can't fly," Momo whispers. "I don't know how. I . . . I never learned."

"What's to learn?" the she-duck whispers. "It's completely natural. Just jump and flap."

"I'm—"

"Like this," says the she-duck, and she jumps in the air, and she flaps her wings, and she's flying away, and it's so beautiful, the way she flies, that Momo forgets about everything else, even his sister, and, once again, his shivering relents.

The she-duck turns a whole beautiful circle over the heads of the delegation, and then she turns a second one that, impossible though it seems, is even *more* beautiful than the first one was, and just as she starts to turn a third one, Momo jumps in the air, as high as he can.

And he flaps his wings as hard as he can. As fast as he can.

And he's . . . No, he's not exactly flying. His bad wing—it's trouble. It's giving him trouble. He can't make it rotate the way he needs it to rotate to get horizontal and follow the she-duck.

He's not exactly flying, but he isn't falling either.

He's hovering is what he's doing. Bobbing in the air. And what had gone back inside him is again outside him, also bobbing—and what a weird, good thing that is! The wind against the skin of it feels just so incredibly, indescribably . . . *wow*. Especially when the she-duck, who continues to circle, gets to the part of each circle where she makes the turn right over his head, and tells him, "Come on! You're getting it!" and tells him, "Come on! You can do it!" and tells him, "Come on! You've almost got it!"

He doesn't. He doesn't almost have it. He knows that. He knows. And he knows, just as well, that he'll never really get it. He'll never achieve any lateral distance, much less fly a circle. He'll never get up any higher, either, but still.

Still.

What's better than this? What's better than her? What's better than bobbing in the air and watching her circle while the penguins below point up at you, amazed, and break into peels of their famously joyful penguin laughter, so impressed with the sight of Momo the god they can't even control themselves? Nothing.

Nothing is better.

Remember when you were whispering all meanly about me? he thinks at the penguins. Well, how about this? he thinks at the penguins. How about: fuck you. How about *that*? Fuck *you*, I can hover! *Fuck* you, I can bob! I'm bobbing, you fuckers! I jumped, now I hover. I hover and I bob. I'm a bobbing, hovering god above you. You can all go eat a bunch of shit and die. No, no. I don't mean it. I swear. I don't. I'll forgive you for that whispering. In fact, I have. Just did. You've been forgiven, and forgiveness is good. You're entirely forgiven, and it's good. *Feels* good. It feels *good* to forgive. Everything does.

Everything feels good.

Everything feels good, and soon it'll end. Already, Momo senses that it's starting to end. He's breathing pretty hard. Straining himself. It's okay, though, he thinks. Really. It's okay it's ending. He'll do it again—and again and again—and for now, he'll make it last as long as he can. That's all there is to do, and so that's what he does. Makes it last for as long as his muscles will let him. Till his wings tire out and he starts to sink and he has to touch down.

Bobs five and six feet above the heads of the penguins, then four and five feet above the heads of the penguins, then three and four feet above the heads of the penguins, and then he's touching down.

Sticks the landing so well the joyful penguins keep joyfully laughing. Laughing and pointing.

As do the beaver chancellor and the other gathered beavers.

As does the king.

As does his mother.

All laughing and pointing. What are they pointing at, these joy-drunken goofballs? The spot where he landed? It wasn't that hard! To land on the spot, that is. He just kinda did it. It just kinda happened. Really. They're really too easily impressed.

"Momo," says his mother, gasping for breath. "Where did you *get* that? Have you always *had* that? It's so . . . *disgusting*. So *mammalian*!—no offense, Mr. Chancellor . . . Oh, Momo, please put it away already! Or no, don't! Yes, do. Or, I don't even . . ." She's choking with laughter.

He looks at the sky. The she-duck is gone. Again, he starts to shake.

"Will you be staying for the ceremony, then, your majesty?" the beaver chancellor inquires of the king.

"No, no," the king says. "I think we've seen quite enough. And, it would appear, we've accidentally lost you your fattened sacrifice. We will find a way to replace her, I assure you."

"Please, your majesty! There isn't any need," says the beaver chancellor. "It's not a problem at all. Not even a trifle. We have others down there that'll do just as well. Are you *sure* you won't stay? We can make a feast."

"Again, thank you, but no," says the King of Chicago. "We'll be on our way, now. May you please the weather thoroughly."

On the way back to the palace, Momo pops out several boners. He doesn't want to, but he can't seem to help it.

The breeze kicks up, waving weeds and flowers and blades of grass that caress his underside and, *pop:* boner.

Or, desperate to shut out the penguins' laughter as they relive and recount—at first in whispers, then in murmurs—the story of witnessing his great humiliation, he remembers the she-duck circling in the air, and *pop:* boner.

He had a sister, his sister was killed, he'll never get to know her, or anything about her, not unless he can find the she-duck and convince her to tell him the stories she said she would tell him, which, considering how much of a loser he's shown himself to be, he probably couldn't convince her to do, and even if he were able to come up with a way to somehow convince her, how can he possibly hope to find her when he can't even fly, when she could be anywhere, when she could have flown anywhere, anywhere she wished, just soared across the sky to wherever she pleased, just soared across and dove through and *commanded* the sky with all the liquid grace and beauty of—*pop:* boner.

And while his boners bob, he shivers and he shakes. And when he doesn't have a boner, he shivers and he shakes. Throughout the whole return, he shivers and he shakes and pops out boners. All the way back to the palace, poor duck.

The king enjoys Momo's boners a lot. He finds them as hilarious as any penguin would, but they aren't, he determines, regal at all. Nor is his own bearing in the presence of the boners—he can't stop himself from laughing. The way Momo keeps on popping them out—it just isn't fit for court. Isn't befitting of a grandson of the king. Not even an adopted one.

Princess Guin agrees.

So when the delegation gets back to the palace, the king has Momo escorted to the marsh beyond the southern curtain wall, and held under guard indefinitely: till someone's able to come up with a solution to the boners.

The marsh is large, and the food is fine, and Momo's granted as much privacy, sleep, and exercise as he wants, but no one visits—visitors aren't allowed—and he doesn't do well in isolation. He gets really lonely.

Within just a few days, he loses his appetite. Stops paying attention to his personal hygiene. His feathers misalign, lie at haphazard angles. There's a crust all along the edges of his bill. His claws get overgrown and flaky.

The only thing he's permitted that he's able to enjoy is swimming circles in the marsh as fast as he can so the swaying vegetation just beneath the surface will tickle him in a particular way that—if, while he's doing this very fast swimming, he also concentrates hard enough on what he remembers of the image of the she-duck flying right above him—can, he's discovered, provoke an intensely pleasant sensation that eventually reaches such a high pitch that his boner is caused to completely spaz out for a number of seconds, then pull back inside him.

Not to understate the matter: he *really* enjoys this very fast swimming—from the moment he discovers it, it's his favorite thing to do—but it's not a thing that he can do all day. After four or five goes, his boner skin tightens and prickles and burns, he has to rest for at least a few hours, and it's during those hours that his loneliness peaks.

Three weeks or so into his isolation, a new guard appears beside the marsh, tells Momo to get out.

Momo's trying to concentrate. "Let me finish exercising first," he says.

"We mustn't keep the princess waiting," says the guard.

"My mommy?" Momo says. "My *mother*, I mean? She wants to see me?"

His boner pulls in.

Momo follows the guard to Princess Guin's quarters, rubbing much of the crust off his bill with his wings, shaking most of the feathers of his breast into place.

"I missed you *so* much, Mommy," he says when he sees her.

She takes a couple steps back and gestures to three of the king's engineers, who are standing behind her, holding weird things. Flappy things. Thin.

"Those are called *pants*," she says. "If you agree to wear them whenever you're in public, you'll be allowed to come and go as you please."

"I can move back into the royal quarters?"

"Eventually, maybe. Well, probably not. If I'm being completely honest here: no. But you will be allowed on the palace grounds."

"Don't you love me anymore?"

"I do. Of course. But it's different now."

"Different? Why? Why is it different?"

"You *know* why, Momo."

"I miss you guys, though."

"We miss you, too. But it's the *old* you we miss. Who you *used to be*. Or who we *think* you used to be. Who we *thought* you were, I guess."

"It's not my fault I get boners!" Momo says.

"It isn't. We know that. We know about boners. I mean, we've seen the swans' boners at least—well, who *knows* how many times?"

"Swans get boners?" Momo says.

"Swans do get boners, yes," says the princess, "and we've seen a lot of them. We've seen the beavers' boners, too. And the boners of the weasels and the boners of the badgers. We've seen bats with boners. Rats with boners. Squirrels and dogs and cats with boners. Once, in a field of overgrown soy past which we journeyed on our way to the coronation of our cousin, the King of Cicero, my brothers and I saw dolphins with boners. They were chasing a walrus. We've seen countless boners, Momo. We are birds of the world. However, we have never seen a boner in the palace. And we've certainly never allowed the boner-capable to reside in royal quarters, or even spend the night. Not in my lifetime. And that won't change. Can't. The king won't let it. But if you wear the pants, you can come and go from the marsh as you please, free as any citizen of the Kingdom of Chicago, and sometimes you can visit us, here in the palace."

"Okay," Momo says. "Okay, okay! I'll *wear* the pants. I didn't say I wouldn't. I'll do whatever I have to to be less lonely—I mean, I'm really going crazy. I've missed you so much. I just . . . I really want things to be like how they were. Between you and me at least."

"That won't happen," the princess says. "Never again will things be like they were. You have to accept that. But an approximation of how things were . . . that's better than nothing."

"Is it?" Momo says.

"It very well might be," the princess says. "It just might be. So one step at a time, son. First step is: try on those pants. Try them on while I go get the king."

There are three pairs of pants, each a different color: fluorescent orange, shocking pink, and electric blue.

Momo goes to the engineer holding the blue pair. The engineer shows him how to put them on. Momo puts them on, walks around a little. There's a roughness. A ragged seam or something. Something rough that rubs against the rim of his cloaca.

For a number of steps, it doesn't feel that bad. It feels almost good. His boner pops out. Well, it tries to pop out, but the seam, or whatever it is, rakes the tip, which *hurts,* and the boner pulls in.

He tries on the orange pair of pants—no better.

Tries on the pink—again, same thing.

All this time, the engineers are laughing. Momo figures it's because he's been walking so haltingly, but then he stops walking, and they keep on laughing.

His mother returns, trailing the king.

The moment they see him, they fall apart laughing.

"It's even . . ." the king says, trying to catch his breath. "I think it's even worse than . . ."

"It's like they're talking!" Guin says. "It's like they're saying, 'Hey, Guin! There might be a boner hiding out in here!'"

"'Your majesty!'" the king shouts. "'Your majesty, please! Help us! Keep us safe! Within us resides a most fearsome boner!'"

"Oh dear," Princess Guin says. "This won't work, will it?"

"I'm afraid not," the king says. "He can't be seen like that." He tells his engineers: "I commend your attempts here, and I'm proud as ever to reign in a kingdom with an educational system that gives rise to engineers who are capable of such cutting-edge innovation as that which has gone into the creation of these . . . *pants,* as you call them. Proud, I tell you. And you *will* be rewarded. However, these pants *are* a failure. They hide the boner, true, but only at the cost of constantly reminding one that a boner's being hidden."

"Grandpa, I don't," Momo says to the king. "I don't have a boner."

"And yet, I can't," says the king, "stop thinking you might. Thinking you do. Even as I speak, I'm imagining your boner."

"The same goes for me," says Princess Guin.

"I'm sorry, Momo," says the king. "The pants are a bust. You'll have to stay in the marsh."

"No, please," Momo says. "*Please no.* It's too lonely. Alone in the marsh—that's so much worse than making people laugh. I feel so much better right now than in the marsh. I'd rather be laughed at any day—every day—than be all alone." Momo isn't just saying it. Isn't even exaggerating. It's entirely true. This is how Momo feels.

The king hates a whiner.

"Get ahold of yourself," he scolds. "You lack force. You lack dignity. Look at how you're shivering and shaking. Your very presence can't help but make a mockery of your surroundings. I can't have that in this palace. I *will* not have that in this palace."

"But you do," Momo says. "You do and you have." Momo's had an idea! An inspiration! An idea so inspired, it stops him from shivering. "You do allow it, Grandpa," he says. "You do allow that sort of mockery in the palace. You allow it *at court.*"

"False!" the king says. "Never have I allowed—"

"Lope!" says Momo. "What about *Lope*?"

Lope is the king's congenitally brain-damaged bastard son.

"Lope's the court jester," says the king of Chicago.

"Yes," says Momo. "I could be like Lope."

"You . . . are not the court jester," says the king.

"I *could* be," Momo says. "Why couldn't I be?"

"Well, for one thing," says the king, "we already have Lope."

"Maybe I'm better than Lope, though," says Momo.

"Lope *has* gotten tiresome," Princess Guin says.

"Perhaps a *little* tiresome," the king says to Guin. "He's been complaining of headaches lately. Or I *think* that's the complaint. 'Lope's melonbobby glumpens and nunkers' he tells me—that means 'I have a headache,' right? That's how I've understood it, at least. I think he's still pretty *good,* though, our Lope. I still enjoy having him around, you know?"

"Of course," says the princess, "and no one's suggesting we cut Lope loose, just: Who's to say we couldn't have two jesters?"

"Two jesters? Hmm . . . that might be interesting, actually," the king admits. "But jesters *tell jokes,* and Momo here . . ."

"I can tell jokes," Momo says. Then he tells a couple jokes. What did zero say to the number eight? Why was six so afraid of seven? Those kinds of jokes.

"See?" Momo says. "My jokes made you laugh."

"Your pants made us laugh. We turned our heads, saw your pants, and we laughed."

"Still," Momo says. "You laughed. You're laughing."

"We are," Guin says.

"Okay then," says the king. "We'll give it a try. Clean your bill, arrange your feathers decently, and you can jest at tonight's hour of entertainment. But before and after both, you have to stay in the marsh. And you're *never again* to leave the marsh without pants. I hear tell anyone sees your boner, you'll be exiled, Momo, to Gary, Indiana."

Momo, overjoyed by this reprieve, thanks his grandpa profusely and reaches up to be hugged. The king doesn't hug him, says that his huggable days are over, and that, furthermore, he has to stop saying *Grandpa*. It's no longer cute. In fact, it's worse than not-cute. It makes a mockery of the monarchy. Henceforth, the king says, Momo will refer to the king and Guin by their royal pronouns. "We're Highnesses," he says. "I'm Your/His. She's Your/Her. Don't forget, or I will fuck you up good, kid."

"I won't forget, Your Highness," Momo says. "Thank you, Your Highness."

So, most evenings, after dinner at the palace, there's this "hour of entertainment," which hardly ever lasts less than three hours, and sometimes goes past sunrise.

It's pretty much the way you'd imagine: Chicago royalty, ambassadors from other kingdoms, and exotic courtesans gather in the throne room to drink fermented herring blood, snort coke, eat opium, and be entertained alongside the king. Usually there's some dancing. Sometimes some athletic feats. Dr. Mike, the Ancient Historian Laureate of the Kingdom of Chicago, queues up and like *deejays* old YouTube and Spotify and Pornhub clips on the throne room's big screen, occasionally accompanies the clips with short lectures no one pays much attention to. Also, of course, the aforementioned Lope is always circulating, making his faces, doing his pratfalls, passing his gases, and telling his jokes, of which he has two.

One of the jokes goes like this: Lope stands erect—Lope's huge, by the way—he stands up as straight as possible and flaps his wings furiously while saying, "I'm a prince! I can fly! I'm the king! I'm a prince!"

And then the other joke is, Lope bends over, shows his cloaca, flexes it repeatedly, causing it to wink, and he either says, "Just kidding! Just jokes!" or "Only me and you know about this! We gonna keep this big secret between just us!"

So maybe the cloacal winking thing counts as two jokes, which would mean Lope has three in total. Depends on how you count, I guess.

Anyway, Momo's an instant hit. He *runs* the hour of entertainment. It's so easy, it's almost *too* easy. He hardly has to even say anything—only enough to call attention to himself—to get the penguins rolling around on the floor, laughing their faces off and applauding. He just shows up in pants—he rotates the colors for the sake of variety—clears his throat, and he's the belle of the ball. The subject of toasts.

Eventually, however, the pants get tired. Enthusiasm dies. The penguins grow bored and impatient with his pants, and start paying more attention to the jokes he's telling, jokes he learns by studying clips from ancient sitcoms and stand-up routines that Dr. Mike has been kind enough to link him through to on YouTube, and Momo isn't, frankly, very good at telling jokes. Often, he doesn't seem to understand what's supposed to be funny about the jokes he's telling—and nearly as often, he *doesn't* understand. His timing . . . sucks. He lacks Lope's magic.

One night, he does a late-career Louis CK bit—it's from the year 2041—that's about pets and children and boners and shame, and Momo doesn't get a *single* laugh. In the video Momo stole it from, the bit *kills*. It's five minutes of material that take Louis CK nine minutes to tell because he has to pause so frequently to allow his audience to quiet down.

The bit takes Momo . . . five minutes.

Momo's bombing so hard with the Louis CK bit that the King of Chicago himself rolls his eyes, appears embarrassed for Momo, and this makes Momo very afraid. Afraid, specifically, that, now that the era of hilarious pants is over, he'll never be thought funny again, he'll be banned from the hour of entertainment, and will have to live the whole rest of his life by himself in the marsh, crazed with loneliness.

He becomes so afraid that, during the last few seconds of the bit, he starts to shiver. Starts to shake.

To Momo's surprise—and great relief—the penguins roar with laughter.

—

All at once, he's got a new schtick: he stands up, performs routines that no one laughs at till he's so humiliated and afraid that he starts to shake, then watches the room just fall apart.

This schtick works for weeks, but then, just like with the pants, it loses efficacy. Momo tries to shiver more thoroughly, to shake with more gusto, but there's a limit to what he's able to do.

Once again, he sees the king rolling his eyes and looking embarrassed near the end of a bit, but this time, the shivering and shaking that provokes in Momo—which is, in fact more intense than it's been in weeks—barely garners a charitable chuckle from his mom.

Maybe the problem, Momo wishfully thinks, is with the bits he's been ripping off—bits written and originally performed by Pryor, Burr, Seinfeld, Dangerfield, Carlin, Rock, the aforementioned CK . . . Comedians who, according to Dr. Mike, were all extremely famous in their day.

Maybe what he needs to do, he thinks, is rip off a routine from a less famous comedian: a routine no one ever found all that funny to begin with.

Like, maybe he could bomb even *harder* than he has been, and after bombing harder, the shaking and shivering will seem funny again.

That doesn't make a lot of sense, not even to Momo, but Momo's sense of humor doesn't jibe with the penguins', and he knows it. Even at his peak, he didn't get why his pants were so funny, let alone why his boner was funny, and he sure as shit doesn't understand how his shaking can be funny— he's scared as hell when he shakes, or angry, or sad. Unless he's faking it.

He *has* learned how to fake the shivering and shaking—to perform it without feeling afraid or angry or sad in order to get the penguins to laugh, and maybe once or twice he thought it was kind of *a little bit* funny to shiver and shake like he was afraid or angry or sad when he was neither afraid nor angry nor sad, but the reason he thought his faked shaking was kind of a little bit funny wasn't, he gathered, the same reason why the penguins found his faked shaking funny, and was maybe even the opposite reason why the penguins found it funny.

What Momo had thought was kind of a little bit funny about his faked shaking was that he was able to pull one over on the penguins: he thought it was kind of a little bit funny that the penguins seemed to think his fake shaking wasn't fake.

Anyway, Momo, hoping to find an act to rip off that'll cause him to bomb even harder than he has been, googles the search terms *comedian* and *Chicago* and *not that funny* and *not that famous,* and gets some hits.

Now, it feels incumbent on me to mention that we've reached a part of this story where you're gonna have to bear with me a little, take a small leap of faith, because this part of the story of Momo the shivering duck in the postapocalyptic Kingdom of Chicago that's run by emperor penguins who chastise the bonered—this is the part of the story where the story might begin to seem impossible to you, or like, strain your credulity or desuspend your disbelief or whatever, because what happens in this part of the story is that Momo finds an audio clip of this performance. The one I'm doing right now.

It's not *exactly* this performance, actually. I'm not *exactly* me. I mean, I look like me, and I call myself Gladman, and I have the same family, same childhood, same career trajectory and so forth, but owing to some multiverse-, eternal return–type stuff, the terrestrial anomaly, in the fictional universe of this bit that Momo's inhabiting—the anomaly hasn't killed everyone I love. It's killed no one I love. It's killed relatively few people, in fact—like thirty people, say. A few delivery drivers, a few police patrolmen, a couple building engineers, and some homeless folks camped out in the park.

Thirty people instead of the however-many thousand it killed in this universe that you and I share.

Same anomaly, geologically speaking, but hardly anyone's around when it happens because, thank God, prior to the anomaly—just, like, a couple-three months prior—a viral pandemic that everyone thought had been dealt with accordingly suddenly reared its ugly head again, killed millions across the world, hundreds of thousands just in the U.S. alone, and the City of Chicago was locked down by the mayor, and the citizens of Chicago were ordered to shelter in place.

So on 11/17, no one went to the Art Institute: the Art Institute was closed. No one went out to brunch: restaurants were closed. Except for those building engineers, hardly anyone went into the office downtown: the offices were closed.

And so this performance was also different. It started the same way it started today, in our universe—me talking about the time I clipped Gogol's claw off—and ended the same way it's gonna end in our universe—with me telling you about the day I got kicked out of kindergarten—but this part we're in now, this part about Momo: it's not part of the performance Momo finds on the internet.

In the universe in which Momo exists, I—however many eons before Momo's birth—I, on the morning of 11/17, realize that the whole duck and pants bit that I've been trying and failing to write for days isn't worth pursuing. It's aggravating me, making my hemorrhoids flare up. So I give up on the duck and pants bit, which depresses me a little, as giving up will, and I go to the bedroom, where Daphne's at her desk, reading a book, and she asks me if I like her shirt, which I do, I like all her shirts, and I say as much to her, and she says I look glum and asks me if I want to take a walk, and we take a walk, and she cheers me up a little, cracks some jokes, makes out with me awhile, and then we decide to order a pizza for lunch, and we eat the pizza and watch some Larry David, and we take a nap, and, while we're napping, the anomaly strikes, and we wake to the news of it, and we're glad we weren't there, and we stay in bed awhile, glad we weren't there.

This Day Zero fundraising concert for the Mount Chicago Memorial Park still happens, but because the loss of life to the anomaly was relatively limited, it's a smaller affair. No pay-per-view or whatever. And because I've already given up on the duck and pants bit, and because I, with my life still intact, see no advantage to ginning up a sense of agency for myself, I don't pursue the duck and pants bit, and so, like I said, my performance is different than the one I'm giving right now. It starts the same, ends the same, but it's different in the middle. There's nothing about Momo. Nothing about LSD or the Holocaust for that matter. Goes from Gogol pretty much straight to kindergarten, and lasts only fifteen minutes or so.

So when Momo hears the clip of my Day Zero performance, there's nothing too weird or meta about it for him. He isn't in it. It doesn't freak him out at all.

And for reasons he doesn't quite understand, he finds the performance really hilarious. He *loves* it. Might actually be the funniest thing he's ever heard. He really doesn't understand why—like with all the other bits he's been ripping off from other ancient performers, he doesn't even know what half the words mean—but there's something about me, something in my voice or something, that, when he hears it, just sets him off. He can hardly stop laughing.

Which is perfect, right? Just what he's looking for. If *he* thinks something's hilarious, the penguins will almost certainly think it's terrible. He'll bomb harder than he's ever bombed before, and then, when he shakes, maybe they'll laugh.

So he listens to the clip about fifty times, memorizes all of it, and at the hour of entertainment the following evening, he performs the whole thing beat for beat.

And he bombs. Bombs harder than ever.

He bombs harder than ever, there are just *unprecedented* levels of hostility in the throne room—like, they want to *murder* him, the penguins, he can feel it, they want to stomp him dead—and when he's finished, he shivers, he shivers and shakes, *harder than ever,* and he doesn't have to fake it, not even a little, and . . . still, no one laughs.

For a minute, it seems—and not just to Momo, but to everyone gathered—that the penguins might actually do it: might actually murder him.

Then Lope—one likes to think deliberately, though one can't be certain—Lope saves the day. He bends over sharply, shows his cloaca, and cuts the tension by cutting the cheese. It's a major squealer. Long and high and multisyllabic. One for the ages.

Classic Lope.

And the penguins expel their rage through laughter. Some of it, anyway. By the time they've recovered from the thrill of Lope's fart, they're just too spent to stomp a duck dead.

Momo's still shaking.

He's pretty sure his career has just ended, and when the king calls him over to the throne, it's confirmed: Momo's no longer welcome at the hour of entertainment. Furthermore, he's never to enter the palace again. In fact, he's never again to leave the marsh. If the princess wishes to occasionally see him, the king won't stand in her way, he tells Momo, but she'll have to visit the marsh to do so.

And the princess does visit him a couple weeks later. She can't explain why. Guilt? Pity? A sense of obligation? A pitiful sense of guilty obligation? She no longer feels maternal toward Momo at all, she feels stupid for having ever felt maternal toward Momo, like she'd been tricked or something, but she did once love him like a son—she loved him *a lot*—and even if that embarrasses her, and even if she's *mostly* past it, love does leave a mark, traces of itself, and to ignore those traces entirely seems . . . She doesn't know, but she thinks she should visit, and so she visits.

The visit is brief. Fifteen-twenty minutes. Little is said. What's said is polite. Neither bird really knows what to say. How's the water in the marsh, how's the mood in the palace, do the guards treat you decent, is the king in good health, fine and good and yes and glad to hear it. It's a tense and cold and sad encounter absent of any display of affection and almost entirely bereft of eye contact, though just before the princess leaves, Momo senses that something like progress is being made, and after she leaves, there is some hope—on Momo's part—that if the princess comes back she might warm up, might remember how it felt to be his mother, and how and why she used to adore him, and thereby come to adore him once again, or at least not feel so uncomfortable around him.

And maybe some or all of that would have happened had she ever come back, but she never comes back. Shortly after her visit, she dies very suddenly from a case of E. coli she contracts from her lover.

And Momo spends the rest of his life all alone, except for on those very rare occasions—usually Halloween—when mischievous young penguins who've heard and misheard rumors about him sneak past his guard and into the marsh to wake him in the night and demand he humiliate himself before them.

"Put on your pants, or we'll murder you," they say.

Or, "Fly like a cripple, or we'll stomp you," they say.

Or, "Show us your boner, or we'll kick your fucken ass."

"Tell us one of your shaky duck stories, or die."

Momo lives for another nine years in the marsh. Lives to nearly eleven—old for a mallard—and although he never encounters the she-duck again, and his brethren are never freed from the beavers, and anyone he's ever loved and anyone who ever loved him is entirely lost to him, it isn't the worst. That is: it isn't any good, but it could be worse.

He's still able to get some respite from his terrible loneliness by eating when he's hungry, drinking when he's thirsty, sleeping when he's tired, and doing his very fast swimming in circles thing. Also, no one stomps him to death. When he dies, it's from cancer of the liver and kidneys, which doesn't hurt at all as long as he's asleep, and takes a long time—long enough to allow him to realize life could have been worse.

Anyway, my family wasn't particularly religious, but we were really *Jewish*—I'm telling you about how I got kicked out of kindergarten now—we were really Jewish, my family, like not so very much *people of the book* as loud, bookish people, who talked fast and laughed a lot and enjoyed a good argument, so I knew how to read and do some basic math before I learned how to hit a ball or ride a bike or mop a floor or whatever.

And so my parents wanted me to start going to school a year earlier than the public school system would let me—my birthday was after the deadline or something—so they sent me to this private Jewish day school for kindergarten. It was a nice place. I liked my teachers. Got along with the kids. It's kindergarten, you know? Private kindergarten. You get your snacks, you get your naps, your arts and crafts, your morning recess, afternoon recess . . .

But one peculiar thing about this kindergarten: its bathroom was, first of all, unisex, and, second of all, didn't have any stalls. And this wasn't some kind of a hippie thing, either. Like I said, this was a Jewish day school. Not all the kids were from religious families—a lot of them had the same kind of family as mine—but all the boys wore yarmulkes while they were there, everyone went by their Hebrew names, the afternoons were spent learning Jewish stuff, and on Friday mornings, we each braided eggy dough and baked a *challah*, dipped wicks into warm, colored beeswax, and braided the wicks up for *havdallah* candles. Friday afternoons, with our braided bread and candles, we got out early so that, just in case the bus broke down, we'd still make it home before the start of the sabbath.

A religious school. Not the kind of place, I'm saying, that you'd think would have a unisex bathroom, let alone toilets without any stalls. Or maybe *exactly* that kind of place. I don't know. If you have great faith in the innocence and purity of little children, maybe you figure, "What do they have to be shy about?"

Either way. Unisex bathroom. No stalls.

There were toilets on three walls of this bathroom, two per wall, then the fourth wall had the doorway and the little sinks. No urinals. Six sit-down toilets at little-kid height, with little-kid depths and little-kid seat widths.

So one day I get diarrhea from too many fruit snacks or whatever, and that's horrible enough, having diarrhea, but I'm, like, *publicly* having diarrhea, okay? For a while. Fifteen minutes. Twenty minutes. Thirty minutes. Hard to say. But I'm sitting there on this little toilet on the middle wall that faces the door and the sinks, and I'm shitting my little-kid brains out, while other little kids are coming in and going out to use the toilets and wash their hands. Soon enough, it's time for sing-along, and I'm still shitting—it just won't stop—and sing-along happens to be my favorite part of kindergarten, I *shine* at sing-along, everyone says so, I have such a sweet voice, and I'm so *enthusiastic* about using it. And dancing, too. Love to dance along while singing along. So I'm shitting my brains out, listening to the other kids singing this song about God—*Ha-Shem* as we called Him—and it goes like this, it goes,

Ha-Shem is here,
Ha-Shem is there,
Ha-Shem is truly everywhere!

Up, up, down, down,
Right, left, and all around,
Here, there, and everywhere,
That's where He can be found!

It's my favorite song that we sing during sing-along, partly because of the bouncy point-and-look dance that goes with the lyrics, and it's usually sung for four or five rounds, sometimes even more. And because it's my favorite song, and because, I guess, I *shine so brightly* when I sing it, the teacher notices I'm missing after just a couple rounds, and she stops the song.

Now I remember hearing her say, "Where is Shlomo Gladman hiding?"

I forgot—that was another thing I used to like to do, was hide from the teachers. I'd hide, they'd call out for me, I'd make a noise, they'd find me, we'd laugh—it was just . . . It was a whole routine. I was a nice little kid. Huggy. Giggly. They indulged my whims. And the hiding was something that happened often enough that it made sense for the teacher to figure I was hiding.

Anyway, "Where is Shlomo Gladman *hiding*?" she says. "Doesn't he know we're singing 'Ha-Shem Is Here'? Does he really want to miss out on singing along to his most favorite song?"

Something like that. I mean, I'm not really sure I heard her say that stuff. I *remember* it, but it might be one of those true-enough fictions you confuse for a memory when you reconstruct an incident frequently enough. Not that I've ever told this story to anyone. I haven't. I've thought about it a lot, especially over the past few months, but . . . Who cares, right? Not the point.

Teacher stops the song, asks where I'm hiding, and this girl, Shulamit Kreingold, she says she thinks I'm hiding in the bathroom, that she saw me in the bathroom just a couple minutes ago.

Which she *did*. She'd pissed in the little toilet right next to mine and *smiled* at me. She was really cute, little Shulamit Kreingold. We were friends, and I suppose I had a little crush on her. She was the only girl in all the kindergarten who I said I would marry. I remember that for sure. It was important to me. A lot of the other little boys and girls would get engaged on a Monday, break it off on Wednesday, and find a new fiancé by Friday. Not me and Shulamit. We broke it off on the Wednesday sometimes, sure, but come Shabbos, it was always she and I again.

Shulamit Kreingold aka Stacy Kreingold. No luck being named in any language, poor girl.

Shulamit Kreingold tells the teacher she saw me in the bathroom and she thinks that's where I am. And the teacher, who must still be assuming I'm doing my hiding game—I don't know what the fuck she was thinking—she dispatches Shulamit Kreingold to find me.

Moments later, Shulamit Kreingold opens the bathroom door, and I don't know if she saw this, or didn't see it, but I haven't noticed it yet, and, what I mean by *it* is this: I've shit so much, so very much, into this little-kid toilet—a toilet that, on reflection must have been clogged or full to begin with, I know I'd run to it, ass in hands, about to explode, and I'm sure I did *not* check if it had been flushed—what it is is that I have shit *so much* into this little-kid toilet that the diarrhea, which is still, by the way, occasionally spraying from my asshole, has filled the toilet, and started to overflow, to *spill over the lip of the toilet*, down the front of the toilet between my legs and onto the floor. And Shulamit, whether she notices this or not, or just sees the straining, suffering expression on my face, she's standing in the open doorway, and she *points* at me—extends her whole arm and points—and says, "Shlomo! No!" and I look down, ashamed enough already, and I see the shit overflowing the lip of the toilet, see some of it has gotten onto my bunched-up pants, that one of my heels is in a puddle of it, too, and I realize that my ass, my *whole ass*, is submerged, my *whole little ass* and my little scrotum, too, are submerged in diarrhea, and right then, *upon this realization*, right then is when I hear some kid shout, "Shulamit's crying! Shulamit's crying!" and the teacher comes up behind Shulamit Kreingold, who still hasn't lowered her arm, and the teacher's looking at me, and she says, "Oh no, Shlomo. Oh no," and soon enough, the rest of the class, all forty-however-many of them, are flying past the teacher, piling into the bathroom, gathering around me, pointing at me and laughing, or pointing at me and looking stricken, and saying, "Shlomo, no. Oh no, Shlomo," and I don't . . . I don't know what to do. What can I do? I mean, I can't get up—I'm still *shitting,* man. I'm still shitting, and I'm covered in shit. I'm literally *dipped in shit,* my own shit, probably also the shit of others who'd shit before me, the shit of one of these kids or even possibly *more than one of these kids* who's standing there, pointing and laughing or looking stricken and saying, "Shlomo, no," and I don't know what to do. What do you do? What the fuck can you do? I didn't know what to do. So you know what I did? I wonder if you know. I think maybe you know. I really think you might know. Do you know me at all? You gotta know me by now. At least a little. At least this much. I think you know already. I think you fucking know, man, but it's the end of my story, it's the last thing I can say, so I'll tell you anyway. I'll tell you what I did. This is what I did:

-shem is here,
Ha-Shem is there,
Ha-Shem is truly everywhere!

Up, up, down, down,
Right, left, and all around,
Here, there, and everywhere,
That's where He can be found!

Ha-Shem is here,
Ha-Shem is there,
Ha-Shem is truly everywhere!

Up, up, down, down,
Right, left, and all around,
Here, there, and everywhere,
That's where He can be found!

Ha-Shem is here,
Ha-Shem is there,
Ha-Shem is truly everywhere!

Up, up, down, down,
Right, left, and all around,
Here, there, and everywhere,
That's where he can . . .

I sang till all of them sang along with me.
    No. Not really.
    No one ever sang along.
    But a couple of the other kids, maybe even three or four—
they danced a little.
    Couldn't help themselves.

Sound Body

1

May 2, 2022

Dear Apter,

You're reading a suicide note. Gogol's yours to look after for the rest of her life. Among some other things I owe you is an explanation, so:

Before now, the longest Gogol had ever been away from me without plucking was four days, unless she was with my sister Kayla. She's been in your care for eleven days and she hasn't plucked. As long as she remains in your care, she won't. I'm as confident of that as one can be about anything.

She's at least as crazy about you as she was about Kayla. She was drawn to you from the very beginning—from the first time you visited us. I would've seen that at the time, had I thought it possible—looking back on that visit, it seems pretty obvious—but it's been so rare a thing for her to even just *not dislike* anybody who wasn't me or Kayla that I couldn't imagine it. So I didn't suspect it till a number of days later, after I noticed her acting strange. Then you came over again, and my suspicions were very happily confirmed. She preened you; you bonded.

Anyway, I used to leave her with Kayla for as many as twelve weeks at a time, and she never plucked, I could've left her with Kayla forever and she wouldn't have plucked, and I'd be leaving her in Kayla's care today if Kayla were still alive, but Kayla died in the anomaly, along with Daphne, my parents, my other sister, Naomi, and Naomi's three children, which I didn't want you to know because I worried that if you knew, you might worry I might be a suicide risk, and that, if you worried I might be a suicide risk, you might not take Gogol home; you might, instead, accurately conclude—for inaccurate reasons (e.g. the only reason I hadn't yet killed myself was that Gogol's presence lessened my desire to be dead)—that if you took Gogol home, the likelihood of my suicide would increase.

So I didn't tell you.

To sum it up: I played a dirty trick on you, Apter. Took advantage of your kindness and admiration. Lied. Said I'd try to do Day Zero with no intention of ever doing Day Zero. Said so in order to get you to take Gogol home so I could see if Gogol would be all right in your care, and then, when it turned out Gogol was all right—more than all right—I ended my life.

I apologize for tricking you. I'm certain you can understand why I had to, or thought I had to. I'm certain you *do* understand why I'm dead. Understanding, though, isn't the same as forgiveness. I hope you'll forgive me. I like to think you will. And I like to think that, even though your feeling obliged—your *being* obliged—to look after Gogol is inconvenient (what obligation isn't?), the looking-after itself provides its own rewards. Thank you for taking care of her.

Enclosed please find:
  1. A thumb drive containing:
    a. An audio recording of my final "performance," which you're free to play or not play in part or in whole on Day Zero if you want. Copyright's yours.

b. Three versions of a short, unpublished novel I wrote called *Play Your Straightman*. One of the versions is better than the others—it must be—but I can't tell which. Do whatever you want with *Straightman*. Publish whichever version you favor, splice them together and publish your splice, or sell the rights to another publisher. I guess you could just throw it all away, too, but I hope you won't do that. I've never shown it to anyone, not even Daphne, and it's either the best thing I've ever written, or could have been. What's more, I think you'll like it. In any case, the copyright's yours.

2. A notarized copy of my last will and testament, which further substantiates the above, and also says that I'm leaving to you:

a. Three unused bird cages.

b. All the books on my shelves.

c. Half a million dollars in cash.

d. Another million and a half or so in local real estate.

Warmly,

Gladman

PS When you call the police to report my death, please let them know that I've stashed a set of keys in the toe of a boot among the mess of footwear outside my front door so they don't break it down or wreck the lock—I'm leaving my condo to a former student, and she'll probably want to sell it. Left boot, tallest pair. Body's in the bedroom.

2

Gladman printed and signed the letter, sealed it in the envelope addressed to Apter, placed it in his bag with the other two envelopes—addressed to his lawyer and Daphne's mother—then swallowed his afternoon dosage of Xanax and left for the FedEx Kinko's on Division.

Outside the FedEx Kinko's on Division, he noticed it was no longer FedEx Kinko's, but FedEx Office Print & Ship Center. He wondered how long that had been the case, how long he'd neglected to notice the rebrand, attempted to recall the last time he'd paid attention to the signage, found this impossible, wasn't surprised to.

He entered the shop, exchanged friendly greetings with the woman at the counter, and paid to post the envelopes. International Express to Daphne's mother, Priority Overnight to Apter and the lawyer. Sign on delivery? Yes please, good. Insurance? Okay. How much? I don't know—never mind the insurance. You sure? I'm sure.

He was in and out in under ten minutes.

It was midafternoon. It was sunny, cool, and dry with occasional gusts. It was spring in Chicago. The trees had leaves. Songbirds chirped. The Xanax kicked in. It was forty-four Fahrenheit. Yesterday was eighty. There were tables on the sidewalk in front of the restaurants, their matching chairs chained together in stacks. Gladman left his cap in the pocket of his parka and raised his hood and pulled the strings.

He felt far more determined than he did sentimental, yet he didn't like the thought of the FedEx Office Print & Ship Center being the last place he'd purposely visit, so he walked a few blocks out of his way to look at the building attached to the Rainbo, which had been Daphne's favorite building in the neighborhood.

He'd always thought the building was nice-enough looking—redbrick, four stories, a big round window up near the top—but he'd never understood why it had been Daphne's favorite, always wished that he could, and, given how he would be dead within an hour, and given that he'd know he'd be seeing the building for the very last time, he imagined his senses might heighten to a point that would help him see what his wife had seen.

He paused at the corner of Division and Damen and looked across the street at a redbrick building that was four stories high and had a big round window up near the top.

Nice-enough-looking building.

He turned around and headed for home.

Near Augusta and Ashland, a car sped past him blaring a song through its zipper-pull-rattling subwoofer system. A song he knew. What was the song? He'd heard only a snatch of it, hardly half a measure, and the sound was distorted, but he knew that he knew. What the fuck was the song?

He had to let it go. He'd never find out if he didn't let it go.

The suicide kit was in a cardboard box at the back of his basement storage space. It was heavier than he'd remembered, or maybe it was more that he'd gotten out of shape. Maybe that was a distinction without a difference. Or was the phrase *a difference without a distinction*?

He stopped to catch his breath on the first-floor landing.

The suicide kit was a tank of helium, a nine-foot length of vinyl tubing, a clear plastic bag with an elastic closure, and a set of instructions featuring diagrams. An amateur darts team composed of hospice workers had given it to Daphne four years earlier.

The team was the focus of a chapter in *Retreat,* Daphne's microethnography about Lena's Tavern, a corner bar in Humboldt Park that was patronized largely by nurses.

Although Verso Press didn't publish *Retreat* till the fall of 2020, the chapter on the darts team, which had originally appeared in the quarterly journal *Cultural Anthropology,* was excerpted in the June 2018 *Harper's Magazine* "Readings" section under the title "The Second-Best Method."

Of the seven *Harper's* columns the excerpt occupied, six and a half were taken up by Daphne's transcription of an increasingly hostile argument between the increasingly drunken darts-playing hospice workers over which was the second-best method of suicide.

About which method of suicide was *the* best, all the members of the darts team had agreed, but on the night of the argument, they wouldn't tell Daphne, even though she kept asking. That was part of the fun of the excerpt.

However, one of the darts players had a subscription to *Harper's*. On encountering the excerpt, he showed it to his teammates, and—whether because they thought it would be funny to do so (it kind of was), or because they thought that their doing so might make it into *Retreat* (it did), or for both of those reasons—they all pitched in to buy Daphne the kit, which they presented to her at Lena's Tavern.

Affixed to the tank was a greeting card envelope containing a photo of the six of them standing shoulder to shoulder in front of the bar.

On the back of the photo, one of them had written, "Six out of six Chicago-area hospice workers recommend suicide by asphyxiation on helium gas with your head in a bag."

As detailed in the second appendix to *Retreat,* in which Daphne describes the gift-giving episode, the body treats helium gas like air. The lungs absorb it without any struggle. There's no panicked gasping, no choking sensation, no pain whatsoever. Owing to the brain's being starved of oxygen, dizziness and/or light-headedness may accompany your first inhalations, but after only five or six you're asleep, and within just another few minutes you're dead.

Gladman unpacked the box in the bedroom. Set the tank on the floor next to the reading chair, fixed the vinyl tube to the nozzle, laid the plastic bag on the seat, and brought the instruction pamphlet to the kitchen.

He poured himself a bourbon. He didn't much want it, but, in an online forum, he'd read an account by a would-be helium suicide who'd inadvertently yanked the vinyl tube from her bag after passing out, and then, "startled awake by [her] own autonomically induced, panicked gasping, [she] frantically tore the bag from [her] head, and [has] ever since had to deal with permanent brain damage."

Gladman doubted the account. The woman didn't detail any of the symptoms of her permanent brain damage, and constructions like *auto-nomically induced, panicked gasping*—though by no means poetry—didn't exactly make her sound like she suffered from any.

The account, Gladman thought, was probably the fiction of a well-meaning Christian or handgun manufacturer, but he couldn't be certain, so he drank the glass of bourbon to potentiate the action of the Xanax in his body, reasoning that the more his muscles relaxed, the lower would become the already-low likelihood of his involuntarily dislodging the tube once he'd gone unconscious.

Especially if, after pulling the bag on, sticking the tube in, and opening the valve, he sat on his hands like the illustrated figure in the pamphlet's final diagram.

Which is just what he did.

And everything proceeded according to plan.

As Gladman died, he had thoughts. The first ones were verbal.

"Picture something good now, in case there's a dream first . . . Is it going? It's going. That's why the temperature drop and the whisper. *Whisper*—corny. Precious. Gothy. Isn't a hiss, though. Really is more a whisper. A shoosh—that's better. It's a shoosh. Doesn't matter. But I'm still . . . Don't be . . . Let it go . . . It's on. It's going. It's on. Now picture Daphne before you aren't able. Daphne. Where? Daphne. Which city? What mood? How old? . . . Room's ugly through the bag. Hazy and dim. Is the plastic kind of grey or is it starting to fog? *Grey* with an *e*. It's a British color. It should be theirs to spell. Stop looking at the room. Close your eyes and remember . . . *something*. A photo. Think of a photo. Should have looked at a photo to remember before you . . . Think of a photo you'd have liked to remember of . . . Photo of . . . *her*. Of the . . . Of *your wife*. Just picture whoah sleepy . . . Spinning . . . Here comes . . . And so picture the person . . . From the . . . Don't be . . . I'm still . . . I'm still . . . It's . . . Of course!"

At that, the words stopped.

Gladman slumped in the chair and heard flute.

Well, he thought he heard flute. He *remembered* hearing flute. Remembered a flute line.

He remembered the flute line from "Jenny from the Block" by Jennifer Lopez, and, in his diminishing state, thought he heard it.

Just before the words stopped—just as he was about to think the words "'Jenny from the Block' by Jennifer Lopez"—he'd realized "Jenny from the Block" had been the song that, thirty-odd minutes earlier, had blared, distorted, from the passing car on Ashland Avenue.

The realization was false in one sense, and true in another.

The song that had blared, distorted, from the car wasn't "Jenny from the Block" by Jennifer Lopez, but the song from which "Jenny from the Block" had sampled its highly prominent flute line: "Watch Out Now" by the Beatnuts (featuring Yellaklaw).

So inasmuch as the song that had blared, distorted, from the car on Ashland was not the song Gladman determined it had been just before the words stopped, the realization was false.

Yet inasmuch as "Jenny from the Block" *was* the song that Gladman had nearly (however mistakenly) recognized *when* he'd heard the distorted snatch of "Watch Out Now" blaring from the passing car on Ashland, the realization was true.

Prior to hearing the snatch of it on Ashland, Gladman had never encountered the Beatnuts (featuring Yellaklaw) song. If he had, he might have enjoyed it. Hard to say.

On the other hand, he'd heard the Lopez song dozens of times, if not hundreds of times, over the preceding twenty years, and, although he rather liked its flute line, which, the first time he'd heard it, evoked for him the flute line of the very first pop song he'd loved as a boy (a Smokey Robinson song called "Tears of a Clown" that had frequently played on the oldies station his father used to listen to while driving), Gladman found the chorus—in which Lopez, singing, "Don't be fooled by the rocks that I got / I'm still, I'm still Jenny from the block," celebrates herself for possessing humility and authenticity—as vexingly catchy as it was perplexing.

So "Jenny from the Block" was not a song he'd have hoped to be one of the last things—or even just one of the last songs—he'd ever think about. But that it *was* one of the last things, and *the* last song, that he'd ever think about was, all told, not so bad a turn.

His conviction, however false, that he'd successfully identified "Jenny from the Block" as the song he'd heard blaring from the car on Augusta provided him with the same kind of tiny, pleasant bolt of relief that normally attends the overcoming of such "tip of the tongue" phenomena.

But moreover, "Jenny from the Block" was a song that connected two of his all-time finest memories, and, although he'd only ever been aware of the role the song played in the earlier of them, it was a moment from the later one, which was the better of the two, that the thought of "Jenny from the Block" caused him to recall (or *relive,* or *inhabit,* or whatever verb best describes experiencing a seemingly all-encompassing experience that, while we're experiencing it, we cannot or do not describe to ourselves—*experience,* perhaps?) during the final few minutes of his life.

Gladman had met his two closest friends a couple decades earlier, at the MFA fiction program they all attended in upstate New York from 2001 to 2004. These were the only two people whose attempts to contact him since 11/17 he'd ever felt any real guilt for ignoring. Not a ton of guilt, because he'd known they would eventually understand; known that they would have, had they suffered the same losses as he had suffered, taken their own lives as soon as possible and avoided him and one another and anyone else for whom they'd have had to socially perform in the meantime. These weren't men given to self-dramatization. They were not the sort of people who, once Gladman was dead, would blame themselves for "not having done enough" or "not having been there" when their friend was "in need." They were rational men.

Gladman's having remained alive for as long as he had in the wake of the anomaly would have in itself upset his friends, though, had Gladman allowed them to witness it happening. They would have wondered how he could have, Gogol or no, lasted through the night of 11/17, let alone lasted nearly halfway into the following year. They were happily married men, his friends, and they came from loving families they enjoyed, and they knew Gladman as a happily married man who came from a loving family he enjoyed, and were they faced with Gladman's continued existence in the wake of losing his wife and his family, every moment of that existence would have—at least a little—chipped away at their belief in the vital importance to their own lives of the women to whom they were happily married and the loving families from which they'd originated. For as long as Gladman remained alive, they would have, despite themselves, been disappointed that he continued to live, and disappointed in him for continuing to live. They would have, despite themselves, found themselves wanting him to die—to kill himself, or better yet die of grief—and they would have been upset with themselves for wanting such a thing. But no one should be able to live with such losses as Gladman kept living with for *any* length of time, they wouldn't have been able to help themselves from thinking. No one should be able to, much less have to, ever live with such losses, they would have thought. Gladman really shouldn't, they would have thought.

Romantic men, these men. Rational men.

And in the six or so months since 11/17, Gladman hadn't doubted for even a moment that avoiding these men was equivalent to being a conscientious friend.

Nonetheless, he had, as mentioned, felt *some* guilt about ignoring all their attempts to contact him. Not a ton of guilt, but a little bit of guilt because he knew that, up until they learned of the deaths of his wife and his family (he was certain they didn't know that Daphne was dead, let alone that Daphne and his family were dead; was certain that, had they any idea at all of what he'd lost, they'd have boarded the first available flights to Chicago; was as certain both friends, had they known, would have flown posthaste to Chicago to grieve at his side as he was certain he'd have flown posthaste to Los Angeles or Philadelphia to grieve beside them had either of them suffered such losses as he had; was as certain they'd have come to Chicago, had they known, as he was grateful that neither of them had), they would believe he was angry at them or sick of them or something, and that would bum them out.

But their being bummed out at mistakenly believing he was angry at or sick of them was far better, Gladman figured, than their having to repeatedly catch themselves wishing he'd die of suicide or grief, and it was nothing that leaving them the increasingly valuable properties he owned on the island of Grand Cayman couldn't make up for. So that's what he'd done.

All of this to say that one night, in fall 2002, at the unofficial grad student bar in the town in upstate New York that was home to the university at which Gladman and his friends were all getting MFAs, the three of them spent the better part of an evening telling useless lies about their families to each other. None of them had announced that this was what they would do, nor had they ever done it before, or talked about doing it. They just started doing it.

Gladman went first. Apropos of nothing other than perhaps a silence he felt impatient to break, he said, "My mother, in the seventies, dated Dick Cheney. I don't know if they fucked."

Without missing a beat, the friend directly across the booth from him said, "My piece of shit uncle's been in prison since Christmas for trafficking underage Middle Eastern boys to DC diplomats through a website called—and this is sick and kinda racist—Imported Dates dot com. An operation worth millions according to the *Washington Post*."

"You know, my great-grandpa," said Gladman's second friend, who sat beside the first, "was the IRS accountant who originated the American style of numerical notation. Before he came along, the number one-million and a half, to use just one example, was written as 'one period zero zero zero period zero zero zero comma five,' which he never thought looked right, so he switched it up to 'one *comma* zero zero zero *comma* zero zero zero *period* five,' and, within a few years, the whole government was doing it, and the textbooks changed. Very charismatic guy, by all reports, my great-grandpa."

"I wonder," said Gladman, "if he might have known *my* great-grandpa, who invented a million. No one ever seems to talk about this anymore, but until he published his call for reform in the pages of *Scientific American,* people called a million 'a thousand thousand' and never thought twice about the trouble it was causing."

"What'd they call ten million?" said the first friend.

"Well, exactly," Gladman said. "I mean, 'a ten thousand thousand.' That's what they called it. And so a number like fifty million, you'd think, would be 'fifty thousand thousand,' and sometimes it was, but then, other times, it was 'five ten thousand thousand' or even 'five thousand ten thousand,' depending on, I guess, the mood of the speaker."

"So was a hundred million," the second friend asked, " 'ten thousand ten thousand' or 'a hundred thousand thousand' or 'a thousand hundred thousand' or . . . ?"

"Actually, a hundred million, get this," Gladman said, "was 'one-tenth a billion.' But you guys see the problem: it was really hard to talk about larger numbers back then. So when he published his call for reform in *Scientific American,* in which he suggested that 'a thousand thousand' be renamed either 'a thoulion' or 'a goolion'—no idea how he came up with 'a goolion'—the world community of scientists and mathematicians, who were more and more frequently finding themselves having to talk about larger numbers, were pretty much all in agreement with my great-grandpa Millard. Then, after there'd been a few months' debate among the experts in the pages of various journals of science and mathematics about whether to go with *thoulion* or *goolion,* Millard suddenly died of cholera, and the young Albert Einstein commemorated him in a stirring front-page op-ed for the journal *Nature* in which, among other things, he said that regardless of how the community of scientists and mathematicians ultimately decided to rename 'a thousand thousand,' he would personally call the number 'a shevillion' in honor of the man who first gave voice to the need to rename it—Millard Shevitz, aka my great-grandpa. It was simply the right thing to do, Einstein said. And all the other scientists and mathematicians agreed it was the right thing to do *in spirit,* but they also thought 'shevillion' sounded 'too ethnic,' so they settled on 'a million.' All of them but Einstein, who kept faith with 'a shevillion' till the day he died."

"So it was really more like a million got invented by Einstein and the world community of scientists and mathematicians than by your great-grandpa Millard," the second friend said.

"Well, Millard inspired it, though," Gladman said. "I mean, I guess they all coinvented it, together."

"I'm actually his distant relative," the first friend said. "Einstein's, I mean. His great-grandson, Fred Durst, is a cousin of mine."

"*The* Fred Durst?" the second friend said. "Lead singer of Limp Bizkit? You're cousins with him?"

"Third cousins twice removed or whatever, but me and Fred Durst, we just say *cousins* 'cause we grew up close, and *brother*'s a little much, even though we're closer than I am with my brothers. Like, after Limp Bizkit sold half a shevillion of that single—what's it called?—the one that goes, 'I did it all for the nookie, the nookie'—I can't remember the title right now, but after it got certified gold, he bought me my Hyundai Accent GL because I was the one who inspired the song (long story), but neither of my brothers ever did anything even half that generous for me is what I'm saying."

"You're really lucky to have a cousin like Fred Durst, man," the second friend said. "A few years ago, my cousin Kristen, who created *Seinfeld* and wrote the first five seasons, made something close to three-tenths a billion off the sale of the syndication rights, and even though I'm the person who came up with the title of the show, which Kristen doesn't even *pretend* to deny, she won't even buy me a mountain bike, okay? She's one of these right-wing, bootstrapper dickheads. Like, she would kill the last unicorn to be Gladman's mom. First date, she'd have fucked Dick Cheney's nuts off."

And so forth, for hours.

And it happened that, at one point, early on, some prankster from a different section of the bar—it was never clear who—paid the jukebox to play "Jenny from the Block" on repeat for half an hour. The song had been released the previous week, and it was the first time—the first dozen times—Gladman and his friends had ever heard it.

The memory of that night did not contain the moment that Gladman recalled/relived/inhabited/experienced during the final minutes of his life, but it was, despite all the "Jenny from the Block," one of the finest memories he had of his twenties.

And *owing* in large part to all the "Jenny from the Block" (although he'd never had any idea that "Jenny from the Block" played any role in his doing so), he once described his memory of that night to Daphne.

And the afternoon on which he described the memory to Daphne turned out to be one of the finest afternoons he'd spent in his forties.

And the moment that he *did* recall/relive/inhabit/experience during the final minutes of his life was one of the high points of that fine afternoon.

Although Daphne's family had been staunchly atheist for three generations on her father's side and four generations on her mother's side, the Bourbons held fast to a set of secular Yuletide traditions of their own design.

On December 24, for instance, Daphne's sister Isabel ran the stereo till everyone was seated for dinner, and her playlists always opened with Jacques Dutronc's "Et moi, et moi, et moi" and closed with Aznavour's "Emmenez-moi," the latter of which the younger of Daphne's opera-trained uncles would sing along with beautifully while rolling his eyes as if embarrassed for himself, and miming through a sequence of increasingly violent and grisly suicides: pills, car exhaust, head in pre-1970s

British oven, bridge, rope, cyanide tooth, razor (wrists), razor (throat), fall-on-own-sword, seppuku (w/ assisted decapitation), handgun (chest), handgun (temple), handgun (mouth), rifle (mouth), shotgun (chest), shotgun (mouth), seppuku (no assistance).

This same uncle would, on Christmas day, just prior to lunch, pass to each person present a plain white envelope containing instant lottery tickets (between three and five, depending on how lean his year had been), and whoever'd won the most the previous year would then pass around larger, fancier envelopes—gold-leafed, usually—each of which contained a single ten-cent piece to scratch off the wax with.

For the most part, though, the traditions were culinary. On Christmas Eve, the *gougères* from Picard—the only packaged food Daphne's mother ever served—came out of the oven and into the living room in three distinct waves from 6 to 7 p.m. The course that followed was presented at the table, featured two kinds of foie gras (fatty, more fatty) accompanied by sliced up *baguettes muesli,* plates of orange salad, and glasses of Sauternes. The main course was always capon, the legs and wings of which went to the uncles and Daphne's brother, with sides of truffled potatoes and asparagus. For dessert, there would be two *bûches* from Dalloyau—one chestnut, one chocolate—as well as a full-size *deux-mille feuilles,* three "individual" *plaisirs sucrés,* three "individual" *Paris-Brests,* and a selection of at least three other "individual" pastry creations from Pierre Hermé (two of each). The cheese was roughly as variable: there was always Crottin de Valençay and Fourme d'Ambert, but Goudas or Bries (truffled or un- or both) could appear, as well as a wedge of Comté or Mimolette (young) purchased special for Gladman, who feared most cheese. And then on Christmas Day, after the oysters and the pomegranate-starfruit-cantaloupe salad, there was venison with cherries and roasted potatoes and turnips, plus all that remained from the Christmas Eve meal, which, except for the *gougères,* was most of every course but the capon.

Gladman objected to none of the Bourbon family Christmas traditions. In fact he thoroughly approved of all the Bourbon family Christmas traditions. However, there was one he had trouble embracing.

On Christmas morning, all thirteen participants gathered at Daphne's mom's to open presents at 9 a.m. sharp. Like most people, Gladman enjoyed presents, both giving and getting them. He especially enjoyed watching children open presents. And his enjoyment of these things was, of course, enhanced when the presents received were presents that the recipients actively desired, which, as far as he was able to tell, was the case roughly 95 percent of the time at Bourbon Family Christmases. Though none of the Bourbons were wealthy, most were gainfully employed, all were generous and thoughtful, and they took their gift-giving very seriously: slyly inquired as to who wanted what, sought out (at times with great difficulty) whatever that was, and saved up weeks (in some cases months) of disposable income to purchase it. They channeled the consumerist impulse toward kindness. It was cheering as hell.

But to make, at 9 a.m., the kinds of sounds and faces that being in the company of others, let alone beloved in-laws, demanded—this wasn't a pleasant thing for Gladman, especially not in the Christmas Day gift-exchanging context, where you were expected to ham it up quite a bit for the benefit of Daphne's adorable niece.

The muscles of Gladman's face, not to mention his vocal cords, didn't, in the morning, easily shift. He and Daphne wouldn't, on a typical day, trade more than a couple-three sentence fragments prior to lunch—e.g. "Sleep okay?" "I don't . . ." "Aw, sucks."—and such fragment-trading only ever occurred when they accidentally met on the way between their desks and the bathroom or the coffeemaker.

And on returning to their apartment just before midnight on Christmas Eve in 2019, Daphne asked Gladman to set the alarm on his phone for 8:30—she'd already set her own for 8:10, but wanted to be sure that if she mistakenly shut it off when it rang instead of sleeping it, they'd have a backup—and he emitted a semivoluntary throat noise.

"Come *on*," she said.

"What?"

"You always act like it's the end of the world."

"Spending the morning smiling—"

"What 'spending the morning'? You show up for thirty minutes, receive pharmaceuticals and bottles of high-end liquor you covet, come back here and sleep more or do *whatever* for the next three hours, then return to eat one of your favorite lunches with a bunch of people you like to hang out with, one of whom is me, and after that we go to your favorite place in Paris."

"But is it . . . I mean does anyone care if I'm there? Really? I'm not talking about ditching your family, or ditching Christmas—just tomorrow morning. I mean, Mathilde turned ten last month."

"Eleven."

"Right. Exactly," said Gladman. "Mathilde is eleven years old now. I really don't think she'll mind if I'm not there to see her unwrap her books and Star Wars Legos."

"Yeah, okay. So forget it," Daphne said. "You're probably right. If you don't want to show up for presents, don't. Just come by at lunch."

"I don't think you mean it."

"Just set the alarm for me, Gladman, okay?"

He set the alarm.

Daphne woke with her own alarm and unset his. After having showered and gotten dressed, she nudged him and asked, "You sure you want to stay? I bet I could get Mathilde to wait twenty minutes, maybe half an hour."

"Well . . ."

"It's fine," she said. "I'll see you at lunch."

"Twelve thirty?" Gladman said.

"Sure," she said, and left.

At lunch, other than to greet him with the news that Mathilde had been concerned that he was ill, that when told he wasn't ill she suggested they wait for him to open presents, and when told that he wouldn't be there till lunch had shrugged and looked confused, Daphne didn't speak to him. Neither did Isabel, who, apart from Mathilde, who also didn't speak to him, was the relative of Daphne's who'd historically been the warmest to Gladman.

The rest of the Bourbons, however, gave no indication that they'd noticed, let alone minded, his having missed the gift exchange. Through much of the meal, as Daphne and her sisters played a word game with Mathilde, and Daphne's mother and uncles talked Spanish soccer and Mexican fiction and Argentine history (or so Gladman gathered from the proper names and cognates he thought he'd heard them using), Mathilde's father and Gladman counseled and teased Daphne's girl-crazy brother about his latest infatuations and entanglements while tasting small pours of the whiskey and cognac and pomace and poire they'd gifted each other.

A little while after the desserts were brought out, and for no reason anyone could have pinned down, all the conversations taking place around the table stopped simultaneously, and Daphne's eldest uncle, the principal cutup in a family comprised near exclusively of cutups, broke the brief silence by putting on a Frenchified Rocky Balboa voice and quoting the punchline of an apocryphal anecdote Gladman had told them all a few years before about a blowjob a hot-miked Sylvester Stallone once got in his trailer from a wardrobe assistant.

"Cap the bowls," said Daphne's uncle. "Cap. The. Bowls."

After the ensuing laughter had abated, Daphne seemed to soften a little. Dug a knuckle in next to Gladman's spine, right where his nearly constant turning to face her brother and brother-in-law for the past ninety minutes had raised a small knot.

But when, twenty minutes later, he noticed the time and said that they'd better start heading for the Tuileries, she acted as though he'd said that *he* had better start heading for the Tuileries.

"Will you go on foot or take the Metro?" she said.

"I," he said. "You," he said. "Metro, I guess."

He said his goodbyes and took a couple of the previous day's baguettes from among the half dozen on the living room credenza. Daphne walked him downstairs.

A kiss on the mouth, a punch in the arm.

Outside, he quartered both the baguettes. Jammed the pieces in the pockets of his fleece and his parka.

From Poisonnière station, he rode the 7 west.

The train was nearly empty and he found a seat easily but couldn't get comfortable. The bread kept stabbing him. He stood back up.

At the next stop, a drunken homeless man boarded. Begged in a mumble.

Except for a twenty, Gladman didn't have cash. He pulled a heel of bread from his pocket and proffered it.

The homeless man slapped it to the floor and started yelling. Gladman caught *encouler, pain, débile,* and *Noël.* The volume kept increasing till the homeless man cut himself off with a sneeze that he directed into the crook of his elbow. He removed a soiled handkerchief from somewhere in his pants, said "*Excusez moi*" twice as he blew and wiped his nose, then walked off to beg at the car's other end.

A young woman across the aisle was giggling, and Gladman made accidental eye contact with her. "It's not at you," she said, in German-accented English. "Or a little, perhaps. He calls you these very bad names, then *vous* you. That is why."

"Oh," Gladman said, and smiled and shrugged and looked at his shoes. He didn't think it was all that funny, but maybe Daphne would. Probably not. She'd probably tell him it was something that happened all the time. The German woman didn't seem to him to be very bright. Maybe *that* was funny? Why would that be funny? Because she was a German, and one expected a German to be an engineer, and engineers were bright? Or because one presumed she was a German engineer, and a German engineer, however bright, was expected to lack any sense of humor, yet here was this likely German engineer thinking she was on to something hilarious? So then would it be funny—assuming that it was funny at all—because she was the opposite of what you'd expect, or because she was *exactly* what you'd expect, or because she seemed to herself to be exactly the opposite of what she was?

Or was nothing here funny?

Gladman really couldn't tell. Gladman was off. Distracted. He was doing something odd. Odd for Gladman, at least. He was trying to feel bad.

He was trying to feel bad about having ditched out on the gift exchange, and he just couldn't get there. He *did* wish Daphne were with him, sure, and he knew that, without her, the visit to the Tuileries wouldn't be as fun as it had been in the past, and he knew that was the point, i.e. Daphne's point: that that's why she was ditching out on the Tuileries—to even the score, to give him a taste of his own ditchy medicine; that's the whole reason he was trying to feel bad—but he also knew he'd never ditch the gift exchange again, that Daphne'd never ditch the Tuileries again, and that, after the Tuileries, he'd return to the apartment and Daphne would be there, and Daphne'd be satisfied.

She'd be at the apartment, satisfied that the score had been settled (and justifiably so, Gladman thought: the visit to the Tuileries, although diminished, would not be ruined by her absence, just as the gift exchange hadn't, although diminished, been ruined by his) and they'd fuck and crack jokes and eat leftover *bûche* and then maybe watch a movie in bed on his laptop.

He was trying to feel bad for having disappointed Daphne but he didn't feel bad because he couldn't feel bad because only an ingrate who was lucky enough to be married to a woman who he loved enough to try to feel bad for having disappointed could end up feeling bad for having disappointed her, especially when her disappointment was a reasonable response to something of which he knew he was guilty, and Gladman was insensitive as often as not, and Gladman was occasionally also a fool, and he wasn't especially kind or charitable, in most interpersonal matters he was lazy, and he forgave himself for the harm he caused others with the speed and ease of an aspiring sociopath, but he wasn't an ingrate.

He'd never been an ingrate.

The tiniest hint of good fortune could thrill him. Right there on the Metro, for example, he began to feel a vague physical discomfort, realized it came from his body's having begun to overheat, took off his watch cap, cooled down instantly, then thought the following word: "Solved!"

And it didn't stop there. He took it even further. He noted that he'd not only solved his overheating problem, but that he'd gotten the cap off before his forehead had started to sweat, thus annulling the risk of his becoming too cold too suddenly, and he thought the following words: "Perfect timing!"

Gladman's gratitude was near perpetual. Were he less of an asshole, he'd have been intolerable. No one would have loved him. And that's me speaking: Adam Levin, inventor of Gladman. I'm asserting that Gladman's near-perpetual gratitude would have rendered him intolerable if he weren't also such an asshole. I'm asserting that nobody would have loved him.

Which isn't to say he himself was unaware of any of the above.

He was *well* aware of all of the above.

He was grateful he'd learned how to be such an asshole.

—

Maybe I've gotten off track a little bit.

Gladman got off the train at Grand Palais station.

As he exited the station onto Rue Rivoli, he replaced his watch cap.

As he replaced his watch cap, a car playing "Jenny from the Block" drove past him. He heard it and didn't.

That is: he heard it, but didn't notice he'd heard it.

Or in other words: inasmuch as hearing "Jenny from the Block" caused Gladman, there on the sidewalk along Rue Rivoli, to recall the night at the unofficial grad student bar in upstate New York described a few pages back, he heard "Jenny from the Block." But inasmuch as his recollection of that long-ago evening with his friends at the bar seemed to Gladman to arise apropos of nothing—except, perhaps, the hypomanic, almost amphetaminic feeling he'd always felt when approaching the Tuileries on Christmas Day—he did not hear "Jenny from the Block."

He just found himself remembering the night—remembering in vivid, spine-tingling flashes. The lies they told, sure, but other things, too. Random things. The hoodie he'd been wearing. The worn length of traction carpet at the entrance. The graffiti Sharpied on the back of the booth: SOMEONE STOLE A PIZZA. The ashtray stack by the popcorn machine. *Using* an ashtray indoors in New York. Lacking a beard. Socks damp in his boots. The candy-colored halo surrounding the jukebox.

And it occurred to him he'd never described that evening to Daphne. He told himself to remember to do so.

And he did so. He remembered.

He told her just a couple of hours later. Started telling her in bed, after they fucked, and continued to tell her while they got half-dressed, and finished while they ate the leftover *bûche*.

Although Daphne didn't really understand what it was about that night with his friends that he thought was so special—over the years, she'd spent plenty of evenings with Gladman and those two, and it sounded pretty much like any of those evenings—she saw how he enjoyed recalling it for her, reliving it a little, and that in itself was something she enjoyed. Plus, before it started to go off the rails, it was medium-funny. *Invented a million.* That one was pretty good.

But none of that would happen for a couple more hours.

In the meantime, Gladman entered the Tuileries through the low green gates by the shuttered concession booths, and, of the two duck ponds, chose to patronize the nearer. There was only one guy there, on the opposite bank, and he didn't seem to be feeding any birds, so: no competition, let alone the usual.

Every previous Christmas at this duck pond, seated in a chair beside the pond's north bank, there'd been an old man in a lumpy umber overcoat whose dominion over the crows was inviolable.

He was always there when Gladman and Daphne arrived, he always outstayed them, none of the crows ever left his orbit, and, because the old man never left his chair, husband and wife couldn't help but conclude that he had trouble standing, so despite their shared desire to consort with the crows—members of a species possessed not only of toolmaking skills, but (as Daphne'd once put it) "especially expressive and individuated faces"—they'd determined together, however reluctantly, that it would have been rude, and perhaps even cruel, to attempt to lure the crows away from the man.

And so they never had.

And now he wasn't there.

He was, in fact, nowhere. He was, in fact, dead. Having died in his sleep at 2:40 a.m. on December 26, 2018, he'd been dead for exactly 364.5 days. Gladman didn't know about any of that, of course. Nor did the possibility occur to him.

The gratitude he felt at the old man's absence was entirely uncomplicated.

Hearing a crow caw behind him, he turned. It was on a low branch. Gladman approached. The crow remained perched.

But as soon as he reached for the bread in his pocket, the crow took off.

He approached another crow in a different tree, this time with the bread already in evidence. As he ripped out a hunk of *mie* from the middle, the crow took off.

Approaching a third crow, who was perched on a bench, he tossed the hunk of *mie* in its direction. While his arm was in motion, the crow took off.

So the crows were skittish. They needed convincing.

A pigeon soared past him, snatched the crumb from the seat of the bench. The crumb was one or two orders of magnitude larger than a pigeon could handle. Half a dozen other pigeons flew in to help. Pigeons were the easiest—easy as ducks.

Gladman liked the pigeons fine. On balance, probably more than the moorhens. He liked the ducks better. Liked the starlings and the sparrows better than the ducks, and, except for maybe the crows—he'd find out soon enough—he liked the seagulls best.

There were reasons for his preferences.

The pigeons were often wounded—missing toes or eyes, sometimes half a leg, or even half a beak—and Gladman fed the wounded ones whenever he spotted them, but the unwounded ones were frequently bullyish. They'd peck other birds if they got worked up. They'd peck their own wounded.

The ducks were bullies, too, but they only ever seemed to bully one another (being the largest birds at the Tuileries, the other birds didn't often mess with the ducks), and the bullying, which sometimes entailed a small measure of shoving, wasn't wounding, and was usually verbal— they'd quack and flap loudly, click their bills like castanets. The worst he'd ever seen a duck do was clap its bill around the back of another duck's neck and dunk its face in the pond. The incident lasted only half a second, and seemed to be noble: the dunked duck, a female, had just shoved a smaller male aside in pursuit of a crumb, and the dunker, another female, after having dunked the shover, didn't go for the crumb; she let the shoved duck have it. Plus as far as wild animals went, the ducks, who'd gotten used to being fed by people, were particularly trusting. They'd trust you more quickly and to a greater extent than the other birds would. Within fifteen minutes of beginning to feed them, Gladman could get them to exit the pond, walk right up to wherever he was standing, and snatch proffered crumbs directly from his hand. Their beaks would graze his fingertips, but never would they pinch. It felt like getting grazed by the tips of closing chopsticks. It felt respectful. It felt polite.

The moorhens were . . . boring. Gladman liked to observe their very weird, almost sci-fi-looking feet—each phalange was a round, flat-bottomed pillow that appeared to be inflated with air—but he rarely got to see their feet. They were scared of everything. They hid in the marshy west end of the pond, among the tall grasses, came out only if the ducks were far away, and wouldn't even eat in front of anyone else. They brought any food they got back to their nests.

With twenty-thirty minutes of concentrated effort (extremely minimal eye contact; fluid but slow, predictable movement) you could convince a sparrow to light on the edge of your thumb and eat from a pile of crumbs in the cup of your palm for as many as five or ten seconds at a stretch.

Starlings wouldn't land on you, but they'd stay within three or four feet of wherever you were, and—if you signaled them to do so by looking right at them and angling your chin in a certain way—they'd jump up to catch any crumb you tossed.

The main frustration, when it came to the starlings, was that the crumbs they sought were the same size as the crumbs the pigeons liked best, and these crumbs, being tiny, were hard to aim properly, especially if the pigeons—who tracked the sparrows' and starlings' movements around the pond so as to steal crumbs intended for the sparrows and starlings—were disturbing the air with their flapping. Concomitantly, there were relatively few things in the world—a thousand at most—that Gladman found more rewarding than seeing a crumb being pulled from the air by a starling to whom he'd intended to deliver it.

As far as feeding birds at the Tuileries went, there was only one thing Gladman found more rewarding: playing catch with the seagulls. The seagulls were easily the most skilled flyers at the Tuileries; they liked bigger, more aimable hunks of bread than all the other birds except for the ducks; and they knew how to cooperate.

Once he'd managed to attract the seagulls, he could guide them, with throws, to circle over the pond. They'd fly in these circles that were ten to twelve feet above the water—as many as half a dozen seagulls at a time would—and pull from the air the hunks of bread Gladman lofted to them. The circles were probably fifty feet in diameter, took about thirty seconds for a seagull to traverse, and if Gladman could deliver a bread hunk to within a three-foot radius of a passing seagull's head (which he managed roughly two-thirds of the time), that seagull would be able to catch the hunk. Even better than that: if Gladman's rhythm was disturbed—if, say, the quarter baguette he was tearing the hunk from happened to resist his fingers more than usual—the seagull next up in rotation would notice, rotate vertically to slow itself down, and hover for as long as a couple-three seconds, right at the point along the circle that was nearest to Gladman, waiting for his throw. If Gladman couldn't manage to loft a hunk by the time those extra seconds had passed, the bird would move on—preventing pileups, preventing collisions—and Gladman would loft it an extra-large hunk when it came back around.

The seagulls all *took turns* was the thing. They took turns and they squealed and screamed and called out to one another, maybe sometimes to Gladman. And although Gladman knew it was probably in his head, it really did seem to him that when one of them made an especially acrobatic catch, the others squealed and screamed and called out louder—it seemed like they were cheering.

You attracted the seagulls the same way you attracted the rest of the birds: by feeding the ducks. You'd feed the ducks, the ducks would quack and flap and click their beaks, and, soon enough, the others all wanted a piece of the action. That's all it took. First the pigeons closed in, then the starlings and the sparrows would appear, and at last would come the seagulls. He never noticed when exactly the moorhens began edging out of the grasses, but when he spotted one, he'd feed it, then watch it flee.

So on Christmas Day, 2019, at a quarter to three in the afternoon, Gladman started feeding the ducks in the pond, the pigeons showed up, and after them the starlings, sparrows, and seagulls.

No crows.

That is: they weren't approaching.

About ten minutes in, just as he'd gotten the seagulls circling, he heard a crow caw behind him, but when he turned to look, the crows were up in the trees, some twenty feet back. All except for one, who stood atop a table even farther back than that. A dozen crows in all.

They continued to caw, but it didn't get louder; they weren't coming closer.

Thirty minutes later, all the ducks were back in the pond, having long since realized that Gladman was pretty much over them, that they'd have a better shot at eating if they waited for the misthrown hunks intended for the seagulls to fall in the water. The starlings and the sparrows had mostly dispersed. A few stray pigeons, however, remained near his feet, and he incidentally encouraged their fidelity by dropping on the ground the sub-seagull-worthy crumbs he tore off by mistake.

The seagulls—there were eight in the circle, highest number ever—were all performing at the highest pitch, swerving and diving and anticipating brilliantly, and Gladman's throws were meeting their mark far more frequently than they had on any previous Christmas. This probably had mostly to do with the weather. The air was still, and, for Christmas Day in Paris—for any winter day in Paris—the sky was clear and bright: so not only were the arcs his bread hunks were traveling less molested by wind than usual, but the seagulls could see the hunks better than usual.

Yes, his unparalleled success with the seagulls that day probably had mostly to do with the weather—Gladman knew that—but he couldn't help but think it was something else, too: something to do with his mood.

His mood wasn't quite as buoyant as it had been on previous Christmas Days. He missed his wife. It wasn't crushing, this missing her—not in the least; his mood was *lovely*—but, especially considering how well things were going with the seagulls, he'd really have preferred it if Daphne were there. She'd have liked to see it, he'd have liked to please her.

And he suspected that the sorts of background thoughts produced by his awareness of that preference—mostly thoughts about how best and most entertainingly to convey to her later that afternoon not just the lies he and his friends had told one another that evening back in 2002, but the accompanying sense-memories as well . . .

He suspected that the sorts of thoughts produced by his awareness of his longing for the company of his wife must have had an effect on the way he was carrying himself; an effect on his posture and the tilt of his head and the shape of his lips and any number of other physical signs he emitted that the seagulls were aware of even as he wasn't, even as he couldn't be: physical signs that the seagulls tuned into to better anticipate the paths of the flying bread hunks.

Anyway, about thirty minutes into feeding the circling seagulls, the pigeons at his feet all startled at once and flew away.

Not a second later, he heard, from behind him, an unfamiliar sound. A scratching sound. And he turned to look, and there they were: the crows from the trees. They were on the ground behind him, just six feet back, a line of them standing side by side.

The nearest one was scratching at the gravel with its beak.

Gladman slowly raised the hunk of bread he'd just torn for the seagulls. The crow stopped scratching.

He tossed the hunk midway between this crow and himself. The whole line jumped back but stayed in formation.

The crow that had been scratching then approached the hunk gingerly, snatched it, flew off. Right past Gladman. It landed on the bank of the pond, dipped the hunk in the water, set the hunk on the bank, stepped on the hunk, ripped half of it off, swallowed the half, took its foot off what remained, swallowed that, flew back to its former spot in the line.

So the hunk of bread had been too large.

Gladman tore a smaller piece off, took a step toward the crows. The crows jumped back. Half of them jumped back as far as they previously had. The other half jumped back not quite as far. He tossed the hunk to the nearest crow in the latter group.

For a number of minutes, Gladman and the crows engaged in repeated approximations of this mutually reinforcing pattern of behavior, and a few other crows from other areas of the gardens, having caught wind of what was happening, had joined them. Except for one tenacious pigeon, who Gladman ignored, not a single bird of a different feather came anywhere near them.

Once they'd gotten about twenty feet from where they'd started, the crows stopped retreating when Gladman tossed the hunks.

They gradually surrounded him until they'd formed a ring, and if he kept those behind him waiting too long for fallen bread, one of them would scratch the ground with its beak, and he'd turn and deliver.

At one point, Gladman addressed a crow who—having just eaten a hunk that he'd tossed it after it had scratched the ground with its beak—had begun to walk away.

"What's *your* fucken problem?" Gladman said to the crow. He wasn't angry or anything, and, at least in his adulthood, he'd never spoken to a bird who wasn't Gogol. It just kind of came out of him. "What's *your* fucken problem?"

And the crow, still walking, swiveled its head to look at Gladman, and it squinted and cawed.

None of the other crows said a thing.

The departing crow's response to Gladman's "What's *your* fucken problem?" marked one of the peak moments of the whole afternoon, which was one of the peak afternoons of Gladman's life, but wasn't the moment that he recalled/relived/inhabited/experienced while dying in the chair with the bag on his head.

Nor were any of the other above-described moments.

The moment Gladman recalled/relived/inhabited/experienced while he died in the chair with the bag on his head occurred .647 seconds later, when he heard a sound that wasn't a scratching sound coming from the right and he turned toward the sound.

EXIT APTER

When, on the first night of Gogol's stay at his place, Apter read, in *Every Parrot Owner's Guide to His or Her Parrot*, that, owing to "the tonsure-like array of light gray feathers amid their otherwise green-feathered crowns," Quaker parrots were also known as *monk parakeets*, he thought about how, if Gogol'd been his, he'd have named her Monkey just to razz Sylvie, whose family's chocolate Labrador and golden retriever had been named Chocolatey and Goldie, respectively.

Maybe after he moved to LA, he thought, he'd buy one, name it Monkey, drive up to San Francisco, and *give it* to Sylvie.

He set down the book to search the web for Los Angeles–area parrot breeders, but by the time he'd gotten his phone's browser open, he knew he wouldn't buy Sylvie a bird—you don't give a girl an animal just to make a joke, even if the joke might win her heart, especially if the joke probably wouldn't win her heart, and most especially of all if you weren't even certain you wanted her heart—and searched "distance Los Angeles San Francisco" instead.

Five and a half hours by car, said the web.
    You'd have to stop for gas, and to piss. Plus traffic varied.
    But then also you'd speed whenever you could.
    So call it six hours.
    Was that longer than he'd imagined, or shorter? What was six hours? A school day, give or take.

—

Three hours, though, was just an hour of music, an hour of news, another hour on the phone with Adi.

He searched "halfway between LA SF."

Coalinga, California.

Scanned the Coalinga Wikipedia entry: Home of Pleasant Valley Prison. Pop. 13k. Monochrome photo of a single-screen movie house demolished by an earthquake. No sign of nightlife. Seemed a little *Killer Inside Me* and Jewless . . .

"Fuck am I thinking?" he muttered to himself.

"Hello," said Gogol.

"She's got a Bobovnikoff," he said to Gogol.

"Gogol," said Gogol.

"What am I talking to *you* about it for?"

Gogol tilted her head and waved.

"You good?" Apter said.

"Good birdie," said Gogol.

Apter pocketed the phone. Got out the Ziploc of almonds from the file box. Dropped a couple in the dish atop the cage.

Gogol climbed on the dish, removed an almond with her beak, removed the almond from her beak with a foot, removed the other almond from the dish with her beak, and, now standing one-legged on the edge of the dish, she said, "Step up" through the beak-clamped almond.

Apter offered her his hand the way Gladman had shown him—knuckles forward, thumb hidden in palm—and Gogol, instead of stepping up, craned her neck to wedge the beak-clamped almond into the crease between Apter's palm and thumb, unclamped the almond, raised her head, and, watching Apter, started nibbling at the almond she held in her foot.

So instantly and thoroughly was Apter charmed that he ate the almond without hesitation; without any of the worries he'd have normally had about ingesting bacteria.

The next morning, a Saturday, he walked to the pet supply shop on Western and bought a bunch of stuff in the exotic bird aisle.

A clutch of popsicle sticks, lollipop sticks, and beetle-size objects made of woven wicker—these intended for Gogol to bend and throw around and destroy.

A small clamp-on lamp with a shatterproof bulb the shop owner said improved mood and feather health.

A plexiglass three-dimensional puzzle called "Ultimate Foraging Challenge for Medium-Size Parrots" that featured seven small compartments, each of which opened differently—either by switch, by dial, by button, or by a combination of two or three of the aforementioned. After locking a treat into each of the compartments, you screwed the whole thing to the wall of the cage.

Gogol went at the destructibles immediately, wicker stuff first, whistling as she twisted and tore at and tossed them.

She appeared not to care about the lamp either way, though whenever she stood directly beneath it, the tips of her feathers iridescently shone.

The foraging puzzle initially frightened her. She screamed a lot while Apter installed it. Bit him twice on the back of the hand. Would have kept on biting had he not removed her to the driftwood perch, which he'd placed on the sill.

When he returned her to the cage, she wouldn't go near the puzzle—stayed on the opposite side of the cage from it—but within a couple days, she grew less shy of it, climbed the wall to which it was affixed, allowed a claw or two to rest on its switches, bit at its dials, beak-bashed its buttons.

Thursday evening, she opened a compartment—the first—and Apter snapped photos of her standing atop it and chomping away at the raisin she'd foraged. He sent one to Gladman along with a text: "The fruit of victory! Our girl here knows how to flip a switch."

Gladman's response was the animoji with the star-crusted rainbow forming in the wake of the upturned thumb that tilts left to right like a speedometer needle.

An underwhelming response.

Which wasn't that surprising.

To all six of the photos Apter'd sent him since bringing Gogol home, Gladman's responses had been underwhelming. Not to say Apter thought that *Gladman* was underwhelmed. Probably more like he was busy writing. Hopefully.

He sent the photo to Adi, Sylvie, and his mom, along with the text "Gogol just discovered how to operate a switch."

MOM
Cute!!!
☺

SYLVIE KLEIN
you're really dorking out over
there, huh?
    you'd be, too!
possible
but would i want other people
KNOWING about it?

ARI EMANUEL
i don't have these kinds of
relationships.
don't want to.
    ?
    oh! me neither
    for sure not with you
    meant to send that to my sister
good.
find a place?
    nabisco bldng loft
    wired yr realtor the deposit this morning
he didn't tell me
    maybe he doesn't want that kind
    of relationship with you.
up yours
plus mazel tov

ADI
v. cute
☺

"That book," Apter said, "says that, on average, creatures like you, when they live in captivity, last three times longer than they do in the wild. Apart from assuming that's true—and there's no reason not to assume it's true—I really don't know what to think about it. I can't imagine how anyone could. Not even you. Still, it seems like I'm sup-posed to have a strong opinion."

Gogol, who'd been cleaning off some residue the raisin she'd foraged had left on a claw, took the claw from her beak and waved the foot it was attached to.

"No, you're right," Apter said. "I'll be back in a while." He covered Gogol's cage and shut all the lights off.

Apter hadn't been to Rainbo, or anywhere, really, except for City Hall, since he'd brought Gogol home. The barmaid from Innertown was drinking alone there. He saw her see him come in then turn away as though she hadn't.

"You," she said, as he sat down beside her.

"I was in a weird mood," he said, "the last time I saw you. I was in a weird mood, and you gave me a hug—it was such a warm hug. Ever since then I've wondered what made it so warm: technique, timing, or technique *and* timing."

"So probably both, then, is what you're thinking."

"Is it?"

"When someone says 'x or y or both x and y,' what they mean is, 'I'm pretty sure it's both x and y.' Usually," she said.

"You some kind of expert rhetorician?" Apter said.

"Some kind," she said.

"What kind?" he said.

"The ABD kind. Computational linguistics."

"No shit?"

"Some shit."

"What kind of shit?"

"I did pass my exams, and I still haven't finished my dissertation, but I'm no longer attempting to finish my dissertation because I'm no longer interested in thinking about computers. How's your mood tonight?"

"Not weird," Apter said.

"Stand up," she said.

He did. They hugged. He said her name. Her name was Nell.

"So x," she said, "y, or both x and y?"

"Can't tell," he said. "I was wrong before. Might even be I lied. I *am* in a weird mood."

For a while after the hug broke off, each kept a hand on an elbow of the other.

The following Monday, Apter told the mayor he'd be leaving City Hall to work at Endeavor.

The mayor tried to talk him out of it at first, but Apter said he couldn't walk away from the money, and named a figure—a made-up figure— that caused the mayor to stare into the distance and shrug repeatedly for most of a minute before he finally said that he had to admit he'd probably do the same thing if he wore Apter's shoes and didn't hate Ari and wasn't living out the childhood dream he'd dreamt for the whole of the entirety of all of his life about being the mayor of the City of Chicago. Then he smiled to himself, poured two more, said Apter would always have a place at City Hall, and offered a toast:

"Live west, young man; go long and prosper."

Nell finished work at eleven that night, and she went straight to Apter's, and they went straight to bed.

A little past two, they startled awake to the sound of a car alarm coming through the window, which Apter'd left open—it was nice outside for the first time in months.

Shutting the window muted the sound, but neither one was able to fall back asleep.

"Am I . . . hungry?" Nell said.

"I have a pint of ice cream in the freezer," Apter said.

They leaned on the counter next to the fridge, eating ice cream and speaking softly, half-naked. They agreed that ice cream tasted better after midnight, and listed the times that they'd previously eaten post-midnight ice cream. Apter's list dwarfed Nell's and wasn't even exhaustive, but whereas Apter remembered just a couple of the flavors of the postmidnight ice cream he'd previously eaten, Nell remembered all the flavors of the postmidnight ice cream she'd previously eaten, which may only have meant that her memory (or her memory for ice cream) was stronger than his, but might also have meant that the postmidnight ice cream she'd previously eaten had in itself *been more memorable,* or, perhaps, that she was better at enjoying eating ice cream after midnight. Maybe better at enjoying eating ice cream in general. Any number of the other possible implications here, many of them implications by metaphor, did dawn on Apter, but they were either too obvious to dismiss out of hand, or too obvious to accept, or contradictory, or paradoxical, or just plain irrelevant—he really couldn't tell—so he thought he should set them aside for later if not forever, discovered they were easy to set aside, understood the ease with which he set them aside to be a sign of something good, and found that he wanted, not for the first time, to invite Nell to move to Los Angeles with him.

Which was not a good idea.

That is: however good it might be to live in Los Angeles with Nell, it was not a good idea to invite her to Los Angeles there in the kitchen, for they'd only just started hanging out with each other.

Unless maybe it *was* a good idea to invite her to Los Angeles there in the kitchen because they'd only just started hanging out with each other.

That is: maybe it was a good idea *because* it wasn't a good idea.

"I guess I've eaten a lot more ice cream after midnight than you," he said, "but, up until now, the number of times I've eaten ice cream after midnight without wearing pants could be counted on the fingers of exactly no hands," in the wake of which statement Nell's face and neck colored (thoroughly enough for Apter to detect, even though the only light in the kitchen came from a streetlamp three addresses west), and she said, "How'd it go with the mayor today? You never told me," and Apter said, "Pretty much like I predicted, but he closed with a toast: 'Live west, young man; go long and prosper,'" and Nell pushed a knuckle against her front teeth and emitted a sound like "Shh-shh-shh," which surprised Apter some—the toast was funny, but it wasn't *that* funny— and she told him, "Go on, say it again," and Apter said it again, and before he was finished saying it again, he became aware that Gogol, from behind the sheet that was covering her cage, was mimicking his whisper, emitting a sound like "Sip, sip, sip," and Apter bit his thumb, made a sound like Nell's, and, after catching his breath and wiping his eyes, he spoke the toast a third time, a fourth, and a fifth.

"Shh-shh-shh," said Gogol. "Sip, sip."

ACKNOWLEDGMENTS

Rob Bloom
Camille Bordas
Jacqueline Ko
Nora Reichard
Christian TeBordo

These people have shown me outsize kindness. Due to their advice, this novel was improved in any number of ways. I owe them more than I'm able to say.

Illustration Credits

All photographs of Matt Dillon are stills from Francis Ford Coppola's *The Outsiders*.

The photograph captioned "Crain Communications Building" is used by permission of the photographer, Jesse Ball.

The photograph of the parrot was acquired from Shutterstock.com/Reimar.

The photograph captioned "Photo 2" and the uncaptioned final photo are used by permission of the photographer, Camille Bordas.

ALSO BY

ADAM LEVIN

BUBBLEGUM

Bubblegum is set in an alternate present-day world in which the Internet does not exist, and has never existed. Rather, a wholly different species of interactive technology—a "flesh-and-bone robot" called the Curio—has dominated both the market and the cultural imagination since the late 1980s. Belt Magnet, who as a boy in greater Chicago became one of the lucky first adopters of a Curio, is now writing his memoir, and through it we follow a singular man out of sync with the harsh realities of a world he feels alien to, but must find a way to live in. At age thirty-eight, still living at home with his widowed father, Belt insulates himself from the awful and terrifying world outside by spending most of his time with books, his beloved Curio, and the voices in his head, which he isn't entirely sure are in his head. After Belt's father goes on a fishing excursion, a simple trip to the bank escalates into an epic saga that eventually forces Belt to confront the world he fears, as well as his estranged childhood friend Jonboat, the celebrity astronaut and billionaire. In *Bubblegum*, Adam Levin has crafted a profoundly hilarious, resonant, and monumental narrative about heartbreak, longing, art, and the search for belonging in an incompatible world.

Fiction

ANCHOR BOOKS
Available wherever books are sold.
anchorbooks.com